Praise for
*Curiosity House: The Shrunken Head*

"Stupendous and stupefying! A riddle wrapped in a mystery inside a shrunken head. If you aren't curious about *Curiosity House*, somebody must have pickled your brain and put it in a jar. Read this book immediately."—Pseudonymous Bosch, *New York Times* bestselling author of the Secret Series and *Bad Magic*

"Step right up! Step right up! Mystery, murder, curses, and sideshow freaks! Or are they superheroes? There's only one way to find out. . . . Read *Curiosity House*! You'll be glad you did!"—Adam Gidwitz, *New York Times* bestselling author of A Tale Dark and Grimm series

"The continuous action, compelling mystery, and dark, brooding illustrations make this book impossible to put down. Perfect for kids who feel they're different or those simply after a freakishly good time."
—ALA *Booklist* (starred review)

"A quick-paced plot is bolstered by the bonds of friendship these unusual yet endearing children form as they try to solve a mystery greater—and more personal—than they ever expected."—*Publishers Weekly*

"From the opening sentence, Oliver grabs readers' attention, enveloping them with strong storytelling and rich language. The first book in a new series, the various oddities, intrigues, and its quirky cast of characters are sure to captivate and become a new favorite for mystery lovers."—*School Library Journal*

"Will have readers lining up for their tickets to the next book."—*Bulletin of the Center for Children's Books*

"The plot abounds with action and mystery."—*Kirkus Reviews*

Praise for
*Curiosity House: The Screaming Statue*

"Oliver and Chester have created another quirky middle grade mystery that will have no trouble drawing a crowd."—ALA *Booklist*

# CURIOSITY HOUSE

## ~THE~ FEARSOME FIREBIRD

## LAUREN OLIVER & H. C. CHESTER

**HARPER**
An Imprint of HarperCollinsPublishers

Library of Congress Control Number: 2016949914
ISBN 978-0-06-227087-0 (hardcover)
ISBN 978-0-06-266102-9 (international edition)

Typography by Erin Fitzsimmons
17 18 19 20 21  CG/LSCH  10 9 8 7 6 5 4 3 2 1
❖
First Edition

*H. C. Chester dedicates this book to his best and most appreciative friend,*
*Trudy*

*Lauren Oliver dedicates this book to her father, for all his support,*
*inspiration, and creative encouragement*

"**S**AM!"

Startled by the voice thundering through the narrow attic room, Sam accidentally tightened his grip on the small, scale-model Viking ship he'd been holding, crushing it to splinters.

"Great." Thomas frowned. "Now what are we supposed to use for a Reverser?"

Thomas and Sam were playing DeathTrap, a complex game of Thomas's own invention that used the swirling patterns of the attic rug as its board and various items pilfered from the museum as its pieces. The Viking ship was critically important: by spinning it and seeing which direction its dragon-headed prow was facing, the player might be forced to move back several spaces or even start over.

"Sorry." Sam carefully siphoned the wooden shards from his hands into a neat pile on the carpet. "I didn't mean to."

"SAM!" Goldini the magician popped up behind the series of interlocking bookshelves that dominated the central part of the attic, looking rather like a deranged jack-in-the-box. His cheeks were a vivid red, and the curled tips of his mustache quivered. "I believe this *monster* belongs to you?" As he held up Freckles, the fluffy white cat that had once belonged to the famous sculptor Siegfried Eckleberger, his face twisted in disgust, as though he were clutching an old, extremely smelly sock.

"Oh *no*." Sam scrambled to his feet. The floor briefly shuddered under his weight. Even though Sam was only recently thirteen and skinny as a beanpole, he had that effect: banisters were pulverized to dust in his hand, doors collapsed from their hinges when he pushed them. It was the decided downside of being the strongest boy in the world. "What'd he do this time?"

In the past two months, Freckles the cat—and, by extension, Sam—had at one time or another made an enemy of nearly all of the permanent residents of

Dumfrey's Dime Museum of Freaks, Oddities, and Wonders. He had chewed Betty the bearded lady's favorite brush to smithereens, had shed all over Smalls the giant's bed less than a day after Smalls had declared that he was hopelessly allergic to cat hair, and had clawed to shreds the shawl that the albino twins, Caroline and Quinn, wore slung over their shoulders during their act. He had terrorized Mr. Dumfrey's pet cockatoo, Cornelius. (Cornelius still shrieked "Murder, murder!" whenever Freckles so much as placed a paw in Mr. Dumfrey's office.) Freckles had even relieved himself into Danny's favorite slippers after the dwarf had been overheard loudly discussing the merits of dogs over cats.

"This time," Goldini said, drawing himself up to his full five foot seven, "that *beast* has been terrorizing my bird." He pointed a pale finger to the cage in which a dove was fluttering frantically, eyeing Freckles as though the cat might at any second claw his way out of Sam's arms and lunge. The bird was an important part of Goldini's newest trick, the Incrediballoon, in which Goldini popped a balloon with a long sewing needle, revealing to a delighted audience a live dove.

"I'm sorry, Goldini," Sam said sincerely. He'd never before heard Goldini raise his voice. Usually the magician spoke in a tone somewhere between a murmur and a bad case of laryngitis, even when he was onstage. "I'll make sure it doesn't happen again."

"It better not," Goldini said with an injured sniff. "How can I make a balloon turn into a bird if the *bird* is passing through the digestive system of your cat?"

Carefully, gently—remembering all too vividly the crack of the little wooden Viking ship in his fist—Sam carried Freckles to his usual spot on Sam's bed, navigating the clutter of objects that had, over time, found a permanent home in the attic: wardrobe racks and overturned chests of drawers, three-legged tables and broken armoires, even a darkened refrigerator.

It was a perfect Sunday afternoon in early September. All the windows were open, admitting a breeze that carried smells from nearby streets—hot dogs and roasted nuts, motor oil and exhaust fumes, florist-shop perfume and a whiff of uncollected garbage.

The museum was, for the first time in recent memory, actually prosperous. The matinee performance had been a resounding success. Nearly every patched felt chair in the first floor Odditorium had been full. Goldini had fumbled not a single one of his tricks. Max's knife-throwing act, which she now performed blindfolded, had earned a standing ovation. Philippa had successfully read all the contents of a spectator's purse, down to the half-empty roll of peppermint Life Savers. After the show, she had been swarmed by a group of single women who pressed quarters in her palm and demanded to know when and where they would meet their future husbands, even after Pippa patiently explained that mind reading and fortune-telling were two distinct disciplines.

On a day like today, it was hard to believe that less than eight weeks earlier the museum had been on the verge of shutting its doors for good. And even harder to believe that Sam, Thomas, Max, and Pippa had nearly lost their lives to Nicholas Rattigan: scientist, fugitive, and monster, whose crimes included the murder of Sam's own parents. It was hard to believe in *anything* other than the beauty of the day and the cozy, shabby comfort of the museum, which was as familiar to all the performers as a pair of ancient slippers, battered over time into the exact shape of the wearer's foot. Even Caroline and Quinn, the albino twins, were in a rare state of harmony, and sat side by side, their foreheads touching, braiding each other's long white hair and humming alternating portions of "Happy Days Are Here Again."

For Sam, the pain of knowing he'd once had a mother and father who loved him was tempered by the relief of knowing for sure that he had not been to blame for their deaths, as he'd always secretly feared. Besides, now that they had names—Priscilla and Joe—he could actually grieve for them. And he had, until grief was nothing but a dull throb, as if his heart were a shoe and his parents' memory a pebble lodged deep inside of it.

In a weird way, it even felt good. Because losing someone meant you'd had someone to lose.

"Whose turn was it?" Sam said to Thomas, plopping down on the rug. Thomas was winning the latest round of DeathTrap. In a brilliant move, he had used the feathered quill pen (supposedly the same one Thomas Jefferson used to signed the Declaration of Independence) to temporarily rewrite the rules, allowing him to capture Sam's pirate hook with a much less powerful U.S. army pin.

But Thomas had apparently grown bored with the game. An enormous book was now open on his lap. Sam just caught a glimpse of the title: *Chemical Compositions and Their Practical Applications*. "Forget the game," Thomas said irritably. "We can't play without a Reverser. We'll have to call a draw."

"Finally." Max spoke up from the corner. She was sitting in her favorite armchair—large and exceptionally comfortable, except for a few protruding springs—and polishing her knives. "If I had to listen to you two squabble about the rules anymore, I might have lopped off my own ears."

Sam felt his face heating up, as it often did these days whenever Max spoke to him—even though she rarely had anything nice to say. Ever since Howie the Human Owl, who could rotate his irritatingly perfect head a stunning 180 degrees, had arrived and then promptly quit (or more accurately, been kicked out of) the museum, Max had been even more snappish than usual. Sam didn't know whether Max was embarrassed that she'd briefly had a crush on Howie, furious about Howie's betrayal of them, or still sad that he had left. He really, really hoped it wasn't the latter.

"Be quiet, all of you." Pippa was draped across a sofa, this one covered in a coarse woven blanket that had supposedly belonged to Geronimo. "I can't hear a thing." And she reached over to turn up the volume knob on the old radio.

". . . You've been listening to *Woodhull's Music Lover's Hour*," said a patchy voice from the speakers, "sponsored by Woodhull Enterprises. *When you need it done well, you need it done by Woodhull.*"

"Did you know," Thomas said, without looking up, "that the human body contains enough carbon to provide lead for nine thousand pencils?"

"Shhh," Pippa hushed him sharply. "I'm trying to listen."

". . . interrupt the program for a special announcement, coming to you straight from Edward T. Woodhull IV, president of Woodhull Enterprises. On September fifteenth, the company will launch the world's largest dirigible. The mammoth airship will fly from a factory on Staten Island to midtown Manhattan, where it will be moored on top of the Empire State Building for a full week . . ."

"Hey, Sam." Max's mouth was hooked into a smile. Sam ducked, trying to conceal a new, furious round of blushing. It felt as if someone had lit a fire underneath his skin. "What's wrong with Freckles? He's scratching like crazy."

She was right. Freckles was furiously scratching his left ear, meowing, whining, and craning his neck to nibble his fur.

"I'll tell you what's wrong with him." The door to the attic slammed, and Danny the dwarf came stomping in from the hall. The tall cowboy hat he had recently taken to wearing—a gift from William "Lash" Langtry, the museum's world-famous rodeo star—was just visible over the bookshelves. "It's those fleas!"

And he rounded the corner into the small common

area where the children were gathered.

Instantly, Pippa gasped. Thomas dropped his book. Even Max stopped polishing her knives and instead stared at him, gape-jawed.

"Wh—what happened to your beard?" Sam stammered.

"What happened to your *eyebrows*?" Thomas blurted out.

Danny, who for as many years as the children had known him had sported a long red beard, thick as copper wire, and a pair of bushy eyebrows so pronounced they looked like russet caterpillars tacked to his forehead, was completely and totally clean-shaven. He looked like an overgrown baby.

"Enough!" General Archibald Farnum stomped into the attic behind Danny, panting a little and leaning heavily on his cane. "I said enough, you hear me? I won't have you mouthing nonsense about my highly trained, highly intelligent—"

"Vermin!" roared Danny, spinning around to face General Farnum. "Awful, bloodsucking, itch-crazy vermin!"

"Vermin? *Vermin?*" Farnum's long white beard wiggled, as if it, too, were enraged. "You listen to me, you sprout. I should have you thrown into jail for slander.

I handpicked each one of those fleas myself, and every one has more intelligence in its speck of a brain than you have in your fat skull!"

"Say that again, you big windbag, and I'll bop you right in the nose," Danny cried, waving a fist—which, unfortunately, only came up to Farnum's kneecap.

"You," General Farnum said, his face by now so red he looked like an ancient, wizened tomato, "are not fit to be a flea on the back of one of my fleas! You are nothing but a—an ear mite! You are a vicious, lying dust mite!"

"Hey now, enough hooting!" Lash Langtry appeared and stepped between the two men only a fraction of a second before they could come to blows. "There are ladies present, don't forget."

Both Caroline and Quinn popped off the bed in unison. "Hi, Lash," they crooned. And then, glaring at each other: "Jinx."

Lash tipped his hat to them and returned his attention to Danny. "What's all this about, anyway?"

"What this is *about*," Danny huffed, "is our so-called General—"

"So-called! I'll have you know I commanded a platoon of Rough Riders while you were still in diapers—"

"—and his collection of miserable skin-feeders! Look at me! Just look at me! I haven't slept a wink in a week."

"All one hundred and two of my fleas are present and accounted for," General Farnum said. "I did roll call just this morning." He gestured with a sweep of his cane toward the miniature circus set, equipped with tiny balance beams, swings, and trapezes, in which his performing fleas were kept. Even from a distance, Sam could see the tiny dark shapes darting between various pieces of equipment.

"Then why"—Danny's voice was cresting again dangerously—"can't I stop ITCHING?"

General Farnum let out a noise that sounded suspiciously like a growl. "Have you considered the possibility of *lice*? Oh, during the war we saw plenty of lice. The dirtiest soldiers were always the most affected."

"You rotten scoundrel, I bathed not four days ago—"

"My point exactly. You stink!"

"Fellas, fellas." Lash once again intervened. "No reason to get so riled up. Danny"—he turned to the infuriated dwarf—"I hate to say it, but General Farnum's got a point. You don't exactly smell like a bouquet of daisies. And General Farnum"—Lash turned to the general before Danny could burst into a renewed round of fury—"ain't it possible that one or two of your, er, *specimens* may've made a break for it?"

"No," General Farnum said stiffly. "I do not lose

men, Langtry—or fleas, as the case may be."

"Well, now," Lash said quickly, before the argument could resume, "what say you both go ahead and shake on it? Come on," he added, when neither man moved. "We're all family here, right?"

After a long second, Danny extended his hand with a grunt. General Farnum clasped it quickly, then immediately turned away, muttering.

"Well, see?" Lash said cheerfully, even as the general stomped off. "All's well that ends—"

"Thomas. Pippa. Sam. Max. Dumfrey wants you in his office." Gil Kestrel, the museum's new janitor, had materialized in the doorway.

It was as if the voice carried with it an arctic chill. Instantly, all the lightness and ease was blown from Lash's face. Slowly, Lash pivoted to face Gil. Everyone was frozen, as if stilled by the sheer force of electric tension in the room.

Gil's eyes flicked to Lash. "Langtry," he said shortly.

"Kestrel," Lash said tightly. As far as Thomas could tell, these were the only words the two men ever exchanged. *Langtry. Kestrel.* And they would pass each other in the hall sticking as close as they could to opposite walls, as if convinced the other one carried an infectious disease.

Lash and Gil had known Mr. Dumfrey from the old days, back when they all traveled the country together, performing for massive crowds in towns across America. But whereas Lash was always telling stories about that time, Gil hardly spoke at all, unless it was to give orders or ask whether anyone had moved the mop. Thomas knew no more about him than he had on the day Gil first appeared at breakfast, clutching a weathered rucksack and moving his ever-present toothpick back and forth in his mouth, like it was an idea he'd been chewing on for decades.

One time, Max had worked up the courage to ask Dumfrey about why Gil and Lash hated each other, but Dumfrey had merely waved off the question.

"Bygones, my dear, bygones!" he'd said cheerily. "Old bones laid long ago to rest."

But it was obvious that whatever the reason for the tension between them, it was anything but gone.

Finally, Gil turned away, and the electric spell that had bound them all in place was broken. Instantly, the air came whooshing back into Thomas's lungs.

"Some family," Max muttered as they followed Gil out into the hall and down toward Dumfrey's office.

2

Mr. Dumfrey's office was accessible only from the performers' staircase, which corkscrewed up the back of the museum before belching its travelers into the attic. As usual, his door was closed, though even from several feet away Pippa could hear Dumfrey's deep, rumbling chuckle emanating from within.

"Well, now, look at that," he was murmuring. "Would you believe I'd completely forgotten . . . and Miss Annie Priggs! How time flies. What a dear she was, what an absolute dear. I wonder whatever happened to Miss Annie Priggs, and whether she ever got the solo act she wanted. Perhaps I ought to . . . no, no."

Kestrel rapped once and, without waiting for a reply, swung the door open. "Delivery for you, Mr. D," he said.

Seated at his desk, his small round spectacles perched on the end of his nose, Mr. Dumfrey was bent over an enormous book so overstuffed with pamphlets, photographs, and loose papers, it looked like an accordion. Instantly, Mr. Dumfrey jumped, slamming shut the book. But as he did, a yellowed photograph was expelled from between its pages and floated down toward Pippa's feet. She snatched it up and nearly choked.

"Mr. Dumfrey," she said. "Is this you?"

"Let me see," Max said, and grabbed the photo from Pippa's hands.

In the picture, Mr. Dumfrey was standing in front of a peaked circus tent between two lean, tall men: Kestrel and Langtry, both instantly recognizable, although Kestrel's face was transformed by a dazzling grin, so different from his usual scowl.

Mr. Dumfrey had a dark mustache, a full head of dark brown hair—somehow, Pippa had just assumed he'd always been as bald as a newborn baby—and, most incredibly, most unbelievably, was about sixty pounds lighter. With one hand raised to his eyes to shield them from the sun and a corner of his mouth quirked into a smile, it was almost, almost possible to see the resemblance between him and his half brother, Nicholas Rattigan.

Except that Rattigan rarely smiled, as Pippa knew too well. And when he did, there was no humor or life in it. It was the smile of a snake as it opens its jaw to swallow a mouse.

Dumfrey pushed up from his desk and leaned over, snatching the photograph back from Max and upsetting a collection of pens with his stomach in the process. "Yes, yes. All very silly. Took a trip down memory lane, I'm afraid to say. Can't blame me . . . having all these old friends around . . . a bit of vanity, I suppose. . . ." His face was the color of a stop sign.

Kestrel's mouth flattened into something less than a frown. "Dumfrey here was the star of the show."

"Mr. Dumfrey, you *performed*?" Pippa squeaked. She had seen Mr. Dumfrey onstage, of course. He often made announcements during the performances of the museum's newest attractions—most recently, General Farnum and his world-famous flea circus. But as far as she knew, Mr. Dumfrey had no special talent beyond his ability to fudge the truth by claiming, for example, that a bunch of dolls with insect wings pinned to their backs was actually a family of Irish fairies; or that an old broomstick decorated with seashells and feathers was in fact an aboriginal Polynesian spear, used in rituals of sacrifice. *Faith begets fact*, Mr. Dumfrey was fond of saying.

"Performed?" Kestrel worked his jaw, left to right, moving the toothpick back and forth in his mouth. In the three weeks he had worked for the museum, Pippa had never seen him without one. Even when Kestrel ate, he merely shoved the toothpick to one corner of his mouth and shoveled food into the other. "Wasn't anybody east of the Mississippi better than Mr. D at what he did, and nobody west, either."

"But . . . what did you do?" Sam asked, a little awkwardly.

"It doesn't matter now," Mr. Dumfrey said quickly. He shot a pointed look in Kestrel's direction, as if cautioning him to stay silent. "It's all in the past."

Unsatisfied, Pippa focused her attention on the scrapbook, closing her eyes. Almost immediately she inhaled the smell of old, sunbaked leather and ink, of tobacco-stained fingers and photographs drying to the consistency of leaves. A second later, various images flashed in her mind: of a young woman, squinting, holding an enormous white cone of cotton candy; of Kestrel and Lash with their arms around each other's shoulders, laughing; of a dusty circus tent and a bearded lady standing in the entryway (not, Pippa thought critically, as fine a bearded lady as Betty; her beard was much patchier and not nearly so long). It was as though her mind had fingers and could riffle through all the pages, one after the other—she was scanning fliers, hopping over notices advertising the Best Variety Show in America, flipping past a dozen pictures of the Priggs sisters, Famed Contortionists and Human Pretzels, fumbling for some evidence of Mr. Dumfrey's special skill. Suddenly, an image of the young Dumfrey began to form. He was holding something over his shoulder, a broomstick, or a shovel, or—

*Slam.*

All at once, a dark wall came down in her mind and she could no longer see. Mr. Dumfrey had shut the scrapbook away and, furthermore, wedged an ornate Victorian cabinet directly in front of it. When she closed her eyes now, all she saw was a confusion of papers and a miscellany of objects—rubber bands, paper clips, old bills.

"I'm sorry, Pippa." Mr. Dumfrey looked anything but sorry as he returned to his desk and sat down with a little, satisfied sigh. "But it really isn't nice to stick your mind into other people's business." He carefully righted the cup of pens he had reversed earlier, slotting each pen back in its rightful spot. "Thank you, Kestrel. That'll be all for now. I do believe Miss Fitch may need your help turning out the Bloody Baron exhibit. That old guillotine is terribly hard to maneuver."

Kestrel's toothpick once again hopped from one corner of his mouth to the other, and without another word, he turned and left the room. Dumfrey turned a beaming smile on the children. "So," he said, "you wanted to see me?"

There was a brief pause. Once again Pippa wondered, somewhat guiltily, what special talent Mr. Dumfrey might possibly have possessed. In his cage, Cornelius preened his feathers and let out a prolonged squawk.

"Actually," Sam said, again apologetically, "you wanted to see us."

Mr. Dumfrey struck his forehead with the palm of his hand. "So I did, so I did. Don't know what's wrong with my mind nowadays. Old age, children, old age. Never say I didn't warn you!" His face turned serious.

"I'm about to entrust you with an enormous responsibility," he said, lowering his voice, as though worried that the large bust of Thomas Jefferson occupying one corner of his desk might come to life just to eavesdrop.

"As you know, the poor Monsieur Cabillaud has taken ill."

"Let's hope it's the plague," Max muttered. Pippa elbowed her sharply, trying to arrange her face into a fitting expression of sympathy.

Monsieur Cabillaud was the museum's resident tutor, and ever since September 1 had insisted that school was back in session. It seemed he had spent the whole summer brainstorming new ways to torment them with agonizingly boring lessons on every subject, from the correct conjugation of the French verb for *somersault,* to the proper application of Epsom salts to cure stiff muscles, to the names of all the Chinese dynasties from 2000 BC to the present day. He had even conscripted Smalls the giant, an aspiring poet, to give weekly two-hour lessons on literature, during which Smalls read aloud from his newest unpublished work, "How Sweetly Doth the Pigeons Coo," and railed against the stupidity of every literary magazine that had rejected it.

"Normally," Mr. Dumfrey continued, having failed to hear Max's comment or chosen to ignore it, "Monsieur Cabillaud takes care of all our expenditures and deposits." Mr. Dumfrey coughed—perhaps because there were usually far more expenses than deposits, if there were any deposits at all. "But this week I must ask you to take his place."

"You want us to go to the bank?" Max asked, in her typically blunt style.

Mr. Dumfrey looked vaguely irritated to have been interrupted. He coughed again. "I would do it myself," he said, "but I'm expecting an important phone call. A once-in-a-lifetime opportunity—a specimen so rare it doesn't yet even have a name."

Pippa and Thomas exchanged a look.

"I would hope that this goes without saying, but it is absolutely imperative that the money go safely into the accounts"—Mr. Dumfrey emphasized the word *safely*, peering at each child in turn over the rim of his glasses—"especially in light of recent . . . events."

In the past two months—ever since Professor Rattigan had vanished, seemingly into thin air, from a shuttered trolley factory into which he had lured them—the number of bank robberies in New York City had spiked a record 250 percent. There was no doubt, at least in Pippa's mind, that the two factors were linked. Rattigan had made no secret about the fact that he was planning something big. And something big meant something expensive.

Unfortunately, there was no way to prove it.

Half the New York City police department and a whole team of special agents were combing the city for Rattigan, with absolutely no success, and every robbery had so far gone off seamlessly, leaving no indications behind of who might be responsible.

Pippa, Max, Sam, and Thomas knew that Rattigan must be behind the bank heists. And deep down, *very* deep down, Pippa was the teeniest bit . . . relieved. Of course she would never admit to it: her friends wouldn't understand, and most of the time she joined them in hoping that he had simply vanished from the face of the earth.

But if Rattigan died, then she would have no chance of asking him about *her* parents. Tom, she knew, felt that the museum was his true home. Max thought having parents sounded like more trouble than it was worth and proudly declared herself an orphan to anyone who would listen. Sam knew that his parents were named Priscilla and Joe and seemed satisfied.

Pippa wanted more. Not just names, but pictures, and facts, and stories. Knowing that she might have had parents who loved her had opened up a need she hadn't known existed, just as the smell of sizzling bacon will awaken a sudden hunger.

Mr. Dumfrey removed the metal cashbox from a desk

drawer and handed it to Thomas. Once again, Pippa couldn't help herself. The contents of the enclosed metal box floated up to her consciousness, as if the material that separated her from them had been suddenly dissolved.

"Three dollars and seventy-five cents?" she blurted out, even as Mr. Dumfrey counted the money into a large envelope. "That's it?"

Mr. Dumfrey had the grace to look embarrassed. "Ah, yes, well. . . . I might have deducted a certain fee for museum development and expansion. Rare specimens don't come free, you know!"

"And"—Thomas took the cashbox and peered into it—"a set of false teeth." He made a face.

"Aha!" Mr. Dumfrey leaped to his feet and, cupping the teeth carefully in a palm, transferred them to one of the many glassed-in cabinets that cluttered his office. "I've been looking for these everywhere. Do you know these fine specimens once belonged to George Washington? An excellent man, and very careful about his dental hygiene. Really, they're in beautiful shape, don't you think? Especially considering his diet—all starch. Really no fresh vegetables or fruit to speak of; I don't know where that business about the cherry tree came from. Now go on," he said, turning businesslike again.

"Straight to the bank and no stopping. Miss Fitch has threatened to serve my head on a platter if we go one more week on cabbage stew."

Max zipped the envelope into her jacket, which was several sizes too large, so as to accommodate the knives and blades she always carried with her. Almost automatically, Pippa counted four of them tucked into various pockets. Just then, the phone began to ring.

"That's your cue." Mr. Dumfrey snatched up the receiver with one hand and waved them good-bye with the other. "Is that you, Sir Barrensworth? Excellent, excellent. Dumfrey here, of Dumfrey's Museum of Freaks, Oddities, and Wonders." As Thomas, Sam, Max, and Pippa retreated from his office, Mr. Dumfrey pulled his mouth away from the phone and whispered, "Be careful."

"Now," he said, returning his attention to the call and gesturing for Pippa to close the door behind her. "About the price we were discussing . . ."

small crowd was gathered just outside the museum, waiting for admission. Hanging over the entrance was a garishly painted banner advertising *General Farnum's World-Famous Flea Circus* and showing vastly magnified fleas wearing elaborate circus costumes while bouncing on trampolines, riding tiny tricycles, and performing various acrobatic routines. The eager customers would likely be disappointed by the real thing—the fleas were so small it was hard to tell where they were, much less whether they were actually backflipping—but Pippa was just grateful that the new attraction had taken much of the attention away from the living wonders of Forty-Third Street, as she,

Thomas, Sam, and Max had briefly been known.

For a short time, they had become unlikely—and largely *unliked*—celebrities, and nearly every day a new article, many of them unflattering, had appeared in the newspapers about them. They had found it difficult to move through the streets without someone shrieking an insult in their direction or whispering or merely staring. But now they slipped into the street happy, unnoticed, and undisturbed.

It was a beautiful fall day, warm but crisp, with the sun sitting high in the sky like a perfectly cooked egg. Across the street, Barney Bamberg was sponging the windows of his new delicatessen, while the smell of pastrami, corned beef, and sauerkraut issued from the open front door. Jumbled displays of wrenches, nails, keys, and hammers gleamed in the windows of Majestic Hardware. Henry, the day porter at the St. Edna Hotel, was napping on the job, as always.

"Hey," Thomas piped up. "Want to hear a joke?"

"No," Max and Pippa said together.

Thomas ignored them. "What do you do with a dead chemist?"

Sam made a face. "Not now, Thomas. You know science makes my head hurt."

"Come on. Just play along."

"Leave him alone, Thomas," Max said. Sam turned so red, Pippa was sure his whole face would combust. When, she wondered, would he 'fess up to his enormous, obvious crush on Max?

"Barium," Thomas said. When no one said anything, he sighed. "Bury him. Get it?"

Sam groaned.

"I'll bury *you*, unless you shut it," Max said, glowering.

"No sense of humor," Thomas mumbled, but fell silent when Max moved a hand threateningly toward her pocket.

Despite the new, sharp-toothed curiosity that nibbled at Pippa whenever she thought about her past, she was happy. She was happy to be walking here, in the sun, side by side with her friends—even Max. She let her mind wander and skip like a stone across the river of people flowing toward Broadway, skimming through pockets and purses, the knowledge coming to her easily now, with hardly any effort, as if the whole world were an origami figure unfolding itself to reveal its secrets. She could see the melted taffy gummed to the bottom of a woman's pocketbook and the man with a sandwich in his pocket; she could see card cases and money folds, loose change and gold-tipped pens.

She could even, occasionally, slip into other people's

*minds.* These images came to her in brief bursts, like camera flashes that left a lingering image, a quick impression of shape and meaning. There! A pair of darned socks strung from a wash line. And there! A memory of a little girl whose fingers were sticky with jam. There! A narrow office space in a tall gray building; the smell of ink and paper. They bubbled up to her consciousness and then vanished again, like items bobbing on a tide.

Then, suddenly, a new image intruded: the breath went out of her, and she felt as if she'd been hurled against a rock. A factory, dimly lit, and someone screaming . . . Rattigan's face, twisted into a cruel smile . . . an arm pinning a wide-eyed girl to his chest . . . pinning *Pippa* to his chest . . . .

She let out a short cry of pain, spinning around, searching the teeming crowd.

Someone—one of the men and women on the street— had been there that night at the factory, the night they had last confronted Rattigan and Pippa had been sure she was going to die.

Almost immediately, however, she began to doubt. She saw no one who looked suspicious or even faintly recognizable: just the usual mass of scowling businessmen and street vendors, women herding their small children, theatergoers craning their necks to look at the billboards. Had she imagined it? Maybe her own memories had intruded—it was hard to distinguish, sometimes, between her mind and other people's, as though they were two sticky masses that sometimes gummed together.

"Move it." A fat man elbowed her roughly, and she realized she'd stopped walking in the middle of the sidewalk. She hurried to catch up to her friends, who had just reached the corner.

"Hey." Sam pointed at the far corner, where a boy with straw-colored hair sticking out of his hat was squatting on an overturned milk crate. "Isn't that Chubby?"

It was. There was no mistaking Chubby's thatch of unruly hair, his nose as thin and long as a pencil, or his bizarre style of dress. Today he was wearing battered boots, unlaced, tongues lolling out; red-and-green striped socks; pants several inches too short for him; and several shirts layered over one another, all of it topped with a floppy woolen cap, so he looked rather like someone who had selected his outfit by diving headfirst into a laundry basket.

They crossed the street, dodging a clattering trolley car. Chubby was sitting with his elbows on his knees, surrounded by various pots and brushes. A sign written in shaky black letters on cardboard next to him said: *SHEW POLISH OR SHINE.*

"Hello, *Leonard*," Pippa said sweetly. Chubby scowled at her. For years, Chubby had been tormenting her by using her full name, Philippa, which she hated. But she had recently learned that Chubby had been born *Leonard* and wasted no occasion to remind him.

"What are you doing?" Sam asked, surveying Chubby's various materials.

"What's it look like I'm doing?" Chubby said, scrubbing his nose with a finger and leaving behind a large streak of black shoe polish. "Read the sign." He gestured to it proudly.

"But what about selling papers?" Thomas asked.

Chubby was an orphan, and proudly so. For years he had ruled all the corners between Herald Square and Forty-Second Street, selling papers and also collecting bets on everything from whether or not the Yankees would win their next home game to the quantity of pigeons that would roost on the Pepsi sign at any time. For a short while he'd even lived with a group of petty thieves and had made his living picking pockets.

But after Rattigan had kidnapped Chubby to try to blackmail Thomas, Pippa, Sam, and Max into cooperating with him, Chubby had vowed to change his ways.

Chubby waved a hand. "I gave Tallboy my corner," he said, pronouncing the name *Tallboy* the way someone might say President Roosevelt or Mickey Mouse, as if everyone should know him. "I got tired of slinging news all day for peanuts. I make twice as much right here, plus I don't got to stand all day."

"Don't *have* to stand all day," Pippa corrected him.

"Will you lay off?" Max said. "You sound like Cabillaud."

"Cabiwhat?" Chubby scratched his head. "So what do you say? Ten cents for a polish, five cents for a shine." He brandished a filthy brush in their direction.

"What's the difference?" Thomas asked.

Chubby grinned and hawked a wad of spit onto the toe of his shoe, then rubbed it in with a thumb. "See?" he said proudly. "Good as new."

Max laughed. Pippa shot her a dirty look. "You're disgusting," she said, turning back to Chubby.

Chubby seemed to take that as a compliment and only shrugged. "Who wants to go first?"

"Err, maybe next time," Sam said quickly.

"How's Von Stikk?" Thomas asked, deftly changing the subject. "She manage to get you in school yet?"

The word *school* provoked an explosion of rage. "It should be illegal!" Chubby burst out, clutching his head as if the very idea of education pained him and leaving a long trail of smudgy shoe polish across his face. "The woman's prosecuting me."

"You mean persecuting," Pippa said. "Sorry," she added, when Max shot her a look.

Chubby frowned. "That's what I said. Prosecuting." He looked over his shoulder, as if worried Von Stikk might be hiding somewhere in the crowd, prepared to jump out at him. "No matter where I go, she's there. It's like she's following me. Yesterday I had to hide in a crate of sausages to avoid her. I smelled like pork for the rest of the day. A dog nearly took my hand off."

Pippa was tempted to point out that Chubby often smelled a bit like pork, but remained silent.

"Tough break," Thomas said, clapping Chubby on the shoulder. Pippa knew, however, that he was relieved that Andrea von Stikk had found a new target. Von Stikk had overseen the Von Stikk's Home for Extraordinary Children until it was closed because children kept disappearing, presumably because they had run away. Her newest project was the Von Stikk School for Underprivileged Youths, and in the summer, she had briefly attempted a legal campaign to remove Thomas, Pippa, Max, and Sam from Dumfrey's care and enroll them at her school. "Take it easy, okay, Chub?"

"I always do," Chubby said cheerfully. "Wait!" he called out as they started to move on. His face turned serious. "Listen. I, ah, never thanked you guys for, you know, saving my life." He extended a hand solemnly to Thomas. "And I want you to know if you ever need anything, I'm your guy."

"That's all right, Chubby," Thomas said with feeling, reaching out to clasp Chubby's hand. "There's no need to thank—ahhh!"

There was a loud buzz. Thomas jumped back with a yelp, shaking his hand as though he'd been burned.

"What *was* that?" Thomas said, his freckles darkening as they did when he was angry: like a small, furious constellation.

Chubby only hooted with laughter. He opened his palm, revealing a small, circular device. "Superdeluxe joy buzzer. I got it from the new joke shop on Fifty-Seventh Street. They got everything—stink bombs and itch powders, dribble glasses and whoopee cushions, loaded dice and fake decks."

"Can I see?" Max said, staring at Chubby with renewed interest.

"Get your own," he said coolly, slipping the joy buzzer back into a pocket that contained—Pippa blanched—one quarter of an old bologna sandwich. "But really," he said, once again extending a hand toward Thomas, his face turning serious. "Thank you."

Thomas cast an infuriated glance at Chubby's outstretched palm. "I'll pass," he said. "See you next time, Chub." He continued scowling as they kept on toward the bank, muttering something that sounded very much, to Pippa, like "revenge."

Located at the corner of Broadway and Sixty-First Street, the New York Federated Savings Bank looked like an ancient Greek temple. It looked like a temple inside, too, with its soaring ceiling, vaulted windows, and a marble floor so beautifully polished that you felt slightly guilty for walking on it. Gray-faced men sat behind enormous gray desks, sorting gray documents into gray folders, all of them moving so mechanically that Pippa thought at first she was looking at the same man replicated over and over.

It was obvious that the bank had taken recent precautions against robbery. An armed guard was stationed next to the front doors, and a second guard paced the room, evaluating customers and keeping one hand on a holstered gun.

A line of people snaked up toward the counters. Pippa, Thomas, Max, and Sam joined the back of the line. Normally, Pippa enjoyed the bank, but she kept thinking of the vision she'd had in Times Square, of Rattigan's leering face and her own mouth open in a scream. He was out there, somewhere, and the key to her past was locked inside of him . . .

She was jolted from these thoughts when the man behind her stepped hard on her heel, nearly sending her sprawling onto the floor. She whipped around.

"That's the third time you've trampled on my . . . ," she started to say, but the words got tangled in her throat. Cold fear gripped her, as if the floor had just dropped away and she'd plunged into freezing water.

The man was wearing a long overcoat with the collar turned up and a low-brimmed fedora hat that concealed his eyes. He had his gloved hands in his pockets.

And in one of them was a gun.

Slowly, the man raised his eyes to hers. They were dark brown, nearly black, and cold as stone. He drew his lips back into a grin, and she saw that beneath his straggly mustache, his teeth were yellowed and rotting.

"Pardon me, your highness," he said mockingly.

"Forgiven," Pippa squeaked. She turned around, her heart beating very fast. She nudged Max with an elbow.

"Stop bumping me," Max said lazily, without looking

up. She was using a gold-tipped penknife to clean her fingernails. Pippa nudged her again, a little harder. Still, Max didn't look up. "I *said* keep your elbows to yourself."

Thomas had just reached the counter.

"Hello," he said to the gray-faced man blinking at him from behind the glass, looking like a somber fish staring out from the murky depths of an ocean. "We'd like to make a deposit."

"Thomas," Pippa hissed.

"Hold on a second, Pip," he said, waving her away. "You have the money, Max?"

"Gave it to Sam," she said, still concentrating on her fingernails.

"I gave it to you," Sam said, turning to Thomas. "I'm *sure* I gave it to you."

"Step aside, please, if you aren't ready to conduct your business," the gray-faced man said in a voice that sounded as if it had been piped out of a tin can.

"You didn't," Thomas said to Sam.

"Did."

"Didn't."

"Sirs, I must ask you to step aside so that our other customers . . ."

"Thomas," Pippa tried again desperately. The

man shifted behind her. She could feel his growing impatience—could see the barrel of the gun, inching upward in his pocket, pointing directly at her lower back.

"Not now, Pippa." Thomas glared at Sam. "You don't think I would remember if—"

He didn't get any further. The man shoved Pippa roughly out of the way, at the same time yanking the gun from his pocket. In an instant, he'd seized Thomas by the collar and jammed the revolver to his neck, lifting Thomas clean off his feet and pressing his face to the window that divided him from the bank clerk.

"Nice and easy now and no trouble," he said in a low voice. The bank clerk's face had gone from gray to sheet-white. "Or else *this one's* brains get splattered on the counter, understand?" He shook Thomas so hard, Thomas's teeth clacked together. "A thousand dollars, small bills, in an envelope. *Now.*"

As the trembling bank clerk began counting out bills, Pippa felt a desperate desire to scream. But she couldn't risk it—not when Thomas was in danger. Max started to reach into her pocket but Sam shook his head.

The man would have to release Thomas, or set down the gun, in order to take the money. And then Pippa would scream. . . .

The clerk sealed the envelope and slid it beneath the glass, drawing his hand away quickly, as if the man were a poisonous snake who might bite.

"Nice try," the robber snarled, and Pippa's heart sank. "Put it in my pocket."

The clerk did as he was told, sliding open the little glass window, reaching forward with trembling hands to stuff the envelope into the robber's coat pocket. And still the guards hadn't noticed or moved, though the customers in line were starting to get impatient.

"P—please," the clerk stammered, keeping his voice low, nervously licking his lips. "L—let the boy go. You got what you wanted."

"I'll think about it, just as long as you don't make a peep," the robber snarled, and Pippa's heart sank. And she knew, in an instant, with that intuition that was more than feeling, but vision, that the man didn't intend to release Thomas—not until he made it free and clear of the bank.

Keeping Thomas in a choke hold, the man spun around.

Pippa didn't have time to think. He was nearly on top of her. She could see Thomas's eyes, big as moons, trying to communicate a message. But she didn't understand. And without thinking, she dropped to the ground, jutted out a leg, and tripped the man as he barreled headlong for the doors.

The robber went flying, releasing his hold on Thomas. They both tumbled to the ground, hard, and the gun skittered out of the robber's hand and discharged with a thunderous—

*Bang.*

The bullet ricocheted off the wall and left a fine web of cracks in one of the glass doors as the guard, letting out a cry of surprise, stumbled backward, fumbling for his own gun. Suddenly, everything was chaos. Women were screaming as they pulled their children to the ground. Clerks cowered under their desks.

By then both Thomas and the robber were back on their feet. Their eyes fell on the gun at the same time. Thomas dove for it first.

At that moment, one of the guards came charging across the floor, roaring for the robber to put his hands up. Pippa watched, horrified, as time seemed to slow down, to grow soupy and almost still: Thomas was in the air, reaching out a hand, sailing, sailing—directly into the path of the oncoming guard.

"Watch out!" Pippa screamed. But it was too late.

The guard knocked the fallen gun with the toe of his boot, spinning it back toward the robber. A fraction of a second later, Thomas hit the ground, colliding with the guard's shins, and the two of them fell into a hopeless tangle of limbs.

The robber bent over to snatch up his gun, his long fingers outstretched, only inches from the weapon—

*Thwack.*

The thief let out a high-pitched scream as a knife—Pippa recognized it as one of Max's favorites, with a fine, needlelike blade and a bone handle—nicked him perfectly between his outstretched fingers. He drew back, cradling his injured hand, leaving a trail of blood across the front of his coat. He must have decided the gun wasn't worth the trouble, because in the next instant he was barreling toward the doors again, easily knocking aside the lone trembling guard who stood between him and the exit, shaking too hard to draw his weapon.

"Quick!" someone screamed. "He's getting away!"

"Sam!" Pippa called desperately.

Luckily, Sam understood. He lunged for the nearest desk—an enormous, hulking thing made of heavy oak—and hefted it in the air, revealing a small knot of people clustered beneath it, whimpering, like mice crammed into a hole. With a grunt, Sam heaved it toward the doors . . .

. . . just as the robber slipped through them onto the street.

*Crash.*

The desk tumbled through the thin glass and spun across the stone steps. Pedestrians leaped out of the way, screaming. An alarm began to wail, so loud that Pippa had to cover her ears. Several curious faces appeared beyond the shattered doorway, peering at the inside of the bank from behind the remaining jagged teeth of glass, so that Pippa had the sudden impression of being an animal in a zoo exhibit.

Outside, the robber had already disappeared into the crowd.

"I should have known," was the first thing Assistant Chief Inspector Hardaway said when he spotted Thomas.

Max groaned. Sam cast a longing look at the door, as if he were thinking of making a run for it. Only Pippa managed to respond.

"Hello, Mr. Hardaway," she said.

"*Assistant Chief Inspector* Hardaway," he snarled. Pippa didn't blink. Thomas was sure the insult was deliberate. He felt an unexpected surge of affection for her. Pippa might act like an overcooked noodle sometimes, but when push came to shove, there was nothing soft about her.

"All right." Hardaway spun around in a circle, hitching up his belt, addressing the room at large. "Does someone want to tell me what the h—"

"Sir." Hardaway's underling, Lieutenant Webb, coughed the word, indicating with a jerk of his chin all the little children just emerging from behind overturned tables and countertops, and Hardaway swallowed back the curse, barely.

"Does someone want to tell me," he said through gritted teeth, "what in the name of my aunt Tillie happened here?"

"We were robbed, sir." An ashen-faced man sprouted from behind his desk, like a particularly fast-growing and colorless flower. He smoothed and resmoothed his tie with hands as plump as dumplings. Thomas immediately identified him as the bank manager.

"Poor Mr. Abner was at the counter—" He gestured toward the ashen-faced clerk who had delivered the money into the robber's hand.

Now that the danger was over, however, Mr. Abner seemed considerably recovered—cheerful, almost, as if invigorated by the whole affair and by his role in it. "That's right, Inspector," he said with great solemnity, puffing up his chest. "He came pushing to the front of the line and grabbed hold of that boy"—he indicated

Thomas—"and that's when I saw the gun." One of the witnesses let out a low moan, as if even the memory was too much. "He told me to put the money in an envelope. I was hoping he would have to put down the gun, or release the boy, to take the money, but he was clever. He made me tuck it into his pocket."

"What did he look like?" Hardaway said, and Lieutenant Webb removed a pad of paper and pen from his back pocket. Beneath the brim of his fedora, Lieutenant Webb's eyes were as hard and dark as two very old raisins.

Now Mr. Abner appeared uncomfortable. "I—I didn't get a good look at him."

"You didn't get a good look at him?" Hardaway repeated. "He was standing less than six inches from you!"

"He was wearing a hat, pulled very low, and a high-collared coat," Mr. Abner said, removing a handkerchief from his pocket and swiping agitatedly at his nose. "He looked a bit like your lieutenant, actually . . ."

Lieutenant Webb let out a low growl.

"In the manner of dress, I mean," Mr. Abner said quickly. "That's all. Like I said, I didn't get a good look. He had a gun . . ."

"I see." Hardaway's frown deepened to a scowl. "So he scared the wits straight out of you. Anyone else?" He looked around the room at the assembled crowd. When no one spoke, he let out a little huff of impatience. "Give me something. Was he tall? Short? Dark? Fair?"

"Tall," a short woman said, shivering. "Very tall."

"Not so tall," a tall man said, disagreeing. "Quite average, really."

"He was wearing a hat, but I could see his hair was dark," said someone else, just as an older woman holding a squirming poodle said, "He was quite fair. Blond, practically white."

"He was ugly," Max said.

"He had a betting slip in his pocket," Pippa said, "and a book of matches."

"He had a mustache," Sam added. "An ugly one."

"Wonderful." Had Hardaway been a dog, Thomas was sure he would have bared his teeth. "So we're searching for a man who may or may not be tall, has either light or dark hair, sports a mustache, likes to gamble, and occasionally requires a match." He wrenched off his hat as though tempted to throw it—instead, he settled for mashing it back onto his head. "That narrows it down to half the population of New York."

47 ☞

"We tried to stop him," Sam said, somewhat defensively.

"I can see that," Hardaway said, shooting a glance at the shattered door and the splintered desk beyond it, around which a crowd was still buzzing like ants over the remains of a picnic. "How much did he make off with?"

Mr. Abner hung his head. The manager spoke up. "A thousand dollars, sir."

"Not exactly." Thomas spoke up for the first time. He dug a hand into the inside of his jacket and revealed a slightly crumpled envelope.

Pippa gasped. "You didn't."

"'Course I did," Thomas said proudly. "You didn't think I'd let that lunatic half strangle me for no reason, did you?"

Thomas wasn't built like other people. His bones were *flexible*. They could bend. As a result, he could squeeze himself into a shape hardly larger than a child's suitcase. He could escape a pair of handcuffs or a thick cable of chains. And he could certainly escape a headlock. As soon as the robber had seized him, however, he knew he would have the chance to recover whatever money the clerk handed over to him.

"But—how?" Pippa said as Thomas gave the envelope

to a still-scowling Hardaway, who looked as if he would have actually *preferred* the money to be gone.

"Max taught me," Thomas said, shrugging. Max grinned and gave him a thumbs-up. Pippa folded her lips together and for once had nothing to say about Max's old habit of picking people's pockets.

Hardaway opened the envelope and peered inside. When he looked up, his dark eyes were glittering dangerously. "Is this some kind of a joke?" he said softly. "There's less than four dollars here."

"See? I *told* you I gave you Mr. Dumfrey's money," Sam grumbled.

"Wrong envelope," Thomas said, digging in his other pocket and producing the correct one.

The bank manager looked as if he was about to swoon from joy. "Miraculous!" he exclaimed. "Amazing! Wonderful!"

"Lucky," Hardaway growled, before dismissing them.

If Thomas was hoping for a peaceful afternoon, he was to be disappointed. Even before they reached 344 West Forty-Third Street, he could hear a commotion from inside. A small group of their neighbors had assembled just outside of the museum, doing a terrible job of trying to appear casual while craning their necks to see inside. The noise had drawn out even the reclusive Eli Sadowski, who lived next door and ventured outside only rarely, and then typically only for a few minutes, to procure another stack of newspapers to add to his vast collection or to visit a doctor for medications to combat everything from dust sensitivity to a fear of cucumbers.

"Hello, Eli," Thomas said as he slipped through the knot of people and put his hand on the gate. Thomas had a soft spot for the man, despite or maybe because of his eccentricities. It was in Mr. Sadowski's cluttered apartment that Thomas had decoded the mystery of one of Rattigan's many pseudonyms and realized his connection to a series of murders that had occurred earlier in the summer.

Eli touched a finger to his hat distractedly but kept his eyes glued to the museum doors. Through them, Thomas could hear the squabbling of angry voices. The crowd scattered slightly when Sam cut through it, allowing Thomas to get the gates open and slip inside.

But before he could reach the doors, they flew open, and a woman in a feathered hat scurried out, gripping the hand of her wide-eyed daughter. Simultaneously, the sound of angry voices crested.

"How dare you?" General Farnum was shouting. "How dare you come in here and—?"

The doors closed with a soft *whoompf*, so Thomas couldn't hear the rest of what he said.

"Come, Delilah," the woman said, when her daughter stopped to suck on her fingers and stare at Thomas. She gave the girl's hand a tug. "I knew we should have gone to Coney Island instead," she muttered, casting a disapproving look at Thomas, as if he were to blame for all her troubles. "*Very* unprofessional, if you ask me, even for a freak show. Such *language* . . ."

Now desperately curious, Thomas flew into the museum, followed closely by Sam, Pippa, and Max.

He was relieved to see that Farnum and Danny hadn't resumed their earlier argument. Instead, a very tall man with the squashy face of a somewhat overripe sweet potato was distributing business cards to the crowd gathered around Farnum's flea circus, even as Farnum lunged after him, trying to snatch the cards back. A card ended up in Thomas's hand before he could refuse it.

"Ernie Erskine's Professional Extermination," the squashy-faced man was saying jovially. "Fumigation and cleansing. Best flea killer in the business for over forty years."

"Flea killer?" General Farnum grabbed back the card from an alarmed-looking old woman. "You murderous monster, I'll have you brought up on charges—I'll have your head mounted to my door—"

"Don't be fooled, ladies and gentleman," Erskine continued, as if Farnum hadn't spoken, working the crowd like a politician on a press tour. Thomas couldn't help but think that if he didn't look so normal, he'd make a very good performer. "Dress 'em up like ballerinas or rodeo clowns, these aren't nothing but pests, pure and simple. Breed like bunnies and itch like poison ivy. Even now, they're probably jumping and skipping all around us, making nests in pocketbooks and pant creases."

"How awful," an old woman said loudly, above the dismayed muttering of the crowd.

"It makes one feel positively filthy," agreed the man next to her.

General Farnum's bushy eyebrows looked as if they might spring off his forehead and launch an attack. "The only *filthy* thing in this room—" he began, but he didn't get to finish his sentence.

Erskine was still talking over him, even as the crowd began backing toward the door, casting suspicious glances at the small black blurs moving within their colorfully decorated terrarium—which, only a minute ago, had been their main reason for paying the twenty-cent admission. "No doubt about it," he said. "Only good flea is a dead one! Call Ernie Erskine's Exterminators, before it's too late!"

And with that, Ernie followed the last customer out the door, leaving the furious General Farnum yelling after him.

"Handpicked—best fleas from San Francisco to Syracuse—slander—"

"Let's go." Thomas nodded to the others. He felt sorry for General Farnum. Farnum was at least twenty years older than Mr. Dumfrey, and even though he often repeated the same stories about his time fighting for Teddy Roosevelt during the Spanish-American War, about the fleas that had infested their sleeping bags, and Farnum's discovery of the insects' remarkable intelligence and acrobatic ability, he reminded Thomas somewhat of the late Siegfried "Freckles" Eckleberger, the closest thing Thomas had ever known to a grandparent. Besides, General Farnum had reason to be obsessed with his fleas. His first wife was long dead, and his second had left him for a French lion tamer. He had no children. Before joining the museum, he'd had no family at all—except, of course, for his fleas.

Halfway up the stairs to the attic, they could still hear the general raging.

*"World famous!"*

"Poor General Farnum." Pippa sighed. "And the flea circus was doing so well."

"Well," Max said, "that's what you get when you go around teaching bugs to do backflips."

*BANK ROBBERY—FOILED!*

When Thomas went out to get the paper the next morning, he found that nearly every headline was the same. Returning to the museum just as the other residents were waking up, he found Pippa in the kitchen, blowing steam off a mug of tea.

"Hello," she said. "Where'd you go?"

"Paper delivery," he said, and slid the newspaper between them. He sat down, and they huddled together and began to read.

There's no doubt about it: New York City is in the grips of a crime wave. A spate of recent bank robberies has the

New York City Police Department spinning in circles, and yesterday, at 11:55 a.m., the New York Federated Savings Bank became the most recent target. As in previous instances, a single man entered, waited on line before producing a gun, and demanded the clerk hand over cash. This time, however, there was an unexpected twist to the story: when the robber attempted to take a boy hostage, he instead got a whole lot more than he bargained for.

"They looked normal-like," said Fred Genovese, who was on security duty at the time, "just like any other kids. But one of 'em—a skinny kid, looked like someone who'd get his teeth kicked in at school— chucked a desk straight through the doors. Musta cleared forty, fifty feet. And those desks are heavy. Solid oak with brass claw feet, probably a hundred, a hundred ten pounds."

Miss Eliza Niefenager, who had come to the bank to withdraw a sum for her monthly meeting of the Women's Midtown Cotillion, added: "And there was a girl—at least, I'm pretty sure she was a girl. She was wild-looking, like an animal. She had on an enormous jacket. And pants! In any case, she threw something—I think it was a knife, but she moved so fast, it was hard to see—and nicked that awful man right in the hand before he could snatch up his gun."

Mr. Gould, the bank manager, was overjoyed. "That small boy got all the money back!" he told *The Daily Screamer* exclusively. "Every penny!"

"Harumph," Pippa said. "Not a word about me."

"Cheer up," Thomas said, giving her a thump on the knee. "At least they didn't say you looked like a wild animal."

"To Max, that's a compliment," Pippa grumbled.

They continued reading:

Not everyone, however, approved of the intervention of these four young Samaritans. Assistant Chief Inspector Hardaway of the New York City Police Department, who has been spearheading the effort to track down the perpetrators of the recent spate of robberies, emphasized that the children's actions may well have endangered the investigation.

"This is police business," he said. "The details are confidential, but let's just say that the NYPD has launched a complex and delicate plan to bring the thief—or thieves—to justice. Now that they've had a scare, they'll take extra care next time to cover their tracks." He added: "Besides, those kids could have got someone killed. Like I always say, leave the job to the professionals."

"Piddle," Pippa said. "They've got a plan like I've got a third eye."

"I knew a woman with a third eye once," Smalls said with a sigh, turning away from the stove. He was holding a large wooden ladle that in his enormous hand looked more like a teaspoon. "Rebecca was her name. A most exquisite creature. I wrote a poem for her. 'Triclops of My Dreams' it was called. I still remember the first line. *O hadst thou three eyes wide to see, the love and care I have for—*"

Thomas cleared his throat and read the last paragraph of the article out loud, so that Smalls couldn't continue.

"'This was not the first time that these four "living wonders," Thomas Able, Philippa Devue, Sam Fort, and Mackenzie (last name unknown), all of whom reside at Mr. Dumfrey's Dime Museum of Freaks, Oddities, and Wonders, have had run-ins with the law. In August, they were on scene when the notorious fugitive Nicholas Rattigan made a dramatic escape from a West Side factory. And earlier this year, they made headlines after a string of murders baffled police and made a former reporter at this very newspaper an overnight sensation.

"'"Born criminals," Hardaway said, when asked for further comment.

"'The renowned educator Andrea von Stikk—'"

"Not her again," Pippa interrupted. "I thought she'd finally gone on to making Chubby's life miserable."

Thomas shrugged and continued reading. "'—von Stikk was quick to stress that it is the fault of the children's education, and not the children themselves.'

"'"It's that madman, Mr. Dumfrey," she stated firmly. 'How many times do those poor children need to end up in mortal danger before the state agrees to remove them from the clutches of that charlatan? The children need discipline and a proper education.'"'"

"Proper education, *ma foi!*" As Thomas finished reading, Monsieur Cabillaud was just entering the kitchen. It was the first time he'd been on his feet in days, and though he still looked quite pale, he was dressed impeccably as always in a fine tailored suit, a silk cravat, and a thin-brimmed hat (which had been designed to unique specifications to fit his pin-sized head). "I shall write to zat terrible lady and give her some *education* of her own."

"Thomas, look," Pippa said, pointing to the bottom of the page, where a smaller headline read: *Police Still on the Hunt for Fugitive Rattigan. For full story, turn to page 12.*

Thomas turned the page—but before he could continue reading, his attention was attracted by an advertisement that dominated the better part of the page. Pippa saw it at the same time and inhaled sharply.

"Is that . . . ?" she said.

"Howie," Thomas confirmed.

The advertisement showed a group of performers clustered in front of a stately old building, above which a giant neon sign indicated the *Coney Island Curiosity Show*. The text, which was liberally sprinkled with capitalization and exclamation points, trumpeted: *New York City's BEST and ONLY LEGITIMATE Freak Show and Dime Museum! Don't be FOOLED by imitators! Don't be FLEECED by impostors! All freaks are 100% AUTHENTIC and you won't BELIEVE your eyes! Come see Howie the Human Owl and Alicia the Armless Knife-Throwing Wonder!—and much much MORE!*

In the photograph, Howie was standing front and center, wearing a typical expression of self-satisfaction and looking, as always, irritatingly perfect. Thomas noted that he had one arm around a girl who could only be Alicia. Like Howie, she had the same kind of chiseled physical perfection typically found only among dolls: cloud-blond hair; big, staring eyes; lips that looked as if they had been drawn on by someone trying to imitate a rosebud. Only the empty sleeves of her blouse, tied loosely at her chest, and the knife handle clutched between the toes of her bare feet betrayed her uniqueness.

"I don't believe it." Pippa's face had grown flushed.

"They practically call us frauds."

"At least they don't mention Mr. Dumfrey by name," Thomas said.

"They might as well," Pippa said. "New York's *only legitimate* freak show? It's offensive. I'd like to find that little worm and twist that great big head of his right off."

Earlier in the summer, Howie had briefly joined up with Mr. Dumfrey's Dime Museum. His startlingly good looks and ability to swivel his head a full 180 degrees had made him a temporary sensation, but Thomas had never quite trusted him. Howie was sly and rude and arrogant, and had boasted constantly of his connections to famous performers on the circuit and even to the United States government: his uncle could supposedly rotate his entire torso without moving his feet, and had worked as a bodyguard to a US president.

Eventually, Howie had revealed his true nature: all along, he'd been looking for opportunities to sabotage the museum. Despite his superficial politeness, he hated Thomas, Max, Pippa, and Sam—despised them not for being different but for having been created. Somehow—they still could not figure out how—he knew that they'd been made, born by Rattigan and his sick experiments. Howie had even started an organization called SUPERIOR: Stop Unnatural Phony Entertainers from Ruining and/or Impairing Our Reputation.

Thomas couldn't help but crack a smile. "You sound just like Max."

She glared at him. "Careful," she said. "Or it'll be your head, too."

"Speaking of heads, we'd better get rid of the evidence." Thomas stood up. "I'd like to keep mine, and if Max sees this, she'll go absolutely—"

"If I see what?"

Thomas froze. Max had just appeared in the doorway, yawning, rubbing an eye with her palm. Her hair was so wild, it looked as though she had styled it by attempting to electrocute herself.

"Nothing," Pippa and Thomas said quickly, at the same time.

Max narrowed her eyes. "What's the matter with you?" she said. "What's the big secret?"

Thomas moved for the trash bin. But Max was too quick. She darted across the room and snatched the paper from his hands. It didn't take her long to find the advertisement.

Thomas braced himself for an explosion of curses or a violent demonstration of temper. Even Monsieur Cabillaud, huddled in the corner over a steaming cup of chamomile tea, had gone still, with one hand tremblingly clutching the spoon he had been using to stir. Only Smalls was oblivious, still lumbering around the stove, mixing and stirring, humming to himself.

After a minute, Max merely folded the paper, her lips pressed tightly together, crossed to the trash can, and stuffed the paper so deep inside of it, her arm all but disappeared.

"What's for breakfast?" she said with a toss of her hair, and Thomas let out the breath he'd been holding.

"What's for breakfast?" Smalls repeated, turning away from the stove with a flourish, holding a dented saucepan in one enormous hand. "Only the sweetest ambrosia! The nectar of the gods! *To taste the gentle moon, and freshening beads/Lashed from the crystal roof by fishes' tails.*"

Seeing the children's blank faces, he coughed. "Oatmeal," he said, setting down the saucepan to reveal its lumpy contents, and shrugged. "It was all we had."

Just then, the heavy creaking of the floorboards announced Mr. Dumfrey's approach. A moment later he stomped down the stairs into the kitchen, leaning heavily on the banister and clutching a handkerchief in one hand. "Well, come on," he said immediately, with an impatient wave of the handkerchief, as if he'd been waiting there for hours. "I've got something to show you. Most extraordinary thing . . ." And he turned and began clomping up the staircase, which was so narrow it barely accommodated Mr. Dumfrey's stomach.

"*What's* the most extraordinary thing?" Thomas called after him. But when Mr. Dumfrey didn't respond, muttering instead about the absurdity of a system that required you to climb down only to climb up again, he shrugged and stood up. Pippa and Max got to their feet and went after him.

When they entered his office, they found Mr. Dumfrey standing beside his desk, which had been cleared of its usual clutter and was now dominated by a large dome-shaped object, covered with an embroidered shawl. Sam was already waiting for them there, but he just shrugged when Thomas gave him a questioning look.

Beckoning them closer, Mr. Dumfrey grasped one corner of the shawl. Then, with a dramatic flourish, he yanked it away.

"Ta-da!" he cried.

The shawl had been concealing a birdcage. Inside was one of the most amazing creatures the kids had ever seen—an enormous bird with dazzling red feathers and a coal-black beak shaped like a parrot's. A golden crest topped its head and its tail blazed with every color of the rainbow.

"Behold," said Dumfrey, his face beaming with delight. "The last living example of the magnificent species *Aviraris igneous*! The Exotic Black-Billed Ethiopian Firebird," Mr. Dumfrey added, when the children only stared at him blankly. "I named it myself."

"A Firebird," Sam said thoughtfully, approaching the cage and stooping down for a closer look. "I've never heard of a Firebird before."

The Firebird turned to face Sam, tilting its head side to side with an air of condescension. For a moment, Sam could see himself reflected in its dark, intelligent eyes.

Then, without warning, the Firebird cried out: "Step away, step away! Big lug, step away!"

Sam stumbled backward, shocked by the voice, which sounded nearly human.

"Oh, yes," Mr. Dumfrey said serenely. "It speaks as well."

"Ugly crow!" Cornelius squawked from his cage, ruffling his feathers in annoyance.

"Now, now, Cornelius," Mr. Dumfrey said, waggling a finger in the cockatoo's direction. "Be nice."

"Where'd you get it?" Thomas asked, taking Sam's place in front of the cage, but staying a good three feet from the bird. Once again, the Firebird looked at

Thomas appraisingly, like a man coolly considering his options at a buffet.

"This magnificent creature is the one I've been waiting for all week," Mr. Dumfrey said. "It was hand-delivered by the fellow who captured it—a celebrated explorer, famous throughout the world, a legend in his own time."

"What's his name?" Thomas asked.

Dumfrey frowned. "Hmmm, seems to have slipped my mind. Wait a moment," he said, patting his pockets. "He left his card somewhere . . ."

Pippa had approached the cage as well. "Check your vest," she said, without turning around.

"Aha!" Mr. Dumfrey extracted a crumpled card from his vest pocket and adjusted his glasses with two fingers. "Here it is. Sir Roger Barrensworth. Funny. Sounds like an English name, doesn't it? But his accent was more Italian. . . ."

The Firebird had apparently made a decision about Thomas. "Shrimp!" it screeched, still in that weirdly human voice. "Silly shrimp! Nosy, noggin-headed noodle!"

Thomas blushed all the way to his ears and backed away quickly. "Not very friendly, is it?"

"Let me see," Sam said, holding out his hand to Mr.

Dumfrey. The card had been folded in half. Inside was a crumpled Tendermint gum wrapper, which Sam flicked off with a fingernail, noting several others like it in the wastepaper basket. Even the card smelled vaguely like mint.

"Sir Barrensworth really likes his chewing gum," Sam said.

"Sir Barrensworth lived for years alone in the wilderness," Mr. Dumfrey said. "If that is the worst habit he acquired, he should consider himself lucky."

Beneath Sir Barrensworth's name was an address, 1270 Park Avenue, and the words: *Explorer. Adventurer. Collector of Rare Speecies.*

Sam frowned. "*Species* is spelled wrong," he said.

Mr. Dumfrey snatched the card back. "Probably a printer's error," he said, waving a hand. "Don't you see how lucky we are? We're saved! The Firebird will be the star of the show—and all for the bargain price of fifty dollars."

Sam nearly choked. *"Fifty dollars?"* That was more than the museum made in a month.

"Cheap!" the Firebird squawked, ruffling its feathers. "Cheap! Cheap!"

"It would be worth more if you wrung its neck," Thomas mumbled.

It was Max's turn to receive an appraisal from the Firebird. This came even quicker than it had for the others.

"Animal!" the bird screeched. "Beastly, untrained animal!"

"You're one to talk," Max said, without seeming the slightest bit offended. And she stuck out her tongue.

Suddenly, with a yowl of pure rage, Freckles bounded into the room and, claws outstretched, leaped directly for the cage on Mr. Dumfrey's desk.

"Freckles, no!" Sam yelled.

Max just managed to catch Freckles by the scruff of his neck and haul him backward before he could work a paw between the cage bars. Even after Max deposited him on the floor, Freckles continued to growl, circling the desk, watching Mr. Dumfrey's newest acquisition with an expression of pure greed.

Cornelius ruffled his feathers in such a way that he appeared to be chuckling.

"Clever cat!" he squawked. "Very clever cat!"

"On the bright side," Pippa said as soon as Mr. Dumfrey had dismissed them and they'd managed to shoo Freckles out into the hall, "if the museum folds, at this rate we can just open a zoo."

6

Even though there was no morning performance scheduled, Max headed straight for the Odditorium after excusing herself from Mr. Dumfrey's office. As always, the big hall smelled faintly of old popcorn and bubble gum. The floor, despite daily scrubbings, was sticky as she made her way down the aisle toward the stage. The lights were dimmed, and in the shadows she saw Kestrel moving between the seats, searching for trash discarded by previous audience members and giving the faded felt cushions the occasional scrub with a large shoebrush.

Max cleared her throat. Kestrel straightened up. His large, dark eyes seemed like holes seared into his face, and Max felt suddenly uncomfortable. She crossed her arms.

"Miss Fitch wants you upstairs," she lied. The museum's seamstress and general manager was so severe that even Mr. Dumfrey didn't dare contradict her. The first and last time Max had made the mistake of seeking Miss Fitch out to ask a question, she had spent *five hours* in the costume shop, getting poked with needles and strangled with yards of taffeta.

Kestrel didn't say a word, but loped immediately toward the door. Max held her breath until he was gone. There was something about Kestrel that made her think of graveyards, or lost cats, or the vacant buildings of the Bowery, sad and skinny and dark. Like he was absolutely *contagious* with tragedy.

Once she was absolutely sure she was alone, she hefted herself onstage. The Odditorium looked different when there was no audience to fill it—sadder but also more beautiful, like an exotic flower wilting behind glass. She moved backstage, blinking in the gloom, and located the large, spinning board she occasionally used in one of her most successful tricks, the Spinning Pinnacle of Death. The wheel was fitted with leather arm- and ankle-straps by which Danny would normally be restrained. While the wheel spun, Max would throw a series of knives—eight or ten, depending on how she felt—so that by the time Danny was released, she had re-created him in metal silhouette.

Today, however, she was interested in a different kind of target practice.

She shoved the wheel across the stage, grunting a little. Finally, satisfied, she stepped back, counting off fifty feet. From her position, the Spinning Pinnacle of Death, with its multicolored rings, looked just like an oversized dartboard.

It was perfect.

After once again checking to make sure that the Odditorium was completely empty, she kicked off her shoes and then, hopping to maintain balance, peeled off both socks in turn, wiggling her toes to get the blood working. Then she removed a knife from the back pocket of her blue jeans—a pair Lash had given her, which fit almost perfectly after she'd cuffed the hems several times—and set it on the floor.

The first difficulty was in merely picking the knife off the floor. She tried with her right foot, and then with her left. She switched back to her right foot. She spread her toes as wide as they would go. She stomped down on the handle. Still, the knife kept slipping.

It was all much harder than she'd thought. And the

harder it was, the angrier she got, and the more desperate to succeed.

Finally, by wedging the knife handle in the space
between her big and second toes, she managed to get
the knife airborne. Now she was standing on one leg,
and she briefly pinwheeled her arms and hopped a little from left to right. When she could finally balance
without wobbling like a top on a floor made of Jell-O,
she took a deep breath, keeping her arms outstretched,
and tried to imagine Howie's face sitting directly in
the middle of the colored wheel, pinned there like
Danny was during their act. That black hair, practically shellacked in place. That smile that was like the
blinding-white grin of a predator. The bright blue of
his eyes.

How had she ever believed, even for a single second,
that he might be the teensiest, tiniest bit cute?

Suddenly energized by a wave of fury, she let out a
half-mangled cry and threw. Or kicked.

The knife arced through the air . . .

Then clattered and skidded toward the wings, landing at least ten feet away from the target.

She tried again. This time the knife slipped from
between her toes too early and went skittering across
the floor like a giant, rotating insect. Her next try was

even worse. She released too late, and the knife soared into the air at a nearly vertical angle, so she had to dive out of the way to avoid getting sliced in two by its descent. The more frustrated she became, the worse her throws (or kicks; she couldn't decide)—until at last, with a short scream of rage, she snatched up the knife with her hand and hurled it straight into the very center of the wheel, and then, for good measure, threw another three knives after it, *thwack*, and *thwack*, and *thwack*, so that the four blades aligned in the approximation of a deeply scowling mouth.

Hearing a step behind her, she whirled around, gripping the last of her knives in one raised hand.

"Don't shoot!" cried a pale, skinny man standing in the door to the Odditorium, holding up both hands.

"Who are you?" Max demanded, keeping her knife raised and hoping that in the dim light the man didn't notice her furious blushing. She wished she hadn't taken off her shoes. It seemed somehow to place her at a disadvantage. "What do you want? How long have you been standing there? Why are you spying on me?"

"I—I'm not," he said. "I mean, I wasn't. I've got a letter, that's all. For delivery to 344 West Forty-Third Street." He held up an envelope as proof, and at last Max lowered the knife, returned it to her pocket, and jumped lightly off the stage.

The man took a step backward as she approached, and she saw that his face was covered with light stubble. He was wearing old clothes that were patched, sewn, and brushed, treated with care that only the very poor give to their belongings. The man's eyes traveled nervously over the room with its vaulted ceiling, speckled with mold; and the low-hanging banner trumpeting the Freak Show to End All Freak Shows!; and the large props visible on the stage, including the Spinning Pinnacle of Death but also a large coffin that Goldini sawed in half during his act.

"Don't be a baby," she said as she reached for the letter in his hand and he gasped and jerked away. "I'm not going to cut your fingers off."

The man looked unconvinced, but he at last allowed Max to take the letter, immediately backing up several paces, safely out of reach.

Despite all of Monsieur Cabillaud's lessons, Max was not yet a very good reader. She didn't understand why *whole* and *hole* sound the same but could be spelled differently, or how *bill* and *bill* could be spelled the same and mean different things. How come *sign* was pronounced *sine* and yet *signal* wasn't pronounced *sine*-al?

Still, she had no trouble recognizing the names written precisely in black ink on the front of the envelope.

*For Thomas, Pippa, Max, and Sam.*

Instantly, she got a very cold, very *icky* feeling, as if someone had just dribbled mud down her spine.

"Where did you get this?" she croaked out. But when she looked up, the man was gone. Obviously, believing his duty done, he had fled the museum and its strange inhabitants.

She opened the envelope with shaking fingers. The *ripppp* of the paper seemed very loud in the empty space. But she could barely make out the words on the page in front of her. It was as though, in an instant, she'd forgotten all of Cabillaud's lessons. Her heart was pounding. Words swam around on the page like fish in a pool of white water. She couldn't get her mind to focus long enough to try to tack them down into any order.

One word, and one word only, jumped out at her, clear as a flashlight beam in the middle of the night.

Max was suddenly overly aware of how alone she was, here, in the vast Odditorium, with all its strange shadows. . . .

She hurried out into the lobby, where the large paneled windows at least gave the room a bright, busy look, and nearly collided with Monsieur Cabillaud.

"Watch where you are going!" he huffed out, in a French accent made even more pronounced by his stuffy nose.

Mumbling an apology, she hurried to the performers' staircase and took the stairs two at a time, stopping on every floor to check for Pippa, Thomas, and Sam. She found them in the attic. Sam was still wearing his pajamas, and he blushed a deep scarlet when he saw her, for a reason she couldn't fathom.

"Look," she panted out, shoving the letter at Thomas and nearly tripping over Freckles, who gave a reproachful meow.

Thomas read the letter and his face darkened. Pippa, who was reading without even looking over the page, went white. Sam took the letter from Thomas, holding it carefully between two fingers.

"Out loud," Max said in a strangled voice. She already knew who it was from. She just needed to know what it said.

Sam read, in a trembling voice:

"'Congratulations, children, on another inspiring display of the powers I gave you. I'm so proud. Soon, I hope, you'll be very proud of me.'"

It was signed with a single name; the word that Max had seen and immediately recognized:

—*Rattigan.*

7

N-U-M-O-N-Y-A.

    N-U-M-E-O-H-N-I-A.

    K-N-E-U-M-O-N-I-A.

Max gnawed on the end of her pencil. Her brain ached from the effort of thinking. Why did spelling have to be so ridiculously complicated? And why did certain words have to be so much longer than other words? If Max ever became president, she would mandate that no words could be longer than two syllables.

Of course, then she couldn't be president. She'd have to be the *present*. Or the *predent*.

Monsieur Cabillaud thwacked a ruler down on Max's paper. "Eyes on your test," he said with a severe glare. "Five more minutes."

It was no use. She couldn't concentrate. Not after the news she'd seen this morning, about Howie and stupid amazing armless Alicia, and certainly not after the letter they'd received.

Pippa had, predictably, wanted to go to the police. "This proves it," she'd squawked, sounding exactly like Mr. Dumfrey's pet cockatoo, Cornelius. "This *proves* that Rattigan was involved in what happened at the bank. That means he's in New York."

Thomas shook his head. "All it proves is that Rattigan reads the newspaper," he'd said. "Look," he added, when Pippa opened her mouth to protest, "*I* know Rattigan's to blame. *You* know Rattigan's to blame. But that doesn't help us, not as far as the cops are concerned."

Sam was still staring down at the page with an expression of disgust, as though the paper was covered not with words but crawling insects. "What about the last bit," he said, "the part about making us proud? What's that supposed to mean?"

Thomas's face was grim. "It means he has something planned," he said. "Something big."

"Three minutes," Monsieur Cabillaud announced, and then sneezed loudly.

Max sighed and gave it one last shot. P-N-E-U-

M-O-N-I-A. She shook her head. Now that *definitely* wasn't right. But before she could erase it, someone began to scream—a high, anguished wailing that rattled up through the floorboards and made Max's teeth hurt.

Monsieur Cabillaud leaped up from the edge of his desk, where he had been perched. "Stay here, children. Keep your eyes on your—*oof*." He didn't finish his sentence. Already, Max had barreled by him, practically knocking him off his feet as she sprang toward the spiral staircase. Pippa and Sam followed quickly after her.

Monsieur Cabillaud fumbled to restore his glasses to his small, sloped nose. "As your tutor, I *demand* zat you all get back here *zees instant!*" he screeched.

But it was too late.

He was speaking to an empty classroom.

From various corners, closets, and rooms, the residents of the museum materialized, pouring down the stairs toward the source of the sound like bits of paper swirling down a giant drain. Lash appeared with a lasso looped over one shoulder. Betty came out from the bathroom with her beard wet and set into pink rollers. Caroline and Quinn, who had been squabbling over a particularly pretty spangled dress, came down the stairs with the item in question still gripped between them.

Max nearly collided with Mr. Dumfrey as he emerged from his office wearing red-toed slippers and an expression of deep irritation. From the faint lines crisscrossing his face and the large ink stain marking his chin, she judged that he had once again fallen asleep on his desk while attempting to sort out the monthly financial reports.

"What in Houdini's name is that awful racket?" he said as first Max, then Sam, then Pippa, then Lash, then the twins, bounded by him.

"Sounds like a prairie dog choking on a prickly pear," Lash shouted back, and Mr. Dumfrey, joining the back of the line, allowed himself to be swept up by the current of motion and carried downstairs toward the lobby.

On the second floor, Miss Fitch, with a thimble on her thumb and several pins in her mouth, emerged from the costume department, neatly dodging a wax replica of the Tree of Knowledge, behind which the door to her quarters was concealed. She was followed by a shirtless Danny, who was being fitted for a new tuxedo to use in the ballroom dancing act.

In the lobby, they found Smalls and Gil Kestrel

already gathered. Thomas had taken his usual shortcut through the walls, and was just brushing a fine layer of dust from his clothing.

General Farnum was on his knees in front of his flea circus, both hands pressed to the glass, leaving smudgy fingerprints. His face was contorted with grief.

Mr. Dumfrey shoved through the crowd. "General!" he cried. "What's gotten into you? What's the matter?" Dumfrey had very little tolerance for dramatics, unless he was the one performing. "Speak, for God's sake."

For a moment, General Farnum's mouth worked up and down, as if he were trying to chew through an invisible bit.

"Go on, General," Lash said, giving him a nudge.

With a deep, shuddering sigh, Farnum finally managed to speak.

"Dead!" he choked out. "All of them—*dead*!"

For the first time, Max noticed that the glass terrarium, usually full of zipping dark shapes, was perfectly still. Peering closely, she saw hundreds of miniature specks freckled across the sand: dead fleas, small as the point of a pencil, piled on the floor of the circus.

Betty gasped. Smalls put a massive arm around her and hung his head.

"Good night, sweet fleas, and may flights of angels

sing thee to thy rest," he said solemnly, wiping a tear from one eye.

"Maybe they're only napping," Caroline suggested.

"Don't be an idiot, Caroline," said Quinn. "Of course they aren't napping." She turned to General Farnum and laid a hand consolingly on his shoulder. "Maybe they've just come down with a bad cold."

Mr. Dumfrey bent forward to more closely examine the fallen insects. "This is *very* unfortunate. And the circus was doing so well . . ." He shook his head and then brightened. "Good thing about the Firebird. With just a little training, it'll be shipshape for the show."

General Farnum seemed not to hear. "All those years of training . . . Handpicked them myself, from Tennessee to Tallahassee and all the way to Tahoe. I'll never find a better group of fleas, *never*."

"Hmmm." Lash removed the top of the terrarium, scooped up a handful of the dead fleas, and began to prod them with a finger. "Nope," he said, depositing the fleas back into their tank. "Nothing doing. Dead as a doornail, each and every one of them."

"It was an ambush." The general sounded as if he were choking on a large and very dry baked potato. "A cowardly sneak attack." Then, in an instant, his face transformed. Gone was the grief, replaced by an expression of such utter rage that Max felt almost frightened. He rocketed to his feet and spun around, pointing a knobby finger at Danny.

"It was you," he spat out. "You killed them, didn't you? To punish me."

"Get your sausage out of my face," Danny said, swatting at Farnum's finger. "And stop talking nonsense."

"You practically admitted it yesterday," General Farnum thundered. "You said you wanted them dead!"

Danny puffed himself up to his full three foot seven. "You better shut your mouth, Farnum, before I shut it for you."

"Oh, yes? You think I'm afraid of you, you murderous sad sack—?"

"That's it, you blundering bag of—"

"Erskine's Exterminators," Thomas said loudly. Max saw he was reading from a business card and remembered that she, too, had received one.

General Farnum and Danny both turned to stare at him.

"What did you say?" General Farnum said.

"Ernie Erskine's Exterminators," Thomas repeated, and then read from the additional message printed on the back: "'*New York's Number One Flea Exterminator. You Got 'Em, We Gas 'Em.*'"

"I told you I had nothing to do with it," Danny grumbled.

Mr. Dumfrey cleared his throat. "Would someone kindly explain to me," he said, blinking, "what you are all babbling on about? What exterminators? Who's Irksome?"

"Erskine," Thomas corrected, and explained how the exterminator had visited the museum the day before, distributing business cards and trying to convince the crowd that the fleas would infest their clothing.

General Farnum squeezed his hands into fists. "That coward," he muttered. "That *criminal*. I'll make him pay for this."

"It might have been an accident," Thomas said. "Some of those chemicals can kill a rat from a distance of a hundred feet. If he touched the glass, even for a minute—"

"No such thing as accidents, sonny," the general cut in, before Thomas could finish, "not when it comes to war."

And before anyone could stop him, he pivoted on his heel and, whacking the floor so hard with his cane even the walls shuddered, stormed out the door.

There was a momentary pause.

"Cowards die a thousand deaths," Smalls quoted somberly, removing his hat and placing it to his heart. "The valiant taste of death but once."

"Oh, will you just shut up?" Quinn burst out. "For goodness' sake. They're just *fleas*."

Max had turned to the windows to watch General Farnum stomping angrily down the street, his coat flapping behind him, like the leathery wings of a bat in flight. "Don't tell Farnum that," she said.

While the other residents of the museum dispersed, Sam volunteered to help Kestrel relocate the flea circus, since it now provided an unsavory picture to anyone who might choose to enter the lobby: all those pathetic little black dots strewn motionless across the sand, in front of miniature balance beams and saw-horses.

"One, two, three, *heave*," Kestrel instructed. But no sooner had Sam laid a hand on the glass than a pane cracked under the pressure of his fingers. He drew back quickly, horrified, as a spiderweb of fissures appeared across the glass.

"Sorry," he said, blushing so hard he could feel it all the way to the very tips of the pimples on his fore-head. "I'm—clumsy—I didn't mean to—" He still didn't know whether Gil Kestrel, the newest addition to the museum, understood what made Sam, Pippa, Thomas, and Max so different.

*Who* had made them so different.

"S'all right," Kestrel grunted, as if he hadn't noticed. "Move aside. I'll get it myself."

When Kestrel braced to get a firmer grip on the large glass terrarium, a rolled-up magazine fell from his back pocket. Eager to help, Sam bent to retrieve it. *Modern Aeronautics* was written in large font across the cover, and, in slightly smaller type: *The Joy and Beauty of Flying.*

"Wow." Sam squinted at the cover photograph, which

featured a man, arms wide, standing on the wing of a small aircraft in flight. "Funny he doesn't get blown clear off the—"

"Gimme that." Kestrel snatched the magazine back from Sam with such force that Sam took a startled step backward. "Keep your eyes where they belong and mind your own business."

With a final glare, Kestrel turned, heaved the glass terrarium into his arms, and teetered off into the darkness of the galleries, leaving a bewildered Sam staring after him. Sam was positive that Kestrel was upset because Sam had seen the magazine. But what was so embarrassing about an interest in airplanes? A few years ago, Thomas had gone through a flight phase. Read about a hundred and fifty books about the physics of flying and went around annoying everyone using words like *propulsion* and *aerodynamic*.

"Don't worry about him, Sam-O."

Sam jumped when Lash laid a weathered hand on his shoulder. When he turned, he saw that Lash's face was grim.

Lash shook his head. "That man's got blood in his veins sour as a lemon and cold as a Rocky Mountain snowdrift."

"What's the matter with him, anyway?" Sam said.

"What's he so upset about?"

Lash sighed. He shoved his cowboy hat back on his head, revealing a long red forehead, grown even longer as his fine blond hair had begun to retreat. "I've known Kestrel a long time," he said, and then stopped, chewing on his lower lip.

Sam was now desperately curious. Lash was many things—but he was never, ever at a loss for words. In fact, it was nearly always impossible to get him to *stop* talking. Even after all the other residents of the museum had gone to bed, Lash was often still chuckling over some past performance or hilarious incident featuring people no one else knew: Sally the human seal, who preferred to eat raw fish and could balance a beach ball on her nose; Jolly Jimbo McCrae, the Minnesota fat man, who consumed 14,000 calories a day to maintain his physique and had to be moved from place to place in a specially designed wheelbarrow; Droopy Dan, the clown who never smiled, and dozens more.

"And?" Sam prompted. "You've known Kestrel a long time *and*?"

"Well, I guess there ain't no harm in telling. Kestrel and me used to work the same circuit, along with Mr. D," Lash began. Sam wondered again what Mr. Dumfrey's act could possibly have been. But now wasn't the time to press for information. "Me and ol' Kestrel were friends, you would say. Good friends."

Sam held his breath. There was something so strange about the way Lash was speaking, about the way he looked—lips tight, face drained of all color, eyes focused on somewhere in the far distance. Sam was gripped by a sudden sense of cold, as if a winter wind had sprung up from nowhere. "So what happened?" he asked.

Lash started slightly, as if he'd forgotten Sam was in the room. "Kestrel was a pilot," Lash said. "Best stunt pilot there was."

So that explained the magazine Kestrel had been reading: Kestrel must miss flying. Sam wondered how Kestrel had ended up here, sweeping up candy wrappers and popcorn kernels, plucking chewing gum from beneath the seats of the Odditorium. He stayed quiet, waiting for Lash to go on.

"We were working the traveling route then. Carny style, set up just south of Indianapolis for a week and a half. One of the tightrope walkers was a girl named Claudette." His voice caught and he cleared his throat. "Prettiest girl south, east, or north of the Mississippi, with a heart of solid gold. She wanted to go up in Kestrel's plane. Wouldn't quit bugging him about it, morning, noon, and night. Finally he said okay." A muscle worked in Lash's jaw, like a miniature heartbeat. In and out. "I'll never forget that day. May twenty-second, bright as bluebells, all clear sky. The kind of day that makes you think nothing bad could ever happen."

Once again, Lash paused. Sam's heart had begun to speed up. He could hardly control his impatience. "So what *did* happen?"

"He took her up, all right. Higher and higher, until the plane was just a little white bird in the sky." Lash's voice had grown very quiet. "Then he started pulling his usual tricks. We were all watching, you know. Free show, and wasn't anybody in the circus who didn't like to watch Gil Kestrel fly. Only . . . only . . ." Once again, his voice broke.

"What?" Sam said.

Lash's face was the color of curdled milk. "Only it turned out poor Claudette wasn't strapped in right," he said. "When Kestrel went into an upside-downer . . ."

Sam's breath got tangled up somewhere behind his tonsils. He could picture it so vividly: the shrill cry of terror, the small dark figure of a girl tumbling through the sky.

Before speaking again, Lash fished a dented silver flask from his front pocket and took a long swig. He drew the back of his hand across his mouth to wipe it. "After that," he said, "Kestrel swore off flying forever."

Now Sam wished he hadn't judged Kestrel so harshly. He tried to imagine what he would do if anything ever happened to Max. But even thinking about it made a space the size of a bowling ball open up inside his chest. And Max barely even spoke to him, except to snap at him for breaking things. "I don't blame him," he said heatedly. "It must be awful, losing your girlfriend like that."

For the first time since starting in on his story, Lash looked at Sam. His eyes were bloodshot, as if he'd gone days without sleeping. "Claudette wasn't Kestrel's girlfriend," he said quietly. "She was mine."

9

"Can anyone tell me," Thomas said, tugging at his collar, "why funeral clothes have to be so uncomfortable?"

It was the following day, and the residents of Mr. Dumfrey's museum were gathered in the courtyard, dressed in their Sunday clothes despite it being only Tuesday, to mourn the loss of General Farnum's extraordinary and internationally famous fleas.

Sam scanned the assembled crowd. "Max hasn't come back yet," he whispered.

"Shhhh." General Farnum, looking extremely regal in a high-collared military jacket with polished brass buttons, hushed them loudly. He was standing next to Smalls—who was similarly dressed in an ill-fitting black suit—in front of a small hole that had been dug between two paving stones in the courtyard behind the museum, a few feet away from the garbage cans. Mr. Dumfrey, sweating in the afternoon sun, was busy lining the small hole with silk flower petals taken from Goldini's trick bouquet.

"You don't think she got into trouble, do you?" Sam lowered his voice even further.

Thomas shook his head. "Max knows how to take care of herself."

"I said quiet," General Farnum said gruffly. But Sam thought he detected a tremor in the general's voice.

At that moment, the door to the kitchen swung open and Max slipped out into the courtyard. She'd left the museum soon after breakfast to try to find out whether anyone among her vast acquaintances of street urchins and message boys knew the person who had delivered Rattigan's note to them. If they could find Rattigan's delivery boy, they might be able to find Rattigan.

But as soon as Sam saw Max's face, he knew she'd failed.

"No luck?" he whispered as she took a place between him and Thomas. She shook her head.

"All right." Mr. Dumfrey straightened up, mopping

his face with a handkerchief. "We're ready to begin." He raised his voice. "Bring out the deceased."

Nothing happened. Miss Fitch—who hadn't bothered to change, since she nearly always looked as if she was going to a funeral—rolled her eyes heavenward. Goldini, shifting in his patent leather shoes, leaned his head toward Mr. Dumfrey and murmured something too low for Sam to hear.

"Bring out the deceased," Mr. Dumfrey said, a little louder.

Behind Sam, the door to the kitchen swung open a crack. Lash poked his head out. "What's all this yim-yammin' about a disease?"

"The bodies," Sam whispered. General Farnum, though doing his best to conceal it, looked absolutely swollen with grief. Even his mustache was droopier than usual. "Bring out the bodies."

"Gotcha." Lash disappeared again.

There were the faint sounds of scuffling from behind the door, followed by a few tentative bleats of a bagpipe. Suddenly the door burst open as the music swelled and became a rhythmic, up-tempo march. Danny came first, face red, his cheeks puffed out around the bagpipe, having set aside his deep dislike of General Farnum just to have an excuse to play his beloved instrument—though Sam couldn't help but feel that his choice of song, "When Irish Eyes Are Smiling," might be inappropriate under the circumstances.

Caroline and Quinn came next, heads bowed, looking quite striking in their identical dark dresses, their skin nearly translucent in the sun, their long white hair threaded with flowers, elbowing each other only occasionally.

Last came Lash. He had removed his ten-gallon hat for the occasion and was wearing, in addition to the beat-up blue jeans and checkered shirt he was very rarely without, a very ill-fitting jacket he must have gotten from the costume department, with tasseled shoulder pads and elbow patches. On his upturned palm he carried a small kitchen matchbox, into which Farnum had previously siphoned all of the bodies of his beloved fleas.

The procession flowed around the miniature grave and quickly filled the courtyard. Sam was forced backward to accommodate the group and wound up placing his foot in a very squishy, pulpy, smelly pile of trash that had somehow gravitated out of the garbage can—a substance, from the looks of it, that might have been either a disintegrating sock or the remains of Goldini's cooking from the night before. On the street level, a couple strolling hand in hand paused to gape.

Danny finished the song, extending the last note so it trembled prettily in the air. In the resulting silence, Caroline let out a dramatic sniffle and touched her face with a handkerchief. Quinn rolled her eyes.

Smalls cleared his throat. "Dearly beloved," he began. "We are gathered here today to pay our respects to the great, the incomparable, the *extraordinary* fleas of General Archibald Farnum's World-Famous Flea Circus. They were friends—"

"They were *fleas*," Quinn muttered. General Farnum glared at her.

"—and, though their time was cut tragically short, our memory of them will be long. In the words of the poet, 'Death be not proud of thyself for killing these fleas—'"

"Yes, yes," Mr. Dumfrey said hastily, before Smalls could really get going. "Very good. *Very* moving. Lash, would you be so kind?"

Lash stepped forward, his face composed in an expression of great solemnity, holding the matchbox. Sam couldn't help but look to Kestrel, who was standing as far from the group as possible, arms crossed, hat pulled low so that his face was in shadow.

What would it be like, Sam wondered, to be

responsible for killing someone else, even—or especially—if you didn't mean to? How were people like Professor Rattigan able to sleep, eat, shave, stroll with the sun on their faces, wiggle their toes in the morning, and watch baseball, knowing all of the pain and suffering they had caused? Sam's earliest memory was of seeing his mother and father, open-eyed and staring, their arms curled around each other as if they'd died in an embrace. Rattigan believed he'd had a good reason to kill them, just as he thought he could end war by creating the most powerful army on earth. All the people he murdered and crimes he committed, he said, were for a greater good.

Despite the fact that the September air was surprisingly warm and he was wearing an old magician's suit, complete with tails, mandated by Miss Fitch, Sam shivered.

Would it be possible that they might someday have to kill Rattigan in order to stop him? Would Sam, too, become a murderer?

That was the problem with violence. Despite what Rattigan believed, it couldn't simply be stamped out. It was a bacteria, a disease. It spread on contact.

Lash kneeled, wincing a little, and deposited the small matchbox in its grave. Caroline let out a little sniffle. The couple had moved on down the street, and for a moment, Sam felt as if he were standing inside a lightbulb, held in a fragile glass container, in the light, with all the people he loved, in the only home he'd ever known.

"Good-bye, good soldiers," General Farnum said, his voice thick with feeling. "You were brave. You were honorable. You—"

"*There* they are."

A voice from the street made everyone turn. Just like that, Sam's sense of peace and calm shattered. Max emitted a noise that could only be described as a growl.

Police officers Schroeder and Gilhooley were standing on the street above the sunken courtyard. Sergeant Schroeder, stuffed into his uniform like a turkey straining within a sock, was staring down at them with a gloating expression, as if he'd caught them in the middle of a crime. Officer Gilhooley, as always, looked as if a hard wind might suddenly blow him elsewhere—looked, in fact, as if he wished that it would.

"Ah, our old friends," Mr. Dumfrey said, imbuing the words with a tone of great sarcasm. "To what do we owe the pleasure?"

"Save it, Dunley," Schroeder said. He came plodding down the steps, huffing, holding up his badge as if it were a talisman that might keep him protected from great evil. "Move aside, please, move aside. Is there an Archibald Farnum here?"

"I'm General Farnum," General Farnum said, drawing himself up. "What's this about?"

Schroeder drew his lips back over his teeth. It was a horrible smile—like the smile of a shark just before it eats you. "Turn around, please, and hands behind your back."

There was an immediate outcry. Everyone began to shout.

"What's the meaning of this?" General Farnum spluttered, even as Schroeder knocked the cane from Farnum's hands and spun him around. In one fluid motion, he unclipped a pair of handcuffs from his belt. "You can't be serious."

"Lay off of him!" Max shouted.

"He didn't do anything," Pippa cried.

Schroeder ignored them. He was obviously enjoying himself. "Archibald Farnum," Schroeder announced, speaking loudly so that he could be heard over the din. "You're under arrest"—here there was a collective intake of breath, and just for a second, it got very still, and very silent—"for the murder of Ernie Erskine."

There was a new explosion of shouting and pro-
testation. Speaking over the din, Schroeder
continued: "You have the right to remain
silent . . ."

"Remain silent!" General Farnum burst out. "I will
*not* remain silent, sonny. You're talking to a decorated
war veteran, do you know that? It's an outrage!"

"Mistake," Betty said softly. "There must be a mistake."

Schroeder went on, undeterred: "Anything you say
may be used against you in a court of law. You have the
right to an attorney. Should you be unable to afford
one—"

At the mention of money, Cabillaud paled and made the sign of the cross.

"—one can and will be provided for you."

Thomas watched it all with a growing sense of nausea. He felt as he sometimes did when he turned a corner in the city and could suddenly, miraculously predict what he would see, as though it had all happened to him before: a woman in a red coat walking a three-legged dog, a blind beggar with a tin cup and a cardboard sign pinned to his coat. Déjà vu—that's what it was called.

But this déjà vu was all too real. Instantly, he was transported back to the spring, when Gilhooley and Schroeder had stormed the museum with handcuffs and accusations. That time, it was Mr. Dumfrey who had been arrested on suspicion of murder.

And Thomas knew in that moment that it wouldn't end. They would always be harassed, accused, mistreated. The police would find any excuse to make their lives difficult, Hardaway and his group of mindless, suited-up zombies especially. Hardaway was furious at them for being different: he wanted them to pay.

"Gentlemen, gentlemen," Mr. Dumfrey spoke up. "Let's not rush to any hasty conclusions. General Farnum is an upstanding citizen and, as he mentioned to you, a veteran of the Spanish-American War, in which he served with great bravery and gumption."

"Look at the man," Danny said. When he was angry his Irish accent became more pronounced. "He's ancient! He's older than a tree stump and twice as useless. Takes him twenty minutes just to get on and off the kettle in the morning, if you catch my drift. He *couldn't* have killed anyone."

"Thank you, Daniel," General Farnum said stiffly.

"Nice try," Schroeder practically snarled. His eyes glinted. He had been trying to pin a bad reputation on the museum for months. This was obviously his big chance. "But we got eyewitnesses who say this creep"—he shoved General Farnum roughly toward the stairs—"was the last person going into Erskine's place."

"Witnesses?" Mr. Dumfrey huffed a laugh. "Louts! Liars! Lowly libelous frauds! We'll have them brought up on charges! You should be arresting these so-called witnesses, not interrupting flea funerals—"

Gilhooley worked a long, skinny finger in his long, skinny ear and spoke for the first time. "Could you speak up, sir? I—I thought I just heard you say flea funeral."

Mr. Dumfrey, who had never once turned down the occasion to give a monologue, barreled on, "—and beating down doors to harass perfectly innocent—"

"Wait," General Farnum said, and Mr. Dumfrey abruptly shut up. It was something about the tone of Farnum's voice. He appeared, far from hysterical, perfectly calm. But that was the terrible thing; he was like a man who, having driven off a cliff edge, relaxes on the plunge toward the rocks. "Wait," he repeated. Even Schroeder released his grip on Farnum slightly, so he could at least straighten up, though he winced in his handcuffs as if they hurt. "Your witnesses weren't lying. I *did* go to see that crook Erskine. I was worked up."

"That's enough, Farnum," Danny growled. "Keep your mouth shut if you know what's good for you."

"That's right." Kestrel spoke up for the first time. His arms remained crossed. He was leaning against the kitchen door, his eyes still shaded by his hat. "These half-wits got nothing on you."

At the same time, Lash said, "These numbskulls couldn't pin a tail on a donkey." For a second, the two men looked at each other, as if acknowledging the similarity of their thinking. Then they both looked away.

"I've got nothing to hide," General Farnum insisted. He directed his words over his shoulder, toward the still-scowling Schroeder. "I did go and see Erskine, like I said. I was mad as a horned devil. But"—this as the babble of voices rose up again—"I never meant to hurt him. I only wanted to have a word about the fleas."

Gilhooley scrubbed at his ear more vigorously. "Sorry," he said, in response to Schroeder's glare. "I keep thinking I hear the word *fleas*."

"There are fleas and there are *fleas*, Sergeant," General Farnum continued. "And my fleas were the special kind. I wanted him to 'fess up to what he'd done—a dastardly ambush when my boys were outflanked, outclassed, and outmaneuvered."

There was a long pause. Schroeder stared at Farnum. Finally, Betty cleared her throat.

"He'd poisoned all the fleas," she explained.

"Aha!" Schroeder cried. "I knew it. A motive!" and he seized Farnum by the wrists.

"No!" General Farnum protested, even as Schroeder propelled him up the stairs and to the street. "I swear on my stars, I never laid a hand on him! He was breathing when I left the building!"

"Save it for the judge, Farnum," Schroeder said, even as they disappeared from view.

Gilhooley hesitated for just a second longer. He removed his hat from his head and pressed it to his chest. Even his hair, Thomas noticed, was long and lanky, like noodles plastered to his forehead.

"I'm, er, very sorry for your loss," he said, and then, replacing his hat, scurried after his colleague.

For a long minute, no one said anything.

"Well." Miss Fitch spoke first. She looked even more unhappy than usual, which—considering the fact that she had once actually modeled for the illustrated dictionary under the word *displeasure*—was saying a lot. "This is very unfortunate."

"I knew no good could come of those fleas," Danny said, stroking his smooth chin. "But did anyone listen?"

"He won't go to prison, will he?" Goldini asked in a whisper. Goldini had a terrible fear of enclosed spaces ever since he had accidentally locked himself in a trick box for three whole days. They'd eventually been summoned by a furious banging and discovered he'd eaten an entire handkerchief for sustenance. "They won't—lock him in a cell?"

"Now let's not get our lasso in a loop," Lash said decisively. "He'll be out in a jiff, you'll see."

"Will he?" Betty shook her head. Her auburn hair glinted, halolike, in the setting sun. "You heard what Sergeant Schroeder said. He had motive *and* opportunity."

"She's right." That was Kestrel, speaking up from

his position by the door. "How do we know he *didn't* do it, after all?"

"Now hold on." Lash pointed a finger at Kestrel. In an instant, his face had darkened with fury. "General Farnum may be a lot of things, but one thing he's not is any kind of murderer. Unlike *some* people I know."

Although the sun was still shining, it was as though an enormous cloud had swept in overhead. Thomas half expected a clap of thunder to erupt over their heads, for sheets of rain to materialize from the blue sky.

Though Kestrel and Lash had finally quit glaring at each other, the sensation of cold discomfort stayed with Thomas. "It doesn't matter whether General Farnum did it or not," he said. "The police will do everything they can to pin it on him."

"Enough." Mr. Dumfrey held up a plump hand. "Enough," he repeated, staring hard at Thomas when he began to protest. "The best offense is a good defense, as they say. I'll just ring up my lawyer, Bill Barrister, and have him scoot down to the station—"

"I don't think he'll be of very much help in this instance," Miss Fitch said. "Mr. Barrister died last January."

"Dead," Mr. Dumfrey repeated, stroking his chin.

"No wonder he never answered my Christmas card. Is it too late to send flowers, do you think?"

Miss Fitch inclined her head as if to say yes, it very much was too late.

Mr. Dumfrey exhaled loudly. "Well, no matter." He squared his shoulders. "We'll just have to find a new lawyer."

"And pay him with what?" Monsieur Cabillaud huffed. "We can barely keep ze lights on!"

"I know a lawyer," Betty said. "She's very good. Remember the Romberger case? That German butcher shop owner, accused of bludgeoning his brother-in-law to death with a meat mallet? Everyone was convinced he was guilty until she proved it was the victim's wife using a frozen leg of lamb."

*"She?"* Mr. Dumfrey's face darkened. "Wait a second. You're not talking about—"

"ROSIE BICKERS!" Quinn and Caroline chorused together. "She'll be perfect," Quinn added.

"She'll be brilliant," Caroline chimed in.

"She'll say yes," Betty said gently.

"Absolutely not," Mr. Dumfrey said firmly. "I refuse to go to that wretched woman. Do you know she once served me with a warrant? Andrea von Stikk tried to have me brought before the courts on a health department violation!"

"Oh, right," Pippa said, making a face. "The Incident of the Three-Legged Chicken."

"That stew was perfectly fine," Dumfrey said irritably. "You're still standing, aren't you?"

"Come on, Mr. Dumfrey," Pippa said. "Think of poor General Farnum."

Mr. Dumfrey only scowled.

"Think of the fleas," Sam added.

Mr. Dumfrey scowled deeper.

"It'll be free publicity for the museum," Betty pointed out. "Everyone loves reading about Rosie."

The words *free publicity* acted on Mr. Dumfrey like a jumper cable to a lifeless battery. Instantly, his posture changed. He straightened his shoulders. He neatened his bow tie, which had begun to gravitate left. He cleared his throat.

"Well," he said, with great dignity, "I suppose for the sake of our friend General Farnum, I can afford to let bygones be bygones. It's settled, then. Rosie Bickers it is, first thing tomorrow!"

11

Rosie Bickers's office was almost directly across town, on a bustling portion of Lexington Avenue just north of the Chrysler Building. Pippa, Max, Thomas, and Sam quickly volunteered to go with Mr. Dumfrey, and Max was relieved when he agreed.

They passed through Times Square, which even in early morning was flooded with tourists. Enormous billboards boasting *Broadway's Best Musical!* and *America's Brightest Stars!* loomed high overhead, eclipsing the sun and casting the streets in shadow, so Max felt almost like a bit of debris floating on a canyon river, tugged along by the current of the crowd. She was comfortable in the buzzing streets, happy to observe without being observed, as she had learned to do during her years on the streets.

Occasionally, she saw something that brought her back to those times: a familiar corner where she had occasionally swiped some oranges from a fruit seller; a beat cop who'd once chased her off the steps of a church; a palatial movie theater where she had occasionally stolen in to watch films for free and sneak bites of popcorn from the theatergoers sitting next to her.

Every so often she missed the freedom that came from belonging to no one—from *being* no one. But for the most part, her life on the streets already seemed vastly distant, as if it had happened to someone else. Mr. Dumfrey, the museum, Thomas and Sam and even Pippa—she belonged to them now and they belonged to her, and she wouldn't have had it any other way.

"We'll have to be sharp around Rosie," Mr. Dumfrey said as they neared Fifth Avenue. "Made a name for herself as the best criminal defense lawyer this side of the Atlantic. Do you remember the Case of the Stinking Mackerel? No? Hmmm. You were too young, I suppose." Mr. Dumfrey sighed. "I was a fan of Rosie's, one of her first admirers—that is, until she threw in with Andrea von Stikk and tried to get me brought up on charges. Ah, here we are, 551 Lexington Avenue."

Max was immediately disappointed. She'd imagined that the best criminal defense lawyer in New York City would have offices that reflected her reputation, in a gleaming skyscraper with marble floors and bodyguards flanking the entryway.

This was a dreary five-story building, its shabby exterior stained with soot. The lobby was narrow, dim, and musty-smelling, and a filthy carpet ran toward a single flight of stairs, at the top of which was a glass-paned door marked *Bickers, Attorney at Law.* Max squinted at the words written underneath the company name, puzzling them out slowly.

*Criminal Investigations, Domestic Defense, and Private Security.*

Then:

*Hopeless Cases Welcome.*

And finally:

*No Solicitation, Suck-ups, or Silliness.*

Max had a feeling she might like Rosie Bickers.

"Remember what I said about Rosie," Mr. Dumfrey said in a whisper, touching his nose. "Keep your wits about you."

Before he could knock on the door, however, it flew open, and a man came barreling out, forcing Mr. Dumfrey to take a quick step backward. His face was very red and his jacket was on in reverse, as though he'd been forced to put it on in haste. Even as he started down the stairs, an outraged female voice carried out into the hall.

". . . And for the last time, if I ever see you in these offices again, I'll take your tonsils out through your nostrils! I'll snip your tongue with a pair of gardening shears! I'll wear your eyeballs as earrings! I'll—"

The door swung shut, swallowing the rest of her words. But almost immediately it opened again, revealing a short, squat, coarse-complexioned woman with a knot of frizzy dark hair, wearing a purple suit that made her resemble nothing so much as a very angry eggplant. She stopped abruptly in the midst of her monologue when she saw Mr. Dumfrey standing on the landing.

Instantly, her demeanor changed. She gave Mr. Dumfrey a toothy smile, stepped forward, and began vigorously pumping his hand.

"Ah, what a surprise. The great Mr. Dumfrey," she said. Her accent was wide and flat and recalled the sailors who unloaded cargo at the Fulton Fish Market. This, too, was not what Max had expected. "I see you brought your little wonders with you, too." Her eyes swept appraisingly over the small group. "Come on in, come on in. Sorry about the greeting. I was just having

a friendly little chat with the tax man. Something tells me he won't be bothering me again this year." She let out a husky laugh.

"Miss Bickers," Mr. Dumfrey said primly as she led them into her office—which, though very large, was just as dingy as the lobby had been, and filled everywhere with stacks of paperwork and overflowing files. In one corner, a secretary with the complexion of a dirty mop and blond hair pinned at the nape of her neck was doing her best to disappear into a typewriter. "You're looking well."

She waved a hand. "Save it, Mr. D. Or did you forget I can sniff out a lie like a bird dog on a duck hunt?" She had to shuffle past various file cabinets and an assorted miscellany of bewildering objects—a pair of crutches, an old-fashioned wicker baby carriage, an umbrella stand in the shape of an elephant's foot, a suitcase plastered with stickers from Niagara Falls—just to get to her desk. She didn't sit down, however. She just leaned over her desk to face them.

"So," she said, her eyes gleaming. "What can I do you for?"

Mr. Dumfrey wasted no time. "You perhaps read about the murder of the unfortunate Ernie Erskine in this morning's paper?"

"Hmmm. Was he the one found half-submerged in the East River, or the body chucked into a cement pourer? No—forgive me. He was the exterminator. Strangled in his office."

"Correct," Mr. Dumfrey said. "And unfortunately, our own General Farnum has been accused of doing the strangling."

Rosie whistled and sat down in her chair. "Has he been arrested?" Mr. Dumfrey nodded. "Is there evidence against him?"

This time, Mr. Dumfrey hesitated. "Witnesses," he said finally. "General Farnum went to visit Mr. Erskine and was apparently the last person to see him alive."

"Except for his killer," Max put in. Rosie raised an eyebrow at her, as though surprised that Max could speak.

"Except for his killer," Mr. Dumfrey agreed.

Rosie whistled again.

"But," Mr. Dumfrey hastened to add, "General Farnum couldn't have killed him. Honor and duty. That's what he lives for."

"And fleas," Thomas muttered.

"Mmm." Rosie spread her palms wide. "What else?"

Mr. Dumfrey started. "What do you mean?"

Rosie leaned forward. "Let's be frank with each other, Mr. Dumfrey," she said. "I'm not one of the half-brained gidbits that wander into your museum, gaping and gawping over a fake mermaid or doctored photograph of an English garden gnome."

"All of my natural specimens are one hundred percent authentic," Mr. Dumfrey said stiffly.

Rosie raised her eyebrows but didn't argue with him. "My point is," she said. "We both know you're here for one reason and one reason only. I take the hard-up cases. The hopeless cases, like it says on the door." She leaned back in her chair. "So what else? The cops must have more ammunition than that."

Mr. Dumfrey cleared his throat and tugged on his bow tie. "General Farnum and the dead man had a disagreement earlier that afternoon. The fight was witnessed by a sizable crowd." Mr. Dumfrey looked deeply uncomfortable. Max didn't blame him. Hearing the evidence out loud made General Farnum's position seem much worse. "General Farnum was in an extreme state of emotional distress. He stomped off, swearing revenge."

This time, Rosie didn't whistle. She sat in moody silence, spinning a fountain pen on her desk. Finally, she roused herself. "I'll take the case," she said. Even as Mr. Dumfrey rushed to thank her, however, she cut him off. "But I'm warning you, I'm not a miracle worker. The truth is the truth. Not my fault if you don't like it. But I'll poke around a bit, see what I find out."

"We can help you," Max said. "We could scout for you."

Rosie smirked at her. "Thanks for the offer, sweetheart," she said. "But I've got it covered."

Max felt her face blush a deep red and decided she didn't like Rosie at all.

Rosie stood up, signaling that the meeting was over. "You can find your way out, can't you? Watch out for the boxes—had a client in here the other week tripped and went headlong down the stairs. We're suing the box manufacturer. Hazardous, if you ask me." She plastered on her toothy grin again and began pumping Mr. Dumfrey's hand, even as she led him toward the door.

"We haven't—erm—discussed the issue of payment," Mr. Dumfey said. "I'm afraid that at this very moment, the museum is in just a bit of a tight spot."

Rosie waved a hand. "Consider it a favor. It's the least I can do for an old friend, isn't that right?" She clapped Mr. Dumfrey so hard on the back he stumbled. "Besides, this kind of case makes publicity you can't buy for the world. No, no. This one's on me. Don't you think another word about payment."

"Wonderful woman," Mr. Dumfrey said, once they were back on the street, blinking in the sunshine.

"Harumph," was all Max said.

12

When they returned to the museum, they found the street even noisier than usual. Two enormous moving vans, parked up the block, were obstructing the flow of traffic. Angry truckers, cabbies, and drivers were blowing their horns and shouting curses out the windows of their vehicles, while men in blue overalls unloaded box after box from the vans, ignoring the deafening din.

"Looks like someone's taking over Cupid's Dance Hall," said Thomas.

"Maybe a decent restaurant," Mr. Dumfrey said hopefully. "We could use one around here."

Drawing closer to number 344, they noticed a

woman standing at the entrance. She unfolded a piece of paper from her pocket, squinted at it, and then stared up at the museum's double doors, as if to verify she had the right address.

"Can I help you?" Mr. Dumfrey said. She started and turned to them.

She was, Sam thought, one of the prettiest women he'd ever seen in his life. Some people, Sam knew, thought that Caroline and Quinn were beautiful, and he judged that this woman must be about their age. But whereas Caroline and Quinn had the soft, pale skin of uncooked dumplings—at least in Sam's opinion—this woman had a complexion of fine ivory, with a strong nose and dark, cascading hair, heavy eyebrows, and a mouth that looked as if it had been stained with strawberry juice.

When Max grew up, Sam thought, she would look a little like that. Immediately, he pushed the idea of Max and her lips away, just in case Pippa decided to drop in unexpectedly on his thoughts, an irritating habit she'd recently been cultivating.

"I'm looking for Mr. Dumfrey," she said, and smiled, showing off white teeth that were just a tiny bit uneven.

"And you've found him," Mr. Dumfrey said cheerfully. Ever since Rosie had agreed to work for no pay, he'd been in a remarkably good mood. "To what do I owe the pleasure?"

"I saw an article about the museum in the newspaper," the woman said. She was wearing a camel-colored coat that reached from her chin practically to her ankles. She tugged on the collar, and Sam wondered how she wasn't burning up. "I was hoping you might have an open position."

"And you are . . . ?" Mr. Dumfrey said.

"Emily," she said, smiling again, "Emily Bellish."

"Well, you see, Miss Bellish," Mr. Dumfrey said apologetically. "Just now the museum is experiencing a few *complications* of the financial variety. That is to say, we're in absolutely no position to . . ."

He trailed off as Emily's whole face transformed. Her smile evaporated. She looked suddenly wide-eyed and helpless, like a child lost without parents in a crushing crowd. The effect was so terrible Sam would have rushed to her and given her a hug, had he not 1) been by nature painfully shy and 2) been likely to crush her ribs by doing so.

Mr. Dumfrey coughed, as if choking back the words he'd been about to say. "But there's always room for more talent! Come, come." Mr. Dumfrey gestured her up the steps toward the doors. "Let's go up to my office.

We'll have more privacy there." And they were gone, disappearing together into the museum.

Thomas shook his head. "She must have an act," Thomas said. "I wonder what it is?"

"I don't know," Sam said musingly. "She doesn't look like a freak, that's for sure." He was still struck by the woman's dark eyes and low voice, and by the idea of Max smiling at him like the woman had, all warmth and twinkle. Then he became aware that the real Max was scowling.

"Did you see that coat?" she said. "Maybe she has scales."

"Or maybe she's a human owl, like your old boyfriend, Howie," Sam blurted out, before he could regret it. He was expecting Max to yell at him—she had expressly forbidden any of the others from mentioning Howie's name, on pain of having their tongues plucked out of their heads—but instead she merely narrowed her eyes at him and then turned, flouncing into the museum.

Pippa sighed. "Did you have to go and mention Howie?" she said. "Now she'll be even nastier than usual."

"Just ignore her," Thomas said.

Pippa glared at him. "Easy for you to say. I share a

corner with her. Last time she got in a bad mood about Howie, she used my favorite hat as target practice."

"I don't know why she's so upset," Sam grumbled. "It's been almost two months."

Pippa looked at him pityingly. "You really don't understand anything, do you?" she said. Then she, too, followed Max into the museum.

Thomas shook his head. "Girls," he said, in the tone of someone who knows all about it. "So what do you think? You going in?"

"Nah." Sam stuffed his hands in his pockets—which weren't, technically, pockets, since the lining had long ago given way to the pressure of his fingers. "Don't feel like it yet." In reality, he was already deeply regretting what he'd said to Max. In his most honest moments, Sam admitted to himself that he had a teensy, tiny crush on Max—but he was also terrified of her, and in no mood to be on the receiving end of one of her rages.

"Come with me," Thomas said. "I'm going to run up and say hi to Mr. Sadowski. You remember how he has all those old newspapers?"

Sam nodded. In addition to old newspapers, Sadowski also had old radios, old coffee mugs, old grocery lists, old socks, old photographs, old piles of furniture . . . In fact, there was very little that Sadowski *didn't* have crammed into his apartment.

"*That's* where we have to look for Rattigan," Thomas said firmly. "Years ago, his arrest was big news. What do you want to bet we find names of the people who tried to spring him?"

"Sure." He was more than a little relieved to have an excuse to delay returning to the museum for a bit. And if the last time he'd accompanied Thomas up to Mr. Sadowski's apartments was any indication, they might be busy for hours. Mr. Sadowski had quite a library. The problem was that he could never seem to find it.

As soon as they started down the street, however, Sam saw something that made him stop dead.

That *something* was a hat—a large, feathered hat, worn by a large, elaborately dressed woman standing in front of the moving trucks, giving orders to the men in suspenders. Her face was concealed by the enormous straw brim, and she was too far down the street for Sam to make out what she was saying, but he recognized her fat bejeweled hands and the sharp cadences of her voice, like an enraged canary.

He felt as if all the blood in his body had pooled into his feet. "Is that—?" he gasped out, but found he couldn't say her name. "That can't possibly be . . ."

Thomas had spotted her, too, and he let out a short,

anguished cry. "Von Stikk," he said. "What's she doing here?"

But it was painfully obvious: both Sam and Thomas stood, stricken, as she hefted a wooden crate in her arms and disappeared inside the old Cupid's Dance Hall, followed by several movers, who'd obviously been ordered to work faster. Thomas started across the street immediately and Sam followed after him, feeling queasy, hoping there must be some mistake, some innocent explanation for the trucks and the cartons and Von Stikk's presence on West Forty-Third Street.

There was, however, no mistake. Many of the cartons were labeled with Von Stikk's name. And the old tin sign that used to hang next to the doors of the dance hall, the one that listed various rules, such as no cursing, spitting, or gambling, had been replaced by a sign that said simply, in elegant cursive: *Von Stikk School for Extraordinary Underprivileged Youths.* It seemed she had combined her two latest educational projects.

Andrea von Stikk was moving in.

Eli Sadowski's apartment might have doubled as a museum for all the broken, useless, and bizarre objects, including old costume mannequins and sawhorses, sewing machines and picture frames, cracked mirrors and grandfather clocks missing their hands—much of it stacked in enormous towers that seemed a bare nudge from toppling over. As usual, Eli greeted them with the offer of milk tea, which they quickly and emphatically declined.

"Well, nice to see you, always very nice to see you," he said, but he seemed even more agitated than usual and Sam noticed he had not taken the time to finish dressing. Normally he wore a suit that might have been lifted from the last century, complete with a top hat and even a cravat. "My brother Aaron sends his regards, as usual."

Thomas and Sam avoided looking at each other. Aaron Sadowski had been dead for several weeks, but Eli insisted on consulting him about matters, such as what to serve for tea and whether it was a good time to begin tidying the apartment (the answer was always no).

"You'll forgive me," Eli said, with an aggressive sweep of his hand that threatened to topple an enormous stack of empty milk bottles, "but I have business outside. A terrible thing, really—I would avoid it absolutely if I could—but very urgent. I've just read that an abandoned rocking chair has been sitting for days on Seventy-Second Street. So you see there's not a moment to lose."

Sam couldn't help but note that Sadowski already had several broken rocking chairs wedged beneath broken card tables and armchairs whose stuffing was largely missing. "Do you need another rocking chair?" he couldn't help but ask.

Eli didn't seem to hear. "Shameful, what people waste," he said, putting one foot into a dress shoe and another into a galosh without seeming to notice the difference. "Shameful," he repeated, grabbing what looked like a constable's hat and wedging it down over his head. "In any case, stay as long as you like. You know the way out." And without another word, he hurtled into the hall, slamming the door shut so that all the towers of objects in the apartment gave a faint, ominous shudder. Dust filtered down from the ceiling, and Sam sneezed.

"Well," Thomas said with fake cheer. "Let's get started."

For hours, they worked their way through stacks of mildewing and yellowed newspapers, looking for news stories about Rattigan and clues about the identities of the people who'd helped him after he made his first, infamous break from prison. But it was no use. The newspapers weren't organized by year—they weren't organized at all—and although they found plenty about

Rattigan, it was nothing they didn't already know.

Finally, Thomas stood up. "This is pointless," he said.

Sam agreed only too happily. His knees ached from sitting cross-legged, and his back was sore from bending over decades-old print. Besides, it had started to get dark, and Sadowski's twisted towers of belongings cast heavy shadows over the floor and reminded Sam of warped fingers, reaching for something.

They retraced their path to the door only to find themselves in an unfamiliar room filled almost entirely with birdcages.

"Hmmm." Thomas frowned. "Maybe we should have made a left at the plaster bust of Beethoven?"

They tried again to find the door, only to end up in yet another unfamiliar portion of the vast apartment: a bathroom, the entire tub filled with bottle caps.

"I told you," Sam said, getting frustrated, "to go straight at the stack of old gramophones."

This time, he took the lead. But barreling around the corner, eager to get out of Sadowski's apartment as soon as possible, he let out a shout: a terrible face was staring back at him, an insect's face with a long, deformed snout, its enormous eyes reflecting his look of terror.

Thomas stepped around him, reached up, and unhooked the thing from the coatrack where it had been hanging. When he swung it in Sam's direction, Sam took a step backward.

"What is that thing?" Sam asked. Even though he saw now that it was not, in fact, a gigantic insect, it was as terrifying as ever to him.

"Gas mask," Thomas said quietly. "From the war. They killed thousands of people with gas." He began to move as though to hook the gas mask over his head.

"Don't." Sam reached out a hand to stop him, and Thomas dropped the mask before he could. "Don't." In the quiet sifting of the dust and the darkness settling all around them, it was all too easy to imagine the ghosts of old soldiers passing nearby.

Thomas replaced the mask carefully. Two more right turns, and they saw the door at last. They hurried home in silence, to the warmth and noise and safety of the museum.

13

As soon as they revealed that Miss von Stikk's School for Extraordinary Underprivileged Youths had relocated to just down the block, Max let out a screech so loud it stunned the other three into silence.

The Firebird, which had been relocated to the attic to help it "integrate" with the other performers—Mr. Dumfrey was hoping that his investment might at last be persuaded to learn words that weren't insulting—came awake with a squawk. Even Freckles, who had been hungrily eyeing the bird from a distance, darted under Sam's bed.

"WHAT?" Max sprang to her feet and began

rummaging through the collection of objects piled around the attic. She opened old steamer trunks and closed them again, cursing. She shoved aside a set of leather-bound books and even overturned a waste-paper basket, which thankfully contained only a single crumpled tissue and a coffee-soaked playing card.

"What on earth are you looking for?" Pippa asked.

"Matches," Max responded, without looking up, as if it was the most reasonable answer in the world. She was on her hands and knees now, feeling beneath the sagging sofa cushions.

"Why? So you can burn the place down?" Sam said it as a joke—but when Max glared at him, he knew she was dead serious.

"Don't be stupid," Pippa said. "It's brick. A fire would never catch."

Max sat back on her heels, seeming to accept the reasonableness of this line of logic. But her face stayed dark and her eyes were flashing like railway signals. *Danger, danger.* "It's all that woman's fault," she practically spat. "Rosie Bickers."

Pippa sighed. "You're just mad that Rosie called you *sweetheart.*"

Max whirled on her, and Sam was grateful that, for once, somebody else had been the one to say the exact wrong thing. "I'm *mad*," she said, her voice getting dangerously quiet, "that Rosie was the one to set up Von Stikk in our backyard, and then *forgot* to tell us about it." She shook her head disgustedly. "What do you want to bet that fat hyena will be banging down our doors morning, noon, and night? What do you want to bet she'll be making up stories about us in the papers?"

"Max is right," Pippa said, gnawing on her lower lip. "She'll never leave us in peace."

"We'll never be in peace, *period*." Now Max's voice was rising again, climbing up a scale of rage. "If it's not Von Stikk coming after us, or the papers calling us monsters, it's the police accusing one of us of trying to bump off a stranger and locking up poor General Farnum, when really they should be trying to keep Rattigan from bumping *us* off."

She lingered on the last note, and Sam had a sharp, painful memory of Rattigan's voice, like the whisper of a silk cord around the throat.

*In the end, you see, your father was weak . . . far too weak to stop me . . .*

He forced aside the memory, but couldn't so easily get rid of the cold feeling that had overtaken him.

Max was right. Even if they miraculously tracked down Rattigan, there would never be a stop to the accusations, the attention, the constant needling feeling of being looked at and judged. They were growing stronger, smarter, more skillful by the day.

But that only meant they were getting further and further from normal.

Everyone settled into a gloomy silence. Thomas sat, frowning deeply, staring glumly at his shoes.

But after a while, he straightened up. "You know, Max," Thomas said slowly. "You're not totally right. There *is* something we can do."

"Do-do!" the Firebird squawked. "That's about all you'll do-do!"

Everyone ignored the bird.

Pippa looked at Thomas. "About Rattigan?"

"I wasn't thinking of Rattigan," Thomas said.

"About Von Stikk?" Despite her turbulent expression, a note of hopefulness crept into Max's voice.

"No, not about her, either." Thomas scrubbed the side of his nose. "I meant that we can help General Farnum."

Sam stared at him. "But the police—"

Pippa immediately made a noise of protest, as if Sam had cursed.

"The police always go for the most obvious solution," Thomas said, shaking his head. "Farnum didn't

133 ☞

kill Ernie Erskine. We're agreed on that, right?"

Everyone nodded.

"But he *did* go see Erskine," Thomas continued. "Which means that the murderer must have seen Erskine after him. Maybe he left some evidence behind."

"Like what?" Max scoffed. "A bloody handprint?"

"Not likely!" the Firebird squawked, ruffling its feathers and giving a convincing impression of laughter. "Not bloody likely!"

"Oh, shut your beak," Pippa said crossly.

Thomas shrugged. "Like *anything*. It's worth a look, isn't it?" No one said anything. "Well, isn't it? Or should we trust Rosie Bickers to do the job?"

"No," Max said emphatically. "No way."

There was another long moment of silence, during which Thomas looked at each of them expectantly. Finally, Pippa sighed. "All right, Tom," she said. "Tell us what you're thinking."

It wasn't difficult to sneak out after dinner. The museum's residents, especially Mr. Dumfrey, had been temporarily distracted by the arrival of Emily. By dinnertime, it became clear what her special feature was.

Every single inch of visible skin—from her anklebones to collarbone, wrist to wrist—was covered in

brightly colored tattoos, so that it looked as if a patterned dress had become grafted to her skin.

Sam caught himself staring at her left forearm, where a woman was cupping a hand to her ear, listening to the whisperings of a snake coiled in a tree. The tableau looked surprisingly similar to the Adam and Eve exhibit in the Hall of Wax, behind which the entrance to Miss Fitch's quarters was concealed.

"That's all right," Emily said, before he could look away. "I'm used to people staring. That's kind of the point, isn't it?"

But Sam couldn't look at her for the rest of the meal.

After dinner, while the other residents argued about how the attic should be rearranged to accommodate Emily and whether Smalls really needed *three* beds laid end to end, Sam, Max, Thomas, and Pippa simply slipped out the front door.

The moving vans were gone from the street, and lights burned on all floors of Miss von Stikk's new school. At the old Cupid's Dance Hall, music might have been piping into the streets through the open window, and women might have been trailing in and out through the doors, laughing and tottering on high heels. But now the street was still, the music forever silenced.

Erskine's store was just off the Bowery, a rough portion of New York, home to pawn shops, saloons, and flophouses. The sun was just setting when they emerged from the subway at Second Avenue and made their way toward the address listed on Erskine's card, and Sam felt a hard squeeze of anxiety: big men leered at them from open doorways, and a whisper followed them down the street like the faint hiss of a snake. He didn't want to fight tonight. He didn't *ever* want to fight, really. He didn't want to be here, period—he would much rather have been sprawled out on the bed next to Freckles at the museum, or laying out a game of DeathTrap with Thomas. Unfortunately, it was starting to seem to Sam that the right thing to do was almost always the thing that was least comfortable.

He wondered where Rattigan was tonight.

They paused at the corner of Chrystie and Stanton, from which they had a clear view of the entire street. There was a single policeman watching over Erskine's shop. He looked as sorry to be there as Sam was himself.

"All right," Thomas whispered. "Pippa, you go distract the policeman—"

Pippa snorted. "And how do you expect me to do that?"

Thomas sighed. "I don't know. Pretend to be lost or something."

Pippa scowled at him, and Thomas rolled his eyes.

"Fine," he said. "I'll do it. Sam, you get us in. But try not to break down the door this time, will you?"

He trotted off before Sam could protest and approached the policeman, gesturing wildly and looking much younger and more confused than he had even a second earlier. Sure enough, after a minute the policeman was guiding Thomas in the opposite direction, leaving the entrance to the shop clear.

"Come on," Max said.

They hurried down the street to Erskine's building. Sam took a deep breath, wiping his palms on his blue jeans, and carefully tested the front door. The lock was old, and the wood groaned beneath the pressure of his hand. It would be nothing for Sam to break down the door, but that would bring the police in after them. He tested the doorknob next and was shocked when it snapped off cleanly in his hand.

"Oops," he said.

"What'd you do?" Pippa whispered.

He turned around, holding up the doorknob. "I didn't mean to," he said.

"That's all right. It isn't your fault. And besides,

it worked." She pushed the door open with an elbow, revealing a dark hallway that smelled like paint and chemicals.

They moved into the shop, closing the door behind them and trusting that the police officer wouldn't look too closely at the doorknob when he returned. It was pitch-black. Sam tried to turn around and Max let out a yelp.

"That was my foot," she whispered. He could feel her warm breath on his cheek and he took a step backward.

"That was *my* foot," Pippa said.

"We need a light," Max said.

"Give me a second," Pippa replied, and Sam heard her footsteps move off. He stayed perfectly still, terrified that if he so much as twitched he would stomp on Max's foot again or break something. A moment later, Pippa had located a lamp, and the room was illuminated in a soft white glow. Sam immediately checked the windows. Luckily, the blinds were drawn. Hopefully the light wouldn't attract attention. Just to be safe, however, Pippa unwound her scarf and draped it over the lamp, dimming the light.

Erskine had three rooms on the ground floor: the first, a kind of reception area with a smelly carpet and a cheap laminate desk; the second, what looked to be a storage room full of cartons labeled with chemical names; the third, a small bedroom with a single very small window fitted high up in one wall.

"Check this out," Sam said, pointing to the bed, which was unmade. "Maybe that means his killer surprised him while he was asleep?"

"Maybe," Pippa said. "Or maybe he didn't like to make his bed."

"Shhh." Max hushed them sharply. "Did you hear that?"

"Hear what?" Sam said. She waved a hand, silencing him. And then he did hear it—a series of soft and muffled thuds from somewhere inside the walls, as if a heavy fist were banging, trying to get out. Sam's mouth went very dry.

Pippa screwed up her face in concentration, and Sam knew she must be trying to see, to feel her way in through the plaster. She was getting better. They *all* were, actually. Sometimes, even lying down, Sam could *feel* his strength pulsing through him, shimmering in his blood and even his fingertips.

Pippa's face cleared. "It's only Thomas," she said, and a second later, there was a rattle and a pop, and an air duct came away from the wall, and Thomas emerged, covered in dust.

"*Oof.*" He swung easily and silently to the ground, dropping the last few feet, and then sneezed. "I need to find a better way to travel."

"How'd you get in?" Pippa asked.

"I had to loop around the back so the cop wouldn't spot me," he said, shrugging. "I went through the heating ducts."

Together, they returned to the storage area, which was piled with boxes. Thomas reached inside and extracted a bottle of something called Fleas-B-Gone, giving it a shake. "Empty," he said. He reached for another one. "All of them empty." He spun the bottle around and let out a low whistle. "No wonder this stuff works. The main ingredient's ethyl parathion."

"Ethel who?" Max said.

Thomas looked up. "Ethyl parathion," he said. "It's a kind of poison. Could flatten an elephant with the right dose."

A chill went down Sam's spine. "What about a man?" Sam asked. "Could that whatever it's called kill a man?"

Thomas shrugged. "Definitely, if he inhaled enough of it. During the war it was used as a nerve gas. Reaper gas, it was called."

"But Erskine wasn't poisoned," Pippa reminded them. "He was strangled."

"That's right." Sam frowned, trying to recall what he'd learned from Rosie Bickers. "He was sitting at the desk."

They returned to the office. The desk was piled with invoices, orders, and unopened mail—stacks and stacks of it, over-spilling the drawers and haphazardly tacked beneath makeshift paperweights: horseshoes, bricks, and empty bottles of Fleas-B-Gone.

"What are we supposed to be looking for again?" Max said as Thomas and Pippa began to sift through the accumulation of paperwork in the drawers.

"I don't know," Thomas said. "But we'll know if we find it."

Half the desk was dominated by an ink-stained blotter, which was covered with a miscellany of mail and newspaper cuttings. Sam began sorting through it, but with every second he became increasingly convinced that they were on a hopeless mission. He thought of General Farnum and the way his mustache quivered when he was upset, how soft his voice became as he coached his fleas through their training exercises, the precise way he polished his boots every morning, and felt a sudden panic. He hadn't known General Farnum for long, but already Sam had grown to think of him as a friend. The museum wouldn't be the same without him. Sam wouldn't be the same.

He'd lost so many people already.

He shifted a stack of invoices and saw a letter, half-finished, penned in handwriting he already recognized as Erskine's.

*Don't threaten me*, were the first words he saw, and his heart jumped into his throat.

*Don't threaten me*, he read again, and then:

*You're nothing but a swindler and the next time I see you I'll be sure and say it to your face. If I don't get either my order or my money back I swear you'll regret it, Benny.* He stopped reading. The name *Benny* rang alarm bells deep inside his mind. It was familiar to him. But the connection eluded him, and so he continued: *Enough with your stories and excuses, you'll drive me out of business and over my dead body will you—*

The letter stopped abruptly, as if he'd been interrupted before he could finish it.

Which, Sam thought with a tiny shiver, maybe he had.

"Guys." Sam's voice squeaked. *Over my dead body.* Poor Erskine hadn't realized how literal the words would prove to be. "I think—I think I found it."

"Found what?" Max said.

Sam took a deep breath. "*It*," he said. "The thing we didn't know we were looking for."

ぞ**A**fter the letter had passed hands, there was a
moment of silence.

"So," Thomas said. "Looks like Erskine
had an enemy."

"Benny," Pippa said. "But who's Benny?"

They returned their attention to the desk, this
time searching specifically for references to a Benny.
They sorted through piles of mail both unopened and
opened—it seemed Erskine *was* in danger of going out
of business, since he'd received multiple complaints
for failing to keep his appointments—and even sifted
through the contents of the wastepaper basket, carefully avoiding the crumpled wads of used Kleenex.

Pippa spent a whole ten minutes standing very still, breathing calmly through her mouth, focusing on the name *Benny* and trying to see her way into the desk drawers and file cabinets to find its twin.

But it was useless. Erskine's shop was *too* full, too crammed with papers and files. It was as if someone had upended an enormous library inside of her mind, and she was left feeling confused and overwhelmed, with the beginnings of a headache.

"Nothing," Thomas said disgustedly, after he'd removed the final drawer from Erskine's desk. "Nothing but junk and junk and unpaid bills."

"And more of this stuff," Pippa said, holding up another empty bottle of Fleas-B-Gone.

Suddenly, Sam straightened up, white-faced, as if a phantom hand had passed down his back. "I knew it," he whispered.

"Knew what?" Max had given up the search long ago and was instead trying to pry loose a quarter that had somehow gotten wedged between two floorboards.

Sam reached into his back pocket and withdrew the battered wallet that was a twin of Thomas's. Pippa knew that Siegfried Eckleberger had bought them each a wallet for Christmas the same year Pippa got a small necklace with a four-leaf clover on it, which unfortunately Freckles the cat had consumed not long after his arrival. From his wallet, Sam extracted a small newspaper clipping. Then he looked up, eyes shining.

"I knew I recognized the name," he said. "Benny Mallett, of Chemical Compounds Incorporated. I wrote to him after Freckles wouldn't stop scratching."

Max stood up, dusting off her hands, having apparently abandoned her attempts to retrieve the money. "What are you talking about?" Max said, snatching the clipping from Sam.

Knowing Max would take forever to tease out the words, Pippa closed her eyes and felt her way down through Max's hand and into the grainy paper. It was as easy now as sliding down a banister—it was as if she could send her brain out to grab hold of objects in the real world. She read out loud: "'Cat Can't Stop Scratching? Try Fleas-B-Gone, the Number One Most Effective Flea Killer in the World.'"

There was a cartoon beneath that, of a happy cat giving the thumbs-up, and then beneath that, in smaller letters: "Send all inquiries, orders, and complaints c/o Benny Mallett, Chemical Compounds Inc., 660 Neptune Avenue, Sheepshead Bay, Brooklyn."

"So let me get this straight," Max said. "Erskine was getting his supply from some guy named Benny."

"And then the supply stopped." Thomas rubbed his forehead. "But why would the supply stop?"

"It doesn't make any difference, does it?" Pippa said. "Maybe Benny decided he didn't like Erskine. Or maybe he went into business for himself and decided to cut out the middle man. Either way, Erskine was *mad*. He started threatening Benny Mallett—"

"So Mallett decided to kill him," Tom finished. He was still frowning. "Seems like a pretty weak reason to kill somebody."

"Maybe he didn't do it on purpose," Sam said. "Mallett came to confront Benny, they started arguing—"

"And Mallett accidentally strangled him?" Thomas shook his head. "It doesn't make sense."

"Look, we don't have to prove that Mallett *did* it." Sam's voice was edged with exasperation, and Pippa knew he was eager to leave the room where Erskine had been killed. He kept casting longing glances at the door. "Just that Farnum *didn't* do it. Right?"

"Right." Thomas nodded slowly. "I guess so." But he sounded unconvinced.

"Tomorrow we'll go to Sheepshead Bay and talk to Mallett," Pippa said, taking the lead.

"Where's Sheepshead Bay?" Max asked.

"Near Coney Island," Pippa answered automatically,

and then immediately wished the words back into her mouth. Coney Island was where Howie had gone and joined up with another, rival freak show. She hoped Max wouldn't remember.

But obviously, Max did. She smiled meanly, narrowing her eyes. "Count me in," she said.

15

They had planned to sneak off to Coney Island just after breakfast the following morning and return to the museum by the one o'clock matinee show. But the day was a busy one. First, Monsieur Cabillaud demanded that they spend several hours listening to his lecture about the brilliant and misunderstood Marie Antoinette, and on the damaging effects of too much butter in the diet, which he claimed had been her downfall.

Then, when Mr. Dumfrey, beaming, announced that Miss Bellish, the pretty tattooed woman who'd been standing outside the museum doors the day before, had agreed to join the show at a reduced salary—a blessing, especially since they still couldn't get the Firebird to do anything but insult anybody who came near it—Thomas was charged with making a last-minute trip to the printer's office twenty blocks away to order new brochures advertising *Emily the Tattooed Wonder*. Caroline and Quinn, meanwhile, upon learning that Emily would precede them in the show's lineup, huffily threatened to quit the museum entirely, and both Pippa and Betty had to spend nearly forty-five minutes soothing their egos.

To further add to the mess, Sam couldn't locate a single steel bar he had not already twisted into a balloon-animal shape or a single concrete block he hadn't split by the light application of his pinkie finger, and Max's costume had several rips in the seam where her knives had been improperly stored. All of this meant that by the time the matinee show was due to begin, Thomas, Pippa, Sam, and Max had no time to do anything but throw on their costumes and hurtle onstage.

The performance, however, went smoothly. Nearly every seat in the Odditorium was full, and the crowd burst into appreciative applause after Pippa had an audience member write down the first and last names of her father's parents on a piece of paper and then successfully guessed them, all from a distance of one hundred feet. It was an old standby, and by this time the paper wasn't even necessary. Pippa could have known about Irma and Egbert Ziegenfelder merely by concentrating, allowing her mind to slip like a hand into the mind of the audience volunteer. But she wasn't certain of her abilities yet. The ability to read minds, really read them, was so far unreliable at best. Besides, she wasn't sure she was ready to reveal it.

Max and Thomas were a big hit, too. They'd recently collaborated on an act that involved a hatbox and half a dozen knitting needles sharpened to daggerlike precision. Max, too, had gotten better. Faster, if that were possible, and even more deadly accurate. Sometimes it seemed that when she threw, she wasn't even releasing her knives: they were simply her fingers, extensions of her body.

Even though Pippa had seen them practice the trick before, she still couldn't watch, and she heaved a sigh of relief when it was all over and Thomas emerged, unharmed, holding the hatbox now perforated with a half dozen holes. Sam performed his tearing-a-phonebook-in-half trick with his usual air of gloomy embarrassment, hurrying offstage as quickly as he could manage it despite a standing ovation and various cries of "Bravo!" returning to the wings with his face flaming scarlet and shedding his costume so quickly he ripped his vest clean in two.

"That's the third one this week," he said glumly, eyeing the torn costume.

Lash did his famous bullwhip act, successfully knocking a pen out of the hand of a man in the front row and a lollipop out of the mouth of a child in another, and receiving a standing ovation for both efforts. He came off the stage with tears of joy in his eyes.

The only trouble came when Gil Kestrel wheeled out the famous Firebird for its inaugural performance. Pippa held her breath as the bird was uncovered and sat preening, seemingly unconscious of its audience, in the middle of the spotlight.

"Behold." Mr. Dumfrey's voice resonated from a concealed portion of the backstage. "The one, the only, the last remaining bird of its species: *Aviraris igneous*, the Ethiopian Black-Billed Firebird!"

The audience gasped as the bird raised its head and shook out its feathers, revealing more fully its remarkable plumage and colorful tail and the dark eyes that appeared to be staring sharply at everyone and everything in turn. Even Pippa found that she was holding her breath—the bird did look remarkable, like something out of an old fairy tale.

Later, Pippa could not have said where Freckles came from. One second he wasn't there and the Firebird was basking in the warm glow of the audience's attention; the next second, the white furball was darting across the stage, fangs bared, claws extended, hissing.

"No, Freckles, no!" Mr. Dumfrey shouted, plunging onto the stage, waving his arms frantically, as the audience roared with laughter and the Firebird began screeching bloody murder. "Stop him! Stop that beast!"

"Oh, no you don't." Suddenly Lash appeared with a lasso circling overhead, expertly hooking Freckles around the tail and tugging the cat backward before he could reach the bird. Pippa exhaled as the Firebird, now squawking curses, was hauled quickly offstage, even as the audience shouted and clapped and stamped their feet, clearly believing that it was part of the show.

Luckily, the performance got quickly back on track. Emily the Tattooed Wonder proved to be a sensation. Even Pippa was mesmerized by her presence, the way she glided silently into the spotlight, clutching her coat to her chin, and then in an instant disrobed—revealing nothing but a swimsuit and skin bursting with color. She did nothing but stand there and slowly revolve, and yet Pippa couldn't tear her eyes away. It seemed to her that the vivid tattooed images were moving ever so slightly, that the horses might break free of Emily's skin and gallop through the air and the fish might wriggle their way after them, that the American flag might start waving in the breeze and little George Washington might lay down his hatchet and start singing "The Star-Spangled Banner." It was beautiful and terrifying at once. When Emily retrieved her coat from the ground and put it back on, there was a sigh from the audience, and then a thunder of applause.

"She's a hit, a smash, an absolute triumph!" Mr. Dumfrey had materialized in the wings to watch Emily's first performance, and he applauded loudly along with the audience. "I knew she would be. The crowd loves her."

Miss Fitch, who was watching, too, only sniffed. "Not much to it," she said, and Pippa wondered whether the coolness of her attitude had anything to do with the fact that earlier, Lash had complimented Emily on the very realistic depiction of a rodeo cowboy riding a bucking bronco on her right forearm. "It's practically indecent, if you ask me. A shame, too. She would have been a very pretty young woman. But now she's painted up like an Easter egg."

"It's the furthest thing from indecent," Mr. Dumfrey said. "On the contrary. Her tattoos are highly educational. Have you looked closely at the scene pictured on her right shoulder? A magnificent depiction of the signing of the Declaration of Independence."

Just then the albino twins took the stage, putting a firm end to the argument.

After the performance, Pippa and Max scrubbed off their stage makeup and went to find Sam and Thomas. This was their opportunity to get to Sheepshead Bay and talk to Benny Mallett, and Pippa knew that they might very well be on their way to speak to a killer. But after coming face-to-face with Rattigan—twice—no killer could scare her.

Rattigan was quite a different breed. He had made Pippa, Sam, Thomas, and Max into monsters— engineered them that way, worked them over in his laboratory like samples of experimental bacteria. But he was the real monster. Even now, she could sense him hovering somewhere just out of reach, like a person waiting backstage to make an entrance—taunting them, plotting his next move.

But where was he? And what would he do next?

There was still quite a crowd milling around the entry hall, many of them clustered around Emily, who was cheerfully signing autographs. Pippa spotted Rosie Bickers in the corner, near the giant stuffed Tasmanian emu, conversing earnestly with Mr. Dumfrey. Mr. Dumfrey had his arms around the Firebird cage, and every so often turned to coo in its direction, apparently trying to calm it after its disastrous appearance onstage. Judging from the way it screeched, flapped, and attempted to nip his nose off, he wasn't having much success.

Before they could make it to the door, Mr. Dumfrey turned and spotted them. "Sam! Thomas! Pippa! Max!" He jerked his chin toward the ceiling, and Pippa didn't have to be a mind reader to know what it meant: *in my office, now.*

"You know, that foul-tempered feather duster wasn't part of the deal," was the first thing Rosie said in Mr. Dumfrey's office as he deposited the Firebird cage onto his desk with a heavy sigh.

"Who you calling feather duster, scrub lug?" the bird screeched. He did have a point, Pippa thought: today, Rosie was wearing a blazer and a skirt that looked as if they'd been assembled from the kind of material used for scouring pots and pans.

"He just needs a bit of training," Sam said optimistically.

Rosie jerked her chin in the children's direction. "I

never said yes to your kid wonders, either," Rosie said. "I'm not here to play babysitter."

"Oh, yeah?" Max fired back, eyes flashing. "Well, we don't need any help from a suited-up loudmouth like you, either."

Rosie turned to Max. Instead of seeming offended, she squinted at Max with renewed interest. "You don't, do you?" She raised an eyebrow.

"All right, Max, that's enough," Mr. Dumfrey said, even before Max could open her mouth. He was seated, as always, in his leather armchair. Rosie was perched on the edge of his desk, having shoved aside the full-scale replica skull of an adult *habeascorpusaur*, a dinosaur said to have existed all the way into the early Renaissance— at least, according to the sign that Mr. Dumfrey had written to accompany the model. "And Rosie, have some faith. I think you'll find that information often comes from unexpected sources."

"So it does!" the Firebird crowed gleefully. "Pretty smart for a fat man!"

Mr. Dumfrey rubbed his forehead. "I'm beginning to have fantasies," he said wearily, "of a roasted bird for dinner. Not you, Cornelius," he said, when Cornelius ruffled his feathers.

That shut the Firebird up, at least temporarily.

Rosie, obviously resigning herself to the children's presence, removed her hat and gave her head a good scratching. "I did some digging. Turned up two locals who say your man Farnum wasn't the last person to visit Erskine on the night he died." She reached into her back pocket and produced a little notebook, like the kind Hardaway had his sergeants carry around for him. "Around ten thirty p.m.—give or take a quarter of an hour—a man slipped out the front door. Skinny, medium height, low-brimmed hat, scraggly mustache. Seemed jumpy." She flipped closed the notebook and replaced it in a pocket.

"Funny," Pippa said slowly. The mention of the straggly mustache had set off alarm bells in her head. "That sounds kind of like the robber at the bank."

"What robber?" Rosie asked, and Pippa explained how she and the others had been witness to one of the recent bank robberies.

"Bank robbery *attempt*," Thomas clarified, swiveling around. He was standing in the corner next to Cornelius's cage, pushing food pellets through the bars. "I got the money back, remember."

"Probably a coincidence," Rosie said. "Lots of men have straggly mustaches. My second husband, for example. Looked like he had a clot of seaweed tacked

158 ☞

to his upper lip. Half the time I was tempted to yank it clean off."

"Maybe," Pippa said. But she wasn't convinced.

Rattigan had been like a shadow, passing across their lives, darkening everything he touched. Could he be involved in Erskine's death, too? But for what possible reason? It didn't make any sense.

"The cops will have to spring Farnum now." Sam looked around the room hopefully. "We'll prove Erskine was alive when he left. All we have to do is bring in your witnesses."

"Yeah, about that." Rosie made a face. "Look, I'd trust my guys with my life. Never let me down and always give it to me straight. But the cops may not see it that way. One spent a few years in Sing Sing for forgery, and the other got called up for stealing apples off a grocery cart. It was Thanksgiving," she added. "Nothing makes for a better pie than stolen apples."

Sam groaned. "Great," he said. "Our star witnesses are a forger and a thief."

"Criminals!" the Firebird screeched. "Misfits! *Losers!*"

Mr. Dumfrey hauled himself out of his chair, snatched a woven Navajo blanket from one of his many shelves, and tossed it unceremoniously over the Firebird's cage, muffling the bird's continued shrieks.

"I've done more with less," Rosie pointed out. "And if we go to trial, I'll make sure everyone on the jury thinks those two men never leave church except to help old ladies across the street."

"We're hoping it doesn't come to that," Mr. Dumfrey said, easing himself back into his chair. "Time is, unfortunately, not on General Farnum's side. The sooner we can get him out, the better." He turned to Pippa, his blue eyes bright behind his glasses, and Pippa had an uncomfortable *shoving* feeling deep in her mind, as if Mr. Dumfrey were trying to read her thoughts and not the other way around. Could that have been his secret talent, all those years ago? Was Mr. Dumfrey a mentalist, too? "Pippa, why don't you tell Rosie Bickers what you found at Mr. Erskine's apartment?"

There was a moment of shocked silence, and for a second, Pippa was sure Mr. Dumfrey *had* read her thoughts. Thomas and Sam exchanged a look. Max busied herself carefully examining a pen cap she'd snatched from Dumfrey's desk as if it were a precious artifact she'd never seen before.

"We didn't . . . ," Pippa started. "I mean, why would you think we—?" She swallowed hard. "We've never even been to Chrystie Street."

"Philippa, please." Mr. Dumfrey removed his glasses

and set them down on his desk, leaning back in his chair with something approaching a smile. "I've known you since you were a child—I've known *all* of you, even if I lost track of our dear Mackenzie for a while."

Max made a face, no doubt because of the combination of *dear* and her full name.

"You don't think I know when you've been up to something?" Mr. Dumfrey continued. "The four of you have been skulking around and whispering in corners for days. It doesn't take a brain like Monsieur Cabillaud's to figure out you might have decided to help General Farnum on your own. Besides"—Mr. Dumfrey did smile now, and spread his hands widely—"you've just confirmed it."

Pippa's face went hot. That, she thought, was Mr. Dumfrey's true talent: even with no special magic, he always understood. Thomas nodded very slightly. She took a deep breath. "We did go to Ernie Erskine's apartment," she said. "We were looking for evidence."

Rosie crossed her arms. Pippa couldn't tell if she looked mad or not. "How'd you get in? Didn't the cops have a guard outside?"

"Well, he was slightly . . . distracted," Pippa said. She didn't mention that Thomas had been the one to distract him by claiming to be searching for a fictional street address on the equally fictional Elmore Street and confusing the cop so entirely that by the end of the conversation he couldn't even point in the direction of the East River. "And then Sam, um, noticed that the doorknob was broken."

"Things are often spontaneously breaking in Sam's presence, I've found," Mr. Dumfrey remarked.

Rosie raised her eyebrows but said nothing. Pippa thought she looked ever so slightly impressed.

Thomas cut in with the rest of the story: "We found boxes of a poison called Fleas-B-Gone. But all of the bottles were empty. Erskine must have been out of the poison." He proceeded to explain about the threatening letter they'd found on the blotter, how Erskine had seemingly been interrupted in the middle of writing it, and how Sam had put together that Benny was Benny Mallett, who manufactured Fleas-B-Gone from his storefront in Sheepshead Bay.

When he was finished, Rosie was silent for a moment.

"Might be something to it," she grunted at last, as if she didn't like to admit it. "Got a full caseload and enough paperwork to start my own newspaper. I'll get down to Sheepshead Bay when I can," she added, rising from the desk and sticking her hat back on her head.

"Actually," Thomas said, scrunching his nose, "we

were thinking of going to see Benny Mallett this after-noon."

Pippa held her breath. It was a gamble. Mr. Dumfrey had previously forbidden them from getting involved in police business, and he'd been touchier than ever since Rattigan had escaped their capture. Of course, even if he forbade them from seeing Mallett, they would go. Still, she didn't like lying to Mr. Dumfrey.

Rosie paused in the act of crossing to the door. She swiveled to face them again. "You may be extraordi-nary," she said softly, "but it looks like your hearing is below average. I said I'll handle it. Murder's no busi-ness for children, extraordinary or not, and I won't—"

"Oh, let them go, Rosie," Mr. Dumfrey said with a little sigh. "They'll go anyway, whether we give our permission or not."

Rosie stood there for a moment, examining each of the children in turn. Pippa found she couldn't even begin to make progress into Rosie's mind. It was par-ticularly well guarded—sharp and spiky and angular. Reading it was like trying to grab a porcupine bare-handed. She knew she should be offended by Rosie's attitude—Rosie obviously didn't think much of them—but she actually found Rosie's blunt speech refreshing.

"Fine," she said at last. "But don't expect me to come

and clean up the mess if you make a bungle of things." And with that, she turned and barreled out into the hall, moving like a linebacker with his gaze fixed on the end zone.

As soon as the door had swung shut behind her, Mr. Dumfrey's expression turned serious. He leaned forward, clasping his hands on the desk.

"Rosie's right about one thing," he said. "As I've told you before, this isn't a game. Mallett may be dangerous. He *is* dangerous, if he killed Erskine. I'm trusting you to tread carefully."

"Why are you trusting us at all?" Pippa asked.

Mr. Dumfrey sighed and stood up, moving toward the narrow window, which looked out over the small courtyard toward the dingy gray faces of the buildings on the opposite side of the street. Absentmindedly, he stuck a finger in Cornelius's cage, and the bird gave it an affectionate nibble. For a long moment, Mr. Dumfrey was quiet.

Finally, he spoke. "Years ago, when I set out to find you—you four, the last of the children my brother kidnapped, or stole, or bought for his *experiments*"—it was rare to see Mr. Dumfrey angry, but he practically spat the word—"I swore that I would keep you safe. That I would protect you."

A shiver went down Pippa's neck, as if a ghost had breathed on her from behind. "The last of the children?" she repeated. "Does that mean . . . ?"

Mr. Dumfrey didn't turn around. But she could see his shoulders sag. "There were others, yes," he said softly. "Dozens. Maybe more."

Pippa felt as if an invisible hand were pressing on her chest. Suddenly, she could hardly breathe. She thought of the nightmares she'd had since she was a child, of a long hallway filled with cages, and a child in every one. Not nightmares, she knew now. Memories.

She'd always believed they were the only ones. Or maybe she'd hoped they were.

"Mr. Dumfrey," Sam ventured, "Rattigan knew my parents' names. He knew all sorts of things about them. He must have had some connection to the people he chose—"

"If he did, I don't know of one," said Mr. Dumfrey shortly, "as I've told you before."

Pippa swallowed. "But why us?" Pippa persisted. "Why any of us? There must be a reason."

Mr. Dumfrey hesitated for only a fraction of a second. And yet in that pause, Pippa wedged herself quickly, seamlessly, into his mind and felt it seize like a muscle, or an animal in front of headlights. "There was no reason," he said quickly. "It was random."

She withdrew quickly from his thoughts, bringing a hand to her chest. It felt as if she'd inhaled ice. Mr. Dumfrey had just lied to them. She was sure of it.

"But that doesn't make sense." Thomas was frowning. "Why would he have gone to all the trouble to get rid of Sam's parents if—"

"I'm telling you, I don't know." Mr. Dumfrey thumped the windowsill so hard with a fist that the glass pane rattled. "I don't know why he picked any of you."

"Wait a second," Max said. "You said there *were* dozens of others. So what happened to them?"

Mr. Dumfrey sighed and brought up a hand to rub his eyes beneath his glasses. He was still turned to the window. Pippa could see his reflection, slivered by the panes.

"His so-called work was dangerous. Playing with blood and brains. Splicing animal parts into humans, and strangers into one another, and more. Playing God." Now Mr. Dumfrey's voice had an edge Pippa had never heard before—a raw, wounded quality, like someone in physical pain. "He treated humans like lab rats. And like rats, they died." Mr. Dumfrey's voice broke a little and he cleared his throat. "That's why I vowed to find the four of you, even if it took a lifetime.

166 ☛

I was hoping you would never have to know about Rattigan and his experiments, never have to know about the past. I failed."

"You didn't—" Thomas started to protest.

Mr. Dumfrey turned away from the window at last, holding up a hand. "Don't argue with me, Thomas. It's true. I failed in my original goal—to keep you safe. To keep you protected. But maybe, after all, that's not such a terrible thing." He looked older, in that moment, than Pippa had ever seen him, and she felt a pain deep in her chest, a quick flash of intuition: they couldn't possibly stay at the museum forever. Someday, they would have to leave Mr. Dumfrey behind. But who would take care of him then?

"You're getting older," Mr. Dumfrey said, as if he'd read her mind. "The world is full of Rattigans, just as it is full of beautiful and wondrous things. You will have to see all of it, and you will have to see it on your own. So go." His smile didn't quite touch his eyes. "Soon, I fear, I will not be able to keep you safe anymore. I will do my best. You should know that. I will always do my best." His glasses were slowly misting over. "I fear that soon, you'll have to look out for one another."

16

Mr. Dumfrey's speech left Thomas with a
lingering unease, a heaviness in his chest
and stomach, as if he'd just eaten too much
of Smalls's lumpy, overcooked porridge. He didn't
want to think of a day when he would have to leave
the museum. Sure, the roof leaked, and someone was
always snoring, and half the time the cashbox was
empty and they had to make do with dinners of fried
bologna sandwiches.

But the museum was so much more than that. It
was Danny playing the violin or, on special occasions,
the bagpipes, and singing ballads about heroic dwarfs
of yore. It was Betty combing out her long beard, and

Caroline and Quinn linking arms to demonstrate the newest dances (when they could be convinced to stop fighting). It was Lash showing off by wrapping his whip around a mop handle to make it skid across the floor and Smalls reciting his awful poetry and Goldini turning cards into goldfish and goldfish into pennies he sank to the bottom of the tank. It was playing DeathTrap with Sam on rainy days or setting up applebowling in the Hall of Wax, using empty soup cans for pins. It was Pippa sprawled out on the sofa listening to the radio and Max doing an impression of Sergeant Schroeder by smooshing her cheeks together with her hands.

It was, in other words, home.

Leaving the museum by the front door, now thankfully clear of lingering audience members, Thomas had a shock that soon drove all thoughts of Dumfrey from his mind. Across the street a tall, skinny boy dressed neatly in a school uniform had just slipped out from Von Stikk's doors and was now moving quickly down the street, loosening his tie as he went and shrugging off his sweater. He would have been totally unrecognizable except for his signature straw-colored hair, which was now plastered to his head with liberal amounts of pomade.

Thomas could hardly believe it. "*Chubby?*"

"No," Pippa said wonderingly. "It can't be."

Chubby turned and winced, as though it pained him to have been recognized. For a second, he looked as if he was considering bolting.

"Chubby." Thomas lifted a hand and waved, though they were standing only about twenty feet from each other. "What are you doing?"

"What are you *wearing*?" Max asked.

Chubby jogged across the street, looking quickly left and right. "Shhhh," he hissed. "Stop yelling my name. You want the whole neighborhood to hear you?" He was still struggling out of his sweater, and for a brief second his head disappeared and he was all pointy elbows distorting the wool. Then he extracted himself again. His tussle with the sweater had left a portion of his hair pointing skyward.

Sam was obviously trying very hard to keep a straight face. "Your hair's messed up," he said.

"Good." Chubby raked his fingers across his head, leaving him looking as if he'd recently been electrocuted. "You wouldn't believe all the rules in that place. Clean your fingernails. Tuck in your shirt. Wash your hands after using the toilet." He shook his head disgustedly. "It's like being in jail, but boring."

"You haven't really joined up with Von Stikk, have you?" Thomas asked. It was impossible to imagine Chubby—who had not only run an illegal betting ring when he wasn't selling papers, but briefly crashed in Chinatown with a bunch of amateur pickpockets—learning multiplication tables and practicing penmanship.

"I had to." Chubby looked tortured. "You hear about that big old dribble they're going to float over the city next Saturday?"

"You mean the *dirigible*?" Pippa said.

"That's what I said." Chubby shot her an exasperated glance. "Anyway, Von Stikk's got the corner on the best seat in town. Roof of this office building right across from the Umpire State Building."

"Empire State Building," said Thomas.

Chubby ignored him. "Half the city's turning out to watch." He scratched his neck, looking slightly embarrassed. "Anyway, I got some, er, interests in the landing."

"Chubby," Thomas said, "are you gambling again?"

"No, no," Chubby said, far too quickly. "Nothing like that. More like . . . estimating probabilities."

Pippa rolled her eyes.

"Don't tell anyone about me going to school, okay?"

Chubby looked around the group anxiously. "I don't want to ruin my reputation."

"Oh no," Pippa said. "We wouldn't want anyone to know you're finally learning to read."

Chubby, who evidently hadn't picked up on her sarcasm, exhaled with relief. "Thanks, Pip," he said, thumping her on the shoulder. "I knew I could count on you."

"It's *Pippa*, Chubby," she said through gritted teeth. "Or should I call you *Len*?"

"But you aren't really learning to read," Max said, before Chubby could respond. From the expression on her face, she might have been saying *you aren't really learning to wrangle poisonous snakes with your bare hands.*

"Nah." Chubby hooked his thumbs into his belt loops, practically preening with pride. "Von Stikk says I'm one of the worst students they ever had. But you know," he continued thoughtfully. "It ain't so bad. Sure, there's lots of learning and numbers and teachers yakking away all day long. And they suit you up like a preacher on Sunday. But the grub ain't half bad and I got my ways of keeping things interesting."

His face took on a crafty expression.

As if on cue, the doors to Von Stikk's institute banged open. Students barreled into the streets, covering their noses, coughing into cupped palms. A high-pitched scream announced Von Stikk herself. White-faced, tears streaming down her cheeks, hair disarranged from its typical pouffy bun, she plunged outside after her students.

"Horrors!" she screeched. "SCANDAL!"

Chubby grabbed Thomas's arm and tugged him around the corner. The others followed.

"Stink bomb," he clarified in a low voice. "Two of 'em, actually, detonated at the same time. I had help on the inside. The Extra-Stink Dirty 5000. Picked 'em up at that joke shop I told you about, the one on Fifty-Seventh Street. Whole place must smell like an egg left too long in a dirty sock."

Even from a block away, Thomas could hear continued sounds of coughing and gagging.

"Er, nicely done?" Thomas thought that was what Chubby expected to hear.

Chubby beamed. "Thanks, Tom." He held out his hand, like he expected to shake. "Always good to see you."

Thomas, remembering the shock he'd received the last time he made the mistake of shaking Chubby's hand, quickly tucked his hands in his pocket. "You too, Chubby," he said. "See you soon."

"And try not to learn anything, Len," Pippa said as they parted ways.

"Don't worry, Pip," Chubby said cheerfully. "I won't."

Sheepshead Bay was as far out in Brooklyn as it was possible to go without plunging straight into the Atlantic. Though just down the road from the kaleidoscope clutter of the Coney Island boardwalk and Luna Park, Sheepshead Bay was a quiet place of shingle-sided houses. Beach grass grew between slatted picket fences and seagulls wheeled low in the sky.

It was, Thomas thought, not the kind of place you expected to find a murderer.

Then again, he knew all too well that murderers hid behind perfectly ordinary faces. How convenient it would be, he thought, if everyone's intentions showed plainly on the outside. Instead, people like Monsieur Cabillaud were judged as being freaks while monsters paraded freely in the streets, wearing normal smiles.

Benny Mallett's warehouse was at the end of a short industrial strip. The building, a brick warehouse of modest size, was painted a surprisingly cheerful yellow. There were even flower boxes in the windows.

Yet there was no smoke coming from any of the several chimneys stacked along the roof, and no lights in any of the windows, no machinery grinding or humming. The whole place had a curiously abandoned feel. Thomas began to feel uneasy.

"You think he's gone on the run?" Pippa asked, lowering her voice and echoing Thomas's thoughts exactly. He glanced at her suspiciously to see whether she was actually reading his thoughts, but she was gnawing on her lower lip, squinting up at the darkened windows.

"If he has, I guess we know who killed Erskine," Thomas said. He took a step toward the door and lifted a hand to test the knob. But a sound from within stopped him and he froze.

"What?" Sam said. "What's the matter?"

"Shhh." Thomas pressed his ear to the door. The sound repeated itself: it was a low moan, as if somebody was in pain. Pippa must have heard it, too. Her eyes went wide.

"Stay here," he whispered to the others. If Mallett was dangerous, he might have someone with him inside—a hostage, another victim, someone who needed help. Maybe Mallett had simply snapped. Either way, it would be stupid to waltz through the front door without knowing what was waiting for them on the other side.

He stepped back, scanning the building facade. His

first move was easy: he sprang onto one of the stone ledges beneath the first-floor windows, skirting the flower boxes carefully, trying to get a look inside. But these windows were covered in a fine metal mesh that completely obscured the view. He'd have to go higher.

Climbing, stretching, bending, squeezing, slithering, and wiggling: Thomas was an expert in all of them. In less than a minute, he'd scaled the facade, finding foot- and handholds in the brick, and reached the second line of windows.

"Be careful," Pippa hissed from the ground.

Thomas waved to show he was okay. Then, crouching on one of the narrow stone ledges, he cupped his hands to his eyes and pressed his face against the dirty glass.

From his position, he had a clear view of a large open space and various vats, compressors, and furnaces that Mallett must use to manufacture huge quantities of Fleas-B-Gone. But, as he'd suspected, no gears were turning, no pipes were hissing steam, no chemicals boiled in great copper tubs, no workers scurried around, white-gloved, wearing masks to protect them from the fumes.

Instead, there was a single person in Mallett's otherwise-empty factory: a man with a bald shiny cap of a head and tufts of dark hair sprouting above each ear. He was slumped over a desk in one corner, resting his forehead on one hand and gripping a tall glass of brown liquid with the other. Even as Thomas watched, he sat up with a sudden lurch, swaying a little in his chair, and threw back the last of his drink. When he tipped his head back, Thomas caught a glimpse of a red and swollen face, and a network of burst capillaries stretching across his cheeks and nose.

He climbed down the way he'd come, wedging his fingers and toes against the brick and shinnying, spiderlike, to the street.

"It's all right," he said when he rejoined the group. Down here, the sound of Mallett's moaning was louder, and Pippa looked anxious. "It's Mallett," he said. "He's not hurt. He's just—"

"DRUNK!" The sudden roar of Mallett's voice made Pippa shriek. Thomas jumped, spinning around to face Mallett, who'd flung open the door and now stood, clutching a bottle, lurching in the door. Thomas was shocked to see that Mallett, standing, was tiny—hardly bigger than Danny the dwarf, and at least two inches shorter than Thomas.

He was wearing a slim pinstriped suit with a matching vest, and had a flashy red handkerchief in his pocket. But now his suit was rumpled and covered with old stains. "Drunk as a thief on Sunday. Drunk as a boiled owl!" He lifted a finger at Thomas, his eyes temporarily crossing and uncrossing. "But who're you?" he slurred. "If you came to be paid, you can scram. I don't have any money. It's gone—all gone! So be gone, fleas! Fleas-B-Gone! Get it?" He took a long swig straight from the bottle and then started to cough, leaning heavily against the doorframe to keep from pitching forward into the street.

Thomas waited until the coughing fit had subsided. "We didn't come for money." He was trying to figure out whether Mallett was crazy or dangerous or just hopeless. Maybe all of the above. He improvised quickly. "We just came to hear your side of the story."

It was the perfect thing to say—a remark so general that nobody could find fault with it. Mallett straightened up as though he'd been shocked. "*My* side of the story," he said, nodding very fast. "Nobody ever wants to hear my side of the story. Nobody cares. Come in, come in." He turned away from the street, waving for the children to follow him into the warehouse.

Inside, it smelled like ancient chemicals and, unmistakably, like whiskey. Mallett trundled clumsily back to his desk and sat down. He was so short that his shoulders barely cleared the blotter, and had he leaned forward he might easily have rested his nose on the stack of paperwork centered there.

"Nice place you have here," Sam said, obviously doing his best to sound cheerful.

"Yeah," Max said, with trademark bluntness. "So what happened to it?"

"What happened?" Mallett's eyes were bloodshot and unfocused. It took him several seconds of blinking and squinting before he could focus on Max. "What *happened* is that someone set out to ruin me."

A shiver moved down Thomas's neck. Was Mallett a killer after all? Was he about to confess? Neither of his hands was visible behind the desk. He could easily have a weapon trained on them.

"Who?" Thomas asked. He waited for Mallett to say Erskine.

To his surprise, Mallett just shook his head. "I don't know," he said sadly. "Wish I did. But I guess it doesn't matter anymore. I'm over and done for. *Ruined*'s what they wanted, and ruined's what they got."

"Talk to us," Pippa said firmly, placing both hands on the desk. "Tell us what happened."

Mallett looked sheepish as Pippa removed the bottle when he tried to reach for it, but he made no objection.

"I've been working this business since I was twelve years old," he said. "Started out with a Bunsen burner and a dream, fiddling around with different formulas. I made my first bottle of Fleas-B-Gone when I was twelve years old. Two or three spritzes of the stuff, bam. Whole colonies of fleas just keeled over. Built the whole place up myself. King of the Flea Killers. That's what everyone called me." His chest, momentarily swelled with pride, now collapsed again. "Then a few months ago some Staten Island kingpin starts buying up all of the primary ingredient on the whole East Coast."

"Ethyl parathion," Thomas said.

Mallett's fuzzy eyes swung to Thomas in surprise. "That's right," he said. "Amazing stuff, ethyl parathion. On its own, it's harmless as milk. But mix it with a little hydrogen and you've got one of the deadliest poisons on earth. Even the military won't use it anymore. Killed too many men—on both sides—during the war. They used to call it the reaper gas, you know."

Thomas decided it was time to go for a direct approach. "Do you know Ernie Erskine?"

Mallett frowned. "Erskine." He slumped back in his chair. "Erskine. Sounds familiar . . ."

"He sent you threatening letters," Pippa prompted him.

Mallett just shrugged. "I get dozens of them every day," he said, waving to the stack of mail on his desk. "Had to stop shipments and couldn't afford to pay anyone back. Well, what can I do? I'm bankrupt."

Suddenly, Thomas had an uncomfortable sensation of something *pushing* directly between his eyeballs. It was a little like getting nudged with an elbow, but directly in the brain. And then Pippa's voice was there, speaking softly to him, as clearly as if she'd whispered in his ear.

*Ask about Rattigan*, the Pippa-in-Thomas's-head said.

*Get out of my head*, Thomas thought back, simultaneously shooting Pippa a death stare.

The real Pippa only shrugged as if to say, *What?*

The Pippa-in-Thomas's-head said, *Just do it.* He was about to ask—or *think* to ask—why, when he remembered that Rosie had mentioned that a man with a straggly mustache had been seen coming out of Erskine's place on the night of his murder, a similar description to the man who'd held them up at the bank.

*I'll ask*, Thomas thought, *if you get out of my head.*

There was a temporary pressure behind his eyelids—and then the weight withdrew, and Pippa was gone. He felt a rush of tremendous relief, followed by irritation. It had been much better, he thought, when Pippa could only read the contents of people's pockets and purses.

Mallett's connection to Rattigan seemed like a big stretch. Still, Thomas kept his end of the bargain—if only because he feared Pippa might otherwise slip herself uninvited into his mind and start humming a particularly annoying song. "What about Nicholas Rattigan?" he said. "Have you ever heard of him?"

Mallett frowned. His eyes crossed and uncrossed. "Rattigan . . . ," he said thoughtfully. "You mean that crazy bat who escaped from prison?"

Thomas nodded.

Mallett shook his head. "Bad news. Read about him in the paper. Heard he used to run tests on living humans, treating them like lab rats."

So that was a dead end. It seemed they had run out of questions—and leads.

"Thanks very much for your time, Mr. Mallett," Pippa said as brightly as she could.

"Yeah. You've been a big help," Thomas lied.

"We're sure things will turn around for you soon," Sam added.

Mallett shook his head. "It's no use pretending. Fleas-B-Gone is finished. Dead."

And then, to Thomas's horror, he leaned forward, thumping his forehead directly on the desk, and began to cry.

After a moment, Sam shuffled forward awkwardly. He lifted a hand as though to place it on Mallett's shoulder—then, obviously remembering how much damage he could do to Mallett's spinal cord if he wasn't careful, merely dropped the hand by his side.

"Don't cry, Mr. Mallett," he said. "It can't be that bad. There's gotta be something else you can do."

"Yeah," Max said. "Maybe you can go into rat poison."

Mallett looked up with a look of such pathetic misery, Thomas couldn't help but feel sorry for him.

"Fleas," he said. "Fleas have been my entire life."

There was, Thomas felt, nothing more to say.

17

Even before it came into view, you knew you were close to Coney Island. As you headed down Surf Avenue toward the great glittering amusement park, you could feel the vibrations of the Cyclone roller coaster as it rumbled along its tracks and hear the excited clamor filling the air: the shrieks of children on the thrill rides; the whistle and pop of the booth games; the roar of the operators as they called to the crowds, trying to tempt them into spending their nickels and dimes.

It was late in the season but crowded nevertheless. In the warmth of the early evening, couples strolled together on the boardwalk while children ran laughing across the white sand beach. In the distance, the lights of Luna Park—250,000 of them, according to Thomas—were just flickering on, though it wasn't yet totally dark. The air was thick with smells of roasting hot dogs and buttered popcorn, all intermingling with salt air and perfume.

For a moment, Sam could forget about poor ruined Mallett and poor dead Erskine and poor General Farnum, still languishing in a jail cell. He could forget about deadly chemicals and bank robberies and monsters like Rattigan, who used people the way people used handkerchiefs. He could forget about everything he'd seen and, instead, enjoy the feel of the late-day sun on his face and the swoops and curls of the great Steeplechase Park rides, like a whole city built in midair.

"Look," Thomas said. "See that Ferris wheel?" As usual, when Thomas got excited, he didn't wait for an answer. "It was the very first Ferris wheel on the East Coast, and named after—"

"Where's Max?" Sam interrupted him. Max had been, as usual, wandering slightly behind the group, as if she didn't want to be associated with them. Every so often Sam sneaked a glance over his shoulder to make sure she was okay—casually, very carefully, so she wouldn't see and plunge a dagger between his eyes. But she'd disappeared somewhere along the boardwalk.

Thomas turned around, scanning the crowd. He frowned. "Weird," he said. "She was right behind us. . . ."

The boardwalk was packed with people—women in dresses and men strolling with their shirtsleeves rolled up and a thousand children carrying balloons or prizes or cotton candy. Where could she have gone?

*Rattigan.* The name was there, like a blade slicing through all of Sam's earlier pleasure. He tried to push the idea away. Why would Rattigan have snatched Max alone? Besides, Max would never let herself get caught so easily. Still, he couldn't shake a bad feeling. He would never fully be able to shake it, not until Rattigan was dead.

"Should we split up to look for her?" Even Thomas sounded uncertain.

"No need," Pippa said.

Sam and Thomas turned to look at her. She was standing with her arms crossed with the weirdest expression on her face—like she'd just swallowed a whole peppercorn. She jutted her chin in the direction of the park. "What do you want to bet I know *just* where to find her?"

Sam turned in the direction Pippa indicated. Extending above the ticket booths that dominated the entrance to Steeplechase was an enormous structure that looked as if it had been assembled entirely from paper signs, cloth banners, and electric lights: a massive, asymmetrical, misshapen monster. Perched at the top of the slanted roof was a huge sign burning with rose-and-white lights: *Coney Island Curiosity Show*, it read.

Beneath that was another sign, this one hand-painted on heavy tarp and hastily tacked to the eaves: *Featuring New York City's Only GENUINE Human Wonders! Don't Be Fooled by Cheap Imitations!*

The creeping heat on the back of Sam's neck turned into a full-blown itch. The Coney Island Curiosity Show, Tom and Pippa had told him, was where Howie had gone to work.

"She wouldn't," he said halfheartedly.

"She did." Thomas pointed, and Sam caught a glimpse of Max's wild tangle of dark hair among the crowd of people flowing through the entrance to the park.

"I should have known," Pippa said, shaking her head. She started moving toward the Steeplechase gates. Thomas followed her.

"Where are you going?" Sam called after them. His concern for Max had turned quickly to irritation. No way was he following her into that mismatched dump of a place so he could watch her ogle her *ex-boyfriend*. Or whatever Howie was.

Pippa turned around, shooting him an exasperated look. "Come on, Sam," she said. "Aren't you just a little bit curious?"

He was—but only a teeny, tiny little bit. Still, faced with the alternative of standing on his own or following his friends, he crossed his arms and shuffled after them, muttering so they'd know he wasn't happy about it.

As they approached the entrance, Sam noted that the cost of admission had been increased to a quarter. He didn't have a penny on him—and neither, he knew, did Thomas or Pippa. He had no idea how Max had slipped in—then again, Max had a way of blending into a crowd. It's what made her such a good pick-pocket.

Thomas had obviously had the same realization. He'd stopped a few feet away from one of the ticket vendors, rooting in his pockets for money.

"Don't bother," Pippa said. "You've got nothing on you but a safety pin and a navy blue button."

Thomas fumbled in his left pocket, extracting the button with a triumphant cry. "I've been looking for this everywhere."

Pippa rolled her eyes. "Follow my lead," she said.

Then, in less than two seconds, she transformed: gone was Pippa-the-mentalist, Pippa-the-mind-reader, Pippa-the-maybe-just-a-little-too-bossy-at-times. In her place was a scared-looking girl with a severe sweep of glossy black bangs, almond-shaped eyes, and a trembling lower lip.

"A quarter a ticket," said the man behind one of the ticket stalls when they made their approach.

Pippa let out a noise so unexpected that Sam jumped and turned to look at her. It sounded as if she had a bullfrog caught in her throat. Then he realized she was pretending to cry.

"Please," she said. "We've lost our parents. They're still inside."

Thomas immediately picked up on the game. "I told you," he said. "We were supposed to meet them outside the Steeplechase *ride*."

The ticket collector looked over each of them appraisingly. They couldn't look less like brothers and sisters. Thomas and Pippa were roughly the same height, but Thomas was pale and blond and so freckled it looked as if an accumulation of dust had become permanently stuck to his cheeks and nose. Pippa, on the other hand, was dark and angular, with creamy skin and glossy, straight black hair cut to her chin. And Sam had at least seven inches on both of them, with a too-large nose and protruding ears and floppy brown hair.

Pippa let out another fake sob. "I don't want to be an orphan!" she wailed. Several people swiveled to look at them and the ticket collector waved them through.

"All right, all right," he said. "Quick, now. Before my manager sees."

Once inside the gates, Sam paused, momentarily overwhelmed by the sheer quantity of people strolling the avenue and lining up for the rides and waiting to take their turns at the shoot-'em-up booths. There were monstrous roller coasters arranged in ribbon-like formations, built on high wooden scaffolding that reminded Sam of an arrangement of bones. Above it all, the Ferris wheel turned majestically in the sky, casting them in its shadow.

But they headed straight for the Coney Island Curiosity Show, which up close was even larger and uglier than it had first appeared from the other side of the ticket booths. Flanking the entrance were hand-painted banners showing a variety of performers—dwarfs, fat ladies, dog-men, Alicia the Armless Knife-Throwing Wonder, a lasso-thrower named Tiny Tex, and, Sam was furious to see, a full rendition of Howie's simpering smile and slicked-back hair, with his head rotated 180 degrees.

"You've got to be kidding me," Pippa said. She pointed to a neatly lettered sign by the door, which announced the Coney Island Curiosity Show as the official home of S.U.P.E.R.I.O.R—the initials of Howie's pompous organization, Stop Unnatural Phony Entertainers from Ruining and/or Impairing Our Reputation.

"I swear," Thomas said, his face flushing so dark his freckles momentarily disappeared, "if I ever see that kid alone in a dark alley, he better know how to run."

At the entrance to the freak show, a carnival barker who might have moonlighted as one of the show's giants was perched on a sturdy three-legged stool, working the crowd, talking so quickly all of his words formed one continuous wave of sound. Sam wondered how he even breathed. Maybe he had gills and doubled as one of the performers.

"Step right up, ladies and gentlemen! Don't be shy! You'll be amazed! You'll be astounded! You'll see

marvels and wonders that you will remember for the rest of your living days! This is a one-of-a-kind show, ladies and gentlemen, the only exhibit of gen-u-wine human curiosities in all of New York City—"

"Now what?" Sam said crossly. He couldn't stop staring at that dumb poster of Howie.

This time, it was Thomas who took the lead. "Follow me," he said.

The barker never stopped shouting, even as they approached. "Just twenty-five cents, ladies and gentlemen! You'll see Derrick the Dog-Face Boy, a perfectly normal lad in every regard except for his uncanny resemblance to a Saint Bernard! There's Alicia the Armless Wonder, who can perform the most intricate acts of manual dexterity using only her feet—"

"Sorry we're late," Thomas said breathlessly, cutting off his speech. "Should we head straight to the theater?"

The barker spluttered, as if he had to physically swallow back his words. "Late?" he said. "What do you mean?"

"What I mean is we got lost, and if we don't get changed in a hurry we'll get roasted alive," Thomas said. The barker was staring at him, openmouthed. "So should we head straight through to the theater? Or is there a faster way?"

The barker shut his mouth with a little click. "You're saying you belong to the show?" he said. His eyes narrowed suspiciously. "Then how come I never seen you?"

Instead of answering the question directly, Thomas just turned to Sam.

"Go on," he said, still feigning impatience. "Show him."

"Me?" Sam squawked.

Thomas nodded, staring at Sam with a look that said *don't mess this up.*

Sam had no idea what Thomas expected of him—clearly, some kind of demonstration of strength. After staring helplessly at Thomas for another half second, Sam pivoted, bent down, and grabbed one leg of the stool with his right hand. Then, with the barker still seated on it, he hoisted the stool into the air.

The barker let out a gasp, pinwheeling his arms to keep his balance. "Put me down," he said. All the color had gone out of his face. "Right now! This very instant!"

Sam did as he was told. As soon as the stool touched down, the barker staggered to the ground.

Pippa smiled up at him. "So," she said brightly. "Can we go in?"

"Go," he said. His face was beaded with sweat. "But be quick about it. The show's about to start."

"That was genius," Pippa whispered to Thomas as they passed into the vestibule.

He shrugged, smiling. "I learn from the best."

The vestibule was long, narrow, and dark and lined on both sides with glass cases like the kind Mr. Dumfrey used to display his curiosities. Sam was shocked to see that all of the one-of-a-kind items that belonged to their museum weren't, in fact, one of a kind. Because here, too, was the coonskin cap worn by Davy Crockett and the goosequill pen used by Thomas Jefferson to sign the Declaration of Independence.

Sam had always known, deep down, that Mr. Dumfrey fudged the truth about his various curiosities. But he had at least believed that Mr. Dumfrey's lies were entirely original. Now it seemed that every unique, priceless, historical relic had its duplicate here. Except that everything at the Coney Island show seemed a little bit—well, actually, quite a bit—*better.*

At the end of the long vestibule a sign pointed them through a set of heavy curtains toward the theater. This, too, made the Odditorium at Dumfrey's Dime Museum look sad and small. The ceiling was gilded with gold leaf and painted on every square inch to depict the fantastical scenes that would, presumably, soon play out on the stage: a strongman bending an iron pipe in two; a contortionist arching her back so far she could peer through her legs; an alligator man with a long snout and sharp, vicious teeth. The chairs were covered in actual velvet—not just brushed felt, repeatedly patched and covered over with shoe polish, like the chairs at Dumfrey's. The stage dazzled with footlights and headlights and spotlights and sidelights. And it was *packed*. All the seats were taken, and a good portion of the crowd was standing, craning to get a better view of the stage.

It didn't take long to find Max. She was standing just behind the last row of chairs, arms crossed, glowering at the stage. When Thomas, Pippa, and Sam finally pushed their way over to her, she barely glanced in their direction. As if she'd known, all along, they would follow.

Sam's annoyance came rushing back all at once. "Couldn't miss the chance to see your boyfriend?" he whispered sarcastically, squeezing in next to her.

Max turned, narrowing her eyes. "You know," she said, raising an eyebrow, "if you're jealous, you might as well say so."

The word—*jealous*—hit Sam like a two-ton ice block to the chest. "*Jealous?*" he repeated. His voice rose to a squeak. "You think I'm . . . I'm not *jealous*. No way. Of

*Howie*? Why would I ever be—?"

But at that moment the lights dimmed and several people hushed him. Sam was glad, at least, that in the darkness, no one would be able to tell that he was blushing furiously.

The show began. Another barker—not the one who'd nearly stopped them outside—strolled onto the stage, dressed like a circus ringmaster, in striped pants and a top hat. He had large protruding front teeth and a black mustache, slicked and curled to perfection, which gave him the look of a particularly well-groomed rat.

"Welcome, ladies and gentlemen"—even his voice was somehow ratlike: silken and hoarse at the same time—"to New York City's only *true* sideshow." Several people whooped and called and stamped their feet. "Don't be fooled, ladies and gentlemen, by imitators and pretenders. Don't be taken by *impostors*." His eyes swept over the crowd and landed on Sam, and Sam had the brief, paralyzing fear that he'd been recognized. "Ours are the only true curiosities in New York. One hundred percent authentic, natural-born *monsters*." More people were clapping and stamping their feet, laughing, calling for the monsters.

Sam now felt as if the ice were in his body, in his *blood*.

They came one by one to the stage: Derrick the Dog-Face Boy, whose entire chin and brow were covered in stiff, bristly hair; a pair of dark-haired conjoined twins who must have been only eight or nine years old; a humongous twelve-year-old wearing a cowboy outfit, advertised as Tiny Tex, the Texas Fatboy, who with several flicks of a wrist lassoed first the hat off an audience member's head and then the lipstick out of his wife's hand.

The strongman was named Trogg, and roughly the dimensions of a water buffalo. However, although Trogg did indeed bend iron pipes onstage, eliciting applause from the crowd, Sam was pleased to see that he did not bend them into any animal shapes, which was Sam's particular specialty. (Iron rabbits were his favorite.)

Trogg lumbered offstage to various cries of "Bravo!" Then Howie the Human Owl was announced.

Sam's stomach tightened. He hadn't seen Owl-Boy since late summer, when Howie had been thrown out of the museum in disgrace after the discovery that he'd been attempting to drive the place out of business for a month. But Howie hadn't changed. He had the same black hair, practically lacquered in place, the same cold blue eyes, the same jaw that looked as if it had been chiseled by a sculptor attempting to render perfect human proportions. Most of all, he had the same smile, halfway between a sneer and a smirk, that made Sam want to drive his fist straight through the roof of Howie's mouth.

As a hush once again fell on the crowd, Howie positioned himself with his back toward the audience. Then, with no warning, he pivoted his head around completely so his chin was positioned directly between his shoulder blades and he was once again grinning into the spotlight. The crowd burst into appreciative applause. He repeated the trick, this time swiveling his head in the other direction, and then held up a hand for quiet.

"Ladies and gentlemen, boys and girls, and"—his eyes landed on Sam then, and Howie's expression changed slightly, becoming narrower and meaner, so he looked not like an owl, but a hunting falcon—"*old friends*." He half snarled the word, and Sam knew they'd been spotted. "Allow me to introduce New York's *premier* knife-thrower." This time, Howie was staring at Max, and Max made a low growling noise and started to move for her pocket, before Thomas held her back.

"It isn't worth it," Thomas whispered to her.

"A tragic story turned to one of triumph," Howie said, "Alicia was orphaned at a young age after losing both arms to the same factory accident that killed her parents." The audience murmured their shock and sympathy. One woman actually dabbed her eyes with a handkerchief. Max rolled her eyes. "Cruelly abandoned to the streets, Alicia survived only by learning to feed herself with her feet. The day she learned to twirl spaghetti with her feet was the proudest of her life."

"What a bunch of baloney," Max muttered.

"A brutal and senseless accident may have cruelly taken her arms, but by virtue of her talent and grit, she has become one of New York City's star performers. Please give a warm welcome," Howie continued, "to the incomparable, the unrivaled, the exquisite Alicia the Armless Wonder!"

Sam could practically feel waves of fury radiating from Max's skin when Alicia took the stage. She was dressed in a trim red jacket with the loose sleeves tied neatly behind her back, dark tights rolled up so her feet were visible, and a pleated skirt. She was as different from Max as could be imagined: all sugary smiles, blond ringlet hair, and pink cheeks. And she was good—there was no denying that. Before starting in on the knives, she shuffled a deck of cards, buttered a slice of toast, and tied a ribbon in her hair. All with her feet.

Next to Sam, Pippa was white-faced, squinting with concentration. Sam recognized now what she was doing: she was trying to read Alicia. But he couldn't imagine why.

Suddenly, even as Alicia prepared to throw her knives and the crowd once again fell silent, Pippa let out a loud snort. Sam stared at her.

"What is it?" he whispered.

Pippa's expression cleared. She slumped backward. "She's a fraud."

"Shhhh." Several people pivoted around to hush them. Howie—who was now serving as assistant to Alicia's act by balancing an apple on top of his head so that Alicia could knock it off with a knife—scowled in their direction.

"What do you mean?" Sam whispered. This time, several more people said *shhh* and glared. She shook her head.

Onstage, Alicia gripped a long-handled knife with her toes, balancing expertly on one leg. Pippa leaned across Sam, cupped a hand to Max's ear, and whispered something. For the first time since entering the Coney Island Curiosity Show, Max smiled.

"Ladies and gentlemen," Howie was saying as Alicia raised the knife, one knee hooked like that of a crane, "please watch carefully. For her grand finale, Alicia will—"

Suddenly there was a sharp whistling sound. For a split second Sam saw two blades crisscross in the air, metal glinting under the stage lights, and he thought, confusedly, that Alicia had must have thrown her knives. But no—the knives had been thrown from the audience.

From *Max*. He hadn't even seen her move. But sure enough, the knives had sailed directly over the heads of the seated crowd, slicing off the feather from a woman's hat in the process, and, like skimming a surface of mold from a block of cheese, perfectly shaved the jacket right off Alicia's shoulders. The jacket, now nothing but rags, plopped to the stage.

The whole audience gasped.

And Sam burst out laughing.

Alicia's upper body was wrapped like a mummy's in what looked like a single long strip of cloth bandage.

And beneath that bandage, held tight to her torso and concealed by her jacket, were two perfectly functional arms.

Howie's face went completely white. Alicia stood

blinking under the spotlight, mouthing soundlessly, even as the audience's protest grew to a roar.

"It's a scam!" someone shouted.

"There's nothing wrong with her."

"We paid to see *freaks*, not frauds!"

The rat-faced barker—whom Sam now assumed to be the owner—hurtled onstage, trying to calm the outraged crowd. And still Alicia stood there, stuttering apologies, with her arms strapped around her waist and Howie staring at her as if she were a three-week-old turkey sandwich.

"Nicely done, Max," Thomas said. The crowd surged around them, rushing the stage, so they were comfortably engulfed in a wave of sound.

Max shrugged. But she couldn't conceal her look of pleasure. "I had help," she said. For a moment, she and Pippa shared a smile. Around them, the audience was still shouting.

"I want my money back!"

"And *my* money!"

"And *mine!*"

"All right," Pippa said. "I think that's our cue."

They began moving toward the exit, fighting the surge of people still flowing toward the stage. Alicia had at last fled into the wings, although Howie was still standing under the spotlight with that stupid apple on the middle of his head, as rigid as a statue. Only his eyes moved: darting back and forth over the crowd, scanning the individual faces. And for a split second, just before Sam reached the exit, Howie's eyes found his in the crowd. His lips were curled back like an animal's, and Sam had a flicker of misgiving.

Howie, he knew, was not the type to forgive and forget.

18

**M**ax barely registered the long subway ride back to the museum. She kept imagining the look on Howie's face when Alicia's jacket had thudded to the stage, revealing both arms wrapped up tightly like meat in a sausage casing. Good old Pippa. Max couldn't remember why she was so often annoyed with her—at this moment, it seemed to Max that Pippa had never once done anything wrong, not even when she corrected Max's grammar or lectured Max on the correct way to make a bed or made a disgusted noise when Max licked her plate.

The sun was just setting when they reached Times Square, and to Max the sky had never looked more beautiful, striped with pinks and yellows and blues like the layered cookies in one of the Italian bakeries on Mulberry Street. As they approached the museum and saw a small crowd gathered on the steps, necks craned toward the sky, Max thought for a second that the other residents of the museum were simply admiring the colors. Then she saw Mr. Dumfrey pointing to something in the air, while Miss Fitch wore her usual expression of faint disapproval.

"What?" Thomas said. "What is it?"

"Just wait and see, my boy," Mr. Dumfrey said, keeping his eyes glued to the sky. "Any second now . . ."

Max looked up. Above them, a prop plane appeared, silhouetted against the blue—and as everyone watched, made a sudden dip and twist in the sky, leaving behind a puff of wispy white cloud that slowly began to resolve itself into a letter. The plane kept going, looping and curling, leaving a trail of puffy white letters in its wake, even as a cheer went up from the assembled crowd. Soon an entire sentence was etched across the sky, and several of the performers read it out loud in unison.

"'Dumfrey's Dim Museum. Home of Emily the Tattooed Wonder.'"

"Magnificent," Mr. Dumfrey said with a happy sigh.

Gil Kestrel grunted. "Looks shaky to me." Max

remembered what Sam had told her: that Gil, too, had once been a pilot.

"Dim Museum," Pippa read out loud. She frowned. "Shouldn't it say *Dime* Museum?"

"Dim Museum, Dime Museum!" Mr. Dumfrey waved a hand. "It's Emily that counts."

Lash chuckled. "Ace O'Toole was never big on spelling," he said. "Good pilot, though. Best crop duster in Oklahoma."

"Crop duster?" Max had never heard the words. "What's that?"

Lash smiled at her. When he did, his eyes crinkled so much they nearly disappeared. "You're a born city slicker, ain't you? A crop duster's a pilot hired to fly low over the fields, spray 'em down with 'secticide to keep the pests away. O'Toole had one of the best reps in the biz."

Max squinted again at the words in the sky, which were even now breaking apart on a faint breeze.

"What about the big orange turkey?" she said. "You going to advertise that?"

"I assume," sniffed Mr. Dumfrey, "that you are referring to my rare Ethiopian Firebird. And about that . . ." His expression cleared. "Ah, here he is now. Sir Roger Barrensworth! Thank you for coming, sir!"

Max turned and saw a man moving deliberately down the street, punctuating every step with a silver-tipped umbrella, despite the fact that it had been sunny all day. He had a sharp, narrow, sunburned face, with an eager expression made all the more pronounced by his large front teeth. His hair was long, dark, and curled at his collar, and he was well dressed in a slim-fitting jacket, highly polished shoes, and a bowler hat. Max disliked him immediately.

"Mr. Dumfrey, a pleasure to see you again," he said, offering Mr. Dumfrey his hand limply, as if he expected it to be kissed, not shaken. His words were tinged with an accent that didn't sound *quite* Italian.

"Sir Barrensworth." Mr. Dumfrey pumped the man's hand vigorously—so much so that Sir Barrensworth winced. "Thank you for coming so promptly, sir. You see," he said, turning back to Max, "I contacted Sir Barrensworth to complain about certain, er, features of the bird."

Pippa crossed her arms. "Like the fact that it can't keep its mouth shut?" she said.

Mr. Dumfrey inclined his head. "Sir Barrensworth kindly agreed to come right over and give the bird a talking to."

"The bird can be trained, on my honor," Sir

Barrensworth said. "We sailed back together from Africa, you know, all around the tip of Cape Home and across the Strait of Gibberish."

Thomas frowned. "You mean the tip of Cape Horn?" he said. "And the Strait of Gibraltar?"

Sir Barrensworth gave Thomas a weasely smile, revealing a wad of gum stuck in the corner of his mouth. "That's what I said, isn't it? The sailors swore up a storm, and the bird picked up the habit. Show him to me and I'll soon set him straight."

"Thank you, sir," Mr. Dumfrey said. He looked as if he might be inclined to shake Sir Barrensworth's hand again. Sir Barrensworth wisely crossed his arms as they started up the museum steps. "I can't tell you how much I appreciate it. I know a man like you . . . with your busy schedule . . ." And together, they disappeared into the museum.

Thomas raised an eyebrow. "What do you think of Sir Barrensworth?" he asked.

"Looks like a cheat to me," Max said.

Pippa sniffed. "Filthy pockets," she said. "It's an absolute *mess* in there. Gum wrappers and pen caps and ferry tickets and tissues." She shivered. "Awful."

Max, Pippa, Thomas, and Sam followed Mr. Dumfrey and Sir Barrensworth into the museum. As soon as they entered the lobby, the phone on the ticket desk began to ring. It was rare for anyone to call the museum. Max was struck by a terrible thought: her little performance at the Coney Island Curiosity Show must somehow have been reported to the police.

"I'll get it!" she shouted, skidding around Lash, who'd already started in the direction of the desk. She practically threw herself on the telephone.

"Dumfrey's Dime Museum," she said breathlessly.

"I have Rosie Bickers," came a nervous squeak from the other end of the phone, "for Mr. Dumfrey, please."

Instantly relieved, Max cupped her palm over the receiver. "Mr. Dumfrey," she called, before Mr. Dumfrey could get halfway up the stairs. "For you."

"You go ahead, Sir Barrensworth," Mr. Dumfrey called unnecessarily, since Sir Barrensworth showed no signs of being inclined to wait. Mr. Dumfrey came trotting back down the stairs. *Rosie Bickers*, Max mouthed, in response to his questioning look. Mr. Dumfrey straightened his bow tie and took the receiver from Max's hand.

"Rosie!" he said with a beaming smile. "To what do I owe the—?" He fell abruptly silent. "Mmm-hmmm," he said, and his smile dimmed and then faded altogether. "Mmmm-hmmm."

Pippa, Thomas, and Sam had all been hanging back, waiting for Max. Now they drew closer to the ticket desk. "What is it, Mr. Dumfrey?" asked Pippa.

Mr. Dumfrey shook his head, holding up a finger. "Yes, I'm still here. Yes, I can hear you. You were saying something about Mallett . . . ?"

A zip of fear raced up Max's spine. Thomas stiffened as if he'd been shocked. And Sam and Pippa exchanged a worried look.

"What about Mallett?" Pippa tried again, this time in an urgent whisper.

But Mr. Dumfrey didn't seem to hear her. Now his mouth had settled into a hard line. "Yes," he said. "Yes, extremely. I understand." And without another word, he hung up. Instantly, his shoulders sagged, as if instead of a telephone he'd been carrying a fifty-pound weight.

The children waited in nervous silence for him to speak, until finally Max couldn't bear it anymore. "What did Rosie have to say about Mallett?" she asked.

Mr. Dumfrey exhaled—a faint, whistling sound that reminded Max of steam leaving the kettle. "Rosie's just heard from one of her friends in the police department," he said. At last, he raised his eyes. "Mallett's dead," he said. "He killed himself this afternoon."

19

"'Benny Mallett, aged forty-seven, was discovered by Sergeant Schroeder and Officer Gilhooley at five thirty p.m. yesterday afternoon,'" Thomas read. He was huddled over *The Daily Screamer*, sitting shoulder to shoulder with Pippa. "'The officers would not disclose the reason for their visit to Mallett's remote warehouse . . .'" He paused to flip a page and resumed, "'seven hundred feet above the ground, to moor directly atop the Empire State Building.'"

"What?" Max wrinkled her nose. "That doesn't make any sense."

Thomas scanned a finger over the line of type.

"Sorry. Wrong column. That one's about the dirigible launch. Here we go. 'The officers would not disclose the reason for their visit to Mallett's remote warehouse in Sheepshead Bay, Brooklyn, but sources say that it was in connection with new evidence that has surfaced in the ongoing investigation into the murder of exterminator Ernest Erskine, a crime for which General Archibald Farnum is currently awaiting trial.'"

Pippa straightened up. "Rosie must have bugged the police about Mallett after all," she said. "They never would have made the connection on their own."

"Fat lot of good it did," Sam said, stretching his arms above his head and yawning.

It was seven thirty in the morning, and the children were the first and only ones in the kitchen. Max had barely slept at all last night, and her eyes were gritty with exhaustion.

Her dreams were a strange collision of past and present: Mallett's face, bloated and red, displayed behind a glass case like the ones in the Hall of Worldwide Wonders next to a placard that read *Murder Suspect, Wrongly Convicted*; a turbulent sea in which she struggled helplessly, her arms tied behind her back, while high above her on the boardwalk a crowd had gathered to point at her and laugh; planes that turned and wrote eerie messages in the sky. *Watch out. I'm coming for you.*

Finally, shortly after four, she'd given up trying to sleep. Still, she couldn't shake the pathetic image of Mallett alone at his desk. According to the paper, they'd seen him only a few hours before he'd ended his life. Could they have stopped him? Could they have helped?

Thomas cleared his throat and continued reading. "'But the police were too late. When they arrived, they found Benny Mallett dead, the victim of an apparent suicide. A preliminary medical examination has concluded that he died instantly of a shot to the chest. The gun that was used to kill him was still in his hand.'" Thomas pushed the paper toward the center of the table. "Look. There's even a picture."

"Ugh. No thank you," Pippa said, making a face. "I've seen enough dead bodies for one lifetime, thank you very much."

"Don't be a baby," Thomas said serenely. "You can't even see any blood."

"Thanks. That's very reassuring. Corpses turn my stomach. *Pass.*"

Max dunked four tea bags into her mug of hot water at once, waiting until the liquid turned mud-black. She took her mug to the table, ignoring Pippa's look of disgust when she dumped five teaspoons of sugar into her tea. Whatever good feeling had existed yesterday between them was now gone. Had ended precisely at four thirty, actually, when Pippa had suddenly thrown off her covers, sat up, and hissed, "If you're going to be tossing and turning every two minutes, can you at *least* have the grace to do it elsewhere? Some of us actually enjoy *quiet* when we sleep."

Max bent over the newspaper, taking a long slurp of her tea. Immediately, she felt more alert.

Thomas was right: you couldn't see any blood. The picture was grainy and showed Benny Mallett, head slumped forward on his desk beside a tower of correspondence. His right hand, still clutching the gun, was visible next to it.

"Poor Benny," Sam said. He had physically recoiled from the newspaper, as if the phantom of Mallett might float off the page. "He really loved those fleas."

"Loved killing them," Max corrected him.

Sam sighed. "Maybe if we'd stayed with him . . ."

"We couldn't have done anything," Thomas said firmly, taking hold of the paper again and bending forward to study it.

"We could have talked to him," Pippa said, snatching away the peanut butter before Thomas could go in for another dip. "He was *depressed*."

When Thomas glanced up, he looked grimly

satisfied, as if he'd successfully answered a question he wished had never been asked. "Maybe," he said. "But it wasn't suicide."

There was a moment of silence. This was the kind of statement that Thomas sometimes made, out of the blue. It made Max want to take his shoulders and shake him until that remarkable brain came out through his nose.

"But," Sam spluttered, "but the paper said—"

Before he could finish speaking, Danny and Smalls came thumping down the stairs, side by side—or as side by side as they could get, given that Danny only reached Smalls's kneecap—and arguing about who had been snoring the loudest the night before.

"Since when has the paper ever gotten anything right?" Thomas adjusted his glasses and stood up. "Hold on. I'll show you. Danny, can you come here for a second?"

Danny's only reply was a grunt. Max had been living at the museum for long enough to know that he required at least four cups of coffee before you could get a single word from him that wasn't an insult or a complaint—five if you wanted more than one syllable. But he begrudgingly came over to the table.

"Sit down, Danny," Thomas said.

"Do I look like your trained monkey?" Danny growled.

"Please," Thomas said. "Just do it."

Grumbling, Danny took a seat on the bench. This required him to clamber up on his hands and knees before sliding into a seated position. He didn't, Max realized, look all that much shorter than Mallett. Danny was insecure about his size, which was a source of tension between him and his other dwarf friends, who felt he was too tall.

Thomas took a step back, squinting, and then grabbed a telephone book that was being used to correct an extremely wobbly table in the corner. He set it down on the bench and had Danny perch on top of it. Now Danny's head and shoulders were visible above the table, just as Mallett's had been. "Much better," Thomas said. "Now pretend to shoot yourself in the chest."

Danny made a gun with his pointer finger and thumb and held it to his chest—or at least Max thought he did, since even sitting on the phone book, most of Danny's chest was invisible and she could see only the very tip of his thumb.

"Bang," Thomas said, and then nudged Danny's shoulder with a hand, indicating that he should slump forward onto the table—just as Mallett had done, so that his forehead was resting on the wood. His gun hand fell unseen on his lap, below the tabletop.

"Alas, poor Danny! Untimely death hath closed

thine gentle eyes!" Smalls recited, clutching a massive fist to his chest.

Max felt a prickling sensation that began in her hands and then spread, as she always did when an idea was dancing just out of range—an itch to reach out and simply grab hold of it. Something was wrong with the picture, but she couldn't make the thing, the wrongness, come to light.

Danny turned his head, still pressed to the tabletop. "Can I sit up now?"

"One more second," Thomas said. He turned to the others triumphantly. "You see?"

Sam frowned. "Not really," he said.

Thomas smiled. "The police report says that Mallett died instantly," he said, and pointed to the grainy picture of Mallett, his forehead resting atop his cluttered desk, with his hand, still clutching the gun, a few inches away. And suddenly the itchy feeling turned, for Max, into a full-on burst of understanding.

"I don't get it," Pippa said crossly.

"Gravity," Thomas said. "Mallett's hand would have dropped onto his lap after he shot himself. But in the picture, his hand is lying on his desk. Which means he would have had to raise his hand—*after* he was dead."

"Murder," Smalls whispered. "Murder most foul."

20

"Murder," Pippa repeated in a whisper. Then she snatched the newspaper, as if she would find evidence in it that Thomas was wrong.

Sam's expression was grim. "Mallett and Erskine's murders *have* to be connected. And there's no way Farnum could have done it—he's been locked up this whole time." He looked around at the others. "We've got to talk to Rosie Bickers. We've got to tell her."

Max made a face. "What's *she* going to do? She's been exactly *no* help so far."

Sam rolled his eyes. "You just don't like her."

"So?" Max fired back.

"So?" He threw up his hands. "You don't like *anyone*."

Thomas expected Max to snap back. Instead, she just turned and made a strange face, as if she'd accidentally taken a gulp of sour milk. "That's not true," she said shortly.

"Oh, sorry." Sam rolled his eyes. "You don't like anyone except for *Howie*."

"If you say his name one more time," Max said in her normal tone of voice, which was somewhere between a grunt and a snarl, "I'll take your tongue out through your nostrils."

"Technically speaking, that's not physically possible," Thomas felt compelled to say, and then quickly shut his mouth when Max glared at him.

Pippa was doubled over the article about Mallett's death, her long black bangs hanging down over her eyes, her nose skimming only an inch above the ink.

"What happened to your sensitive stomach?" Thomas asked.

But Pippa ignored him. Suddenly, she let out a short cry and sprang up from her seat. "A magnifying glass," she said. "I need a magnifying glass!"

By this time, most of the residents of the museum had come down to breakfast, and Pippa's sudden demand provoked a babble of responses. Smalls offered to lend his reading glasses, which proved totally useless. Danny suggested that she use a juice glass, tipped upside down, which proved even more so. Betty said that Pippa would ruin her eyes, and the twins gloatingly implied that she was already getting frown marks just from squinting so long at the newspaper. Nobody had a magnifying glass, in any case, although the children were temporarily encouraged by Goldini's appearance, since he always had a bunch of odds and ends concealed in his vest and waist pockets. But after a thorough search, he produced nothing but some trick coins, five aces of spades, a long multicolored handkerchief, and, in a hidden pocket he had entirely forgotten about, an Easter egg, dyed a mottled red color.

At last Thomas had the idea to look in the chamber of horrors portion of the Hall of Wax and discovered a magnifying glass clutched in the wax fist of the famous surgeon Joseph Bell, on whom the character Sherlock Holmes had supposedly been modeled.

Immediately, Pippa dropped to her knees and flattened the newspaper on the floor, once again peering at the photograph showing poor Benny Mallett's body. They were all alone in the Hall of Wax, which on the busiest days was one of the museum's most popular exhibits. Now, however, in the early morning, it was dark, full of shadows and echoes. All of the dozens of wax figures, many of them created by Siegfried "Freckles" Eckleberger, stared out from their displays with blank, unseeing eyes. Though he knew it was stupid, Thomas couldn't shake the feeling that they really could see him—that they were watching.

"I knew it." Pippa leaned back on her heels. Her face was flushed. "I wasn't sure before, but now it's clear as anything."

"What's clear?" Max said, shouldering Pippa out of the way and snatching the magnifying glass.

But just then there was a loud commotion from upstairs, and they were temporarily distracted by the colorful string of curses coming from the attic. There they found Lash Langtry trying to wrangle the Firebird back into its cage.

"What happened?" Thomas asked.

Lash was sweating as he strained to force the frantically flapping bird to pass through the narrow cage entrance. "Mr. Dumfrey left the cage open after a feeding," he said, grunting with exertion as the bird squawked and protested. "The filthy varmint tried to make a break for it."

"And you brought it *back*?" Max asked in a tone of disbelief. Thomas had to agree with her: so far, the Firebird had proven to be nothing but a pain. Even

Cornelius, Mr. Dumfrey's pet cockatoo, was so angry about the new arrival that he would do nothing but chirp the same song over and over again, an awful dirge called "Why the Caged Bird Weeps."

They got back to reading the newspaper. Max, who still had the magnifying glass, spread the photo on the floor of the attic and kneeled over it. "What am I supposed to be looking at?"

"You're not supposed to be looking at anything," Pippa said, snatching back the glass. "What you *are* looking at are gum wrappers. Five of them, Tendermint brand, sitting right on top of the wastepaper basket."

They took turns with the magnifying glass. Pippa was right. Crumpled at the very top of the collection of old envelopes and unpaid invoices were the same wrappers that Sir Barrensworth had left in Mr. Dumfrey's wastebasket.

"It could be a coincidence," Sam said. "Ten thousand people might chew Tendermint gum. Maybe Mallett liked it."

"I've never heard of it," Pippa said. "Besides"—she wrinkled her nose—"I got the feeling Mallett hadn't gone near a mint—or a toothbrush—in days."

"It doesn't make any sense." Max crossed her arms, blowing her tangled bangs out of her face. "What's in it for Sir Barrenswott or whatever his name is if he bumps off Mallett?"

"I don't know," Pippa admitted. Her chin was inching incrementally into the air. When she was extremely angry, you could see all the way up her nostrils. "Didn't he just get back from Africa?"

"So he claims," Thomas said. Something was bugging him: he could feel a corner, an angle of the picture that wasn't aligning right. Or maybe *he* was the one who wasn't aligning things correctly. He was missing something important.

What had started as a simple enough problem—to prove that Farnum didn't kill Ernie Erskine—had taken so many sharp pinwheel turns to the left, Thomas now felt almost totally lost. And Rattigan was still out there, plotting something, free from police interference. Thomas was sure of it. They should be spending their time trying to find him. But now that they'd started down this road, they couldn't just turn back—no matter how twisty and difficult the road had become.

Pippa shrugged. "Maybe Barrensworth was settling an old score."

"So Mallett and Erskine's deaths aren't related?" Sam said, scratching his head.

Even Pippa had to admit that seemed unlikely. What had felt like an electrifying breakthrough now seemed to be another dead end. Still, Thomas kept having the poky sense that he was missing some fact or connection—but every time he reached and stretched for it, it was like bending backward too far and coming face-to-face with nothing but floor.

He closed his eyes. Sir Barrensworth . . . the Firebird . . . the mess of papers on Mallett's desk . . . mess . . . messy pockets . . .

*Bing.* Just like that, a small alarm went off in his head.

He opened his eyes. "Pippa," he said excitedly, "remember when you read Sir Barrensworth's pockets?"

"Unfortunately," she said, shuddering.

"Can you remember everything he had in them?"

She narrowed her eyes suspiciously. "More of that gum, for starters," she said. "And—I don't know—the usual stuff. Loose coins. Pen caps. Subway tokens and ferry stubs—"

"*Which* ferry?" Thomas asked. Now Sam and Max were staring at him, too.

"Don't be a pill," Pippa said. "You know very well which ferry. There's only one, and it goes to Staten Island. So just tell us what you're thinking."

Thomas felt a warm rush all the way to his fingers, as he did whenever he was closing in on the solution to a complicated math problem, or when he had just managed to free himself from a particularly small and airless space. "Mallett told us he couldn't get any supply of the poison he needed," he said. "He told us some kingpin on Staten Island was buying it up by the truckloads. Well, Sir Barrensworth has been going back and forth to Staten Island."

"You think Sir *Barrensworth* was Mallett's big competition?" Max said.

"Maybe," Thomas said. "Or maybe he works for the competition." He'd only met Sir Barrensworth the day before, and then only briefly, but he hadn't gotten the impression of any great intelligence. The Firebird hadn't shown any signs of improving its attitude, either, despite Sir Barrensworth's offer to help. The bird had spent half the night letting off a stream of words, most of them curses.

Sam shook his head. "But why kill him, then? The poor guy was already deep in the hole. You heard what Mallett said. He was done for."

"I don't know," Thomas said firmly, even as he was making his way to the stairs. "But we need to talk to Bickers. Maybe she can find out." When Max opened her mouth to protest, Thomas quickly cut her off. "I don't care if you like her or not," he said. "It's the only way."

"Who're you calling filthy, you stinking hunk of beef jerky?" the bird shrieked.

"Beef jerky, huh?" Finally, Lash managed to force the bird onto its perch and shut and latched the cage door, but not without accidentally detaching one of the Firebird's extraordinary rainbow-colored feathers. The bird, however, hardly seemed to notice. Puffed up with outrage, it continued insulting Lash in its large and colorful vocabulary, sticking to a theme of Lash's poor personal hygiene and general stupidity.

Lash stood up wearily, dusting off his knees. "Should have let the darned thing fly off, as far as I'm concerned," he said. "Been nothing but trouble since it came through those doors."

"Look on the bright side," Thomas said. "Thanksgiving's not that far away. And I bet Firebird tastes great with cranberry sauce."

"Mmm, I'm not so sure," Pippa said, raising an eyebrow, as the bird continued to huff and swear. "I think it might leave a *very* bad taste in the mouth."

They hadn't taken two steps out the door when Sam stopped short, causing Thomas to run directly into him—which felt a little bit like running straight into a cement wall.

"Ow," Thomas said, rubbing his elbow, which had made impact with Sam's lower back. "What's the matter with you?"

Sam didn't take his eyes off the street. "I don't believe it," he murmured.

Thomas followed the direction of his gaze and saw nothing out of the ordinary. Emily was leaning against the gate—wearing not her typical long-sleeved, ankle-length coat but a simple day dress whose sleeves reached only to the elbow, leaving many of her vibrantly colored tattoos on display—talking and laughing with an unfamiliar man wearing a dusty hat. Every so often, a passerby would swivel around to stare at the coils of color looping around her wrists and ankles—as, in fact, Mr. Dumfrey had hoped they would. He had actually suggested that Emily should start spending part of her lunch breaks outside, as a form of free advertisement for the museum.

"What?" Thomas's elbow ached and he was annoyed about it. "I don't see what's so special about . . ." But then the man in the hat turned slightly, so that the shadows fell across his face differently, and the words died in Thomas's throat. He stood there gaping next to his friends.

The man was none other than Gil Kestrel, the

229 ☞

perpetually foul-tempered janitor. He had been momentarily unrecognizable for the simple but absolutely astounding fact that he was *smiling*.

Never once since Kestrel had joined up with the museum had Thomas ever seen Kestrel crack a smile— not when the twins had fumbled a step during a complicated *pas de deux* and ended up flat on their backs with their legs, still in unison, kicking in the air; not when Smalls and Danny, for a joke, had posed as mannequins in the Hall of Wax and spent the morning jumping out at people; not even when one of Goldini's doves had swooped off the stage and snatched the toupee off of a man in the front row who had been complaining loudly about the poor quality of the acts. So bizarre, so totally unexpected, was this change that it made Kestrel look like a stranger.

Even weirder was the fact that, just after spotting the kids, he immediately waved them over. At least he still had a toothpick wedged in the corner of his mouth. Had he removed this permanent accessory, Sam might have fainted.

"Come here," Kestrel said, still smiling widely, as if all along they'd been the best of friends. "You've gotta see this! Go on, Emily. Show them," he urged her, turning back to Emily and nudging her with an elbow.

Pippa and Max exchanged a smirking, knowing glance.

"Oh, they don't care," Emily said, blushing. "It's just an old story."

"It's better than any story I ever heard," Kestrel said. "Come on, tell them."

"I was telling Gil about Icarus," Emily said. Even the way she said *Gil* was surprising—everybody else called Gil *Kestrel*, except for Mr. Dumfrey, who called him, for reasons related to an old joke on which he had never elaborated, Butter Boy or Bean Shooter. "You know the story of Icarus, don't you?"

"I do," Pippa said importantly, before Thomas could say that he did, too. "He wanted to fly so he made wings of wax. But he went too close to the sun and the wings melted."

Emily turned over her arm so that the soft skin of her inner wrist was revealed. Painted there were vivid blue waves reaching up to swallow a pair of kicking ankles, and a set of enormous, gold-tinged wings.

"How about that?" Kestrel's voice was now lower and more melancholy. "He was a fly-boy, just like me. Crashed and burned, just like me, too."

"Oh, but there's another lesson to be learned, Gil. Here. I'll show you one of my favorites." She hitched her left sleeve even higher. On her bicep, just above her elbow, was a beautiful tattooed illustration of a bird, with flame-colored feathers and a look of pure, soaring joy on its face. It was rising up from what looked like a campfire.

"What is that?" Kestrel asked, making a face. "Another Firebird?"

She laughed and shook her head. "It's a phoenix," she said. "Legend has it that phoenixes live and die in flame. They crash and burn, too. But they always rise again. That's why it's my favorite tattoo. It reminds me that no matter how dark things get, there's always a chance to be reborn."

Kestrel didn't speak right away. When he did, his voice was thick with feeling. "Emily . . . ," he said, and then stopped, as if the force of his emotions was strangling him.

It was time to make an exit. Thomas coughed awkwardly. "Okay. Well, then. I guess we'll see you later," he said as loudly as possible, since he was afraid that Emily and Kestrel might simply start kissing in front of him. But Emily and Kestrel, now gazing deep into each other's eyes, obviously didn't hear.

T he air had a bite to it. Despite the early hour, the
sun was lagging behind the buildings, strip-
ing the streets in shadow, and the wind had the
sharp blow of autumn. Soon the weather would turn,
and the rain would arrive to tumble the leaves from the
streets and turn them to mulch in the gutters, to send
the city, shivering, inside.

It was amazing to think that at this time last year,
Max had been a perfect stranger. Thomas, Pippa, and
Sam had in some ways been strangers to one another—
coexisting without being friends, maybe afraid to admit
to the similarities among them, afraid to acknowledge
what they all suspected: that of all the other residents
of the museum, they were the real and true freaks.

That was before Max had arrived on the doorstep, fierce and proud and perfect—there was no point in trying to deny it anymore; Sam *did* think she was perfect, except perhaps for her tendency to look at him as if he was a squashed bug on the sole of her shoe—before Rattigan had escaped from prison and revealed their awful pasts and ripped a hole in their world. Ever since then, it seemed that trouble followed them everywhere. It was as if Rattigan was a kind of evil eye in reverse. Once he had turned his gaze on them, they'd learned to see as he did and found evidence of evil everywhere.

Could Sam ever forget what Rattigan had done to them? Could he forgive? And would things ever return to normal?

But even as Sam thought the question, he knew that there had never been a normal—not for him, not for anyone at the museum, maybe not for anyone in the world. And he thought again about what Mr. Dumfrey had said: that change always came, that it was bound to come. That Thomas, Max, Sam, and Pippa would someday have to look out for one another.

And maybe, just maybe, they were ready.

As soon as they entered Rosie's office, Sam knew it was a mistake to have come—especially when they almost immediately had to dodge an enormous blizzard of papers that came flying at their heads.

"I told you to *stay* out!" Rosie was bellowing from an unseen portion of her office—a sentence presumably uttered at the young man they'd once again seen fleeing down the stairs—while her harried assistant once again did her best to melt into her desk. A moment later, Rosie's head appeared around the corner and Sam accidentally let out a cry of alarm. Her hair was an enormous frizzled mass around her head, kind of like a giant sea anemone that had become stuck to her forehead and was frantically waving to be let off.

"Oh, it's the kid wonders," she said. She didn't sound exactly upset to see them, but she didn't sound exactly happy, either. She patted down her hair, which had the effect of doing absolutely nothing. "Come in, come in. Sorry for the mess. Busy week. Had a little tiff with the opposing counsel on one of my cases. You might have seen him on his way out. Last time he'll expect *me* to settle."

Sam had not thought that Rosie's office could have grown messier since the last time they'd seen it. But the piles had definitely multiplied. It looked as if someone were making a miniature of the Manhattan skyline in paper.

"How do you find anything in here?" Pippa said, wrinkling her nose. Sam knew how much Pippa hated disorder—she color-coded all her clothing and often sneaked into the exhibits late at night to reorder any objects that had been slightly disarranged.

"Oh, I have a system." Rosie waved a hand vaguely and took a seat on top of the radiator, which was one of the only clear surfaces in the place. "To what do I owe the pleasure?"

Thomas, Sam, and Pippa exchanged a look. Max was staring resolutely at the floor, scowling.

"Well," Thomas said. "It's kind of a long story." He took a deep breath and started in. He reminded Rosie about how they'd gone to Erskine's workshop and found the letter to Benny Mallett. He told her about the visit to Mallett, and about the photograph in the newspaper, and that it proved Mallett couldn't have killed himself. He even told her about the mysterious Sir Barrensworth and his habit of leaving gum wrappers everywhere.

"So you see," Thomas finished, "General Farnum couldn't have done it—couldn't have done any of it."

For a long moment, Rosie said nothing. Then she stood up. "I see," she said. "I see holes. More holes than in a grandmother's pincushion."

"But—" Thomas started to protest. Rosie held up a hand to silence him.

"Listen to me." She shook her head. "I'm on your side. Farnum didn't do it—I know that. But I've got to be realistic. I've got to look at it the way a jury's going to look at it. The connection between Erskine and Mallett? Could be a coincidence. And if the police are saying suicide, that's what most people are going to believe. As for Sir Barrensworth . . ." She shook her head. "A gum wrapper isn't exactly a smoking gun."

"But—" This time, Pippa tried to speak.

"I said *listen*," Rosie said. But then, for at least a minute, she didn't say anything. She turned her back on them and instead stared out the window, where Sam could see cranes and construction, buildings half-finished, stretching for the sky. When she finally spoke again, it was in a totally different voice—hesitating, soft. "You kids are special," she said. "I get that. But what *you* don't get is how lucky you are." She turned back to face them. "Dumfrey's done his best to keep you protected. Maybe he went about it differently than most people would have, but there you have it. So you're smart and you're different and you're strong, and you think you can take on the whole world." She looked at each of them in turn—even Max, who'd finally unglued her gaze from the floor. When her eyes landed on Sam he understood why she could win hopeless cases, why she was one of the most famous lawyers in New York City. He *believed* her. He knew that everything she said would be the truth. "You grew up a little and you learned about evil. Well, now you're going to grow up a little bit more. Evil isn't always obvious. It's not always the people who make headlines. Evil is sometimes in the failure of people to do the right thing. The brave thing. Evil sometimes just looks like going along with the crowd. And you know what? In that way, we're all a little bit evil."

And Sam knew then that somehow she had *seen*. Not like Pippa could see, but with a kind of understanding that was almost like magic. She understood them, and she understood that the world would never consider them normal. And she also understood that their difference was a strength and not a weakness or an excuse.

As always, Sam felt the strength running through him like a current. But for the first time in his life, he wasn't ashamed.

"That's why I like the hopeless cases, you know." For a split second Rosie Bickers, in her fuchsia suit, with her hair sticking out straight from her head, looked beautiful. "I like to go against the crowd. Somebody's got to. And it's a reminder that we can."

For a moment, there was silence. Even Max was staring at Rosie with newfound respect. Then Rosie cleared her throat. Suddenly, she was all business again.

"I want to help you," she said in her usual brisk tone, turning her attention to a stack of papers on her desk. "I do. So I'm going to do my best for General Farnum. As for the rest of it—the theories and the this-and-that . . ." She shook her head. "Sorry, kiddos. You're on your own."

22

"I knew it." They'd barely reached the street when Max allowed her rage to bubble up. "I *told* you seeing that old crow was a waste of our time."

"Come on, Max," Sam said, toeing the sidewalk with a scuffed-up shoe. "Rosie's not that bad, is she? She's just trying to be realistic. She's right. No jury's going to believe us."

Max opened her mouth, then shut it again. It was *so like* Sam to disagree with her. Every time she turned around, he was still needling her about Howie, or telling her to *calm down, be reasonable, don't be so angry*. What on earth, she wondered, was his problem?

So now she didn't bother answering. She just spun

around and plunged back into the crowd heading south.

"Wait!" Thomas quickly caught up to her, and the others hurried behind him. "Where do you think you're going?"

"You said Sir Bottomsworth, or whatever his name is, might be wrapped up in this mess, didn't you?" Max said, tossing her hair. For once, it was her turn to take the lead. "Well, I'm going to ask him."

What she couldn't admit, of course, was that she had no idea what she would actually *say*. She guessed that Sir Butterswhat wasn't very likely to roll and 'fess up to murdering two people, just as a *by the way*—especially not a soggy toast like that, with a *Sir* at the front of a name that sounded like something you'd cough out when you had the flu. He probably thought he was smarter than everybody else. Still, no one objected to the plan—not even Sam, Max was pleased to see.

They hadn't gone half a block when a tall, skinny man with the look of a frightened jackrabbit burst out of the post office, nearly colliding with Max and forcing her to take a quick step backward.

"There you are," he said, and it took Max a second to realize he was deliberately addressing her. "Been waiting for the past forty-five minutes for you lot. Began to think someone was pulling my leg, on account of my being new." He was wearing the uniform of a postal worker. His nose twitched agitatedly as he spoke. "Had my face practically squashed to the window, worried I would miss you."

"Worried you would miss *us*?" Pippa stared up at him.

He seemed not to have heard her. He rummaged in his pockets and produced a small folded slip of paper that Max recognized as a telegram. She'd never received a telegram before and for a moment after she unfolded the slip of paper she stood there blinking, trying to unpuzzle the message, which was written entirely in capital letters and totally without punctuation. Next to her, Pippa gasped and Thomas let out a little strangled sound.

"What is it?" Sam's voice was a low and urgent whisper. "What does it say?"

Max blinked, forcing the words to come into focus.

```
HELLO DEAR CHILDREN STOP HAVE
YOU MISSED ME STOP I'VE MISSED
YOU STOP DON'T WORRY I WILL SOON
RISE LIKE A PHOENIX FROM THE
ASHES AND MAKE BEAUTIFUL FIRE
```

Chop-chop-chop. Her brain churned slowly across the lines of text, chopping the message into phrases that made sense. *Hello, dear children. Have you missed me? I've missed you. Don't worry, I will soon rise like a phoenix from the ashes and make beautiful fire.*

"No." Sam was reading over Max's shoulder. "No, it's impossible."

"Where did you get this?" Max demanded. Suddenly she felt exposed, as if she'd been turned inside out. *Hiding in plain sight.* The phrase came to her abruptly—she didn't know where she had heard it. But that's what Rattigan was doing, and had been doing all along. He wasn't skulking around in the shadows or living under subway tunnels or abandoned apartment buildings, as the police imagined. He was strolling around in the sunshine, smiling, tipping his hat to passing ladies, blending in, doing what was least expected of him.

The man sniffed, as if he was offended by her attitude and had instead been expecting thanks. "Telegram came through direct to me about an hour ago. Short message—just said for me to give the very next telegram to four kids who would be coming out of that building." And he pointed to Rosie's office. The hairs on the back of Max's neck stood up. "A minute later, another telegram came through, so I waited and watched and delivered it like I was told. Just doing my job." And he turned around with another injured sniff and retreated into the post office.

Max crumpled the telegram in her hand, filled with a sudden fury, and took aim at a corner trash bin. Thomas grabbed her wrist before she could throw.

"Don't," he said, gently removing the balled-up paper from her hand.

"He's watching us," Max said. "He's *following* us."

"It's more than that," Thomas said. He unfolded the telegram and read it over, frowning. Even his freckles had gone white. "See this part—about the phoenix? Emily mentioned a phoenix only this morning. Lash was squawking about it to anyone who would listen. It can't be coincidence. Rattigan doesn't do coincidences."

"What are you saying?" Pippa crossed her arms, shivering.

Thomas took a deep breath. "I'm saying he's got a spy," he said. "He's got a spy in the museum."

"No," Pippa said quickly. Sam stared at Thomas, openmouthed.

"Think about it," he said, and began ticking off evidence on his fingers. "He knew we were going to Rosie's office before we even showed up—that's how he knew to call in a telegram across the street. He's been listening in to our conversations—he knows what we're planning just as soon as we do." The more agitated he became, the more quickly he talked. "Haven't you all felt it? As if he's there, breathing on our necks, looking over our shoulders, just laughing at us?"

Max shoved her hands into her coat pockets, comforted by the feel of her knives there. She didn't want to believe it. But Thomas was right. She *had* felt it.

"Emily must be reporting back to him," Thomas finished.

"*Emily?*" Sam shoved a hand through his hair, which immediately swung back over his eyes, curtain-like. "You think Emily's the spy?"

"Who else would it be?" Thomas frowned. "She popped up out of nowhere the moment this trouble started. She's the one who told us the story of the phoenix. She could have easily overheard us talking about going to see Rosie."

Max had to admit it made sense. But she liked Emily—liked her far better than those drippy twins who were always squabbling about a borrowed hairpin or lost eyeliner.

"Poor Kestrel," Pippa said, sighing. "I feel so bad for him."

Max frowned. "What's Kestrel got to do with it?"

Pippa stared at her. "Really?" She threw up her hands. "Really? Am I the only one who sees anything?" And then, turning away, she muttered something under her breath that sounded suspiciously like *blind* and *idiots* and *wouldn't know love if it smacked them in the face with a baseball bat.*

"All right." Sam sighed. Max could tell that he, too, was struggling with the idea of Emily as a spy. "What do you want to do about it?"

Thomas gnawed on his lower lip. "Let's stick to Max's plan," he said finally. "We'll sort out Sir Barrensworth first, and see if he has any connection to Mallett and Erskine. We can deal with Emily later."

They set out again, entering the subway at Thirty-Third Street and heading uptown, a portion of the city Max rarely visited. As soon as they exited at Ninety-Sixth Street, she remembered why.

This wasn't the New York she loved, the New York of trolleys and taxis blasting their horns and the rattle of subways beneath the grates; of crowds and tourists and pretzel vendors and shopkeepers shouting out to one another across the street; of everything crammed together, a mishmash of people and accents and build-ings standing stiff-shouldered and narrow next to their neighbors, as if doing their best to take up as little space as possible.

Here, the buildings were enormous, with fancy scrolled stonework and white-gloved doormen standing at every entrance. They were the kind of buildings that didn't say *please come in* or *thanks for noticing me* but instead *wipe your feet and mind your manners*. Instead of the usual clamor of voices and traffic, it was strangely quiet, as if the whole neighborhood were holding its breath, worried about offending. And everyone they passed gave them a dirty look, as if they were something rotten that had accidentally been carried uptown on the sole of a shoe.

Thomas remembered that Sir Barrensworth's card had listed his address as 1270 Park Avenue. But when they arrived at the correct block, they found that number 1270 didn't exist. There were only two apartment buildings on the street, both of them enormous, with identical green awnings and identically snooty-looking doormen.

"Are you sure you didn't make a mistake?" Pippa asked, staring up doubtfully at the ornate iron numbers, which jumped straight from 1260 to 1280.

"I'm positive," Thomas said firmly. "His card said 1270 Park Avenue. I'd swear to it."

"Maybe we should double-check," Sam suggested gently. "Just to be sure."

"You go, Pippa," Max said cheerfully. "You look like the kind of priss who'd live up here."

Pippa scowled. In Max's opinion, this only completed the effect. "Fine," she said. "Wait here. I don't want you ruining anything." With a toss of her dark hair, she disappeared into the first building, her white shoes slapping loudly on the pavement. She reappeared a minute later, shaking her head.

"No Sir Barrensworth," she said. She tried next at number 1280, with the same result. No Sir Barrensworth had lived at any time at either address. Just to be safe, they crossed the street and tried the apartment buildings there. But no one, it seemed, had ever heard of a Sir Barrensworth.

"What now?" Pippa was growing so impatient she was practically dancing in place.

Thomas's mood had also plummeted. "*Nothing* now," he said, shaking his head in disgust. "That's it. No more. It's a dead end."

"What about the Staten Island connection?" Sam said.

"Do you know how big Staten Island is?" Thomas shook his head. "Forget it. Let's go home. Sir Barrensworth's bound to turn up sometime. He's supposed to be training that stupid Firebird, isn't he?"

"I still don't understand what's in it for Barley-horn," Max said as they started back toward the subway. "Why'd he do it? Why'd he do *any* of it?"

Thomas shoved his hands in his pocket. "Barrensworth, Erskine, and Mallett. Emily and Rattigan." He fell into a moody silence. Max tried to put herself in Thomas's shoes, to see what he was seeing. She wished, in that moment, she had Pippa's ability to slip into another person's mind at will. All she saw was a series of disconnected images: Mallett, red-eyed and miserable, complaining that he was ruined; Emily tracing the outlines of her phoenix tattoo; poor Farnum siphoning his dead fleas into a matchbox.

"And don't forget about the bank robberies," Pippa said. "Rattigan's got to be wrapped up in that, too."

Still, Thomas said nothing. Max held her breath, waiting for the moment that he would figure it all out, when he would give a cry of "I know!" and make sense of everything that had happened, when he would complete the whole puzzle.

But Thomas just sighed and shook his head. "Missing piece," was all he said.

23

Pippa felt as if she'd just been forced to eat one of Goldini's awful dinners: there was a hard knot at the bottom of her stomach that simply wouldn't go away. Rattigan-Emily-Erskine-Mallett-Barrensworth. Erskine-Rattigan-Barrensworth-Mallett-Emily. The names chased themselves around and around in her head, like bees circling endlessly around the same flower. Was Sir Barrensworth in fact responsible for killing Mallett and Erskine? If so, why? And why had Rattigan sent Emily to spy on them? Was it just for fun, to make them feel unsafe? Or was he trying to keep them from discovering some truth, from stumbling onto the connection that, even now, was floating just out of reach?

Thinking this way made her feel as if her brain were tangled up into one of the complex knots from which Thomas freed himself during his acts, and she soon gave up. The fact was that they were no closer to freeing General Farnum than they had ever been. They would have to count on Rosie to do her job, or else . . .

Well. She didn't want to think about the *or else* part.

The others were obviously just as worried and unhappy as she was. She didn't need to be a mind reader to know that. Thomas was unusually silent, and instead of babbling on about the way to mine steel or the chemical characteristics of charcoal or how a dual-compressor engine was manufactured or any of the other billions of facts he'd read in a book, he stared moodily at the ground, biting his lip. Max cleaned her nails with one of her knives, struggling to appear unconcerned—but her hands were trembling, and she nicked herself twice. And poor Sam gripped the subway pole so tightly, he made a hand-shaped indentation in the steel, causing several people to swivel around and stare as the children hurriedly exited, a full two stops early.

"Sorry." Sam blushed deeply. "I was distracted."

"I feel like a walk anyway," Pippa said quickly, so Sam wouldn't feel bad. "It's too claustrophobic down here." The subway did feel close and small after the telegram they'd received. Pippa had the sense of many minds reaching for hers like so many clammy hands. She couldn't relax.

But even the late afternoon sunshine couldn't break up the shadow that had fallen over them. They walked together as a group, but might as well have been alone. They said not a single word to one another. Occasionally Thomas stopped and looked up, and Pippa's heart soared, thinking he'd had a breakthrough. But every time he only shook his head disgustedly and continued on, head bent, kicking at the occasional stray candy wrapper or empty tin can.

They passed the old movie theater where earlier in the summer they'd met with Ned Spode—who had proved, ultimately, to be an agent for Rattigan. Sometimes Pippa still had nightmares about what had happened in that factory, of Rattigan's face illumined by twisted shadows, and Spode's mangled leg, a horrible construction of metal and muscle and skin, remodeled by Rattigan in a laboratory, just as they had been built— remade differently, stronger, *stranger*.

She shook her head, as though she might physically clear her mind of the idea. Just then she spotted a cheerful-looking store across the street. A small crowd had gathered to point at various items—whoopee cushions, trick decks, exploding gum, squirting flowers—arranged in the tiered window display.

"Hey, Thomas." She stopped. The big red sign above the door announced: *McNulty's Novelty Shoppe*. "Isn't that the store Chubby's always going on about?"

Thomas looked up. For the first time in an hour, his expression cleared.

"Come on," she said. "Let's go in." When he hesitated, she nudged him with an elbow. She hated to see Thomas so upset. "You're curious, aren't you? Besides"—she lowered her voice—"you said yourself there's nothing more we can do right now."

"Think they got any more of those stink bombs?" Max said thoughtfully.

Pippa knew enough about Max to be deeply suspicious. "Why?"

Max shrugged. "Was thinking maybe we'd give Emily a reason to want to leave the museum, that's all."

At this, Thomas broke into a smile. "Sometimes, Max," he said, clapping her on the back, "I think you might be the genius of the group."

McNulty's Novelty Shoppe looked, on the inside, like the deranged imaginings of a mischievous twelve-year-old.

Mr. McNulty also gave off the impression of youth, despite the single tuft of gray hair that stuck straight from the top his otherwise bald head, the withered flower he wore in his lapel, and the fact that he walked with a cane.

"Welcome, welcome!" He thumped out from behind the counter to greet them. "What can I tempt you with? A nice rubber chicken? Itching powder? Exploding bubble gum? X-ray glasses? A few trick candles? Or maybe a good old-fashioned slingshot?" And he pointed at each object in question with the tip of his cane.

"We're just looking for now," Pippa said. "Thanks, though."

Mr. McNulty leaned heavily on his cane, which was painted a bright yellow. "Look away, look away," he cried, reaching one hand into his jacket pocket. "Just be careful. It's all fun and games until somebody gets— *Squirt*." The hand inside his pocket twitched and, all at once, a stream of water shot out from his lapel flower— straight into Pippa's eyes.

Pippa shrieked and stumbled backward while Max exploded into laughter.

"That was *not* funny," Pippa said, glaring fiercely at Mr. McNulty, even as she attempted to wipe the water from her cheeks.

"Oh, come on, Pippa." Thomas slung an arm around

her shoulder. All traces of his earlier bad mood were gone. "You have to admit it was a *little* funny."

"A very little," she said. But she still scowled when Mr. McNulty began to laugh.

They circled the shop, stopping every so often to admire one of Mr. McNulty's gags: a jar of peanut butter that released a spring-loaded snake when the top was unscrewed, a fake ice cube containing a cockroach. To Max's infinite disappointment, Mr. McNulty had recently sold the last of his stink bombs and was waiting for a new order.

"But I got something even better." Mr. McNulty picked up a tin from a display beside the register. "Sergeant Schnorner's Superior Sneezing Powder! One hundred percent guaranteed to get the best, the biggest, the tickliest sneezes. Want to hear a neat trick?" He didn't wait for an answer. "Put a little powder into a balloon—just a tablespoon or two will do the trick—and blow the whole thing up nice and full. When you let go, the balloon goes shooting around the room like an airplane, giving everybody a dusting of the stuff. You should hear the sneezes! Like a lion's roar. Like a plane engine!"

"Thanks," Pippa said. "But we were really looking for—" She stopped speaking when she saw Thomas's face, which had gone paper-white. "What?" she said. "What is it?"

Thomas ignored her. He was still staring at Mr. McNulty, transfixed and terrified, as if he'd just seen a ghost. "Airplane," he croaked. "What did you say about an airplane?"

"Sneezes like a lion's roar," Mr. McNulty said. "Like a plane engine!"

"No," Thomas said. "No, before that. About the balloon."

Mr. McNulty picked up at last on the oddness of Thomas's expression. He frowned. "I said it zooms around like an airplane," he said. "Like one of those crop-duster planes, letting off a spray."

"A spray . . ." Thomas closed his eyes and swayed on his feet, as if he was about to fall over.

"What is it?" Pippa hissed. "Are you sick or something?"

For a second, he didn't respond. Then he opened his eyes again, and color flooded back into his face all at once. "The dirigible." He turned to Pippa, grabbing her arms. "Where will the dirigible launch?"

"The dirigible?" This was such a sudden change of topic, Pippa thought she must have misheard.

"Yes, the dirigible," Thomas snapped. "Where does it launch tomorrow?"

"I don't know." Pippa was flustered. She had a sense

of his mind moving quickly—she could feel it, whirling and whirling, like a carousel spinning so quickly all the individual horses became a blur. "I can't remember what the radio said. Some big factory on Staten Island—" She broke off, inhaling sharply.

"That's where all the poison's been going," he said. "That's why Mallett couldn't get any of the ingredients to make Fleas-B-Gone. And that's why he and Erskine were killed—because they were asking too many questions."

"I don't understand," Sam said, even as Pippa did understand. Finally—she knew, she saw it, the missing piece, and a pit yawned open in her stomach.

Thomas dropped Pippa's arms. He turned to Sam, looking suddenly exhausted. "The dirigible," he said, lowering his voice so that Mr. McNulty wouldn't overhear. "He's going to load up the dirigible with reaper gas and let it loose over the city. He'll kill thousands— tens of thousands. Maybe more."

"He . . . ?" Sam's eyes went wide. "You don't mean . . . ?"

"Who else?" Thomas said grimly. "Rattigan."

"He must have been planning this for months," Thomas said. They were on their way back to the museum. Pippa had to jog to keep pace with the rest of the group: Sam's legs were nearly double the length of hers, Thomas was naturally quick, and Max was used to dodging and weaving through a crowd. "It must have cost a fortune to get all the materials together. That's why he's been robbing banks. And calling in favors, too. Whoever's sponsoring the dirigible flight—"

"Woodhull Enterprises," Pippa interjected.

"Woodhull Enterprises, yeah. They must be in Rattigan's pocket. Maybe they owe Rattigan a favor from long ago, before the war. Of course, they don't know what he's planning to do."

"So that rat-faced guy who nearly kidnapped you at the bank—?" Pippa said.

"Working for Rattigan," he said. "Just like you thought. And he was spotted outside Erskine's apartment, too, the night Erskine was killed."

"It wasn't a coincidence," Pippa said.

"But how do we stop him?" Sam said, dodging a man's hot dog cart, hands up so he wouldn't accidentally overturn it. "If Rosie wouldn't listen about Barrensworth—"

"Forget Rosie," Thomas said. "There's no time to try and persuade her. Dumfrey will have to go to the police. I know," he added, when Max made another face. "But we have no choice. The dirigible launches tomorrow. And you heard what Chubby said. Half the city is planning to turn out."

Pippa had a sudden image of the vast dirigible whirring above the city, casting the streets in shadow, and all the people clustered on rooftops and sidewalks to see it—kids, families, babies, grandmothers—as the poison went hissing through the air . . . unseen . . . unnoticed . . .

Her stomach rolled into her throat.

New York would turn into a graveyard.

S am was the first through the front door, shoving
so hard it smacked against the interior wall and
dislodged a large portion of plaster. But he was
so consumed with thoughts of Rattigan and his terrible
plan, he didn't even feel guilty.

Uncharacteristically, the twins were sitting behind
the ticket desk, enjoying a rare moment of peace and
painting each other's nails an awful shade of crim-
son that, against their alabaster skin, looked just like
blood.

"Where's Dumfrey?" Sam burst out. "We need to
talk to Dumfrey."

Caroline barely flicked her eyes in their direction.

"Gone," she said simply.

"Gone?" Thomas parroted. "What do you mean, *gone*?"

Caroline rolled her eyes. "You don't expect me to define the word, do you? Hasn't Monsieur Cabillaud taught you *anything*?"

Max made a growling noise and took a step forward. "Listen, you overcooked piece of—"

"Max." Pippa put a hand on Max's shoulder, presumably to keep her from jumping over the ticket desk and clocking Caroline directly in the nose. She turned back to the twins.

"Where did he go? Please. It's important."

Caroline rolled her eyes. "If you must know," she said, "he's gone to visit Farnum in jail. Afterward, he's going to—ahem—*talk strategy* with Rosie over dinner."

Quinn giggled. "I'll bet he is, the salty dog."

Caroline smirked at her sister. "He told us specifically not to expect him until *very* late."

Max said a curse word that cannot be reprinted on the page. Thomas spun around and aimed a kick at nothing. Pippa stood very still, her lips pinched so tightly together they looked as if they'd been sewn to her face. And Sam's heart dropped, stonelike, to the bottom of his stomach. The cops would never listen to them. They were running out of time—and options.

"We'll have to go to the police ourselves," Pippa said, voicing his thoughts aloud. Sam wasn't sure whether it was related to Pippa's powers, but she seemed always to know what other people were thinking, even when she wasn't reading minds.

"But—" Max began to protest.

"I know what you're going to say," Pippa said, even before Max could finish. "They'll probably just laugh at us. But we have no choice, do we? We can't exactly expect to track down Mr. Dumfrey on his *date*. He could be anywhere in Manhattan!"

"I say we go straight for Staten Island," Thomas said in a low voice. "Woodhull Enterprises owns half of Bay Street. And we *have* to destroy that airship."

"But how?" Pippa cried. "You said yourself, Woodhull Enterprises is in Rattigan's pocket. He has friends everywhere. How are *we* going to stop him?"

"We've stopped him before," Thomas said. His eyes were very dark. "Besides, what other choice do we have?"

For a second, Sam almost hoped that Pippa would continue to argue. The idea of going up against Rattigan was bad. The idea of what would happen if they failed was far, far worse.

But Pippa just gave a small nod, and Sam knew, too, that Thomas was right. They had run out of options. Soon, they would be out of time. It was up to them.

Even as Thomas was reaching for the door handle, however, the door flew open, forcing him to spring backward with a yelp. A glowering Monsieur Cabillaud stood in the doorway, hands on his hips, his tiny bald head mottled with color.

"Aha! *Zer* you are!" he cried. "I have been looking for you everywhere! Naughty, naughty students." He waggled a finger. "You think you can just forget about ze studies, is zat it? You think you can make Monsieur *Cabillaud* forget. But you are in error, *mes amis*! Upstairs, now, and quickly. Zer is still an hour for a lesson before ze bedtime."

"A lesson? *Now?*" Sam cried. Frustration squeezed like a fist in his chest. "But, you don't understand. We can't possibly study now."

"And why is zat?" Monsieur Cabillaud crossed his arms.

"Okay, look." Thomas stepped forward. He took a deep breath. "The truth is going to sound crazy. We're trusting you with a secret. A big secret, okay?" He looked at the others for support, and Sam nodded. "It has to do with Nicholas Rattigan."

Monsieur Cabillaud's neatly plucked eyebrows shot upward. "Ze scientist?"

Thomas nodded. "We know where he is. And we know he's planning something—something big."

"I see," Monsieur Cabillaud murmured. "And I suppose zat you are ze only people who can stop him?"

"Exactly," Thomas said, nodding so vigorously his glasses jogged on his nose. "That's just it."

"Mmm. And I also suppose zer is no time to lose?"

Sam felt a heady rush of relief. Cabillaud understood. "No time at all," he said.

"I see, I see. Zen what I say to you, *mes amis*, is"—Monsieur Cabillaud leaned forward, as though to tell them a great secret, and they all leaned forward with him—"NICE TRY!"

He screeched the last words so loudly that all four children jumped.

"Despicable lies," Monsieur Cabillaud cried. "Unspeakable fictions. Upstairs, all of you, now, or I will see to it zat you are locked into the museum for ze rest of ze month!" He herded them toward the stairs, still shrieking, his chest puffed up in outrage. "*Allez!* Ze dates, please, of ze French Revolution . . ." Monsieur Cabillaud kept them at it all through dinnertime. Soon after, Miss Fitch directed them straight to bed, and they had no choice but to go through the ritual of changing into their pajamas and brushing their teeth and pretending to fall asleep. Sam lay with his blankets pulled all the way up to his chin, as if that might stifle the sound of his heart—which was going so hard he worried the noise might prevent the other residents from sleeping.

And, in fact, it seemed to take everyone far longer than usual to settle down. Sam felt time passing like the crawl of an insect on his skin. But at last, the final light was extinguished and the attic room was filled with gentle snoring and the occasional rustle of sheets as someone turned over.

Sam glanced over at Thomas. Even in the darkness, he could see Thomas's eyes were wide open. Thomas nodded to him, and together they slipped carefully out of bed. Sam peeked over the top of the bookshelves that kept their sleeping area separate from Max and Pippa's and found the two girls already standing in street clothes. Sam had stored his shoes and clothing beneath his bed and changed quickly, hardly paying attention to what he was doing. His thoughts were already outside, flying down the streets, leaping over the water to Staten Island. Would they be in time?

They took the performers' staircase, which carried

the risk of bringing them directly past Mr. Dumfrey's office on the second floor and Miss Fitch's quarters below it, but it was much quieter than the vast, echoey marble staircase used by the general public. Outside Mr. Dumfrey's office, Sam paused, pressing an ear to the door, which was open a crack. Mr. Dumfrey's office was silent. He still had not returned to the museum, though it must have been close to midnight.

They really were alone.

"Come on." Max stood on tiptoe to whisper to him, and for a brief second—a second so quick it might just have been his imagination—he thought she took his hand.

The Hall of Worldwide Wonders was cool, dark, and so quiet Sam could hear Max's breathing behind him. Sam felt as if he were moving through an enchanted tomb. The glass display cases winked in the faint light coming through the windows from the street, and the dark treasures nestled inside of them seemed like buried hearts, pulsing with an invisible energy. On the ceiling above them, the reconstruction of a prehistoric pterodactyl, enormous wings spread midflight, creaked lightly on its suspension wire.

They were about to pass into the lobby when Sam heard something, a muffled cough or a footstep, behind him. He froze.

"Did anyone else—?" he started to say.

Before he could finish his sentence, someone seized him from behind and squeezed. All of the breath went out of him in a whoosh. It was no ordinary someone, either: the arms felt like ten-ton steel belts cabled around his chest. He couldn't breathe. He couldn't get his arms up to fight.

Suddenly, everyone was shouting. Sam saw a figure moving in the shadows. Before he could cry out, a lasso spun through the air and yoked his three friends together.

Then the overhead lights snapped on.

Just inside the doorway, one hand on the light switch, stood Howie.

"Well, well, well," he said. "Looks like you're all in a bit of a *bind*, aren't you?"

"Very funny," Thomas spat. "How'd you snake your way in here?"

Howie raised an eyebrow but addressed his words to Tiny Tex, the Texas Fatboy, who was struggling to keep a grip on one end of the rope restraining Thomas, Pippa, and Max. "You'll want to keep an eye on *that* one in particular," he said, jerking his chin in Thomas's direction. "He's a wiggly one."

"You're going to pay for this." Sam at last managed to draw a breath. But try as he might, he couldn't break free of the hairy arms that encircled him. He realized, to his shock, that he was immobilized.

A foul breath blasted his ear.

"You strong for a boy," said a voice in a low growl, even as the grip tightened around him, so Sam felt as if even his organs were being squeezed. "But Trogg stronger."

It was the strongman they'd seen at the Coney Island show, the beast who was nearly seven feet tall. And Sam knew, with a welling sense of hopelessness, that Trogg was right—Trogg *was* stronger.

"Let us go, you creep," Max cried.

"Oh, I'll let you go," Howie said, making a show of examining his fingernails, which were buffed and newly clipped. "We're just going to take a little stroll first. The Bowery is lovely this time of night, as long as you steer clear of the muggers. And of course, it's the perfect place for a makeover. I'm thinking matching crew cuts. Might as well burn those rags you're wearing, too. Mr. Dumfrey always wants publicity, doesn't he? Let's see what kind of publicity he gets when his prize freaks are parading home in their birthday suits."

"You're out of your mind." Sam was practically

shouting. They didn't have time for this. They didn't have time, period. If they didn't get to Staten Island to stop Rattigan, thousands of people would die. "Let us go, or—"

"Or what?" Howie came forward suddenly, his face contorted with fury and triumph. "You'll call for your precious Mr. Dumfrey to save you?" He barked a laugh. Sam had, in fact, been about to cry out—then he remembered, with a sinking feeling, that Mr. Dumfrey hadn't even returned to the museum. And really, what would Mr. Dumfrey do? "I'm not scared of you, Samson," Howie said. "And I'm not letting you go, either. Not until you pay for making me look like an idiot."

"Please, you don't need our help for that," Pippa said, tossing her hair and doing her best to look dignified despite being trussed up like a turkey. "You do a great job of looking like an idiot all on your own."

"And you deserved it." Max's eyes were narrowed to slits. Sam couldn't believe he'd ever been jealous, believing that Max still liked Howie. She *hated* him. "You and all your Mr. Superior stuff. All along you've been the biggest fraud of all."

"I didn't know about Alicia," Howie snarled. "But better a fraud"—he reached out as if to touch Max's cheek—"than a monster."

Max lunged for him. Pippa and Thomas, lashed together, stumbled forward with her before Tiny Tex managed to rein them in, jerking the rope backward so Max was left wheezing.

Sam's vision went red. Fury pulsed through his body, thrumming in his head. He took a deep breath and, as he felt Trogg relax his grip, flexed and threw his right elbow toward Trogg's face. Trogg, startled, lost his grip on Sam's arm. Howie backpedaled quickly with a small, startled yelp as Sam swung for him. But before Sam could make contact, Trogg had wrestled his arm behind his back again and Sam doubled over.

"Nice try." Howie bent forward. His face hovered only inches from Sam's. "The truth is painful, isn't it?"

Sam was so angry it felt like being inside a stew—something roiling and hot was eating him up. Rattigan would win. Rattigan would *kill*—all because of Howie and his hatefulness. "The only monster in this room is you," he snapped.

"We'll see about that." Howie straightened up. "You know, you should all be grateful to me. Did you ever think about what would happen if everyone in New York found out about Rattigan's little science experiments? You'd be thrown in a cage. You'd be zoo animals. That's if the mob didn't get to you first." His smile was cruel. And worse, Sam knew he was right. "So I suggest you play along, if you want your little secret to stay safe."

They had no choice but to do as Howie said. Tex took the lead, hauling a struggling Max, Pippa, and Thomas forward. Trogg moved Sam forward next, keeping Sam's arms wrenched so far behind his back Sam thought they might tear out of their sockets.

"A fine little parade." Howie wore the same gloating expression that made Sam want to peel off his face. "Just think. If you hadn't—"

He broke off suddenly, holding up a hand for silence, as a noise sounded from the shadows. Sam heard it, too—a faint mechanical click. Trogg froze. Only Tex was still moving forward, straining on the rope, his face red from exertion, huffing loudly.

"Shut up, you idiot," Howie whispered. Above him, the pterodactyl creak-creaked on its thin wire, swaying faintly back and forth, as if it were really flying. Tex at last stopped moving. "Did anyone hear—?"

Crack.

A rifle shot echoed through the room. Tex cried out and dove for cover, as with a clean hiss the thin metal wire keeping the pterodactyl tethered to the ceiling snapped neatly in two—and sent the monstrous, winged creature crashing toward the ground. Howie dove to avoid getting buried, throwing Sam and Trogg off their feet. In the confusion, Trogg loosened his hold on Sam, and Sam shoved him off. With one quick wrestling move, Sam took hold of Trogg's wrists and rammed a knee in his lower back, so Trogg's cheek was squashed flat to the floor.

"You're pretty strong," Sam panted. He was still dizzy from pain and the chaos of shouting and dust. Who on earth had fired the rifle? "But looks like I'm stronger."

Thomas had already freed himself from the lasso. Now, as Howie struggled to climb to his feet, Thomas dove and pinned him to the floor again.

"Let go of me," Howie snarled.

"I don't think so." It was Thomas's turn to smile. The sound of the shot must have woken the other residents, and already Sam could hear footsteps pounding on the stairs, and Miss Fitch crying out, "What is it? For heaven's sake, what's happened now?"

The air was still cloudy with dust from the pterodactyl's spectacular fall. The once-magnificent model lay scattered in splinters, bones jutting from within the wings of heavy canvas, beak pointed to the ceiling as though crying out for help.

A moment later, Miss Fitch appeared on the landing in her nightgown, her hair neatly slicked into its usual bun. Lash was close behind her, scrubbing his bleary eyes.

Then Mr. Dumfrey, dressed in a neat black suit and carrying a vintage Winchester rifle over his shoulder, emerged from between exhibits. "It's all right, Miss Fitch," he said cheerfully, surveying the scene with detached curiosity—as if Tex, Howie, the broken pterodactyl, and Pippa and Max, still struggling to disentangle themselves from the rope, were all part of a tableau he was considering adding to the museum's Hall of Wax. "Just some unwelcome intruders. It's under control."

Sam stared from Mr. Dumfrey to the rifle on his shoulder to the fine wire, hardly wider than a pencil line, that the bullet had severed.

"But . . ." He found he could barely speak. "That shot . . . it's impossible . . . how did you ever manage . . . ?"

On the stairs, Lash snorted a laugh. "Good to see you still got it, Horatio."

Mr. Dumfrey waved a hand. "Oh, well. Some things stay with you, I suppose."

Lash came down into the lobby and made quick

work of disentangling Max and Pippa. "Back in the day, Dumfrey was known from coast to coast as a crack shot," he explained as he curled the rope in his hand. "Could thread a bullet through the eye of a needle at fifty yards. Oh, no you don't." This last bit was directed at Tiny Tex, who'd begun crawling for the door. With a quick flick of his wrist, Lash lassoed him backward. "Just like tying up a steer," he said.

"So *that's* your big secret," Pippa said wonderingly. "You're a sharpshooter."

Mr. Dumfrey actually looked embarrassed. He clucked his tongue. "*Was* a sharpshooter. Now I run a museum. Speaking of which"—his eyes fell on Howie— "can someone explain to me what on earth is going on?"

Sam and Thomas exchanged a look. Sam knew that they couldn't explain why they'd been out of bed—not here, anyway, in front of everybody. More and more of the museum's residents had gathered in the lobby and on the staircase, straining to get a view of the action. And they were in a bigger rush than ever.

"We heard a noise downstairs," Pippa said quickly. "We came down to make sure everything was okay. And then . . ."

"We got ambushed," Max finished, still glaring at

Howie. "They must have broken in."

"We didn't break in," Howie said. Despite the fact that Thomas was keeping him pinned, he still managed to look superior. "The kitchen door was unlocked. Some idiot must have left it open."

"That *idiot* was me," Mr. Dumfrey said calmly. "I knew I'd be returning late and wanted to make sure I didn't disturb anyone. Either way, you're trespassing on private property. Lash, please stay with our new friends while I ring up the police from my office." He handed over the rifle, which Sam now recognized as the one typically on display in the Hall of Worldwide Wonders and having supposedly belonged to Buffalo Bill. "Take this, just in case anyone is stupid enough to attempt a quick getaway."

"Sure thing, Mr. D," Lash said, grinning as he took up the rifle. "Course, I'm not such a crack shot as you. Might blow off a knee or an elbow without meaning to."

"You'll pay for this," Howie hissed, sitting up as Thomas climbed to his feet and then quickly rearing back when Lash took a step toward him. "This isn't over."

"Hmm. Perhaps you should aim instead for his mouth," Mr. Dumfrey said to Lash, raising an eyebrow. "Max, Pippa, Thomas, Sam. In my office, please."

"But Mr. Dumfrey—" Sam began to protest.

"In my office," Mr. Dumfrey said, in a tone that clearly meant *no arguments*. "Now."

Sam's stomach turned heavy again. They would never get out of the museum now. He stood up, leaving Trogg still groaning on the floor. He sidestepped the giant and deliberately avoided so much as glancing at Howie. But Max stopped directly in front of Howie, with a strange expression on her face that reminded Sam somewhat of a cat trying to cough up a hair ball.

Howie's cold eyes glittered. "What do *you* want?"

Max said nothing. Instead, she wound up and clocked Howie straight in the face—so hard that his head spun *completely* around and then, like a watch mechanism unwinding, ticked slowly back around to its correct orientation.

"That," she said with an angelic smile. And Sam had to stop himself from dancing.

The knuckles of Max's right hand still stung from where they had connected with Howie's jaw as she and the others made their way upstairs. But it was the most glorious pain she'd ever known.

"Close the door," Mr. Dumfrey said as soon as they were all crowded inside his office. He didn't even bother to sit. Instead, he pivoted to face them, with a look as stern as any Max had never seen. "As you've just witnessed," he said, and though his voice was steady, it held a fine edge of warning, "although I may be getting older, my eyesight is as good as it ever was. And what I see just at this minute is that you haven't told me the truth. Out with it."

So Thomas told him, and Max, Pippa, and Sam filled in the gaps where they had to: about the relationship of Mallett and Erskine's deaths to Rattigan, and about the dirigible filled with poisonous gas and Rattigan's terrible plan for the city. As they spoke, all the light and color drained from Mr. Dumfrey's face, until he looked almost like one of the wax figurines in the chamber of horrors: pale and hard and terrible.

"So you see," Pippa finished, "it's up to us. We have to stop him."

"Absolutely not," Mr. Dumfrey said immediately.

Max gaped at him. "But Rattigan—"

"It's far too dangerous," he said, raising a hand to cut her off. "My half brother—as much as it pains me to say—has demonstrated again and again that he will stop at nothing and spare no one to achieve what he wants. I hope you're wrong," he added. "I pray that you are. But we can't take any chances. This is a matter for the police. I won't risk your involvement."

"What if the police won't listen?" Sam said.

"They'll have to," Mr. Dumfrey said. But he sounded unconvinced. "Now to bed. All of you."

"You said that we were growing up," Thomas argued. "You said we had to look after one another."

Mr. Dumfrey removed his glasses and stared at them

each in turn. "I said there would come a time when I wouldn't be there to protect you," he said. "Fortunately, that time is not today. You heard me. Upstairs and into bed and no arguments. I'll handle the police." And with that, he pushed the kids out of his office and slammed the door closed behind him. It felt as if he took all of the air with him, too. Max was left with a breathless, frightened feeling.

She shook the hair away from her face. "What do you want to bet the cops take the whole thing as a joke?" she said. "No way are they going to believe Rattigan's going to pull a stunt this big. Not when half the force has been looking for him for months."

"They'll have to do *something*, won't they?" Pippa turned to Thomas.

"I don't know." He put a hand through his hair, making it stand like a head full of exclamation points. "I hope so."

Sam shook his head. "We can't risk it," he said in a fierce whisper. "What if they don't? What if they just laugh?"

"Sam's right," Max said. "There's too much at stake."

"All right, then." Thomas nodded. "We'll stick to the plan and head to Staten Island ourselves."

They couldn't sneak out the front. The doors were

no doubt locked for the night, and only Gil Kestrel had the keys. Besides, Lash was still standing guard over Howie and his band of creeps in the lobby. Instead, they retreated as quietly as they could down the performers' staircase, glided through the hall, ducked into the special exhibits room, and made their way down the set of old wooden stairs that led down into the basement. In the kitchen, faint moonlight came through the narrow windows, illuminating corners and edges, drawing the familiar furniture in broad painted strokes. They moved in a line toward the door that led out to the sunken courtyard where the garbage cans were kept and Farnum's fleas had been buried. Max couldn't believe that had been three days ago: so much had happened.

Pippa reached the door, released the dead bolt, and yanked on the handle. Nothing happened.

"Oh no." She turned, her eyes wide in the dark. "Mr. Dumfrey must have locked up after he came in." There was a second lock, rarely used, that required a key. Mr. Dumfrey kept a copy in his desk.

"Anyone know how to pick a lock?" Thomas asked hopefully.

Max realized that both Pippa and Thomas were looking at her. She sighed. "You got a bobby pin?"

"I have a better idea." Sam stepped forward. He placed a hand on the door and leaned. There was a small groan, and the door popped off its hinges neatly, like a cube of ice out of a metal tray.

"After you," he said, and Pippa giggled.

"Now that's what I call breaking and entering," Thomas said.

"Breaking and *exiting*, you mean," Max said. They passed out into the night, pausing only so that Sam could pop the door back in place.

They reached the ferry dock at a little after two o'clock, and found the ticket office closed. A little sign announced that the next ferry departed at exactly 5:30 a.m.

Max kicked the closed door, ignoring the pain that shot through her foot. "Five thirty? That's too late."

"Maybe we don't have to wait." Thomas pointed to a series of weather-beaten fishing boats bobbing in the shallows.

Max nearly choked. "You want to *steal* a *boat*?"

"Please," Pippa said, already scrabbling down the gangplank toward the rocky beach. "Now isn't the time to sprout a conscience. Didn't you used to pick pockets for a living?"

Max scowled. "Only in the case of emergencies."

"Well, I think this counts as an emergency, don't you?" Pippa hopped into one of the boats and began to untie it from the moorings. "Besides, we'll bring it back. Now come on."

Max had never before been out on the water and found herself gripping her seat as Thomas piloted the boat away from the shore.

"You're sure you know how to drive this thing?" she cried as the boat hit a wave and nearly threw her overboard.

"Sure!" Thomas called back. "Read a book about it once!"

Sam groaned and closed his eyes.

The air stung Max's cheeks and she clutched her seat. Her stomach rolled with every wave and she felt a little like a popcorn kernel in danger of popping right into the water. But after a minute she grew less terrified and began to enjoy the up-and-down motion of the waves and the look of lights reflecting off the inky surface of the bay as they drew closer to Staten Island. Thomas maneuvered them successfully into the harbor, and they climbed onto the dock, securing the boat to a moss-coated piling.

"See?" Pippa turned to Max, smiling. "That was easy, wasn't it?"

"You know what I think, Pippa?" Max slung an arm around Pippa's shoulders. Despite the seriousness of what they had come to do, in that moment, with the silhouette of Manhattan etched against the starry sky, and the waves lapping quietly on the shore, and her three best friends standing beside her, she felt a sense of joy and well-being. "We're going to make a criminal of you yet."

"I suppose, coming from you, that's supposed to be a compliment," Pippa said. But she didn't turn away fast enough to conceal the fact that she was smiling.

Max's happiness was snuffed out as quickly as it had come, replaced by a creeping sense of anxiety. The streets of Staten Island were still, silent, and dark. Max had the uncomfortable feeling of trespassing in an abandoned house. Even the area around Borough Hall, bustling with activity during the day, looked ominous in the dark, everything shuttered and locked, and a lone dog barking somewhere in the distance.

They found Bay Street easily. As the name suggested, the street ran parallel to the water and took them away from the municipal district and into an area of looming industrial buildings, boat repair shops, truck lots, and canneries.

Soon the pavement petered out and was replaced by loose gravel and then, finally, by hard-packed dirt, rutted with deep tire marks and wagon wheels. The trees grew thicker on either side of them, tall pines that crowded out the moonlight, and owls hooted from the branches.

Fear tightened in Max's stomach. She was never afraid in any other section of New York, even in the worst, the dingiest, most dangerous areas. She was at home among the clamor and the filth, the guttersnipes and the street urchins, the hobos and the hustlers. It was here, in this wide-open space, with nothing but the sound of wind through the trees and the crunch of their feet on the road, that she felt truly afraid.

Finally, she couldn't take it anymore. "Are you sure this is the right way?" she blurted, hoping her voice wouldn't squeak.

At that instant, Thomas stopped, sucking in a quick breath. "I'm sure," he said, and pointed.

Just down the road was a break in the trees and a tall chain-link fence that ran parallel to the road. Beyond, the dark silhouette of a group of buildings was just visible, and a large sign, barely illumined by the moonlight, read: *WOODHULL ENTERPRISES. PRIVATE. NO TRESPASSING.*

They advanced more quietly now, sticking close to the shadows, expecting guards to be patrolling. The chain-link fence was at least eighteen feet high and topped by thick strands of spiked barbed wire. The single metal gate, which when opened would have been broad enough to admit two trucks side by side, was locked from the inside. Beyond the fence was an expanse of bare dirt the size of four football fields laid end to end, a small brick building, and a vast airplane hangar that gleamed a pale pearl-white.

"That's where Rattigan must be housing the dirigible," Thomas said, indicating the hangar.

"Okay." Max eyed the fence in frustration. "But how do we get in?"

"I'll do it," Sam said, stepping forward to rip a hole in the fence.

"No," Thomas said, laying a hand on his arm. "If anyone's patrolling, they'll see that someone's inside who doesn't belong. We can't risk an alarm. *I'll* do it." Before anyone could stop him, he sprang onto the fence and began climbing, moving soundlessly, like a spider up a wall.

"Thomas, *no*," Pippa whispered. She turned to the others, wide-eyed. "He'll get hurt."

Max moved to the fence and grabbed hold of it,

trying to shake Thomas off. But the fence was thick and sturdy, and Thomas was already nearly at the top of it. He hesitated, scanning the complex arrangement of barbed wire, searching for a way around it. It looked, to Max, impossible: like a thorny metal hedge sprouting from the top of the fence.

But all at once, Thomas flipped. Max's breath caught in her throat. Pippa gasped. Thomas kicked his legs upward, above his head, so for a second he was balancing in a perfect handstand.

Then he arched his back and his body formed a U-curve as he carefully bridged the first curl of barbed wire. Releasing his grip, he shinnied carefully under the second. Almost immediately, he swept sideways, under a third curl of wire, and somersaulted down onto the opposite side of the fence, so that he was temporarily frozen there, catlike, sweat glistening on his forehead. Then he clambered down the fence and reached the ground safely.

"You did it!" Max burst out, and Pippa hushed her sharply.

Sam, Max, and Pippa hurried to the gate while Thomas worked the lock open from the inside. A moment later, they were all slipping into the Woodhull Enterprises compound. Still, no one had appeared.

Everything was perfectly silent. But Thomas replaced the lock on the gate, just in case.

They started across the yard toward the airplane hangar, bent nearly double and trying to stick to the shadows just in case some unseen guards were watching. Max's instincts were going crazy, firing off warning signals, blazing sirens in her head. Where was everybody? What if the dirigible wasn't even here?

But as they circled the vast hangar they at last heard voices and the muffled sound of heavy equipment being moved. Half a dozen trucks were parked in front of the loading dock. The doors were open to reveal the dirigible, bullet-shaped and enormous, gleaming in the murk. Thomas gestured for them to hang back, ducking underneath a truck bed and concealing himself in the wheel well. Max flattened herself against one of the truck's enormous tires next to the others, trying to calm her frantically beating heart, inhaling the smell of rubber and, beneath that, soft ground. When she was no longer shaking, she risked a glance toward the loading dock.

From one of the trucks, workers in gas masks were unloading crate after crate and disappearing with them into the hangar. As one of the men passed beneath a circle of light, Max saw a skull and crossbones emblazoned on the load he was carrying and the words *Danger! Hazard!* painted in huge black letters beneath that. In their masks, the men looked like enormous insects.

"Are you okay?" Sam whispered to her.

She wanted to say something clever and confident, so he would know she wasn't afraid, but in the end she only nodded.

"There it is." Thomas was nearly invisible, concealed as he was in the dark. "What do you want to bet that's all the gas?"

"What are we going to do?" Pippa whispered.

"We have to get onto that dirigible," Thomas said. "We have to make sure it never gets airborne."

"Now's our chance," Sam said. "Look—the coast's clear."

Sam was right: the workers had all vanished, and the night had once again gone still. *Wrong,* Max's inner alarm was still shrieking. *Wrong, wrong.* It was all this silence: so much of it she felt like she was going to be swallowed.

"Follow me," Thomas said. Before Max could protest, he was on his feet, and Pippa was hurrying after him, staying low to the ground, and Sam slid out from underneath the truck bed. Max tried to stand and found that although she could hear her brain screaming the command at her legs, her legs had decided to ignore her. She would be left alone—she wouldn't be able to move, and the others would leave her here, huddled in a shadow, just waiting for Rattigan to find her.

"You're sure you're okay?"

Max looked up. Sam was still next to her, ducking low to meet her eyes. He hadn't abandoned her after all. All of her confidence came rushing back at once. She reached out, seized the hand he offered her, and wiggled free of the underside of the truck. She checked to make sure that her knives were in her pockets. They were.

"Ask me again," she whispered back, "and you'll be picking your teeth with a pocketknife."

"There's the Max I know," he said, and even managed to smile.

"Pssst." Pippa and Thomas had already crossed to the loading dock, carefully avoiding the light cast by the giant flood lamp on the roof. Pippa waved them forward and they hurried across the yard, Max's heart going like a fist trying to punch through a wall. But she wasn't afraid, not like before. She was focused.

She was angry.

The hangar was cool, dark, and smelled like dust.

Max had the feeling of passing into an ancient tomb, as if the dirigible were a prehistoric creature that had been sealed up forever in darkness, turning white from lack of sun. The dirigible itself was larger, and more strangely beautiful, than she could have ever imagined, like a building turned on its side. For a moment, though they should have been hurrying, Pippa, Sam, Max, and Thomas were all struck dumb with wonder.

There was one problem with the dirigible's design: Max saw no obvious way of getting onto it.

Sam had obviously realized the same thing. "So how, exactly, are we supposed to keep it from taking off?"

"Oh, I don't think you'll want to do that. You'd miss out on the show."

The voice behind them made Max's whole body go to ice, as if she'd been thrown headfirst into a snowbank. They whirled around.

Rattigan. Silhouetted in the light, his face was a dark mask, completely unreadable. But Max knew he was smiling.

"Hello, my children," he said with a happy sigh. "You're late."

26

"You know what I love most about New York City?" Rattigan sighed as a view of the Upper Bay, glittering in the morning light, unfolded beneath the airship's windows. "How *enormous* it is. All of that energy. All of those people! Millions of people. And yet from here, it might as well be a toy city. Like something that might be crushed with a simple footstep."

His voice was light, teasing, but Thomas's stomach coiled up in a knot. He knew what Rattigan was implying: the streets of New York City would be filled by now with all the people who'd come to watch the dirigible float over the skyline of Manhattan. And yet in a single instant, Rattigan could wipe out every one of them.

"You won't get away with this," Thomas said, wishing he sounded more confident. He, Pippa, Sam, and Max were huddled together across from Rattigan and two of his henchmen. One of them, a reedy man with a straggly mustache, named Clyde Straw, Thomas recognized as the same guy who'd shoved a gun against his neck during the holdup at the bank. The other man, Mickey McClure, had been previously known to the children as Sir Barrensworth. He'd dropped his fake accent and let his real voice—gruff, Brooklyn-inflected—come through.

Both men had very large guns pointed precisely in their direction.

"Oh, I already am," Rattigan said airily, with a wave of his hand. "In less than fifteen minutes, we'll reach Manhattan. Thank goodness for all the windows. The view is bound to be spectacular." His mouth twisted into a cruel smile.

"What's the point?" Pippa said, struggling against her bindings. She and Max had had their hands bound in front of them by Clyde Straw, just before they'd been marched onto the airship. Thomas and Sam had been left free—"there's no point with these two," Rattigan had said, smiling pleasantly, "but I think both will have a hard time finding their way around a bullet"—and instead, for the hours they'd sat on the dirigible while the final preparations were made and the sun crept higher in the sky, they'd been watched by a constant procession of armed guards to make sure they had no possibility of escape.

"You're going to gas all those innocent people for nothing," Pippa continued. "You'll be shot out of the sky. Even if you're not killed, everyone in the world will go on the hunt for you."

"I don't think so," Rattigan said, settling back in his seat—a chair made of soft leather, like something that belonged in a cushy office. "Have you ever played chess, my dear?"

Pippa narrowed her eyes. "Of course I have," she said. "What's that got to do with anything?"

"Chess has *everything* to do with it," he said. "In chess, as in life, you have to take out a few pawns before the kings and queens will come into the game." He folded his pale hands, which had always reminded Thomas of things that were dead and fished out of the water, across his stomach. "You see, my dear, I realized I'd been going about everything the wrong way. For example, I'd been hoping that you would see that your proper place is with me. I'd been, perhaps, counting on it. But then I remembered that the people who *get* in this world are the people who *take*. So I changed tactics. I decided simply to take you. And here you are."

"You didn't take us," Max said. "We came looking for you, remember?"

"As I knew you would," Rattigan said smoothly. "How could you miss the opportunity to play the hero? I'm the only true family you have. How could you miss the chance to prove that you belong, that you matter, that you aren't the monsters everyone surely thinks that you are? How could you fail to rush out to save all of those poor, innocent people, all of those boys and girls, fathers and mothers, whose lives will end today? You see," he said, spreading his hands, "I understand you. I'm the *only* one who truly understands. Haven't you ever wondered why I chose you to be my soldiers?"

"You *chose* us because you're crazy," Max spat. "There was no reason for it at all. Mr. Dumfrey told us so."

"And you believed him, I suppose?" For a second, Rattigan's face transformed: all of his twisted hatred for his half brother was revealed. "I don't blame him for lying. If you knew the whole truth, you might not be so fond of your dear old Mr. Dumfrey after all."

"Liar," Thomas said. He felt a black hatred so thick and deep he thought he might suffocate in it. This was Rattigan's effect, his ultimate power. It wasn't only that he was evil. It was that he made you forget that anything in the world was good.

Rattigan's lips curled back to reveal his long gray teeth. "You poor, strange, broken creatures—unloved and unwanted. Unnatural. You deny the truth even when the truth is undeniable. You deny me—the man who made you, who knows you better than you know yourselves. I do," he said, cutting Thomas off before he could object. "I see what you will do before you do it—before you even think it. I know what you dream, and think, and wish, and fear." Rattigan shook his head. "That's another thing about chess, Pippa. To win, you must always be four steps ahead. To be honest, Thomas"—Rattigan turned to Thomas—"I would have expected you to know this. I would have expected *more*."

Rattigan's eyes were strangely inhuman, flat and at the same time calculating, like the eyes of a snake. But Thomas refused to look away.

"Tell us," he said, knowing that Rattigan would never miss the opportunity to boast. Thomas had to delay Rattigan long enough to figure a way out of this mess—to figure out how to turn the airship around or crash it or do *something*. "Tell us how you stayed so far ahead of us."

"You flatter me," Rattigan said, but he looked

pleased. "Most of it, you know. After our last little encounter, I realized I needed a new approach. All of the hiding and lurking, sneaking through the sewers like a common rat . . ." He shivered. Thomas and Pippa exchanged a look. So that explained how Rattigan had managed to escape the old trolley factory. He'd followed a path down into the sewers through the hidden trapdoor in the floor. "But don't worry, I don't hold that against you," he added, as though they'd asked for his forgiveness. "You helped me, you see. You inspired me to attempt more—a single act of greatness, an act of power, that would make the knights and rooks, the kings and crooks, bow to my command."

"Robbing banks?" Max said sarcastically. "That was your big act of greatness?"

"That was a regrettable but necessary part of the plan," Rattigan snapped, looking, for the first time, irritated. Thomas shot Max a warning glance. "Airships don't come cheap, my dear. Neither, unfortunately, do the ingredients to manufacture two tons of reaper gas. Luckily, I had an old friend to help me out on that front." He indicated Clyde Straw, who smiled his weasely smile.

Sweat beaded on Thomas's upper lip. Manhattan was fast approaching. Through the dirigible windows, he could see the tall buildings rising closer. The network of streets was starting to take shape, and he could even see the glint of cars and buses in the streets and small dark spots that must be all the people gathered to watch the dirigible's approach. Among them, Thomas knew, were Chubby and Andrea von Stikk. He pictured all of them with their hands up to their eyes, squinting against the sun, smiling excitedly, totally unaware of the danger that was even now bearing down on them. . . .

They were running out of time.

"But then Erskine started asking questions," Thomas said, fishing desperately for a way to keep Rattigan talking.

Rattigan frowned. "And Mallett," he said. "Both of those idiots had to go. Erskine was becoming just a little too curious. He couldn't understand why Mallett couldn't get his hands on any more of his precious chemicals. I couldn't risk that my *chef d'oeuvre* would be revealed too early. I have spies all over the city, you see," Rattigan said, casting an amused glance at the man the children had known as Sir Barrensworth. "I have spies parroting back every word you say, every single move you make."

Thomas felt as if he'd just swallowed one of Max's

knives. His whole body shook with a violent under-standing. They were almost directly over Battery Park. Now, through the windows, Thomas could definitely make out people, little individual splotches of color crowding the streets and waving from balconies and rooftops.

Rattigan stood up. "Here we are. After today, every-thing will be different. The whole *country* will bow to my demands. The president and the army will answer to me. New York is just the first step. There are other cities. There is more gas. More and more people will die." He shrugged, as if he were talking about cleaning mold out of a bathtub.

Thomas finally understood. Rattigan was going to use the dirigible to blackmail the government into giv-ing him whatever he wanted: money, freedom, even an army, so that Rattigan could perform his sick experi-ments, so he could manufacture soldiers, so he could make the perfect world he envisioned, with Rattigan the creator and commander. The plan was disgustingly simple, and Thomas didn't doubt it would be suc-cessful. And even if it wasn't, how many hundreds of thousands of people would die?

Thomas could feel Pippa trembling. Her eyes were closed. She looked the way she did when she was struggling to think her way into a closed space, like a locked steel drawer—or somebody's mind. Thomas couldn't imagine why she was wasting her energy trying to read Rattigan, when he'd just told them everything they wanted to know. Maybe she was hoping to find information that would help them escape.

But it was too late. They'd reached Manhattan. Thomas saw a family cheering on a nearby balcony, waving streamers and homemade signs. Rattigan waved back at them, cooing a little, as if he were Santa Claus on a sled, bearing gifts.

"Well." Rattigan turned away from the window. His face was practically glowing. "I think it's time, don't you? Mickey, release the hatch, please. It's time to show the world what Nicholas Rattigan can do."

"You got it, boss," said the former Sir Barrensworth, shouldering his gun and moving toward the back of the dirigible. Now there was only Clyde Straw covering them.

Just beyond the tank containing the reaper gas, a giant hatch in the floor of the dirigible opened like a jaw, revealing the colorful patchwork of buildings and people and buses and cars beneath them. Wind whistled through the dirigible, sounding almost cheery.

A bead of sweat rolled off Pippa's forehead and

landed on Thomas's arm. Her lips were moving, as if she were murmuring a prayer under her breath.

And Thomas saw that Straw had begun to *twitch*, jerking his head to the left as though to dislodge a pesky fly.

Suddenly he understood: Pippa wasn't reading Rattigan's mind. She was trying to get into *Straw's* head.

She was doing her best to distract him.

Rattigan extracted a cigar from his vest pocket.

"I don't usually indulge," he said, lighting the cigar and gesturing with it, so the smoke whipped around his head. He had to speak loudly to be heard over the thrumming of the wind, which was growing louder by the instant. "But I think in this instance—" All at once he broke off, frowning. "What *is* that?"

As soon as he spoke, Thomas realized that the thrumming wasn't the sound of the wind at all, but of something mechanical, like an engine.

Like a *plane* engine.

Outside the window, a small, two-seater propeller plane floated into view, pulling level with the dirigible. Lash Langtry was riding in the backseat, his face grimly determined. And in the front cockpit, goggles obscuring half his face, was a man hunched over the controls, his jaw working back and forth, back and forth, as though over an invisible piece of gum.

Or a toothpick.

"Is that . . . ?" Sam said.

"It's Kestrel!" Thomas cried. He couldn't believe it.

Rattigan sprang to his feet, his face contorted with rage. "Open the valves!" he snarled. "Release the gas!" He whipped around to Clyde Straw. "And you—take care of our new friend."

But at that instant, Clyde let out a sharp cry of pain and staggered forward, bringing a hand to his head. At the same time, Pippa slumped backward. Thomas didn't have time to see whether she was okay. Tucking his head to his knees, he hurtled forward like a bowling ball, colliding directly with Clyde's ankles. Clyde went flying off his feet, letting out a spray of bullets that dinged off the metal tank and ripped through the airship's thin shell. Thomas was on his feet again in an instant. Sam had lunged for Clyde's gun and, with a simple series of twists, tied the barrel into a useless pretzel shape. Before Clyde could stand again, Sam gave him a nice plunk on the top of the head, and Clyde once again slithered to the floor.

"Nicely done," Thomas panted. "But where's Rattigan?" Rattigan had vanished, leaving only his cigar smoking in a silver ashtray.

"Sam, Tom, look out!" Pippa cried.

They turned to see Mickey McClure sprinting at them, gun drawn. But before he could fire, Max sprang to her feet. Her hands bound in front of her, she snatched up Rattigan's still-smoldering cigar and fired it directly into Mickey McClure's left eye.

"Aaaaaagggh!" McClure let out a howl, collapsing to his knees and simultaneously releasing a volley of gunfire. Several of the bullets tore through the window directly at Kestrel's plane. Before they could hit, Kestrel sent the plane into a nosedive, then spun skyward, drawing level again with the dirigible

Before McClure could get to his feet, Sam shoved him forward onto his stomach. He removed the rope coiled around Max's wrists and used it to lash McClure to Rattigan's chair.

"Thanks." Max's wrists were bright red and raw from the binding. She winced, massaging them gently, and then bent down to rummage through McClure's pockets. When she straightened up again, she had her knives, the same ones he'd confiscated earlier.

"Rattigan." Pippa staggered to her feet. She could barely stand. She looked exhausted. "We have to stop him from releasing the gas."

"You're too late."

They turned. In that instant, Rattigan looked like a

wild animal: ferocious and desperate, his jacket ripped and his shirt untucked, his ice-blue eyes wild and staring. He reached for the valve on the tank and gave it a quick twist. Thomas's stomach plummeted as he heard the telltale hiss of leaking gas.

"I win," Rattigan said simply. And before anyone could react, he'd thrown on a parachute and hurtled out of the hatch. The dirigible had drifted toward the East River now, and Thomas saw at once that Rattigan intended to land at the seaport, where a crowd of people was cheering him, clearly believing this was all a part of the show.

"No, you don't!" Max leaped, hurling her knives.

For a moment the knives seemed to be suspended, like small metal birds, flashing in the sun.

Then they passed cleanly through the lines holding Rattigan to his parachute. The crowd gasped as Rattigan screamed and began to plummet—straight toward the foaming water of the East River. A second later he disappeared beneath the sparkling water, even as the parachute fluttered, handkerchief-like, down after him.

Sam threw himself at the gas valve and gave it a desperate twist. The knob snapped off uselessly in his hand. He looked up, an expression of pure terror on

his face. The gas was still pouring out of the hatch, a dark gray chemical stream that quickly dissipated in the air. "Oh no . . ."

"And we're heading straight into midtown . . . ," Max said.

She was right. The dirigible, buffeted by the winds, was now veering away from the river and back toward the city.

"How can we stop it?" Pippa cried.

"There must be a way to steer this thing," Thomas said.

They scanned the instrument panel, searching for a way to turn the airship around. But quickly, Thomas saw that the spray of bullets from McClure's gun had blasted the controls into uselessness. The dirigible couldn't be turned. It was going to continue on over Manhattan, spewing deadly poison over everyone who lived there.

And there was no way to stop it.

"Thomas!" Sam shouted. "Look!"

Thomas turned and, through the window, saw Kestrel's plane hovering just below the hatch. Lash—his cowboy bandana tied over his mouth and nose as a makeshift gas mask—had edged out onto one of the wings.

"The mooring rope!" His voice, muffled by the cloth, was just barely audible. "Throw the mooring rope!"

Thomas saw immediately what Lash intended to do. He dove for one of the mooring ropes coiled at the back of the cabin and hurled it down to Lash. Lash snatched it from the air and, edging carefully back along the wing, fixed it to the airplane's tail.

Thomas held his breath as Kestrel leveled out the plane and turned. They were now directly over the east side of the city, so close Tom could make out individual faces turned up to the sky, mouths open, shocked and confused.

"Come on," he muttered. "Come on."

"It's working," Pippa breathed. "Kestrel's turning us around!"

She was right. Slowly, and then faster, the plane was turning. Kestrel was drawing them away from Manhattan, away from all of its people, out over the East River and down toward the open water of the Atlantic Ocean, as the gas continued to hiss and steam, emptying out into the bright blue sky.

27

"I *still* don't understand why Rattigan picked Barrens-worth—or McClure, or whatever his real name is—to spy on us," Sam said, rooting around in an enormous box of mixed chocolates for the caramel. He popped one in his mouth and then made a face. Banana. "Remember how he misspelled his own business card?"

"I still don't understand *how* Mickey *was* spying. He only showed once or twice." Max's voice seemed to be coming from an extremely large arrangement of calla lilies—courtesy of Andrea von Stikk—which dominated the silk footstool in Mr. Dumfrey's office. A second later, her head appeared above it, so that she appeared to be growing directly out of its branches. "Aha," she said, brandishing a small paper-wrapped box. "I knew there was a box of toffee somewhere."

"It wasn't Barrensworth," Thomas said. He was perched on Mr. Dumfrey's file cabinet, one of the few surfaces that wasn't completely obscured beneath a layer of gifts, candies, chocolates, notes, flowers, and other thank-you gifts that still, a week after the almost-disaster, flooded the museum on a daily basis. A specialty cutlery designer had even sent Max a set of knives to replace the ones she had lost during their aerial battle with Rattigan.

"Don't tell me you still think Emily had something to do with it." Pippa, who was modeling a red silk kimono gifted to all of the children by a grateful downtown seamstress, had been angling to check out her reflection in one of the dusty windowpanes. Now she turned around to face Thomas, plugging her fists on her hips. "She wouldn't. She *couldn't*."

"Not her, either." Thomas jumped neatly off the file cabinet and dodged the stacks of unopened gifts. "Ladies and gentlemen, I give to you . . . Rattigan's spy!" With a flourish, he swung open the door.

But there was no one there except for Mr. Dumfrey, just barely keeping hold of the enormous cage that still housed the Firebird. Sam peeked into the hall as Mr. Dumfrey staggered into the office, to see whether someone else was waiting there, but it was perfectly empty. He turned to Thomas, expecting him to look disappointed—maybe he had *intended* for Rattigan's spy to show, but had somehow lost him—but to his surprise saw that Thomas's eyes were practically glowing. And yet the hall was most definitely empty.

"I don't get it," he said. He hated feeling slower than the others and was relieved that, at least, Max and Pippa seemed as confused as he was.

"Is this a joke?" Pippa asked, shaking off the kimono and folding it neatly.

Max stood up, scowling. "Yeah," she said. "What happened to your big theory?"

Thomas opened his mouth to reply, but whatever he said was lost beneath the bird's screams of protest.

"Let go of me, you flabby-fingered frump!" the Firebird screeched. "Let me out, you dwindling dumpling!"

"Quiet," Mr. Dumfrey said, between huffing breaths, "or by tomorrow you'll be feathering my pillow." Elbowing aside another hideous arrangement of flowers—this one, Sam had noticed, addressed specifically to Mr. Dumfrey from *A Secret Admirer*—he set the cage down on his desk with a groan. "You wouldn't think," he said, turning back to the children and mopping his brow with a handkerchief, "that a bird could be so *heavy*."

"Maybe that's because it's not a bird at all." Thomas strutted around the desk, his chest so puffed up that for a second it looked as if *he* might sprout feathers. Then, suddenly, he leaned forward, banging both fists on the desk on either side of the bird's cage. Sam swallowed a yelp. *"It's a rat."*

There was a moment of silence. Thomas glared at the bird. The bird seemed to wither, ever so slightly, under the intensity of his gaze.

"Who you calling names?" the bird squawked, but Sam thought that the bird sounded nervous.

And at last, he understood: Rattigan's spy was, very literally, a bird brain.

Pippa began to giggle. Then she began to snort. Finally, she was laughing so hard, she had to bend over and wrap a hand around her stomach. "I don't believe it," she said finally. "I really don't believe it."

"Think about it," Thomas said. "It was perfect. Someone rung up claiming to have a rare species of bird for sale—Rattigan *knew* Dumfrey would bite."

Mr. Dumfrey looked pained. "My half brother likely

remembers the parakeet I had as a small boy," he said. "Euclid was my very best friend."

"The Firebird was trained to repeat anything it heard. Maybe at first Rattigan just planned to keep an eye on us, make sure he knew what we were up to. But after Farnum was arrested and we began poking around, the Firebird was necessary. Then Barrensworth—or McClure—popped up again, offering to help train the bird for the stage. But instead he's bleeding it for information, so he knew what *we'd* found out about Benny Mallett and Ernie Erskine." Thomas shook his head. "It was lucky that Farnum got pinned for Erskine's murder, actually. Otherwise we would never have known what Rattigan was planning."

Max made a face. "Some luck," she said.

"How did you piece it together?" Sam asked. The Firebird was no longer strutting in its cage or puffed up on its perch. Instead, the bird was huddled by its feeder, looking, to Sam's eyes, extremely nervous and unhappy. In less than ten minutes, it seemed to have shriveled to half its normal size. Sam wondered whether now, knowing its secret was out, it also knew there was nowhere for it to go, no one for it to return home to. After all, the Firebird had known Sir Barrensworth, or Mickey McClure, as its rightful owner.

He felt almost sorry for it.

"Something Rattigan said on the dirigible," Thomas said, and for a second the memory of what had happened high above the city passed over them like the shadow of the airship itself, plunging them all into cold. "He said he had spies parroting information back to him, and he kind of winked at McClure. I knew then."

Pippa sighed. "So Emily . . . ?"

"Is completely innocent," Mr. Dumfrey said firmly.

"I'm glad," Pippa said. "Kestrel will be so happy."

Now Thomas looked puzzled. "What's he got to do with anything?"

"Not *you*, too." Pippa threw up her hands. "How can you be so smart and so dumb at the same time?"

Thomas grinned at her. "Natural talent."

"But what are we going to do about the bird?" Sam asked.

Max was fiddling with one of her new knives and didn't glance up. "Maybe we can let Freckles have a turn with it," she said. "He's had the right idea all along."

The Firebird had, by now, begun to tremble. Sam definitely felt sorry for it.

"Oh, I don't think that will be necessary," he said. He reached out and gave the cage a tentative pat. "I imagine that now Rattigan and his friends are gone, we'll find that with the right training and just a little luck, the Firebird's attitude turns around."

"Go train yourself, you ball of blubber," the Firebird replied, but without any real conviction. It even settled onto its perch and preened in silence as Mr. Dumfrey began to sort the gifts that had arrived since that morning, without once criticizing the way Thomas smelled or calling Pippa an animal.

The Firebird even, Sam thought, looked ever so slightly relieved.

Later that afternoon, Pippa, Thomas, Sam, and Max gathered with the other residents outside the museum to await the triumphant return of General Farnum, who'd recently been cleared of all charges related to the murder of Ernie Erskine. It was perhaps the last perfect day of autumn. Tomorrow, the papers were predicting a dramatic temperature drop and rains that would strip the trees of their singed-gold leaves. But today was perfect: brilliant sunny, sharp and cool, the air just edged with the faint smell of wood smoke.

"What do you think?" Gil Kestrel wobbled a little on the ladder as he gave one end of the museum's newest banner a tug. "Look about right?"

Lash shoved his cowboy hat farther back on his head,

squinting against the sun. "I don't know," he said. "I reckon it's slanted a mite too far to the right."

Kestrel made several adjustments. "How about now?"

Lash gave a noise of appreciation. "Straight as a preacher's sermon."

"It's perfect," Emily agreed, taking Kestrel's hand and giving it a squeeze as he came down the ladder. "General Farnum will love it."

Thomas and Pippa had spent the morning painting a large banner announcing his return, which Mr. Dumfrey proudly proclaimed would hang above the entrance of the museum at least until Christmastime.

*Welcome Home, General Farnum\*!* it read in bold red letters, with a special star next to Farnum's name. Mr. Dumfrey had insisted they add in a secondary bit: *Cleared of all charges related to the notorious and fantastic murder of Ernie Erskine, victim of the murderous Nicholas Rattigan and his plot to take down Manhattan!* This had resulted in a banner rather larger than usual, especially after a third addition became necessary when General Farnum, through Rosie Bickers, had communicated that during his time in prison he'd come up with an idea for a new act.

"Listen to this." Thomas had for days been obsessed

with reading all the newspaper coverage about their role in saving the city from certain disaster. Now he had at least several different editions, including *The Journal-American*, *The Daily Screamer*, and *The New York Herald-Examiner*, spread out on the stoop. He snatched up *The Screamer*:

"'There is no doubt that the police department's grossly incompetent search for Rattigan, and failure to tie Rattigan's reappearance to the string of bank robberies that paralyzed the city, nearly resulted in a catastrophe of unknown proportions,'" he read. "'The police'—*blah blah blah*, hang on, we can skip how Rattigan was able to get an airship all to himself. Wait, here's the good part." He cleared his throat. "'"If it weren't for the *extrapotential* children of Mr. Dumfrey's Dime Museum, who knows what would have happened?" said Miss Andrea von Stikk, of the recently renamed Von Stikk Home for Extrapotential Children. "It's obvious that Mr. Dumfrey's educational methods should be commended for their untraditional approach—an approach, I might add, I've long admired. As for the police—"'" Thomas broke off, grinning. "From there it goes on for four columns."

"Von Stikk's singing a different tune nowadays, isn't she?" Max said.

"Did somebody say my name?" came Andrea von Stikk's sweet, trilling voice. Pippa turned and saw her sailing down the street, dressed in one of her typically ornate outfits, complete with bows and ruffles and lace, so that she looked more like a parade float than a person. Behind her came Chubby, his hands in his pockets, still wearing a badly fitting school uniform, smiling sheepishly.

"There you are, my darlings." Von Stikk squeezed Pippa into a hug so tight, Pippa felt as if she might suffocate in the older woman's layers of clothing. "And *you*." She repeated the performance with Thomas and Sam and nearly went for Max but thought better of it, especially when Max bared her teeth and growled. She obviously hadn't forgotten that Max had once jabbed a fork into her left hand. "And—er—Mackenzie. And *you*." She turned to Mr. Dumfrey and seized his hand. "Our hero! Our savior! Our *saint*."

"A servant, madame," Mr. Dumfrey said gallantly, bending forward to kiss Von Stikk's hand, as if all of the tension between them had never existed. "As always and ever at your service."

"Oh, Mr. Dumfrey." Miss von Stikk whipped a paper fan from the folds of her enormous dress and vigorously fanned herself with it. "You are too, too much."

"And you, my dear, are never enough!"

Max pretended to gag. Pippa had to turn away, clapping her mouth to stifle the laugh that was rising like soda bubbles in her chest, threatening to burst. She couldn't ever remember a time when she'd been quite so happy and when the museum had felt so deeply and totally at peace.

She didn't know what, exactly, had happened between Gil Kestrel and Lash—only that when Mr. Dumfrey realized that the children were missing from the museum, he had immediately guessed that they were heading to stop Rattigan at all costs and had set Gil and Lash in immediate pursuit. Somewhere along the way—or perhaps even midair in Manhattan—Gil and Lash had come to an understanding about what had happened in the past. All Kestrel would say about it now was that Lash was a good man, a fine friend. And Lash, usually so talkative, would say only that Kestrel was a mighty tall hog at the trough—an expression Pippa didn't entirely understand but knew to be a compliment.

But it was more than that. Rattigan was well and truly gone. Even now, the police were combing the river for his remains. The whole museum had, for the past three days, been in a near-constant state of celebration. Max had graciously congratulated Pippa on what she had done in the dirigible and even suggested that mind manipulation become a new part of Pippa's performance—although Pippa had quickly declined, since the effort had left her exhausted and weak for two days.

Gil Kestrel and Emily had quietly announced their engagement, and Lash had expressed his excitement by tossing the sour-faced Miss Fitch in the air and planting a kiss directly on her lips. Although this had of course made the twins unhappy, even they couldn't be sore for long, especially now that Miss Fitch, shockingly, had begun appearing in the morning with her hair loosened in long waves, seemingly too distracted to notice or care if the performers were late to their curtain calls.

Good luck, it appeared, was contagious. Smalls had just received a letter that his poem "How Sweetly Doth the Pigeons Coo" had been accepted into the *Poets of Our Period*. (Smalls was so thrilled, he didn't even care that the magazine's acronym was POOP.)

"What's the matter, Chubby?" Sam nudged Chubby with an elbow, and Chubby took a quick step sideways to avoid being knocked over. "I thought you were done with school."

"Oh, er, yeah." Chubby coughed and rubbed the back of his neck with a hand, feigning an air of casualness. "Turns out Von Stikk's not so bad. I think I might hang out a little longer. I been working on my vocabulary. And reading's not so bad, once you get the gist of it. Plus the free grub and all," he added quickly. Red splotches had appeared in both of his cheeks.

"Good for you," Pippa said. "That's great."

"Thanks, Pippa," he said, smiling at her. It was the first time he'd ever called her Pippa, not Pip or Philippa, and it occurred to her then that he was not so very, not so *absolutely*, silly-looking after all. In fact, the way he blushed was actually kind of . . . cute. As if tomatoes had been crushed beneath his skin. And his nose was sort of fantastic. . . .

All down Forty-Third Street, she recognized neighbors and friends, all of them lingering outside, hoping to catch a glimpse of the four children who'd saved New York City, or to cheer on General Farnum when he made his triumphant return home. There was Henry from the St. Edna Hotel, for once awake on the job; Barney Bamberg, standing outside his delicatessen; Miss Groenovelt, with one of her many cats encircling her ankles; Sol from the sweet shop on the corner; and there was Gus, from the barber shop below Eli

Sadowski's apartment, still holding a bottle of shaving cream. Even Mr. Sadowski himself could be seen at his window—which was amazing, considering that his window was usually entirely concealed behind stacks of things—and Pippa gave him a little wave before turning her eyes back to the street.

And there, just rounding the corner of Forty-Third Street . . .

"Look!" she cried. "It's Rosie! And General Farnum!"

Rosie Bickers and General Farnum didn't make it halfway down the street before they were absolutely swarmed. Goldini was pumping Farnum's hand and Smalls was reciting bits of *The Iliad* and Andrea von Stikk and Rosie were embracing and in the chaos Mr. Dumfrey kissed Rosie right on the mouth not once but *twice*. They moved back toward the museum as a babbling, many-headed creature, everyone talking at once, and Pippa was carried along on a wave of sound and a crush of her friends all around her.

". . . can't believe it . . ."

"Home at last!"

"Justice prevails . . ."

"Well." Kestrel gestured to the banner hanging proudly above the museum doors. "What do you think?"

General Farnum was momentarily overcome with

emotion. His lips trembled. He seemed to have trouble finding the right words. His mustache vibrated so hard that Pippa thought it might fly right off his face.

"What do I think?" General Farnum's voice cracked, and he coughed to clear his throat. "I think I haven't seen anything so beautiful since the Battle of San Juan Hill. I think that I'm *home*."

"The bit about your new act got kind of squished," Thomas said, eyeing the lettering critically. "Sorry about that."

At the very bottom of the banner was a hasty add-on: *Come See World-Famous Farnum and His Cleverly Cavorting Cockroaches!*

General Farnum's eyes were bright. "It's perfect, sonny."

Then the babble of conversation started up again. Everyone wanted to hear about Farnum's time in jail, and all the performers had news to share of their own. Farnum and Rosie were quickly swept up as the crowd flowed into the museum.

Pippa hung back for a bit, reluctant to leave the sunshine. She had the strangest sensation then, that she was watching a scene that had happened years ago—that all of this, the sunshine and the noise of traffic and happy laughter, was already a memory, long-cherished and often relived. Her heart ached with a feeling so strong she couldn't exactly name it: a sense of time stilled and also rushing by too quickly. It was like Mr. Dumfrey had said. There were, perhaps, other Rattigans in the world, other evils she would someday have to face. They were growing up, and couldn't stay at the museum forever.

But for now, Sam and Max were walking side by side, perfectly in sync. Mr. Dumfrey was directing everyone into the Odditorium for chilled sodas and free sweets. And Thomas stopped with one hand on the door, glancing back to where Pippa still stood, watching it all with a sense of love and rightness and belonging.

"You coming?" Thomas said. Pippa nodded and jogged up the stairs to pass before him into the museum.

It was like General Farnum had said. For now, they were home.

# READ THEM ALL!

"With a dollop of Lemony Snicket's hyperbole,
a blob of J. K. Rowling's take on journalism, and a
splotch of sideshow allure, Oliver and Chester have
crafted a wildly imaginative, over-the-top tale."

—ALA *Booklist* (starred review)

**HARPER**

*An Imprint of HarperCollinsPublishers*

www.harpercollinschildrens.com

prudes but supreme sensualists who pursued the art of great love, not just a great lay. True passion was their religion. In contrast to our fast-food sex, which fills the body—maybe—but not the soul, Victorian sex was subtle yet consuming, a banquet to be savored course by course. No one left the table hungry when men and women made love instead of war. We've been looking for love in all the wrong places. This book will help to chart a new direction.

The same road map will guide us to the Victorian home, whose affordable beauty, bounty, and binding ties knocks the stuffing out of all the Cleaver family values. Learn from the past how to create a home where the threads of family are woven together in a tapestry that doesn't unravel.

Bill Clinton won reelection in 1996 by promising to build a bridge to the next century. But we will surely repeat and magnify the tragedies of this one unless we build a bridge to the last. We won't wear hoop skirts again or abandon motor-powered transportation. Above all, we won't revert to denying women and minorities full legal and economic rights. As the architectural and landscape designer Calvert Vaux wrote in 1864, "The past should always be looked on as a servant, not a master."

The bridge I picture is a two-way road where the best of the present and the past will meet. We have already begun to build these roads with popular concepts like cracking down on "trivial" quality-of-life crimes in order to prevent more serious crimes. Slowly but surely, Victorian common sense is becoming our wisdom.

You won't find my bridge on the political maps of prominent liberals or conservatives. As a sociologist, I have grown tired of hearing the right and left battle over the great social issues of our day, oblivious to the fact that many of these very problems were addressed, and successfully so, by the Victorians. Liberals are allergic to history, unless it belongs to specific victimized groups. Conservatives are no better. The columnist Jonathan Yardley observed, "Conservatism as it now exists in these United States is no longer a force for the preservation of the best in the past's legacy but a force for the diminution and elimination of barriers erected by government against the uncontrolled exercise of individual and institutional avarice."[1]

Conservatives just won't leave the Beaver Cleaver ideal behind because their stunted view of the good life began in Levittown, died in Woodstock, and survives only in TV reruns, where history spans less than a half century. Their solutions to our vast social problems and our aching need for personal fulfillment are as modern and ineffective as those prescribed by liberals. Both are chips off the old block of an anti-Victorian century that shaped them and the mess we're in.

So why should we turn our battered faith and our rhetoric-weary ears to the Victorians' distinctive message? Why journey to a past that, for all its glories, had manure in the streets, allowed robber barons to plunder, and discriminated against women and minorities? Why risk traveling yet another promised route to salvation when so many have led us astray? Because for all our travels, this is a road we moderns have not yet taken. Because our own proliferating experts, who always know so much about so little, have failed us. Because Victorian sensibilities worked, and nothing else has worked as well since then. Because Victorian notions of how to live life achieved far more than crime control, civility, and stable families: They perfumed daily experience, and in turn nourished the soul with beauty, grace, and the bounty of layered meanings that found grandeur in fine details while living by grand designs. This holistic vision, this different way of seeing, is our legacy, but we have been robbed of it. We must learn to reassemble all the pieces of this quilt—morals, manners, crime, clothes, aesthetics—that have unraveled since the 1920s. To the Victorians the minutiae of life were never minute.

So let us return to the premodern era and see what treasures we so casually and carelessly tossed out at the beginning of the modern era. Americans pride themselves on being open to new ideas. It is time we tried some old ones.

# PART I

# HOW FAR WE HAVEN'T COME

# I

## The Age of Impudence

Virginia Woolf once said that human character changed in 1910. If so, it took another decade and a cataclysmic war before the radical ideas and lifestyles of Bloomsbury and Greenwich Village affected ordinary people. Critics who confuse history with memory may blame our current epidemic of self-indulgence and incivility on a Reaganesque "decade of greed" or the "me decade" or the Woodstock generation. In fact, its origins lie in the seemingly innocent times of flappers, jalopies, and raccoon coats.

In the 1920s "Victorian" became a dirty word, as the postwar generation set about dismantling their parents' ideals like children attacking a tower of building blocks. As Frederick Lewis Allen recalled in *Only Yesterday,* his 1931 memoir of the 1920s, "It was better to be modern—everybody wanted to be modern—and sophisticated, and smart, to smash the conventions, and to be devastatingly frank. And with a cocktail glass in one's hand, it was easy at least to be frank." In our own day, "Victorian" has become a synonym for sexual repression (but read on!). To those smart young things downing gin fizzes in smoky speakeasies, "Victorian" was still an entire worldview.

## "A CULTURE OF CHARACTER"

What was the worldview that they rebelled against so insistently, and why should we bother to remember it (much less recover it) today? In contrast to the chaotic muddle we now call values, Victorian values were so consistent, and so consistently taught, that they formed what historian Warren I. Susman called a whole "culture of character." This culture was so powerful and pervasive that it did not need to be legislated or litigated; it was internalized.

Clarence Day, who immortalized the age in his 1935 memoir *Life with Father*, said the rules his parents taught him weren't written down in any single book. "It was a code, a tradition. It was to be upright and fearless and honorable . . . and in general always do the right thing in every department of life. . . . In my boyhood, I never had a doubt that the beliefs they taught me were true. The difficulty was to live up to them." Yet Day was not alone or helpless in his struggle. In his youth during the 1880s, he recalled, people talked without irony about "true nobility and noble deeds. The atmosphere that my generation grew up with was thick with nobility."

In our Beavis-and-Butthead culture, it takes a leap of faith to realize that nobility of character was once a widely accepted ideal for young people. When Bill Clinton recently proclaimed a "Character Counts Week," it was a pathetic reminder of how little character does count these days. For this lost nurturing atmosphere cannot be recaptured by presidential declarations, at a time when our role models are celebrated deviants like basketball star Dennis Rodman, who titled his bestselling memoir *Bad As I Wanna Be*. Before we can even attempt to recreate the Victorians' environment of virtue, we need to remember what it was all about.

## SELF-RESTRAINT AND SACRIFICE

What were the nuts and bolts of the remarkable code that sustained the lawfulness and civility we associate with the Victorian era? It had a broad and inclusive religious foundation that was a far cry from Bible-thumping moralism. It stressed hard work, frugality, sobriety, honesty, civic responsibility, sexual decency, good deeds, self-restraint, and self-sacrifice.

To our own generation, equating love with sacrifice and self-restraint is difficult to understand, much less accept. Isn't love a vehicle of individual happiness? If you randomly stopped people on the street and asked them to assess their lives, most would ask themselves, "Am I happy?" But a Victorian would ask himself, "Am I a good person?" In the seamless web of Victorian connections, self-fulfillment required social virtue. Conversely, the fate of the community depended on a view of happiness that transcended a personal wish list of experiences and acquisitions. As Sara Josepha Hale, the influential female editor of *Godey's Lady's Book*, America's leading magazine for women, put it in her 1868 book *Manners; or Happy Homes and Good Society All the Year Round*, "In 'the pursuit of happiness,' the first right step is to seek that which is good to do, not merely for one's self, but for others: ultimately we reach the public good."

The hallmark of Victorian character—self-restraint—was more than a means to test your mettle. It was a key deterrent to crime. The rise of modern industry and big cities, and a consequent weakening of family ties, boosted crime in the first decades of the nineteenth century. Yet in the second half of the century, crime declined rapidly, as a result of what social scientists James Q. Wilson and Richard J. Herrnstein, writing in *Crime and Human Nature*, call "intense efforts to inculcate an ethic of self-control." In contrast, they note that crime rates "rose faster in the twentieth century than can be explained by higher birth rates, owing to a shift from that ethic to one emphasizing self-expression."

More than a hundred years before we needed Ph.D.s to legitimize this insight, Henry James, Sr., warned in a letter printed by the *New York Tribune* that if man is "free not only in respect to outward compulsion, but free also in respect to inward constraint . . . he is essentially devoid of obligation either to his fellow man or to himself; in a word, his own sole law."[1] "His own sole law"—is there a better definition of criminality?

## AIMING FOR PERFECTION

This painful lesson was central to Victorian aspirations for the human spirit and social prosperity. Whereas we have had to pay a heavy price for indulging our "healthy" natural instincts, most Victorians believed with Elizabeth Blackwell that our "natural" state of instinctive desires "is really a state of rudimentary life, which does not display the real nature of man, but only its imperfect condition." As history's most ardent moral self-improvers, the Victorians thought humanity could and should strive toward perfection. They would have been puzzled by the current quest for self-esteem; they sought to create a self that would be worthy of esteem.

In place of this vision of striving upward, we began "defining deviancy down," as Senator Daniel Patrick Moynihan put it.[2] By lowering our social sights, we made it possible to normalize unprecedented levels of antisocial behavior, ranging from petty boorishness to vicious violence. In so doing we lost a philosophy that made crime and incivility the universally condemned exception, not the rule. Even worse, we lost the Victorian "cosmic sense" that underlay this philosophy—the optimistic faith in grand designs and eternal truths that linked every aspect of our lives to something larger than life.

Current-day conservatives may think the "grand plan" drowned in the mud at Woodstock. Actually, it met its end in the 1920s, when a lot more than hair was bobbed. Dumbed-down versions of the works of thinkers like Freud, Nietzsche, and Einstein began to popularize the since then widespread notion that values are relative and rules of morality are made to be broken. Here was the tragic beginning of the moral mobocracy that left everyone free to make and break their own rules. These days, according to a recent poll, two out of three Americans reject the notion of irrefutable moral truths.

The Victorians always knew what we have only recently discovered: When the tides of history wash away our old sand castles of ethics, we simply build new ones to suit our needs. The "bridge generation" of the Roaring Twenties whose members experienced the transition to our brave new world learned this lesson too late. As one bewildered contemporary, quoted by the historian Arthur M. Schlesinger in *Learning How to Behave*, mused in 1926, "It is a new age, new thinking, new ideals. Does it mean no ideals?" The answer was a cocksure, scorched-earth yes!

Even Edith Wharton, famed for deftly skewering the foibles of the old social order, came to regret the loss of its rules and rituals. In her memoir *A Backward Glance* (1933), she lamented how the Great War had swept away this world and rendered its codes unintelligible:

"The unalterable rules of conduct became
. . . as quaintly arbitrary as the domestic rites
of the Pharaohs."

In the hoochy-koochy age, morale
replaced morality. One of the leading psychologists of the day, G. Stanley Hall, called
it a time when "animal spirits" were at "top
notch." The frantic quest for self-fulfillment
trumped the traditional concept of charac-
ter built on hard work and self-denial. Influenced by Freud, people
began to believe that all problems in adulthood were rooted in the
repression of natural instincts during childhood and adolescence.

## THE LOSS OF GRACE

But breaking the bonds of restraint went far beyond a new fascination
with fulfillment. Advice and child-rearing manuals printed during this
era shifted their emphasis from developing character to improving
one's personality. Words like "decency," "truth," "unselfishness," "justice"—the vocabulary of Clarence Day's "atmosphere of nobility"—
were ridiculed. The new lingo shifted the focus from social virtues to
surface gloss. People were told by advertisers, the movie industry, and
cosmetic manufacturers to become fascinating, magnetic, stunning,
and attractive. In sum, the world became one's mirror.

The new ethic of self-expression rode a wave of generational
rebellion that has yet to crest. In the 1920s the etiquette authority
Emily Post declared that each generation was entitled to make its
own rules. Many bashers of Victorian mores denounced their elders'
"stilted formalities" and "worn-out hypocrises." Similar sentiments are
still preached by current historians. Milton Rugoff, in his 1971 book,
*Prudery and Passion,* portrayed the Victorians' notion of character as
"intolerant and unrealistic" as well as insufferably pretentious,
because "it truly overreached itself in the virtues and ideals it set up."
John F. and Robin M. Haller, in their book *The Physician and Sexuality in Victorian America,* called the Victorians "burdened, as no generation before them, with the weight of their own image. . . . They
struggled to gain the highest planes of achievement . . . for their highest duty lay not to themselves, but to future generations." Translation:

How dare they aspire to goals that nowadays might waylay modern pilgrims on their pursuit of self-fulfillment?

Is it any wonder that the mentality of the 1920s, in the words of the historian Paula Fass, "sits solidly at the base of our culture?" Many of us would feel right at home in an era when, as Frederick Lewis Allen claimed in *Only Yesterday*, even the "best classes displayed their worst, and trashing was the order of the day." When morals collapsed, manners quickly followed, as the Victorians knew they would. Allen, a battered survivor of the Jazz Age, recalled that guests couldn't be bothered to speak to them on arrival or departure; that "gatecrashers" at dances became an accepted practice; that thousands of men and women made a point of not getting to dinner within half an hour of the appointed time lest they seem insufficiently blasé.

Sound familiar? Similar complaints about the guests from hell are routinely lodged these days in Miss Manners's and Ann Landers's columns. But we are too far removed from the golden age of civility to notice any but the most egregious offenses. Writing about the twenties in his 1950 book *New Cosmopolis*, James Hunecker lamented not only the spread of alcohol, gambling, sexual frankness, and general bad manners but also gum chewing and sloppy appearance. To the Victorian mind even such venial sins were important, because they "debase the currency of life."

This might seem like ridiculous nitpicking; we all know how fussy those Victorians could be. Yet it highlights a loss more poignant than the etiquette or morals that went bankrupt along with social currency. Before her death in 1937, Edith Wharton pined for the beauty of what she called the the age of innocence, also the title of one of her most famous novels. According to her memoir, she found the new age to be "a world in which so many sources of peace and joy are already dried up that the few remaining have a more piercing sweetness." Gone was that intangible, almost mystical, loveliness of life that still holds the power to enthrall us when we glimpse it in old artworks and photographs or recreated on a movie screen.

## HEDONISM, CONSUMERISM, AND GREED

Wealth of a different kind—our kind—was supposed to adorn the world when all the Victorian gilding was stripped away. The twenties spawned the age of mass-produced goods and the megamall, the all-you-can-eat mentality that measured happiness and achievement in dollars, not good deeds. The spread of movies, radios, autos, home appliances, and seductive installment plans turned savers into spenders and created the modern consumer.

Meanwhile, newly aggressive advertising tactics urged people to gratify their whims by emptying their wallets. They had yet to be told to shop till they dropped, but they would surely have embraced that slogan, along with the current television ad for a discount mall that promises, "You can buy happiness; just don't pay retail for it." The end result, concluded the sociologists Robert S. and Helen M. Lynd in their classic 1929 study *Middletown*, "was that people seemed to be running for dear life in the business of making the money . . . to keep pace with the even more rapid growth of their subjective wants."

The results were obvious even if the implications were not. In their study, the Lynds compared everyday life in the 1890s and 1920s in a typical midwestern city—they called it Middletown. They found that increased consumerism and commercialized leisure had brought a decline in manners, morals, parental control, and community participation. These early social scientists were more concerned with explaining the present than predicting the future. But they were peering through the crack of a doorway that their grandchildren would fling wide open.

Even as the nineteenth century produced robber barons, corrupt industrial monopolies, and unprecedented prosperity, the Victorian ideal of character made it possible to protect the soul from becoming a cold cash machine. But the buying binge of the twenties had no place for the Victorian adage that reckless spending was a form of false pride. The Victorians saw this as a "deadly" sin long before the crash of '29. Believing, as the suffragist Mary Livermore wrote in her autobiography, that "the highest civilization is not material only, but mental, moral, and spiritual," they rightly feared that upsetting this delicate balance meant the triumph of personal greed. In the end, such a triumph would, in the words of Elizabeth Blackwell in 1852, "reduce every phenomenon to the limits of the senses." The mushrooming choice of market goods could never transcend those limits. Today the array of goods has become more dizzying, but no more fulfilling.

The spiritual vacuum created by such hedonism undermined both civility and the moral foundation that sustained it. When Katherine Lee Bates wrote "America the Beautiful" in 1893, she was inspired by the spacious skies and fruited plains that she viewed from Pikes Peak in a moment of epiphany. But her lyrics also expressed an inner vision of her country's spiritual wealth: "America! America!/ May God thy gold refine/ Till all success be nobleness/ And ev'ry gain divine." These sentiments resounded with her listeners three decades before Calvin Coolidge proclaimed the business of America to be business.

When was the last time you heard anyone sing this verse? Even modern conservatives who rail about "traditional values" have been strangely silent on the immorality of greed, of which the Victorians were quite aware. We have grown to expect campaign speeches that promise rising standards of living, with no mention of frugality or the demoralizing toll of rising debt. To the heirs of Reagan, self-restraint applies to crime and extramarital sex, but not to personal spending. But to the Victorians, who religiously connected all the dots to see the big picture, breaking one bound meant breaking all others.

The forces unleashed in the 1920s are in full gallop today. By constantly pushing the envelope of civility, advertising's apostles of narcissism have driven us over the edge. The calculated outrages of Calvin Klein and his ilk are only the most visible symptoms of Madison Avenue's promiscuous willingness to turn the impulses of teenage rebellion and childish self-indulgence to the ends of retail profit. We should wear Nikes because "we're all hedonists and we want to feel good. That's what makes us human." A Nintendo TV spot best sums up this tawdry mixture of infantile narcissism and adolescent nihilism: A boy spits at the camera as an announcer exhorts young video-game customers to "hock a loogie at life."

At the Container Store, I once received a shopping bag with the written instruction CONTAIN YOURSELF. Even as it made me smile, this gentle pun reminded me how farcical Victorian virtues appear to the modern sensibility. No one will ever make a perfume ad defining love as self-sacrifice. In its ceaseless efforts to add value to products by associating them with primitive desires and juvenile fantasies, corporate America devalues all that was once precious in life. Nobility of character and the aristocracy of virtue are no match for the democracy of consumption and the equality of desire.

To the Victorians, the celebration of limitless desire was not just wrong, it was literally childish. Without self-control—the hallmark of

*Strollers on the Coney Island boardwalk on a summer day in 1897 show a sensibility about public dress and decorum that is in stark contrast to the modern era.*

mature adulthood—they believed that morality, civility, and community would crumble. You can hear it in another rarely sung verse of Katherine Lee Bates's anthem: "America! America!/God mend thine ev'ry flaw,/Confirm thy soul in self control/Thy liberty in law." By turning this notion on its head, the Jazz Age laid the groundwork for the mental diapers that still bind us today. "Self," wrote the Victorian poet Henry Van Dyke in *The Prison and the Angel*, "is the only prison that can ever bind the soul." If we are ever to reclaim our souls, we must first recognize how far we have fallen.

# 2

## Buy Now, Pay Later

Shared ideals of character and civility formed the bedrock of Victorian community. In our own day, these standards of personal development and social behavior have been almost totally inverted. Society's moral arbiters, the pop psychologists, exhort us to satisfy childish impulses rather than transcend them. In trifles and essentials, we seek the right to indulge our desires and to be indulged by others when they backfire. Meanwhile, we are tenuously bound together by our shared dysfunctions, addictions, and A-to-Z support groups. What the Victorians called virtue—doing for others—has been replaced by the virtue of victimhood, or what's been done to us. And we flaunt it like a badge of honor, while the word "honor" is now as dated as the notion of character it defines.

### I'M DYSFUNCTIONAL, YOU'RE DYSFUNCTIONAL

We support an army of lecturers and authors, who are always on the lookout for new dysfunctions to cure. Now that nearly half the population either attend support sessions themselves or have friends or family members who do so, a 1995 *New York Times Magazine* article reported that Hallmark has introduced a lucrative line of "recovery cards" offering encouragement for sticking to a diet or a course of therapy.[1] Company officials say that the line is selling "far beyond expectations." The circle of support keeps stretching, but as in the game of "ring around the rosy," all we can do is tread the same narrow turf until we all fall down.

The TV talk show has become a national confessional of addictions and dysfunctions, where we can find forgiveness before the closing credits. Everyone is blamed but "poor little me." We have become a culture of victims.

## PAINLESS LIVING

The modern game of shifting blame was once a favorite of liberals, but all sides have learned to play. For example, in her well-reviewed 1994 memoir *Motherhood Deferred*, the journalist Ann Taylor Fleming faulted feminism for her decision to postpone childbearing beyond her fertile years. Both the careerist feminism Fleming criticized and her high-tech, high-priced procreative efforts stressed the primacy of self-gratification. She needed to bear a child to feel personally fulfilled. Despite the marvels of science and Fleming's professional success, however, she learned too late that in the glittering bazaar of lifestyle choices, nothing is free.

Even though fulfillment so often proves elusive, the prospect of a painless fix is firmly embedded in the modern psyche. Our boundless sense of entitlement is evident in national opinion polls showing that we want to reduce our bloated "nanny" government, but not if it requires trimming the specific programs that benefit us personally. (Let him who is without sin cast the first stone at welfare mothers.)

We expect all our wounds to be tended, even those we consciously inflict on ourselves. Despite well-publicized warnings about soaring rates of skin cancer, we keep bronzing in tanning salons and baking on beaches. This dangerous and disfiguring practice began in the 1920s, when the prized pale complexions Victorian women guarded with parasols and veils became passé. "People wonder why I take the risk," one hardcore twenty-something sunbather recently told a reporter for *The Washington Post*. "But I figure if I need plastic surgery when I'm forty, I'll just go out and get it." When questioned about the possibility of cancer, she replied, "It's off in the future. By then they'll have a cure."[2]

Of course, no age is immune to selfish or self-destructive behavior. The late nineteenth century produced its own share of rascals and rogues, including some whose notoriety has survived to the present day. What makes the current crop of whiners and dysfunction junkies any worse than the charlatans and robber barons of the Gilded Age? Quite simply, the answer is that Victorian miscreants skirted and sometimes flouted the rules, but they didn't try to rewrite them. Even the greatest Victorian villains understood that the moral fiber of a civilized society would fray and break if there were not dire consequences for flouting society's rules.

Consider the case of Jim Fisk. As his biographer W. A. Swanber noted, in an age that revered humility and discretion, Fisk was a flamboyant self-promoter—the Donald Trump of his day. Along with his partner, the reviled Jay Gould, he nearly cornered the country's gold supply in 1869. Their failed attempt did succeed in bankrupting half the brokerage houses on Wall Street. The married Fisk was equally notorious for flaunting his affairs with actresses, dancers, and other "loose women."

Not only was Fisk socially shunned and roundly condemned by prominent preachers and politicians, his sins hit him squarely in the wallet. Many men refused to do business with him because he was not a "gentleman." Fisk expected this and accepted it as a cost of doing business his way. He never thought to question society's right to ostracize him, much less to turn his flamboyant style to his advantage. He broke the rules in good faith and didn't expect any credit for his bad behavior.

Can we imagine the philandering Donald Trump paying such a price for his high-profile affair with Marla Maples? (Of course she had a successor and was later dumped herself by yet another look-alike blonde.) On the contrary, he was rewarded with more publicity, which conventional wisdom claims is never bad. A front-page story in *The New York Times* featured the city's mayor kissing mistress Maples when Trump and she eventually applied for a marriage license. Politicians and celebrities attended the wedding, and the minister who presided claimed no authority to pass any moral judgment on the happy couple since "I'm in a very different place today than I was when I was a young minister."[3]

The difference between the 1860s and the 1990s is that public vice once carried a price, and those who played expected to pay. Jim

Fisk certainly did. According to Swanberg, before Fisk met what society termed his fitting end—the lover of a former paramour shot him—he bowed to the power of the moral code he had consciously breached:

> There isn't any hope for Jim Fisk. I'm a gone goose. . . . I am too fond of this world. If I've got to choose between the other world and this, I take this. Some people are born to be good, other people are born to be bad. I was born to be bad. As to the World, the Flesh, and the Devil, I'm on good terms with all three. If God Almighty is going to damn us men because we love the women, then let him go ahead and do it. I'm having a good time now, and if I've got to pay for it hereafter, why I suppose there's no more fair shakes; and I'll take what's coming to me.

Today, every talk-show therapist worth his sheepskin would tell Jim Fisk or anyone else who thought vice carried a price: "Don't worry; be happy." We have spent a century learning to take things easy. Of course, it is easier to take it easy if you don't have to worry about the hereafter. The Victorians were well aware of this connection. As Catharine Beecher wrote in her 1841 *Treatise on Domestic Economy*, the Victorians saw democracy as the "practical Christianity" of "trained and disciplined good temper that produced a general elevation in the character of the people [and] the highest form of interaction between men and their beliefs . . . in all public and private life."

## SIN NO MORE

Nowadays we order our religion over easy, like eggs. Not that God is dead; He has just mellowed out. We could see His change of heart in the recent movie version of *The Scarlet Letter*, which ends with its lovers freely riding off into the sunset. Perhaps the Hollywood talents that bowdlerized Hawthorne's message about sin and guilt presumed a modern audience would squirm at watching the cowardly Arthur Dimmesdale confess his guilt before dying, revealing a red stigmata on his chest. Or perhaps they found it difficult to deal with Hester Prynne's redemption through suffering for her sins. After all, as the modernized Hester asks in the film, "Who is to say what is a sin in God's eyes?"

The Victorians were no Puritans, but their social code was powerfully reinforced by activating the same sense of shame that was sewn into Hester's scarlet letter. Nor had this approach to punishment gone entirely out of style in the early part of this century. After the San Francisco earthquake of 1906, children who vandalized shops and homes were publicly shamed with placards that announced their crimes. (Adult looters were shot on sight.) Ultimately, the power of shaming rested on the public's acceptance that human conceptions of right and wrong were rooted in divinely ordered judgments of good and evil.

We wouldn't expect the notions of shame and sin to flourish in a world where New Age healers define "spirit" as getting in touch with who you are. But touchy-feely spirituality is no longer confined to fringe groups that walk on hot coals and run with wolves. In the spirit of the age, mainstream religious groups are busily adapting their messages to fit the tailor-made morality of self-affirmation.

Traditional churches are fast losing ground while new feel-good megachurches that cater to "customers" are thriving. Some makeshift churches, seeking space as well as convenience, even rent space in malls. The most successful model for this approach, Willow Creek near Chicago, is the best-attended church in America.

The diligent research staffs responsible for these amenities and activities proudly affirm that they were inspired by Disney World themes. Churches should be "fun" and "user-friendly," declared a

with-it pastor, and "customers" heartily agreed. One resumed attending church after a long absence because "it's like going to the movies." He found this brand of religion "easy," adding, "I like things easy." So theater seats have replaced pews. Crosses are banned so they won't "alienate" those who are still just "investigating Christianity." In fact, actual theaters are being used for church services in a suburb of Washington, D.C. "I advertise [that] we have the most comfortable seats in town," brags the unapologetic pastor, George Beavens.

*Ladder of Fortune*

The like-minded executive director of the Mount Vernon (Virginia) Baptist Association, Bob Perry, explains the appeal of such settings: "Baby boomers and baby busters are just not into the thing of getting the whole family up on Sunday morning and getting dolled up.

They roll out of bed and put on jeans and a T-shirt and go to church. We have a number of churches appealing to that trend." Freed of the once obligatory "Sunday best," many people now wear their worst.

According to a March 1995 ABC News report, "In the Name of God," national surveys say most of us think "something in society is morally amiss." But pollster Daniel Yankelovich warns that people are put off by anything "preachy and abstract."[4] No problem. "Most churches you go to are boring," complained a progressive pastor in an April 20, 1995, article in *The New York Times*. "It's like you're captured behind the stained glass. . . . Our sermon moves. There's no dead time." Gone are the days when people flocked to hear the long eloquent homilies of renowned Victorian clerics like William Ellery Channing and Henry Ward Beecher, and major newspapers routinely printed their texts. Now sound-bite sermons cater to our shrinking attention spans.

In keeping with this relaxed approach, the King James Bible is being ousted for simpler editions stripped of the inspiring lyrical language the Victorians treasured. No *thee*'s, *thou*'s, *verily*'s, or sense of the sacred elevate the common lingo that makes poetry sound like a weather report. In the au courant *Everyday Bible*, God no longer says to Adam and Eve, "Behold, I have given you every herb bearing seed." Now He sounds like an annoyed Valley girl: "Look, I have given you all the plants that have grain for seeds." In the Twenty-third Psalm, the Lord is no longer the shepherd who "restoreth my soul." Instead, "He gives me new strength." What does He strengthen—your gluteus maximus?

An ad for one of the new breed of Good Books promises "God's Word in your words." If that's what we want to hear, we can always talk to ourselves. Perhaps the assumption behind these nursery school Bibles is that we can't tell the difference anymore. As for self-sacrifice— the essence of Christianity and, not coincidentally, Victorian civility— fewer than half of those surveyed call it a positive moral virtue.

While it may feel as comfortable as a Barca-Lounger, our modern amusement-park approach to religion demands a tradeoff. In this cushy chair there is only room for one—no challenges to grow beyond the chair, no moral tests to strengthen spiritual muscles, no links to community, to higher goals, or to the God, Who would hardly be godly if His Word were really reducible to our words. But in a culture where living, not just loving, means never having to say you're sorry, the very concept of sin is itself a sin against humanity, because it lowers our self-esteem.

## THE FALSE RELIGION OF SELF-ESTEEM

The self-esteem movement is a natural expression of our ongoing effort to sanctify self-indulgence in place of that old-time Victorian religion of self-restraint. The gospel of self-indulgence was recently related by a new disciple, in whose writing the link is especially clear. In *Revolution from Within: A Book of Self-Esteem,* Gloria Steinem argues that our paramount problem is having our "preferences repressed" by a racist and sexist society, which fosters obedience to its "external authority" by undermining confidence in our "internal wisdom." Ms. Steinem blames deficient individual ego for crime, violence, drug/alcohol/spousal/child abuse, dropping out of school, and welfare dependency.

Unfortunately, we have yet to taste the proof in this pudding, despite the efforts of countless authors, lecturers, consultants, and the National Council on Self-Esteem. The University of California sociologist Neil Smelser says that after reviewing thousands of studies, scholars have failed to document claims that high self-esteem is a consistent predictor of higher grades or of which kids will experience substance abuse, child abuse, or teen pregnancy.[5] Experts not only failed to document a link between violent behavior and low self-esteem, they found that violence-prone individuals have unrealistically high opinions of themselves. They become hostile when their inflated egos are challenged. Rather than trying to reduce violence with "I am special" prison chants, Roy Baumeister, a Case Western Reserve University researcher, suggests, "Perhaps it would be better to try instilling modesty and humility."[6]

Our insistence that self-esteem is a cure-all is fostered by pop culture venues that feed our hunger for spiritual self-transcendence with "self-esteem makeovers," and gurus who offer easy trade-in terms on exchanging old selves for new ones. Before the final credits rolled, one renovated guest on Phil Donahue's talk show in July 1995 giddily explained that she finally understood why her live-in boyfriend habitually beat her, and why she took it: "He had low self-esteem, I had low self-esteem, and his beating me lowered my self-esteem more."

# ME FIRST

Ironically, many feminists who complain about narcissistic, juvenile men (the "Peter Pan Syndrome") preach their own version—that women can have it all. It has become a cliché that marriage, like work or hobbies, is just one means of self-fulfillment. To the Victorians, the mutual spousal obligations of this institution were so deep that they could "only be discharged through eternity," as Henry C. Wright put it in *Marriage and Parentage*. But surveys show that only a minority of American adults in our disposable age still include "being married" in their definition of family values. Should this particular lifestyle become constraining or displeasing, you take your toys and leave.

Moreover, according to a recent report by the Rockford Institute, "Marriage in America," most adults now *reject* the antiquated idea that the family—the first school of civility—should stay intact for the children's sake. Unfortunately, experts have begun to marshal hard evidence documenting what the Victorians regarded as common sense: the devastating social and personal impact of equal-opportunity self-indulgence. As documented extensively by Barbara DeFoe Whitehead, children suffer, financially and otherwise, when moms or dads get tired of playing adults.[7] And so, after decades of insisting that kids would adjust to divorce, researchers now recant with a boatload of wreckage from broken homes. And there isn't a whiff of self-esteem in this equation.

The Victorians would say that a culture of self-indulgence in which parents don't take responsibility for teaching character and civility eventually takes its toll on children's development of self-restraint and a social conscience. And so the cycle is repeated, as adults expect little of themselves and even less of their children. These basement standards, which are no bargain, have done more than change the relations between parents and their children. They have changed the very relationship between childhood and adulthood.

# 3

## *Alone in the Toy Store*

Young children are naturally, sometimes charmingly, uncivilized.... Selfish and hedonistic, they are strangers to self-restraint. Aggressive and rebellious, they expect unconditional love. They make countless demands, whine endlessly when they're not satisfied, and blame everyone but themselves when something goes wrong. They require constant reassurance but rarely need ego boosting. "Whom do you love more than anyone in the world?" I heard a cousin ask her four-year-old daughter. "Me!" the little girl gleefully replied.

There would be no cause for concern if I had just described an average child who, with age and training, would develop the trinity of a social conscience—civility, duty, and self-control. But Victorian standards of character development have been so inverted that today's parents are expected to satisfy childish impulses and desires, rather than to help their children grow out of them. The results have been as bad for kids, for parents, and for the larger society as the Victorians feared.

# RAISING (UP) CHILDREN

Victorian standards of child-rearing demanded much of parents and children alike, because learning how to use the building blocks of civility was never optional, even in the nursery. When these parents spoke of *raising* children, they meant it literally. As Dr. E. H. Ruddock wrote in *Vitology*, his 1899 encyclopedia of home and health, the goal was to "lead the child gradually from its natural egoism to a reasonable altruism." No corners could be cut in civilizing the selfishness out of the next generation, because every youngster had to be carefully formed "physically, mentally, and morally." This was a full-fledged "parental duty," not a lifestyle choice with loopholes, and its success meant more than personal satisfaction. Raising a moral and mannerly child was "the highest guarantee of the stability of the whole fabric of the state." In this sense, even the smallest child was part of a big picture.

Although well-mannered children doubtless made their parents' lives easier, manners were taught for the children's benefit. However, the Victorians saw manners as far more than a surface gloss that would win friends and influence people. In his 1911 essay "The Decay of Manners," Thomas Nelson Page wrote, "'Manners maketh the man' holds a deeper philosophy. . . . This matter of manners goes much nearer to the heart of life." If that heart skipped too many beats, he warned, we would have "the most intolerable class that any society has ever been called on to carry."

We are carrying this burden now, from shopping malls bulging with children who don't want to grow up to prisons bulging with children who never got the chance. For, as Page predicted, "Having been . . . led to imagine that their own desires can be gratified at any cost, they not unnaturally . . . feel at liberty to pursue their desires at whatever cost either to themselves or to others."

The current crop of parents is not the first to shy away from exercising the duties that Catharine Beecher found so essential to social stability. Researchers such as the Lynds, the authors of *Middletown*, trace this trend back to the 1920s, when modern parents began to behave like "pals." By the 1950s, the ideal family was expected to have what Susan Kellogg in her 1988 book *Domestic Revolutions* called a "carefree, child-centered outlook with relaxed methods of child discipline." This enlightened attitude is popularly identified with Dr. Benjamin Spock, who, according to Kellogg, described his own mother as "very tyrannical, very moralistic, very opinionated," yet "very dedicated to her children." Apparently, she was also very Victorian in her approach to the "inner child." Dr. Spock recalled that he and his siblings "didn't realize that she instilled such a sense of guilt in us that it showed all over when we came in having done something naughty."

Now that we are more concerned with consciousness raising than conscience raising, Mrs. Spock's moralistic approach might be considered psychologically abusive. Indeed, the whole notion of child raising has given way to "parenting." The new term is revealing: The focus is on transforming ourselves into parents, rather than transforming our children into mature adults. And who is the best judge of this effort? Who else but the child to whom we are trying to "relate"? Hence the complaint of one elementary school counselor that parents constantly seek their children's approval of their decisions. This gives new meaning to the phrase "children raising children."

## PASSIVE PARENTS, PERMISSIVE PARENTS

Part of the problem is that many parents don't want to have to be the bad guy, the disciplinarian, preferring to be their children's friend. Even so, the kid down the block often seems to have more authority over the children than the parents do, because parents have abdicated their responsibilities. It's not that Mom and Dad don't love their offspring. Most parents who stay together tell pollsters they want to spend more time with their kids. Yet kid time has decreased dramatically over the last generation. The growth of dual-income families is an obvious culprit, but this fails to explain why an astonishing amount of the waking hours today's go-go family members actually spend together is devoted to watching TV. Lest we think this is the contemporary equivalent of gathering round the campfire to roast marshmallows and share ghost stories, researchers say we relate most directly to the set, not to each other. And even as the size of the average household decreases, TVs proliferate like mold. A growing number of American homes have three or more sets, so we can watch whatever we choose—alone.

According to surveys, parents spend less time talking to their own kids than they do calling telephone operators for information or chatting with gas station attendants (who are not easy to find). Because family time is sliced thin as diet bread, experts tell us parents are reluctant to use it "hassling" their kids to learn discipline. This is the intersection of indulgence and neglect, as "home alone" means free to roam in every sense. In a 1993 Metropolitan Washington Council of Government study of drinking habits, nearly three out of four teens admitted they had gone home visibly drunk, yet only one in five parents said they noticed. When questioned about her own son, one mom admitted to *The Washington Post,* "In the end it all comes down to . . . the realization that I'm very powerless over this person's choices."

*Victorian children were expected to help with the housework from an early age. Through chores, youngsters learned the details of running a home or farm.*

Such a casual assertion of parental powerlessness would have amazed the Victorians. We have experienced a sea change in outlook, which has drastically reshaped what we take to be reasonable or commonsensical responses to everyday problems that parents have always faced. Consider how an advice column called "Family Almanac" responded to the mother of an eight-year-old girl who threw incorrigible temper tantrums and constantly berated her obedient younger sister: "Take the older child out to a proper ladies' lunch at the department store . . . without once reminding her to mind her manners. Talk with her instead as you would talk to a friend, asking her how she has been, and what she thinks about the latest book she's reading, and also confide in her."[1]

The columnist goes on to advise that the parent confess to the child that she is concerned about problems at home, which will cause the girl to reassure the parent: "Your daughter will probably tell you quite seriously that you shouldn't fuss so much, but she will ponder the problem later and try to be better, as long as you haven't blamed her for the problem." Granting the child this "respect" will compel her to behave, and "you'll find her much easier to handle."

Put aside the difficulty of finding that "proper ladies' lunch" in an era when the very idea of being a "proper lady" has become controversial. The premise here is that an unruly child isn't going to behave until she gets some respect. But what is the value of respect that isn't earned but is dispensed like party favors? To the Victorians, respect was granted not as an incentive to behave properly but as a reward for having done so. By giving our children something for nothing, we get what we ask for in return. And so today's parents worry about earning their children's respect, rather than vice versa. Looking back on his youth, the prominent Victorian cleric Henry Ward Beecher recalled being so inspired (not cowed) by his father "that when he said anything to me . . . it was like the speaking of God."[2] We shouldn't be surprised if our kids are more likely to hear the voice of Rodney Dangerfield.

## MONEY TALKS

Unable to command their children's respect, parents increasingly try to buy it. The total discretionary funds controlled by America's kids exceed the annual budgets of most Third World nations. This country's yearly expenditure on toys, not including video games, has sky-rocketed to $24 billion, according to Pennsylvania State University history professor Gary Cross. As he noted in a *New York Times* article titled "Too Many Toys," that represents a 260 percent increase since 1980, at a time when middle- and working-class incomes have stagnated.[3] Experts ascribe the increase to dual-income couples and guilt-ridden divorced parents who spend money on their kids instead of spending time with them.

The apotheosis of this buying binge and the habits it teaches can be glimpsed in a toy for girls called "Melanie's Mall." It contains a mini-Barbie-like doll, her shopping bags, and boutiques where she can charge to her heart's content with her own gold credit card.

To find the intersection of material indulgence and spiritual neglect, take a trip to any upscale shopping mall. Ask the security guards about the runaway parents who leave their toddlers to wander alone in toy stores, while they go off to shop undisturbed. When they return, they comfort the anxious child by buying him or her new toys. Parental desertion became so rampant at a Discovery Zone in the Washington, D.C., area that the manager had to hold parents hostage by requiring them to leave their shoes at the front desk.

This behavior is not just a product of sheer affluence. The late nineteenth century witnessed what was then the greatest explosion of material wealth in history. This fueled a vast expansion of the middle classes and the comforts they enjoyed. But the Victorians believed that perpetually playing Santa Claus, even if you had the means to do so, meant being a bad parent and a bad citizen. As Dr. E. H. Ruddock wrote in *Vitology*, "Such indulgence is apt to lead to pride of person, of position, and of purse, . . . and expose those so educated in false kindness, to the ever present risk of being stranded upon the shoals of utter helplessness by the first unexpected tempest of adversity." Not to mention turning parents into absentee checkbooks for their kids.

Clarence Day, Sr., the eponymous Victorian patriarch of *Life with Father*, was a successful stockbroker who owned a brownstone on Madison Avenue and a pew in the local Episcopal church. But even in this affluent household, Clarence Jr. and his brothers received new toys only at Christmas. Mr. Day was no Scrooge; this was a matter of morals rather than meanness. A popular rhyme of the era spelled out the modest and practical gifts children could expect: "Something to eat, something to read, something to play with, something they need." This presents quite a contrast to contemporary scenes of parents slugging it out in toy stores over the last Tickle Me Elmo or Beanie Baby, and reflects the Victorian ethos that parents show more concern for their children's good than for their goods.

## KIDDIE CONSUMERS

Of course, Clarence Day's parents didn't have to compete with a popular culture obsessed with lowering the age of consumption. It was during the 1950s, a decade now idealized by conservatives, that charmingly innocent shows like *Howdy Doody* and *Walt Disney Presents* began pitching ads directly at children. As Stephanie Coontz writes in *The Way We Never Were,* this was a time when children were "pampered as never before," and everyone thought "you must eternally give to your children: otherwise you are not a loving parent." No left-wing sociological tract ever did so much damage to Victorian values. If you have any doubts, pull out those old Kodak moments of birthday parties and Christmas mornings. Loot was the name of the game.

It was in the 1950s that a TV cartoon brat first screamed, "I want my Maypo!" until Mom quickly fed him his favorite cereal. Forty years later, daily life imitates popular art. We have all stood in line behind some octopuslike child in a shopping-cart seat, as she strained to grab strategically placed toys while wailing at a pitch that could shatter nerves and glass. In my latest such encounter, the mother (who seemed to have far fewer arms than her child) finally distracted her little girl by coaxing her to sing a TV jingle—from a toy commercial. Understandably, Mom seemed too frazzled to recognize either the irony or the cultural hole she was stuck in.

## THE BURDEN ON SCHOOLS AND TEACHERS

With help from Hollywood and Madison Avenue, kids keep upping the ante until parents throw up their hands. It should come as no surprise that teachers are being forced to step in where parents fear to tread, if only to avoid utter chaos when the orbits of these little angels intersect in a single classroom. School officials increasingly report that the babies of baby boomers know all about self-assertion and empowerment but lack a sense of basic decency and key social skills. So the schools must teach them the ABC's of how to raise their hand in class instead of calling out, how to say "Good morning" (rather than some less savory remark), even how to play with each other.

But learning that play has any rules, much less a code of sportsmanship, can be derailed by role-model parents whose own role models seem to be British football fans. An article in the February 23, 1995, *Washington Post* noted that in one wealthy Maryland county, so many parents attending various youth league games loudly ridiculed kids on opposing teams, cursed at coaches, and harassed officials that the recreation department mandated a "Spectators Code of Ethics." This measure barred children from participating in games unless their parents signed a pledge of allegiance to the "principles of decorum."

Sometimes parents even manage to undermine civility in the classroom. They file official complaints, or unofficial ones with their kids, when teachers dare to control chaotic classes by rebuking or ejecting troublemakers. Teaching any values while placating parents has become such a dance on banana peels that teachers are attending special programs and institutes recently established for that purpose. For example, Boston University's Center for the Advancement of Ethics and Character emphasizes teaching "the basics," such as honesty, hard work, decency, justice, caring, and friendship. Who can argue with those? No one, which is why one member of the institute, Kevin Ryan, has said that teachers should "save other issues for later on down the road."[4]

Left unclear is where that road leads or what happens when you hit a pothole. Here's a big one—a values manual for middle-schoolers with the inspiring title *Help! My Teacher Hates Me: How to Survive Poor Grades, a Friend Who Cheats off You, Oral Reports and More*. The book's author, Meg Schneider, states that cheating is wrong but then gives several reasons why people cheat. Instead of explaining why these don't excuse the deed, she cops a plea of relativism: "Can't there be exceptions? In some instances isn't cheating, well, necessary? Perhaps the best answer to [this] question is that there may not be a clear-cut answer. . . . Sometimes people simply have to make their own tough choices."[5]

How can this Swiss cheese diet nourish a child's conscience? According to the author, conceptions of right and wrong are not "clear-cut." So she can only present the menu, then leave the kids to select their favorite dish. At best, you recommend the chef's special, according to Ms. Schneider: "You can't give a kid a moral. You have to help that kid come to the moral on his or her own." This amounts to telling nascent travelers to draw a world map, then crossing your fingers that they don't get lost.

This kind of juggling act was unknown when the public school movement spread during the late nineteenth century. In 1912, the retired president of Harvard, Charles W. Eliot, summarized its gospel, which used to be the gospel truth for most Americans: "Since the safe conduct of democratic society . . . depends on an unprecedented development of mutual good-will, manifested kindliness, and hearty cooperation, the function of common schools in teaching manners and morals is plainly one of the most important parts of public education, and the main reliance of democratic optimism."[6]

Because manners have always been nourished by the oxygen of morals, Victorian educators tried to teach children to forge the connections between them. When teachers wrote simple plays in which students acted out the proper way to respectfully address their elders, they intended to civilize the child, the classroom, and the streets simultaneously. Such lessons were not intended to substitute for those learned at home, unless home was a Dickensian slum plagued with crime and physical neglect. Otherwise, schools built on home base.

In 1899 E. H. Ruddock, a popular writer on civics and child-rearing, could assert confidently, "It may be assumed that all parents . . . will take care that the character of youth is founded in honesty, industry, sobriety, integrity, fidelity, economy, perseverance, and self-reliant determination, which are the weapons in the armory of character by which success is wrested from all conditions of life." This is something we may no longer assume, to put it mildly.

## WHEN CHILDREN RULE THE ROOST

In a sure sign that the spread of overindulgence has reached critical mass, Oprah Winfrey recently devoted a show to it. In one segment a parade of frustrated parents moaned about the extortionary rates charged for household chores by those few kids who deigned to do them under any circumstances. The Victorians would be grabbing their smelling salts. They believed children of both sexes should master and perform every domestic chore, from mending clothes to repairing windows—without compensation. "A child as young as six," said Lydia Maria Child in her 1833 advice manual *The American Frugal Housewife*, "should be taught to consider every day lost in which some little thing has not been done to assist others."

Building character meant contributing to the common family maintenance, acquiring various survival skills for later life, and becoming self-sufficient. Victorian parents showed that they "cared" by giving their children a sense of morality, the tools of civility, and the Golden Rule, which made both possible. If you view the world through Victorian eyes, as a complex tapestry of threads, you'll see why material and even emotional overindulgence can damage more than your credit rating.

These threads cohered for me a few years ago, during a trip to the airport. Waiting next to me at the arrival gate was a woman and her squirming child of five or six. As the child's father deplaned, she shouted, "Daddy, what did you bring me?" The horror on this well-trained parent's face revealed that he had forgotten the expected gift. A promise of swift compensation failed to stop the caterwauls that quickly dimmed the ambient noise of jet engines and public-address announcements.

Finally, sighing with resignation, the woman carried her flailing bundle of hysterics toward the luggage carousel, along with a bag of toys and kid supplies that looked heavy enough to dislocate her shoulder. Dad carried himself and a slim, monogrammed briefcase. With his glassy, tuned-out stare, he was as self-absorbed as his offspring. Though the couple had yet to greet each other, the resentful woman finally tugged her husband into a public therapy session about their squalling daughter. This mutual blame game quickly extended to whose needs weren't being met in and out of the bedroom.

With both of these well-dressed thirty-somethings emoting and sporadically cursing almost as loudly as their little carbon copy, I saw the perverse harmony in that distinctly modern picture. They were truly creatures of their time, three would-be stars equally oblivious to the planets that were supposed to revolve around them. I lost sight of them in the baggage claim area, surviving my close encounter at the cost of a bruised rib. (Not surprisingly, they assumed that their feelings—tired, testy, and wanting to get home—justified wielding their elbows to carve out more personal space.)

"Big deal," an acquaintance remarked when I recounted this experience scene by scene. "Nobody died." Not there; not that day. But something precious that could not be tallied in a body count had died long ago. Even this lapsed Catholic began praying for its resurrection.

# Portrait of a Lady

Victorian women, those constantly embroidering and crocheting seamstresses of history, are uniquely qualified to serve as our teachers. It was they, not their fathers or husbands, who embodied their culture's unified vision of etiquette, values, and morality. Their lives and works still contain the keys to those elevated codes of conduct and aspiration that were orphaned nearly a century ago and are so sorely needed today. To understand what they have to teach us, though, we must first understand how radically our notions of womanhood have changed.

The tragic tally of recent statistics on sexual abuse, rape, and domestic violence brutally demonstrates how the collapse of basic decency levies its greatest toll on women. Less obvious is the story of how modern feminists abetted this tragedy, and their sex's social suicide, by renouncing the broad moral mission of their predecessors, the trailblazing Victorian suffragists and reformers.

This is a tale of two roads—the high and the low. The first was proudly genteel, altruistic, optimistic, visionary, politically pointed yet spiritually driven, and unshakably empowered by the femininity it carried as the lamp of human progress. The second road was crude, negative, self-absorbed, soulless but religiously political, and so sexually insecure that it masculinized the world in the name of helping women, which sent us all down a dark cul-de-sac.

## FEMINISM OLD AND NEW

This divorce between two centuries of feminists, and the two traditions of feminism they represent, can be glimpsed on Gloria Steinem's desk. Prominently displayed there is a framed letter written by Victoria Claflin Woodhull, one of history's most infamous and truly dysfunctional deviants. Woodhull hailed from a family of blackmailers, hucksters, charlatan spiritualists, and murderers worthy of an old dime novel. When not peddling quack lethal potions, the Claflin clan pursued its favorite hobby: constantly suing each other. They were such a social menace that the citizens of their Ohio hometown actually paid them to leave.

According to Johanna Johnston's 1967 biography of Woodhull, she was a shameless self-promoter and publicity hound who became a major advocate of the short-lived Free Love Movement in the 1870s. (On this score, there was nothing new at Woodstock in 1969 but the mud.) She packed them in on her lucrative lecture tours. In a speech in the 1870s, Woodhull declared, "I have an inalienable constitutional and natural right to love whom I may, to love [for] as long or as short a period as I can, to change that love every day if I please!" She proved true to her convictions of the moment by having a string of affairs with single and married men who were discarded when they ceased to further her career. Outdoing even Madonna, she juggled one lover while living with another who had abandoned his wife for her. Like all modern moral arsonists, this very un-Victorian Victoria never cared who got burned. "What does it matter whether the child or anyone knows who its father is?" she asked rhetorically. Nothing mattered but her rights and those of like-minded rebels to breed randomly and recklessly.

Victoria Woodhull's housekeeping arrangements were as elastic as her conscience; she simultaneously shared quarters with her children, her legal ex-husband, and his probably bigamous successor. Following a farcical but headline-grabbing run for president (at a time when women still couldn't vote), this proponent of adultery divorced her second husband for that very offense. Then she sailed for London with a pocketful of hush money paid by a prominent family trying to avert a scandal. England provided her with a soft landing. Previously a professed communist, the versatile Victoria changed her tune after she married a wealthy blueblood. She also denied having preached free love and claimed she had been misused and victimized by men.

Despite Woodhull's pro-suffrage views and acclaimed oratorical skills, Susan B. Anthony, Elizabeth Cady Stanton, and other principled suffrage leaders quickly distanced themselves from her when they discovered she was a trouble-prone hypocrite whose chief cause was herself. But modern feminists rush to sing her praises. For example, in her book *Fire with Fire,* Naomi Wolf applauds this self-gratifying "power feminist" for being "free thinking, pleasure loving, and assertive," instead of the more typical "morally superior" and "self-denying" Victorian reformer whose unpaid "good works" contributed to her sex's "suffocating condition." And Woodhull earned her place of honor on Gloria Steinem's desk, Steinem explained in *Moving Beyond Words,* for "liv[ing] out in public the principles of female emancipation and sexual freedom that were not only unusual in her day but illegal." Ms. Steinem sees an inspiring "strength" in this "rare woman who had escaped all training to be a lady."

~~~

## Goodnight All You Ladies

Though in England the term "lady" was originally a title one had to be born to or acquire by marriage, in the democracy of America any woman could become a "lady" by virtue of her behavior. Alas, the term is now on the hit list. In a recent book on workplace diversity, *Workforce America,* management consultants Marilyn Loden and Judy Rosener decry the word's objectionable implications of white gloves, unflagging politeness, and general "gentility." At a time when such traits are regarded with suspicion, the word "lady" is disappearing from public discourse as rapidly as it is vanishing from the doors of public restrooms. I once witnessed an elegantly attired woman lodge a loud and inelegant complaint with a maitre d' about the sexist labels on his restaurant's facilities.

The most telling inversion of the old lexicon that honored women is that both genders use the universal term "you guys" in barrooms, boardrooms, classrooms, and on network news shows to address absolutely everyone. It seems God retired from the creation business after making Adam. For all their consciousness raising, when women talk to each other, the lingo of guyhood often subsumes their sisterhood. Even Victorian prostitutes would have balked at such a denial of the feminine identity.

In this century, men have patronized women as "gals" and "broads," or compared them to animals from "chicks" and "foxes" to the increasingly popular "bitches." Even women have sometimes called each other by these names, but there is a big difference between a "foxy lady" and a true lady. Any of these terms for women would have horrified the residents of an age that even frowned on the word "female" as insulting, since it describes both higher and lower forms of life.

## THE AGENDA OF NINETEENTH-CENTURY FEMINISTS

That despised label "lady" would keep most Victorian feminists off the desktops of their present-day successors. Victorian suffragists and reformers never toed a single party line, but they shared one quality that today's feminists hate more than hoop skirts. As Julia Ward Howe, who knew and worked with most of these women throughout her long career, wrote in *The Woman Suffrage Movement,* they all had "a great heart of religious conviction and a genuine spirit of self-sacrifice." Elizabeth Oakes Smith, a suffragist and cousin of Elizabeth Cady Stanton, wrote in her autobiography, "Duty was my motto everywhere."

The fight for female suffrage wasn't a mere lifestyle choice for Victorian women, nor was it motivated by sheer self-interest or a desire for redistribution of patriarchal power. The leaders of this hunt were after much bigger game than the ballot. Unlike modern-day feminists who have pushed a totally female-centered rights agenda in

*Suffragettes such as these, shown in an 1899 photograph of The League of Political Education in New York City, had a far-reaching agenda and a moral authority current feminist activists lack.*

the past quarter century, the Victorian-era reformers regarded the vote as a stepping stone to nothing less than "the better development of humanity," as Mary Livermore wrote in her 1889 autobiography *The Story of My Life.* Even when crusading for themselves and their sex, activists of old knew that unless everyone shared in the prize—including men—theirs would be a shallow victory. The suffragists did not promote so-called "women's issues," or demand the vote so that they could usher in politicians sympathetic to their special interests. According to *American Home Life 1880–1930*, the suffragist Julia Ward Howe believed that "[Voting] is a part of the duty which our sex owes to humanity. Religion, purity, peace, temperance are as much in place at the polls as at the altar or the fireside."

The reformer Consuelo Vanderbilt wrote in her autobiography that she found Paris gowns, glittering parties, and charitable dabbling left her as cold as her family's marble palace in Newport, so she abandoned "contemplations of a purely personal nature" for the deeper satisfaction of "higher idealism" and a "life lived for others." Jane Addams, suffragist, peace activist, municipal reformer and founder of the settlement house movement, put her money and herself to work among Chicago's immigrant poor. The robber baron Jay Gould's eldest daughter, Helen, continuously opened her home and her wallet to vast numbers of needy children, some of whom she adopted. Among middle- and upper-class Victorians, a Mother Teresa spirit was the venerated rule, not the exception.

This concept is alien to those feminists who define success as making partner so that male associates have to sleep with *you* to get ahead. NOW's founding manifesto of 1973 urged the liberated to shun traditional volunteer activities because they reinforced women's second-class status. What was once upper-class, even aristocratic, behavior had officially become déclassé. Small wonder that contemporary feminist scholars mock their nineteenth-century Samaritan sister as a masochist who "loved her crosses," as Ann Douglas wrote in *The Feminization of American Culture*. Not only was she "delusive, oppressed, and damaged," but her elevated spiritually driven aspirations were "fakery and crippling for all." Just studying these women is deemed a "painful" and "frightening" task, whose only reward appears to be academic tenure.

In her book *The Second Stage*, Betty Friedan analyzed some of the excesses of feminism's take-no-prisoners first stage. She half-heartedly conceded that it was wrong to denigrate "selfless service," because a "life lived for oneself does not truly satisfy men or women. There is a hunger in America today for larger purposes beyond the self." Once again, modern "wisdom" vindicates the Victorian common sense we had to relearn in the hardest possible way. Although national polls confirm how soul-starved we are, Friedan's revisionist view is not shared by "power feminists" who urge women to channel their energies and Ivy League brains into economic and politically self-interested pursuits. Are bimbos who measure their self-worth by their cup size any more limited than women who define themselves by the size of their résumés or bank accounts?

## Bringing Womanly Virtues to the Public Sphere

Self-described "radical" feminists who want to scratch the entire capitalist system scorn the "womanly virtues" that were once a welcome antidote to the truly rough-and-tumble Victorian economy. Nurture, generosity, religion, and a sense of redemptive mission feminized nineteenth-century culture through the home, or private sphere, which was women's domain. These values were then applied to the "enlarged housekeeping" of the public sphere of society, which was considered men's domain. With a vast agenda that the Prohibition crusader Frances Willard termed "do everything" reform, Victorian women lost neither time nor their dignity by whining about inequality. Before they saw the inside of a voting booth or glimpsed a glass ceiling, they mobilized what Elizabeth Cady Stanton called "a great moral revolution" to improve public sanitation, education, prison conditions, and housing for the poor; build parks and playgrounds; and eliminate sweatshops and child labor, alcohol, prostitution, and pornography.

Even with this overflowing plate of ambitions, the Victorian ladies, as always, had higher goals. These supremely confident "do everything" women were spiritually charged up and hell bent on eliminating "the selfish and brutal elements which lead to war and bloodshed," as Julia Ward Howe put it (according to *American Home Life 1880–1930*). In this the Victorian reformers failed, but their vision will not fail to inspire those who hunger for more than victories they can take to the bank.

### Selfish vs. Unselfish Feminist Agendas

Modern feminists have picked apart the agenda of their Victorian "sisters" as if carving up a chicken to select the tastiest parts. They advocate specific social programs that directly or indirectly benefit women, like child-care facilities that help working mothers. Larger issues with no direct payoff are ignored or given only lip service, and any curbs on sex are denounced as "censorious." After all, our culture is not sexually permissive enough. According to Naomi Wolf, writing in *Ms.* magazine, "There's too much sexual judgment going on."¹ To eliminate such judgmentalism, we have seen feminists advocate axing the word "normal" from sex-ed courses and threaten to sue schools that eject pregnant teens from cheerleading squads.

Victorian crusaders were not sexless schoolmarms who jealously foiled everyone's fun. Their social purity campaign transcended sex, just as sweatshops meant more to them than bad wages or working conditions, and raw sewage in the streets spread more than epidemics. In an age when everything had a moral dimension, these Dickensian-style horrors demoralized people, and were considered evils that rivaled illness or physical hardship. The Victorian reformers would have considered such denial of the moral dimension of these social problems and their effect on human souls the ultimate dereliction of their duty.

They delivered the full punch of this power in the late nineteenth century, when their voices, pens, and petitions defeated efforts by prominent male physicians and police officials to legalize prostitution in many towns and cities. These men proposed licensing prostitutes who were certified as "clean" so they and their clients would not spread venereal diseases. Susan B. Anthony, Elizabeth Cady Stanton, Frances Willard, Dr. Elizabeth Blackwell, and scores of other influential women opposed such laws on grounds that must mystify marketplace feminists who view "lifestyle choice" as the highest goal of a liberated woman's movement. The physician William Acton, in his 1857 book *Prostitution,* echoed the beliefs of the Victorian reformers when he wrote that reducing sex to a mere commercial venture "not only breeds distaste for virtuous society, but causes the mind to form a degraded estimate of the sex, until all women seem mere objects of desire and vehicles of indulgence . . . a toy, a plaything, an animated doll; a thing to wear like a glove, and fling away . . . instead of an immortal being, composed, like himself, of body, soul, and spirit."

This argument illustrates the way Victorian thinking wove together the threads of personal, social, and moral consequences. This kind of needlework was highly valued and effective woman's work, and no one did it better.

Woman were so instrumental in the Prohibition movement that it became known as "the woman's war." Alcoholism was a serious problem in the nineteenth century, especially in saloon-infested slums. Bar owners routinely set out "free" buffets to entice men to spend the paltry wages their families desperately needed on booze that was adulterated at best and poisonous at worst. It was common for men "polluted by drink" to physically and sexually abuse their wives and beat their children. The Society for the Prevention of Cruelty to Children was founded in 1875 to rescue many of these youngsters. One year earlier, praying, preaching, and chanting women shut down hundreds of saloons in the Midwest. The tireless efforts of a broad coalition of female reformers resulted in the passage of the Eighteenth Amendment, banning alcohol, in 1919, the year before women won the vote. By the time the law was repealed in 1933, the invincible "conservators of public and private morals" were extinct.

## THE MORAL AUTHORITY
## OF VICTORIAN REFORMERS

Today we have countless factions of politically active women, but none can claim the moral authority that women shared and wielded so effectively a century ago. The Victorians would view this as a devastating loss of female power that can never be recompensed by political and economic rights. The admirable work of Mothers Against Drunk Driving is based on one of our few shared moral values: that operating a vehicle while intoxicated is a gross imposition on the rights of fellow citizens. But for all its importance, drunk driving is a single self-contained issue, unconnected to a grand design for elevating the human race. I cannot imagine the president of M.A.D.D. or any woman from a "most admired" list publicly warning the nation's men, as Julia Ward Howe did (according to *American Home Life*), that they must "recognize in us not only a moral sentiment which they must respect but a moral determination to which they must conform."

Mrs. Howe could make this sweeping demand because her rock-solid self-esteem was not built on the quicksand of self-worship or the approval of men. Woman as the "nigger of the world," a term coined by Yoko Ono in the early 1970s, expresses a modern attitude, not a Victorian one. Victorian men did not denigrate women; on the contrary, they craved the approval and inspiration of the superior sex. No less celebrated an iconoclast than Mark Twain venerated woman as the "the civilizer of mankind." Comparing the sexes, Henry James called woman "a diviner self than his own." His father brought that notion down to earth when assessing his "slothful, self-willed, petty, obstinate, selfish" character against his wife's: "I should simply have gone to hell long ago if my wife had not saved me . . . by *unconsciously* being the pure, good, modest woman she is" (emphasis added).[2]

What modern male ego would freely confess such faults and credit a woman with his survival? Or admit, as A. J. Ingersoll, M.D., did in his 1889 book *In Health,* that he depends on his wife's "spiritual hand when he goes forth into the hurry of life [where] he may feel its grasp warm and strong to help him rise above the billows of vice and corruption which are everywhere, ready to drag a man down to moral death"? What modern male would attribute this country's "extraordinary prosperity" to "the superiority of their women," as de Tocqueville wrote in *Democracy in America*? Or concede, as Henry C. Wright did in *Marriage and Parentage*, that "men degenerate in every particular when left . . . without the refining and elevating influence of women"?

### Women Did and Can Set the Standards

Occasionally a voice in the masculine wilderness speaks up for Victorian notions of social sanity. The renowned black newspaper columnist William Raspberry wrote in a 1993 column in *The Washington Post* that, as a group, "Young women in low-income neighborhoods have neglected—forgotten—their power to control male behavior. If they could learn again what 'everybody' used to know, they could break the violent young men to the domestic yoke."[3] (Why limit this reclamation of female power to the poor?) At the perilous risk of being called sexist, Raspberry dares to suggest that "unless we can re-induce young women to take on the task of civilizing young men, social chaos may well be both unavoidable and irreversible."

One hundred and ten years before this message was rare enough to be newsworthy, Frances Willard stated the obvious when she said, "It is rather by holding men to the same standards of morality [as women] that society shall rise to higher levels." as Richard Leeman pointed out in his book *"Do Everything" Reform.* Raspberry didn't lay odds on whether modern women would accept or achieve this daunting mission. Victorian men had no doubts. The English art critic and philosopher John Ruskin spoke for his age when he said, "What woman wills will be accomplished."

The source of this distinctive female force of will was nature and what it nurtured. Both sexes regarded motherhood with religious reverence. Because women could be mothers, they were the "better half of humanity," in Mary Livermore's phrase, the natural enemies of

*A lady could expect a Victorian gentleman to assist all ladies in any way he could. This engraving from a Victorian-era etiquette book shows gentlemen the proper way to help a lady into a carriage.*

injustice and the natural allies of the weak and helpless. The stamp of the mother of mankind was first and final. "The standard of manhood really derives from that of womanhood," wrote Julia Ward Howe in her 1881 book *Modern Society.* "The woman's influence comes before that of man and outlasts it."

### Mothers to the World

This influence emanated equally from those who never bore children. Some of the most prominent Victorian reformers and suffragists were biologically childless and unmarried but proudly maternal. Miss Beecher, an ardent advocate of female education, acted as a surrogate mother to her students and helped raised her sister Harriet Beecher Stowe's seven children, enabling the author to write *Uncle Tom's Cabin.* Susan B. Anthony had many informally adopted nieces, and Dr. Elizabeth Blackwell officially adopted a daughter.

Modern feminists have long been split on the importance of the "maternal virtues" Victorian society ascribed to women. The psychologist Carol Gilligan is famous for her controversial argument that women value personal relationships and responsibilities, while men value autonomy and cold logic. Whatever the validity of her conclusions, Gilligan rightly argued that the male-defined standards of her profession branded "women's" traits as deficient in moral development. To the Victorians this sort of double standard would have seemed like heresy verging on lunacy.

## VIVE LA DIFFÉRENCE

Rather than embracing la différence, modern feminists prefer to see gender as merely an artificial label. Yet there is a growing body of scientific research that documents another nineteenth-century precept: that male and female brains function differently. As Anne Moir pointed out in her 1991 book Brain Sex, sophisticated magnetic resonance technology now shows that the left and right brains of women constantly communicate, while men's barely speak to each other. Thus, women excel at language skills, intuition, and judging the subtle cues of emotions. Men, however, use more of their brains when solving math problems, which may explain their greater aptitude for math and for estimating spatial relationships. Women are more likely to recall specific landmarks, not distances. (But no one needs studies to tell us who stops to ask for directions, and which ego-driven mammal would rather drive aimlessly and endlessly than ask for help.)

Some conclusions emerging from this research have lit a short fuse in the gender wars. For example, male brains are more focused and less easily distracted while women have a harder time separating feelings from thoughts. Alarmed feminists who fear they will lose hard-won economic and political ground if science can demonstrate that women don't match men neuron for neuron have tried to suppress this research, although it shows promise in understanding and treating such "female" problems as higher rates of depression. And of course there is a flip side to such male "superiority"—which is female "superiority." If the typical male brain is more focused and logical than a woman's, the typical female brain has the converse advantages: the ability to perform more than one task at a time and consider emotional factors when making a decision.

But the real problem here is not the First Amendment, the pursuit of knowledge, or feminist paranoia—it is a modern tragedy and a travesty of women. The same culture that spreads the gospel of racial and ethnic diversity with an evangelist's fire has desanctified the distinctly female qualities the Victorians revered. This is far more threatening to men, women, and civilized life than a mountain of magnetic resonance pictures of physiological difference in male and female brains.

Long before science could photograph the brain in action, women celebrated their uniqueness and the complementary "strengths" of the sexes. In her book *The Laws of Life* (1852), Dr. Elizabeth Blackwell wrote, "Man is just as dependent on woman as woman is on man. Man by himself is powerless, so is woman; but united both are perfected." The educator and etiquette authority Eliza Duffey agreed, writing in her popular 1873 book *What Women Should Know* that the sexes were "halves of a perfect whole." She believed in a "male and female process of reasoning," though neither was "inferior nor superior."

Even courage had two faces. Writing in 1912 about female survivors of the *Titanic* disaster and the chivalrous men who drowned to save them, a reporter at the time, quoted in *The Titanic* by Wyn Craig Wade (1979), lauded "the courage of woman seeing her dear one standing on the sinking deck" and "the heroism of the woman who would rather see the dear one dead than dishonored."

The differences between men and women, believed the suffragist Mary Livermore, were complementary. Furthermore, she wrote in her autobiography, *The Story of My Life*, "The man is never intended to be measured by the woman, nor the woman to be measured by the man; for they are intended to be different, while, at the same time, one is as important to the whole as is the other."

Contemporary feminists can find few dichotomies more offensive than Livermore's assertion that man was "the head" and woman "the heart." But this heart was more than some frivolous chocolate valentine, and it certainly did not belong to the stereotypical swooning damsel. It was wisdom, strength, inspiration, life, home, and God. It epitomized the ennobling intangibles that were mother's milk to the Victorians.

# THE MODERN MASCULINIZED WOMAN EMERGES

These treasured qualities of "the heart" were lost in the 1920s, as women began to masculinize themselves by drinking, smoking, cursing, and sexually experimenting. In so doing they took as their new models of behavior not just men but "ungentlemanly" men. It was during this period that dedicated social reformers like Jane Addams were displaced on lists of most admired women by movie queens like Mary Pickford. In the twentieth century, we began to admire public figures such as actresses for extremely superficial reasons. Now that we have come to revere image over substance, the enduring marriage of admiration and inspiration is divorced. We are all its damaged children.

When women disempowered themselves by leaping off the moral pedestal, no one and nothing took their place as the "civilizers of mankind" and the visionary agents of "higher growth." Organized religion was no match for the rough, raw, masculine values that conquered every corner of life like an invading army. The breadth of their victory forces modern women to adapt or pay dearly for behavior that was once rewarded.

In *Listening to Prozac*, the psychiatrist Peter Kramer notes that our culture denigrates "overly feminine" Victorian virtues like sensitivity and loyalty. Popular antidepressants don't just brighten moods; they allow women whose "personality styles are no longer socially favored or fashionable" to become more robust, risk-taking, competitive, combative—in short, more like men. Two of his patients, the fastidious Julia and the romantically reticent Sally, illustrate his point:

> Contemporary convention demands that women be more assertive (here meaning aggressive, outgoing, and flexible—not firm in defense of the right to be passive and perseverative), but . . . social circumstances tend to frustrate women who use too cautious a strategy. If Julia is to be happy in a two-career marriage, she will need to tolerate disorder. For Sally to avert depression, it is required that she ask men to dance—that she have a more extroverted temperament. A degree of introversion that might have been rewarded in a different social climate here leads only to deprivation, disappointment, and depression.

Compared to the Victorians, modern women do not have more freedom, just a different kind of freedom. They have a briefcase full of economic and legal rights, but they have lost the right to be women on Victorian terms and to be admired or rewarded for it. We should not be fooled into thinking that women can have it all when old choices have been swept away like discontinued merchandise. While none of us would want to trade places with those who couldn't vote or own property, gaining the right to crash men's-only clubs does not seem like a very good trade-off for giving up the right to be feminine. We never got to vote on the trashing of values that not only empowered women but made them the nation's moral arbiters.

Suzanne Gordon documented the cultural and personal fallout from this loss in her 1991 book *Prisoners of Men's Dreams*. These "prisoners" of male standards were professional women who had learned not to care about coworkers, friends, or family members. These women had adopted the compulsory detached and aggressive attitude of the male-oriented marketplace, which denigrates traditional nurturing feminine qualities. "Over and over again," Gordon writes, "whether they are single or married, with children or without, women

*This engraving from* Harper's Weekly, November 5, 1887, *is an example of the type of courtesy Victorian women experienced as a matter of course.*

say they can't find enough time for their close relationships, or even for civility—the small gestures of politeness or neighborliness that have always been nurtured primarily by women." Now these "successful" women lack the time "to support and sustain one another emotionally, as well as to do the work that kept communities together."

At the turn of the century, Jane Addams summarized this lost sentiment that inspired her labors, and those of many other female reformers: "Woman is responsible for the gentler side of life, which softens and blurs some of its harsher conditions" (as quoted in *Jane Addams: A Centennial Reader* by Emily Cooper Johnson). Similarly, in her 1889 memoir, *Glimpses of Fifty Years*, Frances Willard described a "cardinal doctrine of my creed" when she said "the woman['s] touch is to brighten every nook and corner of the earth."

## FEMININE ROLE MODELS

Women like Willard and Addams would see the problems revealed by Gordon's research as involving much more than a time crunch. Women, especially prominent ones, must be civil before they can civilize. But many of our role models have chucked the female standards of civility that were once a secular religion. Julia Ward Howe paid her sister suffragist Lucy Stone a high compliment when she said that Stone's actions were "always guided by her faultless feeling of propriety." In contrast, in a 1993 *Ms.* magazine roundtable article, Gloria Steinem called mannerly women "female impersonators."

Yet even in pursuing what belonged to men—like the right to vote—Victorian women continued to insist on being womanly. When Susan B. Anthony rented public halls for suffrage meetings, she insisted that the "mannish" appearance of the room be transformed with "ladylike" touches, such as flowers. Julia Ward Howe's daughter recounted the many long train rides to campaign for suffrage, on which Mrs. Howe and her fellow workers always brought all the accoutrements they needed to prepare the consummate civilized ritual: afternoon tea.

### Nice as Vice
Modern feminists would still be chasing the ballot without the efforts of these ultraproper, flower-loving tea drinkers, who softened the

world's harsh edges. Yet they continue to heap contempt on Victorians who had the restrictive social training to be "ladies." Now women are told they can be anything but the dreaded L-word. Female college basketball teams have even begun removing "lady" from their nicknames, which traditionally distinguished them from their male counterparts. In *Fire with Fire,* Naomi Wolf counsels her would-be sisters to "cast off the lace nets of our niceness." The journalist Elizabeth Hilts, author of a book entitled *Getting in Touch with Your Inner Bitch,* believes that "toxic niceness"—putting other people's needs first—foils a woman's happiness. She found her happiness by getting de-toxed. Now a confirmed "bitch," she says, "I don't back down from what I believe in or apologize for saying what I think."

To the Victorians, behaving like a female dog was considered toxic to both personal happiness and social civility. But times change. Now this philosophy is emblazoned on T-shirts sporting the slogan, THAT'S MS. BITCH TO YOU. One mail-order catalog promises that buying this less-than-subtle fashion statement "ensures that you get your due respect! Let all misinformed males know that you have a title to uphold." Such bold demands may seem on the surface to be empowering. Instead, they are not only ineffective but serve to lower women to the status of a barking hound or yapping poodle, easily dismissed as an object of contempt.

### Feminine Power

Victorian women embraced the distinctly feminine qualities that society deemed anything but frivolous. Being exemplars and ennoblers of public and private conduct was widely viewed as their choice, their God-given right, and an awesome responsibility that rivaled any man's. "As women are, so will the whole nation be," wrote Eliza Duffey in 1876. And so we slide toward the sewer via the masculine vulgarity of the gutter that has become commonplace. Leading us there are new feminist "role models": the unennobling likes of Madonna, the queen of in-your-face sexuality, and Roseanne, who considers obnoxiousness a badge of female power.

Current conventional wisdom once again allows us to condemn the growing coarseness that corrodes civility. But we tread on sexist landmines by suggesting that women who embrace the male weapons of aggressive rudeness and selfishness denigrate themselves and bring society to even lower levels of civility. Woe to anyone who believes, as Thomas Nelson Page wrote in his 1911 essay "On the Decay of Manners": "Women make both the manners and the morals of a people. Neither rises higher than the gauge which women set in a community. . . . Where a woman has bad manners, it always has in it an element of vulgarity which is more painful than it could be in a man. . . . The result will be a society hopelessly vulgarized . . . with no end but to sink in an ever deeper abyss of vulgarity."

Now that women have resigned themselves to acting like one of the boys, they have unknowingly brought men to record low levels of masculine coarseness. Sadly, the most hard-hit victims of the new male incivility are women themselves.

# Men II Boyz

"Boys will be boys." With a shrug and that abhorred excuse, too many Americans dismiss a smorgasbord of abuses against girls and women. . . . A 1994 *New York Times* editorial denouncing young males in public swimming pools who surround girls to fondle them and rip off their bathing suits—called "whirlpooling" by some—quoted local citizens who resorted to that familiar if outrageous excuse for despicable male behavior: Boys will be boys. News reports show that citizens also cited the "boys" mantra to excuse the horrendous results of a 1992 nationwide study cosponsored by Wellesley College and the NOW Legal Defense and Education Fund. The study revealed that a staggering 89 percent of girls in elementary and secondary schools were subjected to demeaning sexual comments or gestures. Nearly as many said they had been touched or grabbed—a far and frantic cry from the days when "bad boys" dipped girls' pigtails in inkwells. If girls survive the gauntlet at school, they run into another one at work. Three out of five women executives have experienced sexual harassment in the workplace, according to a recent UCLA survey.[1]

## MALE VIOLENCE IN AMERICA

Feminists widely believe that such boys have been around since the cavemen and that patriarchy is to blame for men's abominable behavior throughout history. As Gloria Steinem put it in her book *Revolution from Within*, "Patriarchy requires violence or the subliminal threat of violence in order to maintain itself." On PBS's prestigious *NewsHour*, the former Carter administration foreign policy official Patricia Derrian stated flatly that women have always been battered; the twentieth century just hid the abuse via a "gentlemen's agreement." Some gentlemen!

Feminists aren't shooting off their mouths when they rail about the physical and sexual abuse of modern women. According to the American Medical Association, two million women are battered each year. A scary 1994 survey by *Esquire* magazine found that a majority of college males would commit rape if they could get away with it. The Justice Department estimates that 160,000 rapes occurred in 1993. While others believe the actual number far surpasses this official figure, most experts agree that the "silent epidemic" of violence against women is drastically underreported to legal authorities.[2]

The problem is all too real. Yet those who attribute it to unchanging human nature or social relations do a disservice to our heritage. They blind us to the real reasons so many boys and men act like beasts, and to the best means to civilize them. The first major fallacy is that the true character of "boys" is to be cruel, selfish, and disrespectful. This is a myth that needs debunking.

The saying "Boys will be boys" originated in the 1849 novel *The Caxtons* by the once-popular English author Edward Bulwer-Lytton. In the book, a father says this in reference to his son's extravagance and gambling debts. The comment had no connection to sexual abuse or any form of violence against women, a connotation added in the twentieth century. While this etiological tidbit may seem trifling, it reminds us that the predatory image of "boys" is strictly a modern one. The Victorians could not revere women as they did and "wink away" crimes against them. On the contrary, such criminals felt the hard hand of justice in two courts—the community and the law.

Writing about rape in *Democracy in America* (1835), Alexis de Tocqueville said, "No other crime is judged with the same inexorable severity by public opinion . . . as Americans think nothing more precious than a woman's honor and nothing deserving more respect than her freedom; they think no punishment too severe for those who take both against her will." If patriarchy or the quest to maintain it causes rape, then the supremely sexist nineteenth century should have been a rapist's paradise. Instead, rape was his passage to prison or the gallows. Until the enlightened 1960s, rape was one of the few violent crimes besides murder that merited capital punishment, a tradition America adapted from English common law.

### The Myth of Patriarchal Violence
The one-size-fits-all patriarchy theory is especially ill fitted to the present day. The rape rate in America is four times higher than Germany's,[3] thirteen times higher than England's, and twenty times higher than Japan's. These rates reflect the comparatively low levels of all violent crimes in these countries.[4] Cathy Young, whose findings on global patterns of rape and domestic abuse appear in her book *Gender Wars*, wrote:

> There are undoubtedly men who enjoy hurting women because they hate them. But in many countries far more male-dominated than ours (Japan or Israel), women run far lower risks of victimization. The "backlash" explanation— men use force to reclaim power when their traditional supremacy is eroded—doesn't hold. "Liberated" Sweden also has far less male-on-female violence. What all these societies have in common is dramatically lower rates of violence in general.

### The Myth of Violent Victorian Men
The historian Elizabeth Pleck of the University of Michigan has studied wife beating in Victorian America. Her analysis of court decisions, state statutes, and other related documents revealed that no "gentlemen's agreement" protected wife beaters. Pleck also debunked the myth that a man could legally assault his spouse if he used a stick or whip no wider than his thumb.[5]

Pleck found that wife beating was illegal in most states by the 1870s. Even in states where specific laws did not address this crime, husbands were arrested on assault charges. Convictions brought heavy fines, imprisonment, or the poetic justice of a whipping. Far from encouraging violence, the sexism of Victorian men protected the "weaker sex." Men's physical advantage, which we still can't legislate away, brought a moral obligation to guard the "weak," not an entitlement to exploit them.

Aside from concrete legal sanctions, Pleck found that women were shielded by "vigorous and extensive" informal networks of friends, relations, and concerned community members. There was a strong "male prerogative to discipline other men." Thus, men in the community frequently flogged men who ignored their warnings or were merely suspected of beating their wives.

Then as now, most abusers were poor or working class. The severity of this problem in saloon-filled slums figured prominently in the Prohibition movement. Many female crusaders, including those who knew and aided victims by working in urban settlement houses and missions, described a causal chain that still holds firm. Drunken men often beat and raped their wives. (Contrary to contemporary stereotypes, middle- and upper-class Victorians believed nonconsensual marital sex was rape.) In every century, a cocktail of alcohol and men could be toxic to women.

Spousal battering was so unthinkable in civilized circles that marriage manuals and etiquette books had no need to mention it. Now public service ads must actually tell women that a man who loves you doesn't beat you. Men used to be stigmatized as brutes, bounders, or worse for what now seem like ridiculously trivial infractions against women. For example, if a male dinner guest failed to bow his head to the lady of the house when raising his first glass of wine at the table, he was deemed rude (the Victorian kiss of death) and would not receive another invitation. Other men—not lawsuits, sensitivity classes, or chanting demonstrations—put the fiercest punch in such stigmas. In the Victorian version of the "big chill," men ostracized the offender from social activities and their sacred clubs, or even refused to do business with him. Duels were fought over insults to ladies that today would not raise an eyebrow—his, or hers.

Just threatening to mistreat women could severely wound a man's career and reputation. The autocratic General Benjamin "Beast" Butler, who became military governor in New Orleans when it was captured by the Union army in 1862, aroused outrage when he issued an order that all women who showed disrespect for the Union flag or Union soldiers would be treated like prostitutes. President Lincoln promptly recalled him.

## THE VICTORIAN MALE

To understand the depth of the Victorians' indignation over General Butler's attitude, we must understand the Victorian concept of manhood. The Victorians assumed that all males aspired to be heroic. The influential *Godey's Lady's Book* editor Sarah Josepha Hale claimed in 1873 that "the true hero worships God and honors women" (quoted in Ruth E. Finley's 1931 biography of Hale). Women were the core of the social religion that raised man to the civilized peak of his potential—the gentleman. Modern males rely on faddish movements, marches, and mountains of conflicting how-to books to define themselves. The Victorians had a single ideal of manhood, whose embodiment was the gentleman and whose essence lay in being masculine without being macho.

### A Gentle Man

The gentleman, as Hale wrote in her 1868 book *Manners*, was first and foremost a "gentle man." She portrayed a gentleman's balanced character: He was "respectful but not groveling to his superiors, tender and considerate to inferiors, and helpful and protecting to the weak."

According to *Arthur Martine's Hand-book of Etiquette* (1866), a gentleman possessed "a high sense of honor—a determination never to take a mean advantage of others—an adherence to truth, delicacy, and politeness" toward all. As Mrs. Humphrey's 1897 *Manners for Men* put it, the Victorian male was "dependable in trifles as well as the large affairs of life." He was fearless but God-fearing, had "self-possession, a gentle manner," and gave constant attention to "the needs and desires of others before his own." And of course, as sure as he drew breath—or deserved to—the gentleman "is always respectful to women."

The constant coupling of manhood with words like *gentle, tender,* and *delicate* may sound effeminate to our ears—which is precisely what they were. The ideal Victorian male was neither a sissy nor a chest-pounding ape but the integrated creature that conflicted modern men claim they want to be. One of the century's Renaissance men, the great English critic and reformer John Ruskin stated his belief that a true gentleman combined "the strength of manhood with the delicacy of womanhood."

Many other writers of that sexually unthreatened era echoed these sentiments, and not just those who penned the rules of politeness for a living. In 1897 a prominent American physician and clergyman, Rev. Sylvanus Stall, said, "In the higher type of man the best and highest feminine characteristics have been fused with the best and highest masculine characteristics. The fighting instinct, for instance, has become moral courage." Ruskin also saw the distinctly feminine features of true manhood:

> A gentleman's first characteristic is that fineness of structure in the body, which renders it capable of the most delicate sensation, and of that structure in the mind which renders it capable of the most delicate sympathies—one may say, simply "fineness of nature." This, of course, is compatible with heroic bodily strength and mental firmness; in fact, heroic strength is not conceivable without such delicacy.[6]

Take that, Iron John!

We've come a long way, baby, since women and "womanly qualities" were essential to defining manhood. Neither sex gained much from the journey. Women lost an incalculable power, and gentlemen devolved into mere men who grew increasingly rough around the edges. The currently prevalent image—with some roots in fact—of men as violent, selfish, commitment-phobic boors feeds conservative nostalgia for the 1950s corporate drone in a gray flannel suit who obeyed the law and supported his family. While he may have scored low on the warmth and personality meter, he was a dependable provider. But he was no Victorian gentleman.

His narrow scope of obligations began and ended with paying the family bills. And his sense of manhood—if one existed beyond his bank account and job description—had no social or spiritual connection to how well he treated women.

## THE SEVENTIES SENSITIVE MALE

Since that "golden age" of the fifties, we have sampled enough brands of ideal men to fill the aisles of a Wal-Mart. The "sensitive" seventies male may seem Victorian at first glance, but as many women came to learn, he was more likely to be a glib, unprincipled wolf in sheep's clothing who schemed to get women out of theirs.

Sensitivity still "plays" for some men, whether they try to score with women or the legal system. One modern marshmallow recently sued the city of San Diego, California, for the "emotional trauma" he suffered at a Billy Joel concert when women grew tired of waiting in rest-room lines and boldly used the men's facilities. The presence of these anatomical aliens in plain sight of urinals was simply too traumatic to bear without financial compensation. Victorian men, who would have held their breath and a lot more to accommodate needy "ladies first," would have promptly flushed away this insult to their sex with all the other refuse.

The rebellious toughs of the 1980s proclaimed, "Real Men Don't Eat Quiche." Real men would never buy in to such slogans. The hodgepodge called the men's movement—a women's movement wannabe—helped men get in touch with their feelings but no one else's. Men are certainly entitled to explore their feelings, but did this emotional masturbation satisfy their "needs"? Not according to Bill Geist, a CBS news correspondent and the author of *Monster Trucks and Hair in a Can.* Geist calls men "dispirited. We've lost track of whether we're supposed to be acting more manly or more sensitive." Victorian men knew how to be both.

There are a few hopeful signs that men are recovering a sense of manhood that incorporates some of the Victorian ideals. The latest masculine flavors of the month are million-man marches and stadiums filled with Promise Keepers pledging to honor God and their family duties. Few would fault these intentions. Yet pledges, like diets, are easily made and broken in an era where only uncertainty is certain and the one constant is change. In 1962, Bob Dylan asked, "How many roads must a man walk down before you call him a man?" The answer is still "blowing in the wind."

## The Ghetto "Man"

Ironically, today's only coherent concept of manhood—one that inverts and perverts everything Victorian—exists in inner-city ghettos. The renowned African-American scholar Elijah Anderson and the *Washingon Post* journalist Leon Dash have written painfully eloquent first-hand accounts of the rampant conscienceless brutality and crime committed by young men and boys with no respect for life, least of all their own.

In this Darwinian environment, the weak, including women and children, are not protected but routinely exploited. Manhood is still defined by females—but only in terms of how badly they are treated. Males gain status from their peers by publicly demeaning their mate of the moment. In his book *Streetwise,* Dr. Anderson describes an endless game of "hit and run" sex, where guys bed, impregnate, and abandon as many girls as possible, who are left with no hope of child support. These nominal fathers show up on "mother's day" to claim their share of welfare checks.

## ADDRESSING MALE VIOLENCE AND HARASSMENT

Meanwhile, feminists urge women to fight for their rights, spurning any assistance from the "enemy," and they have even won a few lawsuits. But the victories often ring hollow in absence of social repercussions for vile male behavior. In 1995 the U.S. Equal Employment Opportunity Commission negotiated a record sexual harassment suit in which one million dollars was paid to fifteen female employees who had been fondled and otherwise assaulted by Dan K. Wassong, the chairman and president of Dell Laboratories. Although the male-dominated company agreed to institute mandatory sensitivity sessions, it added insult to assault by declining to fire Wassong. Apparently the impressive profits he earned during his twenty-year tenure at Dell carried more weight than his outrages against women. Before the advent of imposed sensitivity classes, Victorian males, sensitized by an entire culture of principles that honored women, would have boycotted the offender into professional and social oblivion.[7]

While this upscale barbarian was still enjoying his private-sector perks, four men in upstate New York were convicted of raping an unconscious woman. Their penalty? A plea-bargained misdemeanor charge and a $750 fine. You could get a stiffer sentence for kicking the family dog. The rapists were indicted on more serious charges only after women's groups protested.[8] But where were the indignant men? They may not wield canes or horsewhips anymore, but they still have mouths that might administer verbal lashings. Unfortunately, men's very free speech is more likely to offend women than to defend them these days.

What is worse, few women even expect male support on moral grounds anymore. In place of this lost power and privilege that women once enjoyed, they now have to fight for respect, resorting to the law to protect them from sexual harassment. But rather than concentrating on lawsuits designed to force men to show common courtesy to women, we should be asking ourselves: Is a civilized society possible when even nonviolent men have little moral stake in protecting the physical integrity of women?.

## Where the Boys Are and the Men Aren't

A glaring example of modern men at their apathetic worst is the O. J. Simpson case. Quite apart from his double-murder charge and acquittal, Simpson was an acknowledged batterer. (He subsequently testified that his ex-wife's photographed bruises were self-inflicted. But that is another horror story.) Nicole Brown could have been any man's daughter, sister, or neighbor, yet after Simpson was sentenced to attend group therapy sessions to deal with his violence, he did not lose a single job as an actor, sportscaster, or company spokesman. When he decided to skip the therapy altogether, no judge or policeman enforced the sentence.

In a desperate effort to promote the kind of ostracism Victorian men would have imposed on Simpson, women's groups protested in front of the Los Angeles courthouse, carrying signs that reminded the nation he was "100 percent guilty of wife beating." In October 1995, a male reporter who was covering the demonstration was seen on the news asking the women what right they had to punish Simpson more than the legal system; he neglected to question the justice of a system that failed to punish Simpson for hitting his wife.[9]

Even before the verdict, a Columbia University professor wrote an article for *The New York Times,* entitled "The Morals of Marketing Simpson," in which he speculated on how the trial's outcome would affect the defendant's value as an advertising pitchman. Simpson's chief attorney, Johnnie Cochran, was just being a savvy (if swinish) lawyer when he sloughed off his client's 1989 spousal abuse conviction by telling the jury, "None of us is perfect." (Cochran should know, since his first wife also accused him of assaulting her.) But the good professor's article never even mentioned the abuse. Apparently, it passed beneath the threshold of his moral radar.

If patriarchy is a neat and tempting culprit for this drama of disgraceful actions and reactions, it is also a moribund institution that is as powerless as feminists to explain the rampant mistreatment of women. The problem is not men but modern men and their morally criminal contempt for the women those Victorian patriarchs protected and revered. This self-serving contempt even masks itself with makeshift morality, as we saw at George Washington University in 1995. A highly touted high school basketball star who had pleaded guilty to forcing a fifteen-year-old girl to perform oral sex and had been sentenced to a year's probation was given a full scholarship by the university. The school's male president, Stephen Joel Trachtenberg, justified this as part of its "mission to reclaim lost jewels." When questioned about his star recruit's brutal act, Trachtenberg replied, "I have neither the authority nor the inclination to try to impose my own morality on others." When a public outcry arose, the president tried the less-than-Solomonic compromise of offering a scholarship to the victim as well.

This mentality prevails from the halls of academe to the corridors of power. In 1995 a long overdue investigation by the Senate Ethics Committee documented a disturbing pattern of sexual advances by Republican Bob Packwood against his female staff. When asked to comment on the Packwood case, the Christian Coalition head Ralph Reed said it wasn't proper "to engage in witch-hunts of public officials based on personal or private behavior."[10] Just when are such hunts proper? When the sins are committed by liberals and other political opponents? If all private behavior is off limits to scrutiny, so are rape and wife beating, not to mention abortion. Either Ralph Reed needs a new Bible or I need a new religion.

Even seemingly innocent remarks by conservative politicians betray an anti-Victorian disdain for women that feels like a back-handed slap instead of a frontal assault. When *The CBS Evening News* profiled the Republican senator Richard Lugar during the 1996 presidential primary season, this upright, buttoned-down family man named *Animal House* as his favorite movie.[11] The brothers of this frat house showed as much regard for females as for the beer cans they crushed on their heads. They ogled naked coeds through dorm windows, bedded the dean's sex-starved wife, and left a passed-out underaged girl in a shopping cart on her parents' doorstep after a bacchanalian toga party. All in good fun, of course. Just a comedy. Boys will be boys.

High government officials routinely shrug at the abuse of women and even young girls. In 1995 the admiral who commanded all U.S. forces in the Pacific said three U.S. servicemen accused of raping a twelve-year-old Japanese girl in Okinawa could have hired a prostitute for the cost of the rental car where the crime was committed. Yes, and they could also have shown respect to women by not treating any woman or girl like an object for their use and abuse.[12]

And let us not slight former congressman Bob Dorman (R-California), a chief sponsor of the Defense of Marriage Act, which would allow states to refuse to recognize same-sex marriages. This advocate of family values has been charged by his wife with having "choked, struck, kicked, attacked, and harassed" her, according to documents filed in court.[13]

Our chivalrous national leaders had another chance to shine after the O. J. Simpson trial. *The Washington Post* noted that politicians on both sides of the aisle were reluctant to speak about the verdict for fear of inflaming racial tensions. They could have accepted the verdict, or even proclaimed Simpson's innocence, while still speaking up about domestic abuse. Aren't raped and battered women worth that much heat?

Politicians denounce crime with every breath, but none bothered to ask how men like Simpson can commit serious crimes against women without serving time. When we compare the legal and social penalties they would have paid a hundred years ago, can we doubt how much women have been devalued since then? Will national summits on domestic violence change that? (Simpson was acquitted during Domestic Violence Awareness Month.) The Navy developed a strict and comprehensive handbook on sexual behavior after women were assaulted at the 1991 Tailhook Convention. Yet outside experts doubted it would change the Navy's "ingrained contempt" for women. Meetings and manuals can only skim the surface; nothing runs deeper than contempt.

Shortly after the Simpson trial, Hillary Clinton went on television to urge everyone to participate in a Week Without Violence. This well-intentioned but futile gesture reminded me of the childhood pledge to give up sweets for Lent. What happens when this civilized week expires? Do we congratulate ourselves, then go back to battery as usual? We could build more rape crisis centers and battered women's shelters, as mainline feminists regularly demand. We could fund an infinite variety of after-the-fact Band-Aid measures, like the pilot program in New York City that lends cellular phones and pendant alarms to domestic violence victims fearful of future attacks.

## Women Fighting Back

Alternatively, we could follow the increasingly popular practice of fighting fire with fire. These days Hollywood gives us an endless stream of tougher-than-thou role models, from Linda Hamilton's militant mom in *Terminator II* and Sigourney Weaver's warrior queen in *Alien* to the latest Thelma-and-Louise wannabe in a low budget made-for-TV movie. In real life, women are told to become more aggressive even as they demand that men become more sensitive. Millions of women are enrolling in martial arts classes and packing pistols. It may be a sign of these well-armed times that the National Rifle Association recently elected its first female president.

Those who remain too timid to karate-chop their assailants like a stack of boards, or blow a few holes in their egos and elsewhere, can resort to pepper sprays, stun guns, ear-splitting alarms, or plain old dime-store whistles, if pricier survival tools strain the budget. A farsighted woman with the means to splurge can even deter assailants with the aid of Safe-T-Man. For $99.95, plus $34.95 for his tote bag, you too can own a life-size blow-up doll to place in the passenger seat of your car to ward off would-be attackers. Since the genuine article is apparently too scarce or threatening, "independent" women must settle for a factory-model male. (With a little creative anatomical redesigning, he could do double duty as a lover, thus giving customers twice the "man" for their money.)

Safe-T-Man may fool a few gullible strangers, but the biggest fools are women who believe a bogus escort will offset the modern disadvantage of being the physically weaker sex. Life is not a round of golf. One way or another, crime takes a psychic toll on women. We live behind locked doors, choose a home in a remote but safe neighborhood, wait an eternity for a populated elevator instead of chancing a ride with a suspicious-looking male. If women can't feel safe at home, on a date, or walking on city streets, will they ever feel safe enough to "let go" in their romantic lives?

In this aggressively "liberated" age, it is far easier for a woman to act like a man than to find a man who makes her feel like a woman. The testosterone mind-set seems to be her only reliable security blanket. As Roseanne, the passive-aggressive patron saint of victims, was quoted in a July 1995 issue of the *New Yorker*, "Women should be more violent, kill more of their husbands." Compared to Roseanne's call for vigilante homicide, NOW's form of redress wears white gloves: The organization is currently seeking "test cases" for the 1994 Violence Against Women Act, which entitles victims of gender-specific violence—rape, battery, and assault—to sue assailants for financial restitution. But both throw in the towel on any hopes of reviving mutual respect and social civility.

Even when women "win," they lose by accepting the rules of a man's world. Civility takes a beating, whether the fight is physical, verbal, or legal. Why do we expect so little from men? Why can't women demand—better yet, assume—that men will discipline their own, as the Victorians did? Would we really halt the abuse of women or any other crimes by arming ourselves with guns and the itch to use them? Or do we just stoke the boiler? We should know by now that the brinkmanship of uncivilized behavior will never cure incivility.

The masculinizing of female behavior has resulted in the feminizing of violence and consequently our prison population. According to the National Center for Juvenile Justice, female arrests for robberies, assaults, and other violent crimes rose 23 percent between 1989 and 1993, and male arrests increased by 11 percent during the same period.[14] Recently, the Fairfax County, Virginia, juvenile court judge Jane P. Delbridge expressed surprise at the blatant defiance girls show to their families and the law. "Women wanted equality," she said. "Okay, now they're getting the handcuffs as quick as the men."[15]

Is this the sort of equality that advances the status of women? One probation counselor called this "a major emerging crisis." In Boston alone, girls now account for one in six arrests, but the tentacles of this trend reach beyond our inner cities. In Arlington, a "safe" Virginia suburb, juvenile court judge Joanne F. Alper reported, "There have been days when more than half the kids coming into my courtroom charged with crimes are girls. We've always seen girls not getting along (and lashing out against) siblings and parents, but what's surprised me is the increase in criminal activity the girls are now involved in outside the family circle."[16]

Video games provide a fertile training ground for females who want to kick butt just like the boys do. Game counselors who field calls for Sega and Nintendo say girls now account for 35 to 50 percent of the phone traffic, up from 10 percent just a few years ago. Rejecting the more sedate games that were developed for them, young girls are playing Killer Instinct, Virtual Fighter, and the Metroid trilogy. All feature Rambo-sized female war machines whose only "feminine" feature is their exaggerated breasts. Is this equal-opportunity violence what we want for our young women?

## ENDING THE VIOLENCE

A national women's health group sells a BREAK THE SILENCE T-shirt, subtitled "Stop Violence Against Women." Yet there is no silence to break through anymore. Raped and battered women fill our headlines, movie screens, and TV talk shows. Every facet of this tragic fact of life has been graphically explored, especially since the murder of Nicole Brown Simpson. The phone numbers of crisis hotlines and other recovery programs for victims dot the information boards of libraries, schools, and grocery stores. And the "silence" is routinely shattered by widespread "take back the night" marches on college campuses.

The only silence that still requires breaking is the historical record. The fact is that in the nineteenth century, women did not fear such outrages because they insisted that men treat them with the utmost respect. Ladies set the standards of behavior and did not compromise them, or themselves. Individual women did not have to arm themselves to the teeth or practice martial arts to ensure their safety when all women were accorded respect.

We need to reacquaint ourselves with the idea that safety and respect for women can be more than a wishful slogan on a placard. Oppressed Victorian women had a freedom that we lack—freedom from the fear that anything in trousers was ready to spring like a panther. Even male strangers were regarded with a trust we can scarcely imagine. In her 1898 memoir, *Eighty Years and More,* Elizabeth Cady Stanton remarked that all women and girls could travel throughout America "with perfect civility and safety." Nearly a half century earlier, the educational reformer Catharine Beecher wrote in her book *Letters to the People on Health and Happiness:*

> There are few that have so much occasion as myself to render a grateful acknowledgement of this most chivalrous virtue in my countrymen; for during the last period of my life I have crossed from West to East, or from East to West, not less than thirty times, and have traveled in all Free States and five of the Southern; in all this varied experience—alone. I have never once known a coarse or disrespectful word or act toward myself, or witnessed one toward any other woman.

Even one of this country's harshest critics, Charles Dickens, gave chivalrous credit where it was due. In his famous *American Notes,* published in 1842, he looked down his very British nose at our speech, our clothes, and our manners. Yet he conceded that "any lady may travel alone, from one end of the United States to the other, and be certain of the most courteous and considerate treatment everywhere. . . . If a lady take a fancy to any male passenger's seat, the gentleman who accompanies her gives him notice of the fact, and he immediately vacates it with great politeness."

Perhaps a civilized society can dispense with the female prerogative for a seat on a crowded bus. But it absolutely cannot dispense with the masculine sentiment that once offered it, and allowed women to have a freedom of movement that we so envy today. If women are to regain their freedom, they must reclaim their power. They must demand that men treat them with respect.

# PART 2

# A SENSIBILITY THAT MAKES SENSE

# 6

# The Benevolence of Manners

"There is no fundamental difference between man and the higher animals in their mental qualities," wrote Charles Darwin in his 1859 book *The Origin of Species*. Regardless of whether they rejected the theory of evolution outright as a godless doctrine, certainly on the whole the Victorians believed it was the duty and challenge of mankind to rise triumphantly from the primordial sludge. While our own age celebrates man's animalistic nature, the Victorians looked to manners, morality, and chivalry to humanize nature's most brutal law—survival of the fittest.

## RISING ABOVE OUR NATURE

In 1877 the popular etiquette author Eliza Duffey aptly summarized her generation's frame of mind:

> Civilization . . . calls us out of the natural state in which we are most nearly allied to the brutes, and in which selfish interests alone predominate, and places us in a condition where we may recognize ourselves as belonging to a common humanity, and in which the best good of each is

subserved by permitting many "natural" rights of individuals to be subordinated to the interests of all.

Nature teaches two savages to approach each other as enemies. Each, suspicious of the hostile intent of the other, maintains a natural right to kill that other in self-defense. Civilization teaches each man to respect the right of the other to live, and to refrain from killing him in the hope and expectation that the other will be equally considerate.

By this definition, we certainly have gotten back to nature. The Victorians would say we have regressed rather than evolved. In contrast to today's vague calls for civility, which leave us stranded in the wilderness without a road map, the Victorians' well-marked connection between social theory and personal practice gave strength and sparkle to both:

> Civilization has its laws, civil, religious and social, binding upon the community. Etiquette may be considered as the by-laws of civilization, binding upon each individual in the community. Arbitrary as many of these laws may seem, they are all founded upon some good and sufficient reason, and all intended to make our manners as agreeable and inoffensive as possible to people of refined and delicate tastes—those people, in fact, who have furthest escaped from the state of savagery natural to the [human] race.

The Victorians were proud, not ashamed, of being refined. To us, the blood and guts of savagery may be "real," but so are the deadly diseases we try to cure. You don't have to be a pinkie-crooking tea drinker to see why we need a little less "reality" and a little more refinement for both civility and survival. As Katharine Hepburn told Humphrey Bogart in *The African Queen*, "Nature, Mr. Alnutt, is something we were put on this earth to rise above."

The little courtesies that Ralph Waldo Emerson called "minor morals" were anything but minor. "The power of manners is incessant," he wrote. "It is the beginning of civility—to make us, I mean, endurable to each other . . . to get people out of the quadruped state; to get them washed, clothed, and set up on end.'" (The back-to-nature Woodstock generation retreated big time on this score. In retrospect, the mud that covered Yasgur's farm that weekend looks metaphorically appropriate.) Grace Dodge, president of the YWCA, wrote "Good manners are made up of little things, that taken separately seem very insignificant, but put together make up a very large whole."[2]

## BEHIND THE DETAILS OF VICTORIAN MANNERS

The exhaustively extensive system of Victorian major and minor morals—which made life not just endurable but enjoyable—is legendary. From the prescribed way for a lady to treat a shop clerk to the equestrian rules of the road, all the rules of etiquette shared a logical thread: protection of the weak from physical or verbal exploitation. The rules of the Victorian road may seem overly detailed to us, but the powerful social stigma of breaking such rules served as an effective deterrent to antisocial behavior. With so many dos and don'ts, nineteenth-century Americans knew what to expect in social situations and didn't have to invent etiquette on the spot.

To navigate the complex terrain of Victorian manners required a detailed map as well as a compass. As Eliza Duffey noted in 1877, "Good sense and good nature suggest civility in general, but . . . there are a thousand little delicacies which are established only by custom."[3] But it was precisely these fine points of politeness, the "forms, ceremonies, and rules" that we have abandoned, which "establish and enforce . . . the regulation of the manners of men and women in their intercourse with each other." To the Victorians all this was deadly serious business. For example, ladies would grow apoplectic at the no-show guests we routinely endure with a frustrated shrug. In 1890 the bon vivant Ward McAllister wrote, "A dinner invitation, once accepted, is a sacred obligation. If you die before the dinner takes place, your executor must attend." He may have been joking, but only by half.[4]

## WHEN ETIQUETTE IS DISMISSED

Of course, we don't have such courtesy crises anymore. Or do we? On a New York subway, one enraged rider slashed a woman's face with a boxcutter when the offender bumped into her and failed to apologize. A somewhat more sublimated example concerns the high-

ABOVE AND FOLLOWING PAGE: *These two "do" and "don't" engravings capture some of the specific rules of Victorian parlor behavior. The etiquette errors consist of ( 1 ) standing in the ungainly posture of hands on hips, ( 2 ) leaning forward in a chair, ( 3 ) sitting backward on a chair, ( 4 ) leaning against the wall and casually eating, ( 5 ) placing one's foot on a chair cushion, and ( 6 ) the three-fold error of tipping a chair, leaning one's head against the wall, and smoking in the presence of ladies.*

profile flap that erupted over an alleged presidential snub. House Speaker Newt Gingrich complained that during a long Air Force One flight back from a state funeral, Bill Clinton failed to invite him up to the front of the plane to discuss the budget crisis. Gingrich also had to use the plane's backdoor, while other officials exited through the front with the president. Journalists, pundits, and politicians cited this incident as an example of Gingrich's pettiness and complained that Newt's personal pique had stalled negotiations over the federal budget deficit. Amid all the finger pointing, no one suggested putting the issue of our national manners deficit on the table.

I received a first-hand lesson in the depleted value of this commodity—manners—during a recent visit to Washington, D.C.'s largest bookstore. In the midst of this bibliophilic extravaganza, the few books I found under the ETIQUETTE sign were bottom-shelf crumbs lying beneath the wedding planners. The sprawling children's section offered nothing on manners but an apologetic clerk. (I did, however, note an ample number of children's books on the subject of sex.)

Generation X–ers may find it difficult to imagine a time when pornography was sold under the counter and guides to good manners dominated the bookshelves. Etiquette manuals were so plentiful during the nineteenth century that one historian, John Kasson, called them "a major popular literary genre." Country peddlers and city department stores sold them in abundance, as did the twin giants of the burgeoning mail-order business, Sears Roebuck and Montgomery Ward.

Because learning good manners was the main Victorian route to self-improvement, the maxims in these books had the force of law— and more. "For instance, the law cannot punish a man for habitually staring at people in an insolent and annoying manner," said one self-proclaimed *Guide to True Politeness* published in 1866, "but etiquette can banish such an offender from the circles of good society, and fix upon him the brand of vulgarity." The recovery of civility depends upon reviving the stigma once attached to vulgarity and ranking it as high as "sexist" or "racist" on the scale of social and professional taboos.

## CHIVALRY

But the crux of morality, civility, and the nicest of niceties—what we reduced to the phrase "gender relations"—was how well men treated women. Every advice manual on marriage, manners, or raising children contained the idea that a nation was judged by its citizens' attitude toward women. Even the era's robber barons, those ruthless Darwinian kings of the marketplace jungle, were servants to this sentiment. The English novelist Sir Walter Scott voiced the law of this land when he said that without chivalry—the high-minded and courteous treatment of women—"it would be difficult to conceive the existence of virtue among the human race. It is not what women do for themselves, but what men do for women that marks the true greatness of a people, and their real progress in Christian civilization."[5]

Can we conceive of measuring this nation's progress, no less its greatness, by what men do for women? All we do today is lament what men do *to* women. In the last century entire books were written on the daily courtesies men owed to women. Should we ridicule—or envy—the unquestioned female rights to chairs of choice, decent language, assistance into a carriage, a smoke-free environment, and countless other "ladies' first" privileges?

In the broadest sense, the superior strength of men entitled them to serve, not to be served. Chivalry required that men not only live for women but die for them as well. Chivalry's historic culmination—and its finale—actually occurred eleven years after the Victorian era officially ended. Yet that event was quintessentially Victorian in spirit.

Everyone knows the story of that fateful April night in 1912 when the "unsinkable" *Titanic* struck an iceberg in the North Atlantic. As Wyn Craig Wade recounted in his book *The Titanic,* only a third of the 2,235 passengers and crew survived; most who did were women and children. When one of the ship's officers was asked during a subsequent investigation if this "women and children first" policy was the captain's rule or the rule of the sea, he replied that it was the "rule of nature."

For Victorian men worthy of the name, making the ultimate sacrifice was the rule of nature, as well as civilization's triumph over the primal instinct of self-preservation. The fact that man was descended from the beasts was no excuse to act like one. On the contrary, the capacity for self-sacrifice was seen as a fulfillment of the truly human nature that raised us above our bestial origins. The behavior of the men who went down with the *Titanic* testifies to the power of these ideas to guide their thoughts and actions. We can give an ideal no greater testament than to die for it.

Sworn testimony revealed that several male passengers refused to enter lifeboats because they could not be certain all the women aboard had been saved. One man, when ordered into a lifeboat, not only went under protest but even made the ship's officer sign a statement describing the circumstances, to dull the stigma of surviving a calamity that claimed female lives. Among the few cowards who dashed for the lifeboats, one was evicted and beaten bloody by men who stood stoically on deck, facing death but spared dishonor.

The all-but-forgotten monument to the *Titanic* calamity, a relic of a forgotten chivalrous age, isn't even mentioned in many major guidebooks. Sadly, a similar tragedy today would likely have a less-than-inspiring outcome. By the modern laws of survival, only the fittest cross the finish line. Women would be left to sink or swim—quite literally—unless they were stampeded or pitched overboard by men racing for lifeboats. If push came to shove, no politically correct quota system could preserve a percentage of lifeboat seats for women. It would truly be every man for himself. (I'd like to believe the children would be saved, but I wouldn't bet my life on their chances.)

This scenario illustrates the misogynist peril of the strict gender equality that looks good on paper and makes for stirring sound bites. Victorian civility—not feminist consciousness—conquered the brutality of a kill-or-be-killed world. The twentieth century's march toward every form of liberation has often produced Pyrrhic victories that laid waste the best traditions of the past, and left us to do our atavistic worst.

The smallest gesture of "sexist" gallantry divides women now, and its crowning glory divided women in 1912, when suffrage was a deeply divisive issue. Radical suffragists rejected the chivalrous spirit demonstrated aboard the *Titanic*. One English socialist warned women on both sides of the Atlantic to "consider very carefully whether it is worthwhile to let men assume the entire burden of physical sacrifice in times of danger." But this view posed its own "danger"—making it "difficult to get men to relinquish their heroic ideals."

Modern women have been relieved of worry over men's heroic ideals. What is left of chivalry? Automotive bells and whistles, according to a recent glossy magazine advertisement from Nissan:

"For everyone who's said, 'Chivalry is dead'—we offer this rebuttal: The Nissan Maxima GLE. It opens doors for you, pushes your seat in for you, and adjusts the temperature for you. . . . It's time to expect more from a car."

A century ago, women expected more from men than any machine could deliver, even one that does its own windows. One suffragist declared it "preposterous . . . to confuse the issue of equal suffrage with the problems of the best methods to insure safety in times of panic, and the immemorial usage of seeking to protect the weak and helpless ahead of the strong." In fact, most suffragists praised the "heroic ideals" of men on the *Titanic*—perhaps because they saw the writing on a distant wall

However, the historic valor of those chivalrous men on the *Titanic* was criticized by the Chinese Merchants Association in a public statement issued shortly after the British liner sank. As Wyn Craig Wade recounts in *The Titanic*, a spokesman expressed contempt for a culture that placed the lives of women above those of men. Were the ship Chinese, he said, men and children—but no women—would have been saved. (Although the spokesman didn't press the point, little boys would doubtless have outranked little girls among the children on this survival scale.)

Feminists are still rightly outraged at the inhuman abuse China inflicts on its women. At a 1995 international conference on the status of women held in that country under United Nations sponsorship, vocal American participants denounced China's oppressive birth control policies that result in forced abortions and widespread female infanticide. The Victorians would eagerly join this chorus, while reminding their descendants that honoring women, in small and large ways, is a specifically Western, WASP, middle-class value.

## WASP Bashing

Unlike groups that are shielded from insults based on their past victimization or current minority status, WASPs are openly derided, despite the gradual loss of power that blunted whatever sting they once possessed. WASP bashing began in the 1920s, as Richard Brookhiser notes in *The Way of the WASP* (1991), when influential social critics of the day such as H. L. Mencken reveled in decrediting anything associated with WASP sensibilities. In the public mind, WASPs became "bad dancers," "lousy lays," a "font of pathology," and "an emasculated joke."

Once the arbiters of proper behavior, WASPs are now widely viewed as stuffy, stagnant, and spiritless. After generations of cultural backlash, the onetime high and mighty Episcopalian-born and prep school–bred Anglo-Saxon "ruling class" has been recast as the straight man who sets up a multicultural punch line. But this joke is no laughing matter. Brookhiser argues that iconoclasts like H. L. Mencken and Norman Mailer helped detach all classes from the nineteenth-century WASP principles of conscience, individual responsibility, and civic participation, the very ideals we are desperate to restore.

Notwithstanding our love affair with film versions of Jane Austen novels and Ralph Lauren's preppy clothes, WASP bashing has become a national sport and the inalienable right of every minority. For example, by way of celebrating the growing influence of Latino culture on America, the late actor Raoul Julia could say off-handedly, "We're going to give the whole country salsa, spice. That cold, analytical computerlike Saxon mentality is going out the window." Julia had no need to worry that an Anglo-Saxon Anti-Defamation League might take umbrage at his remark. Had one existed, its members would have been too reticent to criticize him publicly.[6]

Even those who appreciate spice might occasionally crave the taste of Victorian sugar coating. But that choice was struck off the menu decades ago. What is worse, we often confuse the Victorian WASP with Fawlty Towers–like parodies of their purely ethnic descendants. Awkward Basils, giggling Muffies, and tennis-playing Biffs are spineless shadows of a stalwart past. Today,

> WASPs are too guilt-ridden over their "advantages" to understand or defend the moral heritage of civility that has been reduced to collecting matching china and silver services.

The politics of holding doors and giving up seats on the subway may seem irrelevant and petty compared to the drama of life and death on a sinking ship. But to the Victorians, even "petty" courtesies were part of life and death and the whole code of manly behavior. A man would "instinctively" sacrifice his life to save a woman only if he had spent it opening doors for her, tipping his hat, and otherwise expressing his deference and respect. A lazy lout or uncouth ruffian who was unaccustomed to giving up his seat in a train or parlor could hardly be expected to give up his seat in a lifeboat.

Chivalry—the respectful treatment of women—was always the shining centerpiece of Victorian etiquette, even though, of course, both sexes practiced the benevolence of manners. "The universal practice in this nation in thus giving precedence to women has been severely commented upon by foreigners," observed Catharine Beecher in 1869. But this was no apology to plaintive tourists. Beecher called female precedence "evidence of our superior civilization" that should "increase rather than diminish." Suffragist Mary Livermore reflected a widespread assumption of her day—not a gender wars hot-button issue—when she said, "Every boy should be trained to respect womanhood, and in our country this ought not to be difficult. For there are no men so courteous to women as American men."

Fast-forward nearly a century to 1995, when the feminist author and *Washington Post* columnist Judy Mann traced the abusive and disrespectful treatment of females to gender differences in how we raise our children. "Have boys do things for girls," she advised, "such as getting them a drink or fetching a book. The point is to have girls feel entitled to ask boys to do things for them and to develop in boys the capacity to do things for girls, as opposed to expecting girls to wait on them."[7]

Ms. Mann's column merely brushed the tip of the iceberg of all the entitlements her sex has gradually lost. These days mothers, daughters, and significant others grow giddy with delight when guys actually think to pour their mates a cup of coffee when they pour their own. In contrast, Victorian gentlemen rarely stopped waiting on women, especially at social functions. For example, one 1884 book described manly duties if music was on the evening's menu: "Any lady guest being invited to play the piano, it is courtesy for the gentleman nearest her to offer his arm and escort her to the instrument. While she is playing, he will hold her bouquet, fan and gloves, and should also turn the leaves if he can read music."[8] Modern males would undoubtedly label such public displays of attentiveness as unmasculine.

Lest they forget their due, *The Ladies' Book of Etiquette* reminded its readers of the welcome responsibilities a man assumed once a woman accepted his request for a dance:

> Recollect that your partner is for the time being your very humble servant and that he will be honoured by acquiescing in any of your wishes: for instance, you may wish to promenade, to walk from one room to another, to join your friends; you may require a jelly, ice, wine, or any other refreshment . . . in short he will feel honoured by receiving your commands, and he ought to anticipate your wishes on most of the above.

Only a man whose "manners were the index of his soul" would feel honored to be a woman's servant, eagerly accepting her commands and the chance to show himself and the world that he deserved the sobriquet of "gentleman." What modern woman would expect any guy not just to serve her but to anticipate her wishes? Henry James wrote of another time, not another planet, when he described in his novel *Washington Square* gentlemen guests who retreated from a room "in the best order"—walking backward, so as not to turn their backs on the ladies who remained. Now women are grateful if they don't get the backs of men's hands. Misusing those hands on a woman was once considered a sin beyond redemption. Consider the obligation to wear gloves while dancing. According to a 1901 etiquette book,

For a man to dance with a lady and leave the imprints of his fingers upon her dress is anything but creditable to him. . . . Above all things, men should bear in mind that women rule and sway society, and the man who incurs, in any manner, their dislike or enmity, is one of the most unfortunate of individuals who will find that the road he expected would be lined on either side with beautiful, blooming roses is in reality bordered by shrubbery of which the most conspicuous characteristics are sharp, protuberant and long thorns.[9]

Ouch! This painful botanical warning illustrates why the Victorians were so scrupulous about details that escape our notice or regard. The glove rule, which both sexes followed while dancing, is also a prime example of what Eliza Duffey called a "thousand little delicacies which are established only by custom." Yet there is plenty of sense in this custom, even if it isn't common. Wearing gloves allowed partners to comfortably share a dance, not the sweat of their hands.

The city streets, which have become a gauntlet for women, were another arena where civilized rules and ladies once reigned. Bowing and hat tipping were two ways in which men acknowledged and reinforced this fact of life. As Arthur Martine wrote:

The really well-bred man always politely and respectfully bows to every lady he knows. . . . If she expects no further acquaintance, her bow is a mere formal, but always respectful, recognition of the good manners which have been shown her, and no gentleman ever takes advantage of such politeness to push a further acquaintance uninvited.

Since this form of "ladies' choice"—and many others—were etched in stone, no woman had to worry about escaping from the men she knew but wished she didn't. Any man who hoped to win the favor of her further acquaintance had to properly wield his hat. A lazy tap or tickle of the brim was unacceptable. "A gentleman will raise his hat fairly from his head," *The Bazar Book of*

*Decorum* averred, "and not limit his salutation to a mere touch of the rim, like a coachman or a waiter."

A man was also obliged to salute even unknown ladies who were walking with any men he knew. If the man was honored with an introduction to the lady, he would not expect to hear that she was "happy" or "delighted" to meet him. Aren't such trite phrases just the sort we associate with courtesy-conscious Victorians? Not if they compromised a woman's supreme social power: "When a gentleman is introduced to a lady . . . the pleasure is supposed to be upon his part, the condescension upon her side," said Maude C. Cooke, the author of *Social Etiquette* (1866).[10] Hats were tipped to any woman on the street who requested directions or other information from a man. This assumed that women felt safe enough to act in a way we would consider potentially dangerous or provocative. Now there was freedom!

The removal of his hat provided a crucial test of a man's character, and woe unto him who failed it, even if the ladies he slighted

*Hat tipping was serious business to the Victorians. Men acknowledged all ladies, regardless of age, beauty, or class, with this gesture of respect.*

were those most likely to forgive the offense. The 1884 publication *Standard Book on Politeness, Good Behavior and Social Etiquette* reflected the prevailing standard on this issue:

> The man who stands with his hat on in the presence of his mother and sister, manifests thereby a want of apprehension of the requirements of filial and fraternal reverence and affection. . . . If circumstances do not combine to correct him, [they] will in the long-run render him fit for treason, stratagems, and spoils; he sets at naught feelings and principles which would interpose one of the most important barriers between himself and crime. It would not be surprising if such a man were to finish his career in the dock or the hulks; he lacks true nobility and elevation of sentiment without which he will not, and he cannot, come to good."

No man since that time has ever carried such weight on his head. Those who valued their reputations constantly guarded their behavior on the streets. A full century before the song "Girl Watcher" hit the top forty, *Martine's Hand-book of Etiquette* decreed: "No gentleman will stand in the doors of hotels, nor on the corners of the streets, gazing impertinently at the ladies as they pass. That is such an unmistakable sign of a loafer, that one can hardly imagine a well-bred man doing such a thing." The popular imagination had stretched considerably by 1934, when etiquette books were pleading, "Girls, never, never turn at a whistle, to see if you are wanted. A whistle is usually to call a dog." This plunge in the evolutionary scale to canine status definitively demonstrates which gender lost respect, self-respect, and control of the streets when Victorian "delicacies" were swept into its sewers.

To the Victorians, civility depended not just on men who obeyed its rules but also on women who expected men's compliance. Women were entreated to continuously assert their "royal prerogative" in full, as Thomas Nelson Page wrote, and never to "accept with complacency the insolent indifference of the male sex . . . the scattered and scornful crumbs of attention that they deign to let fall before their eager eyes."[12]

If any crumbs are left, we need a magnifying glass to find them. Men are the generic scapegoats of choice—and often deserving ones. But it was women who put us on a starvation diet of manners and courtesies. The feminists who claimed they fought for all women's legal, professional, and economic rights never asked any women but themselves how they wished to be treated by men, or what rights they wanted revoked. Now, many women don't even know what female perquisites they have lost. Morbid curiosity prompted me to ask some Generation X women if any of their male peers still engaged in antiquated rituals such as carrying their packages and holding chairs and doors. They responded with blank stares, as if I were a pointy-eared Vulcan who was just beamed down from a distant prime-time zone. One finally replied, "Like, when did guys ever do those things for girls?" This made me rethink the implications of Santayana's maxim "Those who cannot remember the past are doomed to repeat it." Women should be so lucky.

The perils of liberated living are familiar to every woman, but most of all to pregnant ones. I followed the nine-month odyssey of a colleague whose fate was all too common. After daily bouts of morning sickness, she endured long commutes—on progressively swelling legs—with unencumbered yuppies who never offered her a seat. Twice she was knocked off the sidewalk by tardy young men sprinting toward the office. Frustration, fatigue, and fear compounded the usual burdens of her condition.

Understandably, such women, beleaguered by the death of chivalry, want someone specific to blame for the politically correct incivility that seems more like a crime against humanity. Without the essential chivalrous code that was once man's second nature—the code Lord Chesterfield called "the only protection [women] have against this superior strength of ours"—what laws could have given this woman the unequal treatment she sorely needed?[13] Will we draft affirmative action laws to protect pregnant, package-laden, or merely petite women on federally regulated sidewalks?

Victorian women did not need legislation to protect them from such public abuse and disrespect. In Henry James's short story "An International Episode," the obliging Willie Woodly is described as a man "whose mission in life . . . was to find chairs for ladies." Women today might not choose such a man as a life partner, but all our lives are impoverished when such men—and their mission—cease to exist.

At the turn of the century, Harvard president Charles W. Eliot implied the necessity of chivalry to the very existence of civilized life when he warned that "the chivalrous sentiments . . . of civilized men" would die if women became "coarse, combative, [and] rude."[14] Case closed—right in women's faces. If Victorian chivalry was a ruse to keep women in their places, it was equally effective at keeping men in theirs by defining a large measure of their self-worth and reputations. But as with all things Victorian, chivalry's purpose ran even deeper. Women were entreated to encourage and accept it because it demonstrated not manly "strength" but manly "honor," as Thomas Nelson Page wrote. If men still had this positive outlet for expressing their masculinity, perhaps they would stop verbally and physically brutalizing women and each other.

Echoes of the pathetic quest for chivalry's crumbs laced the controversy swirling around the Nation of Islam leader Louis Farrakhan and his 1995 "Million Man March" on Washington. He told the media one of its intended messages was "to atone to God for the way we have mistreated our women and girls." Unfortunately, he undermined this noble ideal by inviting the proudly unrepentant wife beater O. J. Simpson to the march.

Nevertheless, the sentiment is worth saving. What we need is a sincere national march of atonement by men of all races, and the female equalizers who triumphantly obliterated the sexist chivalry of macho pigs, and left us nothing but the sty. Consider the moral trade-offs made by unliberated women who don't want mud kicked in their faces. Despite Farrakhan's lightning-rod racist views and his "men-only" rule for the march, many black women supported it. Said one female African-American publisher, Frances Murphy,

> Actions speak louder than words. I have yet to walk into a
> room of Nation of Islam members where the men don't get
> up if a lady walks into the room. That's saying a whole lot.
> That makes you feel very, very good.[15]

Once upon a time, such behavior was a mere appetizer in the banquet of courtesy that awaited women. According to modern-day historians, however, women who stubbornly persist in regarding themselves as "ladies" have no right to feel good. For example, in a book called *Prudery and Passion*, Milton Rugoff asserts that the chivalrous Victorian gestures that "converted women into a figure on a pedestal" were not intended to make any woman seem special but were "an unction applied to an entire sex and . . . not a tribute to a particular woman." But current standards are blind to the reason why such "unction" applied to an entire sex. Victorian gentlemen had neither the moral power nor the luxury to choose which women deserved their deference by looks, youth, or any other discriminating criteria. Chivalry implied scrupulous equality. Women were objectified in the best possible sense, because all were entitled to chivalrous treatment. "Women—all women, of whatever age and condition—claim [a gentleman's] respectful care and tender reverential regard," declared the redoubtable Lord Chesterfield. "No provocation whatsoever can justify any man in not being civil to every woman; the greatest man would be justly reckoned a brute if he were not civil to the meanest woman." Many modern women would test even Chesterfield's gentlemanly mettle. But he understood that when a man's mood or hormones dictate his manners, most women will lose the struggle for survival of the fairest.

## WASP SELF-RESTRAINT

The way of thinking that identified manliness with chivalry and self-control rather than self-assertion was characteristically Victorian. This sensibility was expressed in Henry Ward Beecher's maxim "Greatness lies not in being strong but in the right use of strength." But the idea that self-restraint was crucial to the functioning of society was also central to a WASP sensibility that has since been written off as ethnocentric. Never mind that such values served even non-WASP Victorians, who embraced honor and self-restraint as ideals that crossed cultural lines. The Victorians did not call themselves WASPs, although they recognized their religious, racial, and ethnic distinctiveness. Now we use this term pejoratively as a double-edged shorthand for the once-dominant culture of dead white males that we keep trying to bury. (Feminist sensibilities make us more ambivalent about all the dead white females who aided, loved, and inspired them.)

Ironically, even critics of WASP culture like Jesse Jackson have recently joined with such unlikely soulmates as Bill Clinton and William Bennett in calling for a revival of civility. Yet this civility is almost never linked to its distinctly WASP roots. The reason may be simple ignorance or a conscious historical blindness driven by the fear of re-imposing insulting customs on all the hyphenated peoples whom WASPs tried to "melt" before the melting pot was considered cultural homicide. In any case, a return to the central Victorian WASP values of chivalry and self-restraint in action and words is long overdue. "Letting it all hang out" has frayed our social fabric, yet we cannot begin to address our problems until we restore the rules of civil discourse that we abandoned so long ago.

# Keeping a Civil Tongue

To modern materialists, we are what we eat. To existentialists, we are what we do. To the Victorian mind, however, we are as we speak. Our forefathers believed that virtue in words was intimately linked to virtue in deeds. Their concern for the niceties of language reflected their con- viction that outward civility was an agent as well as a reflection of inner nobility. In this they followed the classical aphorism, "Speech is a mirror of the soul: As a man speaks, so is he."

## FIGHTING WORDS

To the Victorians, the intersecting layers of language and life were complex. In 1837, the popular etiquette author William Alcott said:

> The individual who gives himself up to the use of improper or unchaste language, or even to the endurance of it unchecked, is giving up at the same time the out-posts of all human virtue. . . . The vices are all associated; and they who have been introduced to either, or especially to all of these, are likely soon to become acquainted with others, and perhaps the whole brotherhood of them. Let us there-

fore be aware of an improper or indelicate word or look . . .
for it is out of the abundance of these that not only the
mouth speaks, but the hands act.

Any who doubt that language drives behavior should consider a
recent case in which the effects of language were literally incendiary.
In 1995, a black man shot seven people at a Jewish-owned clothing
store in Harlem before setting it ablaze. In the weeks before this
tragedy, the gunman had joined picket lines outside the store, in
which protesters shouted anti-Semitic epithets such as "Bloodsuck-
ers!" The white "crackers" and black "traitors" who patronized the
store were also threatened.

No doubt the anti-Semitic atmosphere created by these epithets contributed to the crime. Few would contest the toxicity of a
link so overt and direct. We see the problem, but we flail about for a
solution.

## SEARCHING FOR RULES OF DISCOURSE

It is no coincidence that "First Amendment absolutism" and "political
correctness" have both become familiar terms in the past decade. A
society that refuses to enforce reasonable restrictions on verbal
aggression will soon discover a demand for unreasonable ones. The
more we encounter egregious exhibitions of coarseness and tastelessness, the more sensitive some become to real and imagined linguistic
slights. Ethnic comedians tell increasingly ugly jokes about their own
groups, but they would be outraged at hearing even the mildest ethnic joke from someone outside their group. We are locked in a downward spiral, as extremists try to fill the void left by the loss of respect
for moderation.

The excesses of PC are easy to sneer at. The state of Massachu-
setts is replacing the traditional SLOW CHILDREN signs with WATCH
CHILDREN, to avoid offending youngsters with learning disabilities. In
the public schools of our nation's capital, there are no "poor" readers,
just "emergent" ones. Real estate agents afraid of being sued for bias
avoid advertising "master bedrooms" (which allegedly suggest slavery), while "spectacular view" or "walk-in" closet are taboo because
they might insult homebuyers who can't see or walk. In 1993, the *Los*

*Angeles Times* issued nineteen pages of *Guidelines on Ethnic, Racial, Sexual and Other Identification.* The offensive terms that were banished as unfit to print included "Dutch treat," "Chinese fire drill," "gypped," and "normal"—a term no one can use anymore without raising someone's ire.

The problem is that while liberals reflexively defend antisocial acts by the "oppressed" and want to repress the speech of loose-lipped "oppressors," conservatives chafe at the muzzle imposed by the sugary euphemisms applied to designated minorities and self-proclaimed victims. We wage our language wars through dueling committees, clogged courts, and last-ditch legislation like Raritan, New Jersey's 1994 effort to pass a blatantly unconstitutional ordinance prohibiting rude or indecent remarks.

The Victorians relied on unwritten laws to civilize language. Etiquette books, the Victorians' social bibles, devoted whole sections to "vulgarisms in conversation." But these tame offenses are a century and worlds away from ours. Unlike our slash-and-burn vulgarisms, which aim at the core of someone's identity, theirs were offenses against proper English, not people—unless you count "folks" for "people," and "old man" for "father." Notably absent were the four-letter word and demeaning names like "bitch," "whore," or their ethnic equivalents. Those who used them were too far down on the food chain to be recognized by readers aspiring to polite behavior.

Writing about her childhood, Edith Wharton recalled in her memoir that in her parents' circle, "Any really expressive slang was welcomed with amusement—but used as slang, as it were between quotation marks, and not carelessly admitted into our speech." Etiquette books, which were rarely amused by any form of slang, frowned on phrases such as "fly off the handle" (when angry, you flew into a "passion"), and "all to pieces" ("entirely destroyed"). And contrary to modern notions of fanatical Victorian prudery, "limb" was considered "a silly and affected expression for leg." Even saying the word "love" could be considered common and unrefined if that serious and venerated sentiment was used as a synonym for "like."

Such semantic quibbling may seem trivial to us, but the Victorians believed that even the smallest erosion of language would eventually result in a landslide of incivility and took steps to check any such downward slide as soon as it could be perceived.

## FROM THE MOUTHS OF BABES

Unfortunately, in our culture the erosion begins in childhood. Researchers and educators lament the staggering rise of obscene and aggressive speech in America's schools. The Victorians assumed and insisted that children address all authority figures as "sir" and "ma'am," "miss," "mister," and "missus." At best, children now address their elders by first names. Moreover, *The Washington Post* reports that female teachers are accustomed to hearing "Shut the ——— up, you bitch," when they try to quiet disruptive students or simply greet them. "Every other word is the F-word," one Virginia school board member said.[1]

Experts cite the obvious culprits—rap music, movies, TV, and especially cable fare like *Beavis and Butthead,* which thrives on brutish and degrading humor. But the chief villains are parents. "Nasty language has become a second language," observes Ronald F. Federici, a northern Virginia school consultant and child psychologist. "Four-letter words are rampant. Parents are doing it at home. They won't admit it, but they do."[2] Richard Gelles, director of the Family Violence Research Program at the University of Rhode Island, has documented that one out of every two parents verbally abuse their children with profanity-laced outbursts at least once a month.

The publisher Madeline Kane cites the increasingly graphic language of today's parents for the widespread popularity among adults and kids of toilet-talk books. The titles of these inspiring works make further description redundant: *The Holes in Your Nose, Everyone Poops,* and *The Gas We Pass.* This last hot seller, which has gone through several printings, is used as a coffee-table book, according to Kane. (Imagine having coffee and cake on that table.)[3]

Susan Lammers, president of a firm that designs computer programs for elementary schools, defends the educational value of materials that make poetry of bodily functions. Since these poems helped her young son "learn rhyming and reading," she argued, "it's worth it." In the same article, Cyma Zarghami, an executive at Nickelodeon, the children's cable channel whose comedies have included *Salute Your Shorts,* says, "A tiny bit of naughtiness never hurt anybody."

Even those who don't turn a profit from hawking untraditional "toiletries" can barely muster a shrug over this trend. For example, *The Wall Street Journal* reported in 1995 that a professor of psychology at the University of Utah would put the brakes on kids' racist or sexist remarks but contends that "vulgarities are not going to harm any child." Besides, he believes, "other issues are more pressing." The same article quotes another credentialed critic, the psychologist Timothy Jay, author of *Cursing in America*, who objects to cleaning up media smut. "Who wants a sanitized, Walt Disney version of street life?" he asks rhetorically. Jay views indecent and coarse language as "a valuable tool for teenagers because it allows them to defy authority fairly harmlessly." But when does that "fairly" become fairly dangerous?

## WOMEN AND COARSE DISCOURSE

Nowhere is the question of the relationship between verbal and physical abuse more apparent than in our ambiguity about the use of coarse and disrespectful language in front of, and by, women. The Victorians, male and female, were outraged by the verbal and physical mistreatment of women. But they would likely trace today's epidemic of abuse of women to women's lost social power and the general decline of civility, not the currently favored (and ahistorical) explanation of sexism.

The current penchant for public crudity inverts the Victorian notion that carefully weighed words preserved freedom, especially for women. Alexis de Tocqueville, our most insightful tourist, found it noteworthy that American men had such respect for women's "moral freedom that in their presence every man is careful to keep watch on his tongue for fear that [women] should be forced to listen to language which offends them" (*Democracy in America*). As the eighteenth-century English statesman Lord Chesterfield observed, the one thing women would never pardon was "a vulgar and awkward air." (Vulgarity was always considered awkward.)

Modern females have lost the vast but intangible power created by masculine fear of giving offense to ladies. Today, female ambivalence toward standards of civility gives off mixed signals that are more likely to confuse than frighten males. For example, a 1994 *Esquire* poll of 1,000 Generation X women found them almost evenly split on whether men should clean up their language in mixed company.[4]

The entry of women into formerly male-dominated careers has only intensified the confusion, as some women try to act like "one of the guys." A female midshipman at the Naval Academy in Annapolis recently complained to a reporter, "I've been called so many names that sometimes it doesn't even register as inappropriate. The lack of respect that the men have here for women is appalling." However, Navy Lt. Lynne Fowler expressed regret that her fellow carrier pilots had become more restrained around her since the infamous Tailhook scandal. "Loosen up," she tells them. "It's okay to tell a dirty joke around this woman at least."

This tug of war among women leaves them pulling both ends of the rope. In a similar case, a feminist college professor recently expressed outrage over complaints filed against a male colleague who opined freely about a student's breasts and often used "salty language." Writing in a *New York Times* essay, she ridiculed the women who objected as "Victorian damsels in distress." She also disparaged the college's grievance committee for its tone of "civility and high moral seriousness" with "echoes of Victorian melodrama." When virtue can be so readily redefined as vice, it is little wonder that women must constantly fight for the respect their great-grandmothers took for granted.[5]

The Victorians believed that social codes, not legal ones, should be used to police and prevent verbal offenses. This, however, requires reticence—the bedrock of Victorian civility that our culture has bloodied and muddied at every turn. Without the unwritten Victorian code that tamed the male tongue like a spirited show horse, women are left protesting, suing, and flailing about for the social power and "moral freedom" they lost by acceding to male standards, according to which refinement is a sign of weakness. The law court becomes the only resort when the sexes clash in the gray zones of behavior. Even if lawsuits and damage awards could solve the problem of our civil speech, the Victorians would have rejected the notion that civility and respect for women should be reduced to a mercenary matter.

Many women would agree with macho-fem Camille Paglia, who derides any attempts to return women to "their old status of delicate flowers," as she wrote in her 1992 book, *Sex, Art, and American Culture*. Paglia credits her beloved 1960s with breaking "the ancient codes of decorum that protected respectable ladies from profanation by foul language." Yet just how free are women who never had their say in revoking the rules of civilized language that once protected everyone from verbal guerrillas? Ironically, women are now accorded special workplace privileges in the guise of affirmative action, but woe unto those who drive trucks without talking like truck drivers. Is this what women want?

At the turn of the century, one social critic warned that women would always "lose more than they gain" by imitating uncouth men. He could not foresee the fat checks gender aping would confer on a few select entrepreneurs and entertainers like Roseanne. But most women gain neither comfort from nor compensation for such behavior.

## Swearing Just like One of the Guys

Now that women can verbally swagger just like "one of the guys," they have lost their right to male respect. Ironically, feminists seeking freedom of speech helped break the last taboos that kept a civil lock on misogynist tongues. By adopting men's rude way of speaking, women lost the formidable power to set the standards that made language a tool of peace, rather than the offensive and defensive weapon we use in our daily wars of incivility.

Even consciousness-raising role models carry us into treacherous currents of uncivil speech, as they remain blissfully unaware of the whirlpool that lies ahead. When a crew from CBS's *60 Minutes* attempted to interview Gloria Steinem about her nemesis Camille Paglia, Steinem told them (and the audience she was lecturing) that she didn't "give a shit" about Paglia's views. Steinem's expletive hardly merits a blink in an age when even professional women, like the judge on the TV sitcom *Courthouse*, routinely pronounce themselves "pissed off." Perhaps that show's writer knew that Steinem was once voted one of the most "confident" women in America. It seems that crudity is now a badge of self-confidence.

Like many old-line feminists (as opposed to many of the young-Turk power-fems), Steinem believes pornography denigrates women and lowers their self-esteem. Connecting the X-rated dregs of "adult entertainment" to Steinem's simple expletive may seem like comparing a heart attack to a hangnail. Yet any woman who ever experienced a hostile environment knows what a wide range this thermostat has, and how easily both victims and aggressors can adjust it.

According to *The Portable Emerson* by Carl Bode, Ralph Waldo Emerson once wrote, "The corruption of man is followed by the corruption of language." Many of his contemporaries would have reversed the order. The Victorians believed that every coarse and demeaning bleep we utter knocks another chip in the crumbling ruins of civility, and invites other vandals to follow suit. So if women don't want to be treated like "shit" by men, they had better start being respectful when they assess and address each other. Their toxic emissions only worsen the hostile environments they encounter in the office, the home, and the street. If women on top of the heap must express themselves through terms for excretory functions, we have nowhere to go but down.

In contrast to today's frequent use of the F-word by women who think of it as a colorful modifier and verb, an 1837 manual on the duties of women (men had their own volume) by William Alcott warned them to avoid "coarse" expressions like "My stars," "By George," and "Good heavens." Those were the days! Fussing over these fusty but innocent exclamations may be a real knee slapper for us, but to the Victorians, they were not only "unbecoming"—a serious social sin—but also "savor not a little of profanity." In a century that noticed every nuance of good and evil, not just their blatant extremes, coarse language was the first rung down the ladder from the sacred to the profane.

If ever a declaration of social mores could seem a relic of a bygone age, it would be Sarah Josepha Hale's casual comment, "Swearing is considered so inadmissible in good society, or in the presence of ladies, that there is little danger of its being introduced in either." Mrs. Hale made that statement in 1868, when she was the editor of this country's most influential woman's magazine. Her misplaced confidence now seems more shocking than the gutter language that daily refutes it.

## THE PROLIFERATION OF PROFANITY

The Victorians could not have imagined how insane profane could get. On a recent visit to New York, I noticed in Pennsylvania Station a souvenir T-shirt covered with silk-screened instructions on HOW TO USE THE F-WORD. The shirt suggests inserting this versatile expression into common phrases such as "Who are you?" and "Pass the salt." And why not? This is but a logical extension of our current approach to language. *Martine's Hand-book of Etiquette* (1866) compared polite conversation to silver: "useful upon all occasions." Now impolite conversation serves the same function.

In 1897 the English etiquette author Mrs. Humphry predicted the fate of "habitually using strong language. . . . It defeats itself; for if the forcible expressions are intended to express disapprobation, they soon become weak and powerless to do so, because they are used on every possible occasion. After a time they lose all meaning." As a good Victorian, Mrs. Humphry assumed that only the "low, arrogant, and ill-bred" used such language. Now the low, arrogant, and ill-bred are the entertainers of choice for the sophisticated, worldly, and well-bred power brokers who make a fine distinction between their dinner-party smut and the streetwise brand they profess to find reprehensible.

Of course, the Victorians had the luxury of assuming that everyone worth knowing would mind their P's and Q's as the rule, not the exception, so they could excoriate barroom language on the sole grounds that such rude discourse was a terrible insult to polite society. The stakes are much higher for us, because the "cream" of society has soured. Once-unspeakable speech is now so common among elite groups such as politicians, leaders, writers, and even educators that it threatens the very survival of the institutions that sustain a civilized democracy.

The great German writer Thomas Mann showed his Victorian-era upbringing when he wrote, "Speech is civilization." To the generation in which Mann was raised, civility meant striving upward in word and deed. Now civility is treated as a "downer," a restriction on our sovereign right to self-expression. The Victorians overruled verbal indecency on the once-obvious grounds that it attracts socially destructive self-attention and expresses disdain for others. The self-aggrandizing urge to shock has led us from the bon mots of Oscar Wilde to the wilderness of trash talk.

## VERBAL FISTFIGHTS AND AMBUSHES

Once ribald language has been sanctioned in private conversation, it soon finds its way into public discourse. Indeed, among the arenas suffering most from the decline of civility are those in which words have the greatest power to inflict harm: politics and the law. Critics note that once-courtly rituals like legal depositions have degenerated into "Rambo-like tactics" aimed at intimidating witnesses and opposing counsels.

On the political front, the circus of TV talk shows is just a poor relation to the weekly televised shouting matches of educated journalists who know their politics but not their P's and Q's. Critics fault these shows for promoting conflict over substance and polarizing political debate. I would add the general debasement of everyday discourse to this list.

The Victorians believed in dousing angry sparks, not fanning them into an inferno. Being modern means acting or blabbing before you think, and never repenting. In 1855, over a century before the apostles of political correctness tried to selectively censor the raw emotions that break their rules, Catharine Beecher explained that the social obligations of civility required everyone to avoid

> . . . all remarks which tend to embarrass, vex, mortify, or in any way wound the feelings of another. To notice personal defects; to allude to others' faults, or the faults of their friends; to speak disparagingly of the sect or party to which a person belongs; to be inattentive when addressed in conversation; to contradict flatly; to speak in contemptuous tones of opinions expressed by another; all these are violations of the rules of good-breeding.

They are also the bread and butter of attack TV, bullet-tongued comics, poisonous music, and the scorchingly candid everyday atmosphere of our offices, homes, and streets that keeps daily life on the verge of boiling over.

In an article entitled "The Triumph of the Yell," the psychologist Deborah Tannen blamed our pervasive "culture of critique" for promoting extremism over compromise and stifling our search for truth. The Victorians were unusually blunt but accurate when they labeled perpetual critics "bullies." Whereas we celebrate the forthright rudeness of radio shock-jocks and tell-it-like-it-is politicians, the Victorians condemned brassy behavior as a barbaric lack of restraint. Even if one was able to win an argument with lungs and intimidation, "could" never justified "should." One etiquette writer acolded those skilled at sarcasm, barbs, and contempt, "Because you happen to have a razor in your possession, that is no reason why you should be allowed to cut the throats of the rest of us who are unarmed." Over a century later, Tannen noted how the Darwinian deck is stacked in today's verbal wars, writing in the aforementioned article that "opposition also limits information when only those who are adept at verbal sparring take part in public discourse, and those who cannot handle it, or do not like it, decline to participate." Can we truly have a democracy when our public, and private, discourse is dominated by bullies?

Blowhards did not fare so well a hundred years ago. The Victorians disapproved of people routinely rumbling like thunder. It was considered selfish, divisive, undignified—and therefore uncivilized—but it was also considered counterproductive. To be convincing, remarked Lord Chesterfield, always state your opinions "modestly and coolly." Losing your temper meant losing more than self-control: "A man who does not possess himself enough to hear disagreeable things without visible marks of anger and change of countenance . . . is at the mercy of every artful knave or pert coxcomb."

Cool-headed civil discourse may not play as well in the Nielsen ratings as getting one's nose broken in a discussion that has deteriorated into a brawl, but we sorely need to return to it if we are to solve any of our serious problems as a society. If we gave all ranters the Victorian treatment—stony silence—they would be forced to pipe down or be tuned out.

## NO MORE SECRETS

Part of the reason we developed our high-volume style is our sadly mistaken notion that intensity, bluntness, and lack of reticence denote sincerity. Talk-show audiences doubt that dysfunctional guests have truly recovered unless tears flow, and reconciling parties are required to produce hugs and kisses. We applaud the "honesty" of bestselling memoirs that lay bare every dark family secret, from alcoholism to incest. Until fairly recently, mothers taught their children, "If you can't say anything nice, don't say anything." When I lamented the decline of this maternal wisdom, one devoted mother replied, "Then no one would ever say anything."

The reluctant renovation of Bob Dole is a prime example of the modern demand to prove that you have guts by spilling them. During the last presidential race, image makers convinced the normally reticent Dole to share in painful detail the pain and permanent debilities of the wounds he sustained during World War II, when his "I feel your pain" opponent was still in diapers. What was really accomplished by our learning that Dole's wife must peel his fruit or that he wears a shoulder pad beneath his undershirt to buttress his shattered frame—except the loss of the privacy and dignity this man had earned in his country's service? You don't need to be a Republican to admire either quality.

## TASTELESS PUBLIC "HUMOR"

If we aren't demanding that people spill their deepest secrets to the general public, we are finding other ways to "democratize" ourselves by dropping our standards of public speech down to the lowest common denominator. Perhaps the saddest sign of our corrupted discourse is the willingness of self-described conservatives to adopt the tastelessness and rudeness that would have appalled their ideological forebears. Howard Stern would strain the needle on any vulgarity gauge. But where was the conservative decency brigade when Republican congressman Martin Hoke publicly remarked on the size of a TV producer's breasts, and talk-radio king Rush Limbaugh went on his television show in 1994 and defended Hoke as follows: "I'll tell you, we're in bad shape in this country when you can't look at a couple of huge knockers and notice it." If his listeners want to ditto that, let them try it in front of their wives.

This attitude illustrates how anti-Victorian modern conservatives can be. Limbaugh built a megabucks career on blaming liberals for America's moral decline, but his crude comment would never pass the most superficial Victorian moral muster. This persuasive preacher could begin his rehabilitation by learning a lesson from *Miss Leslie's Behaviour Book*, a popular manual published in 1859: "Persons who have no turn for humour, and little perception of it, are apt to mistake mere coarseness for that amusing gift; and in trying to be diverting, often become vulgar."

In our deeply politicized culture, crassness crosses all party lines. In 1995 President Clinton and a large collection of Washington's movers, shakers, and reputation breakers were entertained at the prestigious Radio and Television Correspondents' Association dinner by the comic Bill Maher, the longtime host of the humorous talk show *Politically Incorrect*. Putting that spirit into practice, Maher made a derisive ethnic joke about Senator Phil Gramm's Korean-American wife and peppered his racy monologue with four-letter words. Although a few boos were heard, no one walked out.

CNN's bureau chief, who had booked the controversial comic, declared the evening a success because at his table "there was a lot of laughing." Maher claimed, "The President was laughing the whole time . . . and he told me he enjoyed the performance." In addition to presidential accolades, "I got nothing but congratulations from people like Cokie Roberts, Sam Donaldson, Wolf Blitzer, John Sununu, and Ralph Nader." If anyone was offended, Maher said they should learn to take themselves "less seriously."

Compare this to the reaction to a notorious 1877 speech Mark Twain gave at a dinner attended by three cultural icons, Ralph Waldo Emerson, Oliver Wendell Holmes, and Henry Wadsworth Longfellow. The irrepressible Twain concocted a spoof, complete with his signature dead-on dialect, in which these honored guests became grotesque drunken tramps who invaded a miner's cabin. In his comic narrative, they ate the miner's food, drank his booze, cheated him at cards, and stole his only pair of boots.

Twain's wit badly misfired. Witnesses said the entire audience "turned to stone with horror." One attendee described the wall-to-wall silence as "weighing many tons to the square inch." Twain later said that the incident "pretty near killed me with shame." Although he wrote letters of apology to the three revered butts of his joke, one biographer said the event dogged him for the rest of his life. Ten years afterward, newspapers still referred to it as evidence that Twain had "no reliable sense of propriety."

Today professional insult mongers like Howard Stern can literally take their schtick to the bank. Not that the Victorians didn't appreciate humor—Twain was a legend in his own lifetime—but even legends were not excused when they broke the cardinal law best summarized by the late-nineteenth-century poet Will Carleton:

> "Careful with fire," is good advice, we know:
> "Careful with words," is ten times doubly so.

# RELEARNING RESPECT FOR
# THE POWER AND BEAUTY OF LANGUAGE

Propriety was not the only reason the Victorians took care in their choice of language. Like the seventeenth-century English clergyman Robert Burton, they believed "a blow with a word strikes deeper than a blow with a sword." But their posture was neither negative nor defensive. They simply loved and respected language, a loss that has cost us the most effective means of fulfilling our increasingly desperate quest to communicate. As a child, Edith Wharton learned "a reverence for the English language" that was "as authoritative an element . . . as tradition was in social conduct." Both language and friends, she said, were always treated with courtesy.

This sort of testimony belies the modern assumption that the self-censorship required by civility stifles creativity. If anything, it nourished the creative impulse by demanding discipline and discernment from Victorian-era writers such as the Brontë sisters, Edith Wharton, and Henry James. Even common folk spoke and wrote in language that would put to shame many modern writers who earn large sums and critical acclaim for their blunt and unrefined prose. Many people were amazed to hear the incredible richness and eloquence of expression in the letters between soldiers and their wives, which were featured in Ken Burns's PBS documentary on the Civil War. Would that such beautiful language were still a part of our common daily discourse.

Contemporary writers who use literature to shock or deconstruct, rather than to edify or ennoble, might well benefit from less candor and more self-censorship. Restricted expression can be a rewarding challenge, when the restrictions are self-imposed and widely accepted. We have been reduced to a literal but limited vocabulary. Too often, the beauty of tact and subtlety is discarded in favor of cold, brute honesty. In so doing, we have forgotten the value of graceful communication.

## VICTORIAN SILENT LANGUAGES

Consider the lost Victorian legacy of silent languages, which once textured life with nuance. The only silent language we still vaguely remember was the most flirtatious, the language of the fan. The faintest movements of these lace, silk, satin, and feathery confections conveyed a world of meaning that was widely understood. But for the Victorians, life and love, like God and the devil, were in the details. Simply by touching the lips with the fan, holding it in one or the other hand, drawing it across the cheek, or fanning rapidly or slowly, a woman accomplished in its grammar could hold an extensive conversation with an equally literate suitor.

Between expressing the passionate extremes of love and hate, she could apologize for a tiff, ask for a kiss, or declare that her heart belonged to another. A right-handed twirl warned the hopeful swain he was being watched by a disapproving chaperone or parent. If a man requested the honor of escorting a lady home with an equally tactful cue—lifting his left forefinger to his left eye—she could accept the offer by resting her fan on her right cheek or reject it by resting the fan on her left. Tapping the fan with one finger meant an emphatic "My mother says no."

Even the fluttering motion held meaning. In 1832, the magazine essayist Joseph Addison wrote, "There is the angry flutter, the modest

*Fans were not merely fashion accessories; ladies used them to convey the nuances of their emotions to suitors and would-be suitors.*

flutter, the timorous flutter, the amorous flutter. . . . There is scarcely any emotion in the mind which does not produce a suitable agitation in the fan." Many of these gestures were too subtle for the modern eye to perceive. For all Martin Scorsese's attention to period detail in *The Age of Innocence*, he displayed a tin ear—or eye—for its silent languages. In a real 1870s drawing room, Michelle Pfeiffer's indecipherable fits of fluttering would have left Daniel Day-Lewis utterly befuddled.

Nowadays women must register their feelings with the bluntness of a sparring partner if they expect men to understand their intentions. As many women have discovered, the subtlety of a look, a frosty tone of voice, or body language is lost on most contemporary men. If women still had such a powerful and unambiguous nonverbal language at their fingertips, they could indulge their feelings and spare those of rejected men by avoiding mutually humiliating public clashes. The equivalent of a properly wielded fan might even prevent a few sexual harassment suits. It would certainly restore a picturesque and civilized quality to the often ugly exchanges between the sexes.

Before the bestselling author John Gray informed us that *Men Are from Mars, Women Are from Venus*, Victorian ladies and gentlemen shared a single planet, which they adorned with the comprehensive language of flowers. Dictionaries listed hundreds of flowers, plants, herbs, vines, and even weeds with their corresponding meanings. We have condensed this elastic art to the vaguely cheerful "Get well" bouquet, the funeral wreath, and the predictable dozen roses on Valentine's Day. By choosing the appropriate symbols, the Victorians expressed every shade of romance from "You are my divinity" (American cowslip) to "You will be death" (hemlock). One language might even soothe the wounds inflicted by another. Lotus leaves recanted ill-spoken words, while a gift of hazel pleaded for reconciliation. Without a breath of verbal confrontation, you could accuse someone of cruelty, deceit, coquetry, even misanthropy, or admire their bravery, wit, kindness, and the defining quality that separates the last century from ours—grace.

Gems provided an equally acceptable (if more expensive) public means for expressing private feelings. Before Marilyn Monroe taught us that diamonds are a gold digger's best friend, they symbolized the strength of eternity. As such, the diamond has long been a popular choice for engagement rings. But the Victorians also favored colored stones for both romantic and platonic gifts, because they symbolized diverse emotions. Emeralds and sapphires signified fidelity, while red gems such as garnets and rubies expressed affection. Coral was given to children to wish them a happy, healthy life, while death was marked by the bereaved with onyx for spiritual strength and jet for everlasting memory.

Particular combinations and sequences of stones provided a clever alphabet to "speak" in code through necklaces, earrings, rings, pins, and bracelets. In one version, the first letter of each stone's name spelled out a sentiment. Thus, a ruby, emerald, garnet, amethyst, ruby, diamond, and sapphire set in that order spelled "r-e-g-a-r-d-s." For a more impassioned attachment, a lavender amethyst, olivine, violet sapphire, and an emerald declared one's "l-o-v-e." Sadly, many of these bejeweled bouquets were dismantled when tastes changed early in this century. With their disappearance was lost a charming way to speak from your heart without smearing it on your sleeve.

Finally, the antique language that today is the most ridiculed and misunderstood involves the silent dialect of calling-card etiquette. In the Victorian ritual of paying calls, a visitor presented his or her card during the appointed hours when the lady of the house was "at home." Although business cards rule the world today, using one on a social occasion was once considered unpardonably tasteless.

After being admitted by a servant or other family member, the guest had tea with the hostess, an encounter garnished with light conversation. The all-occasion emotional gushing we call communication would have been thought rude and self-indulgent in an era when conversation was an art to be nurtured and savored. In learning to chitchat politely, the Victorians learned to be respectful to a new or casual acquaintance, not just those we gracelessly term "significant others." They did not take the liberty of inquiring about a stranger's religious or political beliefs, state of pregnancy, finances, or sexual behaviors, nor would they have proffered such information about themselves.

There is great need for these lost civilizing lessons in today's world, but it is hard to imagine how we could incorporate them into our modern lives. We regard "wasting" time as the greatest crime, and most Victorian habits would flunk our efficiency tests measured in computerized microseconds. Thus, the custom of calling has been reduced to call waiting. To modern critics, however, such old-fashioned customs even had an insidious side. According to one historian, they embodied the middle-class demands of "polished performance and emotional self-control" that "reinforced class distinctions" and "deference to superiors." Luckily, so these critics' thinking goes, we have since unmasked the authoritarian impulse lurking behind these repressive customs. Today members of all classes can be emotionally uncontrolled, and deference to anyone but oneself is considered dysfunctional.

Since the current mind-set is closed to the benefits of Victorian-style calling, it can hardly grasp the subtler but equal advantages of leaving silent messages via cards. If the Victorian hostess was not at home or unable to receive any guests, the latter could indicate the nature of their visit through the language of folding cards. Turning down a particular corner conveyed congratulations, condolences, or the courtesy of saying good-bye before leaving town. Most important, leaving your card was a safe way to approach someone socially who might not desire your acquaintance. If the person did not return the call, you were gracefully spurned. No one hung up on you or slammed a door in your face. Although today we have technologies such as answering machines and e-mail that could conceivably be used like calling cards, we have yet to develop a reliable and unambiguous system of using them. If a message is not returned, is it a snub or a software problem?

Gentlemen left calling cards when the ladies they were visiting weren't receiving visitors. An unacknowledged card was a clear sign that one's company was not desired.

# THE POLITE SOCIAL DISCOURSE WE LEFT BEHIND

Today we talk endlessly of our failure to communicate. Our ancestors devised ways to communicate politely and precisely without speaking at all. Perhaps if we still practiced the subtle arts of silent conversation, we could do with less of the endless blather from pop linguistics experts and talk-show hosts who tell us how to understand and be understood. But the poignant eloquence of this other "hieroglyphic world" died in the 1920s. Coded Victorian jewels were melted down or reset. Mile-long cigarette holders replaced milady's fan. And flowers still pleased the eye but lost their ability to speak. In this same decade, people began to notice the accompanying decline of linguistic skills, as vocabulary became more restricted.

In her 1953 memoir *The Glitter and the Gold*, the socialite-turned-reformer Consuelo Vanderbilt later lamented the lost charm of the twilight Edwardian years she spent in England, when after-dinner entertainment meant Winston Churchill's distinctive recitation of Shakespeare's plays—which he knew by heart. But even the less oratorically gifted thrived on conversation:

> We talked so much more in those days than we do now, when I find my guests stampeding for the bridge table as soon as they leave the dining room. We talked morning, noon and night, but we also knew how to listen. There was so much to be discussed. . . . We talked endlessly, for the tempo of life was slow, gentle and easy; there was no radio to tune it up. . . . Our endless discussions on politics fostered a sense of civic responsibility, and I began to look beyond the traditional but superficial public duties expected of me.

It is fashionable to bemoan our declining sense of civic commitment; the Victorians would say we lack the words to inspire it. What replaced the spoken and silent communing arts our ancestors treasured? In *Only Yesterday*, one of the best memoirs of the Jazz Age, Frederick Lewis described the unisex taste for "strong language" that developed with the taste for strong liquors, as words like "damn" and "hell" became commonplace:

It was delightful to be considered a little shocking; and so the competition in boldness of talk went on for a time . . . a conversation in polite circles was like a room decorated entirely in scarlet—the result was over-emphasis, stridency, and eventual boredom.

We may have upped the four-letter ante since then, but our desperate attempts to shock are still doomed to end in boredom. Expletives do not fill the void left by the Victorian eloquence that disappeared. Since the 1930s, the courts have gradually narrowed the legal boundaries of obscenity and indecency in entertainment, news, and individual expression until the macho lingo of the meanest streets became our de facto language of the land.

Recent years have witnessed a growing backlash against the resulting debasement of social intercourse. We have a dim but growing perception that we need to establish some rules for discourse. But the absence of a socially enforced consensus on civility has made such efforts either marginal or misguided.

## A RETURN TO CIVIL DISCOURSE

We only delude ourselves by assuming that free speech carries no social costs. But the greatest delusion is believing that plain old vanilla obscenities, which don't insult other colors, can safely slide by without scarring our social fabric. Ever mindful that a deluge always begins with a single drop of rain, one Victorian-era etiquette writer warned, "If you pass over a thing today because it is slight, you will pass over something else of at least—perhaps greater—importance tomorrow."

Those who have recently rediscovered the wisdom of this simple observation now find that studies are required to prove it. Very well. "Language is the first symptom of conflict—the small stuff escalates," said Ronald D. Stephens, executive director of the National School Safety Center in Los Angeles. After two years of interviewing fourth- to twelfth-graders around the country, the center's researchers found that name-calling and cursing were among the most frequent triggers of violent behavior. At the far end of this spectrum, according to police records, homicides frequently begin with verbal provocation.

When mouthing off can lead to murder, we dare not dismiss crude or hostile speech as "fairly harmless."[6]

Julia Ward Howe possessed no scientific data, just the common sensibilities of her day, when she said that all "rude and selfish habits of mind" encourage "great social troubles and even crimes." Inhumane speech was and is a crime against our humanity, a misdemeanor from which felonies follow. Many modern women have been forced to relearn this lesson through firsthand experience. Feminists often insist that verbal aggression is as serious as physical aggression against women, despite concern that labeling verbal offenses as harassment or abuse diminishes the meaning of those charges. Our scant facility for nuanced language may exacerbate the tendency toward catch-all accusations, but women are grappling with serious problems that can threaten first the quality of life and then life itself. Without a common social agreement on what is acceptable speech and behavior, the lives and liberties of all Americans are diminished.

# Hypocrisy, Democracy, and Diversity

Even people whose image of the nineteenth century comes from Scarlett and Rhett think they know the problem with old-fashioned manners: They were phony, wooden, and stifling, reflecting the way the uppity upper crust excluded everyone who wasn't upper crust. At least that's today's party line. In truth, Victorian manners were anything but exclusive and exclusionary. Instead, well-mannered behavior, the great equalizer, was within the reach of all. The renewal of civility depends on our rediscovering how the democracy of manners once stabilized the nation and promoted true democracy.

## THE DEMOCRACY OF COURTESY

In 1869, the very middle-class educational reformer Catharine Beecher defined manners as "the outward exhibition of the democratic fundamental principle of benevolence and equal rights . . . the same courtesy which we accord to our own circle, shall be extended to every class and condition." Victorians like Miss Beecher recognized that within such a democracy of courtesy, judges must exercise authority over their courts, teachers over their pupils, and bosses over their workers. This promoted "the general well-being." But even in distinctly unequal situations, respect and restraint were the rule at every level. This was because, as Miss Beecher wrote in *American Woman's Home*, "courteous address is required not merely toward superiors; every person desires to be thus treated, and therefore the law of benevolence demands such demeanor toward all whom we meet in the social intercourse of life."

## American Manners

Many people's image of Victorian manners is based on toffee-nosed lords and ladies—like those in the novels of Anthony Trollope and the plays of Oscar Wilde—who lounge in the ornate parlors of *Masterpiece Theatre*. What is fiction for us may have been a matter of fact for Europeans, but American etiquette authors of the era scrupulously noted that more than an ocean divided us from the Old World.

Bootlicking and heel-clicking European customs were considered as outré in the New World as primogeniture. "Here the practice of politeness has in it nothing of the servility which is often attached to it in countries where the code of etiquette is dictated by the courts of monarchy," the etiquette author Arthur Martine wrote in 1866. In her book *Modern Society*, Julia Ward Howe criticized English or Continental manners which were "affected by those among us who mistake the aristocracy of position for the aristocracy of character." Similarly, Catharine Beecher, in *American Woman's Home*, emphasized that American civility relied on "gentility in mind," not "birth or fashion." Thus, even those to the manor born could be "vicious coxcombs." "Ruffians" were found "in the drawing room as well as on the street." And Thomas Nelson Page warned against those "vulgarians who use money, not courtesy, as a standard of pre-eminence." Etiquette writers were particularly critical of newly minted millionaires who tried to buy gentility by trading their marriageable daughters (and hefty dowries) to threadbare counts and lords in return for use of the family title.

Even top power brokers could be socially bankrupted if their uncivilized behavior went too far. A notorious example was the publisher James Gordon Bennett, Jr. Dixon Wechter recounted in *The Saga of American Society* how Bennett, the immensely wealthy owner of the influential *New York Herald,* was well known for being "brandied to his top white hat," a habit that eventually cost him his reputation and his wife-to-be. In 1877 the tippling Bennett attended a crowded reception at his fiancée's home. According to startled witnesses, "Suddenly it was apparent to those standing nearest the fireplace that the *Herald's* publisher had mistaken the purpose of that fixture for a plumbing facility, and was extinguishing the flames in a most unconventional manner." Bennett promptly received a bum's rush into the street and was later forced to fight a duel with a young male member of the insulted household. Both men managed to miss each other, but the exchange of fire was required to rekindle the flames of family honor that Bennett had quenched in so unseemly a fashion.

Moreover, even though he was left physically intact, the offender's social position was mortally wounded. A Victorian-bred historian who later chronicled Bennett's antics matter-of-factly stated the only possible outcome in an era when rules were not made to be broken: "Obviously every private residence in New York was forever barred to him." Bennett's disgrace exiled him to Europe for the rest of his years. There his money bought him the high life, but it could never buy back his life in New York.

Even our own willful age has not changed its standards sufficiently to accommodate this kind of personal expression. But the penalties for such behavior have been drastically reduced. In 1995, when the drunken president of an investment banking company was refused additional drinks in a first-class airline cabin, he defecated on a service cart. Far from being tackled by the defenders of propriety, he assaulted a flight attendant. In this case the bum's rush would have been lethal, but I doubt the altitude would have stopped the outraged Victorians. The man was later arrested but quickly released on a personal recognizance bond. With or without the bond, a hundred years ago he would have lost all personal recognizance. Whatever fine this man had to pay, can we imagine his "disgrace" driving him from his country or even his country club?

## Rules of Courtesy for All Classes

A truly democratic code of courtesy once preserved a civilized atmosphere for everyone by punishing anyone who flouted it. Its loss leaves us at the mercy of barbarians from every class, and especially those who can buy their pardons. Despite the egregious inequality of modern mayhem, however, contemporary historians deprecate Victorian etiquette for its alleged elitism. Of course, we have long since lost the emphasis on physical and emotional restraints that, in the words of the historian John Kasson, "assured the individual's deferential participation in the dominant social order." Unfortunately, what is left is neither social nor orderly.

This notion of deferential participation smacks of blatant or subtle coercion from the high and mighty. But it was nothing of the sort. In a study that traced how standards of proper behavior developed, the historian Arthur Schlesinger, Jr., called manners "one aspect of the common man's struggle to achieve a larger degree of human dignity and self-respect." Similarly, the social scientists James Q. Wilson and Richard Herrnstein note that working-class parents in Victorian America enrolled their children in Sunday schools to teach them not just religion but "respectability." They conclude, "The bourgeois world view triumphed in the late nineteenth century largely through consent, not force." At the end of the twentieth century, the brute force of public incivility revokes the very notion of consent. Victorian ideals of courtesy embodied equality and unity because everyone was entitled to learn them and live by them. Victorians of all classes strove to make etiquette habitual and ritualistic, understanding that manners, like discipline, can only be effective if they are applied consistently rather than treated like a set of fine china to be used only when company calls. As Catharine Beecher warned in 1869, "If good manners are not practiced at home, but are allowed to lie by until occasion calls upon their wearer to assume them, they are sure to be a bad fit when donned."

## Courtesy at All Times

What a dreadfully unromantic image of civilized behavior Beecher's is, compared to the "random acts of kindness" movement that burst upon popular consciousness a few years ago. According to the authors, such acts are "those little sweet or grand lovely things we do for no reason." Spontaneous courtesy, the authors claim, means "the best of humanity has sprung exquisitely into full bloom." By buying lunch for a homeless man or a bouquet of roses for an elderly woman "you are not doing what life requires of you, but the best your human soul invites you to do."

Who but a misanthrope would rain on this blooming garden of philanthropies, which should make anyone's day this side of Clint Eastwood? Aren't random acts of kindness the perfect counterweight to our epidemic of random acts of incivility? Not a chance. Both live by the fleeting "I feel like it" factor, like dogs who might lick your hand or maul it. Both are dangerous—incivility for obvious reasons, spontaneous niceness because it leaves civility to the mercy of how merciful we feel at the moment. In contrast, the code of Victorian courtesy did not depend on our moods or biorhythms. It was a daily, demanding, universal obligation, not a whimsy that favored a chosen few. When courtesy was integrated in everyday life, one noticed its absence, not its presence.

Even the "random kindness" movement's founders concede that the main impetus for doing good is to make you feel good about yourself and promote personal growth. This brand of altruism offers another way to wallow in dysfunctions and justify self-indulgence, because learning kindness to others "begins by simple acts of kindness toward ourselves." Whatever window dressing it wears, me-first-ism is toxic to civility.

Our culture is rife with selfish and self-absorbed behavior. The Victorians believed in treating everyone with courtesy at all times. Instead we "treat" everyone to the juicy tidbits of instant intimacy that feed our egos and their ids. Respect and self-respect, not repression, made privacy what Lord Chesterfield called a "sacred right." He understood intuitively that private life would be cheapened and distorted if it became public fodder.

## BARING ALL IN THE MODERN ERA

Baring our all compromises the humanity of those who gawk and those who are gawked at. Proper gawking was once confined to zoos and P. T. Barnum's freak-filled dime "museums." In the 1920s and '30s, disheartened Victorians pined for the days when notoriety was denounced as social nudism, and "people lived with more dignity and sinned more successfully than they do now," as Frederick Townsend wittily put it in his 1913 memoir. Citing the mounting number of divorce cases that the "cheap press" reported in "nauseating detail," he concluded that marriage was becoming "a joke." We need look no further than the tell-all divorces of Britain's royals or the videotaped near brawl in Central Park between John F. Kennedy Jr. and his live-in girlfriend. Royalty, real or presumed, looks uninspiringly plebeian when it goes naked in the world. (As for Kennedy's legendarily private mother, Jackie O., the astounding prices her personal belongings fetched at auction proved, as Maureen Dowd wrote in *The New York Times,* that "in an age of exhibitionism, coyness was a good investment.")[1]

*Newsweek*'s Evan Thomas attributes our current fascination with Jane Austen—via movies and BBC series—to the mannerly reticence that we have lost. He noted that "people have become accustomed to vulgarity . . . and perfect strangers insulting them or, worse, confiding in them. Possibly they are growing sick of it."[2]

Possibly they are rediscovering the not-so-secret wisdom of buttoned lips. Charlotte Brontë wrote: "The human heart has hidden treasures / In secret kept, in silence sealed;— / The thoughts, the hopes, the dreams, the pleasures, / Whose charms were broken if revealed." We may relieve these hunger pangs for a few hours by watching period dramas, but Hollywood cannot bring celluloid civility to life. That requires recasting our modern virtues as the vices they were once considered.

### Public Egotism

We are at our most anti-Victorian when we celebrate ourselves. Our ancestors didn't need the Bible to tell them, "Pride goeth before destruction, and a haughty spirit before a fall." Yet it seems that no fall is too great to dent the egos of today's "masters of the universe." For example, after reversing his business misfortunes, Donald Trump penned a paean to himself in a November 19, 1995, *New York Times Magazine* article. Far from teaching him humility, his brief experience of being down and out taught him that others were unworthy of his beneficence:

> Many . . . lives had been profoundly changed by me, in an extraordinarily positive way. Some had become rich, some powerful, but in all cases they would never have ended up in their high social or economic positions without the

influence of Donald Trump. When crunch time came, however, some . . . were not around when I most needed their help. . . . I view these people as being born with garbage in their genes.

Trump is hardly alone in publicly patting his own back, a trait than which, according to Lord Chesterfield, there was "no surer sign of vulgarity." In the decades since Norman Mailer aptly titled a collection of his essays *Advertisements for Myself*, a generation of self-promoters has learned to follow his lead. During the 1992 presidential campaign, Hillary Clinton told the Washington-based reporter Kathleen Matthews she had "no doubt" she herself would be a "terrific" governor or president in her own right. On the other side of the political spectrum, Rush Limbaugh calls himself "talent on loan from God." Mail-order catalogues offer mere mortals a similar chance to crow via a personalized $34.95 pillow that tells visitors, "It's Hard to be Humble When You're from 'X' college." Even cheaper are bumper stickers that advertise parental pride in having honor students. Advertisements for your children's accomplishments are deemed no more dishonorable than advertisements for your own. For good reason: The latter are extensions of the former.

Occasionally someone comes along to remind us that less is more. Air Force captain Scott O'Grady survived six days in the wilderness surrounded by hostile Serbian forces when his plane was shot down over Bosnia. When he was given a hero's welcome back home, he refused that tribute, conferring it instead on the marines who rescued him. In this "strut your stuff" age, journalists seemed genuinely perplexed by the modesty that used to be a common part of uncommon valor.

It is much easier for us to understand the self-proclaimed "courage" of Rachel Worby, West Virginia's first lady. In a book on the "private struggles" of "accomplished women," Worby revealed details of her extramarital romps, her progress from frigidity to orgasm, and the strategic location of a tattoo. When questioned about the propriety of this truly heroic act of self-revelation, her husband, the governor, seemed puzzled by the controversy, asking: "How can anyone be too honest?" How indeed? The Victorians lived by the adage "Pride and grace ne'er dwelt in one place"—not even in the "almost heaven" of West Virginia.[3]

Even as our popular culture screams for equality at any cost, it demands that we puff ourselves up to prove we are first among equals. "Nothing vilifies more than pride," wrote Arthur Martine in 1866. The Victorians, who recognized a deadly sin when they met one, knew how deadly pride could be to civilized relations, where all are entitled to feel valued, not inferior to big mouths and braggarts. We may call boasters healthy; Victorians such as Arthur Martine considered them "boa-constrictors spewing the vile saliva of selfish vanity." Their view of bragging, not ours, had a true egalitarian spirit. As the 1880 *Manual of Politeness* explained, "To shine in society is more frequently attempted than compassed; to please is in the power of all."

The Victorians believed it was impossible to please anyone but yourself if you turned conversations into rambling autobiographies. Not only was it "conceited" to brag and "make yourself the hero of your own stories," it was boring: "If you are full of yourself, consider that you and your affairs are not so interesting to other people as to you," proclaimed an 1891 etiquette guide, *Don't, or Directions for Avoiding Improprieties*. Alas, this assumption has become a dinosaur in this tell-me-all age. We prick up our ears for private affairs, not ideas. Our ancestors could never have imagined that we would actually boast of failures and dysfunctions along with achievements, or that we would reveal other people's intimate secrets without their consent.

## A COMMENDABLE HYPOCRISY

But isn't this just the price we pay for truthfulness? We assume that honest people hold forth; only hypocrites hold back. We deride those tight-lipped Victorians with their starched-shirt fronts, their saccharine euphemisms, and their plastic compliments. Better to ruffle some feathers and feelings than compromise your own. The social philosopher Hannah Arendt summarized this "virtue" when she called any disjunction between feelings and their expression "the vice of vices." Those who don't tell it like it is are in denial, which always requires some liberating form of therapy. Civility and veracity are considered oil and water. For example, MTV's show *The Real World* was described by this introductory voice-over: "Seven strangers are picked to live in a house . . . to find out what happens when people stop being polite and start being real." Drama is guaranteed, but do not look for these seven strangers to experience a moment of the serenity of civility.

Yes, the Victorians were hypocrites and made no bones about it. Contrary to Arendt, however, there was virtue in this vice. The Victorians practiced what they called "a commendable hypocrisy." As Eliza Duffey wrote in *Ladies' and Gentlemen's Complete Etiquette*:

> We are called upon to make such minor sacrifices of sincerity as a due regard for the happiness and feelings of others demands. True politeness requires us to consider these before our own. A lady who shows by act or expresses in plain, curt words that the visit of another is unwelcome may perhaps pride herself upon being no hypocrite. But she is, in reality, worse. She is grossly selfish. Courtesy, which is the essence of unselfishness, would require her for the time to forget her own feelings and remember those of her visitor, and thus her duty is plain to make that visitor welcome and happy while she remains. If she really does this—forgets self and thinks only of her friend—there is no hypocrisy, but the highest order of Christian charity.

Certainly there is nothing commendable about the hypocrisy of certain public images and image makeovers. But the Victorian brand of social religion, which applied equally to each sex and to give and take alike, is a civilized alternative to using the truth as a bludgeon. Turning the high ideal of honesty to the lowest possible purpose—indulging ourselves—was, as Eliza Duffey wrote, cold-blooded and "only a pretext to introduce something that will wound your feelings." What is candor to us they denounced as survival of the thick skinned.

Most of us are walking wounded, courtesy of a culture that entitles friends, relatives, enemies, and strangers to act as self-appointed Solomons. Defining their opinions as truth, they may ruthlessly dissect every aspect of our thoughts, appearance, and actions as if we were laboratory rats. They generously give us a piece of their mind, even if it robs us of our own peace of mind. Brute truth is always a slippery slope, even when our footing seems secure. Your friend may tolerate or even appreciate being told her new dress makes her look like a parade float. But once the mouth starts its motor, where does it stop? With racial and ethnic slurs? Why censor yourself if that's what you honestly think? One rap musician dismissed complaints about his using the word "bitch" because "you call a spade a spade." If "bitch" is his heartfelt opinion of women, would we want him to sing false but flattering lyrics for the sake of civility? How could we trust his motives, his music, or our judgment if he did? Do we want to trade a "bitch" for "B.S."?[4]

The Victorians carefully distinguished between diplomacy— which used to be valued—and the fawning that Jonathan Swift called the "food of fools." Etiquette authors always vetoed affectation. "There is nothing more disagreeable in the intercourse of civil people than the deference which descends to flattery and obsequiousness," wrote E. H. Ruddock in 1899. Julia Ward Howe thought flattery an "offense against politeness"; those most susceptible to it were "already suffering the intoxication of vanity," she wrote in 1895. Because the Victorians were so attuned to character, the subtle cues of hypocrisy rarely escaped them. "When I hear the soft voice, a little too soft, I look into the face to see whether the two agree," said Mrs. Howe. "But I need scarcely do that. The voice itself tells the story, is sincere or insincere."

Moreover, chilly civility was considered as repugnant as stale hot air. The ideal social temperature was warm without being overly familiar. "Where kindness is rendered with cold, unsympathizing manners, which greatly lessens its value," wrote Catharine Beecher in 1869, it became nothing more than "the payment of a just due." Lord Chesterfield condemned "the mechanical observances of social for-malities . . . the courtesies of life are something real, and not a mere hollow form."

Did that mean you chucked the form if no real feeling filled it? Again, the Victorians had an answer that preserved both integrity and civility. They believed that like an arranged marriage in which love gradually grows, the duty that was an effort at first would become habit. Thus, you subdued your gloomy mood in company because, as Arthur Martine wrote, "To look pleasantly and to speak kindly is a duty we owe to others." But if we focus on their concerns, not ours, practicing selflessness we cultivate sentiments that fill those hollow

forms. This politeness was not phoni-
ness, but "artificial good nature." Conversely, good nature was considered
natural politeness.

If all this sounds like practice-
makes-perfect fancy footwork, it was.
But even Fred Astaire labored long
and hard to achieve his look of easy
grace. His performance was no less
worthy for the effort that lay behind the impression of effortlessness.
Victorian finesse was a labor of love whose essence lay in giving, not
taking. Our ancestors loved the civility that cushioned all of us more
than they loved the self that demanded expression. So they took
pains—which spared others from feeling them. Lord Chesterfield
urged his son to learn "how to conceal a truth without telling a lie."

Sometimes this finesse can be truly heroic. When the French
president François Mitterand died in the winter of 1996, his widow
revealed that he kept his cancer from her for ten years after it was
diagnosed. "He didn't lie, neither to me nor those he loved," she
explained. "He simply preserved our tranquillity of spirit."[5]

This secrecy may seem incomprehensible in an age when truth
routinely tramples the spirit's tranquillity in the minutiae of daily living no less than the drama of life and death. The hardball business of
gift giving provides a sad but fitting example. Miss Manners's and
Ann Landers's columns are filled with hurt-filled stories of gifts blatantly unappreciated by the receiver, returned for cash or exchanged
because they weren't liked or needed. Before detailed gift lists
demanding material goodies of a specific size, color, and style number, gift recipients made the effort to sound grateful even if they
weren't, because to all but the thoughtless the thought mattered
more than the object.

Even in intimate matters, truth was a delicate balancing act.
Arthur Martine urged his readers: "Speak from the heart when you
speak to the heart; only making judgment prune the expressions of
deep feeling without checking the noble sentiments that call them
forth." So a commendably hypocritical lady gently rejected a marriage
proposal by calling it an honor, even if wasn't. Now just asking for a
date—where honor no longer figures—risks a range of bruising

replies: a simple "No!," a more definitive "Not in this lifetime," or a selection from the menu of casual obscenities that have become our unofficial national language.

Our brutal honesty has become sheer brutality. The Victorians aspired to be, in the words of the seventeenth-century essayist Thomas Fuller, "cordial to the soul." We have lost our culture's soul, and even our ability to understand how simple cordiality sustained human dignity. This is illustrated in the classic Victorian novel *The Rise of Silas Lapham* by William Dean Howells. In this 1885 comedy of manners, the bumbling social climber Silas Lapham is invited to dine with the ultrarespectable Cory family. He frantically consults etiquette books to determine what color gloves and cravat he should wear. He becomes farcically obsessed with details, behavior the Victorians themselves derided as the "silver-fork school of etiquette." For all his sartorial pains, he gets roaring drunk at the dinner. He insults his hosts and mortifies his own family.

The next day Lapham bemoans his disgrace to the Cory family's son and asks what the senior Cory said about his boorish behavior after he left the party. The young man answers matter-of-factly, "My father doesn't talk his guests over one another. . . . You were among gentlemen." If Lapham had learned the spirit, not just the letter, of all the etiquette books he read, he would have known that "whatever passes in parties at your own or another's house is never repeated by well-bred people." The Corys' silence may have been hypocritical (just imagine what they were thinking!), but it was also soothing and forgiving.

## LOWERING OUR STANDARDS

While we carry the banner of equality, we practice the reverse snobbery of forcing everyone to bring themselves down to the lowest possible level or risk being demonized as elitist. This is not just hypocrisy but a disaster predicted more than eight decades ago, when Thomas Nelson Page warned that a civilized society could not survive if the lower classes no longer took "their cue and tone" from middle- and upper-class ideals that stressed obligation over self-indulgence.

Today the mainstreaming of lower-class attitudes and behavior threatens to tear society apart. The prominent black columnist

William Raspberry worries about the role-model reversal among American youth, in which lower-class kids no longer mimic the styles of the privileged. Instead, he writes, "The downward pull of the 'bad element' is more and more evident in the pricey suburbs, even in the small towns of exurbia—and among girls as well as boys." Record industry executives report that middle-class white kids are bigger buyers of violent rap music than are blacks. Raspberry, no elitist, prays that "the slovenly dress, unsightly hairstyles and dismaying manners of our children" are not "a prelude to something far, far more deadly."[6] While I am reluctant to discourage any prayer, this one seems particularly futile if we continue on our current course.

Lower- and working-class crudeness also rules over TV's wasteland. Whether shows are set in the streets or corporate suites, they increasingly mimic the nasty edge of *Married with Children* and *Roseanne*. Both on and off the air, the blustery Roseanne torpedoes everyone who fails her down-and-dirty test of character. She has called top actresses like Jodie Foster, Susan Sarandon, and Meryl Streep "castrated females" who are "too middle class." She is clearly proud that more than talent separates her from these women.

While the growing ranks of civility preachers readily denounce her ilk, too few will openly tackle the sensitive but undeniable link between low class and no class. Bulldozers like Roseanne have plenty of defenders among the upper-middlebrow set. They range from the chic *New Yorker* editor who invited her to help "guest edit" a special issue on feminism to the *New York Times* critic who sees the newly belligerent style of prime-time TV as one of "honesty and sincerity, as opposed to the sneaky passive-aggressive style that goes under the name politeness."

The newly popular sports ethic of "in-your-face" is another example of how society's cream sinks to the bottom of the barrel instead of leading the way to the top. *The New York Times* describes the in-your-face approach as the "very fast, very physical, very vocal playground game that came out of the ghetto and now dominates the National Basketball Association. Half the game lies in the art of mercilessly taunting one's opponent during the game, then rubbing his face in the ashes of defeat afterward."

In a truly Victorian assessment of this unsportsmanlike approach to sports, the legendary Kareem Abdul-Jabbar warned that basketball is "moving back to the law of the jungle."[7] (In the last century, when sportsmanship was synonymous with sport, baseball prohibited sliding and stealing bases because they were considered "ungentlemanly tactics.") But life in and out of sports stopped being gentle when it took off the gloves and traded them for cleats. Criminologists note that the violence once confined to the inner city is now increasingly at home in the suburbs. Poverty is not a crime, but emulating the poor at their worst impoverishes our country's soul.

## LOWER-CLASS MINORITIES AND MANNERS

Just as we must acknowledge the distinctly WASP flavor of Victorian etiquette, we must stop pretending to be colorblind if we hope to restore it. Race is the most explosive and divisive issue in America today. But only by discussing it candidly—something we claim to admire—can we reweave the threads of civility that will keep it from tearing us apart. Although civility's vandals come in every class and color, the young black ghetto male personifies the mocking antithesis of Victorian morals and manners.

The renowned African-American sociologist Elijah Anderson has extensively documented the "inability or unwillingness" of lower-class black males "to follow basic middle-class rules about dress and comportment." In his book *Streetwise,* he notes that their behavior is blunt, aggressive, and selfish. To establish dominance and turf rights, they rouse fear on the streets with their swagger, balled fists, boom boxes, cursing, loud spontaneous singing and laughter, and broadcasts about intimate matters. As Dr. Anderson puts it with some understatement, "All convey the impression of little concern for other pedestrians"—particularly women. Many women I know routinely negotiate a gauntlet of threats, dehumanizing comments on body parts, and proposals for their abuse. They will acknowledge this harsh reality only with reluctance and a don't-blame-the-victim dose of liberal guilt.

For all his insight, Professor Anderson faults people like me for clutching their belongings and making other instinctive defensive moves in reaction to any perceived threat. We are branded racists if we fail to distinguish between troublemakers and law-abiding black males, even when both wear the same clothes, such as gold chains, designer warm-up suits, and dark glasses. The logic of Victorian etiquette neatly resolved this problem, since it recognized—correctly—that such distinctions are impossible to draw during brief public encounters.

The Victorians believed that in work, as in life, "Graces do half the business," as Lord Chesterfield wrote. This is why job training programs, however well intentioned, will never make inner-city residents employable, unless they recognize that the right attitude is an indispensable skill. This has become painfully apparent in urban areas across the country. Despite the tax breaks and government grants that create employment opportunities for the poor, foreigners are often hired over needy locals. According to many employers, Hispanic and African immigrants have a strong work ethic, while native minorities lie about their qualifications, show up late if at all, and even assault their bosses. Rather than honestly confront this destructive and self-destructive behavior, urban experts pass this racial hot potato by blaming employer bias.

Basic civility is readily sacrificed to racial doubletalk in manicured neighborhoods as well. At one high school in an affluent Washington suburb, an African-American honor student said that "fear of crossing the PC line" smothers this essential debate: "There is a lot that people want to talk about [such as the fact] that black kids have been allowed to be rude, vulgar, racist because their parents and grandparents have suffered from discrimination. So no one holds them accountable."[8]

We must stop legitimizing the tyrannical, uncivilized minority of all races and classes, while stigmatizing those who want to reclaim safe streets and peace of mind for the majority. Jacob Riis, the great Victorian urban reformer, once said that to help the poor you must sometimes fight against them. Past wrongs and cultural diversity can never justify what Julia Ward Howe, writing in 1895, called "indifference to the divine and contempt for the human." Sixty-five percent of American adults believe "the world is out of control these days," a view shared by 79 percent of blacks—those most victimized by its brutality. In one way or another, we all have the scars to prove that "in-your-face" can never save face; it just leaves us to the mercy of time-bomb tempers.[9]

## RAISING STANDARDS OF BEHAVIOR

Only recently have we rediscovered Victorian methods to diffuse hot tempers. In 1994, Harvard University's Jay Winsten, the creator of the highly effective "designated driver" strategy, turned his talents to the "squash it" antiviolence campaign." "Squash it" is a street-wise gesture based on the "time-out" signal used in sports. Winsten recruited entertainment industry leaders to help find ways "to communicate that it's cool and smart to walk away from a confrontation without a fight."[10]

In an acclaimed bestselling book, Daniel Goleman of *The New York Times* maintains that successful students need more than academic skills; equally important is what he calls emotional intelligence. This includes impulse and anger control, empathy, and harmonious interactions with others; in Victorian shorthand: self-restraint and respect. Students who lack these essential skills are more likely to get poor grades, behave violently, and experience discipline problems, teen pregnancy, and drug abuse. While all children with emotional deficits are at risk, African Americans suffer most. According to many inner-city teachers, those children who try to defy the stereotypes and the odds by pursuing academic excellence are often taunted by peers and accused of acting "white." Goleman's laudable book is another example of our inadvertently claiming past wisdom as our own. Back in 1852 Elizabeth Blackwell noted, "Knowledge alone will never make a people virtuous." Ralph Waldo Emerson put it even more pithily: "Character is higher than intellect."[11]

The growing number of "conflict resolution," "life skills," and "emotional literacy" programs in the nation's schools unwittingly promote this not-so-new idea. They teach the ABCs of civility so that kids won't pull a weapon on whoever bumps into them in the hallway. One largely minority high school in Washington, D.C., extends this approach to the next step by teaching girls to dress, speak, and carry themselves "like ladies." The Victorians understood that how you carry yourself is just as important as what you carry in your head. They believed that a person's posture and carriage expressed to others what sort of person she was. An upright citizen did not slouch and shuffle.

Another Washington-area program for mostly male minority juvenile offenders combines lessons in anger control with proper

English, grooming, and table manners. "I didn't realize how much better I would feel when people started looking at me with respect," said one gratified teenage participant.[12] Like Lord Chesterfield, he learned that "dignity of manners is absolutely necessary to make even the most valuable character either respected or respectable."

### The Downside of Diversity

Ironically, even as we try to civilize (and, however unwittingly, Victorianize) our students, diversity training in the workplace is bucking that healthy trend. As our labor force becomes increasingly less homogeneous, we have an even greater need for shared standards of civility. Unfortunately, the current brand of cultural diversity that is popular in corporate America undermines its own stated goals—sensitivity, tolerance, and inclusion.

Over half of all Fortune 500 companies have diversity coordinators or directors. Business and government spend billions of dollars on such personnel and related programs. Diversity experts write that homogeneous values are "disturbing" and the melting pot is "destructive." The flaw in this approach is not its laudable goal of bringing more women and minorities into the workplace. But promoting the expression of diverse values guarantees continuous conflict by insisting that a wide range of cultural behaviors must be not only tolerated but celebrated.

The diversity consultants rely on a raft of management texts such as *Differences That Work: Organized Excellence Through Diversity, Cultural Diversity in Organizations,* and *Workforce America.* They teach that judging all workers by the "traditional white male yardstick" discriminates against racial and ethnic groups who see it as "foreign to their self-definition." Instead of minorities fitting into the organization, the organization must adapt until everyone has "the freedom and support required to be themselves." The racist white-bread yardstick is replaced by the inviolate assumption that "today's employees want to maintain their unique ethnic and cultural heritage while receiving the respect of their bosses, colleagues, and organizations." This new moral imperative is no less than "the key to solving our most pressing global problems."

There is so much surface sense in this argument that it is easy to buy it, especially if the open-handed buyers are white corporate executives who fear boycotts, bad PR, and lawsuits. Only by candidly assessing the diversity agenda can we see how it exacerbates the tensions, unfairness, and incivility it claims to cure. Consider the scenario, posed by one diversity trainer, of two female colleagues who disagree. A white woman has been socialized to be "conciliatory" in conflicts. As a "peacemaker," she always tries to "smooth over differences. Speaking with a New England regional accent, the volume of her voice will often drop as the pitch rises. She will exhibit more smiling behavior." In contrast, a black woman proudly describes herself as a "feisty battler." Research shows that her racially based behavioral preferences are "highly assertive, even bold by Anglo standards." With an "animated and challenging" style, she will emphasize points of disagreement, her volume rising with the pitch of her voice. "She will also frown or display more emotion."

These women are likely to "misjudge" each other. The white will be seen as "weak and cowardly," while the black will be wrongly viewed as "escalating rather than resolving conflict." The "direct approach" favored by many African Americans "may be perceived by others as inappropriately hostile or militant behavior, a perception that is reinforced by stereotypes of Blacks as being prone to violence." The proposed solution is to educate everyone to accommodate all stylistic differences, "with none superior or inferior." These clashing styles provide the added bonus of making the work environment "more stimulating and exciting."

Problem solved! Is everybody happy? Is everyone respected? Is everyone productive? Only if your ideal work environment is a free-for-all that drains time and money from the bottom line. Only if you believe that customers and clients, as well as workers, are equally "educated" and accepting of whatever behavior they encounter from those seeking to sell them a product or service. The seductive logic of diversity attempts to legitimize the "in-your-face" style that has turned schools, sports, and streets into battlegrounds. How absurd that we must be sensitive to a style that epitomizes insensitivity and obliterates civility.

Furthermore, there's an inherent contradiction in the message. Whites are expected to learn and uncritically accept all aspects of other cultural styles so minorities can be embraced as representatives of distinctive ethnic traditions without being stereotyped. Meanwhile, minorities are pressured to define themselves and be defined in terms of their ethnicity, whatever their personal preference. Is this progress? Isn't this pressure to conform, this compromise of individuality, the despised Victorian gospel we so proudly rejected?

Despite the lofty rhetoric about equally respecting all cultural styles, this stacked deck inherently favors "feisty battlers" over cool conciliators. The latter can either perish or adapt by abandoning their own cultural style to the heat of hostility—what the world needs now. By contrast, the Victorians believed that etiquette was "practical kindness" rooted in common sense. Common sense should tell us civility and hostility are inherently incompatible. Hostility is a volcano, exploding "in your face" at will. Civility presumes you "think before you act." This pearl of wisdom comes not from a present-day Ph.D., but from the quill of the fourteen-year-old George Washington. As a teenager, the future father of our country compiled over a hundred "rules of civility" to govern daily life. The Victorians often cited precepts from this list, which concludes with the all-purpose admonition, "labor to keep alive in your breast that little celestial fire called conscience."

## Manners and Opinions

Victorian manners never precluded voicing opposing opinions, which can hardly be avoided in any workplace. But their artistry, born of necessity, was to keep conflict from destroying "peace and goodwill." Writing at the turn of the century, the educator Charles W. Eliot said, "Long experience among civilized men has proved that good manners are compatible with holding strong opinions and expressing them firmly on fit occasions. They cannot and should not prevent earnest contentions, but they can take the bitterness out of strife, and prevent personal animosities between sincere and strenuous opponents." Imagine how much less hostile and more productive our public and private debates would be if we followed Eliot's advice:

> If a gentleman advances an opinion which is different from ideas you are known to entertain . . . differ with him as gently as possible. You will not say "Sir, you are mistaken!" "Sir, you are wrong" or that you "happen to know better;" but you will rather use some such phrase as "Par-

don me—if I am not mistaken," etc. This will give him a chance to say some such civil thing as that he regrets to disagree with you.[13]

This approach not only preserves dignity and principled disagreement, it discourages the bruising insults that are often exchanged when people get in each other's faces.

## AGGRESSION'S POWERFUL NEGATIVE EFFECT

Not only do manners, as Eliot put it, "take the bitterness out of strife," a value that can't be measured, but they are also essential to physical and economic health. In 1995 New York City launched a $150,000 five-year campaign to teach cab drivers and city employees to be polite to tourists. Why spend tax dollars to reform the rudeness capital of America? Because government surveys again ratified what was once Victorian common sense. Tourists named that legendary rudeness as a main deterrent to return visits to New York.

Etiquette is also good medicine, while hostility can be toxic. Medical researchers found that boiling tempers and loud, aggressive language contribute to coronary heart disease and death by raising testosterone secretions. Dr. Redford Williams of Duke University has characterized anger as a risk factor akin to smoking or high blood pressure. According to Dr. Aron Siegman of the University of Maryland, just speaking loudly can significantly raise blood pressure, while speaking softly eliminates "cardiovascular upheaval." Studies conducted at dozens of medical centers and hospitals show that among those who already suffered a heart attack, angry outbursts more than doubled the risk of having another within two crucial hours after the first. Can we really afford to promote any cultural style that shortens life expectancy and increases budget deficits?

Without the soothing coolness of manners, the Victorians predicted that society would fall apart. But patching Humpty Dumpty back together needs more than desperation and good intentions. It needs the glue of what Arthur Schlesinger, Jr., called the "nationwide consensus of manners" that defined nineteenth-century America. This consensus became more, not less, important as millions of immigrants diversified the country.

# A COMMON COURTESY

The Victorians' rational response to widening class, racial, and ethnic divisions was the common currency of common courtesy that a fragmented country needs to peacefully settle disputes as much as it needs a common language. Imagine the chaos and traffic fatalities if everyone followed their own rules of the road. Responding to those who ridicule rules they had no part in setting, Schlesinger noted that the immigrants' willingness to imitate them "has in the long run had the effect of lessening artificial distinctions."

In 1895 Julia Ward Howe made a crucial observation that would be heretical today: "Perhaps our theory of the freedom and equality of all men leads some of us to the mistaken conclusion that all people equally know how to behave themselves, which is far from being the fact."

Unless corporate America has the courage to put the welfare of all above cultural coddling for some, what hope is there to civilize our streets with a unified code of manners? For business to function efficiently, workers of every racial, ethnic, and religious background must check some part of their identities at the door when they clock in each morning.

A nudist can't truly be himself on company time—and his means of personal expression is far less hostile than those celebrated and mandated by cultural diversity junkies. Not only do they balkanize society, they injure those they seek to help. In our candor-crazed age, we must bluntly admit what many only whisper—they don't object to working with people from different backgrounds, just those who display the brute, threatening, chip-on-the-shoulder attitude that coarsens everyone and drains the grace from everyday life.

The force-fed propaganda that justifies what the Victorians considered selfish and egotistical behavior fosters resentment and hardens whites to the laudable aspects of diversity—bringing more minorities into the labor force and encouraging everyone to learn about other cultures. This brand of diversity is a win-win goal, but diversity in manners guarantees adversity. There is little peace and even less pleasure in a world where equality equals anarchy. Without common rules of etiquette, we will continue to regress to the bullies' rule of the jungle.

Proponents of diversity often complain that their critics focus exclusively on the "here and now" while ignoring the history of past discrimination that unjustly devalued certain groups and cultures. I agree. The Victorian civility we have trashed for nearly a century deserves restoration and emulation, not as an exclusive privilege for a few but as a gift free to all for the taking. Polite isn't white or any other color. It is the key to the colorblind justice we owe each other in our daily interactions. When Lincoln said, "A house divided against itself cannot stand," he referred to the rift between slave states and free. Luckily, that house survived a bloody war. But it may not survive the continuing corrosion of its foundation—civility.

# PART 3

# PRIVATE INTIMACY

# 9

# Babes in Toyland

If our new no-strings-attached sex is so great, why aren't we satisfied? . . . We wander down the aisles of a vast sexual toy store, filling up our carts with experiences and sexual gadgets and techniques but feeling unsatisfied and empty. Having destroyed the cultural climate that nurtures great love, we've been forced to settle for a great lay—if we can find it.

## CAN'T GET NO SATISFACTION

Like shopaholics who try to buy that elusive high, we struggle in vain to fill the void of romance with racy paraphernalia and entertainment. Marketers invade our bedrooms with videos, books, and sex toys designed to cure our sexual ills. In place of poetry, we purchase our inspiration from 900 lines. Mail-order catalogs selling mops, mugs, and laundry stain removers also hawk his-and-hers glow-in-the-dark underwear "guaranteed to light up your love life." *Joy of Sex* author Dr. Alex Comfort tells his readers not to be afraid of reducing sex to a technique. Even conservative Christians Tim and Beverly LaHaye, in their 1976 book *The Act of Marriage*, describe the "art of love" as a product of "practicing mutually satisfying techniques." Yet for all our new moves and fancy footwork, we are still not finding passion.

In our desperate quest for ever higher erotic highs, we have scoured the kitchen, the toy store, the drug store, the burgeoning sex stores, and their mail-order spinoffs. We've had our love-ins, wife swappings, feminist consciousness raising masturbation workshops, scared-safe sex, man sharing, and man hating. We search everywhere but in the century that looks disapprovingly over our shoulders and are convinced there is nothing that we could learn from that era of "repression."

## *Animal Instincts*

After all, isn't such repression of our animalistic instincts unhealthy? "It's scary for a feminist woman to acknowledge that she is also an animal," says Naomi Wolf in *Fire with Fire*, "because it is just our animal nature that a sexist society wants to use to constrain us. . . . At times, the critical mind has got to shut down; we have to become simply beasts, simply mouths, simply sex, even as men are known sometimes to want to be just sex. Let us make room for that need without being made to feel that we are abdicating evolution or revolution." This sounds like a strategy for putting women on top in the boardroom and the bedroom. But it is only another sad example of the delusional freedom that appropriates the lowest male standards. It limits women's choices rather than expanding them, and it normalizes a sexual conformity as sterile and severe as the relentless male bashing it opposes.

Like selfishness and crudity, animal copulation may be natural, but the female of the species naturally gets shortchanged by it. The Victorians knew that unharnessed primal instincts would turn courtship into a cold-blooded contest between the hunter and the hunted. *This* is what they deemed unnatural. Describing the "mean animal passion" of fornication, the physician William Acton wrote in 1875, "Its peculiarity and heinousness consist in divorcing from all feelings of love that which was meant by nature as the . . . intensest expression of unreserved affection to a mere momentary and brutal indulgence."

Sheer gratification of "natural appetites and passion" was never a sufficient reason to indulge. As Henry James, Sr., put it, "No man and woman can do that deliberately without converting themselves into brutes."[1] In her 1876 work, *The Relations Between the Sexes*, the ever-commonsensical Eliza Duffey specified which sex would be more brutalized by free love. [It] reduces man to the exact level of the

cat, the dog, or the bull, which gratifies its animal propensities whenever or wherever it finds a willing female of its own race, and then
goes away utterly oblivious of consequences. . . . As man dropped the
mantle of responsibility in the matter of offspring, it would unavoid-
ably fall upon the shoulders of women."

The current explosion of single mothers and welfare costs fla-
grantly proves her point. But the Victorians didn't need to experience
such egregious consequences in order to reject sophistical doctrines
of sexual equality. They understood biology's inherent double standard, but they responded by imposing women's standards on men.
Their solution stands in stark contrast to our present-day practice of
performing a mental sex change operation on the female psyche. As
with civility, "Women are especially called on to strengthen and guide
the sexual virtue of a people," wrote Dr. Elizabeth Blackwell in *Essays
in Medical Sociology*. The biographers Leon Stein and Annette Baxter
note that Grace Dodge, first president of the YWCA, said any self-
respecting woman "does not allow the sowing of wild oats in men."
Now equality means matching them oat for oat.

## WHAT'S GOOD FOR THE GOOSE

The Victorians, however, had a different sense of sexual equality.
When a self-respecting Victorian woman declared, as Dr. Blackwell
did in 1902, that "a man demands absolute chastity in a wife, and a
woman should be no less in her demands," she was heard and
heeded. In 1899, a prominent male physician, E. H. Ruddock, wrote
in his advice book for husbands, "Society has no right to condone in
man what it condemns in women."

This was no pipe dream or personal preference but a forceful
cultural mandate of true manhood. Among the private period documents unearthed by the historian Karen Lystra is an 1898 letter from
a middle-aged widower seeking to reassure his new love interest of
his honor. During the fourteen years since his wife's death, he wrote,
he "loved no woman," although passions "blaze in my blood as fiercely
as volcano fires [but] break forth only where I love. I will look into
your eyes with a clear, unchallenged soul, Clara, when I meet you."
Subsequent letters confirm that their eventual marriage was both
physically and emotionally rich.

Despite Mark Twain's raucous youth, he was a virgin when he married at thirty-four, according to his biographer Resa Williams. Did inexperience equal deprivation for this man who was an embodiment of worldliness? Not a chance. Always deeply reverential toward women, Twain still sounded like a smitten schoolboy when corresponding with Olivia, his wife of fifteen years. He mourned nothing so much as her grievous loss. The painfully romantic epitaph he spoke at her graveside was not just a tribute to one couple's boundless love but a reflection of masculinity fulfilled in his time: "Wherever she was, there was Eden."

Teddy Roosevelt, according to his biographer Edmund Morris, proudly wrote that he remained "perfectly pure" throughout his bachelorhood. Now onetime basketball star Wilt Chamberlain boasts in his memoirs of bedding twenty thousand women. Which man was more manly? Current NBAer A. C. Green doesn't play the macho game Chamberlain's way. This self-proclaimed virgin intends to remain one until marriage. He preaches chastity in schools and on talk shows, hoping to inspire youngsters, especially those who worship sports figures. He also wants to teach young men to respect young women.

Perhaps if there were more men with an attitude like A. C. Green's there would be fewer women who think their only option is to adopt the male attitude to treat the opposite sex like something to be consumed, used up, and thrown away. Coldhearted consumerism is a sorry substitute for passion.

In retrospect, how many women found sexual satisfaction in the much lauded "zipless fuck," a phrase coined by Erica Jong in her 1973 book *Fear of Flying* to describe an emotionless, guilt-free sexual encounter? Yet the mentality that girls-must-be-boys continues to find its supporters. In a 1994 *New York Times* Op-Ed piece, Celia Barbour claims she has a solution to such sexual dissatisfaction and women's resentment of "men's easy access to sexual arousal," to wit: "[m]ore good pornography for women" to "even the score."[2]

Ms. Barbour is no fringe academic theorist but an associate editor at *Martha Stewart Living*. Now we know the real sublimated yearnings of all those Martha-ites who crackle-glaze floors, renovate lamp shades, and make spun sugar. Tough luck for women who can't or won't follow Barbour's lead. They are the ones who need renovation, says advice guru Ann Landers. Responding to an angry woman who signed herself "disillusioned" after discovering her husband's porno collection, Ann declared that wife, not hubby, needed counseling to get over her "obsession." The Victorians understood that evening the score on such sorry terms guarantees men will still keep score.

At best, this validation of male standards, or the lack of them, blurs acceptable sexual boundaries for everyone. The resulting confusion produces the kind of hair-splitting rules that have taken sex from the sublime to the ridiculous. For example, Antioch College issued a dating code that sounded like a parody and became instant fodder for stand-up comics. Thirteen pages of legalistic dos and don'ts required students to obtain explicit consent for each act of touching and disrobing. This would make sex stilted and awkward, critics complained—as if it isn't now. Not surprisingly, male students were especially concerned that "asking means not getting what you want."

If women are not getting what they want, some experts blame anatomy. The biologist Robert Francoeur of Fairleigh Dickinson University claims that women's brains are better integrated: Their left and right hemispheres are more intimately connected. Thus female sexuality is "whole body," whereas "the male orgasm is much more penile-centered."[3] This helps explain *Women Who Love Sex* author Gina Ogden's finding that women view sex "more holistically, more as a whole person proposition, body, mind, and soul, than men do."

Having reviewed over 200 studies, the University of Vermont psychology professor Dr. Harold Leitenberg has found that women's fantasies focus more on emotional connections, unfold at a slower pace than men's, and involve more nongenital caressing than genital contact. In a poll of 1,000 women, two out of three women said they would choose hugging without intercourse, twice the number who preferred humping to holding each other. Not surprisingly, men's fantasies are more genital, graphic, and impersonal, including strangers as well as friends. One researcher called these scenarios a pornotopia where "sex is sheer lust and physical gratification, devoid of encumbering relationships, emotional elaboration, complicated plot lines, flirtation, courtship, and extended foreplay, where all the women were easily aroused and willing."[4]

Biology may tempt us to capitulate to this soulless, self-centered, penis-centered pleasure principle. The prisoners of this century's hundred-year war between the sexes include all the women who settle for the best they can get, as well as those who make the best of being manless. Yet the Victorians would not allow the worst of nature to trump the best of nurture. The holistic sex we term "female" was their unisex ideal.

## THE TRUTH OF CONSEQUENCES

All sides in the current sexual debate are destined to keep talking past each other, if they remain blind to the fundamental Victorian insight that sexual relations are social relations. Doing your own thing—even in the ultimate privacy of bed—is never just your own business. Free sex is never free, because its salespeople indirectly impose their expectations on conformists and dissidents alike. Just as passive smoke pollutes the lungs of nonsmokers, casual sex poisons the atmosphere that nourishes romance. This equation cheats all lovers of sublime loves, not just superb lays.

Victorian women and their sentiments reigned supreme during the century of romance. The loss of those sentiments reduced most ordinary women to the status of powerless pawns, even as the favored few play at being mistresses of the universe. When Madonna slides a whip between her legs, she is degrading all other woman, regardless of whether they have a penchant for leather. When rapper Adina Howard sings, "I want a roughneck brother who can satisfy me," she invites guys to play it rough even when their partners want it soft and slow.

Among those seeking an alternative route is Christina Kirksey, a teenage intern at the National Political Congress of Black Women. In a newspaper interview, she described Ms. Howard's music as a roadblock for African-American women, not a liberating force: "The lyrics were nasty and vile. I'm striving to get an education and make something of myself. I have to constantly fight against catcalls and sexual harassment on the street and here comes Adina Howard [with] 'I need a freak in the morning.'"[5]

The infamous Tailhook convention also made an entire gender fair game. Although the media focused on female officers and civilians who were forced to run a groping gauntlet and were otherwise assaulted by drunken Navy fliers, a Defense Department report concluded that "many women freely and knowingly participated in gauntlet activities." Some bared their breasts so they could be pasted with squadron stickers, or encouraged men to drink shots of tequila from their navels. Some performed simulated fellatio on a dildo attached to a booze-dispensing rhino.[6]

The women who reveled in this orgy breached the bounds of self-expression (never mind decency) by compromising the choices, the welfare, and the credibility of women with less expansive views of sex and recreation. Those who say they were assaulted are easy to doubt, precisely because others volunteered their bodies to the assaulters.

Although it is men who directly violate a woman's body and peace of mind, other women unconsciously conspire in those crimes. Demi Moore received $12.5 million—the single highest fee ever paid an actress—to unveil her artificially enhanced breasts in the movie *Striptease*. Defending her nudity and her salary, she told a reporter, "The strongest feminine statement I can make is: Be supportive of women who make conscious choices for themselves." It is certainly a commentary not only on Ms. Moore's mentality that this is "the strongest feminine statement" she can make, but also a sad commentary on the milieu in which she thrives.

In this "get mine any way I can" mode of liberation, Moore and her ilk bank the loot while other women get taxed. "We need sluts for the revolution," Naomi Wolf told *Esquire* magazine.[7] But all women who ever shared a neighborhood with streetwalkers know that every woman becomes not only a target for prowling men but also a compulsory competitor in feeding the furnace of male pleasure. Women who feel empowered by appearing nude or seminude in public will never lack for partners, however fleeting, in an era that has drastically defined down romantic expectations from their Victorian peak. Only women who believe in the tooth fairy could imagine themselves in the place of Ellen Olenska, when Newland Archer kneels to kiss the tip of his beloved's satin shoe. You say such scenes could only have existed in fiction? Then imagine receiving a birthday gift like the one the composer Richard Wagner gave his wife in 1870. He assembled a group of musicians, whom he had secretly rehearsed, on the stairs of his house, and directed the first performance of his famous Siegfried Idyll, which he had written for her.[8]

Men do not express such sentiments toward strippers, porno mimics, or sluts, be they pro- or antirevolution. The cold truth is that whatever politically correct mantras men feel compelled to voice, we all know that "slut" is precisely what they're thinking and what they snicker to each other when safe from the propaganda police.

## Prisoners of Sexual Freedom

Moreover, modern women who desire the attention and affections of a man must struggle with new standards of attractiveness. Forget character, bearing, and personality. Beauty is our bait, and the more we see airbrushed, near-naked females on every television screen, magazine cover, and public street in the summertime, the more impossible it seems to be to measure up to this ideal. Current studies by psychologists show that anorectic, computer-corrected images of Barbie Doll models foster unrealistic body images that contribute not only to widespread eating disorders but frigidity among the many women and girls who feel hopelessly flawed. No feminist needs science to validate the destructive effects of "normalizing" impossible standards of beauty, which have bound women to the Stairmaster and the plastic surgeon's table.

Women create for themselves a "falsely styled freedom," as Dr. Elizabeth Blackwell said in 1902, when they lower themselves to the level of male standards, instead of raising men up to their own. When enough women hit the sexual fast lane, others are pressured to keep up speed if they want a second date. But just how free are women who express relief (in private) that the fear of AIDS provides a convenient excuse to abstain from "casual boinking" in their search for the Holy Grail of Mr. Right?

The Victorians believed a woman deserved far more than fidelity and a ring on her finger. Respecting her bodily integrity and freedom was a sacred if implicit vow that a husband took in marriage. However difficult it was to uphold, a gentleman's personal honor and a couple's joint happiness depended on his sexual restraint just as much as social stability depended on controlling the selfish instincts of brute force. With roots in this rich soil of loving monogamy, trust, intimacy, and passion blossomed.

# I 0

## *When Life Was Foreplay*

Nine out of ten people, if asked what "Victorian" means, will include "prudish" or "sexually repressed" somewhere in their answer. It's something everybody "knows," even if they don't know exactly where they learned it. They probably picked it up partly from the popular culture— all those Hollywood films and Harlequin Romances that feature nineteenth-century heroines breaking free of rigid social conventions to find true romance. But this is one point on which Hollywood agrees with most history books.

Generations of historians have taught us to ridicule the Victorians' attitude toward sex as a token of our own enlightened perspective. According to some of these scholars who created today's conventional wisdom, such as historian Ronald Pearsall, our benighted ancestors regarded sex as "vulgar," "deplorable," a "deed of darkness." Desire was "something the well-bred man and woman should not have." Women in particular were supposedly sexless creatures, mere "child-bearing vegetables" who could only "lie still and think of the Empire."

At a time when we are willing to question just about every other piece of received wisdom, and "revisionism" runs rampant among historians, no one ever seems to question the priggish and puritanical image we have of the Victorians. And why should we? After all, one of the most frequently quoted passages on the Victorians' thinking comes from an 1865 work, *The Functions and Disorders of Reproductive Organs*, in which Dr. William Acton wrote, "The majority of women (happily for society) are not very much troubled with sexual feeling of any kind. What men are habitually, women are only exceptionally."

## VICTORIAN SENSUALITY UNCOVERED

Unfortunately, it turns out that Dr. Acton was very wrong about Victorian sexual mores. In 1974 the eminent historian Carl Degler discovered an unknown but extensive survey of married women born between 1850 and 1880. Until Degler found this unpublished gold mine, it was widely assumed that such surveys did not exist before the 1920s. Yet the Stanford University professor Dr. Clelia Mosher, a highly respected female physician, began this research on sexual attitudes in 1892. Even more surprising is that most of Mosher's subjects were the picture of sexual health by modern standards. These ordinary middle-class women freely admitted that they had sexual feelings, enjoyed intercourse with their husbands, and usually experienced what they called "voluptuous spasms"—a term far more evocative than the more prosaic and clinical "orgasm." One claimed that sex rendered "a sense of completeness, a spiritual oneness, which is not gained in any other way." Another described intercourse as "the extreme caress of love's passion," whose "habitual bodily expression has a deep psychological effect in making possible complete mental sympathy, and perfecting the spiritual union."

The spiritual importance of sensuality was not lost on Henry James, Sr., either. In what may sound like blasphemy to some but was a tribute to the supreme importance and scope of Victorian love, he wrote, "The more perfect the oneness" husband and wife attained through sex, "the more like God."[1] Similar sentiments were expressed in the correspondence analyzed by the historian Karen Lystra in her book *Searching the Heart: Women, Men, and Romantic Love in Nineteenth-Century America*. One young husband's awed description for intercourse with his spouse was that it was "solemn and sublime." Another called the act of physical love simply "a sacrament."

In fact, numerous Victorian marriage manuals, all aimed at the general public, celebrated intercourse and female sexuality. *Excessive Venery: Masturbation and Continence,* an 1887 work by Dr. Joseph Howe, described sex as "one of the essentials to perfect health." A generation earlier, Dr. James Ashton wrote in *The Book of Nature* that sex was "essential for good health"; he prescribed lima beans, mushrooms, and shellfish as aphrodisiacs. And in his 1899 book *In Health,* Dr. A. J. Ingersoll called the sexual life "the sustaining life of the mind, as well as every organ of the body" that "controls all actions of humanity." Ingersoll counseled his patients to "love and reverence sex," and he warned that suppressing it "could lead to disease, even the lunatic asylum."

Dr. Ingersoll's tribute to sexual expression appeared in the same year that an unknown young physician named Sigmund Freud published *The Interpretation of Dreams.* The book sold fewer than 200 copies that year, and it would take another decade for Freud's theories to find more than a narrow audience. A century later, it is easy to forget that Freud was not the first medical authority to notice the importance of sex to personal health and marital satisfaction.

Even the prototypically prudish Dr. William Acton believed that "to ignore the bodily and secular aspect of married love would be false and unwise," as he wrote in *The Functions and Disorders of the Reproductive Organs.* Despite his notorious pronouncement on female frigidity, he also commented that some women "have sexual drives so strong that they surpass those of men." Other physicians of the period noted that women often experienced more intense orgasms than men. By mid-

*Victorian prudery has been much exaggerated. Couples expected and experienced passion within marriage.*

century many, such as Charles Knowlton, M.D., asserted (as post-Freudians rediscovered generations later) that the clitoris is "the principal organ of sexual pleasure in the female." In an 1897 work with the provocative title *What a Husband Should Know*, Sylvanus Stall may have stoked more fears than he allayed by describing sex as a "ruling passion" for some women, who should marry only men with "large powers of endurance or risk ruining their health."

Nor did the passionate cravings felt by wives die along with their husbands. Dr. Elizabeth Blackwell recalled witnessing "the severe and compound suffering experienced by many widows who were strongly attached to their lost partners [which is] also well known to the physician, and this is not simply a mental loss that they feel, but an immense physical deprivation. It is a loss which all the senses suffer by the physical as well as moral void which death has created."[2]

Speaking for themselves, both famous and ordinary women affirmed the deep deprivation of an empty bed and the joys of a shared one. In 1835 one lonely Southern wife wrote her husband that she would "drain your coffers dry" when they were reunited. He in turn wrote of anticipating "unspeakable delight in your embrace," as he imagined her "caressing hands" and "voluptuous touch."[3] The English author Beatrix Potter experienced similar exquisite torture, recording in her journal in 1889 that "God knows celibacy is as painful to a woman as it is to a man. It could not be more painful than it is to a woman."[4]

On the other side of the Atlantic, a bride wrote in her journal in 1879, "I am most deeply grateful to God for giving me in my husband a man whose fresh springs of deepest tenderness and love grow fuller and fuller every day, encompassing me with the sweetest life-fountains that a woman's life can ever know."[5]

These warm-blooded women were anything but frigid mummies who were stoically doing their duty to posterity. Even confirmed spinster Emily Dickinson promised some imagined lover, "Wild Nights— Wild Nights! / Were I with thee / Wild nights should be our luxury." And the era's icon of prudery, Queen Victoria, was less repressed than most have supposed. She and her husband, Albert, bought each other nude portraits, and she even drew some. Biographer Louis Auchincloss wrote that the intensely passionate nature of the queen "may explain her near insanity on Albert's death."

Women's consuming yearnings were no surprise to the men who were their object. In an 1853 letter to his intended, one man wrote that he assumed his wife would be his "equal with flesh and blood, with magnetism, electricity, passion." Another gallant swain assured his fiancée that he would not take premarital advantage of "the roused and throbbing nature of your woman's heart, which in its sweetly awakened passion might feel tempted . . . to throw all reasons to the wind and give life, love, thought, being, destiny—everything—to the lover who holds you in his arms."[6]

After his own extensive survey of revealing letters between Victorians of all ages and relationships, the historian Peter Gay concluded in *Education of the Senses* that "the bond that mattered, surpassing all others, was that between spouses. The nineteenth-century middle class wife who pours all her affection into her children and denies her husband all sexual warmth is largely a myth." Gay found that shared sensuality—something we think of as a tribute to our own "enlightened" sexual attitudes—was considered an "indispensable element" of marriage. Many couples undoubtedly found it, for as de Tocqueville noted in the 1830s, America above all countries "is the one in which the marriage tie is most respected and where the highest and truest conception of conjugal happiness has been conceived."

So why has the twentieth century so severely misrepresented the sensual Victorians as fanatical prudes? Carl Degler faults twentieth-century historians for failing to fully survey all the available literature. But the Victorians' artistic legacy is difficult for even the laziest scholar to miss. We needn't read the Victorians' letters and journals to know that nude statues were displayed throughout the century in parks, public buildings, and homes. Copies made in Paris of Hiram Powers's classical undraped maiden, *The Greek Slave*, were among the most popular ornaments for parlors. Another Powers masterpiece, *Eve Tempted*, also celebrated voluptuous female nudity. And what could be more erotic than the embrace of naked lovers in Rodin's *The Kiss*?

Peter Gay, in *Education of the Senses*, blames present-day ignorance of Victorian sexual realities on the legacy of Freud, "a professional skeptic" who based his observations on sexually maladjusted people rather than healthy ones, and was therefore inclined to "underestimate the opportunities for erotic happiness available in the bourgeois world, for women and men alike." Even though revisionists have since made Swiss cheese of Austrian psychotherapy, we still accept the Viennese doctor's dismal view of Victorian sex, or the lack of it.

Our drastic differences from the Victorians feed our suspicions of their ways, along with our occasional awe at their accomplishments. Perhaps it is inevitable that we should judge them on our terms rather than their own. Because sexual reticence is as alien to us as high-buttoned shoes, we erroneously assume, as Gay puts it, that ordinary people in the nineteenth century "did not know, or did not practice, or did not enjoy what they did not discuss."

## A PRIVATE PASSION

In contrast to our own "open-book" attitude, the Victorians drew sharp lines between the public and the private. Sexual intimacy was regarded as just that—intimate, personal, and very private. It was not fodder for budding exhibitionists or salivating voyeurs. William Wordsworth wrote: "Strange fits of passion have I known: / And I will dare to tell, / But in the Lover's ear alone, / What once to me befell."

By contrast, contemporary practice now favors an approach that might be called the public gush. For example, tennis star Martina Navratilova could not confine her sweet nothings to her lover's ears. In an article that appeared in the Style section of *The Washington Post* in July 1996, she announced to the press that she and the L'Oréal model Hunter Reno, a niece of Attorney General Janet Reno, were an item. "I've never been one to hide," Navratilova explained. "I love Hunter in a way I haven't loved before." The Victorians would score this advertised "love" just as tennis does—as zero.

There was far more than finger-wagging prissiness to the old etiquette rule "Make no public exhibition of your endearments." As Karen Lystra noted, "Forbidden expression in Victorian public life . . . attained a special and privileged meaning in private precisely because of public prohibitions."[7] This gave a "special aura" and "heightened meaning" to romantic love that eludes us today because of, not in spite of, our loose talk, loose sex, and celebration of technique. We announce our sexual needs and our bedroom conquests and failings with the boldness of cheap cologne. Victorian passion was an exotic perfume made all the more alluring by its subtle presence.

While we presume that other hidden facets of private life, like wife beating and child abuse, were rampant in the not-so-good old days, we don't apply this "given" to sex. We define sexual extroversion as healthy and diagnose as "sick" an age that loved to love under the covers, not in the spotlight. But making a spectacle of sex not only clouds our historical judgment but also cheapens a treasure, draining it of the intriguing secrecy that once raised passion into the stratosphere of desire and imagination. "Its very mystery," observes Peter Gay in *The Tender Passion*, "often taken as a symptom of the shame with which prudish bourgeois approached the marriage bed, was something of a tribute to their high regard for loving," and for "erotic pleasures" as well.

Mysteries make us wary in this age of nonstop communication. We demand that our potential bedmates put all their cards and transmittable diseases on the table. Anything less is a bluff that derails the brutal honesty essential to building a solid relationship. Didn't the Victorian veil of privacy compromise this candor? Weren't people condemned to marry strangers who revealed their true—and worst— selves only after they tied the knot? Wrong again. The Victorians believed in absolute mutual premarital candor, with full disclosure of every flaw and folly. "To be natural is the great secret of success in love making," advised "An American Gentleman" in his book *Good Behavior for Young Gentlemen* (1848). "To disguise your character and study affectation in courting is the very error of the moon."[8]

It was precisely because the lovers' bond was intensely private that they could reveal all their imperfections to each other. Since they regarded marriage as neither a passing fancy nor a phase of self-development but a lifetime commitment, its stakes were as high as you could go. America's first ordained female minister, Antoinette Brown Blackwell, quoted in *Hands and Hearts*, told her future husband, "You must always say everything to me, darling. Nothing but the utmost confidence can make us quite happy, and nothing but the want of it can destroy happiness."

Victorian lovers often risked all for love by baring their souls— only to each other—so their marriage would not crash on the rocks of false ideals. This theme appears repeatedly in letters and journals from the period, many of which were collected by Karen Lystra: "I have rather ruthlessly shown you my worst traits in a sort of passionate desire to have your love founded in realities and not on dreams," wrote one young woman to her fiancée. Looking back on a misunderstanding with his sweetheart, an attorney offered this defense: "I am not sorry . . . to have let you see whatever you have seen. I want you to marry me and I am unwilling to win you under false pretenses."

Revealing your darkest side was a dangerous test of love. But true love had to be tested with truth, and this was both acknowledged and appreciated. Responding to his fiancée, an architect wrote, "I am very glad you did send me your downhearted letter instead of destroying it as you thought you ought to have done the next morning. . . . It is good to know and share our innermost consciousness and we need more than anything else to get acquainted—to really know our own and each other's true selves."

## THE DEATH OF INTIMACY

In contrast to these sincere confessions, Ellen Rothman found a striking change of attitude in correspondence from the 1920s. As she wrote in *Hands and Hearts,* in that decade "a growing emphasis on personality and physical attractiveness made self-exposure a risky proposition. 'Catching' a mate had become a matter of wearing stylish clothes and knowing the latest dance step, rather than of demonstrating certain attributes of character."

For example, Rothman reports, one disenchanted young man wrote his mother that he "wasn't very favorably impressed" with a girl he met at a dance. She wasn't "a looker" and "her line was weak," he complained. "At a time when young people were expected to woo each other with the right look and the right line, candor and openness were outmoded virtues," Rothman concluded. "This was the message of popular fiction, movie romances, advertisements. Even the marriage counselors of the period advised young lovers to 'get over any habit of thinking that they must be frank and tell everything they know.'"

For all the lip service we pay to letting it all hang out and urging others to follow suit—without hanging them out to dry—we have inherited the line. When sex is the goal, honesty is easily sacrificed to the self-serving sound bites that ease the way into bed. Women especially expect to hear the right noises before they hit the sheets, an exercise that often taxes macho patience beyond its narrow limits. This gender war raged in a much-debated February 1994 *Esquire* article on the rise of the postsensitive male who rejects female standards in the mating game. As one man admitted, "It used to be . . . that you didn't date, you screwed. And when the drugs wore off the next morning, if you could still remember the woman's name, you had a relationship. Today they all expect you to remember their name. . . . I spent most of the last twenty years trying to make the right, enlightened sounds, and there were times I was so convincing, I believed what I was saying."[9]

## Cynicism and Male Bashing

This man's psychological swindle might explain his failed marriage, not to mention the male bashing that has become a national sport among women. No wonder women feel cheated, deceived, and disempowered by all the frauds who made the right sounds. No wonder they are so wary that they increasingly rely on private investigators to "check him out." One advertisement for such a service warns, "He may have a wife, an embellished resumé, a criminal record, or the potential to be a 'fatal attraction.'"

This wholesale mistrust of the opposite sex (which seems more like another species these days) breeds an embittered contempt that is toxic to mutual respect, much less romance. One painfully humorous T-shirt illustrates the seething frustrations of women who keep kissing toads in hopes of finding a prince. The shirt features "The Perfect Man" in the shape of a gingerbread cookie. The caption reads, "He's quiet. He's sweet. And if he gives you any crap, you can bite his head off."

The problem is not that men are inherently deceitful, but that they no longer accept the Victorian ideal that candor in love enhanced their masculinity. Where women now have to dig for the truth through calcified layers of masculine muteness, Victorian men were expected to be willing and equal partners in the give and take of truth. But why should we care about this missed historical footnote and the mincemeat unscholarly scholars made of intimacy in bygone days? What could we possibly learn from a society that lacked vibrators, flavored condoms, and illustrated manuals to sexual acrobatics?

We could start by recognizing the hunger that exists in the midst of plenty. For all our vaunted openness and freedom to experiment, sexual relations seem no better than any other relations between the sexes today.

## NO SATISFACTION

The widespread absence of sexual satisfaction has been documented by numerous surveys in recent years. Women are especially dissatisfied with their lot, which they regard as far too little. A 1994 poll conducted by the University of Chicago found that only 29 percent of women always experienced orgasm with their primary partner, compared to three quarters of men.[10] (If only Woody Allen's orgasmatron from *Sleeper* were more than a futuristic prop.) And over half of 1,000 women age 18 to 25 surveyed by *Esquire* magazine in 1994 admitted to doing what Meg Ryan so ably demonstrated in the movie *When Harry Met Sally*: They fake orgasms.[11] So much for candor. No wonder the popular book *Why Women Need Chocolate* claimed this always satisfying treat outranks sex on the female priority list.

For those who place their faith in the future, there is little hope that the next generation will bridge this intimate divide. A Roper poll of 503 ninth- through twelfth-graders found that nine out of ten boys called sex a pleasurable experience, compared to only six out of ten girls. Even more telling—and disheartening: 62 percent of all girls surveyed regretted not waiting until they were older to become sexually active. These once tender years have become very tough, and the toll this is taking is anything but equal.

Since the 1970s surveys have shown that early intercourse predicts lingering sexual dissatisfaction for females. With the lost age of innocence steadily dropping, their prospects are dim for getting what they want or deserve from men. In a recent public-service ad broadcast on television, a remorseful pregnant teen wishes she had waited for "real love," and girls are urged to believe "you're worth waiting for." At this late date, such efforts are likely to have less effect on unwanted pregnancies than on our sense of irony that the Advertising Council has belatedly discovered the joys of abstinence.

Increasingly, though, it is grown women who have lost their patience. Movies like *Waiting to Exhale* explore a growing intolerance of men's emotional and sexual deficiencies, which range from the Felix Ungers who take forever to unwrap a condom to the bedroom growlers who make women feel like zoo keepers. Yet a generation after Dionne Warwick addressed her pleas to "anyone who had a heart," some experts tell women to settle for anyone who has a pulse. The prominent black sociologist Audrey Chapman advocates *Man Sharing* (the title of her book) for women who lack the energy to fight "reality." Reality means using available men for sex and having no "romantic illusions" about this scarce and undependable commodity.

Ms. Chapman is addressing the plight of a particularly put-upon group of women whose rivals for potential mates all too often include drugs, violence, and the criminal justice system. Yet such concerns are not just "a Black thing." This was evidenced by a national Harris poll of 2,002 adults, in which 70 percent of the men were honest enough to admit that birth control is a "woman's problem" because men are too irresponsible to choose and use a method.

Feminine disenchantment runs deep. "Love," like "soul," has become a four-letter word long since milked of its meaning by modern neglect and our penchant for cruder expressions. This soul, an intangible spiritual essence that transcends any religion, fired Victorian love and passion with a consuming intensity we can scarcely imagine.

Just as we have lost the civility that graced and ordered Victorian public life, so have we lost the mystique that elevated sex and romance beyond a bunch of roses or the almighty orgasms we tally like beans. This loss has impoverished the inner lives of men and women alike, but even as women are the prime victims of modern incivility, women have suffered most from the loss of soulful sensuality. We long to recapture the sensuous rhythms of the dance of romance we left behind. To do so, we must first listen to the lyrics of its swan song.

# 11

# *Backseat Follies*

Like the demise of civility, the death of romance came after a lingering illness. Contemporary conservatives see romance as a hit-and-run victim of the 1960s, the decade that whetted our appetites for loveless love-ins and letting it all hang out. But the sexual revolution merely euthanized an invalid whose fate was sealed long before, when the world stopped waltzing and started spinning out of control.

## WHO NEEDS THAT OLD-FASHIONED ROMANCE?

The devotees of twenties café society and the denizens of speakeasies aspired to "do it" like Cole Porter's amorous birds, bees, and educated fleas. Instead of making love, the bright young things of the Jazz Age just wanted to make whoopee. From the first herd of Miss America contestants parading in bathing suits through Atlantic City in 1921 to the new sensational movies that featured Max Sennett's bathing beauties, sex was suddenly everywhere, and no one wanted to miss out.

In *Only Yesterday*, his devastating chronicle of the Jazz Age, Frederick Lewis Allen described how its new, more permissive mores robbed love of its power and panache:

The intellectuals believed in a greater degree of sex freedom—and many of them found it disappointing when
they got it, either in person or vicariously through books
and plays. . . . Love was becoming too easy and too biological to be an object of respect. . . . The heroine of a postwar novel . . . indulged in 259 amours, if I remember
correctly, without getting the emotional wallop out of any
of them, or out of all of them together, that the lady of Victorian literature would have derived from a single compe-
tently completed seduction.

In his book *Haven in a Heartless World,* the social historian
Christopher Lasch traced the decline of romance that "set impossibly
high standards of devotion and loyalty" to sex manuals of the 1920s
and '30s that prescribed techniques for "stage-managing quarrels, the
technique of mutual agreement on how much adultery the marriage
could tolerate, the technique of what to do in bed and how to do it."
Lasch noted that in the same period the literature of grand fantasies,
consumptive heroines and impassioned suitors went out of fashion,
along with the "unhealthy" music of Wagner, Strauss, and Puccini.

Henceforth, sex, like work, was considered a pragmatic task to
be mastered by adopting a set of practiced skills. Sacraments had no
place in this budding science. "Sex does not need to be elevated into
something else after the fashion of those who advocate spiritualizing
marriage," opined Ernest Groves, a pop psychologist of the period. So
sex traded its magic and its mystique for the thrill of notoriety.[1]

Sex quickly degenerated from a class act into a sideshow. As
Frederick Lewis Allen noted: "Almost every human motive was attrib-
utable to it; if you were patriotic or liked the violin, you were in the
grip of sex—in a subliminated form. The first requirement of mental
health was to have an uninhibited sex life. If you would be well and
happy, you must obey your libido. Such was the Freudian gospel as it
imbedded itself in the American mind."

## Modern Girls

The new looser sexual mores of the twenties cheapened what the Victorians esteemed even more than sex—the worth and self-worth of
women. Hutchins Hapgood observed in his 1939 book, *A Victorian in*

*the Modern World,* that "the future mothers of the race no longer had that self-preservative instinct which is extremely difficult to maintain without the tradition of right living." In the guise of liberation, sexual license was only a means to exploit them, a legacy that lingers like a recurring infection. Then as now, notes the historian Linda Gordon in her 1976 book, *Woman's Body, Woman's Right,* women were offered and often accepted ersatz unions based on "arguments designed to show that love without marriage was infinitely superior to the other kind, and that its immediate indulgence brought the world, night by night, a little nearer to freedom and Utopia."

The Victorians believed that in morals as in manners, man would—and did—follow woman's lead. Our century revoked that feminine privilege when it legitimized the notion of love as a passing fancy. This was accomplished with the aid of a divide-and-conquer strategy, in which some women pressured others to conform to sliding standards. This compromised both all women's honor and the freedom of choice that has become our own religion. Early surveys quoted by Ellen Rothman in *Hands and Heart* show that women born after 1900 were twice as likely as their elders to "forego the sweetness of waiting." Holdouts were derided as "mid-Victorian." Ninety-two percent of Jazz Age coeds engaged in petting, and those who abstained were chronically dateless or on the defensive.

With STDs becoming an adolescent rite of passage as commonplace as acne, our grandparents' concern over petting may seem quaintly anachronistic. But getting to this base and all the others began turning sex into a game in which scoring eventually got boring. By 1936 *Forbes* magazine declared that on blasé college campuses "sex is no longer news."[2] (This same story line, suitably updated and embellished with details of contemporary practices, has proved a hardy perennial of weekly newsmagazines ever since.)

## Out of the Parlor

The key that unlocked the door of the sexual closet was a novel institution called dating. You don't have to be a prude to consider "date" a four-letter word. With the advent of this practice, women traded social power for physical pleasure. Feminist historians who regard women's loss of "virtue" as a gain in freedom should think again. Long before date rape became a movie-of-the-week cliché, the date established an insidious strain of male control that has been fluffed over by the innocent veneer of prom queens, sock hops, and beach-party movies.

Women were literally driven down the garden path. The automobile—that shining symbol of modernity and mass consumption—made dating, and parking, possible. When women began rutting in the rumble seat, it was only a matter of time before men would demand that they do it in the road. The historian Beth Bailey notes, in *From the Front Porch to the Back Seat,* that when wooing exited parlors and porches for restaurants, theaters, and dance halls, "One had to buy entertainment. . . . Money—men's money—became the basis of the dating system and, thus, of courtship. This new dating system, as it shifted courtship from the private to the public sphere and increasingly centered around money, fundamentally altered the balance of power between men and women in courtship."

During the previous century, it was women who, once they came of age, designated their "at home" days to receive gentlemen callers. In this female-governed world, a man needed permission to call, and undesirables were promptly turned away, like the luckless Freddie Hill in *My Fair Lady.* Despite repeated attempts by Freddie, flowers in hand, to see Eliza Doolittle, Professor Higgins's vigilant gatekeeper-housekeeper informed him that Miss Doolittle was "not at home," even when she was. The closest he came was the consoling joy of knowing he was "on the street where you live." Today only stalkers get a high from that knowledge.

If admitted callers stayed too long, made inappropriate remarks, or otherwise behaved rudely, a hovering chaperone would indicate that their behavior and future visits were unwelcome. Describing how the dating system abruptly shifted power between the sexes, Bailey writes:

> "Calling," as either a simple visit or as the elaborate late nineteenth-century ritual, gave women a large portion of control. First of all, courtship took place within the girl's home—in women's "sphere," as it was called in the nineteenth century—or at entertainments largely devised and presided over by women. Dating moved courtship out of the home and into man's sphere—the world outside the home. Female controls and conventions lost much of their power outside women's sphere. And while many of the con-

ventions of female propriety were restrictive and repressive, they had allowed women [young women and their mothers] a great deal of immediate control over courtship. The transfer of spheres thoroughly undercut that control.[3]

Women retained the prerogative to refuse a date, but once they consented, the man controlled the wheel, the purse strings, and the moves. At this late date, it is easy to forget how unthinkable this once was. The etiquette author Eliza Leslie explained in *Miss Leslie's Behaviour Book*:

> In her intercourse with gentlemen, a lady should take care to avoid all pecuniary obligations. The civility that a gentleman conventionally owes to a lady is a sufficient tax— more she has no right to expect, or to accept. A man of good sense, and of true politeness, will not be offended at her unwillingness to become his debtor. On the contrary, he will respect her delicacy and approve her dignity; and consent at once to her becoming her own banker on all occasions where expense is to be incurred.

## Pay Up or Else

The feminist version of the Dutch treat revived this arrangement but not the power women once enjoyed. Men no longer feel obliged to pay the tax of civility. Yet for many women, paying their share of the bill is not a choice but a presumption that is as awkward to negotiate as safe sex. Splitting a check won't change the way a guy treats a chick. That will require resurrecting the old esteem for women whereby they were treated as ladies first and lovers later. Like all matters of heart and conscience, this kind of change cannot be legislated, bought, or sold.

Even gifts from Victorian admirers, however well intentioned, were returned if their extravagance or implications compromised a woman's sovereignty. Eliza Leslie wrote:

> Young ladies should be careful how they accept presents from gentlemen. No truly modest and dignified woman

will incur such obligations. And no gentleman who really respects her will offer her any thing more than a bouquet, a book ... or a few relics or mementos of memorable places—things that derive their chief value from associations. But to present a young lady with articles of jewelry, or of dress, or with a costly ornament for the centre-table (unless she is his affianced wife,) ought to be regarded as an offense, rather than a compliment, excusable only in a man sadly ignorant of the refinements of society. And if he is so, she should set him right, and civilly, but firmly, refuse to be his debtor.

Like so many other aspects of life and love, the Victorians treated gifts as deeply symbolic. So without a permanent commitment (what used to be called "an understanding"), perishables like flowers and candy were the most acceptable tokens a man could give. Only then could a woman reciprocate. Even then, her gifts had to be "handmade and inexpensive," like a "drawing or a trifle from a needle." Like the rules of civility, these norms protected a woman's integrity, a man's solvency, and the uncorrupted value of what they shared. But dating, like prostitution, made all potential mating a balance sheet that debased and commercialized relations between the sexes and set the stage for our endless gender wars. Even old tokens of endearment lost their "sweetness and light." According to one person in the 1920s who reminisced about earlier days:

> The coal dealer and the gas man may fear the coming of summer—but florists aren't much worried over the fact that spring flowers will soon be growing in every front yard. . . . The days have gone by when a young man may pick a bouquet of flowers from his own yard and take them to his best girl. Nowadays she demands a dozen roses or a corsage bouquet bearing the name of the best florist.[4]

Girls lost far more than the gift of sentiment when their suitors began picking the florist instead of the flowers. Men began to grouse about unfavorable rates of exchange from women who reneged on their tacit obligations to those who purchased their meals and entertainment. Popular magazines from the Jazz Age routinely printed male complaints to this effect. The bluntness with which correspondents expressed these sentiments reminds us that women who accept the economic model of courtship had better be ready to give value for money.

For example, in 1924 one unsatisfied customer wrote a letter to a magazine to declare a "one-man buyer's strike" after estimating that, as a "buyer of female companionship" for the previous five years, he had "invested" about $20 a week—a grand total of over $5,000. Finally, he wrote, he had realized that "there is a point at which any commodity—even such a delightful commodity as female companionship—costs more than it is worth." The commodity he had bought with his $5,000 had been priced beyond its "real value," and he had had enough.[5]

Comparing the 1890s and 1920s in the seminal study *Middletown*, the sociologists Robert and Helen Lynd analyzed how such bluntly mercenary relations pressured women and priced them like cattle:

> Necking and petting were integral parts of the dating system, and to participate in the system, one had to meet its requirements. Furthermore, the dating system promoted sexual experimentation not only through the privacy it offered but also through the sense of obligation it fostered. Dating was an unequal relationship: the man paid for everything and the woman was thus indebted to him. According to many, boys and men were entitled to sexual favors as payment for the debt; the more money the man spent, the more petting the woman owed him.[6]

Back then male revenge may have been limited to dumping recalcitrant dates or smearing their reputations with locker-room tales of easy conquest. But the imagination doesn't have to leap very far to see the same perverted sense of entitlement in a Washington, D.C., man who recently unleashed his pit bull to attack a teenage girl who refused to undress on command. Indeed, the crude economics of woman's demands and her relative worth became a staple of advice columns down through the decades:

One late–1940s book for men suggested techniques for winning various "types" of women. For the "prom queen" (which the author considered an overpriced commodity), one must "spend money like water. You don't win prom princesses," he said, "you buy them—like show horses." Public sources, over and over, emphasized that women should be evaluated as if they were show animals. Women's value as dates—so far as they had individual value—lay in the impression they made, in how the possession of them made men look.[7]

Grading women from prime cuts to by-products reversed the cherished Victorian ideal of elevated womanhood. Christopher Lasch noted that sociologists who studied campus life in the 1930s saw "formal modes of true courtship" yielding to "dalliances" that exploited women. Social prestige took precedence over character in choosing a date or a temporary mate. Like smart clothes, smooth lines, fat wallets, and nimble feet that could jitterbug the night away, the human ornament on your arm was another way to gauge your popularity. However much fashions and dances have changed, we are the fruit that fell from this tree and has been rotting ever since.

## The Battle Lines Are Drawn

Lasch wrote that the equally ruthless and mathematical "rating and dating complex" that weighed so heavily in this equation fed the growing yen for thrill seeking at the cost of romance. There were no more Ralph Waldo Emersons to pen poems with titles such as his "Give All to Love." Making your mark on the social scene depended on using the opposite sex and avoiding emotional attachment.

Lasch also notes that the sociologist Willard Waller, who studied collegiate behavior between the two world wars, found fraternity "bull sessions" in which those who displayed dangerous symptoms of old-fashioned romance were "repeatedly warned that they are slipping, those who have fallen are teased without mercy, and others are warned not to be soft."

Waller could have been recounting tales from the trenches of any modern campus when he wrote, "Wary is the only word that I can apply to the attitude of men and women students towards each other.

A fundamental antagonism exists between [them]." One male student Waller interviewed described the cynical shell women developed to protect themselves from cold-blooded males. "They're out for what they can get. That's fine. So are we. Everything is one grand big joke. Many of the girls really fight against liking a boy. . . . One way in which they do this is the use of ridicule." Sound familiar?

This bitter joke turned the sweetness of romance into a struggle for survival of the fittest. Thus Christopher Lasch concluded, "The dating system repudiates those who make the mistake of falling in love and awards its highest prizes to the cynical."

## INTIMATE NEGOTIATIONS

Rather than liberating women, the changing rules left them in a position of being damned if they "did it" and damned if they didn't. By 1948, Kinsey was applauding widespread necking and petting as an essential part of high school and higher education. But then as now, girls remained understandably ignorant of how to cave in to sexual pressures, as popularity demanded, without losing popularity and self-worth by being labeled cheap. John D'Emilio and Estelle Freedman, in *Intimate Matters: A History of Sexuality in America*, report that one teenage girl summarized her dilemma this way: "The girl who permits

liberties is certainly popular with boys, but her popularity never lasts very long with any one boy. You know the saying 'Just a toy to play with, not the kind they choose to grow old and grey with.'"

The progression from women setting the sexual parameters to men making the rules began benignly enough, according to D'Emilio and Freedman. In 1905, the *Ladies' Home Journal's* "Lady from Philadelphia" advice column received a letter from "Sadie" asking what to do "when a man persists in holding your hand in spite of all that you can say." The answer: "No man, who is fit to be welcomed in your home, would refuse to release your hand if you asked him as if you meant it." This advice is the formula that persisted for decades, but with one important difference. Here, the man's liberties are not necessarily the woman's fault. If the woman is truly virtuous, and the man does not comply with her wishes, it is because he is not "fit to be welcomed in [her] home." That conditional term soon disappeared.

D'Emilio and Freedman also note that by 1914, the author of a later *Ladies' Home Journal* advice column, "Girls' Affairs," largely ignored men's possible role. A girl wrote from a coed college asking what to do about boys who refused to date girls who didn't allow "privileges." The adviser, Mrs. Parks, replied: "I think that girls are largely responsible for the attitude of boys in this matter; for if, whenever fun merged into familiarity, the girls would instantly check such conduct, the boys would soon learn what to expect whenever they dared trespass the barrier of a self-respecting manner."

The sagacious Mrs. Parks failed to mention that the maintenance of this barrier presumed not just self-respect from women but also male respect for women—which was steadily eroding in both the private and public spheres. Other historians noted how this devious double standard and the budding gender war persisted through the next several decades, while acceptable boundaries of casual sex kept stretching from necking and petting in the twenties to premarital intercourse by the fifties.

During the *Happy Days* era, girls still set the sexual limits but boys routinely pushed them, according to D'Emilio and Freedman. In turn, many girls were pushed into petting or coitus by "subtle pressure" or "outright aggression." They note that one pregnant sixteen-year-old who was seduced and abandoned poignantly summarized the dangerous rift between the sexes, even as they rocked around the clock together, and the resulting position of women—up against the wall: "How are you supposed to know what [boys] want? You hold out for a long time and then when you do give in to them and give your body they laugh at you afterwards and say they'd never marry a slut, and that they didn't love you but were just testing because they only plan to marry a virgin and wanted to see if you'd go all the way."

The Victorian ideal of sex as a sacred expression of devotion and elevated love became a distinctly female adjunct of virginity. As such, it was doomed to fight a losing battle against the duck-tailed conquistadors who enhanced their prestige among their buddies by cutting notches on their belts. No, I haven't forgotten the "good clean fun" of relatively sublimated traditions of the 1950s such as panty raids. But collecting lacy briefs or running them up a flagpole is hardly the twentieth-century equivalent of Newland Archer's attempt in *The Age of Innocence* to steal Ellen Olenska's parasol just long enough to kiss its handle.

The rituals of twentieth-century coupling replaced the sentimental passion that filled the yearning soul with a system that was designed to scratch an itch. By the 1940s and '50s, Beth Bailey reports, "relationship" experts were telling sexually inexperienced girls that "frigidity" was as bad as promiscuity and were urging them to find a middle way: "The person who is over-inhibited, excessively prudish, or unresponsive to the extent that he or she cannot or will not tolerate overt expressions of affection from a member of the opposite sex has just as great a problem as the person who aggressively goes as far as possible in petting on all dates."

In theory, this was a gender-neutral critique, but every teeny-bopper knew that the gropers and the gropees came equipped with different hormones. Young women learned this lesson every time they watched Doris Day play a repressed ice maiden who only needed the right man to melt her. The male version of this message was made explicit to moviegoers of the following decade, who saw James Bond use his virile charms to redeem a character named Pussy Galore from her lesbianism in *Goldfinger*.

Girls were told to stop complaining about male aggression and instead ask themselves how they had provoked it. Now we call this blaming the victim—the double whammy Victorian women were spared when they encountered cads, rogues, boors, reprobates, scoundrels, and other such swine. The varied pejoratives that were used to describe these offenders demonstrates where the blame was placed. The demise of these labels bespeaks how a serious moral crime became a misdemeanor that eventually required sexual harassment legislation and judicial intervention to restore its punch.

## NOT-SO-NIFTY FIFTIES

Today's conservatives yearn for a counterfeit "age of innocence" dating from the days of their own youth. They cannot look back far enough to see how much power women (along with love and decency) lost when wooing to the slow lyrical creak of a porch swing devolved into make-out sessions in the backseat of a T-bird. As Stephanie Coontz observed in *The Way We Never Were*, the halcyon fifties were no model for abstinence and deferred gratification: "'Heavy petting' became a norm of dating in this period, while the proportion of white brides who were pregnant at marriage more than doubled. Teen birth rates soared, reaching highs that have not been equaled since. In 1957, 97 out of every 1,000 girls aged fifteen to nineteen gave birth, compared to only 52 out of every 1,000 in 1983."

Bed hopping went mainstream in this era, however subtly it was portrayed by current standards. "Wink wink nudge nudge" was the formulaic response of popular entertainment to a public culture caught between an old order that was gone but not forgotten, and the first stirrings of the "anything goes" ethic that we now take for granted. On television during the late 1950s, for example, *The Bob Cummings Show* featured a swinging bachelor whose career as a photographer allowed him to caress his models as he positioned them for shots. His job also gave him the opportunity to play the field, sometimes juggling two or three dates in one evening. His promiscuity was not officially admitted, because he never took the "girls" home to bed in the house he shared with his widowed sister and her teenage boy.

Of course, this offstage denouement was leeringly implied in every episode of the *Cummings Show* (which was later syndicated under the title *Love That Bob*), just as *Three's Company* relied on the sniggering subtext of an unconsummated threesome two decades later. Soon thereafter, the leers began giving way to hoots on the laugh tracks of television's lascivious sitcoms. In the 1990s television gets its yucks from sex-starved newlyweds humping on the kitchen table while their dinner guests wait in the dining room. (All that distinguishes this scene in *Mad About You* from most of the prime-time competition is that the couple was married.) But what is explicit today was already implicit back in the not-so-innocent 1950s.

While television introduced winking innuendo to every family lucky enough to have a set, postwar America was bursting with pornography as well as prosperity. D'Emilio and Freedman point out that the demoralized youth of the land returned from World War I with the first pinup girl posters and cartloads of pornography acquired abroad. By the 1940s, corner drug stores for the first time openly sold cheap paperbacks with cheesecake and beefcake covers. In 1948 Popular Library tempted readers with its lurid "nipple cover" on the book *The Private Life of Helen of Troy*. Pornographic books, photos, movies, and records blossomed into a billion-dollar business by the mid–1950s. In 1952 Marilyn Monroe posed for her famous nude calendar. According to Russell Miller's book *Bunny*, the following year a shrewd Hugh Hefner bought the rights to it for $500 and published the first issue of *Playboy*. Summarizing the creed of the magazine and its founder, Miller wrote,

> Most of *Playboy*'s articles and ads were devoted to the idea that since women were only out to catch a man, men needed to learn how to get as much sex from them as possible without getting trapped. *Playboy* invited men to take over editorial areas of domestic and personal consumption formerly managed by females: food, clothes, wine, and body scents. Men didn't need a "purchasing agent for the home" anymore; all they needed was a nubile partner for the bedroom.

So much for the fabulous fifties. The emblem of this idyllically wholesome decade inverted the entire Victorian philosophy of women by pinning bunny tails on them. Hefner taught America that manhood meant living in silk pajamas surrounded by sex toys and accommodating babes that you proudly collected and displayed. An increasingly permissive culture opened a welcoming door to once-secret lives, making venereal disease (the dreaded "VD") the only remaining risk. If men no longer had honor, at least they had none to lose.

D'Emilio and Freedman note that "after World War II, pornography, as well as other media products that titillated males by sexually objectifying women's bodies, moved beyond their customary place in a marginal underground world." This was exactly where Victorian respectability, obscenity laws, and the veneration of women once kept them, even as purity crusaders like the notorious Anthony Comstock tried to expunge them.

## Sex as a Science

Sex was further brought out into the light of day by Alfred Kinsey and his apostles, who claimed that sexuality was a natural human function on the order of eating, drinking, breathing, and defecating. They waved the banner of animal sex, charted its different outlets like electric sockets, and taught us the importance of frequency, position, and technique. Directly or indirectly, this emphasis on performance justified casual sexual encounters, guiltless affairs, and quantity over quality of sexual experience. Orgasm was no longer seen as a shared glimpse of heaven but an end in itself—a mere physical function, not a transcendent experience.

By the Ozzie and Harriet era, women and men had abandoned the ideal of transcendent love. Ironically, as Christopher Lasch noted in *Haven in a Heartless World*, women's lowered expectations produced a rare gender consensus you could take to bed: "They no more wished to revive the nineteenth-century ideal of the lady than their husbands wished to pose as patriarchs. Both sexes, repudiating the mystical exaltation of womanhood formerly associated with the cult of romantic love, tried to ground marriage in . . . 'charm.'"

Behind the doors of those charming aluminum-sided homes and seemingly happy marriages, however, were some very unhappy women. According to doctors interviewed by Betty Friedan in the early 1960s for *The Feminine Mystique*, many wives were so sexually ravenous that their husbands couldn't sate them. Without a high-octane career—the new-feminist panacea—frustrated females had meaningless affairs, popped pills, or became psychoanalysis junkies. Sex stripped of old-fashioned romance was not a panacea, as Friedan observed:

> Instead of fulfilling the promise of infinite orgiastic bliss, sex in the America of the feminine mystique is becoming a strangely joyless national compulsion, if not a contemptuous mockery. The sex-glutted novels became increasingly explicit and increasingly dull; the sex kick of the women's magazines has a sickly sadness; the endless flow of manuals describing new sex techniques hint at the endless lack of excitement.[8]

The Victorian sexual mystique that led to women being treated with respect and even reverence had been replaced by a "Playboy philosophy" that confused mere rutting with the art of romance. But women lost far more than window dressing when intimacy became a gender impasse instead of a shared religion. Modern marriage was viewed as a sexual partnership, yet husbands and wives often approached the conjugal bed with widely divergent expectations about the meaning of sex. Many women hoped for love and affection; their partners sought orgasmic relief. The companionate ideal posited equality between spouses, yet wives remained economically dependent, aware that failure in marriage spelled disaster. As D'Emilio and Freedman wrote in *Intimate Matters*, in the fifties

> . . . marital ideals prescribed that [a wife] be an erotic companion to her husband, that the happiness of marriage would grow in proportion to the sexual magic generated between husband and wife. By the 1960's . . . wives could look with concern at the sexual competition they faced from women who did not have to change diapers or cook for a family. For her part, the single woman might forever question her own femininity, lacking as she was the central attribute of motherhood. Whether dutiful wife or alluring single, the American woman was left to wonder whether she made the grade.

Some of the conflicts that American women faced were embedded within the new system of sexual liberalism. As the birth control pill lessened the dangers of pregnancy and the media portrayed the glamour of the single life, young women who had helped shape an ethic of "permissiveness with affection" found the rules suddenly altered. Placed on the defensive, they rapidly lost the right to say no that nineteenth-century feminists had struggled to obtain. We have not, it seems, come a long way, baby.

## A COMMENDABLE HYPOCRISY

Of course, Victorian bashers love to point to the hypocrisy of those Victorian "gentlemen" who secretly indulged in dirty books, French postcards, and local prostitutes, disdaining a society that looked away from moral slumming to keep its petticoats clean. But such hypocrisy had a commendable purpose: The Victorians followed La Rochefoucauld's sage maxim "Hypocrisy is an homage vice pays to virtue." We modern sophisticates would eliminate hypocrisy by lowering our virtues until they correspond to our vices. But the Victorians were consummate strivers who kept reaching for the heavens, even when they slipped and lost their footing. They knew that rewriting the script to make ideals conform to reality would only destroy the ideals and degrade the reality.

Even the most inveterate debauchers understood the need to sin discreetly and pay severely if they were caught. For example, the eminent architect Stanford White never dared parade his sweet young things—some of them very young—through the parks and reputable parlors of New York. His was the classic double life. His wife and family resided in the country, while he enjoyed his paramours and his erotica collection in a carefully chosen urban hideaway equipped with mirrored ceilings and a red velvet swing.

White came to what the Victorians considered an appropriate end. In 1906 he was shot and killed by the millionaire Harry Thaw. This self-appointed avenger discovered that several years earlier, White had unceremoniously deflowered Thaw's wife-to-be, the showgirl Evelyn Nesbit, after allegedly rendering her unconscious with champagne. After White's various escapades were exposed in the ensuing sensational trial, denunciations of his behavior issued from the pulpit, the press, and even the presidency. These were the days when death did not redeem a sinner. A resolution introduced in Congress denounced his "loathsome and licentious acts" for their "demoralizing influence on the youth of the land." Today, Mr. White would be driving to the bank to deposit his $2 million advance against royalties for a tell-all autobiography.

Sadly, after all these years of mechanical tinkering with the relationship between sex, love, and passion, we have stripped the gears of romance and left women to walk home. Our flashy new vehicle of casual sex somehow does not work as well as the old reliable romantic monogamy did and we can't figure out what went wrong, or how to get back to where we started.

# 12

# *The Religion of Romance*

The Victorians looked at love in the same way they looked at life—as a holistic fusion of one's body, mind, and eternal soul. It was this transcendent fusion—as opposed to a narrow focus on physical or even merely mortal love—that made their passion so gloriously great, consuming, and complete. This is why we mistake great sex for grand passion.

The Victorians made a religion of love, believing it lifted them up into a transcendent realm of experience. This exalted ideal was commonly expressed in inspirational terms of endearment far richer and sweeter than any "honey"—the best we can muster. To Nathaniel Hawthorne, his wife's love letters were "spiritual food." So ardent was his veneration of the feast that his adored Sophie supplied, writes the historian Karen Lystra, that he wrote, "I keep them to be the treasures of my still and secret hours, such hours as pious people spend in prayer; and the communion which my spirit then holds with yours has something of religion in it." Among the courtship letters of ordinary Victorians studied by the historian Ellen Rothman was that of a college student who told his fiancée, "You have been my very soul."

Today's woman can choose from models of masculinity that range from the sensitive "postfeminist" male to socially sanctioned sides of beefcake. But can we imagine any of them, from Tom Cruise to Fabio, describing sex like the Victorian swain Austin Dickinson, who, when writing to his beloved Mabel, called it a "consecration" and "the white heat that engulfs my being"?

## NOT-SO-GREAT EXPECTATIONS

Indeed, while Victorian passion thrived on great expectations, we bring cynical and dispiriting apprehensions to the tentative venture of love and marriage. This wet-blanket attitude was rampant among welfare mothers recently profiled in an article in *The Washington Post*. "I don't know what people get married for," said one resigned twenty-something woman. "For stability or security or what? That would just make you co-dependent on some man."[1]

Declining marriage rates among rich and poor alike reflect the deep disillusionment with any chance that love is forever. In her book *The Hearts of Men*, the journalist and author Barbara Ehrenreich warns women that their relations with men will be brief, "punctuated by emotional dislocations, and seldom offering the kind of loyalty that might extend into middle age." So use men for sex, she counsels, but rely only on women for friendship, support, and every other human need men are too inhuman to meet. Better yet, rely completely on yourself and the insurance company whose ad tells women to "Be Your Own Rock," presumably with suitable investments. This unchallenged gospel touts the mental equivalent of safe sex—protect yourself at any cost or it will cost you plenty.

We may steel our hearts and bank accounts against assault, but steel is no substitute for poetry, passion, or the love we are supposed to learn to live without. Since Gloria Steinem compared the utility of men to women as that of a bicycle to a fish, women have asserted that they don't need men to be happy or fulfilled. Some actually believe it—independence is loneliness that learns to smile. Many settle for the warmth of whatever hairy body they can find, but I have yet to meet any woman who could imagine a religion of love. "[H]ow can you make the sexes act as if they needed each other to survive when they don't?" asked *Nation* editor Katha Pollitt in a *New York Times* article. "All they need each other for is love, and love is hard to find."

To reweave all the threads we have severed—love, marriage, children—Pollitt says, "We would have to bring back the whole nineteenth century." This threat is supposed to send shivers down your unnostalgic spine, so that you keep the world secure for all the commitment-challenged hedgers and vacillators who cover their rears even when they're naked. Otherwise you might crave the old-time religion, with all its rules and demands, its unbreakable bonds, and its bared and vulnerable hearts.

## Till Divorce Court Do Us Part

Even if you have the best modern knockoff—a sustained relationship—take care to treat it cavalierly. No more "white heat that engulfs my being." Even the Hollywood celebrities who have turned yesterday's "alternative" lifestyles into today's norm can't handle the heat of that kitchen. For example, the actress Susan Sarandon, a sex symbol for the over-forty set, enjoys a long-term live-in relationship complete with children. In an interview with *Cosmopolitan* magazine, she offered this verbal shrug on infidelity: "If someone is very special to you, is it really that important if every now and then he takes off and has a liaison with someone else? I mean, is it really a great catastrophe?"

Yes, but only if your love life is something more than a mutually satisfying arrangement between independent contractors. Not everybody in Lala-land goes along with this enlightened approach. Still, there's no question which values set the tone for the town that sets the tone for towns around the country. Closet monogamists tread lightly in the land of the cutting edge. Even professional tough guy Bruce Willis avoids bruising the feelings of his fellow celebs by not imposing his own lifestyle choice on them: "I believe in monogamy for myself, although it works for very few people."[2]

Cynical about their future, many up-to-date spouses are deadly serious about protecting their possessions and their precious space. Separate finances, separate vacations, even separate homes protect what's "yours" and "mine" from becoming "ours." In the process, they protect you and me from becoming us. Promises that were once etched on the heart are now inscribed in the dry legalese of prenuptial agreements. These contracts provide an escape clause for those who fear being locked into what was once quaintly termed "holy wedlock." One prudent young couple featured on *World News Tonight* specified every particular, from who will keep the budget and fill the gas tank to how often they will have sex. Any breach of any clause extracts a fine—picking up the tab for dinner. Should these parties of both parts ever permanently nullify this agreement, they can take comfort in the current catchword that terms a first union a "starter marriage," where you learn the ropes for the second.

## COMMUNING VS. COMMUNICATING

Unlike today's pop psychologists, who pontificate about how hard it is for "partners" in a "relationship" to really "communicate" with each other, it is hard to imagine Victorian couples expressing their feelings in terms of "soul communing." When souls failed to commune, their failure was not shrugged off as a mere bust in the bedroom or a bad experience to be brushed off like dandruff. It was seen as a moral disaster. Because sex was "the highest part of your nature and should be held sacred," observed Henry C. Wright in his 1855 book *Marriage and Parentage,* sex devoid of spirit was "coarse, selfish, polluted, and necessarily tends to denigrate and profane both body and soul."

This message squarely hit the broken home of an embittered Elizabeth Cady Stanton. According to her biographer Elizabeth Griffith, after separating from her husband, Cady Stanton wrote to a cousin lamenting that she and Henry Stanton no longer shared "the joy of a deep soul love." During their long marriage she relished "connubial relations," but scorching the sheets was not enough. "Soul union should precede and exalt physical union," she said. "Without sentiment, affection, imagination, what better would we be in procreation than the beasts?"

We still ask that question, though the sad state of modern love and the ongoing war between the sexes renders it prophetic rather than rhetorical. It is not only Hollywood hedonism that turns the rhapsodic into the prosaic. While we might expect more talk of souls and sentiment from the religious right, they too offer an erotic wasteland. For example, Tim and Beverly LaHaye's bestselling seventies marriage guide gave this tediously literal take on sacred sex: "Be fruitful and multiply." Keeping up with the times, the LaHayes assured their readers that conception is not the only legitimate purpose of their God-given plumbing: Intercourse is also for pleasure and "marital communication." Where is the poetry in this pious benediction of bodily delights? Where is the passion? This Bible-thumping brand of therapeutic psychobabble is as estranged from the Victorians' "spiritual food" as the low-rent epicureanism of *Melrose Place*.

We have so desecrated sex and love that we find it appropriate instead to consecrate their dissolution. Some ministers now perform divorce ceremonies so couples can feel that untying the knot is divinely condoned. This four-hundred-dollar package includes personalized prayers, a ritualistic burning of the marriage certificate or other related items, and a perverse exchange of rings. For those determined to erase all evidence of their connubial blunder, a service called Divorce X will use the wonders of modern technology to edit your former spouse or any other undesirables out of your wedding pictures. In the ultimate denial of what was once a union "till death do us part," you can even order a pure self-portrait.

## A RICH TAPESTRY OF LOVE

Those serious young couples in Victorian wedding photographs, on the other hand, understood dying for love, as Sidney Carton did in *A Tale of Two Cities*, or dying from its loss, as the eponymous Anna Karenina did. They would not, however, have understood either the Hollywood inamoratas who love and let love or the lawyerly lovers who begin their romance with contingency plans. To our ancestors, love that was ephemeral and divisible was unworthy of the name. But the only eternity left to today's lovers is the one that has elapsed since people fervently believed in the title of the William Morris poem, "Love Is Enough."

In an age where love has become a high-wire act that requires the safety net of divorce and the services of plaintiff's attorneys, we experience a gulf between the Victorians' cup-runneth-over faith in love and our own cup-is-half-empty cynicism. Nowhere is this clearer than in the enormous change in the valentine card.

### *Forever Yours*
Victorian valentines were so lavish and expensive, they were often gifts in themselves. Although simple printed cards like ours could be had for pennies, men tried to buy the best, and women often made their own.

During the Civil War, when many soldiers made about fifteen dollars a month, a smitten suitor would spend as much as ten dollars on a single card. By the 1890s, the price of luxury cards topped twenty-five dollars.

Those costly tokens of love, and the feelings they expressed, became treasured keepsakes that both sexes displayed in the privacy of the bedroom, despite their distinctly feminine look. These intricate confections of filigree lace paper could be painted, gilded, or silvered, even fragranced, and were often so thick they came packed in presentation boxes. Trimmed with silk, satin, feathers, leaves, or dried and wax flowers, they featured universal symbols of love such as hearts, doves, cupids, or bows and arrows. Some unfolded like fans, while mechanical valentines had levers or disks that made figures dance, hands move, and birds flutter their wings. These unique and memorable cards remained popular until the 1920s, when morals, manners, clothes and interior décor converted to a new religion: Less is more. Its believers got less than they bargained for.

The lyrics printed on Victorian valentines were as effusive as their appearance. Whether sent by a steady beau proposing or a secret admirer finally confessing his feelings, these cards were unabashedly sentimental, pleading for the affections of "my sweetheart" or "my one and only." They pledged undying devotion happily ever after, and delighted in complete surrender to the rule of love.

*Victorian valentines were often elaborate and unabashedly sentimental in their verses.*

The sweeping amorous certainties that impassioned the past have dissolved in the ephemeral, evasive, fence-sitting emotions that give modern valentine cards the solidity of a cloud. According to researchers at Hallmark's Val Lab, love is such a traumatizing gamble that the "L-word" is used sparingly, if at all. There is a "real need for a more guarded message," according to one company rep, so cards are designed more to soothe the nervous giver than to please his partner. Such cards "talk about waking up beside you or your touch. Something like that." Alternatively, flippancy or ridicule are easy fallbacks that save face and mask the fears of wading into love's deep waters. "Be my Valentine," says one such card. "I've already told people we're sleeping together."

Even admissions of love are neutralized by turning every body part except the heart into the object of affection. Cards that rhapsodize over a well-shaped butt may be the perfect way to express affection in a Beavis-and-Butthead world. The next logical step is the proliferation of smutty "love" cards, whose sentiments don't bear repeating. All these cards represent the ultimate out for a culture that prefers the upper hand and cool detachment to the terrifying risk of surrender.

### The Lost Language of Love

Today's language of love ruthlessly demeans the intimate experience the Victorians cherished. All the beaux, swains, admirers, the admired, the beloveds are gone. Sweethearts have become the squeezes we wring dry before moving on to fresh ones. Instead of courtship, we have relationships, as we do with hairdressers or tennis partners. Even the meaning of making love has narrowed from all the feelings, stages, words, and gestures of wooing to specific physical acts that lump us in with any other mating beast. How appropriate that sexual malaise drives us to shrinks who help accommodate us to our emotionally downsized culture.

Like prayer, the Victorian language of love was exclusive to itself. By contrast, our present-day sexual vocabulary borrows from the lingo of animals, mechanics, and sports. It seems only too appropriate that scientists are debating the presence of higher emotions in animals while they study the mating behavior of humans. If we share a mailbox and a bed, we "cohabit" like any other domestic animal.

When we copulate, we "perform" like seals. When we do so frequently, the appropriate reference is to minks. An attractive male is a hunk, a female is a piece. Both are available postmortem from a butcher.

## THE SENSUOUS—AND SENTIMENTAL—MALE

Victorian men relished the full menu of tender words and touches that really light a woman's fire. "Days and weeks go by when it would be wine to see even the hem of your dress," one man wrote to his sweetheart in 1883.[3] Women's hands were considered intensely erotic in an age that did not measure arousal in the stretch of a string bikini. Smooth, shapely feminine hands were reproduced everywhere in the form of candy dishes, card holders, ring stands, even drapery tiebacks.

In the days before groping was socially acceptable dating behavior, women expected their hands to be lavished with a lover's kisses, especially as his first physical display of devotion. Thus, at the turn of the nineteenth century, a middle-aged widower launched his courtship of a widow with a letter revealing his desire to kiss her fingertips. Subsequent correspondence shows that they maintained their charms for him even after marriage. Elizabeth Barrett Browning later described in one of her sonnets from the Portuguese the "First time he kissed me, he but only kiss'd / The fingers of this hand wherewith I write; / And ever since, it grew more clean and white."

Every woman knows the earth-moving power of subtle sensuality, even if she knows it only by its absence. Women crave the little things that mean a lot. They want love as a total experience of all the ways and reasons one is loved, like those in this breathtaking letter that still pulses with passion a century after it was written: "I kiss your cheeks, dear Little Girl, and that's for friendship. I kiss your brow, sweet Lady Violet, and that's for reverence. . . . And I stoop to cover the soft warm lips with a lover's kisses—many and long—and lingering Lover's kisses, dear. . . . No one in the world—no one else, can kiss you as I do. My darling."[4]

Men are still enthralled by women's body parts, though not as parts of a glorious whole. We have butt men, breast men, and leg men, like those who favor particular pieces of roast chicken. Fan magazines rate the specific parts of Hollywood stars, while family newspapers like *The New York Times* routinely run steamy clothing ads that zoom in on bare cleavage, half-unzipped crotches, and peek-a-boo rears. Ignored are the feminine features once cherished by literature, art, and life. In his lush poem titled "Ruth," Thomas Hood rhapsodized over the assets that are now shortchanged: "Round her eyes her tresses fell, / Which were blackest none could tell, / But long lashes veil'd a light, / That had else been all too bright."

When men loved women piece by piece, rather than regarding them *as* a piece, their love was exalting rather than degrading because its object was always esteemed as far more than the sum of its parts. A woman was a work of art—rather than an orifice—to be admired from every angle, in every light. Passion was stirred by what seem like "nothings—by an untied shoe-lace, by a glance of the eye in passing."[5] The loss of these sweet "nothings" stripped women's worth to bare meat and bones. By the same token, it deadened men's sensibilities to a treasure trove of pleasures. Today, the mere turn of a feminine ankle no longer turns the heads of males who can go to the movies to look up Sharon Stone's skirt. We have to take Bill Clinton's word as to whether he wears boxers or briefs, but viewers of *Basic Instinct* could see for themselves that Ms. Stone wears neither.

*Part of croquet's immense popularity during the last century was the chance the game offered to glimpse a lady's petticoat or ankle when she placed her foot on the ball.*

When sex is treated as nothing more than a bodily sensation—as "only the thrill of boy meeting girl," in the words of a popular song—the quest for that sensation becomes an addiction in which ever-increasing doses are required to produce ever-diminishing effects. As a character in the crossover soft-core porno flick *Showgirls* observes coolly during a Las Vegas strip-show scene, "In America every man is his own gynecologist." In a society that has ruthlessly physicalized feminine allure, the religion of love is reduced to the physiology of lust.

Explaining the appeal of the aesthetically alien film *The Age of Innocence*, one critic, Andrew Delbanco, noted that in the movie, "The only removal of clothing comes in an intensely erotic scene when Archer, pressed close against Ellen in a narrow brougham, unbuttons and peels back her tight, calfskin gloves and kisses her exposed skin and wrists." Because Newland Archer ventures no further, "He touches a nerve in us."[6] Would a carriage quickie with Countess Ellen Olenska have been as resonant or arousing as these nuanced gestures?

Even sounds have been deromanticized and disimpassioned by our painfully literal view of sex. We understand the grunts and groans of bumps and grinds. But can they fire the imagination like the music of an unseen petticoat? "Drapery but enhances the estimation in which men hold the female attractions of the person," wrote the physician Nicholas Cooke in 1870. "The rustle of a woman's garment is more potent to charm than the lavish exposure of the proportions of a Venus." The fashion historian Alison Gernsheim noted that in 1902 some fashion arbiters decreed that audible petticoats were "vulgar." Yet, as Gernsheim notes, women refused to relinquish their glacé silk and taffeta lingerie for quieter satins and brocades, because husbands enjoyed such suggestive sounds. Can we say the same for the snap of a Spandex body suit?

## A SENTIMENTAL JOURNEY

The open sentimentalism of Victorian men makes their descendants seem like another species. Yet the culture of sentimentality that once nourished great romance has long been a target of historical and rhetorical scorn. Consider our contemporary understanding of this onetime Victorian virtue. *Webster* tells us that a sentimentalist is "unduly" influenced by tender feelings, and *Roget* reminds us that its connotations include the sappy, the syrupy, and the maudlin. The psychoanalytic pioneer C. G. Jung called sentimentality "a superstructure covering brutality." And the historian Milton Rugoff claimed, "There was a tendency to gloss over such primal urges [as sex], to veil, to gild, prettify, idealize or sentimentalize them, or simply push them into the cellars of the mind."

By this myopic logic, sentiment is lethal to sex. But since when did heat preclude warmth? The Victorians had their ultrarich cake and ate it too because both men and women savored every taste of love. The ladies were legendary for collecting immense albums of romantic keepsakes such as pressed flowers and souvenirs of excursions. Favored gents eagerly contributed a sketch or a few lines of poetry. This was an age that courted by the faint flickers of light given off by small domed glass or ceramic fairy lamps, even though gaslight and eventually electricity made candlepower obsolete. An historian of decorative arts calls this nostalgic ritual "incredible." But if we accept the Victorians on their terms, this practice is hardly as surprising as the escalating value of those bewitching little lamps.

The allegedly repressed Nathaniel Hawthorne possessed a singular literary talent, yet his expression of sentiment was far from unique when he slept with his wife's letters next to his heart while away from home. Like knights who took their ladies' scarves into battle, Victorian males carried women's locks of hair or pictures in their pocket-watch cases. You won't find such sentimental tokens on a man's Timex.

Gone are the men who cherished what contemporary males now dismiss as female stuff. In love, as in civility, true manhood melded what John Ruskin called delicate sympathies and fineness of nature with masculine strength.[7] Victorian men lived and died for love in ways as tragically poignant as the heroes who went down with the *Titanic* after escorting their wives and children into the lifeboats. The crusty newspaper editor Horace Greeley died of a broken heart shortly after the death of his wife. When consumption claimed James Tissot's adored young model, the artist took refuge from the world in an abbey, where he died.

Jilted men also bore deep scars. Even love lost was so important that wounded hearts could never grow blasé. The English poet

Arthur Symons wrote: "And I would have, now love is over, / An end to all, an end: / I cannot having been your lover, / Stoop to become your friend." Now sundered couples and spouses boast about remaining friends, and the television series with the name *Friends* celebrates friends who are sometimes sexual partners but never lovers. Our casual attitude toward friendship and love alike would make romantic Victorians cringe. To them love was not a mood or a pair of ships that docked together at their mutual convenience; love, in the words of poet George Henry Boker, was "the orbit of the soul."

## Real Men Say I Love You

How the mighty feelings have fallen. Today talk-show shrinks are constantly urging men to emulate women by expressing their intimate feelings. Although we assume that men have always by nature been emotionally challenged, our national religion of communication is determined to convert them to sissies, despite biology, dysfunctional backgrounds, or whatever else has greased their flies but stitched their lips together. For example, in the hit film *Ghost*, Patrick Swayze can respond "I love you" to his significant other, Demi Moore, only at the end of the movie. Until then, he can only mutter an aloof "Ditto" when she voices her affections.

Like Ms. Moore's character, women know they must pull teeth for something more than a "Ditto" or a grunt. Our impoverished males desperately need a history lesson. Even the manliest Victorian males reveled in pouring out their passion to the women who inspired such sentiments in them. This is one equal right and shared pleasure that women have lost, thanks to the shifting cultural sands whereby true confessions were once encouraged but now "sensitive" men are scorned with peer pressure and ridicule for sounding like the clown-ish characters in Harlequin novels.

## Letters from the Heart

In private love letters, middle- and upper-middle-class Victorian males fairly exploded with feeling, manifesting as much emotional intensity and range as their wives and sweethearts. In the extreme privacy of romantic relationships, men's emotional expression flour-ished, contrary to the stereotype of the emotionally constricted Victo-rian male. The historian Karen Lystra writes, "The range, depth, and intensity of masculine emotional expression in love letters challenges any unqualified generalization that nineteenth-century men were less emotional or less forthcoming about their feelings than nineteenth-century women."

Our minimalist approach to love has had its day in the sun, and it has left us parched and singed. Victorian love was effusive and ageless, not the sole province of smitten young studs with abs of steel. In 1890 the staid sixty-year-old college bureaucrat Austin Dickinson sent this torrential letter to his mistress:

> I must tell you . . . that you are my love, that I love you with a wild, passionate love, with all the love there is in love—the finest, the tenderest, the sweetest, the highest, the greatest, the most dependent, with all my heart, and soul, and mind and strength. . . . That in you in our eight years of closest intimacy, in which we have penetrated the most veiled recesses, each of the other—always with delight—I have found you only fresher, more charming each day—ever new.[8]

A definite step above "Ditto," especially for an old warhorse whom our youth-crazed era would put out to pasture. The fire of this amorous missive cannot be brushed off as a relic from a letter-writing age—writing letters being a lost art that enhanced every part of life—or the thrill of adultery. Only a bloodless cynic would believe this impassioned couple, or any couple, "penetrated the most veiled recesses, each of the other" just on paper. Victorian love existed in the flesh as well as in the imagination.

Mark Twain's connubial affections for his "better half" never cooled through three decades of marriage. In the correspondence that bridged their long separations, this old-school "man's man" bared his captive heart without ever doubting the potency of his other organs:

> I do love you, Livy—as the dew loves the flowers; as the birds love the sunshine; as the wavelets love the breeze; as mothers love their first-born; as memory loves old faces; as the tides love the moon; as angels love the pure in heart. I

so love you that if you were taken from me it seems as if all my love would follow after you and leave my heart a dull and vacant ruin forever and forever.[9]

This was no idle prediction. Losing his beloved Olivia devastated the aging Twain and severely darkened the last phase of his fiction. Recounting the wrenching moment he found her dead after a long illness, he wrote that she was "unresponsive to my reverent caresses—a new thing to me and a new thing to her that had not happened before in five and thirty years." Marriages made in heaven may be a rarity in every century, but without a religion of love, love remains as hopelessly stuck on earth as the tongue-tied young lover in *Ghost*.

## Even Presidents Get Smitten

According to his biographer Edmund Morris, Teddy Roosevelt, the quintessential man's man, publicly and privately indulged his obsession for his first and greatest love, Alice Lee. Before she accepted his pressing proposals, he so feared someone would steal her that he carried a pair of French dueling pistols around with him. When heart sickness sent him on endless insomniac wanderings through frigid winter woods, his alarmed Harvard classmates appealed to the Roosevelt family for help.

It would sorely tax modern minds and male egos to envision this rough-riding big-game hunter reading poetry to his wife or mooning in his journal over his "sweet queen." One critic, reviewing a PBS documentary on Theodore Roosevelt, marveled at TR's ability to combine "the soul of a poet and the hide of a rhinoceros."[10] But Roosevelt's blend of outer toughness and inner tenderness was precisely what men of his time aspired to and admired in him. TR may have been a fool for love, but in his day, only jealous fools would have mocked him. What manner of "today's man" could fill this Renaissance man's boots?

Another Oval Office occupant displayed the same dual nature, although he and Roosevelt were cut from different cloth. The reserved and bookish Woodrow Wilson also suffered the untimely loss of his adored wife. But when an attractive widow caught his fancy, this bespectacled midlife widower sent her countless boxes of orchids and amorous letters, as many as three or four a day. We might label such surface contradictions as hypocritical or crazy, but this duality was fundamental to Victorian romance. As Robert Browning wrote: "God be thanked, the meanest of his creatures / Boasts two soul-sides, one to face the world with, / One to show a woman when he loves her."

## TWO SOULS UNITED AS ONE

The public soul and the private soul were equally real, and equally vital to protecting the exalted creed of love. We too draw lines, but they compromise love's power and uniqueness by exalting individuals above the bond that unites them. Even committed mates jealously guard their space. Women especially are warned by relationship experts that subsuming their identity to a man's promotes low self-esteem and male dominance in the endless gender wars.

This war was as alien as singles' bars in the world of Victorian love. "Men and women . . . viewed each other not as useful performers in the drama of survival, not as antagonists in the battle of the sexes, but as two-in-one, a united being," writes Karen Lystra. Thus, couples reveled in "the deep silent look in each other's eyes . . . the consciousness of nearness, even to the absolute unison of being."

Passion was not a product of contests or separate checks. As civility and morality presumed some sacrifice of personal freedom by each that repaid all a hundredfold, the solid gold ring of love required both the emotional and ritual wedding of two becoming one. Yet there was no short change in this bargain. Although wives were legally subservient to husbands during the nineteenth century, it was men who longed to experience feminine sensibilities. As Ford Maddox Ford wrote in *The Good Soldier*:

> The real fierceness of desire, the real heat of a passion long withering up the soul of a man is the craving for identity with the woman that he loves. He desires to see with the same eyes, to touch with the same sense of touch, to hear with the same ears, to lose his identity, to be enveloped, to be supported . . . to come to her for the renewal of his courage, for the cutting asunder of his difficulties.

This is quite a contrast to the his-and-hers standoff of women anxiously policing their turf and macho watchdogs who could never imagine relinquishing theirs. The most politically correct couples would believe, or at least parrot, this especially progressive 1870 definition of marriage as an "alliance [where] neither is superior, neither inferior. Their qualities mingle by exchange. The wife is strengthened by the husband, who in turn is made better by the wife." Victorian men knew that woman was the key to a sublime high—the kind that men now seek in fast cars, drugs, and sports. Mark Twain wrote, "My whole being is permeated, is renewed, is leavened with this love, and with every breath I draw its noble influence makes of me a better man."

Because women were so exalted—emotionally, sexually, and spiritually—they alone could provide the magic carpet ride that exulted men beyond any other thrill. Masculinity was fortified, not diluted, by the loved and loving woman who fulfilled what Austin Dickinson called "the sweetest, richest dreams of my boyhood, youth, and early manhood. That I found in you what a woman may be to a man, hope, courage, joy, inspiration, rest, peace, religion!"

Victorian men who knew the meaning of true masculinity embraced the wisdom expressed in this line from a poem by John Ruskin: "Lay thou thy soul full in her hands, low at her feet." Now the only entity willing to stoop to those depths is Nike Inc. "You are not a goddess," proclaims their magazine ad for a woman's walking shoe, "and most likely you never will be a goddess, but just because you are human that doesn't mean we can't worship the ground you walk on."

Today most women would jog barefoot over broken glass if only their love were returned in kind. But for Victorian men, simply reciprocating love was paltry gratitude for the precious gift they lived for and would die for. During his dogged pursuit of the suffragist Lucy Stone, Henry Blackwell said that he felt so ennobled by her affections, he would constantly strive to prove himself worthy. "I reverence you, as well as love you," he wrote a few months after their marriage in 1855. "I long for opportunities to manifest to you the love which fills my soul." His forty years of devotion to her and her cause redeemed that promise.[11]

If heaven turned into hell, some Victorians did divorce. But that comparative rarity was not only a personal tragedy and a social disgrace, it was also the morally devastating fall of religious ideals that nourished the highest romantic expectations. For us divorce seems as permanent as roadway gridlock. We will never reduce its frequency or its toxicity to the heart so long as it is plumbed into the architecture of life and love.

An entry from Theodore Roosevelt's journal illustrates the delicious tension and thrill we have lost by divorcing sex from the sacred. Meeting Alice after a long separation, he noted that she had "a certain charm that I do not know how to describe; I cannot take my eyes off her; she is so pure and holy that it seems almost a profanation to touch her, no matter how gently and tenderly; and yet when we are alone I cannot bear her to be a minute out of my arms."

At the core of this antimacho sentiment was an ideal that all men ought to treat all women respectfully, in gestures small and large: chivalry.

# 13

# Wives and Lovers

It was not only maidens who were protected by Victorian notions of chivalry. In an age that venerated women, romance, and the unsundered bonds of those joined by God, even marital sex was regarded as prostitution or outright rape if it was dictated purely by male demands. The author Eliza Duffey forcefully stated this case in 1876, over a century before its belated rediscovery became a talk-show staple: "I see . . . women who feel that they bear the brand of the prostitute within their souls, because they are forced to yield their bodies unwillingly to gratifying that which they can regard in no other light than selfish lust, hallowed as it is by no mutual desire, nor exalted by self forgetting impulse."

To the woman who wondered what to do when her husband wanted sex and she didn't, Duffey advised that she "should give or withhold her favors according to her own best judgment, uninfluenced either by fear or over-persuasion," for a man's only marital rights were "to take what is granted to him freely and lovingly. A woman is no more bound to yield her body to her husband after the marriage between them, than she was before, until she feels that she can do so with the full tide of willingness and affection."

## MUTUAL AFFECTION

Duffey was not alone in condemning what was called the "phallic worship" that threatened the physical and moral integrity of women. Many male physicians and clerics advocated full equality of bedroom perks. Sounding distinctly modern and even politically correct, Rev. Sylvanus Stall wrote in 1897, "As mutual affection is the heavenly bond of marriage, so mutual pleasure should also sanction its earthly bond. . . . No sorer punishment could be inflicted than to be deprived of the right of ruling over one's own body." Any breach of that rule was "conjugal debauchery" and a "gross insult to womanhood."

In his 1881 work, *Sexual Physiology*, Dr. R. T. Trall accused carnally selfish men of turning spouses into "mere machines." Likewise, Dr. Nicholas Cooke asserted in 1870, "Nothing should induce a man to gratify his own desires at the expense of his wife's comfort or inclination." Only rapists engaged in "unreciprocated passional indulgence," wrote Henry Wright in his 1855 book on marriage—a crime deserving of "the gallows or the dungeon."

While shared desire was both expected and considered ideal, the Victorians believed the female psyche and the burdens of pregnancy made woman first among equals. Men might rule the world, but women ruled the bed. (Now, having been liberated, they rule neither.) "The wife must decide how often and under what circumstances the husband may enjoy the passional expression of his love," said marital adviser Dr. Denslow Lewis. In 1902, Dr. Elizabeth Blackwell called woman "the natural regulator of sexual intercourse." The more poetic Dr. Joseph Howe regarded her as "the true guardian and priestess of the temple of marriage."

The undisputed sexual authority of wives was not just preached but widely practiced, as journals and letters from the period reveal. In 1853, one man wrote his fiancée to assure her that "you will be my law" in intimate matters. This was no obligatory promise to some cold fish. The author assumed his life's partner would possess "human passion and susceptibilities . . . [of] a warm blooded girl" who would "lie in a warm blooded man's bosom."[1] Historians cite steadily declining birth rates throughout the nineteenth century as evidence that Victorian gentlemen, unlike their less gentlemanly ancestors (and descendants), understood the meaning of "No." (Fertility rates dropped from 7.04 children per family in 1800 to 3.56 by 1900.[2])

Just as civility depended on curbing brute instincts, "true manliness" meant taming the libido without breaking its spirit. "A strong sexual nature is not a curse, but a blessing," said Reverend Stall. "God made no mistake in making man what he is; but He never intended that the lower nature should rule over the higher and better nature of man." A prominent physician, Dr. Trall, also reflected the Victorian respect for sex as a double-edged sword: "It is very true that nothing can be more vulgar, indecent, and degrading than its abnormal or merely lustful indulgence. But it is equally true that, normally exercised, no act . . . is more holy, more humanizing, more ennobling."

The Victorians believed this humanizing and civilizing view of sex distinguished them from the misogynists and self-centered savages who felt "no moral obligations . . . which compel them to abstain from a natural gratification of their passions." Unless a man could transform his lust to love instead of the other way around, he became his wife's master but not his own.

In those pre-pill days, it was essential for a man to spare his wife from frequent and often dangerous pregnancies—what Queen Victoria, an amorous mother of nine, called "the shadow side of marriage." But in love, as in life, sacrifice was its own reward. Refraining from constant intercourse not only proved a man's love and deepened his reverence for his spouse. By placing her needs above his own, as Bernarr MacFadden, a married female author of several marital guides, wrote in 1918, "his happiness proportionately increased."

## THE MIND-BODY CONNECTION

The Victorians' moral instruction on sexuality was reinforced by the scientific thought of the era, which held that expending an ounce of semen was equal to losing forty ounces of blood. Definitions of "excessive venery" varied widely. In general, however, more than weekly copulation was believed to risk depleting the male's "vital life force." Among the dire consequences invited by overindulgence were muscular degeneration, mental enfeeblement, headaches, nervousness, blindness, heart disease, sterility, and impaired resistance to epidemics.

A few physicians believed that during intercourse, the expenditure of "nerve force" was replenished by the magnetism (energy) of the partner. Yet there was no hope of recharging the batteries of those who descended to the level of "beastliness" by engaging in the "subversive and degrading" practice of "self-pollution" (masturbation). While physicians debated the extent of "physical, moral, and mental" damage inflicted by "self-abuse" (as Dr. Elizabeth Blackwell put it in her book *Essays on Medical Sociology*), all agreed that it violated the essence of sex: emotional and spiritual connection.

The Victorians believed that no artificial substitute could replace this link, a conviction that would put a crimp in the growth of today's burgeoning sex tools industry. For example, amid such articles as "No Mistakes Guide to Home Hair Coloring" and "Trim Down Tune Up in 7 Days," the aptly titled *Self* magazine recently carried an ad for a product its manufacturer calls "The Tongue." The copy reads, in part, "Designed by a woman for women. This incredible product duplicates oral sex with absolute perfection by providing REAL MOVEMENT and tireless rhythm. . . . This amazing wonder has 5 orgasmic speeds . . . is erotic, soft and lifelike." Even if this little wonder did windows as well as women, the Victorians would have questioned the amount of "life" in the cheap thrills it offers for only $39.95, plus shipping.

Because "the God-given relationship is two-sided," even coupling was not regarded as fully legitimate when the sexual act hit for one partner but missed for the other. "It becomes mere masturbation to the body and mind of the one who alone is gratified."[3] Lust was considered toxic to love. The Victorians would not be surprised that in our increasingly macho culture, selfishness is a national disease, although men still take the lion's share, especially in bed.

## A WOMAN'S SENSUALITY

Gory theories about enervating ejaculations may sound like a quack rationale for penis control. They certainly provide a convenient excuse, which many historians use, to dismiss all Victorian notions of sex. But before we start snickering, we should remember that twentieth-century science has spawned its share of junk studies and embarrassing retractions, from the Piltdown Man to cold fusion. Whatever the limitations of their biological knowledge, our ancestors understood and honored the unique intimate needs of women. For all our apparent enlightenment and superior science, we are still struggling to recover that understanding from our own flirtations with the unisex ideology and Pygmalion mentality that impose male standards on women.

Long before researchers discovered that biology makes women more likely than men to contract sexually transmitted diseases, the Victorians recognized the handle-with-care feminine sense of sensuality. They were correct (if not politically correct) in openly admitting the inherent gender inequalities that leave us conflicted and uneasy today. Physically and emotionally, a woman is more vulnerable than the man between her legs. Thus his sensitivity—the hallmark of chivalry—determined her fate in the street and in bed. Elizabeth Blackwell wrote in 1902:

> All that concerns the mental aspect of sex, the special attraction which draws one sex towards the other, is exhibited in greater proportionate force by women, is more steady and enduring, and occupies a larger amount of their thought and interest.... Words spoken, slight courtesies rendered, excite a more permanent interest in women. That which may be the mere passing thought or action of the man, at once forgotten by him, obliterated by a thousand other intellectual or practical interests in his life, often make a quite undue impression upon the woman.

Men were expected to emulate women's superior qualities, not to belittle them or subsume them to basic biological mechanics. This was more than a question of moral high ground. It was a choice between the heat of a once-struck match and that of a well-stoked furnace. Eliza Duffey noted in 1876 that women, unlike men, "do not love lust for lust's sake." For women, she said, passion and love go together. Furthermore:

> This bud of passion cannot be forced rudely open. Its development must be the work of time [or] the bud will be blighted. The husband will have only himself to blame, if he is bound all his life to an apathetic, irresponsive wife. She will be wounded in her deepest feelings, and dis-

gusted and sickened. The apple of pleasure will turn to ashes in her taste. She will become convinced, as this apathy extends through the years, that she was denied all passional feelings by nature. . . . She will feel deep regret that she should have lost out of her life something so essential, which of right belonged to her.

Exactly one hundred twenty years after Duffey issued this warning to men who were "utterly selfish and rapacious," instead of "practicing in lawful wedlock the arts of the seducer," a letter to Ann Landers confirmed the timeliness of Victorian wisdom that so many unsatisfied women still want their partners to learn. A reader explained to men who wondered why their wives were so turned off by sex that women are tired of men's demands after having been ignored, yelled at, and deprived of loving affection: "Do you ever hug or hold us? If you get close enough to touch us, do you grab a part of the anatomy that may have been an erogenous zone in another lifetime? We are not trying to punish you by withholding sex. We're just trying to salvage a shred of decency." Where, the reader asked, did the premarriage tenderness, kissing, and caressing go?

Ann Landers's published reply reflects the widespread sexual illiteracy of males in our sex-soaked society: "Your letter is going to be taped to a zillion bathroom mirrors and placed on a lot of pillows tonight."[4] Zillions of men would not be sharing their pillows or morning shaves with a newspaper clipping if they understood how women ticked as well as those "repressed" Victorians did, and relished the manly challenge to keep the clock running smoothly. Those too egocentric or too lazy to try received blame and contempt from other Victorian men, rather than a friendly poke in the ribs reaffirming that they were one of the guys. Dr. Charles Knowlton observed in 1878:

Passion is forever killed, or, if capable of resuscitation, it is not at the hands of him who destroyed it. It may be that another can reawaken the slumbering spark, and the flame be all the wilder for the rights it has been denied. This is the reason for the fall of married women. . . . You should never forget that this passion is ordinarily slower of growth and tardy of excitation in women than in men, but when fairly aroused in them it is incomparably stronger and more lasting.[5]

Advice manuals of that era, such as *The Gynecologic Considera- tion of the Sexual Act* by Dr. Denslow Lewis (1900), consistently urged bridegrooms (who were presumed to be gentlemen) to be "delicate, attentive, and forbearing" toward their brides (who were presumed to be virgins), even if days or even weeks were required to "cultivate womanly passion" and consummate the marriage. Talk about foreplay! Not only was such saintly patience "due the woman he loves," said Dr. Lewis, but following her sexual tempo was the only way to win her trust and ensure that "perfect and reciprocal happiness would crown the act." To the Victorians, true happiness, like marriage, had to be shared—it never flew solo. Although virgin brides are now as rare as honest politicians, can anyone imagine a "forbearing" modern man enduring days of false starts, even for the woman he claims to love?

In an age when selflessness was a precondition of self-fulfill- ment, any man worthy of the name did not resent his wife's sexual reserve. On the contrary, he cherished it, even as he searched for a way to light her fire. As a Bernarr MacFadden wrote early in this cen- tury, "Responsibilities are a joy to one who has the courage to meet them, and the greatest pleasure in the world comes through sacrific- ing oneself for those whom one loves." Yet even when finally reaching "the fullest abandon . . . and highest exaltation and desire in a physi- cal union," the "female impulse" still determined the frequency and pace of intercourse: "The real lover waits upon every word and look and gesture of the beloved."

The previous century, unlike our own, taught men that it was bet- ter to give than receive both in society and between the sheets. Victo- rian romance had no place for horny hubbies who rolled over on their wives like logs. Whether newly wed or old, an "impetuous husband" who satisfied himself but not his spouse was guilty of "defrauding womanhood," in the eyes of the indignant clergyman Sylvanus Stall. This lesson might have spared John Wayne Bobbitt the ultimate vengeance of his defrauded wife, who told the police she castrated him because "he always have orgasm and he doesn't wait for me to have orgasm. He's selfish. I don't think it's fair, so I pulled back the sheets then and I did it."[6] Feminists who treat Lorena Bobbitt as the patron saint of revenge fantasies miss the point: The problem isn't men, it's modernity.

## Quality, Not Quantity

The Victorians considered anything that compromised what Dr. Nicholas Cooke called "the pleasure to which woman is entitled" to be a "cruel injustice." This included contraception. They had spermicidal douches, condoms, primitive diaphragms, and a flawed notion of the rhythm method. But the most common form of birth control was withdrawal. Many objected to this practice for depriving women of, as Dr. Cooke put it, "full satisfaction." Periodic abstinence was favored as cultivating reverence for women and the sexual act, and most Victorians feared "mechanical methods" would make women "playthings of men."[7]

Few women today would relinquish the modern mechanical methods that make sex possible without making babies in the bargain. But we have yet to solve the stubborn problem of keeping women from becoming male playthings, and the condom hasn't been invented that can separate frequency from mediocrity. The Victorians believed that habitual copulation risked degenerating into sheer habit and boredom. While we can no longer imagine quality without quantity, this was one realm of life where our ancestors thought less was more.

In the 1880s Dr. Joseph Howe voiced the conventional wisdom when he warned that sexual gluttony would ruin "the real charm and zest of married life." As Rev. Sylvanus Stall put it, intercourse was meant to be "an overpowering passion, not simply a source of physical gratification." Because sex was so important, "It belongs only to the hour of highest spiritual communion, when heart and soul are merged in the consciousness of but one existence, one life, one eternity," said Stall. "Then, the whole being may and must thrill in unison with such harmony. Passional intercourse is meant to be an ecstatic expression of the soul. Take from it that significance, and you rob it of every attraction."

## Sexual Junk Food

The twentieth century fulfilled this prophecy. The Victorian version of gourmet sex kept thrills from becoming cheap—the only kind we can buy in today's erotic bazaar of junk food. Temperance not only "maintains the integrity of the sexual," observed Elizabeth Blackwell in 1902, "but heightens its enjoyment, as fasting makes food more delectable." (For proof positive, just ask anyone on a diet.) Keeping the flames of desire burning was "the key to a happy marriage. And while it may seem at first to be a sacrifice, you will soon learn that it is instead a means of adding exquisite pleasure to both your lives that you were formerly strangers to."

Strange as it may seem to our oft-sated appetites, the Victorians knew how to respect and even relish deprivation. Writing to her husband in 1883 after a six-week separation, one wife dwelt on the "great wave of sweet memories and longings and the touch of clinging warm lips, and the still magnetic thrill of your warm body, and I was all lost to the present. Let us be very tender and careful of this physical bliss . . . and not abuse it, but keep it sweet and clear through the years."[8]

When sex and women were both considered precious jewels, rather than costume jewelry, it was not only possible but essential to distinguish mere appetite from passion. "The term 'passion,' it should always be remembered, necessarily implies a mental element," Elizabeth Blackwell said in 1902. "Passion rises into a higher rank than the instinct of physical impulse, because it involves the soul of man. In sexual passion this mental, moral, or emotional principle is as emphatically sex as any physical instinct." Nearly a century later, sexperts have rediscovered that, as we now put it, the brain is our most important sexual organ.

Nevertheless, many self-styled sexual advisers still uphold the twentieth-century standards that treat females as second- class citizens in the realm of the senses. They tell women who crave the crumbs of romance to let men set the menu or risk starvation. For example, the popular TV therapist Barbara DeAngelis asserts that women who want their men to make love must compensate them with more stripped-down sex. For women who don't take this carrot, DeAngelis wields an awesome stick—scary numbers on adultery and divorce.

Similarly, in their Christian marital advice guide, Tim and Beverly LaHaye warn Christian wives who are not always in an obliging mood that husbands denied a "necessary means of relief" will become "irritated." And trendy gender astronomer John Gray is on the same wavelength when advising Venus and Mars on how to navigate their crossing orbits. Since the typical male gives love to get sex while the female gives sex to get love, Gray asserts, women must be willing to dispense fast food in return for the occasional gourmet treat. No wonder he refers to this once-exalted experience as "getting it."[9]

Few women know that their ancestors celebrated more female-friendly ideals of sex and love. But some of them recognize that they're being screwed in more than one sense. When John Gray appeared on *The Oprah Winfrey Show* in June 1995, one female audience member told the good Dr. Gray that his prescription encouraged men to treat women like machines. Call it women's intuition. Even without realizing that history is on their side, women know that a male meal of fast-food sex may satisfy the body but not the soul. They deserve a long-overdue feast with all the Victorian trimmings that made intimacy a banquet to be savored course by course.

## SEX ED AND ROMANCE

We have done sex to death for ourselves and our kids, many of whom are begging for the help we no longer know how to give. In a 1994 Emory University survey of 1,000 teenage girls, 82 percent said the top issue they wanted to discuss in sex education classes was how to say no without hurting a guy's feelings.[10] In fact, "sex ed" is one of the hottest battlefields in the current culture wars. But for all their differences, both liberals and conservatives advocate a modern approach that is equally sterile and narrow.

Former surgeon general Joycelyn Elders exemplified the permissive safe-sex agenda by comparing sex ed to driver's ed: "We taught [our kids] what to do in the front seat of the car, but not what to do in the backseat of the car."[11] What the Victorians once described in the transcendent language of religion has become a technical handbook for rules of the road. Sex ed as a public-health campaign, like those long waged against various diseases, is also the philosophy behind "home health parties" sponsored by Planned Parenthood for low-income women across the country. Combining the giggly atmosphere of a sleep-over with Tupperware-style demonstrations, Planned Parenthood reps dispense nonjudgmental nuts-and-bolts advice on contraceptives, lubricants, and AIDS tests while handing out token prizes like crockpots and compacts.

Some notches up the economic scale, schools such as the University of Maryland and George Washington University give their students "safe break" survival kits for spring vacations that include aspirin, sunblock, and condoms. Thus equipped, students can frolic risk-free on the beach and in bed alike. (The aspirin is presumably for the morning-after hangovers.) More parent-palatable programs in elementary and secondary schools combine contraceptive instruction and condom distribution with lessons on how to resist peer pressure—the chief reason teenage girls say they start having sex.

The sad futility and resignation felt by girls who are sexually used by boys surfaced in a *New York Times* profile of teens in city and suburban schools. The headline says it all: "For Some Youthful Courting Has Become a Game of Abuse." Guess who gives the abuse and who gets it. The article describes how the flagrant mistreatment of girlfriends has become a status-winning male bonding rite. "If you dis a girl you get respect," one adolescent male told the *Times* reporter. "Like, 'Yeah, you dissed her, you're the man, you're the man.' That's how people think."[12] As one indication of just how widely young males think this way, the massive Mall of America in Bloomington, Minnesota, recently imposed a curfew on youths unescorted by adults after a rash of rowdiness in which boys were physically harassing girls and shouting remarks like "Meat!" as they passed by.

Girls too jaded to hope for the thrill of romance, or even the charm of puppy love, have learned to accept being treated like dogs. They don't even expect their boyfriends to acknowledge them in public. "Nobody loves nobody anymore," one girl lamented. "And there's no respect, no trust."[13] I remember a teen telling me she thought courtship had something to do with being sued. Despite all the feminist progress in the professions and education, this century has left male footprints all over women's faces.

Woman's reign in the lost world of romance doesn't appear on either side's syllabus in the sex education battle, where the weapons of choice are frightening AIDS statistics and lectures on the lost opportunities produced by premature parenthood. While liberals throw lubricated condoms at confused adolescents, conservatives bombard them with the dry dust of moral instruction. What both sides neglect are the aesthetics of love. The absence of this dimension would have mystified the Victorians, who knew that beauty was essential to both morality and pleasure.

### Chastity and Passion

Liberals cannot be expected to tout chastity, except on the open menu of choice. But conservatives, who like to think they control the turf of personal integrity, are too busy intimidating kids to explain how early promiscuity can ruin what suffragist Mary Livermore called "the appetite for higher pleasure."[14] ("Appetite" and "pleasure" are not exactly buzz words in the conservative lexicon of sex.) Even the feminist heroine Margaret Sanger, the midwife of the modern birth control movement, voiced her quintessentially Victorian belief in the

*A Victorian woman's chastity gave her power in courtship.*

power of transcendent passion. Writing in 1926, she entreated the young "to refrain from lesser sex experiences and temptations." As Mary Livermore put it, such experiences "render impossible the great drama of love of which all humans are desirous."

The Victorians were too enamored of this drama, a value they sought to instill in their children, to rely so heavily on sin, fatality, and fear to keep their kids out of each other's drawers. Today's pro-virginity apostles lend new meaning to the label Spiro Agnew gave to the media—"nattering nabobs of negativism." For example, in a lengthy newspaper ad soliciting funds, a group named Focus on the Family focused on afflictions such as syphilis, chlamydia, and pelvic inflammatory disease to discourage premarital sex. In this group's view, virginity is not a noble ideal that sweetens and spices anticipated love. It is a "necessity" propelled by studies showing that the microns of HIV can penetrate latex condoms. The only way to survive this growing epidemic is to wait until you marry an "uninfected partner."

Instead of inspiring the young with elevated sentiments of sex and marriage, we try to scare them off with dire warnings of disease and death. Still, millions of easily exploited teens are still getting pregnant by males who get it on and then take off. Those clueless young moms might not have grabbed the first ride that came down the pike if they thought a better one would come along. Instead of instructing them about toxic microns or proper condom use, let kids rediscover how their ancestors once raised the heat of passion to a level we can only envy.

If stamping a skull and crossbones over sex won't stop kids, who assume they're immortal, from doing it, let them read this letter written in 1867 by a young man to his equally chaste but eager fiancée:

> And now, love, you with the warm heart and loving eyes, whose picture I kissed last night and whose lips I so often kiss in my dreams, whose love enriches me so bountifully with ... sweet anticipations ... making my heart beat faster, my flesh tremble, and my brain giddy with delight. . . . Good night: a good night and a fair one to thy sleeping eyes and wearied limbs, the precursor of many bright, beautiful mornings when my kisses shall waken thee and my love shall greet thee.[15]

## FORGOTTEN LESSONS

In a revived culture of romance, deferred gratification would be its own reward. But the modern sex education line, whether it comes from left field or right, is enough to make anyone with heart and soul give up on school programs and return sexual edification to the home, as many conservatives would prefer. Surprisingly, history sides against them. While our ancestors believed home should always be the primary school of the personal and the political, the sexually reticent Victorians wanted outside authorities to supplement these lessons or even to provide full instruction when parents neglected their obligations.

In 1887, Dr. Joseph Howe urged his colleagues to ensure that all their patients knew the score to promote the "health and happiness of the race" and to prevent a "ridiculous performance before the marriage was consummated." In 1902, Dr. Elizabeth Blackwell called for "sexual morality" instruction in schools, and she chastised churches and religious organizations that "are afraid or ashamed to deal with this most powerful force of our God-created human nature." In 1876, the marriage and etiquette adviser Eliza Duffey also saw such candor as the ally of adolescent virtue, and the only way to correct misinformation acquired from friends or the street: "There should be no fables of babies . . . being found under cabbage leaves."

But at home and in school, sex was never intended be taught with today's Joe Friday matter-of-fact driver's ed approach. Sex was "not proper for general or frivolous conversation," Duffey stated. Reflecting the unique and sacrosanct status of intimate relations in her day, Dr. Blackwell explained in 1902 why she assumed this subject would be treated with tender loving care, even in open debate, and why it never should be bandied as

> . . . a topic of idle gossip, of unreserved publicity, nor of cynical display. . . . Happily, in all civilized countries there is a natural reserve in relation to sexual matters which indicates the reverence with which this high social power of our human nature should be regarded. It is a sign of something wrong in education, or in the social state, when matters which concern the subject of sex are discussed with the same freedom and boldness as other matters.

The "something" that is wrong today is the corrosive incivility of relations between the sexes and the resulting infectious debasement of sex, which is proving as fatal as the diseases sex can spread. When Elizabeth Blackwell spoke of "this natural and beneficial instinct of reserve, springing from unconscious reverence" for sex, she could not envision a Parents' Weekend at elite Smith College, where guests and students were invited to enter condom relay races. Contestants tried to put five condoms on a banana without breaking it.

Similarly, at a private elementary school in New York City, a book for seven-year-olds not only discussed orgasm but compared it to the pleasure of jumping rope. The authors certainly succeeded in bringing sex down to a child's level, where it has stuck tight. Sex is just "an exchange of pleasure" like any other, as Howard and Martha Lewis described it in *The Parents' Guide to Teenage Sex and Pregnancy* (1980). Exchanging gifts, business cards, bodily fluids—it's all part of the same flat continuum in a world that sees no natural hierarchy of experience.

Such books assume that even worried parents have "no nostalgia for Victorian standards"—which are exactly what we need for adults and kids alike. Both the conservative mantra of abstinence and the liberals' sexual smorgasbord cheat young people of the "great drama" that elevates love beyond wearing a glove. One high school English teacher in a Washington, D.C., suburb discovered these starved sensibilities in his students, even among those who knew all about condoms but nothing of romance. A movie based on the work of the virgin spinster Jane Austen provided their most enlightening lesson. Teacher Patrick Welsh writes about his students' discovery that "a flavored condom is no substitute for a nosegay": "When I took my class recently to see the movie *Sense and Sensibility* (in which the touching of a female ankle is the most overtly sensuous moment), I was steeled for the hoots of my macho male students. Instead I was pleasantly surprised to find in class the next day that the boys loved the movie as much as the girls. Perhaps there is still hope for civilization."[16]

That hope depends on our desire and determination to rescue sex from the gutter of low expectations and restore it to the lofty heights of romance. To save our future, we must shed our prejudices, fears, and misconceptions of the past. Rescuing the history that it took a century to destroy won't be an easy task, or a quick one. But period books and faithful films are a good place to start. In a recent survey of 750 randomly chosen ten- to sixteen-year-olds nationwide, 62 percent said portrayals of sex in TV shows and films influenced their behavior.[7]

Spurred by populist criticism and concern over mounting welfare costs, many schools now sponsor abstinence classes. In California alone, students in an abstinence program learn practical reasons for not having sex—you can't support a child on lunch money, and condoms don't protect you from herpes, genital warts, or psychological scars. Shifting cultural winds ensured that the bipartisan welfare reform legislation enacted in 1996 allotted $250 million for such programs, along with $400 million in bonuses to states that reduce their rates of illegitimate births.

## THE OVERLOOKED ADVANTAGE OF ABSTINENCE

Some enthusiastic teens are even starting virgin clubs and proudly proclaiming their status on T-shirts. Like most new ideas, this one is quite old. Starting in the 1880s many young people joined White Cross Societies and wore the badge of purity that symbolized their commitment to premarital virtue. The historian David J. Pivar noted that males who took the oath "tacitly agreed that women's moral standards were higher than men's . . . the common goal . . . implied the sanctification of womanhood."

While pregnancy and disease are strong inducements for today's kids to heed this example, many girls are rediscovering and reclaiming the power Victorian females considered their birthright. For example, a counselor at a Maryland high school reported that taking a virginity pledge boosted girls' self-esteem and gave them a greater sense of sexual control. They desperately need all they can get in the down and dirty dating-mating game that stacks the odds against them.

Sex may be instinctive, but love is largely learned, and great love is nurtured. We can either break it or make it what we will. And we had better make it a priority if we ever want family values to be more than rhetoric. All the think-tankers and politicians have forgotten that home is where the heart is. Before preventing or mending broken homes, we must first mend love's broken heart.

# PART 4

# HOME SWEET HOME

# 14

## You Can Go Home Again

What is a home these days? It's a place we go to find our "space," a mail drop where we stash our stuff, a revolving door we rush through to change our clothes and roles. The Victorian concept of home was so alien to the contemporary version that we need a different language to describe it. Home was the very heart of nineteenth-century culture, the central icon for a national creed. It was an emotional and aesthetic environment that provided the essential nutrients of family values, not just the box within which parents preached them. But it was also a physical structure whose design and decor were infused with moral significance.

### THE RELIGION OF HOME

The Victorians regarded the home as a kind of sacrament that rendered the intangible tangible, through the daily rituals of dining, chores, and leisure. In fact, the Victorians often resorted to religious metaphors to describe its significance. For example, Horace Bushnell, the most famous theologian of his time, said, "Home and religion are kindred words: names both of love and reverence; home because it is the seat of religion; religion because it is the sacred element of home."¹ But it wasn't only theologians who talked this way. Julia Ward Howe enjoined her audience to "revere the religion of home," and Harriet Beecher Stowe hoped her readers would cultivate "that most sacred flame, the fire of domestic love."² Even this wasn't enough for the marriage adviser Henry C. Wright, who ranked the home above religion as the centerpiece of human existence. Compared to the home's "power over the organization, character and destiny of human beings," he wrote, "the Church is nothing, the State is nothing . . . government, priests and politics are nothing."

Such accolades may sound excessive or even comical to our own domestically challenged sensibilities, but they represent far more than the Victorian penchant for "flowery" language. Home was a passion

*The Victorian home was considered a sanctuary, and the family, central to one's life.*

you lived daily, as well as an ideal you sought to honor. To the Victorians, a life worth living required just a kind of ineffable charm, and home was the haven where it flourished in ways great and small. At a time when the marketplace was still a man's world, home provided what the physician William Alcott called "his blessed retreat from the turmoil of business." Reinvigorated by this nightly respite, he could return the next day to the business that paid the family's bills.

## THE WORKINGS OF THE VICTORIAN HOME

But maintaining the home was no one-sided affair. Every family member was expected to contribute to creating this prized oasis, and every contribution was respected. Sharing the load fostered reciprocal obligations, reinforcing family ties and reverence for the home that only such joint efforts could enrich and sustain.

It is difficult to overestimate how much the nineteenth century valued the skills and hearts of the women who provided the precious refuge of home. The fifties brought us the famed television show *Queen for a Day*, but Victorian women were queens of the home every day, managing and overseeing the large and small details. Domestic manuals of the period assumed the mistress of the house could master a staggering range of tasks and topics that would now daunt any would-be "supermom." These included the basics—which are not so basic anymore—such as cooking, cleaning, showing all guests "the perfection of hospitable entertainment," and tending to her children's bodies, minds, and souls.

Women were expected to serve as the family doctor and pharmacist, who dispensed home-brewed remedies without the backup help of emergency rooms and all-night drug stores. Preserving domestic health also required a working knowledge of ventilation and heat and lighting apparatuses, plus waste disposal systems and the potentially lethal vermin that carried infectious diseases. As if her plate weren't full enough, she was the household accountant, the seamstress who made clothing, drapes, and linens, and the carpenter who crafted pictures and mirrors. And she had to pull all this together to what Catharine Beecher called a "beautiful effect by the wise disposition of color and skill in arrangement." Martha Stewart, eat your heart out.

Above all, women were the paragons of that defining Victorian virtue, thrift. Frugality was highly respected as a "feminine" accomplishment, and a wife's ability to budget, bargain, and keep her financial house in order determined her family's fate as much as her husband's paycheck. The *Ladies' Home Journal* editor Edward Bok even advocated teaching young girls this skill not only through maternal example—their chief means of all domestic education—but by giving them charge of their father's business ledger. Any Victorian homemaker worthy of the name did not buy now and pay later. She took to heart the widely read advice (and edifying example) of Dickens's immortal wastrel, Wilkens Micawber, who failed to practice what he preached to David Copperfield: "Annual income twenty pounds, annual expenditure nineteen, result happiness. Annual income twenty pounds, annual expenditure twenty pounds ought and six, result misery."

Today's thoroughly modern woman is far more apt to identify with the profligate Nora who was "imprisoned" in Ibsen's *A Doll's House*. Like the *Kramer vs. Kramer* heroine who has to leave her family in order to find herself, feminist prototype Nora is distinctly modern—that is to say, she violates every quality and ethic that principled Victorians admired. A chronic spendthrift, she secures a loan through forgery and then can't pay it off. But she shrugs off her behavior and scoffs at the obligation to square her debts with strangers.

By nineteenth-century standards, Ibsen's Nora personified unfit motherhood and domestic disaster—the doll-wife few men would have wanted or could afford, and no self-respecting woman of her time wanted to be. Yet our liberated age has lionized this narcissistic ninny who abandons her own children. (One Victorian actress refused to play the role of Nora for just that reason.) The Victorians put too much stake in the home to let a self-absorbed child act as its broker (a lesson that David Copperfield learned by sad experience).

Victorian women had so many domestic responsibilities that many had to hire help. During the 1870s, about one in eight families had at least one servant, which was more necessity than luxury in an age when muscle, not gadgets, performed most tasks. Except in the case of the rich, hired help was just that, help—not complete relief from extensive domestic responsibilities.

Although the husband's major contribution to the home was financial, even the king of the castle was expected to reciprocate the devotion of his queen, not his slave, via the dishes or the dustpan when required. Since family love and the home's intrinsic worth gave dignity to chores, whoever did them never compromised his own dignity. As Henry C. Wright explained in a chapter entitled "Home and Its Influence" in his 1855 marriage guide, *Marriage and Parentage*: "The details of domestic economy can never be repulsive to the true husband. On the contrary, to relieve the wants and cares of the wife, in any way, and help her to bear the burdens of household labor, is not to serve as a menial, but to cherish her and sustain her as a husband. However minute the service . . . it seems refined and manly."

It is whining about taking out the garbage that would have been unmanly. Pulling your weight on the home front wasn't just permissibly masculine in an age before that quality meant controlling the TV remote. It gave real substance to the love that "must ever be the one consecrating sentiment of the husband's life. This fathoms the depths of his being, and swallows up all other experiences."

More than any other, this notion that a man should pull his weight at home separated the men from the boys at a time when such distinctions were essential. The now-alien idea that scrubbing the hearth you cherished was ennobling also illuminates the gulf between the genuine Victorian home and Martha Stewart's version of what is often mistakenly assumed to be its current incarnation. In a recent speech at the National Press Club, this multimedia mogul described the crux of her business as "giving women permission to enjoy homemaking."[3] The fact that they need public approval demonstrates that its status is about as low as you can go within legal limits.

In an age when irreverence is our national religion, ridicule is the sincerest form of flattery. Ms. Stewart's boundless energy and exacting standards have spawned a satirical backlash, from a parody of her magazine (entitled *Is Martha Stewart Living?*) to aprons that lower expectations to mortal levels by announcing that the wearer isn't Martha. Such reality checks are needed protection from someone who probably forges her own flatware for dinner parties after personalizing each guest's napkin with their initials. But for all Martha's magic with a glue gun, the real magic is missing. Even her finest feats lack the cohesive transcendent sense of home the Victorians conveyed through simple eloquence, unaided by soft photography or the pristine country setting that costars in her TV show. Martha once unwittingly revealed her great limitation to an interviewer: "My life is my work. My work is my life. I think about it twenty-four hours a day." The single-minded drive of this empire builder is hardly surprising, since she endured a nasty divorce, and her relationship with her only child has been described as "cordial." If something deep and vital is missing from the life she fills with a marathon schedule, it is definitely missing from her sense of home—and ours.

## THE SUM OF ITS PARTS

For the Victorians, impressing visitors with time-consuming decorating projects would hardly have been considered the point. The singularly resonant power of the Victorian home, and one's membership in it whether as breadwinner or breadmaker, endowed the smallest act with shared value and respect. The everyday tasks that made up the bulk of women's work were valued because they were performed out of love for the family.

Life in the Victorian era was always considered more than the mere sum of its parts. Yet each part had meaning beyond the literal functions that still maintain, if not emotionally sustain, the modern home. Catharine Beecher, writing in *American Woman's Home,* wove this uniquely Victorian view through the once rich fabric of domestic life:

> The most minute details of household economy become elegant and refined when they are ennobled by sentiment. . . . To furnish a room is no longer a commonplace affair, shared with upholsterers and cabinetmakers; it is decorating the place where I am to meet a friend or lover. To order dinner is not merely arranging a meal with my cook, it is preparing refreshments for him whom I love.

The Victorians presumed the primacy and integration of home, as opposed to the current presumption of an atomized home, which seems to be less than the sum of its parts. We are not the first to discover that its maintenance can be tedious and taxing. Without mechanical washing machines, for example, for the Victorians the laundry alone could consume an entire day of each week. But whatever the chore, it served a grander purpose: the family and the home. (Our ancestors rarely discussed one without the other; and while we speak of mere chores, they preferred the higher implications of duties.)

Recognizing this grander purpose is an essential first step to respiritualizing the home and restoring the traditional values three quarters of Americans want to strengthen, according to polls. One 1993 *Wall Street Journal*/NBC survey concluded that the country is "vaguely searching for some old-fashioned notion of family."[4] What we long for is a lost sense of home, not just a place but a sanctuary from a world in many ways far meaner than it was a century ago. Without restoring the home to its former elevation, family values are destined to remain an airy hope tossed about by the winds.

## FROM HOME TO THE WORLD

When home provided a refuge from the world, it was also the axis on which the world turned and which kept it from spinning out of control. The influential editor Sarah Josepha Hale argued in 1868, "The moral tone of a people must depend . . . upon their domestic institutions." In her autobiography, the suffragist Mary Livermore echoed these sentiments when she linked the success of her crusade for women's civic rights to their role in the domestic realm: "The real humanizing and civilizing of the world is carried forward in homes, and as the aggregate of these may be, so will the nation be." This is another Victorian lesson we have relearned through the harshest possible means, by encountering an explosion of amoral young predators raised in "homes" that parody the meaning that once inhered in this word.

In retrospect, Frances Willard, president of the Woman's Christian Temperance Union, may sound hyperbolic in her description of home as "the citadel of everything that is good and pure on earth." But the Victorians applied their superlatives to what they valued most for both its personal and public rewards. "The family home, carrying on its proper work, is no narrow circle of selfish exclusiveness," observed Dr. Elizabeth Blackwell in 1852, "but a living centre, attracting to itself and widely radiating healthy social life. Its influence is felt in intercourse with all classes."

Although home may have been the ultimate private domain, it was as omnipresent as oxygen, the one institution that bridged the realms of personal identity and social stability. Men fought wars for God and country, but even in this God-fearing age, home was the linchpin of life. As the sartorial innovator Amelia Bloomer, who popularized "bloomers," wrote during the 1850s in her women's rights journal, *The Lily*, "Without home, without the domestic relations, the love, the cares, the responsibilities which bind men's hearts to one treasury of precious things, the world would be chaos, without order, or beauty, without patriotism, or social regulation, without public or private virtue."[5]

To the Victorians, the primacy of home was accepted by men as well as women. In fact, men even viewed the home as the best barometer of a nation's strength. "In love of home, the love of country has its rise," declared Charles Dickens in *The Old Curiosity Shop*. And no country nurtured this bond more than the United States, as de Tocqueville attested in *Democracy in America*: "Whereas the European tries to escape his sorrows at home by troubling society, the American derives from his home that love of order which he carries over into affairs of state."

Today's impoverished debate over "family values" attests to how much we have lost since then. Our ancestors believed in building a house from the foundation up, not from the roof down. Neither family-friendly legislation nor cloning Martha Stewart will accomplish what needs to be done. In 1852, Dr. Blackwell warned that any country where the family was "degraded," not "cherished as the precious centre of the national welfare," was doomed to "rapid dissolution." That path led us to the place we live now, where liberals and conservatives serve up competing nostrums from workplace flextime and day care to tax-code tinkering and tougher divorce laws. We must retrace our steps and understand our missteps if we are ever to rediscover the road not taken.

# 15

## Home Wreckers

How did our notions of home and its virtues turn so topsy-turvy? The usual suspects look depressingly familiar: historical events such as the Great War, social processes such as mass production and consumption, and technological advances like the automobile. All these historical changes had corrosive effects on domestic life, just as they did on public civility and personal intimacy. But history has a human face. The decline of Victorian ideals is the product of personal decisions as well as impersonal forces. And women themselves bear some responsibility for subverting the domestic ideals that their grandmothers held so dear. Yet like the three witches in *Macbeth*, three early-twentieth-century women were instrumental in bringing the pot to a boil: Charlotte Perkins Gilman, Lillian Gilbreth, and Christine Frederick.

### HOME AS HELL

Ironically, the first oracle (and current feminist icon) Charlotte Perkins Gilman rebelled not only against her time but against the domestic ideal celebrated by her influential great-aunts Catharine Beecher and Harriet Beecher Stowe. Gilman never lost the taste of sour grapes that were a staple of her childhood diet.[1] Abandoned by her father when she was six, she and her mother had to move eighteen times in fourteen years. All she knew of solid family life came from occasional visits to cousins. "I saw how loving [it] could be," she recalled many decades later. "Here was courtesy and kindness." But such rare tender memories could not sweeten the bitter anger and resentment that forever blackened her view of the Victorian home. Her "loathing for the home limited her ability to envision how domesticity and justice for women could be compatible," wrote the historian Glenna Matthews.

A classic ideologue who despised what she could not have and did not understand, Gilman is still remembered for her 1903 book *The Home*, a diatribe against domesticity. In it, she denounced "the sanctity of home," "the omnipresent domestic ideal," and the "cult of home worship." Like a termite, she gnawed at its foundation by doing what Masters and Johnson later did to sex: reducing transcendent values to animal functions. "The beehive is as much a home as any human dwelling," she wrote. "We are merely large animals living in large boxes." Gilman's concept of home was not of a shelter that nurtured body and soul but a virtual torture chamber. "The home is the place where we suffer most," according to this sad, scarred woman. In that "hotbed of personal feeling," love (which it seems she never knew) "grows intense and often morbid."

Despite the greener pastures she had glimpsed, Gilman believed if we were all flies on the walls of Victorian American homes, rather than visitors duped by company manners, "we would see how miserable everyone is." Later feminists would echo this paranoid vision by charging that all those white picket fences hid a national epidemic of spouse and child abuse. The dysfunctional circus of TV talk shows further assures us that domestic hell is the rule, not the exception. But Gilman was far ahead of her time in spewing her fiercest contempt at the women who maintained the home with their labor and their love.

Where Elizabeth Cady Stanton said that women's duties required common sense and wisdom, and Catharine Beecher considered them as sacred and important as any man's, Gilman found them "primitive" and "savage." She labeled the Victorian wife and mother a "parasite" and a "domestic vampire" who lived and worked in a "prison" that "impedes social progress." She ardently supported the inevitable evolutionary march toward socialism, when the state would usurp all functions of the home, from caring for children to preparing meals. While women would work everywhere but the home (unless it was someone else's), all domestic tasks would be performed by hired menials or professionals. This new utopia would not only cool the dangerous emotional heat of the Victorian home, it would replace cherished but "inferior" female traditions with the latest efficient scientific methods.

Gilman's own prejudices seemed to escape examination by her superior mind, perhaps because of her own dysfunctional family background. She married a man who was, by all known accounts, loving and attentive, but she had a complete nervous breakdown soon afterward. Her convalescence in a sanitarium inspired her noted work of feminist fiction, *The Yellow Wallpaper*, which essentially blames men for the heroine's insanity. After divorcing her mate, Gilman recovered, although she continued to suffer from bouts of depression. She eventually married another man who was so incidental to her work-obsessed life that she barely bothered to mention him in her memoir. Had she been born a century later, Prozac or twelve-step programs might have tempered her rancor toward the home and family she never had. But she relished the cultural inferno she sparked with her version of progress.

## HOME AS ASSEMBLY-LINE FACTORY

Gilman's cult worship of science was shared by her two sisters in crime. The most famous and least likely member of this home-wrecking trio was immortalized by her children's memoirs and the classic 1950 movie *Cheaper by the Dozen*. On the surface, Lillian Gilbreth seems worlds removed from Charlotte Perkins Gilman. This matriarch of a family of twelve children was mistress of a cheerfully bustling house she occupied with her adored husband and colleague, Frank. She appeared to have the kind of charm-infused life that inspires wistful nostalgia, down to the treasured but unreliable family car—a Pierce Arrow named Foolish Carriage. But under the skin she was as revolutionary as Gilman in her quest to run the home like an assembly line.

From 1910 to 1921, the Gilbreths conducted some of the earliest filmed time and motion studies as consulting experts for industrial plants. But they didn't stop at the factory door. So they crossed that great Victorian divide between the public and the private by using their home as the primary "school for scientific management and the elimination of wasted motions." That modern mentality needed only time and technology to obliterate domestic arts and sentiments.

With their ever-present stopwatch and their children as ready (if reluctant) guinea pigs, the Gilbreths clocked and dissected every household exertion, from making beds and washing dishes to buttoning a vest. (They found that starting at the bottom rather than the top saved three seconds.) This relentless experiment even extended to filming the removal of the children's tonsils. Individuality, however harmless, had no place in a roost ruled by seconds gained or lost. While your hair was technically yours, sheer efficiency determined how you combed it. (And we think of the Victorians as conformists.)

After Frank Gilbreth died in 1924, Lillian continued to apply industrial concepts to the home. In a 1927 book, *The Home-maker and Her Job,* she defined its ideal as a "well-run business" that could be minutely analyzed, summarized, and governed by charts and graphs. The full fruits of her labors took decades to bloom, but she was confident that the winds of change were blowing in her direction: "So many of the prejudices of an older generation are passing away; and any one who has been through modern laundries, bakeries, and preserving plants will find herself looking with suspicion on the unstandardized procedures of many a home."

## HOME AS CONSUMER BASE

"Scientizing" the home was also advocated by a third home wrecker, Christine Frederick. In her 1929 magnum opus, aptly titled *Selling Mrs. Consumer,* she wrote that households should "run like a clock." During her tenure as editor of *Ladies' Home Journal*, she faithfully chipped away at the domestic vision that had been promoted by Sarah Josepha Hale during her forty years at *Godey's Ladies' Book.* An enemy of what Edith Wharton called "the art of civilized living," Frederick urged women to trade quality for quantity by standardizing each household task "so you can do it everyday in an identical manner without much mental attention." This typified the counsel dispensed through women's magazines by the second decade of the new century. No longer was "the whole process of home-making" an "art and a profession" that required "the best qualities of heart and mind." The new religion rendered it both heartless and mindless.

No one deserves more responsibility than Christine Frederick for turning the home into a home shopping network of family demands, where women acted as the "chief purchasing agent." In *Selling Mrs. Consumer* she equated increased consumption with "the advance of civilization" and promoted the new doctrine of consumptionism as "the greatest idea America has to give the world."

In her recipe for that perfect world, business would emotionally and physically revamp the home until the latter's raison d'etre became buying from business. Frederick's lifelong mission—"the conversion of luxuries into necessities"—hinged on teaching manufacturers how to sell women an endless bill of goods, a mission she fulfilled with blazing success. Unlike Victorian domestic advisers, she believed it was impossible to underestimate the intelligence of wives and mothers. Therefore, ads aimed at them should be direct, visual, and simplistic. For example, Frederick discovered that women initially resisted buying the first generation of radios because they were as intrusively large and aesthetically displeasing as many women find today's jumbo-screen televisions. So she convinced manufacturers to design them like furniture and stress their surface appeal, not their technological sophistication.

She applied the same approach to any salable good (and she treated everything as just that). Even when peddling the staff of life, she highlighted the appetizing look of bread, not the nutritional value that once concerned Victorian cooks. Portray apparel as smart; durability be damned. Indeed, the lack of durability became a virtue rather than vice in Frederick's schema. To keep the corporate cash machine churning, she told producers to focus on developing items that would become obsolete almost as soon as they were made. Nowadays we take this planned obsolescence for granted, but it was heresy to those nurtured on the Victorian creed of thrift. Domestic frugality was no longer an accomplishment and a character-forming lesson for children but a "petty and ridiculous" practice.

Beyond the question of home economics, this represented the abdication of women as moral exemplars both in and out of the home. Like the majority of her sex, Frederick favored Prohibition, but not to protect wives and children from the abuse of drunken husbands. Always the money-minded pragmatic, she feared that earnings wasted on booze "curtails man's consumptive power," especially among the lower classes she wanted to consumerize. But it was loosening women's purse strings that mainly occupied Frederick. She mocked every expression of the old "pinching economy," like rolling tapers from newspapers to start a fire instead of purchasing matches, and using stale bread to make bread pudding, even though hard bread works best. Frederick's thriving legacy of what she blithely termed "creative waste" gifted us with myriad waste disposal and other environmental problems.

The indelible red ink Christine Frederick splashed on the household budget more than half a century ago also robbed us of our rightful inheritance—the Victorian domestic soul. When saving time became the bottom line for home as well as business, every appliance that replaced or expedited human labor became a must. Tradition fell before acquisition. Treasured family keepsakes that embodied continuity and cushioned households against the crudities and pressure tactics of the commercial world became hated hand-me-downs destined for the scrap heap.

## Homemade vs. Store Bought

Frederick denounced any object that had "lasting heirloom" potential, including the signature Victorian ebony piano her mother bequeathed to her. To her mind, pianos became as dated and disposable as hats. So you traded it up and moved it out every few years, like all the other manufactured marvels you couldn't live without, and eventually couldn't live with. Replacing them extracted a financial rather than emotional investment, unless one meant the emotions that were the not-so-whimsical whims that triggered impulse buying.

Perhaps most tragically, women were told they had "better things to do" than engage in the formerly time-honored domestic arts. Frederick deemed it unforgivably passé to prepare meals from scratch instead of opening cans, or to dress your family and your rooms with the unique items you crafted rather than the cookie-cutter goods you purchased. The intricate needlework that gave such distinctive charm to the Victorian home was no source of pride or sign of family devotion, just a "petty medieval accomplishment." And petty is what the home was destined to become.

This lesson that the home is unimportant is not an easy one to unlearn, as I was to discover. Upon completing college in the late 1970s, I was gravely disappointed when my graduation gift from an aunt turned out to be not the check I expected but a set of bed linens my great-grandmother had embroidered in the 1880s for her trousseau. This seemed not only a useless relic but an insult to a newly minted careerist. I shook my head in self-pity and disgust as I imagined all the hours my ancestress wasted stitching those fussy monograms, flowers, and scrolls for some anticipated home her Prince Charming would provide and rule. If I had to keep a memento of a woman I never met, why did it have to be this utterly impractical testament to her domestic bondage? I would have preferred her faded but proud college degree. Alas, she had none.

After burying the linens in my parents' closet, I went off to graduate school with plain, wrinkle-free sheets to pursue a vision of womanhood unfettered by froufrou items I couldn't bank or list on a résumé. I forgot those linens for several years, and by the time I was obliged to reclaim them, my irritation had mellowed to indifference. Yet I toted them from house to house, ignoring them except to unpack and repack them after debating their fate with the Goodwill box. It was only gradually that I came to realize the value of those linens— beyond the escalating prices they command in antique shops. Like Mark Twain's father, who seemed to grow so wise between his son's fourteenth and twenty-first birthdays, the linens too seemed to change over the years as I began to understand why the glue binding Victorian homes and families had cracked and crumbled.

Like other girls of her day, my great-grandmother learned such a reverence for home that she began to craft the things that would warm it with her personal touch even before she had her own home. She knew her efforts would be honored, not disdained, by her family-to-be, because such efforts were almost universally practiced. Far from being quaint creations of small-town provincials, needlework provided inspiration to the most noted artists of her time. The Impressionist Gari Melchers's wife inspired him to paint *Penelope* and *Young Woman Sewing*. Mary Cassatt did a portrait of the same title, as well as *Lydia at the Tapestry Loom*. Women also stitched domestic sentiments into samplers (some now costing thousands of dollars) that were prominently displayed. "Peace to This House,"

*This Currier & Ives print celebrated the feminine art of needlework, which was passed down through the generations. Handmade crafts became passé as mass-produced goods became available in the 1920s.*

"God Bless Our Home," and "Home Sweet Home" were among the messages that would now prompt mostly snickers.

I finally appreciate the meaning of their art, which lies beyond mere artistry, along with the art in the linens I once found useless and now feel unworthy to use. Even without a string of degrees and a key to the executive washroom, my great-grandmother created both a place and a sense of home most of us will never know. By current standards, she may have been an imprisoned victim of sex discrimination, but her descendants are the real losers. I sometimes wonder whether she made Edith Wharton's prescribed "twelve of everything" for her trousseau, and I envy the skills I lack. I owe a much-belated apology to the woman I was never privileged to meet, except through her legacy. But it's too late to atone, as it was decades before I was born.

## HOME AS HOTEL

My grandmother would never have described herself as "just a house-wife," a phrase that first appeared in the twenties, not the sixties. In the Jazz Age, the once-exalted domicile this deposed high priestess had tended was becoming more of a hotel than a home. As the historian Ellen Rothman put it, the altar where the Victorian family worshipped devolved into a "base of operations." And thanks to the latest techno-toys, it is has even become a base for spying on our nearest and dear-est. Almost any object, from planters to coffee pots, can conceal tiny cameras and recorders to catch abusive nannies, drug-using kids, and adulterous spouses. According to industry experts, business is booming.

The writing on the wall could be read without a Dick Tracy decoder decades before your average Joe started playing detective. A 1920s resi-dent of Middletown, the town studied by Helen and Robert Lynd, lamented the "physical service station" that replaced a "sacred institu-tion." Frederick Lewis Allen, who also witnessed this domestic demise, similarly described the home as " becoming less of a shrine, more of a dormitory—a place of casual shelter where one stopped overnight on the way from the restaurant and the movie theater to the office."

Allen detected mounting angst among women as they lost the satisfaction and esteem of creating life's central experience and were demoted to the status of "engineers" who managed an increasingly mechanized house. The model home was scientific and rational, not emotional and transcendent, as the houses of Gilman, Gilbreth, and Frederick became the new model. The historian Glenna Matthews notes that "efficiency had become a goal to be served for its own sake, irrespective of the emotional life of the housewife and her family, rather than a means to serve any larger purpose." Nothing before or since aspired to a larger purpose than the Victorian home, and nothing has been more devastating than its loss.

Instead of providing a haven from the depersonalized cash-based world, the home became just one more commodity. As a result, the legendary Victorian respect for its makers went straight into all those new toilets even common folk acquired. The old-time religion of the home was so weakened by the creeping corrosion of change, it was set to collapse when attacked by the first wave of feminists in the 1960s. Glenna Matthews astutely observed, "The desperate letters sent to Betty Friedan after she identified 'the problem that has no name'—that is the emptiness of many housewives' lives—testify to the damage inflicted by the twentieth-century version of domesticity."

## "JUST A HOUSEWIFE"

Friedan's own experience confirmed the complete demolition of the bridge Victorian women built to the wider world by means of—not in spite of—the moral power they wielded at home. By the time she began writing for women's magazines in the 1950s, it was widely assumed that women had few social, cultural, or political interests beyond the narrow confines of shopping and housewifery.

We wrongly assume that Friedan launched the first full-scale assault on domestic work as an activity that could never compensate for the "emptiness" of women's "narrow lives." She wasn't the first, but she did up the ante by pronouncing the vocation of homemaker as "dangerous" in the extreme:

> In a sense, that is not as farfetched as its sounds, the women who "adjust" as housewives, who grow up wanting to be "just a housewife," are in as much danger as the millions who walked to their own death in the concentration camps—and the millions more who refused to believe that the concentration camps existed.

In fact, there is an uncanny uncomfortable insight into why a woman can so easily lose her sense of self as a housewife in certain psychological observations made of the behavior of prisoners in Nazi concentration camps. In these settings, purposely contrived for the dehumanization of man, the prisoners literally became "walking corpses."

Reading this statement with the benefit of over thirty years of hindsight, we might wonder whether it was Friedan who completely lost her senses. Even if we allow for her anger and hyperbole, her judgments reflected a half century of misguided reforms that transformed queen bees into drones. This proud inheritor of Charlotte Perkins Gilman's legacy believed the sole route to dignity was a distinctly masculine one paved with paychecks. The new working woman's free time—as if there would be any—belonged not to hearth, kin, or self but to volunteering for the correct political causes. Indeed, in Friedan's revolutionary plan, women would breeze through domestic tasks, since any "eight-year-old" could handle the "trivia of housewifery." This presumably included raising children—who now often raise themselves.

By the time *The Feminine Mystique* fired its shot heard round the world in 1963, even Friedan's natural opponents were lobbing grenades at the same Swiss-cheese target. That very year, *Playboy* ran a scathing satirical piece that also portrayed the housewife as an idle parasite:

> Tired of the Rat Race?
>> Fed up with Job Routine?
>> Well, then . . . how would you like to make $8,000, $20,000—as much as $50,000 and more—working at home in your Spare Time? No selling! No commuting! No time clocks to punch.
>> BE YOUR OWN BOSS!
>> Yes, an Assured Lifetime income can be yours now, in an easy, low-pressure, part-time job that will permit you to spend most of each and every day as you please.[2]

These days Gloria Steinem complains that traditional women's work, which nearly all women do, was demeaned during her hardscrabble childhood in East Toledo, Ohio, and during her years at elite

Smith College. She still attributes this problem, and most others, to the "patriarchal rule," existing from time immemorial, that crosses class lines. Aside from having herself helped nurture this denigration of homemaking, she overlooks the fact that in the "patriarchal" Victorian era, the work now demeaned was highly esteemed.[3]

Despite Steinem's call to compensate domestic labor like any other paid occupation, which Victorian women would find insulting, even hints of the emotions once connected to that labor remain favorite cans to kick among feminists. Susan Faludi rails at the "domestic sentimentality" featured in publications such as the hugely successful *Victoria* magazine. She denounces "cocooning" among adult women as a return to the "gestational stage," but fails to notice that the modern cocoon is a flimsy excuse for one. However, movement matriarch Betty Friedan admits encountering many professional women who crave a taste of this forbidden lifestyle. They now ask themselves, she reports in *The Second Stage,* "What do you do about life, children, men, loneliness, companionship, the need to have a real home—things no one thought about when we were so obsessed with liberating ourselves?"

Yet the contempt for traditional domestic skills is still so ingrained that it passes for conventional wisdom, especially among female higher achievers—until they discover they don't know it all. One acquaintance, a supremely self-assured financial executive, decided she would make her daughter's Halloween costume because "any idiot could," including her mother, who sewed on a machine, and her grandmother, who learned to sew without one. After ruining a mountain of fabric and her flawless manicure, she was forced to contribute to the yearly $1.5 billion Halloween business by purchasing the kind of flimsy but overpriced costume every other kid had. Admitting a rare defeat and a new respect for a skill she once mocked, she pronounced herself the "real idiot."

## THE MYTH OF THE FIFTIES HOME

The spiritual and substantive stripping of the twentieth-century home explains why the vague sentimental longings of baby boomers are misdirected if they settle for 1950s nostalgia (where liberals rightly charge that the family values of many conservatives are stuck). The hard truth is that the 1950s home was no longer "the" institution but only "an" institution. It no longer thrived on the wisdom, dedication, and moral inspiration of women whose immeasurable worth was valued on its own terms. Instead, it was based on the crass number crunching of the rat race. The Victorian home was a world and a century apart from what a *New York Times* critic wrongly but all too typically described as a myth "no different in essence from the saccharine family-oriented American television fare of the 1950s."

While we may have loved Lucy, she was a domestic dodo whose home and marriage routinely survived in spite of her efforts, not because of them. We laughed at Lucy Ricardo's wacky hijinks more than we laughed with her; that was the point. Although many security-hungry boomers and their parents fondly recall her antics, and the straightman TV housewives like June Cleaver and Margaret Anderson, nothing about them radiates the combination of strength, solidity, and spirituality of the nineteenth-century home and the women who defined it.

## THE IDEAL HOME

The gap between such women's expectations and experiences and our own allows cynics to dismiss the claim that Victorian home life was the good life. In a recent review of a museum exhibition of Currier & Ives prints, the *New York Times* ridiculed these once wildly popular prints as "kitsch," "idealized," and "impossibly uncomplicated" views of the past."[4] The reviewer simply can't understand that the Victorians bought these pictures by the millions not only because they saw themselves in such scenes but because those endearing prints honored their sentiments of what a true home should be. As one domestic adviser wrote in the 1850s:

> To the Victorians, domesticity seemed as instinctive as breathing, because their first allegiance was the home— creating it, perfecting it, revering it, and, above all, instilling its spirit in the next generation. Since women largely dispatched this duty, home was called "the empire of the mother." Motherhood lost its deepest meaning and its most exalted domain when we lost the Victorian sense of home.

# Throw Momma from the Train

One of the most enduring images of the Victorian era is of the revered mother, whether in famous paintings by artists such as Mary Cassatt, Gari Melchers, and Francis Coates or in popular songs. Mother's Day is a Victorian invention. Anna Jarvis, a teacher who was very close to her mother and cared for her all her life, decided upon her mother's death in 1908 to lobby for an official day honoring all mothers. In 1914 Congress passed a resolution requesting that the president proclaim just such a holiday, and on May 9, 1914, Americans first observed Mother's Day; they have observed it on the second Sunday in May ever since.

In the Victorian era, mothers had a moral authority that was respected not only in the home but also in the public domain. To build this "empire of the mother," as the historian Mary P. Ryan called it in her book by that name, the Victorians didn't begin at the beginning. They began *before* the beginning, at the prenatal stage. Their great respect for motherhood conferred both dignity and privacy on pregnancy. *Household*, a popular magazine of the era, declared, "A modest woman does not publish her sacred secret."[1] While the desire to share one's happiest impending event with the world is certainly understandable, by making pregnancy and childbirth such a public affair we have unwittingly destroyed the very specialness of this experience we so want to celebrate.

## PUBLIC PREGNANCY

Once a Victorian woman began to "show," she abstained from parties and other celebrations, opting instead to quietly entertain family members and select friends at home. The Boston socialite and art collector Isabella Stewart Gardner recalled taking carriage rides while swathed in strategically placed blankets that her husband lovingly arranged. But no one dared rub her stomach as if it were Aladdin's magic lamp. The women of her time understood that discretion, not exhibitionism, inspired general respect for their "condition." You don't get that by breastfeeding in public, or suing for the right to do so.

Just as promiscuous women have turned all women into targets of insults and assaults, expectant exhibitionists make all pregnant women the subjects and objects of often unwelcome personal comments and presumptuous pawing. While no one would ask today's pregnant woman to withdraw behind her parlor doors (especially if she needs a paycheck), there is a gulf of lost discretion and respect between a discreet carriage ride and a spectacle swaggering across a beach in a bikini. Fecundity, like attitude, is now in-your-face, whether or not you welcome its presence. Demi Moore puts it on the cover of *Vanity Fair*, while former CBS correspondent Connie Chung launches a publicity effort to advertise her desire to become a mother. And of course, there is the ever-tiresome Madonna, who considered taking out a personal ad for someone interested in "the fatherhood gig."

### Childbirth as a Public Party

Women who are not celebrities unfortunately can be just as crass. These days brag books of sonogram pictures are passed around at offices and parties like vacation snapshots. Strangers, including reluctant males, are encouraged to feel the baby move. And when the blessed event does occur, the entire town is invited to attend, as if birth were a barn raising. Dad was the first required addition to the delivery. Then came the video camera, so the birth could be shown postpartum. I have heard audiences compare and review these movies like regular theater fare. All that's missing is popcorn.

As birth has become a more public event we have seen an increasing number of "homey" birthing suites in hospitals and birthing centers across the country, which accommodate parties of family, friends, and coworkers. Sometimes these gatherings literally are parties. During one typical fete at the Elizabeth Seton Childbirth Center in Manhattan, Mom breastfed her bundle of joy to the sounds of mariachi music while five guests feasted on takeout.

Siblings frequently witness the arrival of their family's latest addition, although experts are divided on the wisdom of exposing youngsters, even toddlers, to a potentially damaging trauma. Advocates, who naturally believe that nothing natural can be bad, stress the unique opportunity for siblings to bond with the baby, and claim it is especially important for "little girls to see how wonderful giving birth can be."[2]

## Coach Dad

What does it mean to treat this momentous event like a football tailgate picnic, complete with coach, fans, and food? It's no picnic, at least for some women, according to a recent firsthand account by the *Washington Post* contributor Elizabeth Chang. In her opinion,

> . . . when you stop and think about it, the idea of having a coach in the delivery room is really absurd, so completely off-target that people who conjured it up must have been male. . . . A woman in labor already has several coaches: She's got a team of nurses telling her to "breathe, bear down, harder" along with a doctor barely stopping by once every few hours to say coachlike things as "Not there yet" or "That's not very productive pushing."

Chang maintains that men often forget the mother's tribulations and focus instead on their own discomfort. "In fact, men are eager to talk about the pain they endured during childbirth. A favorite topic of conversation is how hard their wives squeezed their hands." Those poor babies. Our ancestors could have predicted Chang's most devastating assertion about turning childbirth into a macho game. "The perhaps not-so-surprising result is that men have begun to treat childbirth like sports, complete with training, statistics, and competition that somehow entirely avoids the mind-blowing point: the emergence of a new life."[3]

## PREGNANCY AS A SPECIAL, PRIVATE TIME

The Victorians believed birth made every baby's family "akin to all humanity." But acknowledging this kinship did not entail debasing it with casual locker-room chatter or the naked proclamations of expectant mothers that make them grist for the mills of standup comics who try to get belly laughs out of belly jokes. Many women cringe at these sordid doings staged at their expense, yet they repress their objections for fear of being labeled repressed.

There is far more at stake than questions of sexual frankness or our cultural compulsion to wallow in the nitty gritty of human biology, which the Victorians civilized and we trivialize. Feminists have long insisted that pregnancy is just another physical condition, like hives, as motherhood is just another "role" we play in our varied acting careers. This means macho moms don't slow down, despite swollen ankles or morning sickness that may last all day.

This mentality, not just the cold corporate bottom line of the health insurance industry, surely contributes to the epidemic of drive-through deliveries. Horror stories abound of hospitals that, until recent legislation stopped them, tossed out mothers as little as two hours after birth. As a result, infants not under the observation of hospital staff sometimes developed potentially fatal ailments. In pressing for remedial legislation, Ralph Nader accused insurance companies of devaluing women and children. This assessment is accurate but sadly incomplete. And neither liberals nor conservatives have a clue about how to re-value this experience. For all their recent hand-wringing over broken families, illegitimacy, and delinquent kids, most conservatives fail to connect them to the denigration of motherhood and home.

# THE HAND THAT ROCKS
# THE CRADLE RULES THE WORLD

To the Victorians, a woman did not simply have a child. As one writer phrased it, "She is adding another and equally essential constituent to the home. Indeed, she is helping, as in no other way so efficiently she can help, to build a home." This home was not her prison, as *The Feminine Mystique* would have it, but her bridge to the outside world. The moral influence mothers wielded in their empire both demanded and legitimized its reach to a wider arena. When Frances Willard, the president of the Woman's Christian Temperance Union, told all women to make the world more homelike—and in so doing protect their homes—the Victorians knew this was no crusade to hang lace curtains in Congress. Willard's agenda, which was shared by many other female activists, included not just Prohibition but suffrage, public sanitation, prison and school reform, and the elimination of child labor and prostitution.

Willard's use of home as a rallying cry was more than a savvy choice of a concept that women understood. It demonstrates both the reverence and the clout that home commanded in every quarter a century ago. The historian Mary Ryan notes: "The home was only the imperial center, the mother country, from which women launched their vast social influence." Because the Victorian home had this "broader, sweeter, grander significance," she writes, mothers were considered a nation's builders, not its menials.

Sarah Josepha Hale specifically traced a country's "prosperity and greatness" to Mother's "character and conduct," intangibles that can't be measured like the GNP. Lydia Maria Child described her "empire of the heart" as the "domain of moral affection" distinct from man's commercial world but the "co-equal sovereignty of intellect, taste, and social refinement."[4] Catharine Beecher felt that it was the mothers of America "in whose hands rest the real destinies of the republic." As with any sovereign, everything she said and did affected her subjects in small but potent ways we no longer recognize or value. William Alcott wrote in 1837:

> She does not take a step which does not educate herself,
> her husband, or others. So surely as she lifts a finger, or
> utters a word, or gives a direction, or casts an approving or

disapproving look, that modifies the feelings, or the conduct, or the health, of those around her, so surely does she
become their educator—the former of their character for
time and eternity.

Today's clueless conservatives tell Mom to just chuck the job
and raise the kids, without first restoring her to her proper premier
place. Without this bridge to the past, mothers who choose that full-
time occupation become family serfs instead of a precious national
resource. Their dominion over an institution that shapes all others
entitles them to a voice in the world. Nor should stepping beyond
their threshold ever diminish the admiration for what they achieve in
the home. Lucy Stone's husband, Henry Blackwell, paid tribute to
suffragists when he said, "Never have I known more affectionate
wives, more tender mothers, more accomplished housekeepers, more
satisfied husbands and children, more refined and happy homes" than
among these women's dominions.[5]

## The Authority of Motherhood

Creating those refined and happy homes was a confidence-boosting
source of pride that Victorian women relished. In contrast to modern
feminists, the Victorians believed they were effective reformers
because of their domesticity, not in spite of it. For all its practical
demands, home, and especially motherhood, was not a burden to be
relieved or banished. On the contrary, to activists like Elizabeth Cady
Stanton, motherhood was an ennobling experience, "an added power
and development of some of the most tender sentiments of the
human heart and not a limitation."[6]

The magazine editor Sarah Josepha Hale lived this fusion of
maternity and reform. Among her many public activities, Hale was
instrumental in establishing Vassar College and preserving George
Washington's home at Mount Vernon. A devoted mother of five, she
wrote with as much frequency and ease—but without apologies—on
knitting infants' socks as she did on raising funds for medical mission-
aries, promoting physical fitness, public playgrounds, improved labor
conditions, and higher education for girls.

Because the importance of homemaking and motherhood were
constantly reaffirmed in print and pulpit, women could apply their

insights and integrity to the gravest issues of the day. For example, the historian Glenna Matthews notes that Harriet Beecher Stowe "used the moral authority of the housewife to justify speaking out against slavery. . . . The political impact of *Uncle Tom's Cabin*, filled as it was with domestic imagery, demonstrated how the influence of home on the world could manifest itself."

Now moms have the moral authority to speak on little more than diaper rash. I learned this lesson uncomfortably up close and personal while dining with a wealthy Republican party activist and his wife, who had quit her job to raise their children. He fancied himself a living paragon of family values, and preached accordingly to those who wished to listen and to those who didn't. Yet when his wife dared to voice her opinions on a political issue he was discussing, he instantly interrupted. "No one cares what you think," he snapped. "You're nothing but a housewife from Connecticut who rides horses and takes her kids to tennis lessons." (This woman also does volunteer work for several educational projects that benefit inner-city kids.)

What happened to motherhood to allow the merchant princes of contemporary conservatism to toss bombs of contempt at the symbol venerated by the Romantic poet Samuel Taylor Coleridge as "the holiest thing alive." Contrary to the myth cherished by those who blame the insidious sixties for all social ailments, Betty Friedan was not the first to whack maternity like a child a piñata.

## DETHRONING MOM

The chronic home hater Charlotte Perkins Gilman, whom we met earlier, fired the opening shot against maternity in 1903. Six decades before Betty Friedan portrayed American mothers as mental midgets who "infantalized" and "dehumanized" their kids, her patron saint accused Victorian women of raising a "huge and growing crop of idiots, imbeciles, cripples, defectives, and degenerates, the vicious, and the criminal . . . the vast mass of slow-minded, prejudiced, ordinary people who clog the wheels of progress." Gilman declared that motherhood was just a "brute instinct" no higher than any other of "nature's processes of reproduction." She saw posterity as doomed by "untaught mothers," programmed to "repeat the mistakes of their more ignorant ancestors," whom she likened to a "dog turning three times before he lies down on a carpet." And Gilman was by no means all talk. She walked the talk by giving her young daughter to her ex-husband and his second wife to raise, in an early form of day-care dumping. The woman who called her own mother "cold" froze out her child until she was a self-sufficient adult.[7]

In her own day, Gilman was a lone voice crying in the wilderness. By the 1920s, though, her swan song for motherhood was becoming a siren's song for a new generation. Analyzing popular literature of the period, Glenna Matthews found a growing chorus of Freudian "scientific" child-care experts who warned against "excessive motherly affection." Some, like the pioneer behavioralist John B. Watson, even questioned "whether there should be individual homes for children—or even whether children should know their parents." Making the most of the bad situation—the still lingering home—the new high priests of parenthood told America's mothers to mistrust their once revered instincts and adopt in their place the severely structured schedules and habits cultivated by "scientific" laboratories. This was the Jazz Age version of test-tube babies.

By 1927, one worried nostalgic wrote in *Ladies' Home Journal*, "'Mother, Home, and Heaven!' used to form the pious three. Now the Home is more of an exception than a rule; Mother is cast down from her pinnacle; and a good many people are trying to take away Heaven." Three years later, Dr. Abraham Myerson echoed these dying sentiments in another woman's magazine. Noting the "devaluation of motherhood," he yearned for the days when "Freud had not yet corroded the delight of the infant's attachment to the mother nor the mother's joy in the child, and [John B.] Watson had not yet destroyed the self-esteem of the mother by making her worse than worthless in her own eyes."

Even female voting power could not salvage all the moss Gilman's rolling stone had flattened. Indeed, historians cite the crippled authority of home and motherhood for women's failure to become a formidable political bloc after finally winning the suffrage battle in 1920. When the Nobel Prize–winning author Pearl Buck returned from ultramisogynist China, she was shocked to find the once-honored female sphere "despised" in her native land. "Women's influence is almost totally lacking in the centers of American life," she lamented in 1941. Unlike the powerful suffragette, she said, the modern housewife "putters about on the fringes of her world which really goes on without her." Even within her own domain, "she is no longer the spiritual and moral influence she was once to man and child."[8]

It was only a single generation—and an even shorter psychic stretch—to *The Feminine Mystique's* demonization of Mom that continues to the present day. Our ambiguity about the role of motherhood is most evident in our struggle to define a "working mom." Potomac Mills, a Virginia mega-mall that is one of the state's top tourist attractions, recently sponsored a tribute to "working women." In TV ads inviting nominations for admired achievers, viewers had to be told that full-time moms were eligible because they too "work." Barbara Bush did not fare even that well when she was asked to give the commencement speech at Wellesley College in 1990. About 150 students objected to the then First Lady as an unsuitable role model for aspiring professional women because she did not work outside the home for a salary.

If women collude in this mental matricide, how can we expect any better from men? And how do we save our nation's troubled children, whom everyone agrees are in crisis, if the truly challenging job of raising them must be justified with every breath?

## SUPERMOMS AND JUST-A-MOM'S

Stay-at-home moms often feel compelled to defend themselves by reciting every nanny and day-care horror story they know, then assuring you they are pursuing a second masters degree in their spare time in order to reenter the work force with added credentials and earning power. Without the cushioning self-esteem of a career plan, their absence from the "real world" seems wasted, because they can't take it to the bank. In the 1989 movie *Parenthood*, a woman whose youngest child is about to start school laments, "Everybody's asking me when I'm going back to work, like I'm supposed to." Though she had a job before she had kids, "I'm better at this. I'm good at it," she says, laughing nervously. But no matter how good she is, "People make me feel embarrassed, like I don't have goals."

Even that old barn burner Betty Friedan expressed belated concern about the defensive and diminished status of mothers. In *The Second Stage*, her 1981 reassessment of feminism's impact, she described many women as bitter, confused, and depleted by "female machismo" and the constant strain of juggling the competing demands of work and family—"the blind spot in feminism." Acknowledging that motherhood was "more important than we wanted to admit," she urged gender cooperation rather than conflict, more male responsibility for domestic tasks, and congressionally mandated corporate policies like parental leave. Without them, women must continue to split like atoms between their jobs, their homes, and Friedan's obligatory commitment to political change. But neither Congress nor the Fortune 500 can stretch the hours in a day. And the superwoman Frankenstein that Ms. Friedan helped create still suffers from the same fatigue, "brittle disappointment," and "disillusionment" that she recognized the second time around.

Women have been told they can do anything; now they feel they must do everything. If they don't, all too often nothing gets done. Small wonder that mail-order catalogs sell caps and shirts declaring "I am woman. I am invincible. I am tired." Not exactly the image the Helen Reddy song was intended to convey.

The news is not that women are too tired to roar but that they're even conscious. In dual-income families, a recent survey found that women did over 80 percent of the shopping and cooking and 70 percent of all child-care activities. In *The Overworked American*, the sociologist Juliet Schor observed that our national time crunch is particularly acute and harmful for double-duty moms. And in a survey by the Families and Work Institute, 40 percent of women said it was hard to get up each morning and face another day at work, and 42 percent described themselves as "used up" by the end of the day.[9] Women who work outside the home often find that in trying to do it all, something ends up getting shortchanged. Too often it is the children.

Scholars warn of a "parenting deficit" that cheats children of their childhoods, with predictable consequences—drugs, alcohol, academic problems, and teen suicide. Couples don't fare much better than their offspring, says Schor. "Growing numbers of husbands and wives are like ships passing in the night, working sequential schedules to manage their child care." No wonder so many of those battered and leaky vessels are sinking.

Beleaguered moms and dads are trying to shrink this growing deficit by becoming "virtual parents" through pagers, fax machines, cellular phones, and voice mail that were once used strictly for business but are now sold by companies that exploit parental guilt. In a *U.S. News & World Report* article titled "Fax Me a Bedtime Story," Beth Brophy cited some heart-tugging examples. In the Motorola brochure "Paging All Families," little Billy contacts Mom when he gets a tummy ache so she can drop whatever she's doing to fetch him.[10] Pager or no pager, can most working mothers just bolt from the office when Billy calls?

## RETHINKING PRIORITIES

Many moms want to stay home to raise their kids in spite of a cultural code that denies social status and self-esteem to women who lack a brilliant career, yet they feel they must earn a salary to make ends meet. In a recent survey, a majority of working mothers polled said they must work to support their families. A Yankelovich poll found that a clear majority (56 percent) would quit their jobs if they didn't need the money. This represents a steady rise from 30 percent over the past two decades.[11]

Whether such data seem enlightening or obvious, they fail to explore a sensitive and neglected issue—the meaning of need versus choice. The historian Stephanie Coontz observed that married women first entered the workforce in substantial numbers during the 1950s. Essentials like rent and food did not spark this exodus from the prefab hearth. Rather, as motherhood was "divested . . . of any larger social and political meaning" that empowered Victorian women, and the home lost its spiritual and physical preeminence, we increasingly stuffed our houses with luxuries that became necessities.

Obviously, some women must work to keep their children fed. But for others, feeding the constantly ballooning appetite for goodies is a diet of choice—one often made without sufficient information or deliberation. Many women forego the decision and dash back to work soon after giving birth. Either the added expense of a child seems to automatically demand two paychecks, or else the loss of a professional identity and status is unthinkable. Some women willing to pay that hefty price are astonished to learn they can remain solvent on their husband's income. These are the women who ruthlessly reassess all their previously unquestioned material priorities, which the arrival of children often reshuffles. Can they live without the apparent essentials they once took for granted? Some say yes.

After scrutinizing the family budget, a former bank vice-president I know traded her coveted corner office for a stroller. It wasn't easy to sacrifice her exotic vacations, upscale restaurant meals, and designer clothes, not to mention her hard-won title. But they could not compete with raising her child. "The more you have, the more you spend," she observed six months after her career change. "The more you buy, the more you think you need. Now I just say no. That's the kind of power I never had before." Creativity became a new necessity; she even learned to cook in the kitchen that she once used mainly to store and reheat doggy bags. And she discovered that coupon clipping did not dent her dignity. Another woman who quit her job to stay home learned to save up for luxuries such as a satellite dish because, as she says, "I look at life differently now. I've learned things like that are not the God-given right I thought they were."

The race to keep up with the Joneses (or Madison Avenue's image of them) has reached breakneck speed, costing health, sanity, marriages, and the precious maternal time the Victorians valued far above frills. Instead, we spend $4 billion a year just on baby products that are a "must" for competitive parents who parade their bedecked offspring like show dogs. Yet not all women enjoy earning the cash to buy such things. In one recent survey of 3,000 women, only 31 percent reported getting great personal satisfaction from their work, and 38 percent wanted more opportunities to work at home.[12]

## A WORKABLE NUCLEAR-FAMILY MODEL

Even after all these years of gender warring, both sexes express surprising agreement on their preferred concept of home. According to an international Gallup poll of 1,000 adults in twenty-two countries, 47 percent of American men polled and 49 percent of American women describe the ideal domestic arrangement as one where dad brings home the bacon and Mom fries it up in the pan, rather than burning the candle at both ends. Of all those surveyed, Americans were among the greatest fans of the traditional family.

Even if men's wages and a family's downsized demands allowed mothers to do that job full time, however, they would still be left scrounging for social validation and self-respect. Neither hubby's megasalary nor generous tax credits can restore child-rearing to what the unmarried Susan B. Anthony called "the highest and holiest function of the physical organism." Though she often had to pick up the slack for sister activists who put maternal duties above their causes, she did not deny the unrivaled importance of training the next generation for the world she labored to change.[13]

Victorian priorities were reversed by those who presumed to continue the mission started by suffragists, yet failed to fill their shoes. Despite their conflicting emotional effect on ordinary women, feminists have scored undeniable and dramatic triumphs in transforming media images and cultural prescriptions for gauging female worth. But for all their rhetoric of freedom and choice, the feminist mentality used its muscle to narrow choice by delegitimizing the old division of labor between Mom and Dad. They redefined success in monetary and masculine terms, and grossly distorted the history of a "woman's place."

The eminent progressive historian Carl Degler, in *At Odds*, says that in the middle-class Victorian family, "The typical husband . . . was hardly the patriarchal father who gave little recognition to his wife. By definition, the companionate marriage placed limits on the power of the husband." Neither was he the nonentity of the Simpsons' cartoon world, where father knows squat. If we want fathers to be more than sperm and paycheck donors, we need to carefully select who sits at one head of the table. The conservative flavor of the current men's and fatherhood movements smacks of *Father Knows Best*. But is the likes of Jim Anderson the best we can do? If his factual counterparts were so esteemed, effective, and manly in America's alleged golden age, why did their authority melt down so quickly?

## The Victorian Papa

Robert Young's paternal archetype may seem Herculean compared with Tim Allen's ineffectual character on *Home Improvement*. But he pales beside the real leading man who inspired *Life with Father*. In both content and style, the actor William Powell's portrayal of Clarence Day, Sr., was remarkably faithful to Clarence Jr.'s famous book. One of the movie's early scenes finds the well-polished clan assembled around an equally well-dressed breakfast table. From where we sit, it already seems like another planet. It would have been unthinkable for Mr. Day to exchange mumbled greetings with his kids or bury himself behind a newspaper—a gross violation of Victorian dining decorum and familial respect.

Papa Day extensively questions his sons about every detail of their lives, from one child's reluctance to eat his oatmeal to violin and baseball practice and the welfare of a finger injured from hugging an unfriendly cat. This is an intensely involved and interested parent accustomed to commensurate responses, not rolled eyes or a generalized grunt. The tenor of the family's conversation shows such queries to be an integral part of daily life. While the children might privately dissent from their father's opinions and admonitions (especially concerning oatmeal), they expected them and respected the concern behind them. They clearly loved their father, but they also revered him as much as the home he defined.

Jim Anderson may have dispensed useful advice, à la Ann Landers, but this mellow marshmallow was hardly the inspirational presence who embodied the meaning of parenthood and home with his words and his bearing. Jim was an unthreatening coaxer, a guidepost on the road of life that points in the right direction. Clarence Day, Sr., was an awesome and dignified traffic cop who enforced the rules of the road. Like that oatmeal his son disliked, he stuck to your ribs through the years. And this potent effect was neither a fluke nor a rarity in his time. Teddy Roosevelt's relations said that he always tried to imagine what his late father would do before making a decision, even during his presidential tenure. Can you picture a middle-aged Bud Anderson doing the same with a comfortable old shoe like Jim?

Victorian fathers could be personal heroes; contemporary fathers are dads. Like every facet of the Victorian home, parents provided the subterranean roots that helped their children to grow. And while the father of old might seem a bit stiff, like the horsehair sofa that scratched young Teddy Roosevelt's legs, he was hardly all work and no play. "It is not only the father's duty, but it should also be his pleasure to look after his own children," said an 1897 marital guide for husbands. Victorian men may not have roughhoused with their children, although some memoirs recall piggyback rides and blindman's bluff. But men were expected to participate in games, read to their children, and put them to bed—all expressions of "the true father spirit." This was indispensable to the meaning of paternity and manhood, not a lesson harried mothers verbally beat into self-absorbed couch potatoes, golfaholics, or robots in gray flannel suits.

*Victorian fathers played an important role in their children's education and development.*

The cold cash–based relationships that have gradually evolved since Pop first handed Junior dough for a date and the keys to the family jalopy would have appalled the Victorians, even though their child-rearing practices were intensely mother centered. "Despite the differences between men's and women's natures, the pleasures and satisfactions of parenthood are as great to the father as the mother," wrote Rev. Sylvanus Stall. Dr. Elizabeth Blackwell noted that when a newborn is laid in its father's arms, "the man awakens fully to the wonder and infinite tenderness of paternity." If Mama had her instincts, Papa did as well, and the two were expected to blend rather than clash in rearing their children. The suffragist Mary Livermore fondly remembered this joint rule in her childhood home, and the prayer her father offered at every evening meal: "Bless the united heads of this family."

## The Wholeness of the Victorian Family

Despite this surprisingly modern message, the Victorian view of parenthood sharply diverged from ours in its unbreachable bond to the sacraments of marriage and home. We like to believe couples can split or remain nominally paired and still be good parents, while warring with or ignoring each other. Even after a savage divorce, we (hopefully) continue to love our children, despite the hated source of half their genes. In contrast, Victorian parents loved their offspring as extensions of their mutual love. Like sex, domestic sentiments, and the countless other links that made nineteenth-century culture a seamless web instead of a patchwork quilt, the romantic love that sired parental love was its essence; they were not paired in a marriage of convenience.

Children were "love's tokens" or "pledges of love," rather than another must-have on one's wish list. In a letter to his wife, Nathaniel Hawthorne described a heart that "yearns, and throbs, and burns with a hot fire, for thee, and for the children that have grown out of our love." These sentiments were echoed by ordinary parents of the period. One woman referred to her child as a "tie to both our hearts" in a letter to her husband. Another man told his undoubtedly gratified spouse, "You are my life Darling, and I cannot look upon our baby, except through you. My love for him does not arise from consanguinity alone, roots deepest in the soil of the love I bear my wife."[14]

## KEEPING THE ROMANTIC FIRES BURNING

Such effusive emotions demonstrate what the Victorians called "keeping your courtship in marriage." Both were expected to endure in an era that thrived on high expectations. Romantic love provided the bricks and mortar of the home that enabled the raising of solid, civilized children. "The presence of one man and one woman, who have mutually chosen each other out of all the world . . . are the common centre of the circle of home," wrote Dr. E. H. Ruddock in 1899. "They make its earliest constituent, and its prime and essential condition. Without this, there may be much that is charming and bright, but there is no home. . . . It is a power so enduring and sacred that death itself cannot quite cancel it."

Not only did such deeply valued home-binding sentiments survive the grave, they infused daily domestic life in ways we can scarcely recall, even less, recapture. But there is no better place to learn them than at the Victorian dinner table, which fed both body and soul.

# 17

# *Soul Food*

Perhaps the most flagrant (and certainly the most fragrant!) contrast between the Victorian home and our own is the frequency and quality of family meals. For evidence of this we need look no further than the shrinking modern dining room and its transformation into an office or walk-in closet. The architectural designer and critic Roger K. Lewis wrote in a column called "Let's Put Real Dining Rooms Back on the Table" that "the contemporary American family meal is often little more than grazing in the kitchen, a ritual of search and retrieval quite different from sitting around a dinner table. Eating has become an adjunct to doing other things: watching television, talking on the phone, reading newspapers or sitting in front of a computer."[1]

## THE DINING RITUAL

Lewis predicts that if this once crucial space continues to contract, like the portion sizes of "lite" foods, it will soon be extinct. But we have lost far more than square footage since the nightly ritual Clarence Day, Jr., recalled from his youth: "Every evening from six to seven o'clock, while Father and Mother were having their dinner, this dining room became as sacred a scene, in my eyes, as a high court or shrine. . . . I sometimes leaned over the banisters in the narrow hall outside, looking down in through the doorway."

On his seventh birthday Clarence was "promoted" from the basement kitchen, where he ate with his younger siblings, to the sanctum where his parents took their meals. This generational division was typical at dinner. Sharing it with adults in its proper setting was considered a privilege earned with age and civilized behavior. Like the first teen in the house to obtain a driver's permit—now the prime symbol of domestic liberation—Day reveled instead in the tighter domestic integration of his newfound status. "I strutted around in the nursery beforehand, with my hands thrust into my pockets, saying good-bye to my brothers, who, as I condescendingly explained to them, were still little boys."

The religious aura of dining in Victorian times extended to the symbolism of popular Gothic-style sideboards that resembled altars. But the reverenced meal was a daily affair instead of a special rite to be displayed and then mothballed like holiday decorations. Just as civility was not reserved for guests, the everyday family table rated the same care and attention to detail demanded by lavish parties, which were a recipe for disaster without the right ingredients. Whatever the event, with or without servants, every meal deserved to be treated as a special event. Even simple family dinners were treated with the same formality of meals prepared for company.

Guests were always treated to the best service and food your budget would allow. The notion of potluck would have stunned the Victorians, who placed reflective "butlers' balls" on sideboards so servants could see subtle signals from the master or mistress without interrupting their work by looking over their shoulder or staring at guests. Even families who couldn't afford their own Jeeves expected and received far more than leftover aesthetics at their daily meals. Every meal was served on the obligatory white tablecloth, be it plain oilcloth or the finest damask. Both were respectable and equally respectful of domestic sensibilities. In this hallowed arena, it was the thought, not the cash, that counted.

Leisurely family meals were so important that they merited the special space now often occupied by multimedia entertainment centers. The hours we spend with a remote control or a mouse our ancestors devoted to dining together two to four times a day. Even if

*In the Victorian home, the dining room, not the multimedia center, was the central focus. The formality of the room echoed the formality of the family ritual of dining together. In this picture from 1897, a family is gathered for a birthday party.*

clashing schedules precluded sharing lunch and afternoon tea, breakfast and dinner were a must. Long before dietitians preached the importance of a good breakfast to physical development, job productivity, and weight control, the Victorians realized that how they broke their fast could make or break their day. Because cookbooks of the era assumed their readers understood the crucial link between meals and school or work performance, they mentioned this link only in passing and focused instead on suggested menus that today's food police could almost love. These usually included modest portions of fresh fruit, whole grain cereal like oatmeal, eggs, and bread items such as waffles, biscuits, or toast. Today six in ten children fix their own breakfast—if they get any—which is more likely to run to high-sugar superhero cereals than a measured medley of the major food groups.

## What Was on the Table

While we may think our shortened menus have spared us pounds of that stereotypical Victorian plumpness, just the opposite has occurred. According to researchers at Tufts University School of Medicine, just 15 percent of the population was obese in 1900, compared to 33 percent today. Diamond Jim Brady and Edward VII notwithstanding, most adults refrained from compulsive raids on the cookie jar. In the modern era, we have grown fat not on the fat of the land but by becoming potato chip–consuming couch potatoes, paying for overpriced convenience foods with calories as well as cash. Despite our image of multi-dish Victorian meals that would take more time to describe than we take to eat, the typical family dinner was a three- or four-course affair that included soup, meat, vegetables, a starch, and some dessert like pie or pudding— not an endless gravy train of evening snacks and fast-food "meals."

Our ancestors used meals to nourish both body and spirit, right down to the elegant flowers that graced every proper table. As the *Ladies' Home Journal* proclaimed in 1894, "Elegant serving is the soul of living." Even in winter, "accomplished ladies" of any means could force bulbs indoors and create attractive arrangements to complement meals—another lost domestic art. In his famous turn-of-the-century forays through New York's slums, Jacob Riis found blooming bits of beauty in window boxes, just as his memorable photos reveal china and linen neatly displayed in the glass cupboard of a one-room hovel. Even the fiercest destitution could not kill the home sensibility that Victorians considered a religion. No one had to tell them to stop and smell the roses, even if they were only daisies.

## Civilized Dining

Like sex and etiquette, the dos and don'ts of Victorian dining were considered a mark of triumphal evolution over man's primal roots. The McMeals that we gobble like slaughtered prey in our cars, offices, and on sidewalks prove that man can devolve as well. (At least the lower orders have fresh kill.) "Animals eat; only man dines," declared cookbook author Isabella Beeton. And the way he dined revealed nothing less than a country's history and its destiny:

> Dining is the privilege of civilization. The rank which a people occupy in the grand scale may be measured by

their way of taking their meals, as well as by their way of treating their women. The nation which knows how to dine has learnt the leading lesson of progress. It implies both the will and the skill to reduce to order, and surround with idealisms and graces, the more material conditions of human existence; and wherever that will and skill exist, life cannot be wholly ignoble.

Like the web of civility, the quality and aesthetics of family meals shaped the individual's temperament as well as the nation's.

Our "new age" discovery of the mind-body connection was sheer common sense in an era when the world was viewed as a tightly woven whole, not a motley mess of fraying threads. A century before we gratefully goldplated the bank accounts of Eastern gurus who showed us the light, the educator and cookbook author Mary B. Welch noted without fanfare, "One of the weightiest influences which determine the life of the individual is the nature of the food he eats." Improper nutrition "undermines both intellectual force and physical vigor, and, as upon the combination of these two depends the advancement of the world in any direction, religious, social, political, or commercial, some notion can be gained of the responsibility of those who prepare food."

We tend to ignore this responsibility except when contaminated supermarket products are recalled during the media scare of the week. Yet even in the throes of terror, we assume that preparing appealing and healthy meals at home requires little more than a minute to spare and a microwave. We respect the paid hamburger flipper more than the uncompensated domestic cook, unless she becomes Mrs. Fields. Many gadget-laden yuppies with drop-dead kitchens have turned into amateur chefs. But showing off the wares of a high-status hobby to friends on weekends as you show off your tennis backhand hardly qualifies as nourishing the home spirit or the family's health.

## DINING AS A SHARED FAMILY EXPERIENCE

On the rare occasion when families sit down together for a meal today, the experience is often spiritually barren, aesthetically disinfected, picked clean of the cherished moments and memories that defined and anchored our ancestors' lives. Family meals once provided children with essential nutrients for their character, not just their constitution. Everyone, but especially the young, dined for improvement. Meals had a social, intellectual, and religious element, and children learned daily lessons in these areas as they participated in and listened to dinner table conversations.

Victorian children didn't buy their meals from a vending machine or a mall food court. They earned them through doing their part, and by being part of something that transcended the food on their plates. "Every child should have some specific duty to the progress of the meal," noted Mary Welch in her cookbook, which was typical in dispensing general advice along with recipes. "They will early come to enjoy and be proud of the perfect smoothness of all the routines of a well-ordered table."

Family meals were intended to teach children both obedience to parental authority and the selflessness of assisting younger siblings. Along with the basic table manners and conversational habits they would carry beyond the home, they learned to appreciate and emulate the efforts of a meal well prepared and presented in a clean and pleasant atmosphere, which they were obliged to reflect in their conduct and personal appearance. All this took time and work, but the Victorians knew there was no free lunch. You always get what you pay for, and we've paid plenty for living on the cheap.

In a half-baked nod to the importance of breaking bread together, a TV public service ad announces, "If you want better kids, you've got to be better parents." This announcer pleads for one family dinner a week at the kitchen table, which is shown poignantly surrounded by empty chairs. The family-first Victorians would gasp at this thin-as-gruel formula for bonding, and would wonder whether adults who require such instruction should be anyone's parents. They knew that children's habits were formed by habitual contact with parents, not by sporadic meetings. If kids got the Sunday Christian treatment, vice was certain to outrun virtue in the formative years and thereafter.

Contrast the meal-time experience of an average working mom today, Lori Lucas, a car-repair shop manager from Shrewsbury, Missouri, who was recently profiled in *Time* magazine. She is determined to prepare dinner every evening for her year-old son and his live-in father figure, but a photo of the actual event shows the limits of her good intentions. Instead of sitting at the table, she is crawling under her son's chair to retrieve the food he spilled. Her significant other, clad in a cap and T-shirt covered with advertisements, seems completely oblivious to both of them. Their meals are more or less homemade, yet the table is a littered mess of plastic wrappers, condiment jars, and soda bottles, a fitting complement to Dad's billboard attire.[2]

While this rushed, middle-class family technically satisfies the quality-time mantra, it is hard for the viewer to detect the seeds, no less the fruit, of the home spirit that was mother's milk to the Victorians. Such poor proxies lose something fundamental in translation, leaving a hole in the soul that can never be filled.

Our bottom-line society has sacrificed the very intangibles we grope for—the immeasurable "otherness" of aura and aesthetics that former generations revered. They understood why frills like crisp table linens, flowers, and sprigs of parsley were not frivolous, and how the sensibilities children learned, or failed to learn, at meals could steer a nation's fate. Without the living cultural memory of that intensely domestic past, we are left trying to spice a stew that "needs something" we cannot name because it has become so foreign to our modern palate.

I sampled a small vicarious taste of this "something" through a ninetyish lady I met at a retirement home I visited twenty years ago. As a child, she asked her father why he always changed his collar and cuffs (which used to be separate from shirts) when he came home from work, even if they weren't dirty. This was the prescribed custom of the time, but her father also explained why it was no empty formality: Wearing a collar and cuffs as fresh and white as the dining-room tablecloth was, first, a mark of respect to her mother and the food she carefully prepared on a modest budget. Many years later, that elderly lady I met wondered whether her own grandchildren would have divorced so quickly if they had experienced family dinners that fed not only the body but the soul.

## THE BEGINNING OF CONVENIENCE FOODS

The Victorians' shared repasts, and the skills that produced them, were a distant memory to most Americans by the time Hillary Clinton declared her disdain for staying home to bake cookies. The contemporary palate, along with family meals, was doomed to gradual canned standardization by modern marvels such as the birth in 1916 of Piggly Wiggly, the first self-service grocery chain. Commercial sliced bread, whose nutritional value was processed to a pasty death, appeared in 1928. (So much for what Catharine Beecher called the "divine principle of beauty" in creating the staff of life; the Jazz Age literally traded wheat for chaff.) During that same decade, Clarence Birdseye introduced prepackaged frozen food. These antiseptically sealed blocks taught the public to detach vegetables from their natural roots in every sense of the term.

Another pivotal first of that era—the franchised drive-in restaurant—arrived with the automobile in the guise of the White Castle. It was just a matter of time (thirty years, to be exact) until McDonald's made food fit for a clown. Wherever people went, they could be assured of finding the exact same hamburger bun (three and one half inches) and a total preparation time of fifty seconds for their burger, shake, and fries. Countless younger siblings like KFC and Wendy's put our meals in Styrofoam and cardboard, instead of on the dining-room table, and turned the most ethnically diverse country on earth into one of culinary accidental tourists.

The home economics movement, which started early in this century and came to symbolize the dreaded domesticity of the fifties, was instrumental in destroying the Victorians' craft traditions and cultural admiration for the women who practiced them. Comparing the Middletown of the 1890s and the 1920s, Robert Lynd noted a decline in the quality of food preparation, "one of woman's chief glories." As a local butcher told him, "The modern housewife has lost the art of cooking. She buys cuts of meat that are easily and quickly cooked, whereas in the nineties her mother bought big chunks of meat and cut them and used them in various ways. Folks want to eat in a hurry and get out in the car."

By the twenties, the hours women once lavished on unique and memorable dishes were spent instead on congested roads and the task of chauffeuring offspring to a burgeoning smorgasbord of sports, hobbies, and other activities. After all this obligatory driving, which still drives Mom crazy, she had a stiff back and frayed nerves but no gratifying masterpiece to show for her efforts. External activities for both kids and adults cut so severely into mealtimes that one father told Robert Lynd, "A fellow has to make a date with his family to see them."

A second comestible casualty of this decade was the ritual Sabbath dinner for the extended family. Putting extra leaves in the table to showcase the "great Sunday roast" and to accommodate relatives and close friends was becoming obsolete. These are the kin we now "know" via yearly Christmas cards. Social life was increasingly becoming family-free. Thus did Middletown's, and every other town's, grand feasts of old contract into "quick bites."

In Christine Frederick's 1929 book *Selling Mrs. Consumer*, she pronounced elaborate cooking from scratch as "a social accomplishment of the dark eras before the auto, the movie, the radio, and other inventions came to provide more interests." While deriding Victorian cookery as "conspicuous consumption," Frederick worked for food manufacturers such as General Mills designing labels, recipe booklets, and enticing advertisements. These taught benighted women how to substitute "scientifically correct" canned soups and other packaged products for "inferior" homemade fare. Such blandishments also undermined the authority of lessons learned at mother's knee, making everyone, especially women, distrustful of their own taste-buds and vulnerable to corporate manipulation and deception.

Even Betty Crocker was a crock. An ad man for a flour-milling company that eventually became Gold Medal invented this fictional sage in 1921 to answer letters from customers seeking baking advice. But of course, Betty's bottom line was peddling the goods. By the time she earned a face in 1936, the male executives of food conglomerates had substantially rewritten the menu American women once controlled. These thriving kings of heat-and-serve ransacked not only the larder but also the aesthetics of the family meal. In her bittersweet 1933 memoir, Edith Wharton pined for the lost household arts, which she described as ". . . a most important and honourable part of the ancient curriculum of house-keeping . . . swept aside by the 'monstrous regiment' of the emancipated young women taught by their elders to despise the kitchen and the linen room, and to substitute the acquiring of University degrees for the more complex art of civilized living."

Mercifully, the soul-starved Wharton had departed from that brave new world by 1940, when Emily Post started to lecture her countrymen on the declining manners she traced to the prevalence of dirty tablecloths and diners who ate in their undershirts or curlers. Gone was the dining room "shrine" of Clarence Day, Jr.'s boyhood. But such slovenly clothes increasingly fit the fare. Our military victory in World War II was a crushing defeat for our tastebuds and the Victorian concept of family meals. Along with aluminum siding and tail-fin cars, the public was avalanched with processed foods. Many, including the infamous Spam, were adapted from rations developed for GI Joe, who had more pressing priorities than fine dining. But what was our excuse?

### TV Dinners and Wonder Bread

In 1952, America met the mother of microwave meals in the first frozen TV dinner of turkey, cornbread, potatoes, and peas. Eating à la tube, which got top billing, became the order of the day that many conservatives now hold so dear. Ralph Kramden and Lucy Ricardo supplied the conversation while mute munchers ingested the crusty contents of compartmentalized trays that were eerily reminiscent of those shown in prison chow lines from 1930s gangster movies. As the individual TV table began competing with the communal table, even "shared" meals ceased to be truly shared, since each family member could choose his own poison.

Ads for Wonder Bread—the signature sandwich bookends of baby boomer adolescence—now pursue this target audience with carefree images of its lost youth. That polka-dotted plastic era not only taught us the "wonder" of bread that tore like tissue paper, it reached what the historian Glenna Matthews calls "the nadir of American cookery." "This was the heyday of prepared foods and the cream-of-mushroom soup school of cuisine where the cook could pour a can of this product over anything that was not a dessert and create a culinary treat according to the standards of the day."

Matthews's review of women's magazines from this period found that most recommended meals were mere blends of manufactured goods. Typical recipes from *Ladies' Home Journal* contained frozen vegetables, and salmon, potatoes, and pears—all as canned as the TV laugh tracks that became another staple of prefabricated mass consumption. Matthews notes that by 1960, the "creativity" of a once esteemed and highly personalized craft "consisted in combining a pudding mix with a cake mix." After the Second World War, "The level of skill involved in cooking—no doubt that area of housework with the most potential for inspiring job satisfaction—declined to an all-time low."

Those of us who had some living link to our Victorian-era relations witnessed this sad decline and its implications for the gradual fraying of family life. When I was a child, my grandmother had a kitchen that seemed a wonderland of simmering soups, fresh-baked scents, and carefully selected produce waiting to be transformed by her magic hands. She measured ingredients by instinct instead of using the scientifically precise cups and scales that always remind me of high school chemistry class. Everything she made drew acclaim (or least satisfied sighs) from her husband and children, no matter how often she served a dish.

Although she dutifully taught her daughters to cook, their efforts never approached her art, and they knew it. By the time they grew up between the wars, cooking was just another household task. Most of their meals were dependable but forgettable. Although they sometimes ventured my grandmother's sauces and breads, the factory foods that never dared darken her shelves were right at home on theirs. They did preserve many of her recipes on the three-by-five index cards she never needed. But their own eat-and-run kids never voiced a whisper of the appreciation she had rightly earned.

*Instant Meals*

Today there is a booming market of dinner kits that give the illusion you're cooking without reading a recipe, slicing, dicing, or measuring any ingredients. Even processed spices and herbs are now combined into single containers to spare you the trouble of unscrewing more than one bottle. With manufacturers determining the balance of garlic powder and paprika, forget finesse. We are fooling only our deadened palates and the souls we have robbed of food's sentimental meaning when we forfeit our cultural history. Researchers at Chicago's Smell and Taste Treatment and Research Foundation found that for those born before 1930, fond images of youth were triggered by the aroma of freshly baked goods, especially bread. In contrast, later generations grow nostalgic from the scent of Cocoa Puffs and SweeTarts.

Ironically, bread machines represent the only real growth area in the "home baking" industry. While sales of raw ingredients such as flour are dropping like ruined soufflés, "no- bake" desserts have become bestsellers. "Today, many people think the term 'baking by scratch' means opening a box of mix," concluded a *New York Times* reporter who recently profiled this phenomenon. Those willing to turn on the oven need only water the mix like a plant—something a trained chimp could do.

Studies show women now spend on average a scant quarter hour "preparing" dinner. This meal was once the bread and butter of domestic life. It embodied high esteem for a distinctly feminine craft, the continuity of the generations that had bequeathed their precious culinary legacy, the nourishing of family bonds, and a deep sense of all that home implied. It is this loss that enables us to apply the bastardized label "meals" to fortified candy bars and canned drinks.

The twentieth century surrendered the power of home traditions to the almighty god of convenience—the main reason American adults visit fast-food restaurants an average of six times a month. (Perhaps the accumulated hours spent waiting in their not-so-fast lines could be applied to some home cooking worthy of the name.) Not only do we increasingly "dine" out or carry out, we are now eating solo on wheels. Vehicular techno-wonders like the jumbo cup holder have mutated into lap trays for motorists. Nine dollars buys you five separate sections to hold beverages, food, and utensils. The standard money-back guarantee does not include the promise you will taste what you eat, nor does it reimburse you for staining your clothes and upholstery.

The National Restaurant Association estimates that Americans spend forty-four cents of every food dollar for edibles (or inedibles) prepared outside the home. The attractions of that "special sauce" notwithstanding, working women don't have time to cook anymore, and no one has filled their shoes or their aprons. We may well ask whether we have lost more than the welcoming scent of some delicacy simmering on the stove after battling like gladiators through rush-hour traffic?

## DEPERSONALIZED FOOD

A harried professional woman I know whose mother recently died confided that she still missed the comforting smell of the soup her mom used to create from scratch. It made her feel special because it could be had only at home for love, not for money. With no time to cook such intricate dishes, she lamented, "I have no smells to leave my children."

We have traded the intangible but irreplaceable sentiments of home for hollow "McMemories." Like burgers, shakes, and fries, their immortal incarnation can be purchased from the official McDonald's Collectibles Club. For $39.95 you can own a three-and-one-half inch "authentic replica" of the first McDonald's franchise, which opened in 1955. Ever since then, claims the ad for this "hand-painted" model, "McDonald's has been a beloved part of the American scene—the place where good food, fun and family come together." If this whets your appetite for more, you are invited to view additional memorabilia at the McDonald's Museum in Des Plaines, Illinois.

Popular Victorian sculptures also enshrined food and family—if not what we consider "fun." But they portrayed parents and children gathered together, not the golden calf of the Golden Arches. That is the crucial difference between bona fide memories and McMemories. The first is warm, filling, and sustaining. Its pretender has the staying power of a Chinese meal that leaves us emotionally starved. Those raised on this meager diet are destined to confuse quality food with whatever commands hefty prices in restaurants. But not even the wealthiest gourmands can buy a substitute for the home fare they have missed. Like those who yearn for great romance, they'll always sense that something vital is missing from their lives, even if they can't define it. Another acquaintance of mine said she had come to realize that the parsley her mother used to garnish the meal on the family china "meant something more than a small green sprig." But she can't articulate its meaning.

The need for this personalized "something" is increasingly being catered to by professionals who perform every domestic chore, from ferrying the kids to sports events and purchasing their birthday presents to decorating their rooms and even arranging family photos in albums. And while Grandma is probably touring the country in her RV, new moms pay a substitute to give them a crash course in breast-feeding, bathing, baby rocking, and the lost maternal wisdom of the ages. As an added service (and expense), these surrogates will even prepare a home-cooked meal, whose origin is part of someone else's home.

Can families survive if these functions are narrowed like genetically altered plants and livestock, stripped of the skills, frills, quirks, and traditions, however small, that indelibly stamp our character?

The anthropologist David Murray worries that reducing the unique, defining aspects of family life to "sterile, rational transactions with strangers" teaches children that even the most intimate service is a matter of mere dollars and cents. (Of course, the same applies to prostitution.) Even for those women who still cook for their families, cooking has become little more than just another hassle, another chore best dealt with quickly and efficiently.

### The Lost Art of Home Cooking

In contrast to today's back-of-the-box cooks, Victorian women needed smarts to separate the wheat from the chaff because adulterated foods were rampant in their time. As it did other domestic duties, their culture respected their culinary talents, giving them a source of self-esteem women lack today. Victorian cast-iron stoves, which were fed by wood or coal, had mercurial temperature ranges that demanded human vigilance and judgment. With the bells and whistles of progress came contempt. Glenna Matthews notes that by the 1920s, "experts" who assumed that home cooks had the wits of adolescents advocated the quickie processed foods that a budding industry hawked for an age of "compressed living." Two decades earlier, Fannie Farmer had warned that cooking would descend to "mere drudgery if one does not put heart and soul into the work."[3] Both were compressed into extinction by this new brand of living.

The Victorian mistress of the house was expected to master the art and science of cookery, to have a thorough working knowledge of herbs, spices, meats, fruits, breads, and vegetables. Without packaged foods, refrigerators, preservatives, or a counter cluttered with time-saving appliances, the Victorian home cook had to employ far more elbow grease, planning, and imagination than modern-day homemakers do. Yet however much drudgery the work could involve, they understood that their work was extremely important for the health and well-being of the family and, by extension, the world.

In contrast, the extent of contemporary gastronomic illiteracy today is attested to by the success of cookbooks with titles like *The Complete Idiot's Guide to Cookery* and *Cooking for Dummies.* The culinary historian Karen Hess notes disdainfully, "In the [nineteenth] century, the books were written by cooks for cooks. In the [twentieth] century, mainstream cookbooks were written by dummies for dummies."[4] Describing the proliferation of "dysfunctional cooks" as the kitchen equivalent of "Why Johnny can't read," cookbook author Elaine Corn complains that only "conversations with waiters" keep a substantial part of the population from starving. Weinraub concluded that since so many baby boomers grew up eating canned soups, frozen veggies, and TV dinners, "today's books are aimed at an audience that often hasn't learned to cook at home, and doesn't come equipped with treasured family recipe books."[5]

Kitchen-dummy syndrome is not just a prescription for heartburn or a lifetime sentence of leftovers. It is poison to the psyche. The holistic Victorian view of food traced the influence of the table far beyond the dining room. Sour stomachs produced sour tempers, and coarse food was thought to produce coarse natures.

The intangible effects of what and how we eat were noted in a recent *New York Times* article on the decline of baking. One of the few women interviewed who continues this fading tradition struggled to describe the psychological impact of homemade bread:

> If I serve some of my banana or pumpkin bread at the meeting, people seem to interact better and tend to be more relaxed. It helps to stimulate dialogue and bring out the best in people, maybe because they connect it with images of family and home.

Future generations may experience these images only via history or virtual reality unless we revamp our agenda. Even Betty Friedan, writing in *The Second Stage,* asks, "Shouldn't [homemaking] be valued somehow? And what about the rest—arranging the flowers, baking the cookies? It makes life more pleasant, surely, even if it's not necessary or paid for. What would life be like if no one did that work?"

It is a question many of us have already answered, and our conclusion is that we have definitely lost a great deal along the way. It is no wonder that interest in Victoriana is increasing, as we try to buy and decorate and read our way back to a sense of artful living that has escaped our grasp. Yet a few well-laced doilies and a Jane Austen video-fest offer us only a tiny glimpse of the well-ordered, harmonious lives the Victorians lead. To truly regain their sense of grace, we must look, as they did, at the larger picture. We must, like the era's greatest sleuth, Sherlock Holmes, look carefully at the details if we are to reconstruct the whole.

# PART 5

# LOST ARTS AND FORGOTTEN RITUALS

# 18

## The Art of Living

We live in an age where we document all of our customs in as much detail as we can, through high-tech gadgets that allow us to capture every Kodak moment, from birth to the after-the-funeral beer bash. For all our endless fascination with recording our modern rituals, however, we are intrigued by Victorian customs because they are so very different from our own. Moreover, they baffle us. Why such attention to time-consuming detail? Why such morbid displays when a loved one died? How quaint their wholesome parlor games and croquet matches seem to us now. But for the Victorians, who lived in a holistic and integrated world, there was great meaning and even great love behind many of these rituals and ephemera that we dismiss as curious relics of a bygone era.

### MODERN HOLIDAY CELEBRATIONS

We are most aware of our forgotten customs at holidays, when we long for an old-fashioned celebration that emphasizes God, family, and love over want lists, office parties, and social obligations. Although ornate Victorian holidays required extra effort and preparation, they were natural extensions of what Isabella Beeton called the "ceremonials for common days" that "joyfully united families, adding beauty, grace, and charm to life." Our holidays are anything but, as we struggle to compensate—via added obligations, aggravation, and maxed-out credit card balances—for the patchwork daily "ceremonials" that impoverish our lives throughout the rest of the year. We trim our Christmas trees with reproductions of Victorian ornaments and deck our holiday mantels with a picturesque "Dickens village" that includes steepled churches. We put out the extra effort to do it all, but no matter how much we spend, we can't achieve the feeling of that old-fashioned Christmas/Easter/Passover we seek.

In contrast to the past, modern holidays are more stressful than special precisely because they require not just the time but the domestic skills we lack. Some experts claim that such stress, combined with alcohol, contributes to increased spouse and child abuse during the "ho-ho-ho" season. In addition, frayed family ties mean we never develop the facility and patience to peacefully coexist with difficult relations. As a result, the "shock" of occasional forced family togetherness unleashes endless backbiting, bickering, and complaints about long lines to use the bathroom.

Ceremonies that were once de rigueur for holiday feasts are increasingly shunned. A national 1995 survey commissioned by Lenox China found that over one third of all families planned to serve the Thanksgiving meal in their kitchen instead of the dining room. Kitchens allow even special celebrations a casual air, and they are far less threatening to a culture that has lost the art of dining and views any hint of formality as a hanging offense. But as those sensibilities disintegrate, like Miss Havisham's wedding dress, we forfeit the beauty, grace, and charm that drive us to period movies, where we get a tantalizing whiff of the bounty we cannot taste.

Even as we recognize that such holidays as Thanksgiving, Christmas, and Passover afford us rare opportunities to convene the gasping patient we call family under an oxygen tent, we frequently subcontract to strangers the unique and unifying rituals that gave holiday spirit its meaning. Hired Santa's helpers thrive in the Washington, D.C., area and other regions populated by upscale working couples with more money than time to spend. These all-purpose elves will write your season's greetings cards and select the perfect personal gifts for your friends and relatives, whom they've never met.

This is a true Christmas miracle; I'm still struggling to find acceptable presents for people I've known forever. Even when we take the pains to choose presents for our nearest and dearest, instead of using hired hands or resorting to increasingly popular gift certificates, just how thoughtful can these gifts be when at least a third of all shopping is done the week before Christmas?

If your bank balance is sufficiently merry, all your holiday decorations will be erected and dismantled by a service hired for the purpose. (No more nasty pine needles to pick out of the carpet.) And a feast will be prepared as big as your budget—not your culinary skills—will allow. One upscale catering service reports that requests for complete holiday meals doubled every year between 1990 and 1993, at prices that can surpass $100 for just two people. For some harried consumers who want to have it all, painless soup to nuts won't do at any price. A growing trend in the catering industry called "speed scratch" does all the hard, heavy prep work while allowing buyers to pretend they created the "vittles." These gourmet shops and services offer fully stuffed and roasted turkeys that need only reheating.

Many women realize how their cheated families pay with more than cash when the aura and accoutrements of holidays are ordered like takeout pizza. Indeed, if holiday fare can be so casually obtained, it is no big deal—what is these days?—to schedule or reschedule the meal around football games. This macho madness would have stunned Victorian males, for whom being a man meant actually practicing the family values we preach. They also took pride in presiding over the dinner table and demonstrating the art of carving the turkey or goose as expertly as it was prepared.

Among fifty pairs of mothers and daughters interviewed for a recent *New York Times* article on declining domestic holiday traditions was a grandmother who remarked wistfully, "The rich close relationships my family enjoys took hours and hours to develop." While she admires her daughter's professional achievements, "I worry that the demands on her time may be detrimental to the next generation." One baby boomer mom recalled her parents and siblings constructing an entire miniature village beneath their Christmas tree, an experience her kids will never share. "I don't have the time," she lamented. "I take my children to the mall. So what will they remember?"

"I'm not giving my children the same memories," said another rushed but candid mother who had abandoned all the elaborate Christmas baking that once lovingly linked the generations. "I feel real bad about that." Others assuage their guilt with mail-order remedies designed for just this purpose, like the prefab, prebaked gingerbread house kits that families can assemble with the aid of enclosed instructions. Even if the finished product looks Christmas-card perfect, it is just another cookie-cutter version of those made from every other kit.

## VICTORIAN HOLIDAYS

Whether your tax bracket is Bloomies or Wal-Mart, the memory of freshly baked homemade gingerbread or challah cannot be catered or ordered by phone, fax, or Internet. This is why even wealthy Victorians made their own decorations, gingerbread, and other treats filled with symbolism as well as taste. The goal back then was not look-at-me razzle-dazzle but a rich, if simple, experience to share.

The Victorians' Christmas preparations began right after Thanksgiving, and not by running to the mall. Fruitcakes (light and dark) were first on the agenda because they required time to age—though not into the fossilized teeth-cracking versions we love to hate. Making plum pudding was another prized tradition. Every family member took turns stirring it from east to west to commemorate the journey of the Three Kings. The circles represented eternity while the pudding's spherical shape signified the family's connection to the wider world. The heavy symbolism of this dessert was leavened by the hope of getting a slice containing a penny or a silver charm, both omens of good luck.

Rather than purchasing holiday decorations by the box, the Victorians made theirs from bits of yarn, lace, ribbon, and fancy papers everyone saved throughout the year for just that special purpose. This moneyless moral Christmas club emphasized the venerated virtue of thrift; we might call it recycling. It also made holiday celebrations a slowly savored mutual treat, not a shock suddenly sprung on us, like those first gray hairs we spot in the mirror. Children learned to appreciate both the beauty of nature and the value of home by helping to adorn the house with wreaths and garlands of assorted evergreens, leaves, and pine cones they had gathered. They took particular pride in making Christmas tree trimmings such as ropes of cranberries and popcorn, crocheted snowflakes, cotton batting figures, and cornucopias—the ornate tasseled cone-shaped ornaments that were filled with assorted nuts and sweets.

Holidays of long ago involved more active creation than passive consumption. The former instilled treasured memories often recounted in written recollections of that era. Passive consumption taught us to discard the effortless expected booty we received because the novelty wore thin so quickly. Thus Victorian youngsters usually made gifts for their parents and siblings—a muffler for Father, a sachet or pin cushion for Mother, dolls or doll clothes for girls, carved blocks and soldiers for boys. Why were all these time- and thought-consuming rituals so essential to the Christmas spirit? The editor Sarah Josepha Hale answered this question with one of her own in 1868: "Are not these enjoyments the bread of life and the wine of love that strengthen the best energies of the soul that give beauty and enjoyment to our homes?"

## PARLOR GAMES AND
## OTHER VICTORIAN RECREATION

This enriching soul food also nourished family recreation throughout the year. We run to our separate televisions after dinner, but the Victorians gathered in the parlor to read to each other and play word or board games based on literary classics and Bible stories. Religious images were especially popular for inexpensive jigsaw puzzles, another joint activity that promoted patience. While both have fallen from favor since then, I recently saw an ad for a company that turns the photo of your choice into a "personalized puzzle" for sixty-plus dollars. The ad featured an attractive couple with three young kids. But rather than emphasize the potential for togetherness, this item was hawked as a "conversation piece" for your coffee table. Like coffee-table books, the pleasure it provides is measured by the number of your friends it impresses.

Almost every Victorian parlor had a piano to accompany frequent family sing-alongs. This prized possession was considered a necessity rather than a luxury, and plain or secondhand models were affordably priced. Music could be shared by all, even the tone-deaf, and it was considered morally uplifting. All children, especially girls, were encouraged to master the piano, but pleasure was more important then perfection. Although Clarence Day, Sr.'s renditions of Beethoven and Bach were "limited," according to his son, his feeling for music was "deeply rooted. . . . It gave him a sense of well-being."

*Because singing together was a favorite form of home recreation for the Victorians, many homes had a piano and most young ladies could play and sing. Note the gentleman standing by to turn pages and assist the lady in any way she needed.*

Like most women of her time, Mrs. Day also did her musical best. "We often heard her sweet voice gently singing old songs of an evening. If she forgot parts here or there, she swiftly improvised something that would let the air float along without breaking the spell." The off-key female songbird at family gatherings later became a figure of derision to a cynical century that devalued traditional notions of feminine accomplishment and domestic skills. Like the savory smells of Victorian meals, we have lost the endearing sounds that once made homes not just a place but a state of mind.

Family time also provided cleverly instructive outlets for sibling rivalry, while cultivating the love of learning we wish our kids would acquire. Victorian children competed with each other to memorize and recite passages from Shakespeare and the classics. In his autobiography, the journalist Hutchins Hapgood called this exercise "the chief civilizing influence of childhood." Private theatricals were another favorite pastime. Mark Twain's family and neighbors often dramatized scenes from his novels. Performances could be simple and spontaneous or involve extensive preparation and homemade costumes.

In tableaux vivants the actors staged a famous painting, statue, or story, while onlookers tried to guess its name. Edith Wharton immortalized this form of entertainment in *The House of Mirth*, where Lily Bart represented Joshua Reynolds's portrait of Mrs. Lloyd. "It was as though she had stepped, not out of, but into, Reynolds' canvas, banishing the phantom of his dead beauty by the beams of her living grace."

Fun in our gluttonous age is merchandise-dependent, but the roots of this syndrome predated our addiction to the tube. The authors of *Middletown* noted that by the 1920s, the rich range of shared home entertainments had severely declined. Dancing to recorded music that divided the generations, as opposed to music you made and all enjoyed, became the major domestic amusement—when families weren't going their separate ways. And increasingly, they were. Living meant living it up, which demanded cash and a car. As one person interviewed by the Lynds observed, "It almost seems as though family members simply couldn't wait to get out of the house and away from one another."

We have been deserting the hearth ever since, despite the proliferating video toys that feed us processed leisure while starving the creative "mental vision" Edith Wharton so poignantly described. Even when we technically nest together, like strangers in a hotel, no one is really home. Instead we surf solo on the waves of cable television channels or the World Wide Web. We need to disentangle ourselves if we are ever to go home again.

We have cut away at the ties that bind us not just to each other but to the very rhythms of life itself. We surrounded ourselves with creature comforts and entertainments in order to fend off the hard realities that we try to wish away. This is nowhere more evident than in our inability to deal with death.

## A TIME TO MOURN

In an age when we can't stop talking about sex and our appetite for personal revelations seems boundless, the subject of death is taboo. One ultrasensitive town in Colorado replaced its DEAD END street signs with NO OUTLET signs because the former were considered too macabre. In abridging the classic novel *Little Women,* a book publisher eliminated a section that dealt with heaven in the context of Beth's death. According to the abridger, Laurie Lawlor, today's ten- and eleven-year-olds have "too little life experience" to accept the "very Victorian concept" that Beth's family believes she is "well at last."[1]

The squirming silence that greets the topic of death not only denies an undeniable reality, it also deprives us of the acceptable ways Victorians had to publicly express their grief or offer comfort to the grieving. Without clear etiquette guideposts to follow, we are confused about what to say when people die, how to express sympathy without giving offense, and whether to visit the family or leave them alone.

Most people would say good riddance to Victorian mourning rituals—the dull black crepe worn by female survivors, the family's withdrawal from social activities, and the various death mementos they made. Contemporary historians label these customs grotesque, macabre, grim, creepy, and necrophiliac. Our own method of "dealing" with death—going on, keeping active, jumping back into the swing of life—is much healthier. Or is it?

The "stifling" Victorian formality that so many scorn prevented such awkward situations, as it was intended to do. Ten days after the funeral, friends and acquaintances left their personal calling cards with a handwritten note of condolence at the "mourning house." When its residents wanted to begin receiving guests, they sent out their own black-bordered cards as a signal people should come. Discussing the loss with the bereaved might be tearful, but it was natural and expected. And no one's face turned red.

Today, the voices of self-expression turn suddenly mute in the face of life's final challenge. We struggle just to select some mass-market sympathy card to express our condolences. But you'll have to search high and low for cards that dare to mention death. Hallmark executives report that the word makes us uncomfortable. And since funerals are also discomforting (not to mention inconvenient), attendance is steadily shrinking, according to funeral directors. Some who do attend come as they are without apology, if basic black doesn't suit them. After all, the departed won't notice.

The Victorians would have found our casual response to the death of a loved one as appalling as we find their formal rituals. Widows wore black for the prescribed two years, only gradually adopting "colors" as they passed through three phases of mourning. (Because the typical male business suit was black, Victorian widowers wore armbands.) A widow's entertainment agenda was limited to quiet gatherings of family and friends. If she partied hard before the mourning period ended, she was considered a disgrace and a disrespectful spouse.

Though such limitations may look excessive to modern eyes, they expressed a central tenet of the Victorians' social code: Respect was the heart of civilized life; it did not stop beating at death's door. Queen Victoria, the queen of mourning, wore "widow's weeds" for her forty remaining years after her adored Albert's premature death. This deeply romantic response to one of history's great romances would now be called dangerously dysfunctional, if not deranged. We would press mopey Victoria to get a makeover and take a singles' cruise. Had she outlived the age that bears her name by only a few years, etiquette books would have told her that such extended grief was sheer "self-pity." By then, broken hearts were passé.

In his bestseller, *Listening to Prozac*, the psychiatrist Peter Kramer documents the successful use of antidepressants to treat (mostly female) patients suffering from prolonged bereavement. Then he wisely asks a culturally loaded question: What is prolonged? These days the answer is beyond one year, according to most experts. But is this calculation of the mourning a dead spouse merits any less arbitrary or intrinsically healthier than the Victorian rule of two years (or a lifetime, if needed)?

And is forgetting a past love too slowly any healthier than forgetting too quickly? For decades after the death of his young fiancée, Washington Irving could not bear to hear her name mentioned, and even thirty years after her death, he was so upset by the accidental discovery of some of her embroidery work that he was unable to speak. Though he never awoke from his grief, it nourished the talent that gave posterity Rip Van Winkle.

*An example of a Victorian-era memorial picture, which incorporates the hair of the deceased.*

## Mementos of the Dead

Where we would clean house of any depressing reminders of the dead, the Victorians memoralized them with a variety of personal objects that were treasured and proudly displayed. These living mementos included mourning portraits, embroidered pictures, and custom-made rings and lockets and jewelry woven from the hair of the dead.

The most morbid type of memento to modern eyes is also the most sentimental. While we barely blink when body parts fly across our movie screens, I've observed many visitors at museums and antique shows gasp openly at the necklaces, earrings, men's watch chains, and women's bracelets woven from the hair of the dead. The Victorians made and wore these intimate objects as symbolic links to their loved ones in the hereafter. Hair art also expressed affection among the living. Sweethearts often exchanged locks of their hair, and hair wreaths and floral bouquets created from the mingled strands of family members were common ornaments in the parlor—where funerals were held. A century ago, death came into the household, instead of being shunted into sterile hospital wards. There was no denial of death's role in the cycle of life when it was so much a part of people's everyday experience.

The Victorian way of mourning helped people cope with grief in an age of high infant mortality, when the average life span was less than two thirds of our own. Science and technology have bought us time, but they have yet to make us immortal. While many of us outlive our ancestors, we live without the rituals and trappings that sweetened their sadness, and made leaving this world or being left behind a little easier.

## The Victorian Cemetery

The transcendent meaning that elevates life beyond ashes and dust derives from our ability to forge the connections that the Victorians saw. Those who make them will feel inspired and elevated, rather than alienated or repelled, by visits to Victorian graveyards. Far from being reminiscent of creepy Charles Addams cartoons, they are peaceful havens whose monuments and headstones speak a silent language all Victorians understood. Here eternal souls symbolically rest in urns or in the cradling hands of angels. Crowns promise future

*Victorians, accepting that death is a natural part of life, often went on picnics in cemeteries, which were beautifully landscaped parks for the dead and the living. The Victorians saw themselves, their ancestors, and the physical beauty around them as creations of the same divine grand plan.*

glory, while oak and ivy leaves affirm religious faith. So many infants' graves are marked by empty cradles or lambs of innocence, but their sadness too is an enriching part of this walk through the not-so-distant past.

A distraught woman recently wrote to Ann Landers for advice on how to derail her sister's "morbid" wedding plans. The bride-to-be wanted all her guests to join her at the cemetery after leaving the church so she could lay her bouquet on her father's grave. Ann said the bride could she do as she pleased, but nixed taking the guests as "a downer." My heart ached for that misunderstood bride who wished to honor the father she had lost twenty-one years before. The point of her lovely gesture was to demonstrate connections the Victorians would have instantly understood. This wedding-day visit to a grave fuses the past and the future, the love for a lost parent and the love for a new spouse.[2]

## VICTORIAN CLOTHING

Weddings, of course, bring out the Victorian in many of us. Young women don romantic Victorian gowns for their special day and rent restored Victorian mansions for their receptions. Brides—and grooms—find comfort in the old rituals of something borrowed, something blue, and the flowing, lacy dresses from the previous century capture a sense of old-fashioned romance while they drape beautifully across the female figure.

The line of such gowns was not lost on the Victorians, but their clothing styles were not inspired by such shallow aims as showing off one's figure or one's money. A woman who adorned herself in a beautiful gown was sending a message to her friends, family, and neighbors, which was not about her taste so much as about her state of mind, and her respect for others.

In the modern era, our problematic relationship with clothing reflects a contradiction of contemporary sensibilities—we use our clothes to express ourselves, but we balk if others use them to judge the self we choose to express.

The Victorians, however, were untroubled by such contradictions. Their consensus on morals and manners extended to the meaning of the wrappings in which they chose to show themselves. As Mary Eliza Haweis, author of *The Art of Beauty*, explained in 1878, "Dress bears the same relation to the body as speech does to the brain; and therefore dress may be called the speech of the body."

Like its vocal counterpart, dress could either bolster or batter civility. Appropriate dress was no mere personal preference but a social obligation, said Eliza Duffey, "a duty . . . we owe to others because we have no right to put our friends to the blush by untidiness or uncouthness." Indifferent or slovenly appearance was considered selfish contempt; dishabille was considered a sign of moral laxity. Now it is considered fashionable, which explains why many churches must post signs barring visitors in shorts, halter tops, or other revealing garments. Even many high-end restaurants have abandoned the tie-and-jacket rule for fear of losing patrons. In some cases their sartorial standards have sunk to the point of admitting any bipeds who still wear socks and shoes. Can entreaties to use utensils be far behind?

## Transcendent Clothing

Like all aspects of Victorian life, clothing was invested with a significance that was more than material. It had a transcendent quality, which had an elevating and even refining influence on the wearers and those with whom they came in contact. Everyone was obliged, within their means, to contribute to this aura rather than debase it, because to be slovenly was considered an affront to the feelings of other people. Compare this to the gruesome trend in the fashion industry of "heroin chic": Magazine spreads celebrate the ugliness of heroin addiction and feature pale, thin, drugged-out-looking models slumped on the floor. If we are outraged by the dangerous message this sends to youth, we should remember that, as Michael Gross, the author of *Model*, explained in *The Washington Post*, "Fashion is amoral. Fashion doesn't care what messages it is sending out as long as the message sells frocks." Presumably, this amorality also applies to the people who create these reckless images.

In our search for comfort we sneer at the impracticality of clothing from an era we see as hopelessly restrictive. True, men wore stiff and starched shirt fronts, while some whale-boned women wore up to thirty-seven pounds of clothing, with nineteen pounds suspended from the waist alone. It should be said, however, that corsets were quite controversial in their day, and, Hollywood movie images notwithstanding, many women of the era rejected them. Any modern smugness toward Victorian dress should also be tempered by our fondness for Wonderbras that are as tight as any corset, and the masochistic decades-long devotion to spiky high heels—our version of Chinese foot binding. Fashion demands its due in every age and many seem more than willing to pay the price, which explains why after decades of being relegated to the darkest corner of the lingerie department, girdles and foundation undergarments have come back in vogue.

We also dismiss Victorian dress as too conformist: all those women in long dresses and men in black top hats and tails. It is ironic that in the modern age we claim to value dress as a vehicle of self-expression while sporting designer logos or on everything from underwear to luggage and company brand names on T-shirts and hats. What is more conformist than this "body advertising," which the Victorians relegated to men who were paid to wear placards in public places?

At least the sartorial conformity the Victorians practiced balanced rhyme and reason. They were attuned to how clothing "fit" different surroundings and occasions—a lost sensibility.

*The Victorian ideal in dress was to look modest, not ostentatious or dowdy, and clothes suited the activity and surroundings.*

The Victorians admired utility in clothing as in design, but they also valued form as much as function. In 1880 William Morris stated his "golden rule" for all types of artistic expression: "Have nothing . . . that you do not know to be useful, or believe to be beautiful." A century later the tawdry and the crude are equally at home in discount outlets and pricey boutiques. The runways of New York and Paris have recently featured shirtless suits and dog collars for men, as well as entire outfits of "S and M" leather straps for women. Not many consumers will be attracted by such self-conscious emblems of sexual perversion. But today's designers do their best to debase rather than elevate everyday life. Their fin-de-siècle creative spirit manifests itself in styles that combine what one news report calls "cheesy fabrics, loathsome colors and obnoxious patterns." They are modeled by spindly, hollow-eyed runway walkers and made fashionable by customers like the actress Uma Thurman.

Brooks Brothers and Lands End–type clothing is more typical garb for mainstream America. Neither shocking nor seductive, these clothes are simply bland. But whether we practice exhibitionism or a clothes-in-the-crowd philosophy by what we wear or bare, we have lost all sense of personal appearance as a source of social uplift, signifying self-respect and facilitating mutual respect. The Victorians, however, were very conscious of both functions of dress. In the succinct but potent words of Sarah Josepha Hale, "Dress is both a cause and consequence of civilized life." The idea that clothes could have a civilizing or higher moral power became one of many discarded Victorian "pretensions." Where *Godey's Lady's Book* melded a philosophy of dress and life, the burgeoning fashion magazines of the twenties, fed by advertising dollars from the new cosmetics industry, sold women on a perfectly polished surface as their highest goal.

Now such polish is reserved by most for only the most formal occasions. Flying in an airplane has become so commonplace that many make themselves comfortable and dress in cutoffs, flip-flops and tank tops. Recently, a new disincentive to poolside lounging appeared when a 300-pound woman announced on *The Montel Williams Show* that she wears bikinis because they make her feel good. No word on how her fellow bathers feel.

Now, earnest reformers can do little more than complain, and "serious" discussions of fashion are confined to a narrow clique of sanctified designers and their wannabes. Yet a century ago, the style and meaning of clothes occupied eminent critics of architecture, art, and life. The English philosopher John Ruskin wrote of "true nobleness in dress," while the poet and playwright Oscar Wilde asserted that reforming dress was more important than reforming religion. (Like all the best Wildean mots, this comment was at once facetious and deeply serious.)

Constantly changing fashions used to provide endless fodder for serious debate. The swinging-cage crinoline was denounced as a "monstrous caricature that vexed the artistic eye" or was praised as a "visual charm." The bustle was deemed both a "contorting rigidity" and a "delightful invention." Some praised the "sweeping dignity" of trains, and Tissot's painting *The Stairs* celebrated the flowing beauty of a tea gown. Others denounced trains as "dirt catchers." (Sensible ladies compromised by wearing their trains indoors.) Of course, the incessantly controversial corset "murdered the muscles," even as it "lent the grace of curves to figures lacking the fullness of rounded outlines."

Critics would verbally duel to the death on this subject because the Victorians thought of dress not just as a badge of individual expression but as a collective experience that could help civilize society and elevate the quality of life. By contrast, the solipsistic function of modern self-expressive dress was epitomized for me by a twenty-something man clad in a bright yellow sweatshirt that proclaimed in bold black letters, "Me, Myself and I." At least it wasn't obscene.

We will never again fuss with twenty-button gloves, even though it is just these nuances of Victorian life that charm us in the telling. We may scoff at the antique notion of clothing as an "index and prologue to character" that could ennoble or degrade the nation, but to recapture the sense of community we all claim to want, we need to view community spirit as more than prodding people to vote or do volunteer work. We must rediscover the commonsense wisdom that recognizes how individual appearance subtly colors the aura of our goals and behavior.

The value of this lesson has prompted a growing number of schools, especially those in the inner city, to adopt traditional uniforms and restrict oversized jewelry, gang colors, and other items that feed conflict and distract clothes-conscious kids from their education. Not only have disciplinary problems declined as a result of these reforms, student performance has improved, and the general environment is more controlled. A year after schools in Long Beach, California, mandated uniforms, officials reported a 50 percent decrease in incidents of students fighting, a 36 percent drop in overall student crime, and 32 percent fewer suspensions. In a national survey of secondary school principals, 70 percent favored uniforms. Even President Clinton cast his vote for them in his State of the Union Address.[3] All across the political spectrum, people are beginning to recognize what the Victorians knew: Clothes, like reading and writing, are potent tools of civility.

Social obligation does not demand bankrupting ourselves to mimic the Victorian wardrobe that included a specified outfit for every occasion and hour of the day, but we need to raise our clothing consciousness. Eventually, we might even aspire to a graceful life again, to wear something simple or grand that is worthy of art for the ages. But first we must establish shared standards for acceptable dress, like those we are trying to develop for civility and education. The indispensable foundation of that wardrobe is not a navy blazer or a little black dress, but a sense of respect.

Even more than Victorian elegance and charm, we have lost what might be called the Victorians' environmental fashion sensitivity—how people complemented and completed their surroundings with what they wore and how they wore it. The contrast is perhaps most obvious when twentieth-century sensibilities come into physical contact with nineteenth-century environments. On a recent architectural tour through restored Southern plantations, I joined parades of tourists clad mostly in shorts and T-shirts or jogging suits, tramping through those meticulously crafted treasures. Only the unpaid volunteers leading the tours seemed to harmonize with the homes, even though they wore modern attire, not period costumes. Although they were friendly and gracious, the occasional tight-lipped look betrayed their opinions of their rumpled charges. One docent cast an apologetic glance at the portrait of an antebellum matron before politely giving a gum-snapping, spandexed visitor directions to the nearest McDonald's.

Any attempt to reform the "no-rules" rule of our inflexibly informal dress code will undoubtedly be criticized as snobbish and undemocratic. We prefer to practice the reverse snobbery of dressing as low as we can go. In contrast, the Victorians' attentive care to dress and manners was profoundly democratic. Because it asks more of us than we usually ask of ourselves, civility is always more demanding than self-indulgence. Appearance was never a substitute for virtue; etiquette advisers often warned that image could be deceptive. But as one who held such sentiments said, it gave an "additional lustre to real merit." We need to rediscover the importance of aesthetics so that civility can shine again.

# 19

## Art and Soul

The Victorians' sense of aesthetics reached beyond their person to their surroundings, encompassing their buildings, their public spaces, and the people who inhabited them. They understood that they were a part of their fellow humans' environment, and they believed that all people, of all classes, were entitled to surroundings that were uplifting and inspiring.

Of course, regardless of how it resonates symbolically, a house is first of all a physical structure designed for a very practical purpose. But the inhabitants of a Victorianl-era house understood how physical forms could shape our spiritual as well as our material existence. When the great English philosopher John Ruskin wrote, "There is religion in everything around us," he did not expect people to sing hosannas to their carpets or drapes. Yet as a man of his time he naturally presumed the home environment shaped the moods, the minds, and the hearts of its occupants.

### ART, AESTHETICS, AND THE HOME

Across the Atlantic, Sarah Josepha Hale spoke of the "perpetual influence [which] emanates from [the home] upon those who see it and those who inhabit it." Many other architects, designers, and household advisers extensively discussed and debated what we dismissively label "bric-a-brac" or "stuff." The celebrated critic A. J. Downing explained that next to worshipping God, all "beautiful forms" of furniture, paintings, and sculptures "most tend to purify our hearts and our lives." Such purification cannot be obtained at starving artists sales of paintings held at a hotel by the airport.

Where we see mere objects on our floors, walls, and tables, our ancestors saw "the chief nourishers in life's feast." "It is no trifling matter," asserted Clarence Cook in his 1881 book *The House Beautiful*, "whether we hang poor pictures on our walls or good ones, whether we select a fine cast or a second-rate one. We might almost as well say it makes no difference whether the people we live with are first-rate or second-rate."

Designer extraordinaire William Morris reflected the domestic religion of his day when he observed in an 1882 lecture: "It helps the

*The free-flowing flowers in this early William Morris wallpaper design ("Fruit," 1864) are a product of Morris's belief that nature is the basis of good art—and good art is the basis of a moral society. Morris was no elitist; his designs were often found in middle-class homes.*

healthiness both of body and soul to live among beautiful things." In this view, physical objects were never just "things." Like his hero John Ruskin, who compared the social responsibilities of artists to those of preachers, Morris believed all forms of art had a distinctly ethical dimension and a grander purpose than the selfishness of self-expression. That is why he judged "any decoration futile if it does not remind you of something beyond itself, craftsmanship involving not only the mastery of technique, but the evocation of spiritual qualities of breadth, imagination, and order." In short, Victorian art imitated Victorian life!

Like so many other aspirations of Morris's era, this was a tall order that seems to have stretched beyond our reach. Yet he fulfilled it so brilliantly that his designs endure a century after his death. Believing, as many of his contemporaries did, that home decorations should unite the useful and the beautiful, Morris created his signature natural motifs of leaves, fruits, flowers, animals, and birds, which flowed through his wallpapers and fabrics. This prolific genius also created highly collectible and much copied furnishings, tapestries, stained glass, carpets, and even richly ornamented books based on medieval printing techniques. Morris was far more than a Victorian Ralph Lauren; he had grander ambitions than merely beautifying the home with his designs. Indeed, can we imagine contemporary aesthetic tastemakers also writing poetry or political essays, as Morris did?

Collectors of Victoriana eagerly buy Morris's products and those of his contemporaries, but many are oblivious to their deeper intent and value for the home. Morris's ideas about the importance of aesthetics were echoed by nondesigners as well. Although the dynamo crusader Jane Addams never believed that art alone could cure poverty or an impoverished spirit, when she opened Hull House in 1889, she decorated the settlement house—not with Elvis-on-velvet equivalents but with European artistic treasures that would spiritually nurture its inhabitants. Addams knew that even the most far-reaching reform legislation wouldn't nurture the cultivated citizen that a healthy democracy required.

Ordinary Victorians owned reproductions from Renaissance masters, especially those with religious themes, like Raphael's numerous Madonnas and Tintoretto's *Last Judgment*. They also favored morality plays on canvas, including the series done by Tissot and

William Powell Frith. In five paintings executed in 1887 collectively titled "The Road to Ruin," Frith unfolds the story of a young gentleman's downfall through gambling. Nothing curbs his dissipation, and a few years later his family is shown reduced from solid domestic comfort to drab, modest lodgings. Finally we see the gambler distraught and alone in a dingy garret, with a pistol that bespeaks his impending doom.

Such paintings may now seem insufferably self-righteous, yet at the time they instilled and reinforced core values through the constancy of aesthetics. Are the sporadic and futile lectures we give our kids to counter the "values" of pop music and trash TV more effective?

Even those unable to afford the cheapest prints had attractive options for creating a home that provided inspiration and education. Beauty, like civility, was not exclusive but democratic. For especially pinched purses, advisers extolled the art of nature. Simple flowers, said the legendary Rev. Henry Ward Beecher, "appeal to the power within us which spiritualizes matter." Andrew Weil, author of the bestselling book *8 Weeks to Optimum Health*, is simply revisiting our Victorian past when he recommends keeping fresh flowers in one's home to nurture the spirit.

## NATURE AND THE HOME

The ever resourceful Catharine Beecher offered several ideas for making botanical displays. Her directions were much less complex and costly than Martha Stewart's. She suggested training ivy over curtain brackets crafted of common pine, or making hanging baskets and wall pockets from empty coconut shells. Filling this indoor grotto with plants, rocks, minerals, and shells created a "magical, charming effect" that would teach children "to enjoy the beautiful, silent miracles of nature."

The Victorians enjoyed tending their own outdoor gardens as well. In Dwight Blarney's 1901 painting *Hollyhock Garden*, family members lavish care on the colorful bounty surrounding their cottage. This simple scene illustrates family values that relied not on shallow platitudes or politics but on a deep and enduring network of small acts with grand meanings, of home as a place in the world and a place in the heart.

Am I reading too much into the image of a little shared mulching? Not if you think like the Victorians. For example, complementing the overtly moralistic paintings just described were subtle yet sublimely spiritual landscapes, like those of the Hudson River School. Its founder, Thomas Cole, regarded nature as a direct divine manifestation "fraught with high and holy meaning." Cole hoped his art would

Kindred Spirits *by Asher Brown Drand, 1849, is an example of the popular Hudson River School of painting. The Victorians liked to bring the spiritually uplifting influence of nature into their homes through art.*

give "your souls . . . a sweet foretaste of heaven."' Sadly, the assessment of Cole's art has turned it into kitsch while aesthetically impoverished consumers can now buy their self-described "glimpse of heaven" in the just-invented Window-lite: a backlit plastic window designed by the Bio-Brite Company to cheer windowless rooms and office cubicles. All you need is a picture hanger, an electric outlet, and a minimum of $150 to get a surrogate view of an English garden, a golf course, or a Hawaiian beach. (Studies, which have replaced common sense, show that people are happier, more efficient, and recover from surgery faster when they can look at nature instead of walls.)

When beauty was still taken from reality, and not concocted by Bio-Brite, it was expected to provide moral inspiration and seed the imagination, especially in the formative years. As we devalued the importance of home and its aesthetics, we did the same to the women who were responsible for all the little details that enriched and beautified family life. Before the Jazz Age threw those priorities into the shredder, home was considered the place where people were happiest, and therefore home decorations were of great importance (This importance also applied to those who did the adorning.) Now home is the trifle, and our happiest hours are more likely passed at the mall or on the golf course.

## SHOCK ART AND THE TRIUMPH OF UGLINESS

In 1882 William Morris warned that "the extinction of the love of beauty and imagination would prove to be the extinction of civilization." The twentieth century proved him a prophet. I needn't recount the ugly triumph of Dada, Surrealism, and all the other motley modernists who lit the fuse of the current raging conflict between two camps of artists and critics—the outrageous and the outraged. The former was epitomized to its full in-your-face effect by a 1993 exhibit at the Whitney Museum in New York City. Interpreting gnawed cubes of chocolate and lard, and photos of hookers, gangs, and transvestites, curator Lisa Phillips proudly called them "crude, tawdry, and lacking finish. It deliberately renounces success and power in favor of the degraded and dysfunctional."[2]

Such anti-art fairly begs for indignation, especially if your tax dollars help foot the bill. It is easy for conservatives to lambaste the

National Endowment for the Arts when it awards grants to "performance artists" who smear their nude bodies with food, or to bargain-basement provocateurs who proffer portraits of a crucifix suspended in urine. The sensibilities of average Americans are probably just as offended by all this as they were by the Pentagon's purchase of $640 toilet seats. But even on this no-lose issue, the conservatives' hold on the high ground is shaky, because they lack the ennobling vision of art that made it a fundamental Victorian family value. It is pointless to rail at a Serrano or Mapplethorpe unless you extol a Titian or a Thomas Cole.

Do conservatives advocate art education or mercilessly slash it from school budgets? Do they orchestrate voluntary efforts to democratize access to art by bringing it directly to disadvantaged people (or vice versa), as Jane Addams did? For all their rhetoric, do they even discuss ways to enrich the lives of the ghetto-bound poor whose behavior they rail against? Do they fill their own homes with inspiring prints and paintings, and take their kids to museums to teach them the religion of art? Or is their religion limited to finger-wagging forbiddens and telepreachers who use God as the ultimate marketing tool?

## ART FOR ALL CITIZENS

True to their distinctly modern brand of nostalgia, many conservatives view historic art (not to mention history) through the myopic lens of the Jazz Age. Their opponents have given up on convincing them of the intrinsic value of art. NEA Chairwoman Jane Alexander and her allies push the value of museums and concerts as economic stimuli, a virtue to which free marketeers can relate.

By the 1920s the disheartened authors of *Middletown* noted that even educated people had ceased regarding art as "a thing of unusual merit." They used it instead "almost entirely as furniture," which had also lost its aesthetic and symbolic meaning. Art became mere decoration, and decoration was all about show, not substance. In her 1930 work entitled *Personality of a House*, Emily Post counseled women to choose household goods that would enhance their own appearance by matching their eyes and hair. You tailored your "setting" like a wardrobe, and damn the rest of the family if their features clashed with yours. Another adviser of the 1920s, quoted in *American Home Life 1880–1930*, pronounced every room just "the background of the people who live in it, " as if we were comic-strip figures inhabiting backgrounds.

Since our domestic investment today is chiefly financial, whatever hints at an earlier sense of home is derided as deceptively nostalgic. For example, the writer Holly Bruback, in a *New York Times* article on "Mail-Order America," criticized the L. L. Bean catalog for selling a romanticized image of an earlier age in its pitch for sampler quilts and crewel-stiched sweaters. Those who sneer at Victorian aesthetics might ponder the metaphor to be found in the fate of the 1950s Tupperware collection at New York's Museum of Modern Art. Not only are its "museum-quality" plastic bowls disintegrating into shapeless blobs, but they began to smell so rank that they had to be encased. Thus far all salvage operations have failed to preserve the miracle material that was supposed to last forever, or the foam and Naugahyde furniture that made the fifties home an aesthetic chamber of horrors. In commenting on their quality, a candid curator finally admitted, "The fact is they weren't so great in the first place." (Better late than never.)

## RECAPTURING ENVIRONMENTAL AESTHETICS

This obsessively sensual age is finally beginning to rediscover its senses. Many people swear by aromatherapy to alter their moods with an alphabet of fragrant oils. And retailers, convinced of scents' merchandising power, are piping them into their stores. Researchers at institutions like Johns Hopkins University have found that music influences how much and how quickly we eat, and colors affect everything from casual purchasing decisions to suicide rates. Beauty products in bright containers sell faster than those wrapped in brown. A prison in New York reduced aggressive behavior among inmates just by painting its common rooms pink. And when a bridge spanning England's Thames River went from black to a calming blue, fewer people jumped to their deaths.

If you need more proof that aesthetics is the diet of the soul—that there is more to our environment than saving trees—consider the Chinese practice of feng shui. The art of arranging interiors to enhance creativity, harmony, luck, and prosperity has gone from New Age to mainstream. Several major corporations, such as Motorola, utilized its principles to design office layouts. Individuals also hire feng shui consultants instead of standard decorators. These people are searching for more than coordinated pillows and drapes, even those that match their complexions. Satisfied clients say their homes not only feel more orderly and peaceful but also have changed how their residents interact with the world. At last we can reclaim this Victorian legacy, even if we had to go by way of China to find it.

## Aesthetics of Exterior Architecture

The deep significance our own ancestors vested in a house's decor also applied to its exterior. Because we view architecture as mere style, Oliver Smith may sound completely off the walls he constructed when he wrote in 1852 that, "Nothing has more to do with morals, the civilization, the refinement of a nation than its prevailing architecture." Just as manners were a hallmark of morality, architecture was its face.

Even if twentieth-century Americans had preserved instead of trashed the Victorian aesthetic religion, not to mention its art of living, America, of course, would not be Shangri-la. But it would be a safer, saner, more civilized place, unblemished by an epidemic of eyesores from Levittown to erector-set office towers with windows that don't open. (Mobile ones might tempt their prisoners to jump.) We attack our growing laundry list of social problems with money, legislation, and technical fixes, while ignoring what Calvert Vaux called our abused and deadened senses.

Vaux collaborated with Frederick Law Olmsted in gifting this country with some of its greatest parks, including New York's Central Park. But the wisdom of this landscape artist stretched far beyond the garden gate. He understood that if we are what we eat, drink, and smoke, we are also the buildings we inhabit. "Good architecture," he wrote in 1857,

> must spring up in any society where there is a love of truth
> and nature, and a generally diffused spirit of politeness in
> the ordinary habits of thought. Wherever, on the other hand,
> there is a widespread carelessness as to the development of
> the refined and gentle perceptive faculties, there inevitably
> must be a monotonously deficient standard of existence and
> a very paltry architecture as a necessary consequence.

*This park at Saratoga, New York, captures the Olmsted aesthetic with landscaping that encourages casual walking and intermingling.*

We can imagine what conclusions he would draw from our concrete-slab, near-windowless buildings.

Although the Victorians did not believe design alone determined the state of a nation's civility or morality, that century of subtlety understood how beauty—or its absence—affected attitudes and behavior. This recognition made it natural and essential for prominent members of the clergy like Timothy Dwight to preach on the moral effects of architecture, something it is hard for us to imagine a man of the cloth concerning himself with today.

A house was considered to have a nearly mystical, potent impact on its residents and their neighbors. As one midcentury architect put it,

> No man . . . could live the life in a well-proportioned and truly beautiful dwelling that he would in a mud shanty or rude log cabin. Certain elevating influences would steal into him unawares . . . that would lift his life above its otherwise lower level. . . . And so, too, the power of the tasteful is seen very often in the influence which a single dwelling will exert upon almost all in the neighborhood.

## THE URBAN BEAUTIFICATION MOVEMENT

Given the Victorians' strong ethos regarding environment, it is no surprise that starting in the mid–nineteenth century, a variety of reformers, urban planners, and artists united to combat the blight of factory pollution, ugly billboards, and carelessly discarded trash. They were part of what historians term the "city beautiful" movement, although it wasn't limited to cities. But for the aesthetically minded Victorians, purging the unsightly and the toxic was a mere first step. Because they assumed the visual shaped a country's ethics and civic spirit, that country needed more than breathable air. It needed broad boulevards adorned with flowers, trees, and shrubs, and it got them.

Above all, reformers thought, we needed public parks. Like his partner, Calvert Vaux, Frederick Law Olmsted claimed the elevating powers of nature had "a harmonizing and refining influence . . . favorable to courtesy, self-control, and temperance," especially in cities, where they were scarce. He also hoped bucolic settings where rich and poor could mingle would reduce class conflict. Until his death in 1903, Olmsted applied his theories to creating parks around the continent, from Brooklyn and Boston to Buffalo, Chicago, and Montreal. By then the nation boasted more than two thousand "improvement societies" in small towns and cities.

The World's Fair of 1893 accelerated this beautification movement. A coalition of the century's artistic giants transformed six hundred acres of Chicago swampland into the White City, a palatial extravaganza of classical, French, and Italian Renaissance buildings and fountains. Because the Victorians so richly mined what the architect Daniel Burnham called the "social possibilities of municipal architecture," many of our most inspired and inspiring public buildings, with their equally impressive interiors, were begun or completed during this era. It gave us some of Washington, D.C.'s greatest monuments and institutions, such as the Library of Congress, the Lincoln Memorial, and the Museum of Natural History.

### Recovering Our Environmental Aesthetic

Does this mean our most promising prescription for urban ailments is to give our sterile modern cities a massive architectural makeover? Financially strapped municipal budgets guarantee that will remain a fantasy. Yet in our quest to control crime and our slip-sliding quality of life, we have already borrowed bits and pieces of the past to save our future. Increasingly, cities and neighborhoods are implementing policies based on Victorian atmospherics, unaware of their origin or age. For example, the sociologists James Q. Wilson and George Kelling are often credited with coining the "broken-window theory" of crime and urban decay. In essence it states that ignoring small infractions, like the breaking of a window that stays broken, can propel a snowball of similar offenses that eventually devastates an area physically and morally. As vandalism spreads, residents become apathetic and withdraw from public places. Once predators see that no one is in charge, drug dealers, gangs, and assorted thugs claim the turf.

The "innovative" notion that minor crimes trigger progressively larger ones harks back to the holistic Victorian philosophy we have seen applied in many other contexts. The fashionably "novel" idea that reversing physical negligence and destruction reduces crime is pure old-fashioned aesthetically flavored common sense. It worked then and it works now. New York City has been especially aggressive in targeting the petty "quality-of-life" violations it once ignored, such as graffiti, ear-splitting boom boxes, subway turnstile jumpers, panhandling, and urinating in public. Gone are the infamous squeegee men, who cleaned the windshields of cars stopped at red lights, then extorted money from intimidated drivers. The crime rate in the city has plummeted, and, not surprisingly, police discovered that many of those arrested for misdemeanors were wanted felons or had links to them.

## MORE THAN MEETS THE EYE

The Victorians were convinced that even the most trifling incivility laid a cobblestone on the road to crime and social chaos. This steadfast certainty may now seem puzzling when viewed against the constantly shifting background of Victorian architectural trends. How could our ancestors preach a religion of beauty when its standards kept changing? The answer is that beneath the contrasting complexions of restrained Federal houses and exuberant Queen Annes is a shared foundation. The substance of buildings transcended style, and structures spoke a language the Victorians understood, just as they understood the language of flowers. Consider two major architectural movements—Greek Revival and Gothic Revival.

## Greek Revival

People usually describe the Greek Revival, which had its heyday from 1820 to 1860, as embodying imposing, grand, formal architecture, along the lines of Margaret Mitchell's fictitious Tara. Our ancestors would probably second those comments, but they also actively envisioned the ancient Greek roots of the democratic ideals their young nation cherished and won through the Revolutionary War (which some could still remember). They also sympathized with the recent Greek struggle for independence from the Turks. The Victorians were familiar with all three orders of the Greek Revival's signature columns (Doric, Ionic, Corinthian), and the culturally diverse races that developed them.

## Gothic Revival

The "passionless repose" of Greek Rival's simple rational lines suited public buildings, as A. J. Downing pointed out, but was inappropriate for homes. Domestic architecture, he said, "should be less rigidly scientific, and it should exhibit more of the freedom of play of feeling of everyday life. . . . There must be nooks and crannies about it, where

*Chairs in the classical/ Greek style and the Gothic style, from A. J. Downing's 1850 book* The Architecture of Country Homes. *Home furnishings enhanced the popular styles of architecture.*

one would love to linger . . . cosy rooms where all domestic fireside joys are invited to dwell."

Borrowing designs, history, and folklore from medieval Europe, especially England, Downing became the most eloquent apostle of Gothic Revival houses. In contrast to the flat, predictably balanced proportions that characterize the classical, Gothic was proudly quixotic. It emphasized asymmetrical facades, irregular placement of doors and windows, clustered chimneys, and steep gabled roofs. Other typical features included wooden or iron tracery, gingerbread scrollwork, and soaring towers.

This was a picturesque and contagious style suited to free spirits. Washington Irving revamped his sober seventeenth-century Dutch farmhouse until it seemed to its owner "all made up of gable ends and as full of angles and corners as an old cocked hat." The finest Gothic dwellings were sheer enchantments, passports to another place and time.

*An example of a cottage in the Gothic Revival style, designed by Alexander Jackson Davis, featured in A. J. Downing's guide to country homes. Downing noted that "the character expressed by the exterior of this design is that of a man or family of domestic tastes, but with strong aspirations after something higher than social pleasures."*

## A Proper, Yet Affordable, Home

Downing believed that a "proper house" had to satisfy "all the rational desires of the senses, the affections, and the intellect." Yet his books also extensively discussed practical subjects such as lathing, heating, window sashes, and the thickness of floor boards. When he hit the bottom line—money—he paid equal attention to those who had it and those who had to scrimp. He printed plans for both sumptuous villas and modest "working men's cottages" of three to four rooms. Because the democratic spirit of Victorian manners led straight to the hearth, many house pattern books were published for those of limited means.

Downing assured the readers who took his few books through more than twenty editions that "the peculiar charm of a cottage is as great as that of a villa." And he made good on his promise. A generation before William Morris, he advocated melding "the useful and the beautiful." He showed how even a tight budget could stretch to the "charm of bay windows, gabled and bracketed roofs, beckoning porches and vine-covered trellises." What now seem like frills were then considered essentials. Downing wrote, "There is no building, however simple, to which either good forms or something of an agreeable expression may not be given." Of course, he never saw tract housing.

## THE SOUL OF ARCHITECTURE IS DESTROYED

Victorian architecture was not just structure and style but an encounter with the soul. That is why Downing argued that every house must have "something in its aspect which the heart can fasten upon and become attached to, as naturally as the ivy attached itself to the antique wall, preserving its memories from decay." Nathaniel Hawthorne called that something "moral charm." Across the Atlantic, Goethe described it as "frozen music."

The guns of World War I forever silenced that song. When form became function, architecture lost its charm, its sentiment, its soul—and we lost a large chunk of ours. The budding blight of the anti-Victorian International Style had none, except to its elitist advocates. Replacing aesthetic inspiration and high aspirations were cold glass and concrete towers, along with the minimalist philosophy that less was more. And we got more and more of less and less, until the unprecedented building boom after World War II gave us American homes that were, as described in Malvina Reynolds's song "Little Boxes," "little boxes made of ticky tacky . . . little boxes all the same."

Goethe's "frozen music" became a screeching monotony that stretched from cheap Cape Cods to ostentatious but cheesy tract mansions. Now we had living rooms with built-in TV's that could be financed on a mortgage like other appliances. As Dolores Hayden pointed out in *Redesigning the American Dream,* this new ideal of living centered on "the bright, beady eye of the baby-sitting machine [which] reassured both children and adults that the scant physical community of the mass-produced sacred huts was redeemed by the magical electronic community created by national television."

## Material Comforts Dominate

In the postwar period, homeowners began to have higher expectations for material household comforts and conveniences. Gradually, any remaining expectations of home as a source of morally elevating beauty and binding emotional fulfillment disappeared. The 1948 film *Mr. Blandings Builds His Dream House* made light of this change. In it, Cary Grant struggles endlessly to satisfy his family's suburban dream of private baths and separate rooms for the children without going bankrupt. Confronted with a growing list of such demands, the frustrated architect declares that the Blandings don't want a house so much as "a series of little bungalows." This was a fitting metaphor for family togetherness in its touted golden age.

Such domestic sentiments—or the lack of them—still thrive unquestioned, as I recently learned while touring the sole surviving Victorian mansion in a neighborhood of glossy new undistinguished office buildings. When the guide identified a bright spacious room as the one the family's two daughters occupied until they left to marry, a shocked woman gasped. "Those poor girls," she said to her sympathetic husband. "With all the rooms in this place [over thirty], imagine making them share one." What now seems like child abuse was a widely practiced custom that made the house a home, not a series of little bungalows.

In his 1993 book *The Geography of Nowhere*, James Howard Kunstler dissected the process that morphed the transcendent Victorian home into a "spiritual deformity" during those delusive "happy days" of the fifties:

> You could name a housing development Forest Knoll Acres, even if there was no forest and no knoll, and the customers would line up with their checkbooks open. Americans ... had more meaningful relationships with movie stars and characters on daytime television shows than they did with members of their own families. They didn't care if things were real or not, if ideas were truthful. In fact, they preferred fantasy. They preferred lies. And the biggest lie of all was that the place they lived was home.

The structure and spirit of the buildings Nathaniel Hawthorne and his era admired for their "moral charm" were bulldozed, along with the virgin countryside, by magicians who produced instant pre-fab wastelands. Few mourned the demise of those heirlooms. The glories of historic architecture were despised for the very details and artistry that distinguished them. Many older houses were abandoned and left to rot, while Charles Addams cartoons and the movie *Psycho* made the Victorian home the emblem of the macabre.

Those houses that survived amid the frosty gleam of new developments were ridiculed by neighbors who practiced the national religion of contempt for old things, including their owners. With skyrocketing property values, decaying old mansions became a last resort for those financially strapped yet desperate to escape city crowds and crowded quarters. In the 1960s comedy *Please Don't Eat the Daisies*, Doris Day jokes that she and her hubby had to buy an aged white elephant in Connecticut because they "couldn't afford anything smaller."

## GETTING BACK TO THE ENVIRONMENTAL AESTHETIC

Luckily, the tide began to turn before the juggernaut of modern sprawl completely buried the beauty of the past. A few enlightened souls simply saw homes that merited saving, while aesthetic rebels like Kunstler championed a larger and nearly lost cause to revive the moribund legacy I have described. In typically Victorian vein he writes, "Americans wonder why their houses lack charm. . . . Charm is dependent on connectedness, on continuities, on the relation of one thing to another." Similarly, Robert Wilson of the National Trust for Historic Preservation criticized contemporary public buildings for being "utterly charmless, utterly lacking the capacity to inspire," a quality once deemed essential to civility and community participation:

> Our civic leaders who are responsible for our public spaces seem clueless as they inflict artistic atrocities on us. The prestigious hundred-thousand-dollar Pritzker Prize, awarded by architects to their peers, recently went to a home with a windowless wall made entirely of reinforced concrete. Similarly, a prizewinning "park" in a middle class area of Queens, New York, exemplifies "design excellence," according to the American Institute of Architects. Unfortunately, those who encounter it daily see only a concrete slab studded with oddly shaped steel benches, sparse greenery, and garish lights. The locals pronounced it a "strip park" and a setting "generated from a computer."

So hostile is this latter environment to its original intent of providing recreation and promoting community ties that it is frequently used as a dump for shabby furniture and garbage. The residents have done everything but firebomb what they thought would be "a traditional park with old-fashioned benches, gardens, and lots of shade." The benefits of such a park are more than aesthetic: Researchers who measured the effects of foliage and open vistas on commuters found they had better respiration, blood pressure, and heart rates than those who battled roads hedged by billboards and strip malls, a legacy of the 1950s.

Of course the Victorians relied on aesthetic intuition, not environmental psychologists, to tell them that beauty matters. For example, it was the Victorians who began New York City's Fresh Air Fund. Following the common sense of his age, Frederick Law Olmsted believed exposure to nature brought "tranquility and rest to the mind." This observation was recently certified by an official Justice Department report that concluded our deserts of high-rise slums breed crime, fear, and demoralization.

In the twentieth century, place has become mere space filled by corporate brands of houses that offer no home to the senses or the soul. Meanwhile, growing numbers of tourists flock to our nation's living museums of historic architecture, from Charleston, South Carolina, to Saratoga Springs, New York. Can you imagine tourists a hundred years from now spending their time and money to visit the buildings our age leaves behind—if they're still standing?

## Rediscovering the Beauty of Older Buildings

Happily, some people are recovering our long-lost environmental aesthetic. At the University of California at Berkeley, a school better known for protests than for drawing-room behavior, the chapter of Sigma Phi fraternity occupies an Edwardian-era Arts and Crafts mansion in a neighborhood laid out by Frederick Law Olmsted. In this shingled Gothic-style delight, not just toga parties but even putting tacks on the walls are verboten. The same goes for all the other college pigsty habits that could mar the delicate friezes painted on Belgian linen, the original amber glass lighting fixtures, or the rare Burmese teak and Honduran mahogany trim. (Before any party, the walls at Sigma Phi are covered temporarily with protective particle board.)

The fraternity members are not only obliged to respect the house (a lesson few kids learn at home), but every week each must contribute some serious elbow grease. Students polish the paneling and carefully scrape through multiple layers of paint to find the original wallpapers. Moreover, they don't mind the labor or the time spent raising the hefty sums that renovation requires. Although those interviewed by *The New York Times* struggled to articulate how they are affected by the house, they are certain they are so affected. One called its craftsmanship "an epiphany." So potent is its aura that at a dinner where new members were introduced, the others snapped their fingers instead of applauding because, as the fraternity's president noted, "It's quieter."

If architecture can coax such remarkable behavior from Berkeley frat boys, controlling crime seems like a walk in an Olmsted park— but only if you think like a Victorian. We often do, even if we don't know it. When James Howard Kunstler asked visitors why they came to stroll through historic Woodstock, Vermont, most fumbled for words before settling on some version of enjoying its "old-fashioned feeling." Kunstler notes gloomily that these tourists were "members of a culture that had long ceased to value place except as a sales gimmick, and they had no vocabulary with which to think about it."

Happily, our gut response to architectural treasure troves like Woodstock reveals the spark of our forgotten aesthetic conscience— a lost concept that is ripe for recovery. As A. J. Downing said, "The Beautiful is an original instinct of the sentiment of our nature. It is worship, by the heart, of a higher perfection manifested in material forms . . . an instinct as strong as for life itself." Similarly, in her 1889 work *The Art of Decoration*, the English author Mary Haweis called the "eye for form" a "birthright."

We forgot how to "see" when function buried form. But its light was dormant, not dead. We are searching for that transcendent experience of place that enriches both body and soul. This is why people increasingly crave what Kunstler calls the "organic wholeness" of historic towns, with their "everyday attention to details, of intimate care for things intimately used."

## Neotraditional Buildings and Communities

There are signs of revival of the Victorian aesthetic so memorably summarized by Winston Churchill: "We shape our buildings, then they shape us." Innovative architect Andres Duany and his partner-wife Elizabeth Plater-Zyberk are designing neotraditional communities explicitly modeled on nineteenth-century designs. Following their commercial and critical success in Florida's Seaside and Maryland's Kentlands, they have designed and built 135 such projects throughout the world, and their vision has inspired many others.

Exactly how do these new-old places differ from typical suburbs? Gone is the signature sprawl of isolated office, retail, and residential pods linked only by the almighty automobile. King car has been toppled, and its throne—the garage—moved from the front of the house to the rear, where the Victorians once erected their carriage houses. Residents are encouraged to use their legs, not their wheels, on tree-lined streets that lead to nearby jobs, schools, shops, and restaurants, where you actually stop and eat rather than drive through. Such conveniences not only reduce traffic, pollution, highway construction, and its accompanying destruction of the natural landscape, but also those eternal commutes that steal time people once devoted to family, socializing and civic activities.

Unlike vehicular solitude, walking promotes human contact. When the social scientist Philip Langdon interviewed residents of Kentlands and other neotraditional towns, he found "a different, more neighborly, social life" compared to that in standard developments. "If you're out doing yard work, everyone stops and chats," one Kentlands homeowner told him. "After a big snowfall, we helped each other shoveling the driveways and all had chili afterward. There's more of a sense of community than anywhere else we've lived."

In these communities, designs that promote "we" instead of "me" extend to public space as well. Land usually devoured by vast parking lots is used for playgrounds, parks, or village greens. Commercial buildings have the human scale of those they are meant to serve, not the intimidating presence of looming corporate towers and cavernous malls. In neotraditional towns, the tallest structures are usually city halls, civic centers, and churches that have a shared public function and anchor the community in their purpose and appearance. A century ago, soaring church steeples, the highest points in even the largest cities, were points of orientation for those who had lost their souls or just their way. Today's skyscrapers thrust far above them, yet fail to reach their heights.

Residents of these new old-fashioned towns are inspired to mingle because the buildings around them, whether public or private, mingle comfortably without seeming crowded. There are no remote islands ringed by asphalt or acres of lawn that tell passersby to keep their distance. All structures are set near the street, connecting them physically, aesthetically, and symbolically with each other and the people who have a stake in what they represent. Homes feature front porches rather than isolating backyard decks or the barbecue pits where 1950s males in chef hats and aprons expressed their dwindling sense of masculinity by charring burgers and steaks. Porch life was a Victorian institution. What could be more inviting or pedestrian-friendly than the visual delight of its flowering baskets and roomy white wicker chairs that were made for sipping tea or homemade lemonade sweetened by casual chatter and the lull of a gently creaking rocker? Porches subtly mediate the zone between the house and the street; they also permit discreet vigilance of local children and any sign of potential crime.

It took us almost a century to see the light. But porches are just the frosting on the architectural cake of neotraditional towns. Even expensive modern suburbs assault our senses and our sense of direction with their relentless monotony. Locating "individual" houses can be a logistical nightmare. Consider the contrast in getting directions to a house in a typical tract development with doing so in the old neighborhoods we now copy. How could you possibly miss the Queen Anne with the square turret and the tri-colored fish-scale roof? Yet how could you help but miss the third house on the left, distinguished only by its red shutters—until the neighbor paints his red?

Like their ancestors, neotraditional towns have a refreshing variety of historic styles that harmonize without sacrificing the uniqueness that is the essence of Victorian charm. You can see it and feel it wherever the past is preserved, from Rhinebeck, New York, to Savannah, Georgia. Richmond's majestic Monument Avenue, America's Champs Elysées, is a feast of Romanesque, Tudor, Colonial, and Greek Revival mansions, while in the tiny jewel of Lexington, Virginia, more modest but equally striking Southern raised cottages share the shady streets with classic Queen Annes and compact Gothic fantasies worthy of Sir Walter Scott.

This diversity is more than skin-deep. Like the genuine communities that inspired their aesthetics, the neotraditional heirs have revived zoning codes that encourage a residential mix of age and income groups. Instead of the typical suburban ghetto, where a fairly narrow span of prices attracts families in a single tax bracket, the assortment of detached houses, row houses, and apartments, some above garages and shops, offers a broad selection of accommodations to everyone from singles and families to seniors and empty-nesters ready to shed extra space. Naturally size and cost will vary. Yet even the cheapest homes feature details that complement their more extravagant neighbors. In true Victorian spirit, there are no architectural also-rans and afterthoughts.

Charleston, South Carolina's mayor, Joseph Riley, believes "there is no reason for government ever to build something that is not beautiful." So the city cooperated with developers to build houses that break the standard high-rise ghetto mold—and hopefully its mentality—by echoing the porches, materials, and rooflines of the city's historic homes.

Domestic beauty was a core Victorian family value because it solidified families and communities, which we are desperately trying to patch together with social policies and rhetoric. These efforts will continue to miss the target until we realize that home is at the heart of this matter. For our ancestors, the home was a national religion with a very practical creed. As A. J. Downing wrote in 1850, "Home's moral influence . . . is more powerful than any mere oral teachings of virtue and morality. . . . The mere sentiment of home, with its thousand associations, has, like a strong anchor, saved many a man from shipwrecks in the storms of life."

As we drift about, seeking the security our grandparents and great-grandparents took for granted, we must put aside our shortsighted, narrow views that reduce homes to houses and art to mere decoration. We must reclaim our public space and public art for all the people, even as we reclaim our lost sense of home, family, romance, and civility. We are the most forward-looking nation on earth, but it is time for us to look back in order to move ahead. The greatest hope for our future lies in our past.

# Conclusion:
# Back to the Future?

Eighty-nine percent of Americans say civility is a serious national problem, yet 99 percent claim their own behavior is civil. To pursue the ideal we need to get real. Change, like charity, begins at home. Having your cake and eating it too is a childish delusion that lures us to the hot stove where we keep getting burned. As comedian Joan Rivers says, "Grow up!" We can't cut taxes and balance the national budget while we gorge on government goodies. We won't find charm in a world that shrieks at a thrusting post-Elvis pelvis. We can't build solid families in emotionally hollow homes. We can't make true love while the sexes are making war. And we can't have a civilized society that celebrates "attitude," self-expression, and self-obsession, while brushing off blame like dandruff.

The qualities our culture calls healthy are personal and social poison. How do we detox? By reversing course a hundred years and switching the labels on our virtues and vices. We've done it before. Smoking used to be glamorized; now it is stigmatized. (Every ration kit the U.S. Government issued to troops during World War II contained the cigarettes that have now become federal public enemy number one.) We no longer shrug when someone drives under the influence of alcohol, thanks to the efforts of Mothers Against Drunk Driving.

Let's stop laying back, and straighten up physically, morally, and verbally. Let's get used to the sound of words like "genteel." If we respect all words as potential weapons, we might actually cultivate the art of language again. Free speech is never free; someone always pays a price. Victorian reticence—self-censorship—is no pathology but the bedrock of civility. Let's stop blowing all those noisy horns. In a civilized society people have a stake in each other; let's live that way, instead of driving stakes through each other's hearts. A cohesive code of civility is still the best internal V-chip for kids and the adults who act like kids. Let's start saving others' faces, rather than getting into them, whatever our mood or circumstances. Like the law, true civility is a constant, not a random I-feel-like-it act of kindness. If a social obligation is treated like a crap shoot, someone is bound to get shot.

In the 1800s everyday courtesies saved not just bloodshed but time, money, and general misery as well. Ralph Waldo Emerson said life was never too short for civility, and life was a lot shorter back then. Yet even Emerson could not have imagined how much time, money, and grief civility could save. Endless lawsuits and costly sensitivity training sessions that aggravate sexual, racial, and ethnic divisions, to name just a few. Let's replace narrow concepts that selectively discriminate, like politically "correct" and "incorrect," with more inclusive and equitable terms, such as "rude" and "polite." But semantics alone won't do the job. We must become as outraged by violations of civility as we are by racist or sexist acts and expressions. This would diffuse hostility while broadening and strengthening everyone's civil rights.

We must also apply appropriate punishments to civil wrongs. Legislative efforts and lawsuits should only be used as a last resort. The notorious Victorian frozen silence effectively tied loose tongues prone to crude or insensitive comments. It still works wonders with dirty jokes if the audience, male and female—or rather gentlemen and ladies—unites in its reaction. This is precisely why an established set of manners is essential. We have learned the hard way what happens when we improvise.

More serious offenses demanded fitting penalties, and the Victorians had them. Those committing ethical or criminal violations were ostracized socially and professionally by respectable folk. The effectiveness of this measure rested on several extinct assumptions we must revive. In the past, people had reputations to lose. Every community and class, not just the bluest bloods, followed a powerful moral code instead of a mercurial mishmash of laws. This culture of character—the backbone of civility—"counted" every day in every way, not just for a government-sanctioned "Character Counts" week or when some celebrity-studded interest group decides to make it their cause of the month.

This century turned "character" into a synonym for "odd," "eccentric," or "peculiar" and a reference to actors who didn't play romantic leads. The meat of Victorian character and morality—hard work, frugality, sobriety, nonbrutal honesty, sexual decency, civic participation, self-sacrifice, and self-restraint—got charred beyond recognition when the Jazz Age turned happiness on its head, making it self-centered instead of centered on others. We've been tinkering with the recipe for happiness ever since. Each dish may have seemed palatable when fresh, but they have all given us indigestion.

We have finally begun to nibble at the Victorians' table, without knowing where we are. But we won't find the healing nourishment we need unless everyone gets equal treatment by our unwritten laws, as well as our written ones. For example, the latest trend in crime control pushes the "new" idea of shame. Using mandated signs and newspaper advertisements, judges are stamping updated scarlet letters on the likes of men who solicit prostitutes, drunk drivers, and deadbeat dads. But should we brand only those who can't afford a wily lawyer to spare them such humiliation? We must stigmatize and ostracize across the board, without playing political favorites. If conservatives condemn rap music for demeaning women, they should also tune out Rush Limbaugh until he cleans up his act. If we fine Dennis Rodman for his outrageous behavior on the basketball court, corporate America should stop rewarding him with lucrative offers for product endorsements, and consumers should stop buying whatever he is hawking.

What happens when former Clinton adviser and confidant Dick Morris lets his prostitute listen to private calls with his boss? He is forced to resign, but that blow is substantially softened with presidential sympathy, a fat book contract, and continued access to journalists eager for a good sound bite. When pinstriped executives are guilty of sexual harassment, drum them out of their jobs and their country clubs. As we've seen in recent media scandals, lowly army drill sergeants are promptly court-martialed when their hormones run amok.

Our kids have seen enough double standards. We must teach them level Victorian values as our ancestors would, with a positive spin. Another simplistic "Just say no" campaign won't work because it lacks direction. Speak the snappy lingo kids understand—hypocrisy is commendable, not expendable; uptight is all right; discreet is neat; act fine, not like swine; the Golden Rule is cool.

To make these lessons stick, kids must see their parents faithfully practice what they preach. Parents must be exemplars, not pals with open checkbooks. Of course, popular culture should bolster, not sabotage, their efforts. Here the creative possibilities are as endless as the benefits all of us can reap. Imagine the sports superstars kids idolize bowing to their opponents like Victorian gents, instead of showing them up by showboating after making a slam dunk or scoring a touchdown. That would be a victory for everyone, no matter who won the game.

Recent celebrity "milk mustache" ads actually increased milk consumption. This same approach could promote basic courtesy, a nutrient essential to our social health. No matter how little else they wear, many Hollywood stars never fail to don their AIDS awareness pins. A similar pin might raise civility consciousness, and it needs raising. Let's borrow some of the star power poured into public-service campaigns to make sex safe, and keep kids safe from drugs, booze, and tobacco. Restoring civility requires the high-profile moral force of such crusades. Like secondhand smoke, the lack of that core Victorian value pollutes everyone's air.

Plugs for designated drivers have become a staple of prime-time shows. The TV elite could do as much for civility if it would just get over its anti-elitist bias that consistently portrays bad manners as good. We cannot afford any more Roseannes in fact or the fiction that so easily colors it. With or without a laugh track, the low-class ass as a national role model is no laughing matter.

The nineteenth century was civil because the Victorians lived up to solid standards. They did not go slumming for fashions, morals, or the manners that embodied mutual respect and self-respect. Instead of downscale chic, there was nearly universal pride in acting like ladies and gentlemen. Yet even as they raised the ceiling instead of lowering the floor, the Victorians invited everyone along. Contrary to the stereotype, manners were not elitist but inclusive and democratic. Every person was entitled to courtesy and fairness, not the

intimate details of others' lives. It is time to exchange that entitlement for one we can use, not abuse.

Like the constitutional rights that are free to all Americans,
manners were meant to unify the classes, creeds, and colors. The
chaotic WASP-phobic cultural diversity we practice breeds a divisive
reverse snobbery that costs us plenty. Its only standard is conve-
niently two-faced. We selectively condemn other countries for rituals
like public flogging, animal sacrifice, bought adolescent brides, and
dowry murders. Yet at home we selectively justify some of the worst
attitudes and practices of historically victimized groups as their cultural best. This form of compensation is really toxic discrimination.
Yes, we must acknowledge our legacy of shamefully exploiting minorities and the poor. But we can't continue to allow past sins to excuse
destructive self-indulgence. Ultimately, we sink or swim together.

The Victorians understood that the more diverse a nation, the
more it needs a binding code of civility. This is a common language of
comportment that lets us talk to, not past, each other. Without these
rules of the road, the most aggressive call the shots, and the most vulnerable get hit. This is especially important to women. Beginning in
the Jazz Age, the progressive march of "liberation" succeeded in making the world safe only for those women who act like the dregs of
men, and are treated in kind. Ironically, we have debased and masculinized the world even as we emasculated males.

The twentieth century's brand of equality did not expand
women's rights; it took with one hand and gave with the other. We
should protect, celebrate, and extend the greater educational and job
opportunities that a limited segment of women now enjoy. But we
must also recognize that all women have lost the fundamental rights
of personal safety and respect that the Victorians took for granted.
Rape, violence, harassment—every way women are mistreated—
cannot be blamed on patriarchy or biology. The problem isn't men but
modern men, the culture that tolerates misogynist behavior, and the
women who collude in their own degradation. They will never re-
empower themselves with laws, rhetoric, or karate courses but only
by raising their minds, their morals, and expectations to Victorian
heights, and demanding that men meet them. Likewise, men should
redefine themselves in Victorian terms. This "new" masculinity is
measured by honor, restraint and self-control, and by how well (not

how badly) men treat women. Above all, those who act macho instead of manly must be shunned, not admired, by other men.

Rather than subordinating women, this resurrected chivalry will shield them from verbal, emotional, and physical beatings. A positive means of demonstrating manhood is a realistic and long-overdue recognition of the facts of life—namely, men are still top dogs when it comes to money, sex, and raw muscle. To thrive or even survive, women need old-fashioned equalizers, the sort that encourage a man to give up his seat on a bus (if not a lifeboat). Ask women, especially pregnant ones, if they consider this gesture insulting. A woman could decline any chivalrous offer—politely. She would reinforce general civility and avoid being a "spoiler" for those women who would welcome a taste of the treatment their great-grandmothers routinely savored. This may be sexist, but it's a healthy sexism, much like the good cholesterol that protects the heart from bad cholesterol's artery-clogging fat. We don't need a survey to tell us which type of man most women would rather encounter in a dark alley.

Perhaps when women are once again valued for their "otherness," men will feel free to reclaim the "feminine" side of manhood. Victorian men took pride in being sensitive to others' feelings and the fine points of romance. Love was not a "woman thing" that men grudgingly gave or pretended to give in order to score. It was a unisex ideal, publicly prized but privatized to protect it from degrading exhibitionist displays. A century ago manly men were intensely sentimental. They effusively opened their hearts to their heart's desire, whom they treated like gold, not dirt. They lived for love, visibly suffered lovesickness, and sometimes died of it. Men gave all to love, because it made them feel like men.

The Victorians' holistic vision of life also applied to sex and love. You loved and were loved with the body, mind, and soul, not in bits and pieces. For real men and women, sex was no casual hit-and-run game of techniques and gadgets but a banquet that satisfied "the appetite for higher pleasures." Even the elusive great lay we pursue was no substitute for grand passion. The Victorians made a religion of love. We need to get religion again to connect us to ourselves, to each other, and to the hopes and aspirations that keep us striving instead of settling for second best. This is the one true religion that can fill our empty hearts and restore our ailing homes.

Family values need that home to flourish, as plants need nourishing soil. Our homes and the women who make them must once again have the dignity they deserve. What makes a home? The very intangibles we have shrugged off and cut corners on until we bled dry the very essence of the Victorian home. Those "little niceties"—the frills, the rituals, even the chores—gave the home a deeply emotional sense of place, not just a label or an address. It can't be restored by the tax cuts touted by conservatives, liberal calls for expanded day care, or Martha Stewart's how-to kits.

We have learned the hard way that home is more than another institution, as parenthood is more than a role. It was the sovereign solidity of the Victorian home that strengthened and linked individuals, communities, and the country. The twentieth century tried and failed to trade that strength and the effort it entails for the easy mass consumption that stuffed the home with material goods while stripping its soul.

Financial prosperity alone cannot create or sustain healthy homes or sound nations. Despite our booming stock market and low unemployment, we still face severe social problems born and bred in the homes lacking Victorian sentiments that were enriching beyond measure. We need a new-old way to judge our standard of living and the one we want our children to enjoy. There is nothing wrong with wanting to give them more than what we have, or what our parents gave us, if "more" means more than trendy sneakers, a blue-chip education, or bible-thumping family values lectures. Instead we should try to give our kids the ideal and the reality of a loved and loving home, however modest. This is a precious life-giving gift, and one they can pass on to their own children.

Consider this book not an end but a hopeful beginning. And there is hope. Several months ago I received a thank-you note for a gift I sent to a member of Generation X. As if her uncommon courtesy weren't sufficiently shocking, her monogrammed off-white paper would meet even Edith Wharton's standards. Real success will come the day we notice such gestures by their absence, not their presence. That progress won't be gauged by declining rates of crime, divorce, or out-of-wedlock births. These will naturally follow when we fully reclaim the legacy we have started borrowing piecemeal.

Yes, we can go home again, and not just to the hearth but to the art of love, and the art of civilized living. We have a lot of broken windows to fix, and there are long-rotting timbers beneath our shaky foundation. But history has given us the tools to do this job. All we need is the courage to use them.

No, our world won't be perfect. But courtesy will be common. Love will be our favorite four-letter word. And home will be sweet once again. People will be more sentimental than cynical. Beauty and grace will be noble pursuits that are real, not impossible ideals. We can get there from here. Ralph Waldo Emerson said, "A healthy discontent is the first step to progress." We are already plenty discontented. Now we must take the second step and open our eyes as wide as we can to a different way of seeing.

Adieu!

# NOTES

## Introduction
1. *The Washington Post,* May 23, 1994.

## Chapter 1: "The Age of Impudence"
1. Henry James, Sr., in a letter that was part of a series of articles in 1889 in the *New York Tribune* that was a running dialogue on free love and marriage sponsored by Horace Greeley.
2. Daniel Patrick Moynihan, "Defining Deviancy Down," *American Scholar,* Winter 1993.

## Chapter 2: "Buy Now, Pay Later"
1. Gerry Hirshey, "Happy [ ] Day to You," *New York Times Magazine*, July 2, 1995, p. 20.
2. Justin Blum, "Conventioneers Gather to Bare Witness to the Joys of Nudism," *Washington Post,* July 23, 1994, p. B84.
3. Dr. Arthur Caliandro, pastor of the Marble Collegiate Church, quoted in Todd S. Purdum, "Trump Pledge: In This Plaza, I Thee Wed," *New York Times,* December 18, 1993, p. 1, col. 2.
4. *ABC News* report, "In the Name of God," broadcast March 16, 1995.
5. Neal Smelser quoted in Laura Sessions Stepp, "A Full Head of Self-Esteem: Praising Kids and Putting Stars on Their Work Isn't Enough," *Washington Post,* February 21, 1995, p. D5.
6. Roy Baumeister quoted in Richard Morin, "Unconventional Wisdom," *Washington Post,* February 11, 1996.
7. Barbara DeFoe Whitehead, "Dan Quayle Was Right," *Atlantic Monthly,* April 1993.

## Chapter 3: "Alone in the Toy Store"
1. "Family Almanac" column, *Washington Post,* February 24, 1994.
2. T. J. Ellinwood, *Henry Ward Beecher: Autobiographical Reminiscences,* published in 1898.
3. Gary Cross, "Too Many Toys," *New York Times,* November 24, 1995.
4. Roger Rosenblatt, "Teaching Johnny to Be Good," *New York Times,* April 30, 1995.

5. Meg Schneider, *Washington Post,* August 21, 1995.

6. Eliot, "Democracy and Manners."

## Chapter 4: "Portrait of a Lady"

1. "Let's Get Real About Feminism," roundtable discussion by multiple authors, *Ms.* magazine, September–October 1993.

2. Henry James, Sr., in a letter that was part of a series of articles in 1889 in the *New York Tribune* that was a running dialogue on free love and marriage, sponsored by Horace Greeley.

3. William Raspberry, *Washington Post,* November 24, 1993.

## Chapter 5: "Men II Boyz"

1. Korn/Ferry International and UCLA Graduate School of Management, *Decade of the Executive Woman,* 1993.

2. According to the American Medical Association, two million women are battered each year.

3. A scary 1994 survey commissioned by *Esquire* magazine found that a majority of college males would commit rape if they could get away with it. Results of poll published in *Esquire,* February 1994. The Justice Department estimates that 160,000 rapes occurred in 1993.

4. Margaret Bonilla, "Cultural Assault—What Feminists Are Doing to Rape Ought to Be a Crime," *Policy Review*, Fall 1993.

5. Elizabeth Pleck, "Wifebeating in the Nineteenth Century," *Victimology Journal* 4 (1979).

6. John Ruskin quoted in Duffey, *Ladies' and Gentlemen's Complete Etiquette*.

7. Marilyn Goldstein, "Dell Labs Shows It Still Doesn't Get It," *Newsday,* September 25, 1995.

8. Evelyn Nieves, "Despite Acquittal, Woman Vows to Press on in Rape Trial." *New York Times*, March 27, 1996.

9. *NBC News*, October 10, 1995.

10. Ralph Reed quoted in Richard Berke, "Politicians Woo Christian Group," *New York Times*, September 9, 1995.

11. James Warren, "Lugar Looks Back on a Campaign that Never Caught Fire," *Chicago Tribune*, March 10, 1996.

12. Admiral Richard Macke quoted in Mary Jordan, "In Okinawa's Whisper Alley," *Washington Post*, November 23, 1995.

13. See Frank Rich, "I Got You, Babe," *New York Times,* May 25, 1996.

14. Leef Smith, "In Suburbs, Concern Grows Over Girls' Criminal Activity," *Washington Post*, October 30, 1995.

15. Judge Jane Delbridge quoted in "In Suburbs, Concern Grows Over Girls' Criminal Activity," *Washington Post,* October 30, 1995.

16. Judge Joanne F. Alper quoted in Leef Smith, "In Suburbs, Concern Grows Over Girls' Criminal Activity," *Washington Post, Ibid.*

## Chapter 6: "The Benevolence of Manners"
1. Ralph Waldo Emerson quoted in Eliot, "Democracy and Manners."
2. As cited in Stein and Baxter, eds., *Grace Dodge: Her Life and Work.*
3. Duffey, *Ladies' and Gentlemen's Complete Etiquette.*
4. Ward McAllister quoted in Wechter, *Saga of American Society.*
5. Sir Walter Scott quoted in Duffey, *Ladies' and Gentlemen's Complete Etiquette.*
6. Raoul Julia quoted in the *New York Times*, November 1, 1991 (obituary).
7. Judy Mann, "New World Daughters," *Washington Post*, February 26, 1995.
8. Duffey, *Ladies' and Gentlemen's Complete Etiquette.*
9. John Coulter, *The Hatless Man* (1901), cited in Sarah Kortum, *The New Century Perfect Speaker* (New York: Viking, 1995).
10. Maude C. Cooke, cited in Arthur Martine, *Martine's Hand-book of Etiquette and Guide to True Politeness*, published in 1866.
11. *Standard Book on Politeness, Good Behavior and Social Etiquette*, cited in John Coulter, *The Hatless Man*, published in 1901.
12. Thomas Nelson Page, "On the Decay of Manners," *Century Magazine* 110 (April 1911).
13. Lord Chesterfield quoted in Root, *Lord Chesterfield: Letters.*
14. Eliot, "Democracy and Manners."
15. Frances Murphy quoted in Marc Fisher, "Million Man March: Behind the Scenes, the Women Count," *Washington Post,* October 14, 1995.

## Chapter 7: "Keeping a Civil Tongue"
1. DeNeen Brown, "It's About Respect, Say Students Who Curse Teachers," *Washington Post*, April 18, 1993.
2. Ronald F. Federici quoted in DeNeen Brown, "It's About Respect, Say Students Who Curse Teachers," *Washington Post, Ibid.*
3. Madeline Kane quoted in Don Oldenburg, "Great Expectations," *Washington Post*, April 4, 1995.
4. Results of poll of 1,000 women age 18 to 25 commissioned by *Esquire* and reported in the February 1994 issue.
5. Stephen Dobyns quoted in Francine Prose, "Bad Behavior," *New York Times*, November 26, 1995.
6. *Wall Street Journal*, July 17, 1995.

## Chapter 8: "Hypocrisy, Democracy, and Diversity"
1. Maureen Dowd's column, *New York Times,* October 25, 1996.
2. Evan Thomas, "Hurray for Hypocrisy," *Newsweek*, January 29, 1996.

3. Megan Rosenfield, *Washington Post,* July 20, 1995. Rosenfield got the story from Carolyn Curry's book *Divided Lives: The Public and Private Struggles of Three Accomplished Women.*

4. Rap musician quoted in *Washington Post,* August 15, 1993.

5. Mme Mitterand quoted in *Washington Post,* February 29, 1996.

6. William Raspberry, *Washington Post,* September 30, 1994.

7. Kareem Abdul-Jabbar, speaking on CBS's *60 Minutes,* broadcast November 26, 1995.

8. Patrick Welsh (high school teacher), *Washington Post,* March 3, 1996.

9. George W. Cornell, *Washington Post* (AP), March 13, 1993.

10. John Carmozy, "The TV Column," *Washington Post,* February 4, 1994.

11. Ralph Waldo Emerson quoted in Duffey, *Ladies' and Gentlemen's Complete Etiquette.*

12. Cortland Malloy, *Washington Post,* September 17, 1994.

13. Eliot, "Democracy and Manners."

## Chapter 9: "Babes in Toyland"

1. Henry James, Sr., in a letter that was part of a series of articles in 1889 in the *New York Tribune* that was a running dialogue on free love and marriage, sponsored by Horace Greeley.

2. Celia Barbour, "Looking at Pictures" (Op-Ed), *New York Times,* April 23, 1994.

3. *New York Times,* June 14, 1995.

4. Results of poll of 1,000 women age 18 to 25 commissioned by *Esquire* and reported in the February 1994 issue.

5. Lonnae Parker, "The Body of Her Work," *Washington Post,* September 5, 1995.

6. Tailhook information from the February 1993 Department of Defense report "Events at the 35th Annual Tailhook Symposium."

7. Naomi Wolf quoted in Tad Friend, "Yes," *Esquire,* February 1994.

8. This story recounted by Deryck Cooke in a booklet written to accompany a 1969 Decca recording of "The Ring of the Nibelungs" by the Vienna Philharmonic Orchestra.

## Chapter 10: "When Life Was Foreplay"

1. Henry James, Sr., in a letter that was part of a series of articles in 1889 in the *New York Tribune* that was a running dialogue on free love and marriage, sponsored by Horace Greeley.

2. All quotations of Dr. Elizabeth Blackwell in this chapter are from Blackwell, *Essays in Medical Sociology.*

3. Quoted in D'Emilo and Freedman, *Intimate Matters*.
4. Beatrix Potter quoted in Gay, *Tender Passion*.
5. Quoted in Gay, *Education of the Senses*.
6. Both letters quoted in Rothman, *Hands and Hearts*.
7. Lystra, *Searching the Heart*.
8. *Good Behavior for Young Gentlemen* cited in Lystra, *Searching the Heart*.
9. Tad Friend, "Yes," *Esquire*, February 1994.
10. University of Chicago poll discussed in Barbara Vobejda, "Survey Finds Most Adults Sexually Staid," *Washington Post*, October 7, 1994.
11. Results of poll of 1,000 women age 18 to 25 commissioned by *Esquire* and reported in the February 1994 issue.

## Chapter 11: "Backseat Follies"

1. Ernest Groves quoted in Seidman, *Romantic Longings*.
2. *Forbes* magazine, cited in Bailey, *From the Front Porch to the Back Seat*.
3. Bailey, *From the Front Porch to the Back Seat*.
4. Lynd and Lynd, *Middletown*.
5. Cited in Bailey, *From the Front Porch to the Back Seat*.
6. Lynd and Lynd, *Middletown*.
7. Bailey, *From the Front Porch to the Back Seat*.
8. Betty Friedan, *The Feminine Mystique*.

## Chapter 12: "The Religion of Romance"

1. Tracy Thompson, "Unhitched But Hardly Independent: Having No Husband Complicates Escape From Welfare," *Washington Post*, May 13, 1995.
2. *Washington Post*, May 23, 1995.
3. Austin Dickinson quoted in Longsworth, *Austin and Mabel*.
4. Quoted in Lystra, *Searching the Heart*.
5. Ford Madox Ford, *The Good Soldier* (1915).
6. Andrew Delbanco, review of *The Age of Innocence*, *New Republic*, October 25, 1993.
7. John Ruskin quoted in Duffey, *Relations of the Sexes*.
8. Longsworth, *Austin and Mabel*.
9. Wechter, *Love Letters of Mark Twain*.
10. *Washington Post*, October 6, 1996.
11. Wheeler, *Loving Warriors*.

## Chapter 13: "Wives and Lovers"

1. Quoted in Rothman, *Hands and Hearts*.
2. Hartman and Banner, *Clio's Consciousness Raised*.

3. An 1898 report by the Physicians' Club of Chicago, cited in Reed, *From Private Vice to Public Virtue.*

4. Ann Landers's column, July 17, 1996.

5. Dr. Charles Knowlton, *Fruits of Philosophy.*

6. *Washington Post,* January 12, 1994, p A10.

7. Sears, *The Sex Radicals.*

8. Quoted in Lystra, *Searching the Heart.*

9. John Gray, speaking on *The Oprah Winfrey Show,* June 13, 1995.

10. Marion Howard, professor of obstetrics and gynecology at Emory University, *Washington Post,* May 1, 1994.

11. Former surgeon general Joycelyn Elders quoted in William Raspberry's column in *The Washington Post,* September 8, 1993. Raspberry noted that Elders said this in a video presented to the National Council on Children.

12. "For Some Youthful Courting Has Become a Game of Abuse," *New York Times,* July 11, 1993.

13. Karl Vick, "Mall and Order in Minnesota," *Washington Post,* September 18, 1996.

14. Livermore, *Story of My Life.*

15. Letter quoted in Lystra, *Searching the Heart.*

16. Patrick Welsh, *Washington Post,* April 28, 1996.

17. *Washington Post,* February 27, 1995. The poll was conducted by the polling firm Fairbank, Maslin Maulin & Associates.

## Chapter 14: "You *Can* Go Home Again"

1. Horace Bushnell, cited in Matthews, *"Just a Housewife."*

2. Julia Ward Howe and Harriet Beecher Stowe quoted in Mary Durant, "The Devoted Beecher Sisters: Guardians of Home and Family," *Victoria,* April 1993.

3. All material on Martha Stewart from Annie Grower and Ann Gerhart, "The Reliable Source," *Washington Post,* November 13, 1996.

4. Survey cited in *St. Petersberg* (Florida) *Times* (Scripps Howard News Service), October 4, 1993.

5. Amelia Bloomer quoted in Ryan, *Empire of the Mother.*

## Chapter 15: "Home Wreckers"

1. Material on Charlotte Perkins Gilman from Matthews, *"Just a Housewife."*

2. *Playboy* ad for homemaker position cited in Matthews, *"Just a Housewife."*

3. Gloria Steinem's views on traditional women's work from Steinem, *Revolution from Within* and *Moving Beyond Words.*

4. Holland Cotter, *New York Times,* July 14, 1996.

## Chapter 16: "Throw Momma from the Train"

1. Quote from *Household* cited in Mildred Jailer-Chamberlain, "The Highest Calling," *Victorian Decorating and Lifestyle,* October–November 1994.
2. Lena Williams, "The New Birthday Party," *New York Times,* October 17, 1996, on the Elizabeth Seton Childbirth Center and children watching their siblings being born.
3. Elizabeth Chang, *Washington Post* (Style section), November 24, 1996.
4. Sarah Josepha Hale and Lydia Maria Child quoted in Ryan, *Empire of the Mother.*
5. Henry Blackwell quoted in Matthews, *"Just a Housewife."*
6. Elizabeth Cady Stanton quoted in Griffith, *In Her Own Right.*
7. Material on Charlotte Perkins Gilman from Matthews, *"Just a Housewife."*
8. Pearl Buck quoted in Matthews, *"Just a Housewife."*
9. Survey cited in Michaud and Torg, *Total Health for Women.*
10. Beth Brophy, "Fax Me a Bedtime Story," *U.S. News & World Report,* December 2, 1996.
11. Yankelovich poll cited in Alecia Swasy, "Are Their Kids Better Off?" *Wall Street Journal,* July 23, 1993.
12. Poll conducted for Philip Morris by Roper Worldwide.
13. Susan B. Anthony, cited in Barry, *Susan B. Anthony.*
14. Quotations from Lystra, *Searching the Heart.*

## Chapter 17: "Soul Food"

1. Roger K. Lewis, "Let's Put Real Dining Rooms Back on the Table," *Washington Post,* October 19, 1996.
2. Nancy Gibbs and Michael Duffy, "Desperately Seeking Lori," *Time,* October 14, 1996.
3. Fannie Farmer quoted in Matthews, *"Just a Housewife."*
4. Karen Hess quoted in Judith Weinraub, "Our Consuming Passion for Cookbooks," *Washington Post,* December 11, 1996.
5. Weinraub, "Our Consuming Passion for Cookbooks."

## Chapter 18: "The Art of Living"

1. Editorial criticizing the revised book, *New York Times,* February 4, 1995.
2. Ann Landers's column, August 16, 1995.
3. George Will, column in *Washington Post,* January 28, 1996.

## Chapter 19: "Art and Soul

1. Howat, *Hudson River School.*
2. Ken Ringle, "To PC or Not PC," *Washington Post,* December 26, 1993.

# BIBLIOGRAPHY

Sources that are listed in the Bibliography are cited by author's last name
and short title of work.

*Everyday Bible: New Century Version.* Ft. Worth, Texas: Worthy Publishing,
1988.

An American Gentleman. *Good Behavior for Young Gentlemen.* 1848;
reprint.

"The Censor." *Don't, or Directions for Avoiding Improprieties in Conduct and
Common Errors of Speech.* 1891; reprint, Chapel Hill, N.C.: Algonquin
Books, 1984.

Acton, William, M.D. *The Functions and Disorders of Reproductive Organs in
Childhood, Youth, Adult Age and Advanced Life Considered in their Physiological, Social and Moral Relations.* 1865? or 1875; reprint.

————. *Prostitution.* 1857; reprint, New York: Praeger, 1969.

Alcott, William. *The Young Wife; or, Duties of Women in the Marriage Relation.* New York. 1837; reprint, New York: Arno Press, 1972.

Allen, Frederick Lewis. *Only Yesterday: An Informal History of the 1920s.* New
York: Harper & Brothers, 1931.

Anderson, Elijah. *Streetwise: Race, Class, and Change in an Urban Community.* Chicago: University of Chicago Press, 1990.

Arendt, Hannah. *On Revolution.* New York: Viking Press, 1963.

Ashton, James, M.D. *The Book of Nature.* 1865; University of Nevada.

Auchincloss, Louis. *Persons of Consequence: Queen Victoria and Her Circle.*
New York: Random House, 1979.

Bailey, Beth. *From Front Porch to Back Seat: Courtship in Twentieth-Century
America.* Baltimore: Johns Hopkins Press, 1988.

Baker, Paul R. *Stanny: The Gilded Life of Stanford White.* New York: Free
Press, 1989.

Barry, Kathleen. *Susan B. Anthony: A Biography of a Singular Feminist.* New
York: New York University Press, 1988.

Beecher, Catharine Esther. *Letters to the People on Health and Happiness.*
New York: Harper & Brothers, 1855.

Beecher, Catharine, and Harriet Beecher Stowe. *The American Woman's Home; or, Principles of Domestic Science, Being a Guide to the Formation and Maintenance of Economical, Healthful, Beautiful, and Christian Homes.* Boston: Brown & Co., 1869. Although Harriet Beecher Stowe is listed as the coauthor of this book, historians generally agree that Catharine Beecher wrote the book and Harriet's name was added to help sales.

Beeton, Isabella. *Mrs. Beeton's Victorian Cookbook.* Topsfield, Mass.: Salem House Publishers, 1988.

Blackwell, Elizabeth. *The Laws of Life: With Special Reference to the Physical Education of Girls.* New York: G. P. Putnam's Sons, 1852; reprint, New York: Garland Publications, 1986.

———. *Essays in Medical Sociology.* 1902; reprint, New York: Arno Press, 1972.

Bode, Carl, ed., with Malcolm Cowley. *The Portable Emerson.* 1946; reprint, New York: Viking Press, 1981.

Breathnach, Sarah Ben. *Mrs. Sharp's Traditions: Nostalgic Suggestions for Re-creating the Family Celebrations and Seasonal Pastimes of the Victorian Home.* New York: Simon & Schuster, 1990.

Brookhiser, Richard. *The Way of the WASP: How It Made America, and How It Can Save It, So to Speak.* New York: Free Press, 1991.

Bulwer-Lytton, Edward. *The Caxtons.* 1849; reprint, St. Clair Shores, Mich.: Scholarly Press, 1971.

Carter, Rosalyn. *Random Acts of Kindness.* Conari Press, 1993.

Child, Lydia Maria. *The American Frugal Housewife.* 1833; reprint, ed. Alice M. Geffen, New York: Harper & Row, 1972.

Cook, Clarence. *The House Beautiful: Essays on Beds and Tables, Stools and Candlesticks.* 1881; reprint, Croton-on-Hudson, N.Y.: North River Press, 1980.

Cooke, Nicholas Francis, M.D. *Satan in Society.* 1870; reprint, New York: Arno Press,,1974.

Coontz, Stephanie. *The Way We Never Were.* New York: Basic Books, 1993.

Cox, Taylor, Jr. *Cultural Diversity in Organizations: Theory, Research, and Practice.* San Francisco: Berrett-Koehler, 1993.

D'Emilio, John, and Estelle B. Freedman. *Intimate Matters: A History of Sexuality in America.* New York: Harper & Row, 1988.

Day, Clarence. *Life with Father.* 1935; reprint, Boston: G. K. Hall, 1984.

de Tocqueville, Alexis. *Democracy in America;* reprint, trans. George Lawrence, ed. J. P. Mayer and Max Lerner, New York: Harper & Row, 1966.

Degler, Carl. *The Other South: Southern Dissenters in the Nineteenth Cen-*

*tury.* New York: Harper & Row, 1974.

———. *The Democratic Experience: A Short American History.* Glenview: Scott, Foresman, 1974.

———. *At Odds: Women and the Family in America from the Revolution to the Present.* New York: Oxford University Press, 1980.

Dickens, Charles. *American Notes.* 1842; reprint, Gloucester, Mass.: P. Smith, 1968.

Douglas, Anne. *The Feminization of American Culture.* New York: Knopf, 1977.

Duffey, Eliza. *What Women Should Know.* 1873; reprint, New York: Arno Press, 1974.

———. *The Relations of the Sexes.* 1876; reprint, New York: Arno Press, 1974.

———. *Ladies' and Gentlemen's Complete Etiquette.* 1877; reprint,

Ehrenreich, Barbara. *The Hearts of Men: American Dreams and the Flight from Commitment.* Garden City, N.Y.: Anchor Press/Doubleday, 1983.

Eliot, Charles W. "Democracy and Manners," *Century Magazine* 83 (1911–12).

Ellinwood, T. J., ed. *Henry Ward Beecher: Autobiographical Reminiscences.* 1898; reprint, New York: Frederick A. Stokes Company, c. 1898.

Faludi, Susan. *Backlash: The Undeclared War Against American Women.* New York: Crown, 1991.

Fass, Paula. *The Damned and the Beautiful: American Youth in the 1920s.* New York: Oxford University Press, 1977.

Finley, Ruth E. *The Lady of Godey's: Sara Josepha Hale.* 1931; reprint, New York: Arno Press, 1974.

Fleming, Ann Taylor. *Motherhood Deferred: A Woman's Journey.* New York: G. P. Putnam's Sons, 1994.

Ford, Ford Madox. *The Good Soldier.* 1915; reprint, New York: Octagon Books, 1981.

Foy, Jessica H., and Thomas J. Schlereth, eds. *American Home Life 1880–1930: A Social History of Spaces and Services.* Knoxville, Tenn.: University of Tennessee Press, 1992.

Friedan, Betty. *The Second Stage.* New York: Dell Publishing, 1991.

———. *The Feminine Mystique.* New York: Norton, 1963.

Gay, Peter. *The Bourgeois Experience, Victoria to Freud.* Vol. 1, *Education of the Senses.* New York: Oxford University Press, 1984.

———. *The Bourgeois Experience, Victoria to Freud.* Vol. 2, *The Tender Passion.* New York: Oxford University Press, 1986.

Geist, Bill. *Monster Trucks and Hair in a Can: Who Says America Doesn't Make Anything Anymore?* New York: G. P. Putnam's Sons, 1994.

Gentile, Mary C. *Differences That Work: Organized Excellence Through Diversity.* Boston: Harvard Business School Publications, 1994.

Gernsheim, Alison. *Victorian and Edwardian Fashion: A Photographic Survey.* New York: Dover Publications, 1981.

Goleman, Daniel. *Emotional Intelligence: Why It Can Matter More Than IQ for Character, Health and Lifelong Achievement.* New York: Bantam Doubleday Dell, 1995.

Gordon, Linda. *Woman's Body, Woman's Right: A Social History of Birth.* New York: Viking Penguin, 1977.

———. *Control.* New York: Grossman, 1976.

Gordon, Suzanne. *Prisoner of Men's Dreams: Striking Out for a New Feminine Future.* Boston: Little, Brown, 1991.

Gray, John. *Mars and Venus in the Bedroom: A Guide to Lasting Romance and Passion.* New York: HarperCollins, 1995.

Griffith, Elisabeth. *In Her Own Right: The Life of Elizabeth Cady Stanton.* New York: Oxford University Press. 1984.

Hale, Sarah Josepha. *Manners; or Happy Homes and Good Society All the Year Round.* 1868; reprint, New York: Arno Press, 1972.

Hall, Florence Howe. *Julia Ward Howe and the Woman Suffrage Movement.* 1913; reprint, New York: Arno Press, 1969.

Haller, John S., and Robin M. *The Physician and Sexuality in Victorian America.* Urbana, Ill.: University of Illinois Press, 1974.

Hapgood, Hutchins. *A Victorian in the Modern World.* 1939; reprint, Seattle: University of Washington Press, 1967.

Hartley, Florence. *The Ladies' Book of Etiquette and Manual of Politeness.* 1880.

Hartman, Mary S., and Lois W. Banner, eds. *Clio's Consciousness Raised: New Perspectives on the History of Women.* New York: Octagon Books, 1974.

Haweis, Mary Elizabeth. *The Art of Beauty.* New York: Harper. 1878.

Hilts, Elizabeth. *Getting in Touch with Your Inner Bitch.* Bridgeport, Conn.: Hysteria Publications, 1994.

Howat, John K. *The Hudson River School and Its Painters.* New York: Viking Press, 1972.

Howe, Joseph, M.D. *Excessive Venery: Masturbation and Continence: The Etiology, Pathology and Treatment of the Diseases Resulting from Venereal Excesses, Masturbation and Continence.* Bermingham & Co., 1883.

Howe, Julia Ward. *Modern Society.* Boston: Roberts Brothers, 1881.

———. *Is Polite Society Polite? And Other Essays.* 1895; reprint, Upper Saddle River, N.J.: Literature House, 1970.

Howells, William Dean. *The Rise of Silas Lapham.* 1885; reprint, Bloomington, Ind.: University of Indiana Press, 1971.

Humphry, Mrs. *Manners for Men*. London, England: James Bowden Publishers, 1897.

James, Henry. *Washington Square*. 1880; reprint, ed. Gerald Willem, New York: Crowell, 1970,

Johnson, Emily Cooper. *Jane Addams: A Centennial Reader*.

Johnston, Johanna. *Mrs. Satan: The Incredible Saga of Victoria C. Woodhull*. New York: Popular Library, 1967.

Jacobi, Jolande, ed. *Psychological Reflections: An Anthology of the Writings of C. J. Jung*. New York: Pantheon Books, 1953.

Kasson, John. *Rudeness and Civility: Manners in Nineteenth-Century Urban America*. New York: Hill & Wang, 1990.

Kellogg, Susan, and Steven Mintz. *Domestic Revolutions: A Social History of American Family Life*. New York: Free Press, 1988.

Knowlton, Charles, M.D. *Fruits of Philosophy*. 1878; reprint, Austin, Texas: American Atheist Press, 1980.

Kramer, Peter. *Listening to Prozac*. New York: Viking Press, 1993.

Kunstler, James Howard. *The Geography of Nowhere: The Rise and Decline of America's Man-Made Landscape*. New York: Simon & Schuster, 1993.

LaHaye, Tim, and Beverly LaHaye. *The Act of Marriage: The Beauty of Sexual Love*. Grand Rapids, Mich.: Zondervan Publishing House, 1976.

Lasch, Christopher. *Haven in a Heartless World: The Family Besieged*. New York: Basic Books, 1977.

Leeman, Richard W. *"Do Everything" Reform: The Oratory of Frances E. Willard*. New York: Greenwood Press, 1992.

Leith, Elan, and Susan Leith. *The Secret Life of Victorian Houses*. Washington, D.C.: Elliot & Clark Publishers, 1993.

Leopold, Allison Kyle. *Allison Kyle Leopold's Victorian Keepsakes: Select Expressions of Affectionate Regard from the Romantic Nineteenth Century*. New York: Doubleday, 1991.

Leslie, Eliza. *Miss Leslie's Behaviour Book: A Guide and Manual for Ladies*. 1859; reprint, New York: Arno Press, 1972.

Lewis, Denslow, M.D. *The Gynecologic Consideration of the Sexual Act*. 1900. Weston, Mass.: M & S Press, 1970. Reprint.

Lewis, Howard R., and Martha E. Lewis. *The Parents' Guide to Teenage Sex and Pregnancy*. New York: St. Martin's Press, 1980.

Livermore, Mary Ashton Rice. *The Story of My Life*. 1899; reprint, New York: Arno Press, 1974.

Loden, Marilyn, and Judy B. Rosener. *Workforce America! Managing Employee Diversity as a Vital Resource*. Homewood, Ill.: Business One Irwin, 1991.

Longsworth, Polly. *Austin and Mabel: The Amherst Affair and Love Letters of Austin Dickinson and Mabel Loomis Todd*. New York: Farrar Straus & Giroux, 1984.

Lynd, Robert S., and Helen M. Lynd. *Middletown: A Study in Contemporary American Culture*. New York: Harcourt Brace, 1929.

Lystra, Karen. *Searching the Heart: Women, Men, and Romantic Love in Nineteenth-Century America*. New York: Oxford University Press, 1989.

MacFadden, Bernarr. *Womanhood and Marriage*. New York: MacFadden Publishers, 1918.

Martine, Arthur. *Martine's Hand-book of Etiquette and Guide to True Politeness*. New York: Dick & Fitzgerald, 1866; reprint, Bedford, Mass.: Applewood Books, 1996.

Matthews, Glenna. *"Just a Housewife": The Rise and Fall of Domesticity*. New York: Oxford University Press, 1987.

Michaud, Ellen, and Elizabeth Torg. *Total Health for Women: From Allergies and Back Pain to Overweight and PMS, the Best Preventative and Curative Advice for More Than 100 Women's Health Problems*. Emmaus, Pa.: Rodale Press, 1995.

Miller, Russell. *Bunny: The Real Story of Playboy*. New York: New American Library, 1984.

Moir, Ann. *Brain Sex: The Real Difference Between Men and Women*. New York: Carol Publishing Group, 1991.

Morris, Edmund. *The Rise of Theodore Roosevelt*. New York: Coward, McCann & Geoghegan, 1979.

Ogden, Gina. *Women Who Love Sex*. New York: Pocket Books, 1994.

Page, Thomas Nelson. "On the Decay of Manners," *Century Magazine* 83, (1911-12).

Paglia, Camille. *Sex, Art, and American Culture: Essays*. New York: Vintage Books, 1992.

Pearsall, Ronald. *The Worm in the Bud: The World of Victorian Sexuality*. New York: Macmillan. 1969.

Pike, Martha V., and Janice Gray Armstrong. *A Time to Mourn: Expressions of Grief in Nineteenth-Century America*. New York: The Museums of Stonybrook, 1980.

Pivar, David, Jr. *Purity Crusade: Sex, Morality, and Social Control 1868–1900*. Westport, Conn.: Greenwood Press, 1973.

Post, Emily. *Personality of a House*. New York and London: Funk & Wagnalls Company, 1930.

Reed, James. *From Private Vice to Public Virtue: The Birth Control Movement and American Society Since 1830*. New York: Basic Books, 1978.

Root, R. K., ed. *Lord Chesterfield: Letters to His Son*. 1969.

Rothman, Ellen K. *Hands and Hearts: A History of Courtship in America*. New York: Basic Books, 1984.

Ruddock, E. H., M.D. *Vitology: An Encyclopedia of Health and Home*. Chicago: Halsey Bros., 1885.

Rugoff, Milton Allan. *Prudery and Passion*. New York: G. P. Putnam's Sons, 1971.

Ryan, Mary P. *The Empire of the Mother*. New York: Copublished by the Institute for Research in History and The Haworth Press, 1982.

Sanger, Margaret. *Happiness in Marriage*. 1926; reprint, Old Saybrook, Conn.: Applewood Books, 1993.

Schlesinger, Arthur Meier. *Learning How to Behave: A Historical Study of American Etiquette Books*. 1946. reprint, New York: Cooper Square Publications, 1968.

Sears, Hal D. *The Sex Radicals: Free Love in High Victorian America*. Lawrence, Kans.: Regents Press of Kansas, 1977.

Seidman, Steven. *Romantic Longings: Love in America 1830–1980*. New York: Routledge Press, 1991.

Shiveley, Charles, ed. *Love, Marriage, Divorce, and the Sovereignty of the Individual: A Discussion Between Henry James, Horace Greeley, and Stephen Pearl Andrews*. Weston, Mass.: M & S Press, 1975.

Sommers, Christina Hoff. *Who Stole Feminism? How Women Have Betrayed Women*. New York: Simon & Schuster, 1994.

Stall, Sylvanus. *What a Young Husband Should Know*. Philadelphia: Vir Publishing Co., 1897.

Stanton, Elizabeth Cady. *Eighty Years and More: Reminiscences*. New York: Source Book Press, 1970.

Stein, Leon, and Annette K. Baxter. *Grace Dodge: Her Life and Work*. New York, Arno Press, 1974.

Steinem, Gloria. *Moving Beyond Words*. New York: Simon & Schuster, 1994.

———. *Revolution from Within: A Book of Self-Esteem*. Boston: Little, Brown, 1992.

Stowe, Catharine Beecher. *Treatise on Domestic Economy, American Family Home*. Boston: Marsh, Capen, Lyon, and Webb, 1841; reprint, New York: Source Book Press, 1970.

Susman, Warren I. *Culture as History: The Transformaton of American Society in the Twentieth Century*. New York: Pantheon, 1984.

Trall, R. T., M.D. *Sexual Physiology*. New York: M. L. Holbrook. 1881; reprint, New York: Arno Press, 1974.

Vanderbilt, Consuelo. *The Glitter and the Gold*. 1953.

Vaux, Calvert. *Villas and Cottages: A Series of Designs Prepared for Execution in the United States*. 1864; reprint, New York: Dover Publications, 1970.

Wade, Wyn Craig. *The Titanic: End of a Dream*. New York: Atheneum.1979.

Wechter, Dixon, ed. *The Love Letters of Mark Twain*. New York: Harper, 1949.

———. *The Saga of American Society: A Record of Social Aspiration 1607–1937*. 1949; reprint, New York: Scribner, 1970.

Wharton, Edith. *A Backward Glance*. New York: D. Appleton-Century Co., 1933.

Wheeler, Leslie, ed. *Loving Warriors: Selected Letters of Lucy Stone and Henry B. Blackwell, 1853–1893*. New York: Dial Press, 1981.

Willard, Frances. *Glimpses of Fifty Years*. 1889. New York: Source Book Press, 1970.

Williams, Redford. *The Trusting Heart: Great News About Type A Behavior*. New York: Times Books, 1989.

Williams, Resa. *Mark and Livy: A Biography of Mark Twain and the Woman Who Almost Tamed Him*. New York: Maxwell Macmillan International, 1992.

Wilson, James Q., and Richard J. Herrnstein. *Crime and Human Nature: The Definitive Study of the Causes of Crime*. New York: Simon & Schuster, 1985.

Wolf, Naomi. *Fire with Fire: The New Female Power and How It Will Change the 21st Century*. New York: Random House, 1993.

Wright, Henry C. *Marriage and Parentage*. 1855. Reprint, New York: Arno Press, 1974.

Wyman, Mary Alice, ed. *Selections from the Autobiography of Elizabeth Oakes Smith*. Lewiston, Maine: Lewiston Journal Co. 1924; reprint, New York: Arno Press, 1924.